Renaldo

ISBN: 1-4196-3918-8

To order additional copies, please contact us.
BookSurge, LLC
www.booksurge.com
1-866-308-6235
orders@booksurge.com

JAMES
McCREATH

RENALDO

To Carl,
Great to meet you
Rock on!

2006

Renaldo

For My Ladies: Annie, Kari, Carly, Christie, Coco, and Isabella.

You Are The Sunshine Of My Life.

CHAPTER ONE

Córdoba, Argentina. December 5, 1977.

The young Porteño had never been this terrified in his life. The monster surged from behind, almost engulfing them at times. He knew that he could easily outrun the deadly creature, were it not for the slower members of his group who stumbled and groped their way down the narrow alley.

Gordo was the worst, far too obese to keep up the frantic pace. The red and black torrent was gaining on them, hurling insults along with rocks and bottles. The boy knew all too well what would happen should they be overtaken, for this monster was both human and inhuman.

A narrow lane intercepted their path, and he could see that his amigos had swung off to the right. But Gordo had missed the turn and plunged straight ahead, knocking over several refuse cans in the process.

It was hard to believe that just thirty minutes earlier, this same corpulent straggler, now panting and pallid from exertion and fear, had taunted a stadium full of enraged Córdobans. With cocky bravado, he had boldly questioned their mothers' virtue, the size of their cojones, and worst of all, their team's penchant for dull, defensive football. The first two insults the locals could dismiss from this fat fool, but the third, perhaps because it was bitingly true, set the mob upon them.

Gordo was a well-known lawyer back in Buenos Aires, a self-important, larger-than-life figure with an overinflated ego. His sharp tongue had often gotten him into uncomfortable situations, but this was by far the most serious.

Like the majority of his peers that had made the journey to Córdoba, Gordo was a Porteño, or 'person of the port.' He was an Argentine national, born and bred in Buenos Aires. Born and bred or not, all the men that had accompanied him this day were impassioned supporters of the Newton's Prefects Football Club. A trainload of fans had traveled the five hundred miles to this quaint provincial capital for the championship game of the Argentine premier soccer league.

The atmosphere had been electric as the Prefect partisans staked out their tiny corner of the menacing Córdoba Stadium. Deep inside the lair of the monster, seething with forty-five thousand rabid adversaries, the brave few hundred manifested their colors defiantly to the hordes on the terraces.

"Preeeeeefects! Preeeeeefects! Preeeeeefects!" was the call to battle that accompanied the brandishing of their inflammatory black-and-white flags, scarves, hats, and banners. This display summoned even louder venom-filled jeers, taunts, and shouts from their hosts. Gordo led the rebuttal with a boisterous Prefect fight song. That made him a man marked for 'special' attention.

Throughout the game, the Prefect supporters in general, and Gordo in particular, were subjected to bottles and smoke bombs, insults, and incendiaries. The visitors remained steadfast in their resolve, however, with an unflinching belief in the ultimate destiny of their team.

They had waited so long in obscurity for a chance to, once again, reach the pinnacle. That moment was now at hand, and in the minds of each and every Porteño, the championship trophy belonged back in Buenos Aires, not in this city of peasants and farmers! Perhaps that is why the less refined Córdobans truly hated the arrogant, urbane boasters from the nation's capital. They were so impudent in their team's support!

It mattered little to the hometown fanatics that the Prefect organization was one of the most tradition-steeped clubs in the entire nation. As a founding member of the Asociacion Del Futbol Argentino in 1893, the Newton's Prefects Football Club was originally formed to offer a recreational outlet to the offspring of British scientists and investors who had played such a large part in developing and modernizing this vast country.

The very first teams were made up exclusively from the graduating class or 'prefects' of the Sir Isaac Newton Academy of the Sciences. This renowned English language preparatory school in Buenos Aires was established in 1865 as an old-world safe haven, intent upon salvaging a proper 'English' education for the male children of United Kingdom transplants.

Newton's all-British professional side was the dominant master of the game in the early years of formal competition. But as so often happens in sports, a glorious beginning eventually gave way to mediocrity, then near obsolescence as native-born players took to the game of football with unbridled Latin passion. The foreigners finally succumbed to using a sprinkling of home-grown Porteño talent to increase fan support and stave off bankruptcy, but by the 1920s, the once-proud side had been relegated to third division status, a place where it would remain for nearly five decades.

The team's fortunes began to change for the better with aggressive new ownership in the mid 1970s. The purse strings were opened to acquire more highly skilled players. This rekindled the long dormant interest and affection for the 'Black and White.' The signing of two world-class professionals at the start of the 1977 campaign, striker Ruben Gitares from the River Plate Club, and defender Jorge Calderone from the Boca Juniors, turned out to be just the tonic needed to raise the efforts of the team's supporting cast to their highest levels.

The Prefects had finished fourth in the premier division standings, then upset the highly favored first place Independiente club in a brutally rugged semifinal fixture that saw several people killed in its acrimonious aftermath. The victory over Independiente set the stage for this pilgrimage to Córdoba, whose heroes had disposed of River Plate in the other semifinal game.

Now, with the ultimate prize beckoning, the event set to take place inside this boiling concrete cauldron was far more than just the playing of a football game. This was blood sport! The blood of your ancestors and family against the invaders. Pride and passion. And so it would be on this beautiful afternoon in Córdoba.

The home team, Talleres F.C. of Córdoba, clad in their all-red strip with black numerals, showed a stubborn willingness to defend their honor and their goal with great spirit and courage. For a while, the 'Reds' did manage to bring the Córdobans to their feet, but it was all in the realm of the negative . . . defense!

Little by little, the tension in the ranks of the red defenders grew. Their goalkeeper, a gangly, mustached custodian named 'Puente,' made several inspired saves, but he was also quick to chastise his cohorts. The finger-pointing and verbal dressing-downs escalated with every Prefect sortie into Córdoban territory. Puente pleaded for some offense from his teammates, but the best the Reds could do was to clear the ball either out of play or far upfield, yielding possession to the waiting Prefect midfielders.

Finally, in the twenty-first minute, Gitares, the brilliant Prefect striker, was sent through on a pinpoint pass from Calderone. One-on-one with the keeper, he feinted to his left, then sure-footed the ball into the top right corner of the net from twenty yards out. The spirit of the huge crowd seemed to deflate en masse, except for that tiny corner filled with the now even more vocal visitors. There, Gordo was waving his monstrous all-black flag while shouting insults at his enemies just beyond the eight foot high, barbed wire topped barriers.

Three more Prefect goals followed in the second forty-five minute half, sending the majority of the local patrons on their not-so-merry way before the conclusion of regulation time. Not the Newton's Prefect supporters though! They remained on the terraces to soak up every blissful moment. At the final whistle, Gordo managed to avoid the disinterested security forces standing idly on the warning track and marched onto the pitch, his huge flag waving defiantly to and fro above him.

His Newton's Prefects were the champions of Argentina, and the celebrating would start right now! Taking the fat man's lead, more and more

Prefect supporters converged on their victorious heroes at midfield, singing, hugging, dancing, and scavenging pieces of the lush green carpet.

From where he stood on the terrace, Renaldo De Seta could see the trouble coming. In the far corner of the stadium, a mob of vocal, young Córdobans was also making its way onto the pitch, angered at the insult of having these buffoons on their sacred turf. The security forces remained stationary on the perimeter of the field, allowing the Córdobans to swiftly set upon the still reveling visitors.

In an instant, elation became hysteria. An incendiary flare exploded in the midst of the Prefect supporters, and the screams of the burnt victims could be heard by Renaldo fifty yards away. He could barely see the mêlée through the thick, maroon smoke, but he knew that his compatriots were in serious trouble. The observer quickly looked for the nearest escape route, then leapt into action. Gliding over the barriers, he soon reached what looked to be a senior officer in the National Guard.

"Why do you stand here and do nothing? People are going to get hurt! Surely you have eyes, you must be able to see that yourself! Please do something!"

The officer looked at Renaldo with disinterest and disdain, shrugged his shoulders, then started to turn away. The commotion on the field was getting louder by the second, and it was only the report of several gunshots that startled the officer into action.

"Please help them get out of the stadium," Renaldo pleaded.

There was a fire in the young man's eyes that the officer could not ignore. He looked past the youth out onto the pitch. At that very moment, a Prefect supporter staggered out of the smoke bleeding profusely from a gash to his head.

The visitor is right! the officer thought. If he didn't save these rabble-rousers it could ruin his career, and they certainly weren't worth that.

A piercing blast of the military man's whistle brought several subordinates running to his side. Renaldo stepped back as the uniformed group held a brief conference. A lieutenant screamed into his walkie-talkie as the officer turned to Renaldo.

"We will try to separate them and cordon off an escape route through the nearest tunnel. After that, you are on your own."

The warning track that surrounded the field was now teaming with guardsmen, bayonets affixed to their carbines. A corporal handed the lieutenant a loudspeaker, into which he screamed several commands. As one, the soldiers then advanced toward the smoke-obscured chaos.

Renaldo, having done his best to get help, sprinted past the guardsmen to see if he could find his friends and get them started toward the escape tunnel.

It was pandemonium on the field. More smoke flares had been ignited, and the boy could hardly distinguish the Córdobans from his own companions. Some groups were engaged in hand-to-hand combat, while others stood staring each other down, using verbal abuse as a prelude to a more physical display of their machismo. Renaldo had wisely discarded the black-and-white scarf that he had worn all afternoon, and he was able to streak through the midst of his would-be assailants without being detected as a Prefect invader.

Confusion reigned supreme until miraculously, through a clearing in the smoke, the boy caught a glimpse of what he thought was Gordo's huge Prefect flag surrounded by both friends and foes. Renaldo pushed his way further into the maroon mist until he found himself face-to-face with Gordo and a throng of his dazed blood brothers. The men had formed a tight circle around Gordo's insolent object, for to lose the colors would be a great dishonor no matter what the outcome of the game had been.

Gordo, although sweating profusely, had lost none of his loud, aggressive bearing. He continued to insult his detractors, all the while taunting them with his sacred cloth.

"We must get out of the stadium now or we won't have a chance!" implored Renaldo.

"I would not give these peasants the satisfaction of driving us from this place. This is our field of victory!" spat the fat man defiantly.

"It will be our field of doom if we do not leave right now!" the newcomer retorted.

Gordo did not stand convinced, but just as he was about to resume his verbal tirade against the provincials, the first jet of water slammed into the group of men immediately to their left.

"Water canon!" screamed one of the combatants.

All at once, it seemed as if the sky had opened up and let loose a torrential downpour. Men were thrown to the ground or propelled into one another with terrifying velocity. The National Guard officer had made good on his promise to separate the antagonists, but he was employing a most vicious method of doing so.

A water canon mounted on an armored military vehicle was randomly sweeping the pitch with devastating effect. The National Guardsmen had halted after advancing only a few paces, then formed a corridor leading to the escape tunnel. The officer in charge was no fool. He would not risk the safety of his soldiers by sending them into the smokey fray. Besides, the water canon made for great spectacle, something to amuse his troops and take their minds off the sad defeat that the home team had suffered.

Renaldo knew he had to act quickly or his friends would be separated and left alone to make their way to safety. In one swift motion, he grabbed the flag from Gordo's grasp, pushed him around, and pointed in the general direction of the tunnel.

"Brave amigos, follow me to glory!" he shouted.

To think that he was leaving the field in glorious fashion was somehow satisfying to Gordo, and he motioned for the group to follow Renaldo and the fluttering standard. That was not altogether an easy task, through the jumble of men, the spray of the canon, and the dissipating smoke. The flag, however, served as their beacon, and most of the Porteños made it to the warning track where the guardsmen stood nervously awaiting their arrival.

Only Prefect supporters were allowed through the corridor of soldiers formed where Gordo's pennant swung proudly as a rallying point for the men from Buenos Aires. Many of those assembling there had been bloodied, but their wounds were looked upon as proud souvenirs of a great and glorious victory.

When Renaldo was satisfied that a full complement of the Prefectos, as they called themselves, were in the narrow tunnel, he led them swiftly down the passage and out into the stadium concourse. From there it was an easy walk past the entrance gates and into an open air plaza.

Relief swept over the rescuer as he watched his fellow Porteños file into the bright sunshine. It was an emotion that would be short-lived. Renaldo still held the giant battle colours in his right hand. As he stood surveying the ranks of the rescued and talking to a member of his group, the standard was suddenly torn from his grasp. A young street urchin clad in Córdoban colors sped away down the plaza into a gang of hostile ruffians. Instantly, the flag was set ablaze, then waved defiantly at its owners as it disintegrated into flaming pieces.

The stunned Prefectos could only watch in silence as their colors turned to burning embers. But mute disbelief was soon replaced by Gordo's booming voice, chiding and chastising the vile arsonists. The locals returned Gordo's salutations with their own invectives, and it was all too evident that the situation could rapidly deteriorate into more violence. As the tension mounted, the words of the military officer flashed in Renaldo's mind.

Once you are out of the stadium, you are on your own.

There was neither a policeman nor a guardsman in sight. The situation inside the stadium was still the focus of their attention. This was not the time for more of Gordo's verbal contempt. This was the time to save themselves!

The mob of Córdobans was growing in size by the second and projectiles started to rain down into the midst of the wary visitors. The hunters were now edging closer to their prey, and a repeat of what had just occurred inside the stadium was all too likely.

The men from Buenos Aires had chosen to travel to Córdoba by train, primarily to allow themselves the freedom to party as a group on both legs of the journey. But that decision was now responsible for their present peril. No motor coaches stood at the ready to whisk them away to safety. Most of the Porteños had walked the mile from the train station to the stadium in a large, vocal mass. The remainder had hired taxi cabs, not one of which was anywhere to be seen now. With absolutely no means of transportation available, the conquerors had no alternative but to swallow their pride and flee to safety on foot.

But where? None of the visitors were intimately familiar with the lay of the land, for a police escort had herded them along the route to the stadium before the game. It was glaringly evident that they had to go somewhere, however, for to do nothing and wait for help to arrive at their present location would be suicide.

"We must go now!" Renaldo shouted emphatically to the group.

Gordo was about to offer some resistance to that plan when a piece of brick grazed his left shoulder.

"Mother of Jesus!" he cried out, clutching his collarbone.

"Do you believe me now? Let's go!"

The only escape route available to the Prefectos lay behind them in the narrow passages of an open air marketplace. This confined space would offer some form of protection to the swift, should the Córdobans try to follow them in an unwieldy posse. But subtlety and stealth would be required to disengage from the impending punch-up.

Slowly, so as not to promote panic and tip their hand to the enemy, Renaldo sent small groups of men off at a brisk walk in the direction of the market. He was working in the midst of his companions as if he had done it all before, as if crisis management were, in fact, his calling. But nothing could have been further from the truth. Renaldo De Seta was by far the youngest of all the Porteños that had made the pilgrimage to Córdoba, but at this moment in time, he was their leader, one cool hand amongst the hotheads.

This journey to Córdoba was supposed to have been his special reward, a gift of gratitude handed out to the youngest traveler for past services rendered. Barely eighteen years old, Renaldo had captained the Prefect's under twenty-one feeder squad to a national championship of their own. For his immense talent and leadership beyond his years, he had been invited by the professional side's chairman to travel to Córdoba along with his coach, Estes Santos. His leadership skills were, once again, being called upon, but this time for reasons that shocked and disgusted the youth. Renaldo De Seta loved to play the game of soccer, but the events that had followed the final whistle in the stadium were nothing short of insanity!

It didn't take long for the monster to realize its prey was slowly slipping away to safer ground. A full beer bottle exploded only feet from where Renaldo stood. He knew it was time to throw caution to the wind and run for their lives. Further persuasion was offered in the chilling shouts rumbling from the bowels of the dreaded ogre.

"Get them! They are trying to escape! Don't let them get away! Kill the bastards! We want Porteño blood!"

Even Gordo knew that their lives were in great peril. He called out over his shoulder as he barreled past Renaldo on his flight to the market.

"Save yourself, young man. This is no time for heroics."

With the last of his companions now departed on their dash into the unknown, Renaldo took flight and soon caught up with the fat man and the slower members of his band. He sped ahead, wanting to make certain that there was some form of refuge waiting for them under the colorful awnings of the market stalls. A quick glance confirmed that the lead Prefectos had found an opening beyond the jumble of wooden tables and carts. There was a narrow passage between two buildings, and it was down that corridor that their only hope of escape lay.

A rush of adrenaline caused the usually soft spoken and painfully shy boy to be loudly vocal as he waved his fellow Prefectos on past him, into the confines of the alleyway. Renaldo waited to access the escape route until all but one had passed, pleading with the final Porteño to make all possible haste to save himself. In Gordo's case, there was not much haste to be made.

The lawyer carried almost three hundred pounds on his stocky frame, and his girth rolled and jiggled as a result of his frantic, waddling gait. The gleaming crown of his head was totally bald, with only wisps of greasy salt-and-pepper hair shooting back from his temples. His oily olive skin was, once again, dripping with sweat from exertion and sheer panic. He seemed to be half crying, half reciting some mystic religious incantation as the monster nipped at his heels. In contrast, the younger man who waited anxiously to escort Gordo to safety seemed cool, rational, and totally in control.

Standing well over six feet in height, Renaldo De Seta possessed a swimmer's torso, lean and well-proportioned. But it was the boy's legs, particularly his powerful thighs, which distinguished him as an athlete to be reckoned with. His fair complexion and ice-blue eyes were a gift from his English grandmother, but these features were framed by a curly black mane that was worn to below shoulder length. The overall image of this man-child was one of strength and determination covered by angelic beauty. He would have been teased unmercifully as a 'pretty boy' in his early prep school days were it not for his incredible skill with a soccer ball. It was this particular skill that had earned him respect and changed the course of his life in those formative years. But now it seemed that his affection for the black-and-white spheroid had landed him in a potentially tragic situation.

The events that had led the Prefectos into the narrow maze of alleys had not gone unnoticed by Estes Santos. As fearful as he was for his own safety, he could not help but marvel at the maturity and take-charge demeanor of young Renaldo. The boy had surely never experienced anything as daunting as the events that had just transpired, yet he seemed in complete control, not only of himself, but of the entire entourage of Prefect supporters. To Estes' dismay, that situation was disintegrating rapidly before his eyes.

As Renaldo's coach had fled through the snake-like alleys with the main pack of men from Buenos Aires, he continually tried to keep Gordo and the boy in his sight. Santos had seen that they had failed to negotiate the last turn and quickly realized that the two were in deep trouble. The monster exploded into Estes' view in hot pursuit, making it impossible for him to retrace his steps and offer any help. He sped ahead, remembering several doors opening into the dead-end alley that now held his friends captive. Those doors were his only hope.

Suddenly, the cramped enclosure he was running through spilled out onto a large square. There, right in front of him, stood soldiers in full riot gear, police mounted on horseback, and an array of armored military vehicles. Would they be friend or foe? Were the Porteños caught in a deadly vice between two legions of hostile Córdobans?

In this instance, luck was with the men from Buenos Aires. The soldiers were there to protect them and to assist in the evacuation. Military buses lined the curb, and Santos could see that the first of the Porteños to arrive on the scene were already being escorted onto them. To his left he saw an open air café.

The innermost walls of its kitchen area must back onto that dead-end alley, Estes surmised. In a heartbeat, he tore through the neatly arranged tables and chairs towards the kitchen and what hopefully would be the service entrance from the alley. The café was almost totally deserted, with all but a few curiosity seekers having been scared away by the arrival of the soldiers.

The startled kitchen staff could only stare in amazement as this seemingly madman burst into their midst screaming, "Where is the door? The door to the alley. Where is it? The door, the door!"

One of the dishwashers pointed to a small hallway, barely visible through the stacked bags and metal cans of garbage. The pregame festivities must have been much more lively here than those of the postgame, judging from all the refuse. Estes flailed bags and cans out of his path as he frantically made for the blockaded exit. Finally reaching the wooden door, he could hear the screams and insults from beyond. This must be the right place, but would he be in time?

"Dead end! There is no escape. We are doomed!"

Gordo was screaming, urgently wrestling with one of the locked doors that stood between him and safety. The blind alley was now filling with their pursuers, edging forward slowly and cautiously. They sensed that their prey was trapped and anticipating the kill, started mocking the fat man with a dirge-like rendition of the famous Prefect fight song that Gordo had sung triumphantly all afternoon long.

Renaldo could clearly see the weapons. Baseball bats used as clubs, broken bottles, lead pipe, knives, and even what he thought was the silver plating of a revolver. Gordo had given up trying to force the doors and was now pleading for his life. First he begged Renaldo to save them, to find a way out. He then implored the monster to be merciful and spare their lives. Sarcastic laughter and then a hail of missiles greeted Gordo's display of humility.

The younger man tried to shield the former arrogant boaster from the wrath of the crowd, but the Córdobans wanted the loudmouth's blood first. As one of the closer attackers lunged at Gordo with a broken beer bottle, Renaldo picked up a metal trash can and hurled it at the man. The aggressor fell sideways, his thrust at Gordo's ample torso falling just short. Several of the pursuers were bowled over by the impact of the metal object and the bottle-wielding assassin's subsequent stumbling.

Renaldo grasped a second trash can and hurled it into the front ranks of the ogre as well. The beast seemed to retreat a few paces as a result of the confusion that the boy had created. The intimate confines of the alley, which now overflowed with people, produced a domino effect on the closest assailants once the metal object struck pay dirt.

Curses and screams for the blood of all Porteños filled the reeking cul-de-sac. But at that moment, before the monster could recover its equilibrium and finish off its nasty business, Estes Santos appeared, like the Savior himself, in the doorway behind the two men from Buenos Aires.

It was over in an instant. In unison, Santos and Renaldo grabbed Gordo, one pulling, the other pushing his enormous bulk through the tiny doorway. Renaldo used the larger man's momentum to carry himself to safety. It was as if he were an appendage of Gordo, the way the two were propelled into the opening as one.

Once through the portal, the three men managed to close and bolt the door shut before their antagonists were able to jam the passage open and continue their fun. Gordo's generous weight made closing the opening behind them a much easier task. Santos quickly led the two men through the kitchen and out into the open café. There, much to their mutual relief, they were met by one of their traveling companions who had with him a captain of the National Guard. All four of the Prefectos were swiftly placed aboard one of the waiting buses.

Once settled inside, they were able to watch the scene unfolding before them from behind bulletproof windows covered with steel bars.

The angry crowd had, by now, made its way into the open area surrounding the café. Here they were confronted with the same sight that had brought relief to the hearts of those they had pursued. But it was a totally different emotion that swept over the thwarted aggressors. They had been robbed of their entertainment by the rescuing of these intruders, and they now sought to vent their frustrations on the local militia.

A familiar pattern repeated itself. First taunts and verbal abuse were hurled in the direction of the military men, then objects of every description seemed to take flight. Chairs, tables, bottles, bricks, anything that was not permanently secured became a messenger of hate. But these soldiers were in a foul mood as well, thanks, in part, to the loss that their beloved soccer team had suffered only minutes before. For it was their team, too, and now men that had cheered together for a Córdoban victory were facing each other, about to play a much more serious game.

The buses containing the Prefect disciples were surrounded by two rings of armed soldiers. As soon as all the visitors were sequestered, a colonel of the army could be seen gesturing to the lead driver to remove his vehicle and its volatile cargo from the area. As the buses started to snail their way around the congested military ordinance parked pell-mell in the roadway, the initial burst of a water canon slammed into the unsuspecting locals.

Bloodthirsty barbarians, all of them! Renaldo thought to himself as he, once again, witnessed the canon's devastating effect. Most of these Córdobans had left the stadium before the on-field rumble had commenced, and they were not prepared for the impromptu soaking.

As Renaldo's armored coach gained speed in its departure, the men inside remained silent. Even the verbose Gordo was intent on catching a final glimpse of the brutality that they were leaving behind. It was Gordo, nevertheless, that broke that silence with the all too familiar fight song. Renaldo's emotions were playing tricks on him now. Fear, anxiety, and anger ebbed. Relief, satisfaction, and pride flowed. One by one, the men around him picked up the chorus of the song. Soon the entire group had regained the vocal authority and bellicose attitude of champions.

Song after boisterous song filled the air. The youngest passenger sang along as well, finally succumbing to the prodding of the fat man to join the festivities. At the end of one particularly uplifting rendition, Gordo raised his arms and whistled above the racket for silence. Making his way down the aisle to where Santos and the boy were seated, he addressed the entire bus.

"These two men saved my life this afternoon, showing great courage and true Prefect spirit. I will be indebted to them from this day on, for I will never forget how they put their lives at great risk to save mine. Especially young Renaldo, who fought off that mob with his bare hands! I salute you both, and I want you to ride with me on our return journey to Buenos Aires."

So this is how fate would have it. This is how young Renaldo De Seta would be enticed into the complex, multilayered web spun by Astor Armondo Luis Gordero. The boy was about to step into a world far beyond his wildest dreams, for Gordero, or 'Gordo' as he was derisively called behind his sizable back, was a man unlike any he had ever imagined.

Astor Gordero's vast wealth and political dexterity had placed him in a position of favor with both the essential elements necessary to ensure survival and prosperity in modern-day Argentina: firstly, the ruling military junta that ran the politics of the country with an iron fist; and secondly, the influential Porteño business and social communities that controlled the nation's wealth with a velvet glove.

At forty years of age, Gordero was the beneficiary of one of the largest family fortunes in the southern hemisphere. As a result of his diverse business career, he wore many hats . . . lawyer, investment adviser, political strategist. He acted as private counsel to some of the country's best-known celebrities and dignitaries, was an extravagant philanthropist, a trustee and governor of the Sir Isaac Newton Academy School (of which he was a graduate and class valedictorian), and a ranking colonel in the National Guard Reserve. But most importantly to his traveling companions on this day, Astor Gordero was the chairman of the board of directors and majority owner of the Newton's Prefects professional football club.

Although his weighty proportions had prevented him from playing football in his youth, he was, nevertheless, swept up not only in the game's excitement and passion, but also in its profound cultural teachings. From his earliest days as a fan, he had developed an analytical enthusiasm for the sociological ramifications of the sport. It was his ultimate goal to give the privileged, respectable people of capital city a team to which they could relate. A team rich in tradition, with old-world ties that instilled a certain aristocratic arrogance, a team that reflected the 'attitude' of the Porteño oligarchy, unlike those that catered to the masses in districts such as Boca and Avellaneda. When his floundering, old school team suddenly became available for purchase, it provided the wealthy elitist with a chance to make a lifelong fantasy into a reality. The Newton's Prefect Football Club had the proper pedigree, even for a snob like Astor Gordero.

Stories of the man's immoderate and excessive indulgences were often the topic of discreet gossip at high society gatherings. Discreet was the key word, for no one spoke publicly of Astor Gordero in a derogatory manner without suffering the consequences.

There were rumors of his dark side, whispers that he embraced his ancestors' code of honor to the point of having to seek satisfaction if his name was besmirched. To that end, paid mercenaries usually acted as his angels of retribution, for Astor Gordero was incapable of forgetting a personal insult. Moreover, he would not tolerate failure of any kind. Once he set his mind to achieving a desired goal, the man could not be deterred, even if it meant using the most unscrupulous of means. And heaven help anyone who stood in his way!

Many people actually hated the man, but those who did were careful to hide their feelings and hold their tongues in public. Life in Argentina was fraught with hidden dangers, and to speak out against a man of such influence and power could very easily bring disastrous results.

El Hombre Gordo 'The Fat Man' was one whom it was better to befriend than to antagonize, even if that friendship was purely superficial.

A course of cheers and bravos for Gordo's protectors rang through the bus, accompanied by much back slapping and hand shaking. The residual effects of such lavish praise from a man as well connected as Astor Gordero had not been lost on Estes Santos. He was well aware of The Fat Man's propensity to cosset those whom he thought warranted his attention. Many a career had been accelerated by a simple well-placed word from this porcine dealmaker.

Perhaps now the one thing that the minor league manager craved above all else would be within his grasp at last. But Estes Santos' sixth sense told him that it would be folly to impatiently seek a reward under the present circumstances. He must bide his time for the right opportunity to state his case to El Hombre Gordo. Good things could be derived from Gordero's appreciation and attention in due course. Until then, he would enjoy his newfound celebrity and the fruits that his actions of this day had borne him.

Santos and his team captain did not have to wait long for certain of those fruits to come into bloom. The Prefect supporters soon arrived at the Córdoba railway station and proceeded to embark on their special charter back to Buenos Aires. The station was heavily guarded by more soldiers whose officers quickly orchestrated the visitor's departure off the buses, through the station, and onto the waiting rail coaches. The two 'men of the moment' had traveled to Córdoba in normal tourist class railcars, along with the majority of their fellow Prefect supporters. But not Astor Armondo Luis Gordero. His personally customized coach had been attached to the rear of the train, affording Gordo and his cronies the ultimate in mobile comfort, luxury, and privacy.

Astor Gordero made sure that his two saviors stayed right by his side as they walked down the platform to the last car. His guests were in for "the train ride of their lives," he boasted. The Fat Man was in great spirits now that they were safely out of harm's way. Once Renaldo boarded the Pullman and entered its lavish interior, he was certain that Gordero had not been exaggerating. Before him, stretching two-thirds the length of the coach, spread a sumptuous buffet containing the finest delicacies Argentina had to offer. A fully stocked mirrored bar attracted his attention as well, for the moment the Prefect's chairman of the board came into view, two stewards beside it uncorked magnums of Dom Pérignon.

That popping sound was greeted by a hearty "Ola!" from Gordero, as glasses were quickly filled and passed first to the patron, then to his privileged guests. Their numbers had swollen to about ten men with the addition of the two new arrivals. Before Renaldo had even been offered a sample of the sweet nectar, something else caught his eye. Two of the most gorgeous women he had ever seen, resplendent in the sheerest of boudoir attire, pushed their way past him and embraced their gregarious host.

The trio's lusty gropes and wandering hands held the young boy spellbound. When the chairman had consumed his fill, he gestured for the señoritas to circulate amongst his amigos and make them feel at home. The Fat Man then headed directly for the buffet. Renaldo tried to make himself as inconspicuous as possible and retreated to the far rear of the coach. He knew that he would feel more comfortable back in the obscurity of tourist class, but there was no escaping Astor Gordero. The boy took a glass of champagne, resigned to his captivity. Estes Santos was quickly by his side.

"This is the most incredible thing I have ever seen!" he chortled.

"Yes, truly incredible," was Renaldo's half-hearted response.

"Those women are unbelievably beautiful, especially for putas."

'Yes, they certainly are an eyeful!' Renaldo thought to himself.

Up to this moment, all of his contact with prostitutes had been at a considerable distance. There had been times when he had passed them plying their trade on the streets of the capital, but he would just smile at their overtures and go about his business. He was not particularly worldly about the opposite sex, and Santos knew this well.

"Do not worry, Renaldo. I will take your turn with them if you like."

"Be my guest, Estes. I have had enough exercise for one day."

"That's my boy, save your strength for the soccer pitch."

The train lurched into motion, spilling a small quantity of Renaldo's champagne on the plush carpet. Embarrassed, the youngest of the imbibers tried to find something to soak up the stain.

"Don't worry about it, Renaldo." The booming voice of Gordo could be heard above the crowd. "I am sure that there will be many more stains before we reach Buenos Aires. I will simply replace the entire carpet, or perhaps we will have so much fun that I will have to replace the entire coach." Gordo laughed at his own frivolity. Nothing was going to put a damper on his celebration!

As the train sped through the dark Argentine night on its way back to the capital, a carnival of carnal delights was unfolding before the novice observer's eyes. Several of the youth's traveling companions had become very friendly with the two 'hostesses,' as Gordo referred to them. Individually and in groups, the victors were taking their spoils.

Renaldo sat quietly sipping his champagne on a sofa that was far enough away from the action so as not to be bothered. A reefer was lit and shared amongst the participants. It never made it to the young voyeur. He was fascinated to observe how each of the men acted. Some were ravenous with passion, others more theatrical, performing and demonstrating their technical proficiency for the appreciative audience.

Santos was in the thick of things, having the time of his life. Renaldo's coach had a reputation as a ladies' man, and now the player was seeing why firsthand. Before today, the two men had been strictly business in each other's company. Teacher and pupil, the knowledgeable veteran instructing the promising prospect in the intricacies of the game of football.

But there was a trait of Estes Santos' personality that he carefully guarded from public scrutiny, certain raw and animalistic urges to which he from time to time succumbed. The stories of his prowess with the gentler sex were legend despite his best attempts to stifle them. Renaldo hoped for his coach's sake that word of his present display of physical education would never transcend the walls of this rolling pleasure palace.

Estes was still in excellent condition at age thirty-seven. He had left the playing fields just one year earlier after a triumphant career as an Argentine first division goalkeeper. His thinning black hair was etched with grey now, but he still had a lithe physique that was the envy of men half his age. Yet the man's ultimate goal at this stage in his life had little to do with his physical qualifications. Estes Santos was consumed with procuring a managerial posting to a first division team now that he had retired from the on-field battles. Everyone knew what he could do physically. It was now time to prove that he possessed the technical capacity and mental fortitude to survive in the pressure-cooker atmosphere that was indigenous to premier division football. His actions back in that dead-end alley in Córdoba had certainly seemed to add value to his stock, at least in the eyes of Astor Gordero.

The Newton's Prefect Under Twenty-one team was considered a good point from which to launch a major league coaching career. Santos had attained the posting for many reasons, not the least of which was the fact that he had finished his playing days with the Prefect's second division club. The veteran goalkeeper had been one of Astor Gordero's first acquisitions after he gained control of the Prefect organization. Santos had earned three consecutive championship rings with River Plate in the premier division before his age made him available on the transfer market. Instead of taking the demotion as a slap in the face, Estes Santos had endeared himself to his new employer by shutting out the opposition in his last five games and elevating the Prefects into the first division after decades of relegation.

The keeper's good looks and swashbuckling style had made him the darling of the Argentine press for a time, but Santos had gotten his girlfriend pregnant when he was barely eighteen years old, and was by now quite thoroughly married with three children.

The press had focused on the 'perfect family man' angle when Estes was fêted after his amazing shut-out string. As an aspiring big league manager, he was smart enough to realize that it served him well to keep certain aspects of his personal life hidden very deeply underground. But the rumors of his voracious sexual appetite persisted, nonetheless. When questioned on those terms, he would simply smile demurely and respond,

"Can I help it if the señoritas are attracted to me? It is all fiction, the rest!"

Santos proved to be a fine teacher of the game, and he had helped Renaldo realize its subtleties from the opposing goalkeeper's point of view. He was a stern taskmaster with his charges, remaining detached from their emotional stream as a unit. But he possessed the uncanny ability to reach out and touch just the right nerve to ensure a player's peak performance. His warriors respected him immensely, for he was a champion in his own right, and he had made them champions in his first season at the helm. The Newton's Prefect organization was, at this moment, the most dominant force in Argentine football, and its former star goalkeeper knew exactly why. It all had to do with the shrewdness and perfect timing of the football club's guiding light, Astor Armondo Luis Gordero.

But everything had almost been lost that very afternoon. Estes Santos had arrived at the door of salvation within a split second of real tragedy. A chill swept over the manager every time his mind latched on to the reality of how vastly different the situation could have concluded back there in that fetid alley. Had either Gordo or his young captain been badly hurt by those maniacs, he would have been vilified rather than celebrated. The Fat Man could very well have been hung, drawn, and quartered by now, and then what would all his hopes for a favorable career word from Astor Gordero be worth? Absolutely nothing . . . for dead men are worthless!

Even worse things could have evolved because of the boy's circumstances. Santos was Renaldo's coach, his protector. The young player was a brilliant prodigy, with a bright football future before him. He was a musician and scholar as well. His safety on this 'enlightening expedition to a provincial capital,' words that he had spoken to convince Señora Florencia De Seta of the educational value of the outing, rested squarely on the coach's shoulders. Had he not gone out of his way to convince Renaldo's overprotective mother that her son would not be in the slightest bit of danger? And should any unpleasantness arise, that he would personally see to it that the boy stayed safely out of harm's way?

On this day, Estes Santos had been a terrible protector. The victory celebrations had gotten the better of him. He was totally unprofessional and certainly out of character for a man said to have nerves of cold steel. By the time he remembered to look to his charge, the boy was nowhere to be seen. Gordo's huge flag had brought them together again momentarily, but he had not waited to save The Fat Man's hide outside the stadium as his captain had. Estes Santos had run for his life and forsaken his sworn responsibility. All these thoughts swirled intermittently through his mind as he tried to suppress the guilt of his shortcomings in the arms and between legs of the two 'hostesses.'

Renaldo was both amused and shocked by the performance taking place only a few feet from where he sat in the rear of the luxurious coach. The boy had never imagined, let alone witnessed, such a lewd spectacle. He had no urge to partake of these particular pleasures, preferring, instead, to focus on his host, who was at that moment holding court at the end of the buffet table.

Astor Gordero took on the role of director for this extravaganza, but he never indulged in its antics. He sat in his special easy chair choreographing, cajoling, and encouraging the actors. A large plate of food rested constantly in his lap, and a steward stood attentively by his side, the Dom Pérignon at the ready. Every once in a while, his eyes would connect with Renaldo's across the room, and the older man would nod his approval of the festivities.

Gordero made sure that the boy was left in peace, the second steward warding off any enthusiastic reveler that ventured too near. Champagne, cigars, and repast were Renaldo's for the taking, but the events of the day still occupied most of his thoughts. He remembered the fear that permeated every ounce of his being when he and Gordero had been trapped in the alleyway. But try as he might, he could not recall the exact actions that supposedly saved their lives. Renaldo concluded that he had acted instinctively, much as any trapped animal would have to ensure survival and self-preservation. What had made his acts of valor so distinct and unusual was that he had saved the life of not just an ordinary football fan, but one of the richest, most powerful men in Argentina.

Surely Astor Gordero could have been seated in the president's box at Córdoba stadium, surrounded by dignitaries and other officials of similar status. To see his unmistakable form on the terraces with the Barras Bravas, the 'Brave Bold Ones,' was truly a puzzling sight.

"He prefers to rub shoulders with the real followers of the sport at important games such as this," Santos had explained. The power and passion of football could cut across all social and economic barriers. There on the terraces, wealth and social status meant nothing. A loud voice and a fearless constitution meant everything!

But Renaldo was not as presumptuous as Estes Santos. He felt certain that The Fat Man's gratitude would not extend a minute beyond the end of this entertaining train ride. They would be two forgotten heroes once they disembarked in Buenos Aires. That assumption was discarded forever when Astor Gordero waddled over to the couch were Renaldo continued to sit in the early morning hours.

"So, my newfound friend, are you enjoying yourself?" the chairman inquired. The boy nodded politely.

"Very much so, Señor Gordero. Especially the food and the floor show."

"I am glad that you decided to remain a spectator to all of this. I would have thought less of you, quite frankly, if you had joined in. A fine young man like you should always hold yourself above such public displays. It is all very amusing, of course, but I find it somewhat degrading in the end, very animalistic and messy. I guess that I will have to replace the carpet after all," he chuckled surveying the predawn dénouement.

"Our meeting is not by chance, Renaldo," The Fat Man continued. "As a matter of fact, I was the one who arranged for you and Santos to be here today. I had hoped to meet you personally and congratulate you on your fine season, but I hadn't anticipated the rather trying circumstances under which we became intimately acquainted."

Gordero spoke in a soft fatherly tone, a look of real concern planted on his moon-shaped face. He didn't wait for the boy to respond. Pointing his right index finger at his audience, he smiled warmly. "I know your family background. An illustrious history that helped shape modern-day Argentina. The general and your grandfather, what men of vision they were! I knew your father personally. He was a great surgeon." The tone of voice was suddenly remorseful, with just the right amount of profound respect thrown in. There was a pregnant moment of silence. "I have met your mother on several occasions. She is a cultured, beautiful lady! As for you, my sources tell me that you want to enter university next semester, that you stood at the top of your graduating class academically at Sir Isaac Newton. Well done!" Gordero clapped his hands in approval.

The two men sat silently for a brief moment as the chairman adjusted his position to lean closer to the young scholar.

"Of greater interest to me, however, is the fact that while you could still be playing schoolboy soccer, your level of proficiency in the sport has earned you the captain's band of our semiprofessional, under twenty-one team. Both your coaches and your fellow players have nothing but good things to say about you . . . unusual, for someone so young and wet behind the ears to achieve such positive accolades. On the whole, you've achieved quite a well-rounded list of accomplishments to date. Your mother must be very proud of you." The patron paused to let the compliments sink in.

"I am told that you have achieved all of this while still retaining your humility and your levelheadedness. That is a great asset! Men respect that, they will follow a man like you. I have seen today with my own eyes that you have a special ability to handle men in difficult situations. Keep your head about you and you should expect great things, my boy."

The chubby index finger jabbed the air in front of Renaldo's chest.

He felt uncomfortable listening to The Fat Man's praises and tried to tell his host several times that his actions did not deserve such attention. Astor Gordero would have none of it.

"I have watched you play the sport, Renaldo. That game against Racing Club in which you scored two goals and set up a third? A stunning performance! It was a shame so few people got to see it. But I did, and I haven't forgotten it either."

The rotund barrister turned his attention momentarily to the empty champagne glass in his left hand. The ever-present steward needed only a raised eyebrow as instruction to top the vessel up. When Gordero started to speak once again, his face was masked in a tight, serious expression.

"You are, no doubt, aware that the greatest sporting event the world has ever seen will take place in Argentina in six months' time. The generals and politicians that run this magnificent land want the World Cup to be Argentina's when it is over. Frankly, they will stop at nothing to appease their egos. In this case, that means a world soccer championship. To achieve that result, no stone will be left unturned to find the right players for our National Team. But in spite of the positive lip service the men at the top espouse, at the moment, things could hardly be in worse shape. Scandal, dissension, corruption . . . the men that are running the program are nothing but braggarts and blowhards! They have achieved nothing positive at all. They mouth optimism, but look at the record. Far too many losses on the field in warm-up games. The press is all over the team and its managers. Many of our best players don't even want to play for fear of getting caught up in this mess." A look of disgust shrouded Gordero's meaty face. He shook his head silently for several moments before his eyes once again brightened and he proceeded.

"There is, however, a movement afoot to straighten out the problems by bringing in Octavio Suarez as supreme manager in charge. It would be his job to clean house and start anew. I believe that you know Suarez, is that not so?"

Gordero had certainly caught Renaldo's attention once the topic had changed to the World Cup and Argentina's National Team. The whole nation was obsessed with the daily soap opera that was unfolding in the newspapers and on television. Even more urgent than the team itself was the infrastructure debacle. Would FIFA, the governing body of world soccer, even allow Argentina to stage the event? Construction of the major stadiums to be used was months behind schedule. The same could be said for the modern telecommunications facilities that would beam the games around the world. Adding salt to these internal wounds was the fact that Brazil had offered to stage the tournament should Argentina fail to meet its commitments by the appointed time. This was considered a slap in the face from a South American neighbor, and hostility toward the country to the north saw many effigies clad in the yellow jerseys of the Brazilian National Team burned in the streets. FIFA representatives were to arrive in Buenos Aires the following week to hand down their decision after a final inspection tour. The resulting chaos would be too horrible to imagine if the games were taken away from Argentina.

"Yes, I have taken clinics and trained under Señor Suarez. He has an excellent tactical knowledge of the game. I found him very inspiring," Renaldo recalled.

"He would not take the position of National Team manager when it was initially offered to him because of the interference he anticipated from the bureaucrats," Gordero continued. "I always thought that he was the only man who could do the job. Señor Suarez remembers you as well, Renaldo. He told me once that you play the game as if your head and your feet are connected as one."

The Fat Man held up his left index finger at the same time he said the word 'one.' Renaldo noticed the size of his entire hand for the first time. It was massive! The speaker then gently rested his palm flat on the boy's right thigh, placed his index finger on top of his middle finger, and then crossed his forth finger over top of the other two. He removed his hand from the boy's leg holding up three perfectly entwined fingers, his thumb holding down his crooked little finger.

"Head and feet perfectly connected as if one entity, perfectly connected!" The ham hock appendage continued to be displayed for the prolonged viewing of Gordo's captive audience.

"Renaldo, I want you to come and see me at my office. We can talk in private there about how I may be able to help you. These are dangerous times for timid men, my young friend. But danger brings opportunity to the courageous, the risk takers. I have seen how courageously you behaved today, and if you have the strength and the desire to be even more courageous, I can make great things happen for you! Do you have that strength and desire, Renaldo?"

An emotional wave swept over the boy, bringing tears to his eyes. It had been a long time since he had let his inner feelings come to the surface, but Gordero's fatherly demeanor had instilled in him such a sense of trust and security that Renaldo blurted out his deepest secret with gut-wrenching introspection.

"I have a mission, Señor Gordero, a mission that has never been revealed to anyone. It concerns my late father and something that I would like to achieve on his behalf, something that would bring pride to our family name. It is the reason I continue to play the game of football instead of concentrating one hundred percent on my studies. My mother has difficulty understanding my desire to play. I simply tell her that it's to stay in top physical condition, that it stimulates my mind as well, and she leaves me alone for a while. But it goes much deeper than that. It is for my father's memory, for his unfulfilled dreams."

Renaldo was trying desperately to regain his composure as the tears rolled slowly down his cheeks. He choked out his final few words as the older man held out a napkin to stem the saline flow.

"It is my dream to play for the National Team of Argentina in the World Cup one day, and yes, Señor Gordero, I can find the strength and desire to be courageous. If you can help me, I will not let you down!"

Astor Gordero held Renaldo's brimming eyes intently with his own. He was touched by the show of emotion. The lawyer felt as if he could have gone on talking to this fine young man for hours, but alas, Estes Santos staggered over to the couch and announced their imminent arrival in Buenos Aires. The patron was at first put off by this intrusion, but he was quick to remember that it was as much the actions of Estes Santos as those of young De Seta that were responsible for his still being among the living.

"Estes, I want you to bring Renaldo to see me this week, and we can discuss the future . . . a future that I hope will unfold to our mutual benefit. Here is my business card. I will inform my executive assistant to make sure that you get the first available appointment."

Gordero also gave the handsome athlete a card, just in case the obviously hungover Santos were to lose his, or fail to remember this conversation altogether. The Fat Man had no doubt that Renaldo De Seta would remember their conversation, and that the talented, sensitive youngster would pay him a visit . . . with or without Estes Santos.

The men said their good-byes on the station platform and took leave of each other just as the first rays of sunlight set the eastern horizon aglow. Renaldo then helped his coach to the taxi that would take them both home. Estes Santos had celebrated with too much abandon, and now he was paying the piper. His gait was an off-balance stagger as he made his way to the curbside taxi stand. The two men initially sat without saying a word as the black and yellow Fiat sped through the Sunday morning dawn. It was Santos who first broke the silence.

"Do you think he is serious about our meeting? I mean, really, why would such a powerful man want to talk to us about 'a future that will unfold to our mutual benefit'? There is nothing that we can do for him now. He is just leading us on. The clear light of dawn shines reality on my great expectations. Oh, well, such is life!" Santos sighed, resting his head against the leather upholstery of the cab's interior.

"I would not be so certain about that meeting never happening," the younger man responded. "I have a strange feeling about Señor Gordero. There was something about the way he talked to me. He sounded so sincere and frank. I am confident that we will, at least, be granted an audience with him."

"Oh, for youthful optimism!" snorted Santos. "The only audience I want now is with my bed. Those putas and that champagne were a lethal combination. I feel like shit!"

Estes looks as terrible as he must have feel, thought Renaldo. He wondered how a man could go home to his wife and family in such a state, for the residue of Estes' carousing was all over his face and clothes. But Estes Santos was a careful man. He instructed the cabby to let him off at the Newton Academy sports dormitory, where he could shower and change into the fresh clothes that he kept there for exactly such an occasion as this. The coach gave his captain an enthusiastic hug before stepping out of the cab, and made certain that the boy did not want to be accompanied home.

"If my mother were to lay eyes on you now, she would ban me from ever playing football again. What's more, she would do worse to you, Señor Santos."

"You are wise beyond your years, my captain. Now, not a word of what you have seen on this adventure must ever pass your lips, or I will make certain that it costs you more than just your football career." The smile on the older man's face contradicted his stern tone of voice.

"Adios, coach Santos. Make sure you call The Fat Man!" Renaldo called after him.

"From this day forth, I will refer to the gentleman as 'Señor Astor Gordero, my most benevolent benefactor,' at least until he refuses to see us. If that happens, I have names much worse than 'Gordo' to call him. I will talk to you tomorrow."

Finally the schoolboy was left alone to collect his thoughts. He sank back into the corner of the cab's rear seat, closed his eyes, and replayed the events of the past twenty-four hours in his overworked mind. No one would believe what he had seen and done, especially his mother. Heaven help him if she ever found out that he had been in the least bit of danger. But he was safe nonetheless, and would arrive home in one piece, on schedule.

Throughout the haze of his early morning recollections, the face of Astor Gordero kept coming to mind.

Fate works in strange ways, he reflected. *Or had Gordero really intended for us to meet all along, just as he had alluded to on the train?*

It really didn't matter now, the fact was that they had met. But an unanswered question lingered. Renaldo had the distinct impression that Astor Gordero, should he choose to acknowledge his debt to the two men that had saved his life, would ask for something substantial in return. The young player wasn't at all certain what that something might be, but The Fat Man just seemed like the type that never gave anything away for free.

"Head and feet as one," he mumbled, somewhat amused. *Had Octavio Suarez really said that about him?* Renaldo looked down at his right hand which was resting limply on his thigh. He tried several times to braid his fingers the way the chairman had.

"Head and feet as one."

"Qué?" the cabby responded.

"Oh, nada. Nothing," Renaldo shot back.

Finally, out of sheer frustration, he arranged his fingers in the crisscross pattern with the help of his left hand. Even that took several attempts.

My head and feet might be as one, but my fingers have ten separate minds!

CHAPTER TWO

Florencia De Seta could see the yellow and black Fiat cab pull up to the front gate of Casa San Marco from where she sat at her desk in the second-floor study.

She had barely slept. The news of the soccer riots in Córdoba had transformed her mildly fretful demeanor into sheer panic. She tore from the desk and was downstairs and out the front door in mere seconds.

As she flew through the casa, she screamed to her eldest son, "Lonnie, get up! Get up! Your brother is home."

Renaldo had just dispatched the taxi when he turned to face his mother, who was opening the large wrought iron gate. She was fumbling with her crucifix and reciting her personal thanks to the Almighty as she ran to embrace him.

"Hail Mary, full of grace, the Lord is with thee. Blessed art thou among women and blessed is the fruit of thy womb, Jesus. "

"Mama, what's the matter? Is someone ill?"

"Yes, I am sick, sick in the head for letting you go to that godforsaken place. It has been all over the television and newspapers. People were killed and injured. They said the train to Buenos Aires had to leave half the Prefect supporters behind or it wouldn't have made it out of Córdoba at all. Lonnie and I haven't slept all night. That Estes Santos! I will have his head if you were in the slightest bit of danger. You look tired. Are you all right? Anyway, come inside and we will talk." Florencia De Seta hugged her youngest son.

"I am fine, Mama, nothing happened. As a matter of fact, the train ride back home was quite educational, and I met some very interesting people."

"Football scum, hoodlums, and no-goods were the only people I saw on television last night!" Once they were in the front door, Florencia called for hot coffee and fresh orange juice to be brought to the patio, where they would sit in the early morning warmth.

It was going to be a hot, humid day, and this would be the best time to take in the garden's splendor. The chirping of the birds and the beautiful, full scent of the fruit trees reassured Renaldo that he was truly home as he sank into one of the overstuffed patio chairs. Now all he had to do was survive the Florencia inquisition.

"Alright, I want to know everything! So start!"

"Well, our team won! It was a good game, very exciting. Gitares scored three goals and . . . "

"I don't care about that rubbish! I want to know about the riots. Did you see them? How close were you to them? Did anyone you know get hurt?"

It was Florencia De Seta's nature to get right to the point. When she was serious, there was no getting around her. She was as tenacious as a pit bull until she was satisfied that the truth had been spoken.

Renaldo realized that he had better come up with a good story right away or his mother would pry the truth from him eventually. Heaven forbid!

"Yes, Mama, I saw the riots, but only from the other end of the stadium. The soldiers were everywhere to protect us. All the people that got hurt were Córdobans who were mad that their team lost. Our group was escorted out of the stadium and into special buses by the soldiers. We were on the train when most of the trouble was still going on, I guess, but I really can't be certain. Anyway, here I am, and I am fine! See, no marks or bruises!"

He couldn't help but think how pretty she looked sitting in the soft morning sun. The adventurer noticed that his story was working on her, for she was visibly less tense. Her facial features had become soft and delicate with the waning of her anxiety, and the return of her color and sparkle convinced the wayward son that he would pass her test without further provocation. He focused on her coiffeur as the two sat silently during a pause in their dialogue. She always wore her jet black hair tucked up in a neat braid with a colorful hair piece if she were receiving guests or venturing beyond the walls of the casa. It was long and naturally straight, without a hint of grey these forty-seven years, and when she wore it down, as it was at this moment, to Renaldo, she was, without doubt, the most beautiful woman in the world.

His thoughts of beauty and tranquility ended abruptly when Lonnie De Seta strolled wearily through the patio door.

"So, little brother, did you beat up any Córdobans for me? It looked like a lot of fun!" A well-placed jab to Renaldo's upper arm prompted mock fisticuffs between the two brothers until Florencia had had enough and called for quiet.

"You will both accompany me to mass this morning to help me pray for your misguided souls. I want you ready in one hour."

Disbelief and despair filled the siblings' faces.

"Mama, I have hardly slept all night, and after what I just went through I thought that . . . " Renaldo wasn't allowed to finish.

"You just told me everything was fine. 'Educational,' didn't you say? One hour!" With that she was gone, and in her wake she left two dumbfounded sons.

"Thanks a lot, hotshot! First she keeps me up all night, thinking you had been killed, and now I have to give up the better part of my Sunday to pray for your misguided soul?" Lonnie chided.

"I think your soul is more misguided than mine, big brother. What were you doing at home on a Saturday night in the first place?"

"Celeste has her final term papers to mark by Monday, so I was a gentleman and left her alone. I was at a movie with some of the guys for awhile, but when I saw the papers on the street about the riots in Córdoba, I begged off home. I knew Mama would be frantic if she was watching the news. So, what really happened up there? Did you take any scalps?"

"Like I told Mama, it was all very calm. But I did meet an interesting man on the train ride home. Have you ever heard of Astor Gordero?"

"Who hasn't heard of Gordero? How on earth did you get hooked up with the likes of him?"

"He is a one-man spectacle. I guess I just helped ensure that the spectacle would be around for awhile longer. Estes and I were in the right place at the right time. We got to ride home from Córdoba in his private rail coach. It was quite the ride! Anyway, I need to shower and change for mass. I will tell you the whole story later."

As Renaldo started to make his way toward the patio door, he was met by Oli, Casa San Marco's native Indian housekeeper. She was carrying a silver tray loaded with a pitcher of fresh orange juice, a carafe of steaming coffee, and a basket of pastries. Her face lit up when she saw the younger brother.

"Señor Renaldo, thank heaven you are home safe. Your mother, she worry so much last night."

"I'm fine, Oli, just fine. But I could use some of your coffee right now. Didn't sleep much last night . . . I guess none of us did."

Oli placed the breakfast tray on the table and poured both brothers large cups of coffee, Renaldo's black, Lonnie's with milk. "Café con leche," the elderly lady proclaimed handing Lonnie his cup. She had worked for the De Seta family for over thirty years, like her mother before her. Oli's husband, Olarti, was the resident houseman, chauffeur, and gardener. The housekeeper knew every whim and fancy of the De Seta brothers and understood the boys' innermost desires even better than their mother.

"Thank you, Oli. Would you please take the tray up to Mama's bedroom? She may want something. We are all going to mass in an hour." Renaldo grabbed a warm croissant and juggling his coffee, slid through the door into the house.

"Anything else for you, Señor Lonnie?"

"No, thank you, Oli, I am fine." With that, she picked up the tray and disappeared into the dark depths of the casa. Lonnie sat alone in silence, his head back, catching the rays of sun on his unshaven face.

At twenty-two, Lonnie De Seta cast a formidable shadow over the garden where he sat. He was six foot three inches tall, weighing two hundred and thirty-five pounds. His torso was solid muscle, built up by years of lifting weights and training for his passion, rugby football. He was ruggedly handsome, with strong features and straight black hair worn much shorter than his brother's.

He was now in his third year of political science studies at the University of Buenos Aires and had been a great success for the university rugby team. He had an aggressive, almost mean streak in him, and he preferred to mix things up in the scrum trenches, as opposed to playing the back positions that his coaches wanted him to play.

Lonnie would more likely than not face opponents much larger than himself, but he rarely surrendered an inch of turf. His strength was amazing. His first two seasons at university, he played every position on the field. He became somewhat of a legend on campus, his athletic prowess matched equally by his amorous adventures. Lonnie's tall, muscular physique coupled with his dark good looks meant that this De Seta brother was seldom without an entourage of admiring señoritas nearby.

His coaches noticed the changes in Lonnie before anyone. By the start of his third season, he didn't seem to have the same drive or spirit for the game. He was giving up so much ground in the scrums that they moved him to fly half permanently. Even there, he seemed uninspired, passing off the ball more and more frequently. He started being late for practice, and whenever there was a break in their training, Lonnie was always involved in some heated political discussion. The coaches tried to tell him that he was taking his political science courses too seriously, that he should leave politics to the politicians and concentrate on his rugby game, but it was no use.

The end of the season came early for Lonnie when he was thrown off the team for starting a fist fight with one of his own teammates after practice one day. Unfortunately, the player that he beat up was the son of one of the junta's more prominent generals. It was in the best interest of the university that the incident be resolved to the satisfaction of the general and his son, thus, Lonnie De Seta's rugby career came to an abrupt end.

The strange thing was that none of this embarrassment mattered anymore to Lonnie. He had found something much more important to him now than rugby. That was just a game. Child's play. There were far more relevant matters taking place at the University of Buenos Aires in the spring of 1977.

One of them was the political awakening of many of the upper-middle-class students to the anarchy of successive dictators and military juntas. Another was the rape of the Argentine economy in favor of an ever-expanding military. A third was the escalated suppression of leftist and liberal expressions. But more than anything else, there was Celeste Lavalle.

He had met her as his tutorial leader in a course dealing with the Argentine foreign trade deficit. She was a graduate student from San Miguel de Tucumán, a beautiful city situated in the northern foothills of the Andes Mountains. She had completed her preliminary courses at the Tucumán University and had come to Buenos Aires to research trade factors for her thesis.

Despite her small stature, standing barely five feet tall, she took control of the tutorial group from the first day. Celeste Lavalle placed her cards squarely on the table right from her opening address to the tutorial students. Her passionate speech on the legacy that future Argentines would inherit if the economy was not shifted away from military largess opened many eyes for the first time.

"More butter, many less guns!" she had said that first class.

Lonnie listened to her in awe. Whether she spoke the truth or not, just espousing such views was very risky anywhere in Argentina these days. You never knew who your fellow students were, and the police had been known to sneak plainclothes officers into any situation that might become a breeding ground for dissident opinions. Student informers were frequently paid to provide information on individuals, groups, or courses that were not sympathetic to the junta's right-wing doctrine.

Professors had disappeared from the campus without a trace. Certain vocal students would suddenly have to drop out for 'financial' or 'family' reasons. There was an undercurrent of suppression running throughout every facet of university life. That made Celeste Lavalle's opinions even more daring, and Lonnie was amazed at the passion that those opinions evoked in this fiery, self-assured woman.

But it was more than words and thoughts that stirred the big athlete. This señorita had a beauty that Lonnie had seen in few women. Different, hard to describe. Nothing like the multitude of mindless coeds that he had spent so much time with over the past two years.

Celeste's was more a natural beauty. Lonnie would come to say a 'provincial beauty,' unlike the made-up girls of Buenos Aires. Her cropped black hair and dark complexion were complemented by the saddest brown eyes that he had ever seen. The student knew at once that those eyes held secrets, deep mysterious secrets.

Celeste had made much of the fact that she had come from the provinces and promised to give the Porteños more than just their usual navel gazing view of the problems facing modern-day Argentina. Lonnie was certain after that first tutorial that she would endeavor to do so in an outspoken, candid manner . . . if she were not stopped by the authorities first!

Their relationship had started testily, with Lonnie often defending what Celeste called the 'Porteño Bourgeoisie' attitude toward solving the problems of the Argentine people. It did not take her long to discover that Lonnie De Seta came from a privileged background, and she often used Lonnie as her pet example of how the ruling and advantaged classes were responsible for the current economic and moral bankruptcy of the nation.

At first, the verbal sparing infuriated Lonnie, and had the tutor been a man, he would have simply throttled him with his fists. After that, he would either have sought out another course, or waited for a replacement tutor. But these tactics could not be employed with Celeste Lavalle, and the more Lonnie was forced to debate and listen, the more his understanding and admiration for this 'Tigress from Tucumán' grew. He had never known any woman to have such strong feelings about politics, and he would find himself captivated by her as she spoke in their tutorials, wondering if she carried her passions as far as the boudoir.

The Porteño would stay after class was over, often engaging in heated debate, until one or the other of them would storm off in disgust. He was obsessed by her spirit, and she knew it. Finally, in desperation to take their relationship to another level, Lonnie asked his tutor if she would accompany him to an underground lecture by one of the nation's leading trade union leaders, a man who happened to have a huge student and left-wing following.

She had refused at first, citing the awkward relationship between teacher and pupil, but had finally succumbed from a combination of curiosity and sheer frustration over his relentless pleadings.

The speaker, a thinly disguised Marxist from Rosario named Raphael Squeo, had to be spirited in and out of Buenos Aires to avert arrest for a number of outstanding warrants. These related to what the junta referred to as 'provocative activities and conspiring to commit insurrection against the state.'

The lecture was held in the basement of one of the undergraduate dormitories in University City. Heavily armed security teams were very much in evidence, but what seemed incredible to Lonnie was the fact that they were comprised of his fellow students. He knew many of these gun-toting scholars personally. Had the police or military decided to raid the proceedings, the outcome could have been a blood bath. He was also shocked at the passionate response from the audience to the rhetoric of Señor Squeo.

Much of what the man proclaimed to be the only path to an enlightened Argentina would have meant the downfall of the upper-middle classes. That would include the family and the fortune of Lonfranco 'Lonnie' De Seta. He sat in silence trying to take the pulse of the gathering. Lonnie knew that he was not the only Porteño present that came from an established, well-to-do family. He had seen many others, both young men and young women. The former rugby player watched their enthusiasm and vocal encouragement peak as Squeo skillfully built his ninety-minute speech to a crescendo.

At the conclusion, everyone was standing and applauding, stomping their feet and whistling. It seemed like a football pep rally, with Squeo carried from the room on the shoulders of his supporters.

He preaches pure anarchy! Lonnie thought to himself. It seemed to him that the overall theme of Squeo's lecture was that 'Argentina must be ruled by the will of its common people, with free elections. This must be achieved by any means possible, even civil disobedience and violence!'

That could not be accomplished without even more retaliatory violence on the part of generals who currently controlled the military, and therefore, the country. It was a vicious circle that just seemed to perpetuate itself, recurring every few years with a different cast of characters.

Lonnie was relieved to find no military police at the university that evening as they walked to his car. The audience had been asked before the lecture began to disperse as quickly as possible, so that the location of the event could remain secret and secure for future use. The crowd seemed to be heeding those wishes.

Once they were alone in his car, Lonnie finally sought out a reaction from his learned companion. He was shocked at her diatribe.

"That man knows nothing about what is best for this country! He is a fool and a coward. He has never killed anyone in the name of his revolution! All he does is talk and line his pockets. No one asked him how much he is paid by the unions to stir up unrest, or how much he takes under the table from the junta to keep things peaceful. He is playing both sides against the middle, and his bank account is the middle! We have had dealings with him in the past, and I tell you, the man is a snake!" She sat back forcefully against the seat and caught her breath. "And what must you think, mon petit bourgeoisie, about a man that would take away your heritage, your fortune, and your family's good name? You can't have me believe that you want these people running Argentina the way that they aspire to. They are dreamers, men who do not act except in speeches. Where I come from, we let our actions do the talking."

It was true, of course. All of Argentina was aware of the destruction and havoc that the Perónista guerrilla group, the Montoneros, had wrought, not only in their home base of Tucumán Province, but also right in the heart of Buenos Aires itself. Murders, kidnappings, extortions, and outright firefights with the army had produced a death toll running into the thousands. It all seemed so distant to Lonnie, unless, of course, a bomb exploded in Buenos Aires or a local politician or general was abducted and murdered. Then, at best, it was just a quickly forgotten news headline. But that attitude had changed from the moment he met Celeste. She had succeeded in filling his head with doubt. Doubt about his lifestyle, his family, his country, and also about his prowess with women.

He was certainly not used to the cool aloofness with which Celeste deflected his advances. Other women, they were his for the taking. But not this one. This one drove Lonnie to distraction!

He found himself laying awake at night thinking of political arguments that would impress her in the next day's tutorial. Even his mother had noticed the change in him, proclaiming at the dinner table one night that "Lonfranco has lost his appetite because he is in love."

Following Squeo's dramatic oration, the student had dropped his tutor off at her apartment building with a formal handshake and a thank-you. But something deep inside his being forced him to call out to her impetuously before she disappeared inside.

"What do you want me to do?"

Celeste remained on the stoop of her building staring at him for several seconds, then disappeared without saying a word. Lonnie slammed his fist into the hood of his car.

"Damn, that woman is driving me out of my mind."

No one could have been more surprised than he was when Celeste asked him to have coffee with her after their next tutorial. They had sat and talked for hours in a café near her apartment, and to Lonnie's delight, she did not want to talk politics. She wanted to know about his family and his background and promised to keep the biting comments that she would often make in class out of their conversation. The señorita seemed truly interested in him for a change, and the soft night air along with several carafes of wine made for relaxed, expressive dialogue. When it was time to go, she did not hesitate to ask him back to her flat so that he could "borrow a copy of a book by her favorite left-wing author," as she so coyly put it.

It would be a seduction unlike any Lonnie had ever experienced. Celeste set the mood and controlled the flow of events. With candles lit and soft guitar music on the stereo, they smoked a marijuana joint that Lonnie had been carrying, followed by a bowl of Nepalese hashish. Celeste revealed that the hash had been a present from a student looking to better his grades.

Lonnie's skin was on fire with pent-up lust. When Celeste brushed his arm with her fingers while handing him the hash pipe, he thought that his body would explode. She sensed his arousal and let her hand fall to his inner thigh. Slowly she began to trace the outline of his quickly growing manhood with her fingers.

She leaned forward and kissed his lips. Unbuttoning his shirt, she swiftly ran her tongue down his chest until she was able place his nipple in her mouth and bite it. When he did not shy away from the sweet pain, she continued to playfully explore his hidden secrets.

She orchestrated their coupling from start to finish, bringing Lonnie to heights of ecstasy he hadn't known existed. He was shocked that they fit together so well, considering their disproportionate size. She seemed to meld to him like a second skin.

Her passion knew no boundaries, and in this tutorial of the flesh, she exposed him to new horizons for the first time. When they were spent, she did not demand that he leave. Instead, she asked if he was hungry, then prepared a huge feast of 'vermicelli mixto,' a pasta dish with pesto and tomato sauce. Fresh green salad and hot bread were joined by a new bottle of Chianti. Lonnie was convinced that this was the closest he had ever been to finding contentment in his life as they ate and talked and snuggled.

When the aggressive athlete took too much liberty with his roaming hands, the object of his affection would hit him with the wooden spoon she used to stir the tomato sauce. The telltale red splotches on Lonnie's face and torso finally convinced him that this woman was totally in control of the situation, and that he had better wait for an invitation to continue his advances.

Over the next two days, they stayed entwined with each other, body and soul. It was Celeste, however, that set their course and pace. They would eat, talk, make love, and then repeat the whole routine again at her discretion.

Lonnie did not mind, for he had totally succumbed to her knowledge and power. He had never felt so helpless, yet so connected to any woman in his life. Sometimes they spoke of politics, but mostly of themselves, their backgrounds, their families, their dreams.

She was the descendent of French immigrants who settled in Tucumán Province as sugar cane sharecroppers when the railway expanded into the northwest region of the country in 1875. That same rail line opened the province to trade markets in Buenos Aires and beyond, and Celeste's ancestors became well-to-do sugar merchants.

Tucumán had been one of the first settled regions in the country, with the Spanish Conquistadors arriving from Peru in 1553. The cities in this region served as livestock and agricultural centers to support Peru's nearby silver mines. The city of San Miguel de Tucumán rose to such prominence that the first national assembly representing all regions of what was then considered to be Argentina met there in July of 1816. These representatives declared their independence from the corrupt regime of Ferdinand the Seventh of Spain and established the united provinces of the Rio de la Plata.

This was easier contemplated on paper than it was to achieve in fact. A central Cabildo or 'municipal council' was set up in Buenos Aires, but several disgruntled provinces, including modern-day Paraguay, Bolivia, and Uruguay, quickly gained independence in a series of bloody battles. Spanish loyalists in the Tucumán region fought from bases inside Peru, using terrorist tactics to keep both the military and the local population wary of this new independence.

This in many ways, Celeste explained, was the birth of the continuing antigovernment movements that seemed to flourish in Tucumán province. The cost in human lives and suffering over the last one hundred and fifty years had been immeasurable. From pitched military battles to murder, extortion, and kidnapping, nothing had changed up to the present. There was always a new cause to champion and fight for, and thus, to die for.

It wasn't so much to attain independence or autonomy from Buenos Aires. It was more to achieve a sharing of the national wealth along the populist philosophy. But for those innocents caught in the deadly political crossfire, it didn't matter in the slightest what the current cause was.

Celeste's family had made and lost several fortunes as a direct result of this turbulent history. Scores of her relatives had been arrested and executed or had simply disappeared. Everyone tried to lead as normal a life as possible on a day-to-day basis, but there seemed to be a constant undercurrent of uneasiness due to the likelihood of impending flare-ups.

Lonnie was captivated by the story, but every time he would delve for current family information, Celeste would skillfully shift the conversation to his roots.

He had learned that her parents were retired and living on their country estate, some hours from San Migel de Tucumán. Her two brothers, one older, one younger, were running what was left of the family export business.

The student also received some insignificant facts about his lover's undergraduate studies at the local university, but further information was not forthcoming. Lonnie was too much under her spell to push the point, and subsequently, found himself talking about his ancestors with more feeling and emotion than he had ever done before.

With the gentle encouragement of his tutor, Lonfranco Ernesto De Seta painted the tableau of his family's history in Argentina with a graphic, insightful brush.

CHAPTER THREE

My paternal grandfather and namesake, Lonfranco Guissepe De Seta, arrived in Buenos Aires in 1898 as a fifteen year-old immigrant from Livorno, Italy. He was alone and had only the name of an old family friend to contact."

With those words, Lonnie embarked on a journey through his family's history in Argentina, a history that would take several hours to relate.

He went on to explain how his great grandfather, Alberto De Seta, had shipped his young son off to establish a base in Argentina, with the intention that the rest of the family would follow later if the reports from 'the land of silver' proved promising.

Alberto De Seta had been a traveling porcelain and dry goods merchant/ importer working the northwestern provinces of Italy, with Florence as his main market. The constant travel had taken its toll on Alberto. In spite of the help of his two sons, Lonfranco and Pietro, both of whom he conscripted into the business as soon as they could count money, his health and vitality had failed him.

Seeking a new frontier for his family in retirement, he had sent his eldest son across the Atlantic to establish a foothold for the future. This was not an uncommon practice in Italy at the time. Young Lonfranco would often sit down by Livorno's bustling port, watching the tramp steamers carrying deck loads of his excited countrymen off to the adventure of a lifetime. It was with great enthusiasm that the youth awaited the day that he could be one of those men on the steamer deck, waving and blowing kisses to adoring, tearful relatives below.

That day came in the fall of 1898. Alberto had told the boy that this was the best time to go, for it would be spring in Argentina, and the prospects for work would be much improved. He gave his son the name of a prominent Italian builder in Buenos Aires as a contact. This wealthy gentleman had been a longtime customer of the elder De Seta before immigrating to Argentina.

That information and a few gold coins were all that Lonfranco De Seta had at his disposal to establish a foundation in the land his family aspired to adopt. The boy would have no way of knowing as he stood on the deck of his westbound steamer that none of his loved ones would ever join him in the promised land.

The passage to Argentina was pure hell, with food and sanitary conditions at an intolerable level. Several passengers died outright from disease or malnutrition. Others simply disappeared, jumping overboard to end what seemed like perpetual sea sickness and claustrophobia.

Lonfranco was young and strong, however, and able to endure the first of many hardships he would encounter on his journey to success in the new world. When he finally disembarked on Argentine soil, some four weeks after his departure, he was shocked to find that Señor Pugliese, who was to be his mentor, had died several months earlier and all his businesses sold or terminated. Pugliese's widow had been aware of the communication from Lonfranco's father, but was in no position to offer any assistance, except for the location of a cheap immigrant hotel.

She did mention that there was a lot of construction going on in the well-to-do 'Palermo' section of Barrio Norte, where ambassadors, generals, and the elite of Buenos Aires society were settling and building palatial homes.

Lonfranco was able to find an inexpensive room that first night in his new country. He was thankful that his homesick sobs of anguish could not be heard over the snoring of the dozen or so men with whom he shared his cramped space on the floor. The next morning, the boy ventured off on his own at daybreak, anxious to seek out whatever employment was to be had in this new land that he was forced to embrace.

The sights, the sounds, the smells . . . they all bombarded his senses. More than anything though, it was the humidity that caught him unprepared. His heavy woolen fall clothes were drenched with perspiration within minutes. Nevertheless, his spirits were buoyed by youthful curiosity. There was a newness to the city that was not to be found in any part of Italy that he had traveled.

The similarity of Spanish to his native tongue made communication with the Porteños relatively easy. Within a few hours, he had traveled by lorry and by foot deep into Barrio Norte, where he finally rested at the edge of an immense, open, green space.

One quick inquiry revealed that what he was gazing at was the Jardin Zoologico, or Buenos Aires zoo. The park stretched well beyond the zoological buildings, however. Lonfranco was told by a helpful passerby that what he saw before him was Parque Tres de Febrero. It encompassed over ten thousand acres of land. Along with the zoo, it contained a state-of-the-art race track with grandstands, polo fields, several lakes connected by navigable streams, playing fields, botanical gardens, and picnic areas. He was informed that it was the center of the universe here in Buenos Aires on the weekends, when thousands of Porteños would flock to its soothing, open expanses.

Another local told the boy that construction gang foremen often sought day laborers at the Plaza Italia, not far from where he now stood. Lonfranco was heartened to find that the plaza's dominant feature was a statue of Garabaldi, the famous Italian patriot. To his delight and relief, most of the fifty or so men that had congregated at the base of the statue were from his homeland. Each was after the same thing. Work!

He didn't have to wait long to learn how the system operated. As soon as a prospective employer announced his arrival in the plaza, every man went to great lengths to make sure that he was noticed. They would surge around the foreman, calling out their given names and attesting to their physical strength and willingness to work. Often they were beaten back by overseers that the foreman had brought along, both for his own protection from the would-be workers' enthusiasm and also to have some brutal fun at the expense of these displaced peasants.

Most of these 'bosses' had a keen eye for strength and stamina, and often the old or the frail would be passed over in favor of younger, fitter prospects.

At fifteen, Lonfranco already stood in excess of six feet, and his tight, angular body was well muscled as a result of his labors for his father over the past eight years. His straight black hair was slicked back with pomade and despite his tortuous journey overseas, he looked as robust and fit as any man in the plaza.

Jimmy Shaunaker, the big Irish foreman, must have thought so as well, for he had chosen the youth to join his pick and shovel brigade with a wave of his baton. The half-dozen men that were selected bid farewell to their less fortunate compatriots and were marched out of the plaza.

Lonfranco marveled at the size of the homes as they wound their way through streets bustling with tradesmen, merchants, and well-to-do residents. Each estate was surrounded by a high wall or fence, often affording only a glimpse of the residence and grounds. The styles and architecture varied dramatically from lot to lot, Italianate beside French colonial, beside English-style tutor. Lush gardens and fountains could be seen in the front courtyards of many. *Perhaps one day . . .* Lonfranco thought to himself.

Finally, the procession came to a halt in front of a large vacant lot on Calle Arenales. Tools were issued to the newcomers, and they were told to jump down into the excavated hole and take instructions from the line boss.

Tucho Ortiz was not a man that Lonfranco would enjoy taking orders from, for his methods and his demeanor were as ugly as his face. The work was backbreaking and relentless, with only a half hour break for lunch. Each man was assigned an area to dig. If their progress was insufficient, Tucho's baton, a larger version of Shaunaker's, would come crashing down on his backside accompanied by a stream of invectives.

Lonfranco made sure that he kept up a favorable pace, even though his hands were becoming swollen and blistered. He was able to make it through his first day without facing Tucho's wrath, and to his delight, he was asked back for the next morning with a promise of long-term employment if he made it through his first week. He collected his pay and set out to find good work gloves and bandages with a noticeable spring in his step.

Despite the severe condition of his hands, he completed his first week as a common laborer by keeping his mouth shut, his eyes and ears open, and his shovel constantly moving. Many of his co-workers were not as fortunate, often being physically expelled from the job site with harsh words or even a beating by Tucho and his underlings. The conditions were barely above slave labor, but there were always men anxious to take the place of anyone who fell into Tucho's disfavor.

They worked six days a week and rested on Sunday. Lonfranco had been asked by one of the married workers he had befriended to come for Sunday dinner, and he spent his most enjoyable evening to date in his new country at the small flat of Luigi Monza and his family.

Monza had been an immigrant laborer for almost three years, since arriving from southern Italy. His wife worked as a seamstress, and with their combined income, they were able to maintain a modest lifestyle. They were a fountain of knowledge for young Lonfranco, outlining local customs and habits, as well as recommending where to get cheap food, clothing, and lodging. The boy had found a good friend in the older, more worldly Monza, and he began to feel more secure and at ease about fulfilling his father's wishes than at any time since he had left Italy.

By the start of his fourth week on the job site, his hands had become tough and callused, his back strong and tanned. The foundation of the mammoth home was being formed with concrete, and the work was proceeding at a frantic pace.

Tucho was ever-present, but he never bothered Lonfranco. As a matter of fact, the boy became one of the crew's most able workers, catching the eye of not only Shaunaker, but his peers as well.

The home that they labored on was being built for one 'General Figueroa San Marco,' a hero of the Indian wars whose victories had opened up the rich agricultural hinterland known as the Pampas for settlement.

General San Marco was by now the preeminent figure within both military and political circles in Buenos Aires. It was the ongoing use of his wide-ranging influence that allowed the current regime to stay in political power these last several years. Without support of a united military, no president had ever stayed in office more than a few months. San Marco's enormous popularity with the soldiers serving under him, as well as the romanticized folklore surrounding his combat heroics, made him exulted by the masses.

Figueroa San Marco, it could be said, was the most influential man in all of Argentina.

General San Marco would often visit the sight of his new home to make inspections and update or change architectural plans. There were no beatings or dressing downs when he was on the job site. Tucho and Shaunaker were on their best subservient behavior.

If the general was pleased with the progress, he would sometimes speak directly to the assembled workers, thanking them and giving them encouragement.

He is a man of regal bearing, Lonfranco thought.

Perhaps fifty years of age, the general was not an overly tall man, rather more bowlegged in posture from too many years of cavalry service. He was barrel-chested and powerfully built, however, with a large, hawk-like nose, piercing eyes, and a shock of full, grey hair.

More than anything, it was his voice that inspired respect. One could just imagine the booming baritone imploring his troop to 'push on, push on to glory!' in the face of overwhelming enemy odds. His talks always left the men with uplifted spirits. Even Tucho would be in a good mood for a few hours after the general's departure.

On the few occasions that work had fallen behind schedule due to excessive rains or the unavailability of certain material, the general would quietly walk off the sight. He would simply say to Shaunaker that he was sure that the foreman would have the building timetable back on track soon.

This mild reprimand was translated into escalated proddings and beatings by Tucho's bullies. They would drive the men incessantly, often late into the night. There was some talk among the workers of revolt on these occasions, but each man needed this work, and no one was willing to actually put his job on the line.

It was during one of Tucho's foul moods that Luigi Monza accidentally overturned a wheelbarrow of cement when its front wheel became bogged down in the mud. Tucho was there in an instant, flailing away at Monza with his baton while screaming insults and kicking the legs out from under the startled, apologetic Italian. The cruel man's gang now joined in, and Monza was picked up and passed from bully to bully, pelted, beaten, and insulted.

Lonfranco's blood was boiling. There was a ringing in his ears that he had never experienced before, and he stood, shaking with rage.

Unable to control himself, the youth lunged at Tucho, knocking him into the wheelbarrow and stumbling on into the mud. As the line boss tried to regain his balance and composure, three well-placed punches to the face sent the Argentine reeling backwards again, this time covered in his own blood.

Lonfranco turned to face the other tormentors. As they came at him one by one, he was able to dispatch each, in turn, into the muck. His co-workers cheered him on heartily, but offered no assistance. Even Monza was too stunned to come to Lonfranco's aid.

Tucho, now brandishing a knife as well as his ever-present baton, had maneuvered behind the boy and was about to strike a telling blow to his head when a pistol shot exploded a few feet away. The combatants stopped dead in their tracks.

There on a scaffold propped against cement blocks stood General Figueroa San Marco. He motioned for Tucho to drop the knife, but the overseer was so incensed at the loss of face he had suffered that he hesitated momentarily, gesturing at Lonfranco to continue their dance of death.

A second shot struck the gleaming blade just inches above the handle, carrying it out of the Tucho's grasp. San Marco ordered the bully and his followers off of his property at once, for he had witnessed the entire episode. Loud cheers from the workers greeted this news, and they ran to congratulate Lonfranco. They were silenced by the general's booming voice.

"Be still, you men! You there, the fighter. Come up here. I want to have a word with you." Lonfranco was now filled with dread, fearing the same fate as Tucho. Slowly he made his way to the scaffold.

"Hurry up, boy, I don't bite. Not unless I'm hungry, and luckily for you, I've just had my lunch."

Finally, the worker stood only a few feet from the general, and he launched into a course of humble apologies.

"Be quiet, young man! Is it your habit to always think with your fists, or do you have a brain in that handsome head of yours?"

Lonfranco stood there dumbfounded, unable to answer.

"That was a fine bit of work you just did there, trying to help your friend and all, but it would seem that you have left me without a line boss to finish my home. What do you expect me to do now?"

Lonfranco found his tongue instantly.

"The men will work better with that ogre gone, Señor General. We do not have to be beaten and insulted to work hard. It is for every one of us a great honor to work on the general's residence, and we will prove to you that Tucho and his likes will not be missed. Besides, Señor General, those men were stealing supplies from you. Back in Livorno where I come from, I used to help the dock foremen count cargo containers as they came off the ships. When I started to work here, I noticed that every morning there was less material on the site than the evening before. So I started to count stacks of lumber and cement blocks. I am very good with numbers, Señor General. Tucho and his men were thieves, as well as tyrants. They will not be missed here, believe me."

"Well, Mister Shaunaker, what do you think? Should we give them a chance to see if they can do it their way?" the general queried. "It's your neck on the line as well!"

"The boy is a good worker to be sure, General, and the other men all like him," Shaunaker confirmed. "Why don't we let him be the line boss for a few days and see what happens. In any event, it will take me some time to round up another group of overseers."

"Very well. You have five days, young man. Let's see if you and the others can pull things together and stay on schedule. I will be back for your report at that time, but from now on, my visits will be unannounced and spontaneous. Things seem to be much more revealing that way."

With that, he abruptly turned about-face and was gone. The men stood in silence, the image of the general in his crisp military uniform, polished knee-high boots, and ostrich-plumed kepi etched in their minds.

Shaunaker addressed them all, indicating that he would go along with the plan only if he could see progress. The men were more than glad to be rid of Tucho and his gang, and a new spirit was born on the job site that afternoon.

Lonfranco continued to do his share of the physical work, but he also encouraged and reassured the others in their toil. Not wanting to see the return of the likes of Tucho, each man seemed to find new enthusiasm and pride in his work. When General San Marco appeared on the site five days later, he was full of praise for Shaunaker and his 'lads.' He specifically asked about the young prize fighter whom he had promoted on his last visit.

"The boy seems to have a handle on things," the big Irishman assured the general. "The men are working harder than ever, probably out of fear of Tucho's return. Nevertheless, all is running smoothly, so I see no need to make a change. By the way, the boy was right about the stealing. I was about to make a report to you myself when the topic came up unexpectedly that day. I have placed an armed night guard on the site. There will be no further theft, General."

"Good, I will save some money not having to pay the likes of that rabble to steal from me. Get the boy. I want to talk to him."

Lonfranco had awaited the general's arrival with trepidation. If things were not to San Marco's liking, he felt sure that the burden would rest on his shoulders, and it would cost him his job.

"So what do they call you, young man?" the general inquired of the boy.

"Lonfranco Guissepe De Seta, Señor General."

"Shaunaker says that the men are working better than ever before, but do they not resent you for being so young? You have the face of an angel, but the body of prize fighter."

"They fear the return of the line bosses more than anything else, Señor General, and I think they are willing to accept any leader that does not use a baton on them for inspiration."

"You were the only one willing to stand up for your friend. You are a man of action, they saw that. Where do you come from? Is your family with you?"

"Livorno, Italy, Señor General. My family is all still there. They do plan to join me in Argentina as soon as possible though, within the year, I hope."

"Well, Lonfranco Guissepe De Seta, you have a way of attracting attention to yourself, it seems. You have caught my eye now, and I would hate to have you disappoint me. There will be no more line bosses for the time being, but both Shaunaker and I will be watching you! And my wife will be watching me, so make all possible haste to finish this damned house. She is extremely anxious to move here, and she is driving me crazy! So off you go, and keep your men working smoothly. Prove that you can do this for me, Lonfranco Guissepe De Seta."

The boy's feet hardly seemed to touch the ground as he walked back to the site where his co-workers waited for the news.

"No more Tucho!" he said with a broad grin as the men broke out into spontaneous celebration. "But it is up to us to keep it that way. We will be watched all the time, and every man must pull his weight. Does anyone have a problem with that?" Silence was all that could be heard in the cluster of men. "Good, now let's show them what we can do!"

Over the next few months, the Casa San Marco took shape in record time. Other contractors from all over the city came not only to inspect the beautiful structure, but also to see for themselves the unheard of process of building without strong-armed line bosses.

When most of the physical labor had been completed on the exterior, the majority of the workers were released in favor of skilled interior craftsmen. The general continued to employ Lonfranco as Shaunaker's assistant as a reward for his diligence in completing his tasks so efficiently. San Marco would frequently seek out the boy and ask him personally for his appraisal of various situations.

Their relationship grew to be somewhat like uncle and nephew, for the general had conceived four daughters but no sons. He would say to Lonfranco that he wished for just one son to carry on the family name and provide him with some manly companionship around his home.

"Surely you must get all the male company you want in the military?" Lonfranco had questioned.

"It is true that I am surrounded by men every day, but they are not my blood. They are not family. Unfortunately, my wife cannot have another child. I have fought my wars, and now it is time for me to enjoy the fruits of my labor with the ones I love. But as much as I love my wife and daughters, I can't teach them how to play polo or kick a football."

"Do you play polo, Señor General?" Lonfranco asked in amazement.

"Of course I do, my young friend. That is why we have moved to Palermo, to be close to the polo fields and the race track in the park nearby. I breed and raise both race horses and polo ponies. My polo team is one of the best on the continent."

As one of his chores back in Italy, Lonfranco had been charged with the care of his father's team of horses that pulled their goods to market. He had an intimate knowledge of the animals and had enjoyed riding alone in the open country every opportunity he could seize.

His father's team consisted of large draft animals suitable for pulling the heavily laden wagon that held their livelihood. He had never ridden a thoroughbred in his life and had never before witnessed a real polo match. Nevertheless, his love of horses endeared him to the general even more, and it was only a short time later that Lonfranco was invited to join San Marco and his family for a Sunday afternoon picnic and polo match.

Life for young Lonfranco would never be the same in his adopted country after that enchanted afternoon. The general greeted him with great warmth upon his arrival. He was introduce not only to the San Marco family, but to many of the city's prominent socialites as well.

Whenever the general brought his polo team to play, it was a major social event. Beautiful carriages with their formally attired drivers and footmen lined the perimeter of the playing field. Musicians wandered through the audience, playing any and all requests. The entire scene reminded Lonfranco of the carnivals he had attended with his father years before in Italy.

Señora San Marco, a poised and beautiful woman, was congenial and helpful in explaining the rules of the game to the young Italian. The general's four daughters were in attendance as well, in the company of their governess. The eldest daughter, Maria, caught the boy's eye right away. Her smile made his heart jump when they were finally introduced.

"Papa says that you are a good worker, very willing and smart, too. You must be something special, for he never asks his workers to come to social gatherings," she said as they shook hands.

"I have the greatest respect for your father, Señorita, as does everyone I have met in Buenos Aires," he replied.

"You are from Italy, is that so? I want to study abroad when I finish school here. I was thinking of the Sorbonne in Paris, but maybe you could tell me more about your country. I have read of its great art and architectural treasures."

She was seventeen years old, and Lonfranco could see that her mother's beauty had not been diluted one bit in the following generation. Flowing brown curls, deep hazel eyes, and a figure that was straining to be let loose from the confines of the formal white garden chemise. The total package had a telling effect on the young Italian's hormones. He struggled to keep his composure.

"I am not well educated' Señorita San Marco, but there are many things about Italy that I am sure you would enjoy seeing. I would be happy to tell you about them, at your convenience."

Maria was intrigued by this handsome, well-built youth. The boys that her father allowed to court her were mostly society or military men, usually much older than herself. Thank heavens the general did not prescribe to the prevailing habit of arranged marriages at an early age for his daughters. He wanted Maria, in particular, to see the world and spread her wings a bit before settling down. That was just as well, for his eldest daughter had a mind of her own and had never met a man that she was even mildly interested in.

She and Lonfranco talked for hours that Sunday afternoon, and the young lady was shocked to find that her new acquaintance had not celebrated his sixteenth birthday yet.

"You look nineteen or twenty at least," she demurred. "Are all the young men as mature as you back in Italy?"

"Only the ones that have to go to work at a young age. That forces you to grow up in a hurry!"

As captivating as Maria was, Lonfranco also had eyes for the fine horse flesh that was on display at the park that day. He had never seen such regal mounts, and the men that rode them displayed skill and courage, the likes of which he had never seen.

The game caught his fancy at once, and he sat there daydreaming that perhaps one day he would ride with the general's team. He liked the physical aspect of the sport. The melding of man and mount, the ability to ride like the wind, yet the necessity of having a sharp eye and a true stroke around the goal kept Lonfranco intrigued for the whole afternoon.

A chorus of 'bravos' greeted the general as he rode triumphantly to the podium to accept his team's prize ribbons. Lonfranco ran to his side and took the reins of his stallion as he dismounted.

"Well, my young friend, did I not tell you that I have the best team on the continent?"

"General San Marco, I am truly in awe. Such beauty and yet so physical."

"Would you like to try it, Lonfranco?" Without waiting for an answer, the general called for two new mounts to be brought up. A squire assisted the boy by taking his jacket and giving him a leg up.

"Now, let's see if you can stay on that animal!" The general laughed as he gave Lonfranco's mount a slap on the rump with the flat of his palm. The horse bolted off at once, the general following close behind.

The boy was able to rein in the steed almost immediately, and once he felt in control, he gave the animal its head with a few chortles and a soft kick to the flanks. Never had he been astride a horse with such agility and speed. The equine charger responded to his every command, and the two men raced all over the playing field, seemingly as one with their mounts. It was only the persistent urging of Isabella San Marco to join the family for luncheon that brought an end to their fun.

"You have a fine seat, Lonfranco. You sit aboard a thoroughbred as if you were born on one," the General proclaimed as the two men dismounted.

"I have never ridden like that in my life, Señor General. Thank you for the opportunity."

A steward handed the riders cold drinks as two squires lead the horses away. Both men were soaked with perspiration.

"I am too covered in sweat to eat with your family, Señor General."

"Don't be ridiculous, my boy. Women have to learn how to appreciate good clean sweat and the smell of horse flesh. It is how I have raised my daughters. Each of them can ride like the wind, even my wife. A good horse has saved my life many a time in battle, and they know and respect this. Come now, let's join the women and eat."

Lonfranco tried to stay on the perimeter of the assembled guests who were partaking of the picnic, for he was embarrassed at his malodorous state. Maria was at his side as soon as she located him, spurning the requests of several dandified society boys to join them on their blankets.

"You are full of surprises, Lonfranco! You have a real touch with those animals, that is obvious! You had better watch out or my father will give you a mallet and conscript you onto his team. He has taken a real liking to you. Now, come and eat your picnic with me!"

Lonfranco seemed to be floating on air the remainder of that magical afternoon. The warmth of the general and his family made him at ease. For the first time, he felt a sense of well-being in his new country. It was over all too quickly for the boy's liking, but the general's parting remarks made his heart soar with anticipation.

"I am in need of a handler for my stock that I keep on our estancia in the Pampas, Lonfranco. It would mean relocating, for it is a long train ride from the city. But it is some of the most beautiful land in all of Argentina, where one can ride to the horizon and still keep going. I found it during the Indian campaigns, its owner having been run off for good by the savages. Perhaps you would be interested in the position? Think about it, and we will talk in a few days. Thank you for joining us today. It would seem that you have made a good impression with the whole family, especially Maria. She is strong-willed. Be careful of her charms. I myself have trouble resisting them. She knows how to get what she wants, even from her father, the general! Take care, my boy."

His feet barely seemed to touch the ground as he made his way home that fateful evening. His euphoria did not last long, however, once he reached the modest boarding house that he called home in working-class Avellaneda district.

His landlady, Señora Chazaretta, handed him a manila envelope as he walked through the parlor on his way to the room he shared with two other Italian immigrants. Lonfranco did not recognize the handwriting on the envelope, even though it was postmarked in Livorno, Italy. The return address stated the name of one of Livorno's more prominent legal firms.

He waited until he was alone in his room before he tore open the seal. He slowly tried to decipher the handwritten contents, for reading was a skill that his parents had not stressed in his working-world upbringing. He clearly understood one word, however, and it brought an icy shiver to his spine. 'Morto.' 'Dead!'

He could make out the names of his father, mother, and brother, but he had no idea how they were related to that dreaded word. He started to shake uncontrollably and sat on the edge of his bed to calm himself. It was at this point that Mario Togneri, the elder of the two men that he shared the room with, walked in. He was almost fifty years of age and had befriended the young boy from the day that they were assigned as roommates by Señora Chazarretta. He had a kind, soothing manner, and he would often ease Lonfranco's homesickness with wild stories of his youth in the old country. The two had become very close, which was a good thing, for the young immigrant had never before been in such need of a broad shoulder.

"What is the matter, Lonfranco? You are as white as a ghost."

"Can you read our native tongue, Mario?" he held out the letter clasped in a white-knuckled, shaking hand.

"Of course, I can. My wife was a schoolteacher back in Brindisi for many years, God bless her departed soul."

"Please read this to me, Mario. I fear it contains terrible news, and I am shaking too hard to hold it."

The older man took the document and stared at it intently. Lonfranco could see the blood drain from his weathered face. Tears filled Togneri's eyes as he spoke ever so softly to the boy.

"Your family has been wiped out, back in Livorno. All of them, dead! Influenza! It has apparently ravaged the whole district. They say it came off the ships landing from the Orient. Thousands have died. Your father, being the most frail, succumbed first. After he died, your mother seemed to lose her spirit to resist anymore, and she passed away within a fortnight. Your brother, Pietro, would not leave her side, caring for her until the end. That was his undoing, as he died a few days later. The rest of the letter deals with legal matters concerning the disposal of the family assets. The lawyer gives you two choices: One, to go back to Italy and assume ownership as the sole beneficiary of their estates, or to sign this paper allowing him to liquidate everything and send the proceeds to you here in Argentina. He sends his condolences and asks for a prompt reply. That is all."

Tear-filled, disbelieving eyes met the older man's gaze.

"It can't be true. I just received a letter last week that said everything was fine, and . . . and that they were planning their passage to join me. See, the letter is right here." The boy fumbled uncontrollably with his small valise.

"Here it is . . . read it! Read it! It is all lies from the lawyer! Why would someone do this? I have sent them money, not a lot, but enough to start saving for the voyage. It, it . . . oh Mama! Pietro! Papa! I have let you down. Don't be dead, God in heaven, don't let them be dead!"

He was now screaming at the top of his lungs, and the commotion attracted the attention of Señora Chazarretta and the rest of the boarders.

As she entered the room, the landlady started to berate the boy for his unbecoming behavior, but she was stopped in mid-sentence by his shocking appearance.

"Señor De Seta, it is hardly . . . What on earth has happened?"

Mario Togneri handed her the letter while he explained its contents. Señora Chazarretta cast it aside and grasped the boy lovingly in her arms. He was whimpering softly now in Italian, words and phrases she could not clearly make sense of. She stayed with him for hours, comforting and reassuring him about his future. She let Togneri and the other man that shared the room sleep in her flat that night so that she could keep a watchful eye on her newly orphaned boarder.

Although alcohol was forbidden in the boarding house, she produced a small flask of cognac when she brought him some soup and bread in the early morning hours. The cognac was all the boy desired, and it succeeded in calming his overwrought nerves enough to induce a fitful sleep. When he finally awoke late the following afternoon, he was still in a state of delirium. Nothing he said made sense, speaking half in Italian, half in Spanish. The young immigrant thrashed wildly at times in his bed, shouting the names of his lost loved ones. He refused all food, and with the exception of the cognac that Señora Chazaretta discretely supplied him to bring on sleep, he took no nourishment for three days. Lonfranco remained in his bed for that entire time, unable, or unwilling to talk to anyone.

Finally on the morning of the fourth day, as he lay curled in the fetal position, the drapes and blankets that had been used to keep all light out of the tiny room were cast aside, and brilliant sunshine filled the chamber. Lonfranco reacted immediately to the glare that struck his disheveled form, and he gingerly raised himself on one elbow and protested vigorously.

"Qué pasa? 'What are you doing?' "Cover those windows up and get out! Leave me alone!"

He had to shield his eyes to see the form that stood in front of him more clearly, and even at that, he did not recognize who it was. His head felt as if it would explode any moment. His mouth was parched and dry, and although he had no food in his stomach, he thought that he was about to throw up.

"Who are you? What do you want with me? Please go and leave me in peace, I beg of you."

"So that you can spend the rest of your life in bed feeling sorry for yourself? I think not! I have seen too much good in you to let you throw it all away in self-pity." Although his eyes were still unable to focus, there was no mistaking that voice of authority. He strained to rise to a sitting position.

"General San Marco! How, how did you find me here? Why did you come? I, I am just a worker, not worthy of your time and . . . "

"Be quiet, my dear boy. Your roommate, Togneri, came to my home to tell me of your tragedy. Unfortunately, I was away for two days on military matters. It was three days before I was able to read his note relating your perilous condition. I came at once! So, you have lost your family back in Italy. Tragic! May God have mercy on their souls. I will pray for them, but that is all anyone can do for them now. You, my young friend, are an entirely different matter. You will come with me now, to my home. I have sent for my personal physician to attend to you. He is awaiting our arrival. My carriage is downstairs. Señora Chazarreta will gather your belongings. You may have lost one family, Lonfranco, but you are about to gain another. I have talked it over with my wife and children. You are welcome to stay with us in our new home! Heaven knows, you were the one responsible for completing the casa in record time. As for your future, we will talk when you are of sounder mind and body. Now, my friend, let me help you up."

CHAPTER FOUR

So ended the first phase of Lonfranco De Seta's life in Argentina. He never could have imagined that out of such tragedy would arise such opportunity. His recuperation from the depths of despair was accelerated by the affection and attention that were showered upon him by the general and his family. To be a resident in their home, a home that Lonfranco had helped to build with his own hands, was a wonder that never ceased to amaze him during his entire stay.

And what a magnificent residence Casa San Marco had turned out to be. Covering two complete building lots, the neoclassical structure rose three stories to a summit where four chimneys, one in each quadrant, anchored a wooden balustrade. An open-air walkway skirted the entire second level of the building, protected from the elements by the overhanging roofline.

The casa had an independent and dramatic presence, with its formal, white stucco exterior and symmetrical design. An oversized, double thick steel doorway was a concession to the general's security-minded staff, but to minimize its strength, it was flanked by Tuscan columns and capped by a large paladin window and a cartouche with festoons.

The interior of the casa was no less spectacular. The two-story entrance hall merged perfectly with the Italian marble winding staircase leading to the private second story. The main floor's principal rooms were all meant for entertaining, with the pièce de résistance being the Louis the Fifteenth-style ballroom that could accommodate two hundred or more guests. No expense had been spared in detail or finishing materials. General Figueroa San Marco intended to play host to the most powerful and influential men in all of Argentina. Under the imported Spanish-tiled roof of his new home, he was confident that his guests would be instantly impressed.

The casa's rectangular shape enclosed an enormous central garden that was a horticulturist's delight. Flora from across the land displayed their magical beauty and wafted their fragrant aromas. A large reflecting pond and grassed games pitch gave the captive area a different personality with every meandering turn of its pebbled walkways.

More than anything else, it was the long walks in the garden with Maria that made Lonfranco De Seta feel that there was hope, that all was not lost. The peacefulness of this botanical setting, and the charms of the pretty Maria enabled the youth to once again ponder his future with some optimism. Finally, about a fortnight after his arrival, the general called his houseguest into his study to discuss that very future.

"I have taken the liberty of corresponding with the attorney back in Livorno on your behalf. My instructions were for him to liquidate your family's assets and to send the proceeds to a new account that I have opened in your name at the Banco Central. I hope that you have no objections, Lonfranco, but there is nothing in Italy for you now, and your future truly lies here in Argentina, with me." The boy could say nothing, so he just nodded his head affirmatively in silence. "I think that I did mention to you that I own a large estancia in Pergamino, some two hundred miles from here. The operation has over one thousand head of stock, and I am constantly in need of good men that not only have knowledge of the animals, but are also trustworthy. I am graced with a very good head gaucho, but he is old and has arthritis. He can't stay in the saddle the way he used to. This man would be an excellent teacher, however, if you were to decide that you had an interest in that kind of life. And what a life it is! Miles and miles of the finest land in Argentina. The gauchos are great people, once you gain their confidence. They are brave and fearless men, men who pride themselves in their uninhibited way of living."

The general's eyes seemed to glaze over as he reflected upon past adventures. "In any event, I must make a journey up there in a few days. If you like, you can accompany me and see what you think. It is to this estancia that I plan to retire eventually, if the government can see its way clear to relieve me of all the responsibilities it keeps piling on my shoulders. What do you say? Is it worth a trip to the Pampas to see if that is where your future lies?"

"I would be honored to do anything in the General's service! If that is where you can use me, that is where I will serve."

The smile on the boy's face was the first one the general had observed since that tragic Sunday.

"Good. And don't worry, Maria and the others visit for the entire summer season, so you won't have to be lovesick for too long."

Lonfranco could feel his face redden at the general's last remark, but he kept silent for fear of putting his foot in his mouth.

The general was an astute and observant man, and he obviously knew that his daughter had stolen this young man's heart. At least the infatuation that Lonfranco felt was much easier to bear than the anxiety that filled that same heart whenever he thought about his dearly departed family. He was ready for this new adventure. Whatever the future had in store for him, he knew that there was great opportunity to be had in the shadow of a man like General Figueroa San Marco.

Four days later, the two men stood on the platform of Recoleta station, the general in a dapper civilian outfit, with Lonfranco in a new blue blazer, cotton trousers, crisp white shirt, and cravat.

General San Marco was fastidious about his appearance in public and relished the occasions when protocol did not require him to be in uniform. Lonfranco thought of him as a truly elegant and dashing man.

They would ride in the general's private command coach, which had been customized to his specifications. This innovative idea allowed the military to use the general's expertise in any theater of operations to which Argentina's rapidly growing rail network extended. The coach was equipped with the latest in telegraphic and electronic devises, maps and cartographic tools, working desks for aides, and a private office and bed chamber for the general.

It could only have been by coincidence that this day happened to be the boy's sixteenth birthday. He had told no one, for he did not feel it his place to create a fuss over himself. The San Marco sisters were already calling him their brother and were constantly gawking at his every move and mannerism. Señora San Marco said that it was because they had never had a brother, and no other male except their father had ever lived under the same roof.

Lonfranco was very fond of the sisters in return and would talk and play with them at every opportunity. Despite this mutual fondness, he never overstepped the boundaries of propriety, and made sure that he was discreetly absent if private family matters became a topic of discussion.

So there would be no birthday party, but the young immigrant did not care. It was the adventure that lay ahead of him that captivated his whole being. That and the memory of sweet Maria's good-bye kiss.

The travelers sat in San Marco's office initially, aids serving beverages and light snacks before a full luncheon was offered. The general, sitting behind his desk in an overstuffed swivel chair, undid his tie and waistband. Then he placed his spat-covered, black leather shoes upon the desk.

He began to describe the estancia in great detail, first the history of all the buildings, and then the working mechanics of operating one hundred square miles of land as a profitable business. Cattle, sheep, and crops were the staples of economic stability, and he detailed each segment extensively. But it was the thoroughbred horses that made his eyes light up when he talked. They were obviously his pride and joy.

He spoke of the gauchos at great length, their robust spirit and free, open lifestyle. It was not the same now as it had been years before, when the general first fought in the Pampas as a young private. Agriculture, immigrant farmers, and sheep herders had changed the face of the region. Cities and towns had sprung up where only pulperias, or small villages, once stood. The gauchos were forced to live under a different set of so-called civilized rules, on ever-shrinking ranges. They were men of fierce passion and loyalty, once a person had gained their respect. The general had used their skills to scout against the Indians many times, and had learned their traits and customs, as if he were one of them.

Propped against the wall in the corner of the coach sat a beautiful cherrywood guitar. San Marco reached out and caressed it gently now. He said that one could not understand the gaucho without listening to their music.

Lonfranco looked on in amazement as the general's fingers moved with velvet strokes over the strings and a plaintive chorus flowed from his lips. He had never heard anything like it before and was surprised by the richness of the general's voice. The hours passed too quickly for his liking, but he soon found himself in an elaborate carriage at the gates of estancia 'Buenos Recuerdos.'

"Good Memories," the general explained while pointing to the carved wooden sign that arched between two huge stone gateposts. "That is what I have when I think of life here, so the name seemed fitting."

They sat on a slight rise, overlooking a vast expanse of checkerboard fields. As far as the eye could see, there were only wide open spaces. The country air was exhilarating to Lonfranco, and he basked in the view that the warm sun illuminated before him, filled with wonder and anticipation. He had found a new home, a new vocation, and a new family, all within a month of receiving that terrible letter from Livorno. There could not have been a better birthday present imaginable, and Lonfranco De Seta considered himself to be the luckiest sixteen year-old alive.

The ensuing six years brought days of magic and merriment, mixed with hard work and hands-on education in the operation of the estancia. Lonfranco was placed under the watchful eye of old Roc Sena, the legendary head gaucho. It was under his tutelage that the Italian received all the knowledge and training required to immerse himself in his new lifestyle.

The newcomer bunked in a small one-room adobe ranchero with several other men, not in the main residence with the general and his family. It was the way both the general and the young boy preferred it. Lonfranco had to prove himself worthy of the general's trust and confidence, and he neither asked for, nor received any special privileges. He had in Roc Sena perhaps the greatest living mentor of the Pampas lifestyle in all the country.

Orphaned as a young child, Roc had stolen his first horse to escape incarceration in the provincial youth facility at the age nine. He killed his first man at twelve, fathered his first child at thirteen, and signed on as a military scout in return for whisky and rifles at sixteen. Years of Indian wars and political revolutions increased his folk hero status. It was said that he had more wives and children than even he could remember. Whenever responsibility became too constricting for his liking, he would simply saddle up and move on.

He had met General San Marco when the future general was a young captain seeking to end the Indian raids on the estancias once and for all. San Marco relied on the famous scout's ruthlessness and daring to bring about a swift, but extremely brutal, end to the hostilities. The natives that survived the slaughter were driven south to Patagonia or west into the Andes, never to return to the Pampas.

The general was hailed as a hero by the Porteños, and this popularity ensured a meteoric climb through both the military and social ranks of Buenos Aires. Nevertheless, he could never forget the man that made his fame possible, developing a deep friendship with Roc Sena, offering him a home and employment as foreman on the new estancia that he had acquired.

The gaucho was tiring of his rogue's life and found the general's offer to be timely. The two men became inseparable, each learning from the other about a different way of life. It was General San Marco, however, who became totally absorbed in the culture and habits of the gaucho lifestyle. He rode, sang, drank, and caroused with Roc Sena and his men on every occasion that presented itself.

He drank maté, the intoxicating herbal tea, partook in the asado, or range barbecue where an entire steer would be devoured except for horns and hoofs. He learned to play pato, the physical basketball style game played on horseback. He became proficient with the bolla, knife, and revolver, and picked up a whole new vocabulary of foul language that could not be put to use in the parlors and ballrooms of Palermo.

All of these things were passed on to Lonfranco De Seta under Roc Sena's guidance, and the boy was a willing, eager student. He took the initial hazing from the other ranch-hands in good humor, for he knew that they found it strange for a young Italian immigrant to ride in their midst.

Whatever hurdles Lonfranco had to overcome because of his background or any perceived favoritism on the part of the general were conquered with sheer tenacity and a will to learn quickly. It was not long before the boy was able to pull his full weight in the eyes of his peers.

Other forms of education were being administered to the newcomer at the same time. These lessons were given not only by the general, but also by a private academic tutor named Alveara Alcorta, who was brought in from Buenos Aires.

The general would talk at great length about agricultural facts of the Pampas and the need for alfalfa to be cultivated to feed the more productive English cattle that he had recently purchased. Also the need for cash crops of corn, wheat, and other grains to augment the sheep and cattle. He also spoke of the need for new, efficient methods of marketing the products that they produced, that is, an expanded rail system tying the Pampas to the ports in Rosario and Buenos Aires.

There was no doubt that the general did not consider Buenos Recuerdos as a leisurely pastime. Properly run, and with the right amount of innovation, he was certain that it would maintain his family's economic security through whatever political upheaval should shake the ruling classes of Buenos Aires.

The general would eventually place a lot of trust in Lonfranco's judgment, but first the boy had to read and write so that he could comprehend financial figures and statements. This was the role that Alveara Alcorta played in the making of Lonfranco De Seta. The books were a lot more difficult to master than the bolla or the saddle, but Lonfranco tackled them with the same driven determination. After two years, Señora Alcorta was no longer required in the employ of the general.

The San Marco ladies would be in residence at Buenos Recuerdos for most of the summer months of January and February, and during those months, it seemed to Lonfranco that the estancia was turned into a continuous garden party or ballroom soirée. Guests from all over the countryside and the great cities would enjoy the hospitality of the general and his family for days on end.

The boy's relationship with Maria remained extremely cordial, but his newfound maturity and the worldly stories of the gauchos tempered the infatuation that had made him giddy with love when they had first met. She was, after all, the general's eldest daughter, and he did not want to risk his emerging identity on any indiscretion that he might be lured into because of his naiveté. Affairs of the heart must wait for now, for the affairs of business were uppermost in Lonfranco's mind.

That aside, he was a constant visitor in the main residence, either talking business with the general, or playing some spirited game with the younger sisters as time permitted. He continued to be treated as if he were their favorite cousin, and even Maria seemed to accept that their personal relationship had to remain of lesser importance than their mutual educations.

It was for that reason that Maria and a French governess set sail for France in August of 1902. Maria was about to fulfill her desire to study at the Sorbonne in Paris, and the entire family, including Lonfranco, joined her on the continent the following May for a two month family reunion.

The first-class passage to Europe was a far cry from what the young Italian had experienced on his initial crossing of the Atlantic. The other passengers reveled in his stories of hardship and deprivation as they sipped champagne from the finest crystal. How things had changed for the boy from Livorno. Steerage-class hardships were a distant memory. Only the best available amenities were acceptable for the general and his entourage.

The family traveled on to London after their stay on the continent, where Lonfranco and the general set about acquiring some of the best polo ponies that money could buy. The general made a special gift of one fine grey Arabian mare to Lonfranco, a gesture that brought heartfelt tears to the young man's eyes.

They even managed to play a few chuckers of polo at an exclusive club on the outskirts of London, the president of the club being very willing to rub shoulders with an Argentine war hero and businessman. Lonfranco had played the game with great enthusiasm many times since that first day at the picnic in Buenos Aires, and he had displayed such talent that the general now included him in his first-team lineup.

The polo ponies were not the only business matters that the general tended to while indulging himself at the sport he loved. The man responsible for San Marco's presence at Hocking's Squire Polo Club was none other than the president of British Rail Overseas Limited, Wendel Barrington Thompson.

Thompson, a retired cavalry officer in the Queen's Dragoons, was, like much of the British public captivated by the stories of daring from the American Wild West. Several famous frontiersmen were now touring the continent, displaying their polished western skills with a six-shooter, lariat, and carbine.

Wild Bill Hickok, Sitting Bull, and Annie Oakley were only a few of the characters that had leapt out of the periodical pages into the arenas and fairgrounds of Europe. Although less widely publicized than its American counterpart, the Argentine struggle against its native Indians had followed a similarly bloodthirsty path. The romantic image of the gaucho and the fabled tales of Argentina's most successful Indian fighter raised the profile of General Figueroa San Marco to celebrity status during his visit to England. It also opened some extremely coveted doors into the inner boardrooms of British commerce and finance.

The general, through Wendel Thompson's influence, had made an impressive presentation to the corporate board of directors of British Rail Overseas Limited. The thrust of his message stated the case for extensive expansion of the rail lines that the British company owned or controlled into the Pampas heartland of Argentina.

The facts spoke for themselves. Improved agricultural techniques and revolutionary mechanical devices, combined with the staggering influx of knowledgeable farmers and astute scientists from Europe, meant that the fertile Argentine plain was ripe for tremendous expansion and development.

Vastly improved beef cattle were successfully being bred and nurtured on the Pampas' endless expanse. Slaughterhouses needed direct lines to the ports to enable timely export of their highly sought-after products. Sheep, cotton, grains, and vegetables were all there as well for any person with foresight to capitalize upon the idea.

The general offered his wide-reaching influence in any and every way possible to the Englishmen, and the fact that he backed up his enthusiasm for their investment dollars with a spectacular display of polo skills was not lost on several polo-playing board members. The British Rail Overseas Corporation promised to send high-ranking officials to Buenos Aires on the next available crossing to further discuss the matter with their associates there. The general was assured that his expertise and connections would be invaluable to the corporation and that contact would be made immediately upon his return to South America.

The horn of plenty spread its bounty over the rich lands of Buenos Recuerdos for the next three years. Through the general's diligence and painstaking attention to detail, a modern industrial and agricultural revolution took place right there in Pergamino.

Figueroa San Marco had been able to convince the Englishmen to use his own expansive lands as an experimental testing ground. Some seventy miles of track were laid as a trunk spur from the main estancia compound to a site on the Parana River, just south of the town of San Nicholas de los Arroyos. This location became the terminus and deep-water port for the general's own exported goods. A slaughterhouse, tannery, grain mill, and cotton gin all became integral operating facets of 'Port San Marco.'

The financial viability of such a project quickly became evident to the British Rail operators. They were dazzled by General San Marco's resourcefulness. One full year had not elapsed since the first railway tie had been laid at Buenos Recuerdos, but Wendel Barrington Thompson had already seen enough. He pleaded with the general to open negotiations immediately with the Argentine government to secure vast tracts of land for rail expansion.

At this point in his life, Figueroa San Marco had all but retired from active military duty. He preferred to spend his time overseeing the hands-on toils at his rapidly developing estancia and seaport, and when necessary, traveling to the capital to lobby government officials in an effort to achieve more favorable trade tariffs for foreign governments.

It was in his new capacity as a paid lobbyist that the general first opened discussions with President Julio Argentino Roca concerning the tremendous economic benefits that Argentina could derive should the Pampas be extensively and efficiently connected to the ports of Rosario and Buenos Aires by means of expanded rail service. Roca was impressed with the forecasts and statistics and promised to inform the Minister of the Interior of the British Rail proposal.

Lonfranco De Seta was the general's constant companion in each and every aspect of this complicated puzzle. The boy had learned to type, and this enabled the general to dictate and courier off memos or dispatches on a moment's notice.

The former 'pick and shovel man' was appointed executive assistant to the general at a large formal dinner in his behalf at Casa San Marco in Buenos Aires. There was no area of the family business of which the young Italian did not have intimate knowledge.

Still, the newly appointed executive assistant had trouble understanding why he deserved to be so fortunate, when he had really given the general and his family little more than devotion and hard work in return. The continual affection and respect showered upon him made the equation even harder to solve. There was not one thing that he longed for, be it spiritual, emotional, or material. He could honestly say that he had never been happier!

Nothing could have prepared him for the explosive end to this idyllic life one beautiful Sunday morning, in November of 1905.

CHAPTER FIVE

The Argentine political landscape at the turn of the century was, for the most part, one of 'peace and efficient administration,' brought forth by the ruling National Autonomist Party.

This was definitely a pro-capitalist regime and broad expansion of the economy was courted with the use of foreign capital. But not everyone prospered during the mandate of President Julio Argentino Roca, and civil unrest intensified under the guise of a new populist political party, The Radical Social Union.

Initially, the R.S.U. was nonviolent in its attempts to lure voters to their platform, but 1905 brought rampant inflation and an economic downturn to the country that hit the working classes the hardest. Demonstrations and minor disruptions of public services gave way to bombings of government facilities and kidnappings of high-ranking officials. In desperation, President Roca turned to the one man he felt could take charge of the situation and restore law and order, General Figueroa San Marco.

The general had initially protested that he was all but retired from military affairs and preferred to have a younger man cut his teeth on this latest crisis. President Roca could not be swayed, however, insisting that the general's high profile as a war hero and economic miracle worker could allay the peoples' fears of a full-scale revolution.

Roca was also aware that the general possessed the ruthlessness to use whatever force required to achieve the destruction of the R.S.U., if he was pressed to do so.

To sweeten the reward, Roca promised the general all remaining lands required by the British Rail investors if he succeeded in bringing an end to the upheaval. Roca swore that this would enable San Marco to retire to his business interests full-time, with an even greater public profile.

"Perhaps a great political career could be in the general's future, if he so desired. Why, even the presidency could be within your grasp. I certainly do not plan to be here forever!" Roca eluded.

There was nothing San Marco could do but heed the call of his president in a time of great turmoil. An assassination attempt on the life of the Minister of the Interior the very next day brought home the urgency of the situation. The general mobilized the army, arrested thousands of suspected subversives, placed a curfew on the streets of Buenos Aires from dusk until dawn, and banned all public gathering.

The harsh measures were supported by the majority of Porteños, who were anxious to restore economic stability and not discourage the influx of foreign capital.

It was one bloody confrontation with a large group of R.S.U. activists that turned the tide of the struggle in the government's favor. The army had been tipped off by a paid informer that the leadership of the R.S.U. was holding a strategy meeting at an old bull fighting stadium in the Monserrat Barrio. Several hundred supporters would also be present to handle security.

General San Marco gave the orders to allow the meeting to take place. Once the subversives were inside the stadium, the army closed off all the escape routes, jammed the streets in the surrounding area with artillery loaded with grapeshot, backed the artillery up with mounted cavalry, then set fire to the stadium. The result was nothing but a slaughter. There were only a handful of survivors when all the shooting stopped. The hierarchy of the R.S.U. was wiped out completely, and it ceased to be a political or terrorist force from that day on.

General San Marco was hailed as a hero and the savior of Argentina's economic prosperity by President Roca. For his part, the general did not relish the means by which he had accomplished the demise of the R.S.U., but he was happy that the ordeal was concluded, and that he would be able to retire fully from military life as the president had promised.

Because of the spring planting season, Lonfranco had remained at Buenos Recuerdos to oversee the work schedule and tend to other business in his employer's absence. He was mildly troubled by the general's last visit to the estancia, just days before he assumed his new military duties for President Roca.

There had been something different about the man, a melancholy sentiment that Lonfranco had never witnessed before. He had left his assistant an extended list of duties to fulfill, leaving behind his personal diaries and notes in Lonfranco's care for 'safekeeping.'

Their last night together was spent under the stars, with Roc Sena and his guitar along to provide musical accompaniment. The three men sang and drank and talked about old times with a lingering sadness rather than the usual lusty bravado. At one point, without saying a word, the general turned to Lonfranco, extending his hands. The younger man was stunned for a moment, but he finally extended his own, grasping those of the general. They sat in silence for more than a minute before San Marco spoke.

"You will never know how much pleasure you have brought me, Lonfranco. You are the son I never had. As God is my witness, there is no man that ever meant more to me than you."

Their eyes met for an instant before the general withdrew his hands. He called for his favorite guitar medley, "Estilo Pampeano," from Roc Sena to make the mood more upbeat, but Lonfranco swore that he had seen tears in the older man's eyes as the general turned to put another log on the fire. When Lonfranco arose the next morning, the old warrior had already departed for the capital.

Señora San Marco insisted on staying in Buenos Aires with her three youngest daughters so that they could complete their school terms and lead as normal an existence as possible during the hostilities. The general grudgingly acquiesced, insisting on around-the-clock military guards and escorts for his family. Only Maria, who had returned to France for her final year of studies two months prior, was unaffected by the political situation at home.

The first Sunday after the slaughter at the bullring, President Roca extended an invitation to the general and his family to worship with him at the Cathedral Metropolitana. He told the general that it would be a good display of public unity and also allow his adoring public one last glimpse of the famed military hero before he withdrew into the private sector.

It was an offer that the general could not readily refuse. He adorned himself in full military regalia, hitched up his most ornate open carriage, and with his four ladies in their resplendent Sunday gowns, set off for what he hoped would be his final command performance.

All went according to plan initially. A large, friendly crowd lined the streets surrounding the cathedral in anticipation of the arrival of the president and his revered military guest. Usually the general and his family worshipped at the smaller basilica in Palermo without much fuss or bother. But his daughters were enjoying the pageantry of the morning, with many of the city's social elite joining the procession of carriages that inched towards the foot of the great cathedral's steps.

Soldiers held the swelling crowd back from the edge of the plaza that surrounded the great building. Officers in their finest uniforms, along with mounted police of the President's Guard, formed a corridor through which each of the dignitaries would pass.

As the general's carriage neared the point of embarkation, a commotion erupted in the throng of people to their immediate right. Several gunshots rang out and screams of panic filled the air. While a platoon of soldiers converged on the troublesome area, a man on the opposite side of the plaza stepped out of the crowd and followed the flow of the extra troopers. He took a long drag on the cigar that he was smoking, then reached into his sachel and lit the short fuse of a melon-size bomb.

The man was now beside the general's carriage, and he calmly tossed the explosive device onto its floor. The general, who was standing but facing the opposite direction, turned just in time to meet the man's glare, and hear him snarl, "Death to all enemies of the people!"

The explosion was ear-shattering, and its effects horrific. The general and his family didn't stand a chance of survival. In total, twelve people were killed by the deadly blast.

The subsequent investigation showed that the attacker was a member of the R.S.U., who had lost two brothers during the bullring massacre. He did not survive the bomb's devastation either, which was obviously his intention. The gunshots and commotion in the crowd had been a planned diversionary act which had worked to perfection.

No arrests were made at the site of the assassination. However, President Roca imposed a city-wide curfew for two days that enabled the security forces to incarcerate several hundred suspects. Many never walked the streets of Buenos Aires as free men again.

General Figueroa San Marco, his wife, and their three daughters were given a state funeral of the highest honor and laid to rest in a hero's crypt in the elite Recoleta Cemetery.

CHAPTER SIX

The telegraph operator at the train station in Pergamino sat in disbelief staring at the notepad on which he had been transcribing an incoming message.

"Surely there must be a mistake, this could not have happened." He asked for verification, for the full transmission to be repeated. The message came through exactly the same the second time.

'General Figueroa San Marco, his wife, and three daughters have been assassinated by a terrorist bomb in front of the Cathedral Metropolitana in Buenos Aires today, Sunday, 12 November, 1905. Stop. Notify Lonfranco De Seta to inform the staff at Buenos Recuerdos. Stop. Señor De Seta is then to make all haste to Buenos Aires. Stop. Contact the sender at once upon arrival. Stop. Signed Señor Lopez Bucharo, Attorney at Law, 1538 Avenue Paseo Colon, Buenos Aires. Stop.'

Tears welled in the telegraph operator's eyes as he called for his young apprentice to saddle a horse and ride like the wind to fetch Lonfranco De Seta to the station. He told the boy only that an urgent message awaited De Seta, and that the Italian must come at once to retrieve it.

The operator refused to transmit any further communication for the next two and a half hours. He pulled the blind down on the door, locked it, and hung out the closed sign. He then sat down behind the keypad and wept. Only when the young apprentice was heard pleading with him to open up did he rise from his chair. An irritated Lonfranco De Seta stood before him in the fading sunlight. Silently he handed General San Marco's executive assistant the cablegram.

The following week was the bleakest time in Lonfranco's life. He operated in a numbing vacuum, always efficient, but somehow detached emotionally from the events that swirled around him. Throughout the torturous days and nights, two questions never left his mind.

The first was whether he could have saved the general and his family had he been present at the cathedral. The second, what should be done about informing Maria in Paris about the tragedy?

Was it too cruel to inform her by telegraph, so far away and with only a paid governess to comfort her? What else could be done?

He would gladly have booked passage immediately to bring her home, but the newspapers would certainly break the story on the continent before his arrival. If he didn't notify her of his plans, he might in all likelihood pass her traveling in the opposite direction, if she had already heard the news. That was too great a risk, so he decided to send a cable informing her of the tragedy as gently as possible. He would remain in Argentina and attend to the mountains of bureaucratic documentation that was piled on his desk.

He assured Maria that he would stay by her side until she felt that she had a sufficient grasp of the estate matters, and requested that the general's only surviving heir cable him with her travel arrangements, so that he could be prepared to meet her.

As for his own future, he was certain that his involvement with the San Marco family was at an end, and that he would be seeking employment elsewhere as soon as Maria had a working knowledge of the general's business ventures.

Señor Bucharo had been most helpful in explaining the terms of the general's will in a very broad sense. It stipulated that until any of the San Marco's surviving issue turned thirty years of age, their share of the estate was to be administered by the appointed executors, whose number included Bucharo himself. What he didn't tell Lonfranco about was a far more contentious clause in the will that could change the interpretation of the entire document.

Lonfranco was given the impression that once a reconciliation of the estate's assets had been completed, his services would no longer be required in the management of the San Marco business interests. After all, he was only twenty-two years of age, with no formal education, and an immigrant as well.

Bucharo was unaware of the faith that the general had demonstrated in the young Italian's business acumen. Their personal relationship was not documented in any of the papers at the lawyer's disposal. Lonfranco was not mentioned in the general's will, an instrument which had been executed some thirteen years earlier on the birth of his youngest daughter.

The more knowledgeable that Bucharo became about the intricacies of the San Marco holdings, the colder and more offhand he became with Lonfranco. He finally told the young man that he should start to look for new lodging in Buenos Aires, that it would now be inappropriate for him to reside in the guest suite of Casa San Marco, as he had done in the past, whenever business brought him to the capital. The general's unmarried daughter commanded more respect, he had been told.

Lonfranco took the advice and moved his belongings into a one-room flat in the San Telmo barrio. It seemed to him that Bucharo wanted the general's trusted assistant totally out of the picture by the time Maria arrived from the continent. She had cabled Lonfranco of her scheduled arrival date and had told him that she was holding up as well as possible.

The last function that Lonfranco would perform for the general was to carry his saber in the state funeral procession that wound its way through the streets of the capital.

President Roca had declared two days of public mourning, during which time the casket would lay in state in the Cabildo, the national legislature.

Newspapers hailed San Marco as a great hero, a man of the people who gave his life so that Argentines everywhere could be free of terrorism. The funeral procession was the most elaborate seen in the capital in many years. Full military honors included squadrons of soldiers on foot and on horseback, military bands playing sorrowful laments, and dignitaries and socialites in their carriages. In addition, masses of common citizens marched to the cemetery to pay their final respects.

Lonfranco marched beside President Roca, carrying the drawn saber at waist level, horizontally, between his two hands. They followed directly behind the casket that sat on an artillery caisson, covered by the national flag of Argentina and surrounded by elaborate wreaths of flowers. Behind the President and Lonfranco followed the hearses carrying the remains of the four San Marco women.

The Italian's distraught mind thought most often of the younger daughters, and how they had played and laughed during their all too short friendship. He would have laid down his life for those beautiful children, but now they were gone from him forever.

Lonfranco was distressed to see Lopez Bucharo standing on the pier the day that Maria's ship arrived in Buenos Aires. The two men eyed each other coldly, then Bucharo broke the silence with his condescending upper-class accent.

"You need not stay but a few minutes, Lonfranco. Señorita San Marco will accompany me directly to my office to attend to certain legal matters that are of urgent importance. Please keep your condolences brief. I am sure that she will be in touch with you once she is has adjusted to her new circumstances."

"Perhaps we should let Maria decide where she wants to go and with whom," Lonfranco replied curtly.

"I have been in touch with Señorita San Marco prior to her departure from Le Havre. She is aware of the importance of a smooth transfer of the family assets to the trust that the executors have set up. She will keep this appointment, and I will not tolerate any interference from you. Good day to you, sir!"

The lawyer turned on his heel and walked haughtily down the quay.

Maria looked surprisingly composed as she descended the gangway. Lonfranco had ingeniously tipped a porter several hundred pesos to borrow his red cap and jacket. These would enable him to gain access to the restricted embarkation area. He was standing at the foot of the ramp as she touched Argentine soil again. At first she did not recognize him in his disguise, but as soon as he removed the cap she fell sobbing into his arms. Bucharo, who was watching the scene in a rage from behind the fenced visitor's area, tried calling her name as loudly as possible, but to no avail.

As soon as Maria regained her composure, Lonfranco spirited her and the real porter to the baggage area where they were able to engage in a lengthy conversation while they awaited her luggage. Señor Bucharo had little success in bribing the police officer that stood at the entrance to the secured baggage compound. He was told that he would be arrested if he tried to enter the restricted area and to remain with the other visitors behind the fence. Humiliated and seething with anger, he retreated as ordered.

The lawyer was able to control his temper, however, when he introduced himself to Señorita San Marco with a great flourish as she and her two porters swept past him on their way to the carriage that Lonfranco had hired for the day.

"Señorita San Marco, my deepest sympathies. I am Lopez Bucharo, attorney-at-law. We were in communication before you left the continent. I trust you had as pleasant a crossing as possible under the circumstances. I am the chief executor of your father's estate, and as I informed you, we have some very pressing matters to address right away. If you would be so kind as to accompany me in my carriage, we can proceed directly to my office where the documentation is all prepared and awaiting your signature."

Maria could barely control her disgust at what she considered an untimely intrusion.

"Señor Bucharo, I realize that this is all very important to you, but I am tired and heartbroken, and I am going home now and nowhere else. I will see you at Casa San Marco tomorrow morning at ten, if you can make it there. If not, you may call and book an appointment at a later date. Good day, Señor."

Bucharo stood slack-jawed in amazement as Maria and the two men continued on their way past him. Never had he been talked to in such an insulting manner by a mere snippet of a girl.

This must be De Seta's influence, the attorney ruminated. *He must be removed from the picture at once. As for the señorita, I will deal with the haughty little puta in my own way, when the time is right!*

Lopez Bucharo stood in the entrance portico of Casa San Marco at exactly ten o'clock the following morning. He was shown into the general's den and asked to wait. Several minutes later, Maria entered the oak-paneled room with Lonfranco De Seta right behind her.

"Señorita, thank you for seeing me so promptly. I do hope that you found your homecoming comforting. This business will only take a short time. I do, however, insist that we have our discussion in private. There is no assistance that Señor De Seta can provide for me." Bucharo could not mask the look of contempt that he focused on the Italian.

"That may be true, Señor Bucharo, but he can certainly be of assistance to me. Señor De Seta was my father's personally appointed executive assistant, as well as being a longtime family friend and confidant. There was no aspect of my father's business dealings of which he was not aware. We have discussed several topics since my return to Buenos Aires, not the least of which is your virtual dismissal of Señor De Seta from every facet of responsibility. Perhaps you would rather that I seek independent legal counsel before the will is read, so that I am fully aware of its contents and my rights."

"That . . . that will not be necessary, Señorita," the stunned visitor professed meekly. "I assure you that I have only your best interests at heart. But there are certain legal facts about your father's estate that are plainly and simply the law. You need sound legal advice to deal with them. I am your father's appointed executor. Nothing can change that. I am the one you must deal with, and none of this concerns Señor De Seta!"

Bucharo was becoming more and more irritated by the second. He had been warned by some of his colleagues that the young San Marco girl had a mind of her own, as well as being a finely bred, well-educated beauty.

"Señor Bucharo, those are your choices. We can continue with Señor De Seta present, or we can postpone this meeting until I have sought outside counsel. What will it be?"

"Very well, Señorita, let us proceed."

Bucharo figured that De Seta was the lesser of two evils as far as implementing his plan was concerned. The immigrant would have to be taken care of right away, though. The lawyer spread several documents on the general's large desk, arranging them with meticulous care. When he was finished, he stepped back and motioned for Maria to assume the general's chair. Once seated, Maria stared down at the documents, all of which were turned to the last page, the page requiring her signature.

"Are you not going to explain these papers to me, Señor Bucharo, before I sign them?"

"I have prepared a synopsis of the will and its effect on the estate. I also cover the new trust that has been set up on your behalf. I have it right here for you to read at your leisure. I did not want to burden you with legal details at this very difficult time. All that is required at the moment is your signature on these documents, then I will be able to administer the estate without concerning you about unimportant details."

"Señor, you must think me a fool!" Maria responded. "You bring me a synopsis of my father's will instead of the actual document? I will sign nothing until I have read the original last will and testament! Do you think that I was studying needlepoint and flower pressing on the continent, Señor? This is the twentieth century, and women everywhere are awakening to opportunities never before available to them. The world of commerce and finance is opening up to people like myself. Women who don't have to live under the yoke imposed on them by domineering, arrogant men! I want to learn about my father's business interests, and Señor De Seta has agreed to stay on and help me acquire that knowledge. The first thing I want you to do, Señor Bucharo, is to bring me the original copy of my father's will, so that I may study it. Then, and only then, will I allow you to explain these papers which you are so anxious to have me sign. Be forewarned that you are not dealing with some mindless female who is content to receive an allowance once a month, or whenever some stuffed-shirt lawyer decides she can have a few crumbs. Do I make myself completely clear, Señor?" Bucharo stared blankly at Maria before answering in his most haughty tone of voice.

"Very well, Señorita, we will do it your way. But you will see that you are at the mercy of the estate's executors. I would advise you that your personal relationship with those executors is of the utmost importance as far as your financial well-being is concerned. I have the original will in my briefcase right here. I will leave it with you, as I have another original at my office. Please give this matter your immediate attention, as there are decisions that have to be made right away. Good day to you both. I will let myself out."

Bucharo had gathered up the documents on the general's desk while he spoke and had replaced them with a single manila envelope containing the will. He was flushed with anger as he strode through the door out into the foyer.

Lonfranco, who hadn't uttered a word throughout the meeting, was in shock over what he had just heard Maria say. He had always known that she was not afraid to speak her mind, but to say such things to a man of Bucharo's stature was unheard of, especially from a lady.

"Maria, I don't believe what you just did. You must be more careful if your future depends on that man. He could ruin you! And what is this story about me staying on to help you learn the business? You did not discuss that with me last night, and Bucharo has made it painfully clear that there is no position for me as far as the estate is concerned."

"Lonfranco, I do not trust that man. I have known him since I was a small girl. He would come to the casa to deliver documents to my father. Mama hated him! He was always so condescending, so phony. I think I am seeing the same Señor Bucharo that my mother saw. My father switched lawyers several years ago, but like many people, I imagine that once his will was signed he just forgot about it. He should have changed his executors, but he obviously put the matter out of his mind. I will send for Señor Orlando Houseman, my father's lawyer for the past few years, to read the will and advise me of its contents."

"Yes, that would be a good idea. I have had dealings with Señor Houseman, and he has impressed me as an honest man. Your father would often seek his counsel on various business opportunities. He was very involved in the British railway dealings. You should read the will yourself before you see him, though."

"Yes, Lonfranco, I fully intend to read it, but seeing as you have met Señor Houseman, perhaps you could go to his office right away and persuade him to see me as soon as he has an opening. Would you do that for me?"

"I will leave this instant. With any luck, you will be able to have an audience within a day or two."

Several hours later, Lonfranco returned to Casa San Marco with a portly man dressed in a vanilla cotton suit and a straw boater. He made the man comfortable in the library, then went to find Maria.

"May I present Señor Orlando Houseman, Señorita Maria San Marco."

"Señor Houseman, how good of you to come on such short notice," Maria said in a surprised tone. "I had not expected to be able to talk to you for days."

"My heartfelt condolences, Señorita San Marco. Your father's death is a national tragedy. Señor De Seta explained your predicament to me, and I think I have some timely information for you. Your father was a good friend of mine, as well as a client. I asked him every so often about his will, but he found the subject distasteful and would always change the topic of conversation. I am certain that the general thought that he would live forever. Do you have the will ready for me to take a look at?"

"Yes, Señor, it is right here. I have read through it once, but there are several areas that you could help me with."

The meeting continued well into the night. Maria arranged for the evening meal to be served on trays in the library so that the three of them could continue their studies of the document. Señor Houseman explained each paragraph in detail and made certain that both Maria and Lonfranco understood its implications.

Because Señora San Marco perished along with the general, a large section of the document's contents were not applicable. What was pertinent was the clause dealing with surviving issue under the age of thirty years, should both parents predecease them.

The will clearly stated that until the surviving beneficiaries attained age thirty, the estate was under complete control of the appointed executors. These men, of which Señor Bucharo was the most senior, had absolute control over business decisions inside the estate, and also the amount of income that flowed annually to the heirs. It was exactly as Bucharo had stated, Maria was at their mercy, with one exception.

"Clause twenty-six 'C' is your only escape from this arrangement, Maria," Señor Houseman explained. "Should any surviving issue marry before attaining the age of thirty years, then said issue's entire portion of the estate shall be deemed vested upon her wedding day."

"So the only way I can rid myself of Señor Bucharo is to get married?"

"Exactly! Other than that action, you are stuck with your father's appointed executors running your affairs for the next six years, approximately. Now I must tell you about some matters that have come to my attention concerning the dealings of Señor Bucharo since your father's death. As Señor De Seta can confirm, I was working with your father on the expansion of the Pampas rail lines. The British interests were very high on the project. Thousands of acres of land were to be acquired to accommodate the railway. General San Marco insisted that the property owners be made aware of the impending expansion and be paid a fair price for their land. As a result of the events of that tragic Sunday, I have had to turn all your father's business files over to Señor Bucharo as legal executor of the estate. I have since heard through the legal community that Bucharo plans to run the owners off their land using vigilantes and paid henchmen. He would, in turn, purchase the land through one of his shell companies, and then sell it to the British at a great profit. He is a man of no moral conscience, and he has done similar contemptible things in the past. That is why your father dismissed him. I am certain that this is not his only diabolical plan to benefit from the general's shrewd business acumen. Be extremely wary of that man, Señorita San Marco. He has the ethics of a serpent."

After Señor Houseman had departed, Maria and Lonfranco remained in the library for over an hour discussing the gloomy situation that confronted the General's daughter and her clouded future. It was Maria that shattered the dismal mood with a profound statement that sent Lonfranco reeling.

"Well, my dear friend, it seems like there is no other solution than for you and I to be married immediately, before that bastard can ruin my inheritance and soil my family name! Do you accept my proposal?"

Lonfranco's ears were ringing so loud he was not certain that he had heard her correctly. His stomach was full of butterflies. He thought that he was about to faint.

"What was that you just said? Are you serious? Please, Maria, do not trifle with my emotions. The death of your family is more than I can bear. It devastated me even more than the loss of my own family. I could not stand being treated in a frivolous manner by you now. Perhaps I should just go."

The heiress was at his side in an instant. She grasped his face gently with her two hands and pulled his lips down to meet hers without saying a word. Her kiss was the tenderest sensation that Lonfranco had ever experienced. It seemed to last forever, and his brain swam in a sea of conflicting emotions while his manhood felt the soft pressure of her thigh for the first time.

He was truly speechless when the embrace concluded. He turned from her to conceal his passion from her eyes.

"We have always been fond of one another, Lonfranco, ever since that first day we met at the polo match. I have always had a special place in my heart for you, and I have watched you grow into the fine man that my father thought the world of. I think loving you will be easy if I let myself do it. Up until now, I had other goals to achieve before I could allow myself the indulgence of loving someone. That is why I have kept our relationship platonic all these years. I did not want to end up like so many of my girlfriends, married with three children and dreadfully unhappy by the time they were twenty. Don't you see, Lonfranco? This could be the solution to all our problems! Marry me, and we will be done with Señor Bucharo and his despicable schemes. I promise you that I will be a good wife and business partner, and bear you many sons."

"I am sure that your father would have wanted better for you, Maria. I can offer you nothing. You deserve a brighter future than to be married to a virtually penniless immigrant. There are men of wealth and social standing that are far more suited to be your husband."

"Do you not think that I have had every opportunity to settle down with scores of suitors? Men that looked attractive on the surface, but in reality were just looking for a healthy dowry and a prize chattel. I will be no one's possession! You know me, Lonfranco. All those young dandies that were always trying to win Papa's favor to get close to me, they made me sick! Even on the continent the men were no different. I want an equal relationship with the man I marry. Partners in life, in business, and in love. Is that too much to ask? You are the one man on this planet who understands me, and I know that we can make things work. Please, Lonfranco . . . will you marry me?"

His mouth was so dry that the answer to her question was little more than a croak. He looked into her beautiful dark eyes and gently took her hand. It felt so tiny wrapped inside his.

"Yes, Maria, I will marry you . . . if it is truly what you want in your heart. I have loved you since the first day I saw you. But please, do not take this action because of some business arrangement or to spite Señor Bucharo. Please, only consider marriage if your love for me is pure and untainted by grief or revenge. I could not stand to be used as a pawn in a chess game of the heart."

Maria said nothing. She simply pressed her lips to his again. Her kiss told him everything that he wanted to know and set his heart at ease.

The wedding caused a great sensation and somewhat of a scandal among Porteño society. Lonfranco and Maria were quietly wed the next day in the Basilica de Nuestra Señora del Pilar in Recoleta. Maria had been able to make the arrangements on short notice with the parish priest, Monsignor Augustin. He not only had christened her, but also had been a close personal friend and confessor of General San Marco.

When Maria had walked into the narthex of the basilica, Monsignor Augustin had assumed that she was there to seek solace because of the great tragedy that had befallen her. He was shocked to discover the real reason for her visit, and it was only after intensive questioning of her mental state and her motives that he was persuaded by this very self-confident lady to give the marriage his blessing, pending a chat with the perspective groom.

Lonfranco had waited anxiously outside. After what seemed to him an eternity, Maria bid him into the chapel. The Monsignor asked some very pointed questions of the Italian, but the two men had met before, both at this place of worship and at the general's residence on social occasions. He was aware of the high regard that the general had for Lonfranco, and of the position of trust that the former executive assistant had enjoyed.

He gave the couple his divine permission to proceed and told them to return at nine o'clock that evening. Only Maria's closest friend, Señorita Avril Galaria, was present as a witness. A senior monk of the Franciscan order that founded and ran the basilica would act as Lonfranco's witness.

The service was concluded without pomp and circumstance in under thirty minutes. The newlyweds were then ushered back to Casa San Marco, where the full staff was assembled and told of the news. The couple would be moving into the General and Señora San Marco's master suite that evening, and from that moment on, Maria would be addressed as Señora De Seta.

The last request that the couple made before retiring was for a coachman to be at Señor Lopez Bucharo's office at eight a.m. sharp the following morning and to await his arrival. Señor Bucharo's presence was requested at Casa San Marco at his earliest convenience, and the coachman would provide transportation should he wish it.

The only thing that made cutting short their private wedding celebrations with an anticipated early morning meeting palatable was the chance to rid themselves of the arrogant Bucharo once and for all.

Whether it was their unbridled passion or the excitement of their newfound freedom that the morrow would bring, neither of the lovers slept that night. Both were dressed and waiting when the maid announced Bucharo's arrival shortly after ten o'clock.

"Señor Bucharo, how good of you to see us on such short notice. Would you like a beverage or some fresh pastries?" Maria asked in her sweetest voice.

"No, thank you, Señorita, I have a very full agenda today, and I must be on my way as soon as these documents are signed. I trust that you have come to your senses and will now allow me to carry out the duties that your father bestowed upon me as his executor."

Bucharo shot a contemptuous glance at Lonfranco as he stood by Maria's side.

"Most assuredly, Señor. I have never been so clearheaded and certain of the tasks that lay before me. I have reviewed the will in detail with the assistance of Señor Orlando Houseman, whom I have retained as my personal attorney. I believe you have made Señor Houseman's acquaintance, have you not? In any event, it would seem that you were correct. The estate is to be administered by yourself and the other executors, and I have almost no alternative but to sign the papers as requested."

The color had left Bucharo's face when Maria mentioned Houseman's name, and he began to tremble slightly. He was able to regain his composure as he perceived Maria's compliance with the terms of the will.

"It is a wise decision, Señorita San Marco. These were your beloved father's wishes. I promise you that I will be at your service, to assist you in any way I can. Now, please have a seat and let us get the documents signed." Bucharo turned the chair behind the large desk invitingly toward Maria.

"That will not be necessary, Señor. When I said that I had almost no alternative but to sign the papers, that is exactly what I meant. Señor Houseman went into great detail over the ramifications of clause twenty-six 'C,' I believe it is. Would you mind reading that clause to me, Señor?"

Lonfranco could hardly keep his amusement from becoming evident. Maria was playing the game to the fullest, taking great pleasure in baiting this lowlife before she reeled him in for the catch. Bucharo's voice was a meek stammer when he finally retrieved the document and turned to the appropriate page.

"Señorita, I . . . I don't see how this is of any relevance to the matters that are before us. Can we kindly proceed with the signatures?"

"Read the clause, Señor!" There was a coldness in Maria's voice that Lonfranco had never heard before. There was also fire in her dark eyes, and Bucharo sensed for the first time that something was amiss. He quickly read the clause, then closed the document and returned it to his briefcase.

"Now may we proceed. Señorita? That clause is of no importance at this time. When, in the future, you choose a husband and marry, it is true, the estate will vest in you personally. But we cannot concern ourselves with this provision of the will until such time as you do get married."

The lawyer was trying hard to maintain his composure, but his stomach was turning and a general uneasiness filled his whole being.

"Señor, would you be so kind as to take a look at this scroll. Take your time to digest its contents." Maria handed Bucharo a rolled piece of parchment bound by a purple ribbon. The lawyer's hand began to shake uncontrollably as he looked aghast at marriage certificate.

"No! This cannot be true. This . . . this is some sick joke you are playing. Your father is barely in his grave and this is how you sully his memory? You married this immigrant? Are you mad? I will have you committed! I will have this annulled! You cheap little whore. I will..."

Suddenly Bucharo could no longer breathe, the force of Lonfranco's powerful grip around his throat making him gasp and sputter for air. He felt his feet lift off the carpeted floor, and he was held aloft as he clutched at the Italian's arm in an effort to break the hold.

"Listen to me now, you slimy piece of filth," Lonfranco's voice was barely audible speaking between tightly clenched teeth. "This is the last time I ever want to see your disgusting little act. Señor Houseman will be at your office this afternoon to verify that document. The marriage is legal, and under the terms of the will, it is you who have no recourse. If you do not cooperate to the fullest, there are certain business dealings relating to the Pampas railway lands that will be made public. I don't think your career or your social standing could withstand such a blemish. Now take your lecherous schemes and leave our home forever."

As the last word passed his lips, Lonfranco hurled the lawyer into the general's empty chair with such force that it toppled over backwards, sending Bucharo sprawling head over heels. It was all the newlyweds could do to keep from bursting out in laughter as this once-arrogant man sought to maintain some semblance of composure while he tried to right himself and collect his belongings.

It was like watching a live performance of slapstick comedy. Bucharo strained to avoid Lonfranco's reach, trying to locate his spectacles, circling the desk, dropping papers, and fumbling with the latch on his briefcase. The new husband kept taunting him, pretending to lunge in his direction. Finally, the pathetic little man scurried through the doorway without a backward glance. Despite all the threats, the De Setas were never bothered by Lopez Bucharo again.

The announcement of the De Seta - San Marco nuptials that appeared in the Buenos Aires newspapers within a few days of the wedding sent shock waves through Porteño high society. The reactions ranged from compassionate empathy for the grieving daughter and sister, to contempt and scurrilous gossip about the social climbing Italian immigrant.

Even the general population was intrigued by the suddenness of the event. Had Maria returned from the continent pregnant? Had this been a marriage of convenience to avoid Señorita San Marco giving birth to a bastard? Speculation was fired not only on the streets and in the drawing rooms of high society, but also in the press on a daily basis.

Reporters camped outside Casa San Marco for any storyline that would appease the public appetite for information. Crowds gathered alongside the newsmen, anxious for a glimpse of the most famous couple in the city. Servants were accosted as they left the walled compound. What was the true story? Was Maria pregnant? Was it the truth that the Italian was a peasant, eating only with his hands, that he had no refinement whatsoever, and was abusive to his new wife and the household staff?

It was only after invitations to a giant reception in honor of the memory of General Figueroa San Marco and his family were sent to every person of prominence in the capital, as well as the working press, that the situation surrounding the De Setas calmed down to a large degree. The invitation also announced the union of the general's only surviving heir to his former trusted executive assistant. The celebration would combine both homage to the fallen hero and acceptance of his daughter's marriage.

The affair was to be held three weeks hence at the elegant Alvear Palace Hotel's ballroom. Along with President Roca and a host of government officials, the top echelons of business and the military were invited to the fête. Failure to receive an invitation meant humiliation and a virtual exclusion from the social register. The unkind gossip stopped at once, and the event was anticipated with great excitement.

Lonfranco and Maria kept a very low profile in the days leading up to the reception. The idea of such a gathering had been Maria's. She was not bothered in the slightest by the gossip surrounding her marriage. Instead, it was her intention to use the occasion to cement relationships with potential and existing business associates. She thought it an opportune way of showing the people that mattered just what her new partnership with Lonfranco had to offer them.

With the help of Orlando Houseman and Lonfranco's precise notes of the general's business and social dealings, Maria was able to put together a guest list of the most influential and highly placed people. Over two hundred couples received invitations, and there were only a handful of regrets.

The evening was a major triumph for the newlyweds. Masses of people thronged the streets surrounding the Avlear Palace. Security was extremely tight due to the president's acceptance to attend, but there were to be no incidents on this moonlit night.

The breathtaking crystal chandeliers of the ballroom seemed to captivate the guests with their shimmering light. The mood was one of pure enchantment.

The host and hostess made their entrance down the sweeping circular stairway that intersected the edge of the huge dance floor. Maria looked positively radiant in her new Parisian gown. She had made certain that the fit was extra tight around her midsection to dispel any talk about her being in the family way.

Lonfranco was a presence in his formal tails. A red carnation appointed his lapel, and he had the appearance of a society rogue with his tall firm frame and his handsome good looks. Many a lady swooned at the sight of him as he expertly waltzed with his new bride to the traditional first tune of the evening. He never felt ill at ease or out of place, despite all the unflattering things that had been said of him.

He and Maria charmed everyone with whom they came in contact, and even President Roca was seen dancing with the new bride. The orchestra was the most renowned in all of Argentina, and the food the most lavish delicacies from three continents.

President Roca addressed the throng of revelers briefly to remind them of the loss of one of the nation's great patriots and defenders. He declared that a prominent public square in central Buenos Aires would be renamed Plaza San Marco, and that he had commissioned a mounted statue of General Figueroa San Marco to adorn its center. Tumultuous applause and a course of 'bravos' greeted the conclusion of the President's speech. There was hardly a dry eye in the ballroom.

Behind the scenes, Maria and Lonfranco would engage in short, productive conversations with many of the guests that they had preselected to seek out. Kind words and best wishes were greeted with gracious acceptance and exchanged for the hope of a more intimate discussion on whatever matter was of mutual importance to the two parties.

It was like holding a series of business meetings between intervals of a sporting event. Interviews were given to the press, the newlyweds danced the tango to a cleared dance floor, and a giant wedding cake was wheeled in at midnight to an accompaniment of fireworks in the hotel's garden terrace. When all was said and done, the Lonfranco De Setas had attained a place in Porteño society that would have them the most sought-after couple of the decade. But it was the business contacts they forged that evening that would secure their future and make them wealthy beyond their wildest dreams.

The first piece of business to conduct after the lavish soirée was to obtain a personal audience with President Roca to remind him of his promise to the general. Since complying with the president's wishes to return to active military duty had cost the general his life, Lonfranco was hopeful that President Roca would honor his pledge that the rail lands in the Pampas would be freed for development.

The general, who was a meticulous man and wrote minutes of all his meetings both private and professional, had told his executive assistant of the president's offer. As added insurance, Lonfranco took along the general's diary containing his handwritten notes when he and Maria were granted a few brief moments with Roca later that week. It was evident from the beginning that the president very much wanted the expansion of the Pampas economy.

"The area must blossom quickly as a means of economic stimulation and also to get the population working instead of politicking!" Roca proclaimed.

Maria, who had been thoroughly briefed by Lonfranco about all the general's business ventures, assured Roca that the De Setas were perfectly capable of negotiating and managing the deal with the British Rail interests. They reminded the president that Lonfranco, and no one else, had been with the general in England when the initial presentation was made to the British Rail Overseas board. The Italian had had his hand in every aspect of the negotiations. He was familiar with, and known to, the British agents in Buenos Aires that would be reporting back to London regarding the viability of the project. Some encouragement delivered to the British from the presidential office was certain to firm up the deal. The president agreed with that hypothesis.

Roca was so impressed with the De Setas that he signed a presidential decree that week authorizing the expropriation of thousands of acres of land by a newly formed state tribunal.

Working closely with the Minister of the Interior, the appointed head of this new tribunal was none other than Lonfranco De Seta. Assisted by a team of high-ranking civil servants and government officials, Lonfranco set about opening the fertile heartland of the Argentine Pampas to the world.

Once the rail deal was signed, sealed, and delivered by the British Rail board, the floodgates were opened for investors, both corporate and individual, to flock to the new promised land. Millions of pounds sterling poured into every sector of the Argentine economy.

With its technology and skilled personnel, Great Britain had developed and still controlled the gas, water, and telephone systems. The British population began to swell in the capital, reaching a very prominent pinnacle of over one hundred thousand souls by 1920. English schools, restaurants, social clubs, and political societies became very noticeable on the local landscape.

In the midst of all of this, whenever problems arose, the man most often contacted by the British business community to make inroads into the Argentine bureaucratic labyrinth was Lonfranco De Seta.

Directorships on several boards of foreign-owned companies followed success after success for the young immigrant. The final hurdle in attaining respectability came with the acquisition of his Argentine citizenship papers, which had been aided by a few well-placed directives from President Roca.

Lonfranco was eternally thankful for the chance that he had been given to prove himself, and he never forgot the one who had made it all possible.

Out of both respect and pragmatism, he styled his business persona after that of General Figueroa San Marco, always negotiating shrewdly but in good faith. His honesty and forthrightness elevated him to a position of trust and high standing in the foreign business community. It was said that Lonfranco De Seta's word was his bond, and a gentleman's handshake often replaced reams of legal documents.

Never far from the center of things was Maria, who was updated nightly by her husband on the latest activities. It was much easier for a man to stroll the corridors of influence in chauvinistic Argentina than a woman. Thus, it was decided that Lonfranco would be the more visible of the two partners.

Maria had her own staff that worked behind the scenes to plot strategy and integrate any social niceties into a scenario that might be in need of some extra attention. The arrangement worked to perfection, and there was not a more influential and respected couple in all of Argentina.

Domestically, the couple always seemed to find time for romance and adventure. They traveled alone to England and the continent extensively, combining the business of cultivating new investors and cementing old ties with her passion for antique furniture collecting and his for fine horse flesh.

Maria was also very active in the women's rights movement that was gathering momentum across the European community. Lonfranco gave her his blessing in this regard, but he warned her to keep in mind that they were seeking investors from the same male ruling class that she and her fellow 'suffragettes' were vocally denouncing. The two would joke incessantly about who got to wear the pants in the family on any particular day. It was all taken in the spirit of growing together as two separate, yet united people. Their life and love together was every bit as exciting and stimulating as they ever could have asked for, except in one regard.

By the year 1915, Europe was embroiled in the Great War. Travel to that region of the world was far too dangerous, and the De Seta's business interests had expanded to the point where they needed constant attention from the principals.

The most modern rail lines in the world now carried Argentine exports to nearby ports. Foreign investment in machinery, factories, and technology were at an all-time high. Prosperity abounded. Yet, there was an unmistakable absence in the lives of Señor and Señora De Seta.

Maria had been unable to bear any children in almost ten years of marriage. She had been able to get pregnant easily enough, but three miscarriages over ten years had left her frustrated and drained of much of her self-esteem as a woman. Lonfranco was totally devoted to her and tried to be as compassionate as possible. There was talk of adoption, but Maria would have none of it. In the fall of 1915, Maria became pregnant for the forth time and managed to carry the baby for seven months.

Late one night she awoke to a wet sensation in her lower midsection. Her scream startled Lonfranco. He had leapt out of bed to fetch his pistol and was about to run into the hallway to investigate for intruders when her sobs for him to return to her registered.

His heart sank as she held a bloodied hand out to show him. They were losing their baby! Immediately the panicked husband dispatched a coachman and carriage to fetch the family doctor. In the hour that it took the physician to arrive, the profuse bleeding had not subsided. The look on the doctor's face told Lonfranco that not only was the baby's life in grave danger, but that his wife needed emergency medical treatment as well.

She was taken to Hospital Rivadavia in the family carriage. Although the trip took only minutes, Maria was already unconscious by the time the first surgeon reached her side.

Lonfranco was ushered into a waiting area and told to try to stay calm. Doctor Lujan, the family physician, stayed by the distraught husband's side for the next hour until finally, Dr. Mercedes Plata, the head surgeon of the hospital, appeared in the room.

He asked the two men to accompany him, then turned and proceeded to walk away. Lonfranco was frantic for information and raced after the doctor, physically grabbing his shoulder and spinning him around.

"What is happening here, doctor? My wife and child, are they alright? I must be with Maria! Where is she? Where is she?"

It was only after the last question had passed his lips that Lonfranco was able to focus clearly on the surgeon's face. The tears that had been welling in Mercedes Plata's eyes were freed to fall slowly down his cheeks by the irate husband's jostling.

"Please, Señor, kindly step in here." The men entered a small room containing cleaning supplies, obviously not the original intended destination of doctor.

"Señor De Seta, in all my years of medical practice, I have never gotten use to conveying the news that I must tell you now. Your wife and unborn child have left this world to be with our Savior, Jesus Christ. May God have mercy on their souls! I have called for a priest to attend to their last rites. He may be of some help to you tonight as well, Señor . . . "

The baby had been stillborn. The medical cause of Maria's death was a condition known as 'placentia previa.' Lonfranco was told that this was a tearing of the mother's placenta away from the wall of the uterus, causing massive hemorrhaging. She basically bled to death internally.

Lonfranco could not fathom such a thing. He had rarely heard of birthing problems among the privileged classes in Buenos Aires. He assumed the finest surgeons and medical equipment were only blocks away from Casa San Marco. He and Maria had given lavishly and unselfishly to the Rivadavia Hospital's modernization campaign. Society ladies never had trouble giving birth, not that he had ever heard of.

It was left to Dr. Lujan to explain the realities of life to Lonfranco. "There are far more problems with conception and birthing that are sanitized and left behind private drawing room doors than any member of the male Porteño society will ever know about. The male's job is to induce conception, then step back until it is time to pass out the cigars. Everything in between is left to the women and their specialists. It is not within the realm of a gentleman to want to know the intricacies of what goes on during childbirth. Besides, it is a frightfully messy ordeal, much like fighting a pitched military battle. When things go wrong, especially with those people in the upper strata of society, a trip abroad or to their estancia is planned for several months until the perceived scandal dies down. Thus men hear nothing of these things, and the women gossip and speculate until word is sent from the grieving family that such and such happened a few months back, and that they would be returning to the capital in time for the next social season. I have personally attended to, and been instrumental in carrying off, more of these deceptions than I care to remember."

All of this gibberish did nothing to appease Lonfranco's ire. There must have been some terrible mistake at the hospital for them to allow Maria to die. Someone would pay for this. He would not rest until the person responsible was hung, drawn, and quartered.

It was Maria's lady-friends who were responsible for convincing Lonfranco that her tragic death was an act of God, and not due to incompetence by the medical staff. Avril Galaria, Maria's maid of honor at their wedding, spent many torturous hours at Casa San Marco consoling and reassuring the desolate husband.

"Sometimes these things are necessary, so that those left behind can follow the true path that God has ordained for them."

Lonfranco was not a religious man, but he found solace in the tender words of Avril Galaria. By the time Maria and their unborn male son were placed in the family crypt beside the general, his wife, and their three daughters, Lonfranco was at peace with himself and the world. He would accept Maria's passing as something that must have been necessary, for whatever reason. He would never fully understand why, but he knew that the Roman Catholic Church would provide him with spiritual answers if he ever chose to seek them out.

The widower returned home to Casa San Marco alone after the funeral and began charting out the course that his life must now follow. Certain adjustments were easier to make than others. Death had been a factor in Lonfranco's life before, but to lose a baby, a son that was his own flesh and blood, that was something that was especially hard for him to come to grips with.

"Maria is in heaven, reunited with her family," or so his religious friends told him. *Perhaps a gross oversimplification*, thought Lonfranco, *but the idea seems to give solace to so many people that possibly their theory has some virtue.*

Eventually, Lonfranco convinced himself that this train of thought was the only way to ease his heartbreak. He decided to focus on his business activities as a means of escaping the pain in his heart. The last thing on his mind was his social standing, yet paradoxically, the tragedies that had befallen him had only elevated his status within the Porteño social set. He was sought after with great fervor as a distinguished guest at many of the finest tables in the capital. Lonfranco, while not really caring for all the pretensions that accompanied so many of those 'puffed-up' people, was wise enough to play their games to his own advantage. When it suited him, he could be the host of some lavish fête at Casa San Marco, or he would invite a select group to visit Buenos Recuerdos for a long weekend or holiday. He not only catered to the local Porteño establishment, but also entertained throngs of foreign investors. His connections with the succession of politicians that followed President Roca in the nation's highest office were always based on his ability to drum up the appropriate amount of foreign capital for whatever project the government of the day had in mind. He traveled extensively through Europe and the Pacific rim over the four years following Maria's passing, but his preferred investors remained the British.

The feeling was mutual, by all accounts. Along with their financial interests in Argentina, the British had established a foothold in Buenos Aires and its environs that was beyond anyone's wildest imagination. Scientists, technicians, and manufacturers were joined by bankers, tradesmen, and teachers, many bringing their entire families with them. The British community inside Argentina had attained with pound sterling what they could not accomplish some years earlier with saber and cannon.

Initially, the British had arrived in Buenos Aires from the high seas during the later part of the eighteenth century. Most of them were smugglers or pirates. During the Napoleonic wars in the early nineteenth century, British Commodore Sir Home Popham decided to invade the city, claiming it in the name of his king. The arrogant Europeans were rudely expelled by the local militia and citizenry, but they soon recognized the bounty that extended peaceful relations with this unexplored and untapped market could reap for them. Overtures of peace and economic aid were offered in place of armed aggression, and this time, the Porteños welcomed the Brits with open arms and wallets.

English preparatory schools, or private schools, became established to educate the children of the United Kingdom transplants. St. Andrew's Scots School, the English High School, and a school that Lonfranco would give his particular attention to, the Sir Isaac Newton Academy of the Sciences, were all flourishing in the post-Great War era.

As an adjunct to all their business interests, the British had also brought with them a peculiar game that seemed to be quite the rage among all levels of society. Originally, according to one of Lonfranco's English acquaintances, the sport was meant to be played by gentlemen of the upper classes as a means of keeping the body as well as the mind physically fit. The more prominent teams in England came from famous schools such as Eton, Oxford, or Cambridge.

The sport was called soccer by the gentlemen. It soon became apparent that such good-natured physical release could benefit the toiling masses in various industries. Form a company team, keep the men in top condition, keep them out of the pubs and free of shenanigans, and give them pride in their work through association with that company team.

The factory owners and gentlemen were soon rubbing shoulders with the average working man out on the playing fields, the common denominator being the love of the sport the workers called 'football.'

The Italian immigrants that had arrived in ever-increasing numbers in Argentina had added their passion to the sport as well. It was not uncommon to see groups of young boys and men kicking a ball, or whatever object they could find, into a makeshift net.

The Argentine Football Association had been formed in 1883 by a group of Englishmen with Alexander Watson as its founding president. This was the first organized soccer association on the South American continent. The initial teams all had a link to the British community, whether it be an industry such as the railway club, an English suburb such as Quilmes Athletic Club, or a school team such as the English High School Alumni.

Over the years, the English role in the local version of the sport diminished as football was embraced as the national passion by Argentines of diverse heritage and social standing.

Teams sprang up throughout the country. Boca Juniors were supported primarily by the Italian community, while Racing Club was founded by French residents of the capital. Rosario Central Football Club was a British endeavor, as were the River Plate and Independiente clubs. The first international match pitting Argentina against neighboring Uruguay was played in 1901.

Lonfranco's involvement with the Isacc Newton Academy of the Sciences started as a result of the academy founding the first veterinary college in Argentina. Both equine and bovine studies were of particular interest to the scientific community at the academy. Several of the top practitioners and researchers in the field had arrived from England, having been lured away to join the impressive faculty.

Through a philanthropic foundation that he had set up in Maria's name, Lonfranco gave generously to the academy. He was consumed with perfecting a breed of beef cattle that would not only become the finest stock in Argentina, but would also stand as a premium export product. In addition, he had acquired the general's passion for thoroughbred racehorses and polo ponies, which he continued to breed at Buenos Recuerdos.

Lonfranco spent so much time at the Newton Academy that he was offered a seat on the board of governors by his close friend and fellow polo enthusiast, Dr. C.W. Reynolds, who was its chairman. The widower graciously accepted the appointment.

The Newton Academy was a school of two separate entities, the lower school and the university program. The lower, or preparatory school, catered to highschool-aged male students who had a propensity for the sciences, particularly medicine. While there was a sprinkling of liberal arts courses to round out the scholastic character of the young men, the emphasis was definitely on the sciences.

Admission to 'the prep,' as it was called, was the most highly sought-after placement in the entire country. The entrance examination took an entire weekend to complete. With the aid of an extensive scholarship program, boys from all levels of Argentine society were put on equal footing in the selection process. Preference was given, of course, to English families if there was a tie for a placement opening, but the applicants were never aware of the unwritten regulations that really determined admission.

Upon graduating from the prep, a student had the opportunity to continue on to the academy's university level programs that were affiliated with the University of Buenos Aires. This institution turned out the finest medical doctors, veterinarians, bio-chemists, and researchers on the continent. With a faculty that was world-renowned, students were guaranteed the most thorough and up-to-date educational experience available.

Like all the other English schools in and around the capital, the Newton Academy believed in a sound body as well as a sound mind. The prep soccer team became an attraction in itself, traveling the length and breadth of the country to showcase its skills and teach the sport to anyone who cared to learn.

The team played under the name 'Newton's Prefects,' a prefect being a senior student that had the responsibility of directing the academy's student body in the proper ways of being a gentleman. Prefects enforced the code of ethics and honor at the academy. They could act as disciplinarians among their peers, and their authority ranked just below that of the faculty. They were the most astute in the classroom and the most proficient on the playing fields. They were the elite of the elite. To be a Newton's Prefect was to be a deity among the general population, a perception that their prowess with a football did nothing to diminish.

The faculty, as well as the students at the university level, was also keenly interested in the sport. It was decided by the board of governors that as a means of promoting the academy, a senior team would join the newly formed football association and also play at the professional level as 'Newton's Prefects.'

The popularity of the senior team was immediate and beyond anyone's imagination. The team had acquired so many enthusiastic supporters that the board of governors immediately set about building their own stadium adjacent to the campus. The infusion of some fine Porteño players allowed the team to expand its base of support into the poorer barrios of the city, and even citizens who had no knowledge of the academic institution became fanatical followers of the football side. National championships became the norm, and the trophy cases in the rotunda of the academy's administration building were constantly being enlarged to accommodate the spoils of victory.

A soccer pitch was constructed at Buenos Recuerdos to honor Lonfranco's British friends. Even the gauchos seemed to be taken by the game, and many a lively contest was held between the foreign visitors and the local plainsmen. It was all in good fun, and Lonfranco made sure that his staff did not insult the guests by running up the score, as they were usually capable of doing.

A fortunate visitor to the Pergamino estate would be treated to a thrilling polo match featuring Lonfranco's internationally acclaimed team. Named to honor the memory of General Figueroa San Marco, this fine collection of men and mounts had traveled the world displaying their talents. More often than not, the team's patron used his polo playing sojourns abroad to entice an investor or to explore a new business scheme. Thus the costs of playing his favorite sport were likely to be paid in full by his shrewd knowledge of how to play the financial game as well as the game of polo.

One such trip to England in the spring of 1919 brought developments for which Lonfranco was totally unprepared.

The prime reason for this trip abroad was to buy a prize bull to augment to his stock of beef cattle. The breeder was a gregarious character by the name of Liam Peters, and it took little more than a few pints of stout for the two men to strike a deal on the animal's monetary value. After that, it was a night of lies and tall tales that concluded with Mr. Peters having to carry a very intoxicated Señor De Seta to his lodgings.

Lonfranco was insistent that the Englishman turn out the next afternoon to watch him make a fool of himself at a charity polo event. Peters at first scoffed at the idea, saying he might be interested if the game were played on more practical beasts of burden, such as his Holsteins. Finally, however, he admitted some responsibility for his guest's inebriated state and grudgingly accepted the invitation.

The pounding inside Lonfranco's head had not subsided by the time he sat astride his mount for the opening chucker of the match. A large crowd had gathered to witness the dashing Latin side, but the only thing Lonfranco felt like was dashing to the W.C. He was having difficulty focusing his eyes and was barely able to remain upright in the saddle. His mallet overshot several perfect balls that he normally would have converted easily to goals.

The English team won the day, and at the conclusion of the match, just as Lonfranco was about to collapse into an armchair some distance removed from the festivities, who should appear but Liam Peters with a bottle of champagne and two glasses.

"So, me boy, it looks like ya would have preferred to be ridin' old bossy today. She could have slowed things down fer ya a tad, until ya got yer sea legs back. Here, have a snort o' the hair o' the dog that bit ya."

Peters expelled the cork from the bottle of bubbly, poured two overflowing glasses, and handed one to Lonfranco.

"Mr. Peters, this is hardly what I need to make me whole again. Perhaps you might direct me to a chemist and then a dark, quiet room, a long distance from any beverage hall."

As Peters began to chide the Argentine for his reluctance to drink a toast to the victorious English polo side, he was interrupted in mid-sentence.

"There you are, Father. I've been at my wits' end trying to find you. Doctor Murphy, the vet, seems to be missing a bottle of his champagne. He says that he was engaged in a conversation with you just before the end of the match, and then both you and the bottle disappeared. So what is that object you are hiding from me behind your back? Why, you shameless old billy goat! Don't you know that these society people don't take kindly to . . ."

Lydia Peters left her scolding unfinished. Her father had tried to conceal the open champagne bottle, and in doing so, had turned to face his twenty-year-old daughter, blocking Lonfranco from her view.

As father and daughter engaged in a lively little jig over possession of the libation, Lydia almost fell into the lap of the seated visitor from Argentina.

"Ohhh! My apologies. I did not see you sitting there. My father can be a hand full after a night on the town, and I sometimes have to resort to stern measures to keep him in line."

Lydia pretended to be fully intent on her conversation with the stranger, but as her father tried to take a fast swallow of his precious treasure, she swept the bottle from his grasp and away from his lips.

An anguished cry of protest was all Liam Peters could muster as he watched the liquid gold soak into the turf. When the bottle was empty, Lydia again addressed her father.

"Now, we won't say a word to Dr. Murphy about this little incident, will we?" She slid the bottle quietly into a nearby refuse bin.

Lonfranco had sat watching this whole scene as if being entertained by a theater troupe. But even with his senses dulled by the alcohol consumed the night before, there was no mistaking the breathtaking beauty of this young woman. He was unable to move, mesmerized by the lilt of her accent, so soft and melodic, even when chiding her recalcitrant father.

Her sparkling blue eyes contained the same mischievous twinkle as her father's. Combined with her flaxen hair, she stood before Lonfranco as an image of feminine pulchritude unlike anything he had ever seen in South America. He shook his head to clear the cobwebs away.

"Oooooooohh laaaa." The pain shot across his forehead.

"Are you alright? Can I be of any assistance? You look quite peeked." Lydia's voice was the first soothing sound Lonfranco had heard all day.

"The lad's a wee bit under the weather this mornin', Lydia, as I expected. He's the one I told ya that might need some carin' for. Señor Lonfranco De Seta of Buenos Aires, Argentina, allow me to introduce my daughter, Lydia Anne Peters, R.N. That's registered nurse, if you don't know, my friend. I asked Lydia to come along today in case you fell off one of those hay burners and did yourself in. You weren't movin' too well when we said our good-byes last night. Matter o' fact, you weren't movin' at all."

The words that Peters spoke were not registering in Lonfranco's brain as he struggled to rise from his seat to take the lady's hand.

"It is my pleasure, Señorita, to make your acquaintance. I apologize for my lack of manners. I am not at my best at this moment."

"Father, were you out drinking with this poor man last night? A visitor to our country and this is how you welcome him? Sir, it is I who must apologize to you for my father's lack of consideration and contemptible behavior."

"On the contrary, Señorita, your father was most hospitable . . . from what I can recall. We had the pleasure of doing business yesterday afternoon, where, in fact, your father and I concluded a transaction involving one of his prize bulls. As gentlemen are wont to do, we then retired to the nearest establishment of good tidings to cement the deal. It would seem that I consumed a bit too much 'cement.' Believe me, no harm was done. I am the proud owner of a pedigreed steer, an acute hangover, and an embarrassed polo team. What more could a visitor to your country ask for, except maybe some buffer salts?"

He noticed how delicate her hand felt as he raised it to his lips for the traditional Latin greeting. His words brought a sweet smile to her lips.

Sweet Mother of Jesus, she is a beauty, he thought to himself. His heart was pounding in time with his aching head, and he was unsure if the lightheadedness that he felt was due to his current situation or his former intoxications.

"Well, if it's salts ya be needin', Lydia's the one to find them fer ya. As I said, she's a registered nurse. Served in the army field corps in France during The Big One. You'll be an easy job to patch up after what she's seen! Why don't you take Señor De Seta past the apothecary and then on to his inn to recuperate. I'm sure that Mrs. Peters and I would be honored to have you at our table for dinner tomorrow night, if you have the strength for it."

Lonfranco knew that such an invitation would be difficult to refuse, but he surprised himself at the speed of his acceptance. His business in England was all but concluded, his last polo match played, and he had a week to kill before his departure for South America. He had planned to travel on his own, perhaps to France for a few days, but nothing had been etched in stone.

How strange he felt climbing aboard Liam's small carriage, forced by circumstance to sit scandalously close to Lydia. A brief word with one of his fellow teammates as to his plans for the next forty-eight hours, and he and Lydia were off to Hillingdon Inn.

Liam preferred to remain behind and partake of the buffet that the Hillingdon Polo and Hunt Club had organized in honor of their Argentine guests. He would pass along Lonfranco's humble apologies and regrets due to a sudden illness and offer to assume the place of his old and intimate friend at their sumptuously set table. He instructed Lydia to return for him once Señor De Seta was feeling more comfortable and to remind him of his commitment the following night. With that, Liam Peters was off to join the revelry.

A crack of the whip sent the carriage on its way. Lonfranco's whole being was swept up in a rainbow of the senses. The sights, the sounds, the smells, and the feel of his thigh against the soft material of Lydia's dress all assaulted his clouded mind. He wanted to capture this moment and stop it in time so that he could analyze what on earth was happening to him when he had his full faculties back intact.

Since Maria's death, there had been no feeling in his heart except emptiness and resignation to a life alone. He had rationalized against another marriage as a means of protecting himself from further emotional disappointment. His work became his first and only love, and after his persistent refusal to socialize in a romantic context with members of the fairer sex, the Porteño society matchmakers grudgingly gave up and left him alone.

He had thought himself incapable of the feelings that he was experiencing at this moment, the giddy infatuation that this wisp of a girl was causing him. And he had known her less than an hour!

Her voice was like a lullaby as she made small talk. The early afternoon sun fell flush on his face as they traveled, and he closed his eyes and basked in its warmth.

Lydia asked if he preferred to ride in silence and apologized for "cackling on like a magpie." Now it was his turn to apologize for being such bad company and encouraged her to continue to soothe him with "the voice of an angel."

Lydia laughed and sang a lilting Irish tune that had often been useful to hearten the wounded soldiers in her care, or so she sadly imparted. Lonfranco could not fathom such a delicate creature in the midst of the slaughter that had become known as 'The Great War.' He had been an ocean and a world away from it in Argentina.

Images and impressions of Liam Peters kept popping into his mind. The old man had told him during their liquid shenanigans together that he had "a bit o' the Irish in him, a bit o' the English in him, and a lot o' the Scotch in him, preferably Glenlivet!" He certainly did have the latter in him that night, perhaps two full bottles worth by Lonfranco's best guess.

The South American had warmed to the British hybrid from the outset. Their initial meeting took place in the Peter's barn at 'Lowliam,' his sprawling farm northwest of London. The nearest town of any notability went by the name of High Wycombe. It was said that Liam's Irish grandfather and namesake renamed the dairy establishment and the surrounding lands that he purchased after himself as a way of mocking his snobbish English neighbors.

Liam Peters the Third was now the owner and overseer of one of Britain's most modern and successful livestock operations. He had been introduced to his newest friend and business associate from Argentina by Percy Pellet, a professional livestock broker from London. Pellet's services were retained specifically to search for premium breeding stock, in both beef cattle and thoroughbred horses.

The prospective purchaser found, within seconds of their meeting, that there was absolutely no pretension about Liam the Third. When Pellet introduced the two, the Brit was in a stall, mucking out one of his 'beauties.' The hand that he extended for Lonfranco to shake was covered by the most unsightly effluent. The visitor didn't flinch. He grasped the hand with a strong, full grip, and continued to hold on and shake it vigorously as Pellet made the usual salutations with a shocked, disgusted look on his face.

Liam smiled broadly as he invited his guests to join him for a close-up look at his champion stud. It was only Lonfranco who accepted the offer. The two men inspected the bull from every possible angle, standing knee high in excrement and shavings.

When all was said and done, both men knew that the other had a profound knowledge of the 'whys' and 'wherefores' of the bovine world. No one would be taken advantage of here. A price was stated, Pellet was consulted briefly, and a deal made in a matter of minutes.

Lonfranco had noted that the stout, blond-haired breeder seemed to have a number of personalities and dialects that he used as suited his purpose. He was perfectly capable of intoning the King's English in a thoroughly convincing nasal whine when addressing the haughty Mr. Pellet of London. Yet he seemed to prefer the blarney of an Irish leprechaun or the biting sarcasm of a Scottish warlord when scrutinizing the private parts of his four-legged loved ones. He had the South American doubled over in laughter on more than one occasion. There was no way of refusing to join him for a cleansing ale once the deal was struck and Pellet sent on his way to draw up the formal papers.

After a short stop at the chemist, it was on to Hillingdon Inn for Lydia and Lonfranco. Despite his condition, he was disappointed when the carriage ride was over. He would have gladly stayed by her side the rest of that fine afternoon, just to listen to her hypnotic voice.

Lydia made certain that her charge took the prescribed medicine she had purchased for him. She ordered some strong coffee and fruit juice to his room, soaked a cloth in cool water for his forehead, then made ready for her departure.

"Would you like me to send a carriage for you tomorrow evening, Señor De Seta?"

"Only if you will be in it, Miss Peters," he responded.

"Well, Señor, as much as I might like to be, my place at that time tomorrow will be with my mother and sisters, preparing the evening meal. Father doesn't believe in servants! Besides, with ten siblings and my parents around, there is hardly room for another soul. I would imagine that one of my brothers could fetch you around five o'clock. Does that sound suitable?"

He didn't want to have to wait that long to see her again, but tried his best to hide his impatience.

"That would be fine, Señorita, and thank you for your kindness today. You have made me a new man, or, at least, I hope to be a new man when this medicine takes effect."

"It is the least I could do, Señor De Seta. Someone must make penance for the evil that my father hath wrought upon you. Demon rum, the scourge of the weak and godless!"

Her soft smile told him that she meant her last comment as a jest. After the barbarism that she must have witnessed in France, it was a wonder that she still believed that there was a God at all.

Lydia closed the door gently behind her as she left, and her new admirer listened to the footsteps receding down the hall. Lonfranco reclined on the bed, closed his eyes, and tried to conjure up her enchanting image in his mind. Nothing did her justice. He awaited the following evening with great anticipation as he fell into a deep sleep.

Liam Peters loved to preside over a boisterous and bountiful table. The fare this evening was traditional English roast of beef, Yorkshire puddings, fresh vegetables galore, and a well lubricated trifle for dessert. A new wine preceded every course, and there was ample ale, stout, and bitters, not to mention the host's favorite, Glenlivet, to quench everyone's thirst. It was evident, just by looking around the table, that Liam Peters was as productive a sire as any of his prized stock. He had fathered eight sons and four daughters, much to the delight of the Catholic priest in the village. The old stallion had put all of his children to work at Lowliam when it did not conflict with their schooling, and each child now took a keen interest in the operation and preservation of their thriving enterprise.

The Great War did not leave Liam's brood unscathed, however. Liam the Fourth, once a muscular, towheaded youth, had returned from the front in 1916 severely gassed. The former Coldstream Guardsman was now just a mere shadow of his former self, confined to a wheelchair and unable to function without round-the-clock assistance. The family rallied to his side, and Mrs. Peters would often say that "It was their duty to care for him, just as it had been his duty to go to France to protect them."

Then there was young Will, sweet Will. He had been under the minimum military age, unable to cross the Channel in uniform. But he had inherited his father's ingenuity and began saving his money to purchase false documents that could be obtained on the black market. The lad had left a note, asking forgiveness from his parents and assuring them that he would be 'just fine.' From the day he left until the day the telegram was delivered, his mother knew that she would never lay eyes on him again.

'Missing in action,' was the way the Home Office described it. Did those words mean that there was a chance that he could be 'found' again? It all seemed so uncertain at the time.

Lydia and two of her sisters joined the British Expeditionary Force nursing corps, eventually heading to the continent with high hopes of finding their brother. It never happened. Sweet Will was lost to them forever.

There was also Betsy, Lydia's youngest sister. Bright, inquisitive, a virtuoso on the piano, little Betsy had succumbed to dysentery while serving near the front lines in Belgium at the end of the conflict.

Two dead, one gassed and disabled. It was a tragic toll for any family to suffer, but Lonfranco was impressed with how well everyone had picked up the pieces. Each member seemed ready to face the future, with Liam's contagious optimism. He had toasted his departed children in a heartfelt and emotional blessing as the family gathered around the table. That said and done, his ruddy face lit up like a lantern, and the stories and refreshments continued into the wee hours of the morning.

The guest of honor took every opportunity to engage Lydia in conversation. When that was impossible, he would steal a glance in her direction. Occasionally, Liam would catch him and let loose the canons.

"Be there something wrong with your neck, Señor De Seta? I see that you seem to be facing in the opposite direction whilst I be recounting this extremely informative discussion on cattle suppositories. Perhaps an injury from yesterday's match? I should send for the doctor if the condition persists. On second thought, I know the precise cure. Lydia, come sit beside your loving father. That way our guest will not do himself further damage as he tries to sneak a peek in your direction."

Lonfranco had been found out and could feel the flush of his face. He tried in vain to change the topic of conversation back to cattle suppositories.

Lydia, for her part, played the evening very coyly. She was always polite, but never gave any indication of a spark in her heart, while an inferno raged in Lonfranco's. At thirty-seven years of age, he felt ridiculously child-like. This behavior was certainly not becoming to a man of his age and stature. Try as he may, however, he was unable to get control of his feelings. The slightly tipsy visitor ended up staying the night in a guest room at Lowliam and was in no hurry, whatsoever, to depart the following morning.

Lydia and her sisters had been brought up to love music by their mother, who had trained at the Royal Conservatory in Dublin. Good fortune would have it that Lonfranco was greeted the following morning by the sound of sisters engaged in recital. This particular piece was a sonata for flute, piano, and violin. The melody sent his spirits soaring as he listened discreetly, hidden from sight.

When Mrs. Peters found the shy foreigner listening tentatively in the hallway, she invited him to take a seat in the parlor and listen in comfort. All the men of Lowliam had long since departed to their daily toils, and Lonfranco was 'forced' to spend the morning in the company of the ladies.

When the recital concluded, it was Lonfranco's turn to entertain the Peters women. Toby, the fifth eldest brother, had in his possession an old, badly tuned guitar that the guest had spotted the night before during a tour of the household. After delicately retuning the instrument, the man from South America launched into an emotional love song from his adopted country. The voice was strangely melodic for one with no formal training, and the effect on the women was dramatic. Tears welled in Lydia's eyes. Lonfranco stopped at once upon seeing this.

"Ladies, my humble apologies if I have upset you. I will cease this at once."

He began to put the guitar down when Lydia reached out and touched his arm.

"Please, Señor, do not take offense. Your music reminds me so much of the young men I once knew, over there. We used music to give them hope and peace after everything else had failed. Please, Señor, please continue. It was wonderful. It . . . it touched me deeply."

There is a spark there after all, Lonfranco thought. Music could be his bellows to fan the flames of passion.

A stroll in the garden gave them a chance to be alone, before the men returned for the noonday meal. He confessed the obvious to Lydia, that he was smitten by her and would like to stay in contact with her if she would not be offended.

Lydia countered by asking endless questions about his life in Argentina. She had already been told certain facts by her mother. Señor De Seta was a widower with no children, extremely wealthy, and a man of great influence on both sides of the Atlantic. But she also wanted to know the more personal details. Where did he live? How had he adapted to a life alone? What was Buenos Aires like? Was there room for another woman in his life? His kiss both startled and reassured her that there was.

Lonfranco stayed on at Lowliam for the next four days. When it was time to depart for Southampton to catch his passage back to Argentina, Lydia and Liam made the journey with him. His bond to the Peters family had cemented quickly, and he invited whichever of the troupe that could make the crossing to visit him in Argentina the following February. Liam Peters was heartened by the suggestion, for that disgusting month happened to be bleak midwinter in England, but midsummer in Buenos Aires.

Liam pretended to be interested in the structure of the ship's hull while the two lovers said their passionate good-byes on the wharf. The next time Lonfranco set foot on English soil again, it would be one year hence, on the occasion of his marriage to Lydia Anne Peters.

CHAPTER SEVEN

The nuptials followed eleven months of ardent transatlantic correspondence and a month-long visit to Argentina by Lydia and her father. The young English woman had taken to studying Spanish in preparation for her journey, and Lonfranco was surprised at her fluency and ease with the language.

The visitors were escorted on grand tours of the capital and the surrounding environs, with an accommodating stop at one of the many British pubs or cafés always on the itinerary, lest Liam suffer from liquid culture shock. Lonfranco's special guests were treated to a performance at the Colon Opera House, a boat cruise on the Rio de la Plata, a gala ball at Casa San Marco, and a polo match at the very British Hurlingham Club, where Lonfranco vindicated himself for his poor showing in his last match in England. All this and much more were crammed into a very exhausting two weeks.

Finally it was time to depart for the much anticipated trip to Buenos Recuerdos. Liam in particular had had his fill of the city life and the transplanted snobs from 'over 'ome.' He told Lonfranco that he longed to fill his nostrils with the smell of manure again.

Pergamino was just the place to satisfy his desire. Liam seemed a new man as he spent hours inspecting livestock and learning about South American breeding techniques. He was constantly in the company of Hector Brown, the bilingual grandson of transplanted English stock. Brown had attained the position of head overseer of the cattle operation at Buenos Recuerdos, and was Lonfranco's most trusted employee. This, of course, freed the proprietor of the estancia to spend as much time as he pleased exploring the Pampas on horseback with his ladylove. A guitar was always in evidence on these outings, and often after a picnic lunch and several soulful tunes, they would make love on a blanket ensconced in a world of their own.

Lydia's attitude toward her sexuality had been strongly influenced by her wartime experiences. Life had seemed so insignificant at the time, and pleasures so fleeting. She had given herself first to a young captain in the Blackwatch regiment, and then had heard of his death less than a month later. There had been others after him, but she never considered herself promiscuous. She wanted to give, to soothe, to comfort these poor boys to whom life had dealt aces and eights. A dead man's hand.

Lydia had not resisted Lonfranco's amorous advances as they strolled in that wooded glen near Lowliam many months before. She was afraid of losing him, as she had all the others, but she also felt a stronger passion for this Latin lover than she had ever previously experienced. After their relationship had been consummated, she confessed her past liaisons with a forthrightness that surprised, but did not offend her suitor. The slate was clean as far as he was concerned, and he had told her so. The past was in the past, and it would stay there forever. The topic was never discussed again.

Their parting was excruciatingly painful, and the months leading up to the wedding seemed to move with the speed of a tortoise. When the wedding party finally arrived from Argentina, it included several members of Porteño society whom Lydia had preciously met, as well as a sprinkling of polo players and business associates. In total, thirty-six people made the voyage from the Southern Hemisphere to take part in the most talked about, widely publicized social event in High Wycombe since the end of the war.

Lonfranco's English business associates turned out in full force, kidnapping him on his last night as a single gentleman, and forcing him to take part in their loss of bachelorhood rituals. It mattered not that he was a widower, not a bachelor, as he loudly protested.

"A red herring, old chap. Now come on, another pint and chug-a-lug this time!" came the anonymous reply.

The ceremony, while Roman Catholic, did not offend the vast majority of guests who were Church of England followers. The priest welcomed them warmly, and even inserted a prayer and one hymn from their solemnization of matrimony service so that the Anglicans would feel at ease.

As expected, Liam Peters saw to it that no one left the reception hungry or thirsty, and the festivities continued until dawn. The newlyweds stole away to the Hillingdon Inn just after midnight and took up lodging in the room where Lonfranco had stayed the year before. It was the room in which they had been alone together, ever so briefly, for the first time.

A honeymoon in Italy followed, then a short visit to Lowliam to say their good-byes, and it was off to Argentina to start a new life together. That life would be blessed by a baby in September of 1921, and Lonfranco finally felt that his life was complete and fulfilled with the birth of his infant son.

Named Peter Figueroa De Seta, after the Peters' surname and Lonfranco's mentor, the boy would be the shining star in his parent's constellation. The only cloud that appeared in the De Seta's bright and happy life together was Lydia's inability to become pregnant again, due to complications during Peter's birth.

Lonfranco was not upset in the least at this news, for having lost a wife and baby during childbirth already, he was thankful that he would not have to experience that ordeal again. He had his son, and the bloodline would endure. What more could a man ask for?

The years passed quickly, with good health and financial success blessing the De Seta household. Peter grew to be an intelligent, sensitive young man with a faculty for the sciences. He was enrolled in the Newton Academy at age six, and graduated twelve years later, cum laude and class president. He continued on to medical school at the academy and became one of the top pediatric surgeons in the country.

Life for Lydia and Lonfranco was idyllic during those years. Their love for each other never faltered, and they doted on their son as if nothing else in the world mattered. Lonfranco taught him to ride and play the guitar, much as old Roc Sena had done for him. The boy was instilled with a love of the land and its wildlife, as well as a respect for the almighty peso and the benefits that hard work could reap.

He inherited his gentleness and tranquility from his mother. She read to him in English, so that he would become fluent at an early age. She taught him of the great poets and writers, and also of the wonders of the world and beyond. She shared with him her stories of the horrors of war and warned him to always avoid armed confrontation as a solution to a problem. She imbued him with a true love for children with the many stories of her own childhood as one twelfth of Liam Peters' offspring.

It was with Lydia's blessing that Peter decided to practice pediatric medicine instead of pursuing a career in the family business, as his father would have preferred. Lonfranco was not unduly upset about his son's chosen vocation and actually found the fact that there was an esteemed surgeon in the family, a source of great pride.

The three De Seta's traveled to England and Europe on many occasions to renew old acquaintances with family and friends. All that came to an abrupt halt in 1939, the year that Peter entered medical school and Adolph Hitler entered Poland.

England was at war with Germany for the second time in two decades, and, once again, the Peters family would encounter the grim reaper.

Brothers Edward and Toby, the guitar enthusiast, would perish in the insanity that swept across Europe and infested the Pacific Rim. Argentina again remained neutral, although the advances in mechanized transportation, especially in the aviation field, made the world a much smaller place.

'Splendid isolationism' had become a phrase borrowed from the Americans before their entry into the first Great War. Both the Allied and Axis powers exerted enough pressure on Argentina to make the reality of the phrase far from splendid. Nevertheless, by 1945, the storm had been weathered and life returned to normal for the globe-trotting elder De Setas.

As always, Argentine politics remained volatile during this period, with a succession of governments attaining then losing the favor of the masses. Lonfranco continued to use his influence wisely, and this allowed the family assets to continue to prosper.

In February of 1946, an opportunistic army officer by the name of Juan Domingo Perón swept to power and began what would become the most remarkable political career in Argentine history.

Perón had great appeal with the common people, but he also had a firm grasp of the economic realities of the time. The military was a valuable asset when it came to dealing with dissidents or troublemakers, but it was the bankers and financiers that would determine the real fate of his regime. The master politician played all the angles to perfection. Despite several well documented public atrocities, Perón remained in the presidential palace for the next nine years.

Juan Perón's ascent to the presidency occurred in the same year as Peter De Seta's ascent to the surgical staff of the Children's Hospital of Buenos Aires. A kind and sympathetic practitioner, Peter was at his best in the company of ailing youngsters.

Always wanting to do more for his young patients, he easily convinced his philanthropic father to establish a summer camp for terminally ill children on the banks of the Rio de la Plata, north of the city near Tigre.

The camp, optimistically named 'No Se Preocupe' or 'Don't Worry!' was Peter's pride and joy. Every spare moment he could find was spent planning further expansion or fundraising for new facilities.

His two other passions were the classical guitar, with which he often entertained his adoring charges, and surprisingly for such a gentle man, the Boca Juniors football team. Hard times had fallen on his alma mater's professional club, and Newton's once lofty Prefects languished in the depth of the Argentine third division table.

It was the pride, the color, and the passion of the Boca Junior's fans that were the siren's call to Peter. The first time he ever witnessed a match at the Bombonera, their raucous, rollicking, intimate stadium, he knew that he was hooked. Perhaps it was his Italian roots finding a home and a cause, for there was real passion in the heart of Peter De Seta, too, and on game days he would often become one of 'the bad and the brave' on the Bombonera terraces.

He would buy blocks of tickets and give them away to the soccer mad parents of his patients. It was not unusual to see a star player visiting one of Peter's wards in the hospital or teaching the children the game they loved on the beach at No Se Preocupe.

One of the more prominent local families in Tigre happened to have a direct connection to camp No Se Preocupe. Ernesto Robillar owned several ferries that plied the waters of the Tigre delta as tourist vessels. On weekends, when hundreds of Porteños took the hour-long train ride to Tigre, they would most likely step aboard one of Robillar's boats. There they would continue their escape further out into the delta, where parks lined with weeping willows embraced small restaurants and hotels. It was a profitable livelihood for Robillar, and it allowed his family to enjoy a lifestyle unlike anything available in Buenos Aires.

Unfortunately, Ernesto Robillar's youngest son, one of three sons and a daughter, had come in contact with the polio virus. The disabling disease had wasted the youngster's body to the point where he was paraplegic. The child had spent several months in the Children's Hospital in Buenos Aires under the care of Dr. Peter De Seta.

When the reality of the boy's terminal situation was relayed to his parents, Peter tried to lessen the shock by inviting them to bring young Ernesto Jr. to No Se Preocupe as often as he was able. The staff at the camp was particularly adept at counseling both parents and children on how to face death with peace in their hearts and the joy of being with their God in the afterlife.

Even at ten years of age and in spite of his disability, Ernesto Jr. was a big football fan, a supporter of the River Plate team. He and Peter would engage in spirited discussions on the merits of their respective loyalties. The boy's mind was still as sharp as a tack, and he displayed a knowledge of the strategies of the game that left Peter scratching his head in amazement.

Ernesto Jr. also had a very earthy sense of humor. That, combined with his wandering hands, would often cause him to be reprimanded for telling off-color stories to the other children on his ward or pinching the behinds of the female nursing staff.

Privately, Peter would recount Ernesto's antics to his male peers at the hospital, and the boy became quite a celebrity in the medical circles for his youthful lustiness.

When the illness began to overwhelm the lad and Peter could see the bright light that had shone in his eyes slowly extinguishing, the doctor still had one last trick up his sleeve.

He promised Ernesto Jr. a big surprise if he would visit him for a few weeks at No Se Preocupe. Irrepressible boyish curiosity, along with Peter's blunt talk to the dying youngster's parents, paved the way for Ernesto Jr.'s arrival at the camp one week later. He was accompanied by his mother and sister, Florencia, whom Peter had never met before.

The staff greeted the Robillars with open arms, and after a tour and a light noon meal, Ernesto Jr. was shown to his dormitory, where he was to meet his three other roommates. Instead of other patients, however, he was welcomed to his quarters by Dr. Peter De Seta and a man that the boy recognized instantly.

That man was Omar Canas, the legendary goalkeeper for River Plate and the Argentine National Team.

Ernesto had lauded Omar's skills to such an extent that the doctor had asked the goaltender to make a special trip to his camp. Canas had accepted the invitation without a second thought, for Peter De Seta had saved his young daughter's life a few years earlier by performing an emergency appendectomy on the child. If the good doctor had a special patient who was a fan of his, the very least he could do was to give the child some hope and encouragement.

Ernesto's jaw almost hit the floor when he saw his idol standing before him in the camp dormitory. Their private meeting lasted over an hour, and Peter was sure that he saw the brightness shining full strength in Ernesto's eyes once again. The Robillar women were duly impressed as well, and they thanked Peter at great length for giving the boy the thrill of his lifetime. It wasn't until after the women had left that Peter began to reflect on the dark-haired beauty that was Ernesto Jr.'s sister.

The doctor had never really had the time to engage in the frivolities of romance, much to the dismay of his parents and a legion of single Porteño girls. He had dated sporadically, mostly out of deference to his mother, who kept reminding him that any man over the age of thirty who was still single should be drafted into the priesthood.

Florencia Robillar had initially been slotted into the 'relatives of patients' category in the doctor's mind when they first had been introduced, but he recognized the same fire in her eyes that he had seen in Ernesto's. While patient and football star were allowed to converse privately, Florencia took Peter aside to ask for the real prognosis on her brother. The news was not hopeful, but Peter promised to make the boy as comfortable, spiritually and physically, as was humanly possible.

He invited her to return to the camp any time she wished, for family were always encouraged to be involved in the therapy process. But Peter had been far more enthusiastic in requesting Florencia's assistance than was normally the case. He tried to conceal his interest from young Ernesto, but the boy immediately picked up on the doctor's seemingly offhand inquiries about his sister.

"She's hot stuff, isn't she, Doc?" the boy said with a leer. "When I was able to walk, I would sneak into her bedroom and hide behind her curtains until she came in to change for bed. I would position the mirror on her bathroom door so that I could see her undress and take her bath. Ooh la la, she has some set of knockers! I tried to . . . "

Peter feigned disgust at such language and reminded the boy that he was talking about his sister. "There will be no more of that talk, young man, as long as you are a guest here at the camp. The lady is your own flesh and blood, not some puta. Let's concentrate on our football discussions from now on, OK?"

Peter wondered if the boy had seen him blush at the mention of Florencia's anatomy. He was also thankful for the clipboard that he was holding which enabled him to cover his swelling instrument.

Florencia Robillar became a frequent visitor to the camp while her brother was a patient there. Peter would always find time for a lengthy discussion about Ernesto's condition, often as the two walked along the shores of the Rio de la Plata. They found themselves talking about many other topics as they became more comfortable in one another's company. Finally, it was the doctor who asked permission to escort the señorita to a concert in one of the local parks the following Sunday.

Peter was definitely smitten for the first time in his life, and fortunately for him, the young señorita from Tigre reciprocated his feelings. A yearlong euphoric courtship followed their first date, saddened only by Ernesto Jr.'s tragic passing a month after their announced engagement.

Lonfranco and Lydia threw their son and his bride-to-be a succession of grand parties to introduce Florencia to Porteño society. To be the wife of a famous surgeon was a position that could not be ignored or taken lightly. The couple was married on a beautiful spring night in early December, 1954, an evening that was proclaimed the fête of the year in the social columns of the Buenos Aires dailies.

The Peter De Setas settled into a comfortable flat on Calle Pellegrini in the Recoleta district, only minutes' walk from the Children's Hospital and not far from the home of Peter's parents in Palermo. Florencia adapted to her new surroundings and prominent social position with ease. She and Peter were constant visitors at Casa San Marco, where Lydia and Lonfranco always made the young lady from Tigre feel welcome. She returned their warmth by delivering to them their first grandson, Lonfranco Ernesto De Seta on June 1, 1955.

Again the political tide that constantly ebbed and flowed in Argentina was ebbing for Juan Perón and his Perónista government. The death of Perón's popular political wife, Eva, in July 1952, marked the beginning of the end. Students, restless for more extensive populist reforms, and the church, which felt that Perón was usurping its powers, led the opposition. In September 1955, Perón, fearing a bloodbath when the loyalty of his army came into question, fled to Spain in exile. He was replaced by a succession of military dictators, all of whom, like those before them, maintained their high office by using less than democratic means.

Lonfranco had weathered the Perónist regime by playing both ends against the middle. For the most part, the oligarchy, or privileged classes in Argentina, were vilified and tormented by the Perónists, but the De Setas had kept a low public profile for fear of attracting the attention of Perón's watchdogs.

The president was a charismatic figure who was able to charm many of his most vocal detractors. Perón also had a taste for the good life as well. He had found that Porteño society, with its network of fundraising capabilities at home and international business contacts abroad, was a means by which he could spread his influence into the upper reaches of the global financial strata. As long as you were not his enemy, you could be his friend, and he was welcomed into many of the oligarchy's lavish homes and estates. This enabled him to be perceived as a president of all the people, rich and poor.

Lonfranco had met the president on several occasions, and while he was not fond of his political ideals, he admired the man and his beautiful, intelligent wife. Cattle exports had become the main staple of the Argentine economy, and the president had a high regard for the men that were making this possible, men like Lonfranco De Seta. So in the end, there was no disruption to the De Seta business empire under the Perónists, due in a very large part to Lonfranco's ability to adjust to the climate of the times.

It was shortly after the birth of his grandson that Lonfranco began to experience migraine headaches. At first they were an infrequent annoyance, but they tended to get stronger and more persistent as time went on.

Peter was the first physician consulted, but being a pediatric specialist, he was quick to recommend a visit to the leading neurologist in Buenos Aires. A battery of tests was conducted, with no positive diagnosis formulated. Fresh air and rest were prescribed, meaning an extended stay at Buenos Recuerdos. The industrialization of the capital and the resultant pollution had made living in the heart of the city unsuitable for many of those in frail health.

It was agreed that Lydia would stay at Casa San Marco initially, for she wanted to be close to her new grandson. A team of private nurses would accompany Lonfranco to Pergamino, and his condition would be monitored constantly. The rest of the family would visit the estate on holidays and whenever their schedules permitted.

Buenos Recuerdos had, by now, been overseen by Hector Brown for several years. He remained Lonfranco's right-hand man, responsible for all facets of the operation. The two men had an unspoken understanding of the way life should be on the estate, and they were extremely close.

At age seventy-two, Lonfranco had begun to curtail many of his overseas business activities. This enabled him to concentrate on matters at home. Those damned headaches also had a great bearing on his daily routine. Hector was constantly by his employer's side, ready to carry out his bidding. In the beginning, the doctor's recommendation proved effective. Rest and fresh air had accomplished the desired result of controlling the migraines.

Unfortunately, it was only a temporary reprieve. After almost one full year at Buenos Recuerdos, it was suggested that a trip to New York City be arranged to see the world-renowned neurosurgeon, Dr. Gideon Spence, at the Sloane Kettering Institute. Passage was booked for the entire family at Lonfranco's request. He wanted the trip to be a happy, enjoyable adventure for his clan, no matter how much he feared the news that would ultimately await him there.

While the rest of the family had the time of their lives in Manhattan shopping, sightseeing, taking in the best Broadway had to offer, and residing at the fabulous Sherry Netherland Hotel on Fifth Avenue right across from Central Park, Dr. Spence put his Argentine patient through four days of exhausting tests, x-rays, and scans. Lonfranco did not include Lydia in any of the medical proceedings, preferring, instead, that she enjoy herself and help out with his grandson. Each evening the family would dine together, either out at a five-star restaurant, or, if Lonfranco was too exhausted or suffering an attack, from the room service menu served in their palatial suite.

On the morning of the fifth day, a concerned Dr. Spence held counsel with his patient.

"You have a baseball-sized tumor at the base of your brain, Señor De Seta. How long it has been there is anyone's guess. The procedures from here on are very precise, however. With the frequency of your migraines increasing, we estimate that the tumor is growing rapidly. Immediate surgery is the only option. Hopefully, the mass is not malignant, but if it is, we hope to arrest any further growth with radiation. I would urge you to make your decision quickly, so we may book you a bed."

Lonfranco had known in his heart that this would be the news he had to deal with. He thanked Dr. Spence and informed him that a bed would not be necessary, that he would return to Argentina to live out his remaining time.

At a family meeting that night in their suite, he repeated the doctor's diagnosis and recommendation. He told his loved ones that if there was to be any surgery, it would be done in Buenos Aires, close to his home and the people he loved. He was not willing to disrupt everyone's lives to stay in a New York hospital for what might be months. His wishes were respected without argument, and a few days later, the De Setas set sail back to their homeland.

The surgery was performed in Buenos Aires less than a month later, the pain having become intolerable. The tumor was found to be malignant, and the prognosis for full recovery, very slim. Friends and well-wishers rallied to Lydia's side, and what was anticipated to be a death vigil took place in the corridors and waiting rooms of Hospital Rivadavia.

Lonfranco, however, did not cooperate with the doomsayers. His recovery shocked everyone in the medical profession. Within three weeks of the operation, he was recuperating back at Casa San Marco.

That was the good news, that he was alive. The reality of the situation was that the family patriarch was unable to walk unassisted, and that his speech was slurred and garbled. He would spend his days in the garden, sitting in a wheelchair, a nurse constantly by his side. His frustration with his post-operative condition was hardly ever evident. Only on the rare occasions that his requests could not be deciphered would he raise his voice and shout some unintelligible command.

Radiation treatments, as had been recommended in New York, commenced a short time after surgery. Six months later, Lonfranco was given as clean a bill of health as was possible under the circumstances. His speech and motor movements would never return to him, and Lydia was forced to work in concert with Hector Brown and various other business associates of Lonfranco's to enable her to get a grasp of the family assets and operations. She proved more than equal to the task.

Peter De Seta remained somewhat removed from the day-to-day routine of running his father's assets. A hectic schedule of his own, both at the hospital and the camp, kept him constantly on the run. He had never really liked Pergamino that much, if the truth be known, preferring, instead, the urban lifestyle to the wide-open spaces. He was, nevertheless, very attentive to his father and assisted his mother whenever he was able. It was Florencia who Lydia grew to rely on the most. She and young Lonfranco would spend many a night in one of the guest suites at Casa San Marco after a full day and night of meetings and planning sessions.

Lydia wondered constantly about the future of Buenos Recuerdos, given Peter's lack of interest in stepping into his father's shoes. But the English lady had been born and raised on a farm, and the smell of manure was not foreign to her nostrils. She determined in the end that the cattle business and the estate would be kept, at least for the immediate future. She and her husband would simply commute between the city and the country as matters required.

Lonfranco's condition stabilized to the point that he was no longer in any discernible pain. He constantly wore a hat to cover the scars of surgery on his now fully bald head, but that was the only visible sign of his past trauma. He was generally content to sit quietly and ponder whatever was going on inside his mind. For three years he lived in his own world, watching his grandson grow, the flowers bloom, the rains come and go, all with little or no sign of anxiety or grief.

In May of 1959, an infant was placed on the elderly patient's lap that he had never seen before. Lydia whispered in his ear over and over again, "your new grandson . . . your new grandson." She swore that she saw Lonfranco's eyes brighten before the tears cascaded down his cheeks. His new grandson, Renaldo Figueroa De Seta, had been born on the fifth of May, and named after Peter's mentor and world-famous pediatrician, Dr. Renaldo Las Heras.

As so often happens, "the good Lord giveth, the good Lord taketh away." Those were the words of the priest that was summoned the next morning to Casa San Marco to administer the last rites to Lonfranco Guissepe De Seta. The patriarch of the family had passed into the next world, quietly, peacefully, in his sleep. A smile of contentment graced his angelic face.

CHAPTER EIGHT

Immediately following the funeral, Lydia set about the task of sorting through the myriad of business ventures in which her husband had been involved. She did so, reassured and comforted by the tributes that were accorded to Lonfranco, both locally and in the international press.

The once penniless Italian 'pick and shovel' man had been heralded widely as one of the forebearers of the modern industrial revolution in Argentina. Telegrams from old friends and acquaintances in many parts of the globe attested to his vision and achievements. Even the new president of Argentina, Arturo Frondizi, stated that he wished that he had someone with Lonfranco De Seta's international business contacts to help him spearhead a new push for increased foreign investment in his country.

On a personal level, there was little remorse or regret in Lydia's heart when it came to losing her mate of almost forty years. Their time together had been pure magic, the stuff that dreams were made of, but seeing him in his weakened condition broke her heart. She knew that he was at peace, and that she would be with him again one day. It was now her duty to look after the well-being of the De Seta family.

Lawyers and accountants became constant fixtures at Casa San Marco. Lonfranco had been wise enough to use the same legal and accounting firms for all his ventures, but even so, the complicated web of share stakes and minor interests in smaller companies took weeks to untangle. Lydia never complained though, for she found that she was fascinated by the way her husband's business mind had worked.

The cattle business, for example, began with the breeding of livestock. Simple enough. To get that livestock to the slaughterhouses and tanneries required railways, which were British-owned and controlled. But the rail cars that actually transported the cattle were manufactured in Argentina by a company in which Lonfranco had a seventy percent stake in.

He also had major units of the slaughtering and tanning segments, as well as a shipping company and a small airline. When everything was finally tallied, the estate of Lonfranco De Seta held assets totaling nearly one hundred million U.S. dollars.

Lydia was astounded when the totals became apparent to her. She had known that the family was well off, but Lonfranco rarely discussed the financial details of the businesses with her. Even during his extended convalescence the past year or so while she was working in concert with his advisors, the magnitude of the investments had never really become evident.

Many of Lonfranco's corporate interests had been shielded from scrutiny by an elaborate scheme of shell holding companies, to prevent them from becoming targets of a populist nationalization plan. With the political climate still very tenuous, such precautions were deemed necessary, even critical, to the survival of the family fortune.

The problem that Lydia faced was unsettling. With two young grandchildren on the scene, she much preferred their company to that of the cigar-smoking "suits." After consulting with Hector Brown and receiving his assurance that he would remain at Buenos Recuerdos for an indefinite but lengthy time, Lydia summoned the estate's executors and, as the sole beneficiary, instructed them to liquidate all the interests in each and every company.

The family would remain in the cattle breeding business in a somewhat scaled down version. The capitol raised by the sale of assets would be reinvested in separate trusts for Peter, Florencia, Lonfranco, and Renaldo. Lydia, herself, would hold a certain portion of the proceeds for her own personal use. This plan was not questioned by the executors, for President Frondizi had, once again, opened the doors to foreign investors, and the plums of the De Seta empire would fetch a healthy price for Lydia and her family.

Meanwhile, Lydia urged Peter and Florencia to gather up the children and join her permanently at Casa San Marco. The house was far too large for one person. It also contained too many memories of the happy times when the rooms were alive with the sounds of parties and children, and most of all, of him!

With two growing boys to raise, Peter's once spacious, convenient flat was now, by his own admission, cramped and somewhat constricting. Florencia was all for the move, and so it came to pass that the De Seta family closed ranks inside the high stucco walls of Casa San Marco. They enjoyed the next seven years developing a bond that made them as close as a family could be.

The eldest son, Lonfranco, came to be known by the nickname 'Lonnie,' primarily to avoid confusion with his late grandfather. His proper name seemed to be used only when he was in trouble, as he frequently was.

Lonnie was a bruising, active, vocal child who liked the sport of pushing adults to the brink of frustration. By contrast, his younger brother, Renaldo, was a quiet, studious youngster who was always seeking the approval of his elders. The boys got along together in a typical brother-to-brother relationship, sometimes the best of friends, but more often than not, full of the petty squabbles that make a home with children such a challenging place.

Lydia adored both her grandsons and spent hours reading them stories and telling them tales of their grandfathers. Liam Peters had died shortly after the end of World War II, some said of a broken heart caused by the loss of his two sons in the conflict. Lydia knew the cause of death to be cirrhosis of the liver, brought on by a far too intimate relationship with Mr. Glenlivet.

The stories of England, in particular, thrilled the boys, and their favorites seemed to always revolve around the monarchy, in particular, the recently crowned young Queen Elizabeth the Second. Lydia promised that when they were a little older, the family would book passage to the British Isles on one of the modern ocean liners. They would spend a month or so visiting their great-aunts and great-uncles whom they had never seen, and work in a visit Buckingham Palace, the Tower of London, and Big Ben.

Peter continued to work long hours at the hospital and his camp, but he always made time for his sons. He tried to instill in them his two great passions: the guitar and football. Lonnie had little success with the former, being far too impatient and rambunctious to sit still long enough to make his fingers cooperate. The latter endeavor, football, turned out to be the boy's saving grace.

Finally he had a focus and an outlet for all his pent-up energy. He accompanied Peter to every home game that the Boca Juniors played in the capital, and he was in awe, like his father before him, of the color, the noise, and the passion. To encourage his sons' interest, Peter set up a goal net on the sodded portion of the inner garden at Casa San Marco and spent hours with his boys practicing dribbling, passing, and shooting.

The ladies of the household found it hilarious that he made his sons waddle like ducks around and around the perimeter of the enclosure, then upon his command, leap as high in the air as they could. He told the boys not to worry about the women's silly comments, and that this game of 'ducks and frogs,' as he called it, would give their legs the strength they needed to score many goals.

The younger son, Renaldo, seemed to be the exact opposite of his older brother. He took to the guitar right away, spending hours plucking at the strings, for his tiny hands were still too small to make all the proper cord maneuvers. The first professional football game he attended with his father turned out to be a disaster.

Playing against local rival River Plate, the Juniors fell behind two goals to nil, and this prompted several fights to break out adjacent to where the De Setas were sitting. Confused and upset, Renaldo started to cry for his mother. All the assurances in the world by his father and older brother did nothing to calm him, nor did they stop the nearby brawling in the stands. Peter finally left the stadium at halftime, determined not to return with his youngest until the boy had matured considerably.

Young Renaldo did have one startling attribute concerning football, however. When playing in the garden with his brother or father, he seemed to have the uncanny ability to be able to make the ball do exactly whatever he wanted it to do. If Peter was in the goal and told Renaldo to shoot for the top left corner of the net . . . zip, the ball was there.

When the boys played alone with the ball, Renaldo could always dribble it away from his older brother and keep it in his possession. This usually lasted until Lonnie became frustrated and tackled his younger sibling, thus gaining title to the prized sphere. Peter would often watch his offspring play from a concealed vantage point. The moves that his youngest son displayed filled his mind with visions of Renaldo De Seta scoring the winning goal for Boca Juniors in the Argentine National Championship. Such are the dreams of fathers who have sport for their passion.

This same passion would ultimately be Peter's undoing. In July of 1966, the World Cup of soccer, the Holy Grail of the football world, was being contested in several cities in England. The Argentine National Team had qualified for the tournament and there was great anticipation and excitement in the streets of Buenos Aires, and, indeed, throughout the entire country.

Tours to England were being organized, with airfare, hotel accommodations, and tickets to Argentina's first three games as part of the package. A group of Peter's colleagues from the hospital had secured a number of places on one of the more deluxe tours, and they didn't have a great deal of difficulty persuading Peter to join them.

The subject was broached at dinner the next evening, and Peter was surprised to find little or no opposition from either Florencia or Lydia. His wife did not share Peter's passion for football, and, therefore, had no interest whatsoever in accompanying him. Lydia was enthused that he might be able to visit some of her relatives at Lowliam, which had remained in the family all these years. He would be gone from ten days to two weeks, depending on the fate of the National Team, but he promised to call home on a regular basis.

The tour was staying in Birmingham, an industrial city several hours by train northwest of London. It was here that the Argentine National side played two of their first round fixtures.

So it came to pass that Peter De Seta departed Buenos Aires on July 10, 1966, on the overnight flight to London. He had promised to bring back many souvenirs and gifts for the whole family as they hugged and kissed him good-bye at the airport. He was gone with a wave of a hand and a broad smile, and Florencia caught herself yelling out to him after he had disappeared from view, "Look out for yourself. Be careful!"

She found these words unsettling and was aware of a knot in her stomach. What did all this mean? Why was she shaking? Her sons, age eleven and seven, wanted to go for the ice cream that she had promised them once their father departed, and they quickly brought her focus back to the matters at hand. She tried to put the strange feeling out of her mind.

Peter called home for the first time on the night of July thirteenth. He was in high spirits, as that afternoon, Argentina had defeated Spain 2-1 in an exciting match played in a heavy downpour.

Florencia complained that Peter had been drinking, but his rebuttal was that he needed the brandy to ward off the chill that he had obtained at the match.

"Besides," Peter exclaimed, "it was a great victory that almost certainly assures us a passage through to the quarter finals. The whole tour is celebrating enthusiastically, but we are also watching our manners."

He bid his wife good-night, and told her that he would call again on the sixteenth, after the next game.

It was a different Peter on the end of the receiver the next time he called home. His voice had an edge to it that Florencia had never heard before. He sounded stone-cold sober.

"We had some trouble today at the stadium. Nothing serious, just unpleasant. We are not a very popular group here in England right now. The game today against West Germany was very rough. Many yellow cards and one ejection from the game to our side. The English fans started to taunt us about the rough play. Luckily, they hate the Germans much more than they hate us. It must be leftover from the war, but they are crazy, those English! In any event, we managed a draw with the Germans, which puts us in a good position to advance. I am fine, don't worry about a thing. I have been keeping my eyes open for any trouble. I will call on the nineteenth, after our next game against Switzerland up in Sheffield. Give the boys a kiss for me. Everything alright there? I'll call, must run. Love you."

The receiver went dead. Florencia had not said one word after "hello." The feeling from the airport returned, and this time it stayed long enough to give her a sleepless night.

The evening of the nineteenth came and went without word from England. Florencia passed another sleepless night, comforted only by Lydia's insistence that the Argentine victory that the ladies had watched on television that day must have sent Peter and his friends out on a giant bender.

Argentina had beaten the Swiss 2-0 and had advanced to the second round quarter-finals. Horns, drums, and fireworks could be heard everywhere in Buenos Aires that evening.

"So just imagine what it must be like to have witnessed the victory in person," Lydia said. "Peter was probably too drunk to find a telephone, and even if he did, he probably would be too intoxicated to give the dialing instructions to the overseas operator!"

The call Florencia had agonized over came early on the morning of the twentieth. Peter was warm and enthusiastic, although somewhat sheepish about not calling the previous evening. Lydia's assumption had been correct.

After Argentina's victory over the Swiss, the South American supporters had let their collective hair down and partied until dawn in any watering hole that would have them in Sheffield. It was now afternoon in England, and Peter had needed that extra time to get his feet back on the ground, in other words, rid himself of one giant hangover.

The good news was that he would now be able to visit Lowliam on his way south to London. He and the rest of the tour would be staying on until after Argentina's game against England at Wembley Stadium on the twenty-third. Once they were settled in London, he would seek a means of heading out to High Wycombe to see his many relatives that still resided in the area.

He was extremely excited about spending some time in and about London, but Florencia felt that unfamiliar edge creep into his voice when he briefly discussed the upcoming match with England.

"The British press have been very uncomplimentary to our football team. We were warned by FIFA, the world body that governs international soccer, for rough play against the Germans, and the English fans were heavily for Switzerland in our match against the Swiss. Hopefully, our team will rise to the occasion and play good, clean, football against the English. Heaven help us if they don't! Give my love to mother and the boys. Tell them that I will call again at the same time, two days from now. I love you very much. Adios."

The words 'heaven help us if they don't,' stuck in Florencia's mind. She cradled the receiver for several moments before putting it down. *Well, I shouldn't get worked up about some silly soccer game*, she thought to herself. *After all, Lydia had been right about the other night's festivities in Sheffield, hadn't she?*

It was Lydia who picked up the receiver on the first ring two mornings later. She was overjoyed that her son was going back to visit her birthplace, but the surprise he had for her was beyond expectation. The call had been placed from Lowliam itself, and huddled around the receiver were a score of Lydia's relatives, ranging in age from seventy years to seventy days.

The transAtlantic connection was surprisingly good, and the conversation lasted over an hour. Florencia was becoming impatient with her mother-in-law's silly questions to an endless list of people she had never heard of before. She wanted to talk to her husband, to make sure he was alright! Finally, the opportunity came.

"Peter, please, promise me you will be careful tomorrow. Stay with the group wherever you go. Keep your eyes open and stay out of trouble! I love you, my dear one. Come home to me safely."

He was nonchalant with her about his safety this time. Perhaps it was because he was in a room full of people and taking considerable ribbing from his English relatives about the thrashing that England was going to lay on his team in tomorrow's match. He seemed happy and confident that all would work out for the best.

Peter told her that he loved her and mentioned the great shopping that he intended to do for her before the tour departed for home. That was the last conversation they would ever have.

The whole family sat glued to the television screen at Casa San Marco the evening of the game. Wembley Stadium, the national shrine of football in Great Britain, was full to its one hundred thousand capacity and basking in glorious sunshine. The constant singing of the English fans all but drowned out the Spanish-speaking television commentators, and the sea of Union Jack flags made one feel that there was only one team contesting the match.

Television viewers in Argentina had to be content with the British video feed of the game, consequently there were little or no shots of the small Argentine faction that had been relegated to seats in one end zone corner, high up under the roof.

The game was a disaster from the outset for the South Americans. The British press had vilified the Argentines for their late tackling and cheap shots after the whistle during their previous matches. The visitors from across the Atlantic seemed to make a point of not letting anyone, the press, the fans, the referee, or the English players, intimidate them!

Right from the opening whistle, their overzealous tackling sent a succession of English players writhing to the green carpet. Warnings went unheeded, and the West German referee kept up a constant dialogue with the Argentine captain. Finally, in the thirty-sixth minute of play, having been pushed to his limit, the referee showed the South American's leader the red card, meaning expulsion from the match!

Howls of glee could be heard rolling down from the giant terraces filled with delighted Englishmen. The Argentine, however, refused to leave the pitch and carried on an animated discussion with several English players, the referee, and lastly, FIFA officials, who were forced to take to the field to escort him to the showers. This incident served to fan the flames of contempt and hatred that the British fans at Wembley harbored for their opponents, and the hostile mood of the spectators could be felt right across the Atlantic Ocean.

The knot returned to Florencia's stomach as she sat in stunned silence, watching these events unfold. Her countrymen seemed incensed at their captain's ejection and became even more physical and hotheaded once play resumed. The game remained scoreless through the seventy-eighth minute, when a substitute destined for stardom, Geoff Hurst, glanced in a header from winger Martin Peters. Pandemonium erupted throughout Wembley Stadium, and in the spacious living room of Casa San Marco several thousand miles away, Florencia De Seta felt a sense of relief surge through her.

Please let the English win. Please let them win! Then my Peter will come home to me safely. While she sat repeating her plea silently over and over, young Lonfranco suddenly smashed his cola bottle on the marble floor.

"Goddamned English, they have no balls! They are just a bunch of crybabies. They must have paid that referee off! If I were there, I'd show them. Goddamned English!" With that, he stomped out into the garden before his mother could say a word.

Lonnie was the least of Florencia's worries at the moment. She called for Oli, the housekeeper, to clean up the broken glass, and turned her attention back to the last twelve minutes of the game.

As it turned out, her prayers were answered with a one to nil English victory. Argentina was eliminated from the competition, and Peter would be coming home. Now she would deal with Lonfranco!

Florencia waited anxiously for word from England that Peter was safe and exactly when he would be returning to Buenos Aires. The telephone never rang that entire evening.

She tried to remain calm, resisting the temptation to call his hotel in London, perhaps because she dreaded the thought of not being able to reach him. Señora Florencia De Seta passed yet another sleepless night, with the now familiar knot ever-present in her stomach.

July twenty-fourth dawned clear and unusually humid for the time of year, and Florencia had Oli serve breakfast on the patio for her and the two boys. She hardly touched her coffee or toast, and as the boys kicked a soccer ball around the garden, she sat contemplating her course of action if there continued to be no word from Peter.

The persistent ring of the doorbell brought Oli running from the kitchen. She opened the large, steel-plated door and was about to scold the person on the opposite side for being so impatient. Bue she stopped after her first word, inhaling deeply and standing with her mouth agape.

The elder of the two men, an aristocratic-looking man dressed in a finely cut business suit, spoke immediately.

"I am Dr. Renaldo Las Heras, and this is his Holiness Monsignor Robitaille. Where is Señora De Seta? We must see her at once!"

Oli was barely able to mumble the word 'garden' as she pointed to the rear of the house. A fervent Catholic, the sight of the Monsignor at the door had left her breathless. She crossed herself as the two men brushed passed her and strode purposefully toward the rear of Casa San Marco.

Florencia had put on her sunglasses to shield her sleepless eyes from the bright rays. She couldn't help but think that she might need them for another reason today. The sight of the two men entering the patio confused her at first. She suddenly became lightheaded, as if she were watching the scene unfold from outside her own body. Her palms became covered in perspiration, and she was unable to rise from her chair to greet them. The knot tightened in her stomach.

Monsignor Robitaille was at her side before she could move, and as he grasped her hand, looked down at her with large, sorrowful eyes. Once again, it was Dr. Las Heras that spoke.

"Señora, please pardon this untimely interruption, but we have tragic news from England. There has been an accident. Your husband, Peter, Señora. Oh, sweet Jesus! Señora, I am afraid your husband is dead! It was a traffic accident, but further details are still unclear. I have been in touch with the authorities in London, and I have taken the liberty of making the arrangements to return Peter to you in Buenos Aires. I loved that boy as if he were my own son, Señora. It is such a tragedy, such a waste! Please accept my heartfelt condolences. The Monsignor will remain with you as long as you need him, and please, please Señora, let me assist you in any way I can."

Florencia had sat in silence as Dr. Las Heras spoke. She wasn't taking in his words, for she already knew what he had come to tell her. She had become fixated on his appearance. So dapper and well turned out. *He must be close to eighty years old*, she thought to herself. *How good he looks for his age.* It wasn't until he had finished talking and stood waiting for several seconds for a response that she finally found the strength to reply.

"Peter? My Peter? Is dead? I, I knew something . . . Peter! Oh, my Peter! No . . . not . . . Peter!"

Her voice rose audibly each time she pronounced his name, to the point where she was literally shouting. Then suddenly, a deadly silence hung over the beautiful garden, Florencia having collapsed back into her chair.

The boys, who had stopped their play to stare at the two strangers talking to their mother, ran to her side.

"Mama, Mama, what's wrong? What's wrong? Where is father? What's the matter with my father?" Lonnie pleaded.

Lydia appeared on the patio at that moment, Florencia's screams of Peter's name bringing her in full flight from the far end of Casa San Marco. She had remained in her suite late that morning before venturing downstairs for a light breakfast, preferring to write a few lines to her relatives in England, thanking them for being so hospitable to her son during his trip.

"Florencia, what on earth has happened? Why were you calling Peter's name like that?" She ran to her daughter-in-law's side. This time it was the Monsignor who spoke.

"Your son, Señora. I am terribly sorry. It seems that he was hit by a lorry while leaving Wembly Stadium after the football match. Dr. Las Heras has spoken directly to England. He was told that your son died instantly, painlessly! I am at your disposal for as long as you need me, Señora."

Lydia couldn't help but notice the Monsignor's large, sad eyes. She had prayed at his masses many, many times. Both these men were longtime trusted friends of the family. It was only fitting that news such as this be delivered by men that shared the family's grief and sorrow.

Dr. Las Heras drew a chair to Lydia's side. She refused to sit. Instead, she gathered the two scared, weeping boys in her arms and knelt down so she could look directly into their confused, anxious eyes.

"My special boys, you will have to be strong now. Your father has had a very bad accident in England. He will never be coming home again, but I am certain the Monsignor here will tell you that he is sitting with Jesus right this minute up in heaven. He is not alone. God and Jesus will look after your father forever now! I bet he is looking down at us right this minute, and hoping that we will all help each other to keep on going. We must all be strong, that is the way your father would have wanted us to be!"

Lonnie pried himself free of his grandmother's grasp and throwing the soccer ball as hard as he could against the stucco garden wall, screamed at the top of his lungs,

"I don't want to be strong! I want my father back here now! It's those goddamned English. They did this to him! Your people, Gramma! Your people. I hate them! I hate them! They killed my father. Don't touch me! You're one of them. Those Goddamned English. I hate them all . . . even you!" With that, he fled the patio, tears streaming down his cheeks.

The staff had gathered on the edge of the covered terrace, keeping a respectful distance between themselves and their employers. There was not a dry eye among them. Young Renaldo held his grandmother tightly. He whispered in her ear after Lonnie had left.

"Don't worry, Gramma, I know Lonnie didn't mean those awful things. He loves you very much, just like I do. Don't worry. If father is with Jesus, he will be just fine. Will he write us some letters though?"

"No, my dear boy. You can't write letters from heaven. But when we say our prayers at night and when we go to mass, I know that he will hear every word we say to him."

The Monsignor helped Florencia upstairs to her room. Doctor Las Heras then administered a sedative to the new widow and put her to bed. Lydia stayed with Renaldo and tried her best to make him understand all the things that would be happening next.

They talked about what a funeral was and how his father's body would be put inside a large metal box and laid to rest beside Renaldo's Grandfather Lonfranco. The boy was full of questions, and yet, seemingly calm and under control. He was, in truth, Lydia's strength in this dark hour. The grandmother understood death well, having been touched by its hand so often in the past. She would grieve for her only child, but she would do it on her own terms, behind closed doors. The matriarch must be the pillar of the family! She must teach the boys, and their mother, life's cruelest lesson. But above all, she must show them, by example, that life does go on.

Dealing with Lonnie over the following days was agonizing for everyone. He locked himself in his room, and when a pass key was used to open the door, Oli found that it still would not budge. Lydia suggested that her grandson had probably barricaded all the furniture in the room against it. All entreaties to either come out or let someone in failed for two days. Finally, in the early hours of the third morning, Olarti, the long-serving chauffeur-handyman, placed an extension ladder against Lonnie's window and was able to force an opening large enough to gain entry.

The sleeping boy didn't stir until morning. Olarti had sat calmly in an easy chair, waiting for him to awaken. The two had been fast friends for years. Olarti sometimes let Lonnie drive the servant's old pickup truck on the quiet side streets when no one was around. Of all the people at Casa San Marco, Olarti had the best chance of helping Lonnie come to grips with his father's death.

The grieving child awoke startled and angry. He ordered Olarti out of his room, but the sly servant had pushed the ladder away from the building and down onto the lawn. The only way for him to leave, he told Lonnie, was through the bedroom door. They spent the entire day alone, talking, and in the end, a ravenous Lonnie De Seta finally emerged from his sanctuary to confront the cruel world.

He was a changed youth, however, and no one felt the sting of his bitterness more than Lydia. He would not be in the same room with her unless it was absolutely necessary, and at that, he would not look at or talk to her. Lydia, for her part, was as gracious and understanding of the boy's feelings as any human could possibly be. Again it was Olarti that finally got through to Lonnie about how he was hurting his grandmother for something in which she had no part. He used a personal example to drive home the message.

"Oli and I have worked for your family for many, many years now, Señor Lonnie, just as my mother worked for the famous general that built this casa. You know that we are native Indians from the Pampas region. Well, General San Marco, your grandfather's best friend, was a great man. A brilliant soldier! But it was his job in the army to drive all the Indians from our homelands so that the railways and cattlemen could use the land. My parents were driven from our home when I was just your age. It was very hard for them. My father was a proud man who would not leave what he felt was rightfully his. So he fought the soldiers, and they killed him! My mother, sister, and I had nowhere to go.

"By chance, we happened to come across General San Marco as he was taking possession of Buenos Recuerdos. He was in need of servants and laborers to work on the estate in his absence. My mother could speak fluent Spanish and was a hard worker. She was able to get employment not only for herself, but also for my sister and me. Now, it would have been easy for us to hate the general for what his soldiers had done to my father, but he was a fair and benevolent man. I could not hate all the soldiers for the acts of a few who were following orders.

"It is the same with your feelings for your grandmother. Your father's death was an accident. There was no English plot to kill him. Only one Englishman was involved in his death, the one that was driving the truck that hit him. Your grandmother was not driving that truck. She loved your father very much, and now you are breaking her heart. You must see that this whole tragedy has nothing to do with her. Go to her and tell her that you love her, for there is nothing so pure in this world as the love of a grandmother for her grandchildren."

Olarti's talk had the desired effect on Lonnie. He was able to mend his relationship with Lydia and carry on with his life. He was, however, prone to fits of violence that were extremely unpredictable. He became a patient of one of the leading psychiatrists in Buenos Aires, who recommended sports, specifically rugby football, as an outlet for his emotional and physical demons.

The Newton Academy happened to have an excellent rugby program, and the sport became Lonnie's passion. While he struggled academically, always in need of private tutoring to make a passing grade, he excelled on the rugby pitch. He led the academy team to three consecutive city championships in his final three years there, but his grades were such that he was forced to transfer into an arts program at the University of Buenos Aires upon graduation. This did not concern him in the least, for his goal in life was to make the Argentine National Rugby Side and compete at the international level.

The sport had been a perfect outlet for his explosive temper, and through weight lifting and extensive workouts, he had grown to be an imposing figure. Lonnie De Seta turned the heads of both sexes wherever he went.

Renaldo's reaction to his father's death was totally unlike his older brother's. There were no fits of temper, no angry outbursts. He was inquisitive about the family's future, asking question after question. Lydia, in particular, reassured the boy that the family would be fine, and that they would be able to remain at Casa San Marco and Buenos Recuerdos as long as they wanted.

The younger brother spent many hours alone in his room practicing his acoustic guitar, in time requesting additional lessons on the instrument. He also demonstrated an increased interest in soccer, asking to be taken to another Boca Juniors game, with the assurance that he would not be scared this time. He would play the game with his brother at every opportunity, but Lonnie seemed hesitant to engage in the sport that he felt had caused his father's death. Renaldo could be found in the garden for hours at a time, alone but happy as he dribbled, headed, and shot against an imaginary opponent. The boy would carry on a dialogue with himself as if he were a sports announcer calling the play by play of a Boca Juniors game. He was always victorious and often scored the winning goal. Whenever he could, Renaldo would conscript Olarti to be the opposing goalkeeper, but the old Indian proved too slow to stop all but the most direct shots from this young wizard with a football.

By the time the youngest De Seta son was old enough to play on the academy's lower school side, his coaches and instructors were amazed at the boy's proficiency and athletic skill. Renaldo was an inquisitive and talented student as well, and despite his awkward shyness, maintained a standing near the top of his academic class. Math and science were his forte, just as they had been his father's before him.

The same psychiatrist that had been seeing Lonnie interviewed Renaldo on several occasions, just to make sure the boy had no hidden demons that he was harboring. The doctor's conclusion was that Renaldo had accepted and adjusted to his father's passing very well. There was some concern that the boy was trying to emulate his father by focusing too strongly on Peter's interests, namely math and science, the guitar, and soccer. Taken as a whole, however, Renaldo's progress in school and his social behavior with others convinced the psychiatrist that there was no need for continued therapy unless problems arose in the future.

Florencia took a long time to come to grips with Peter's death. She was barely able to attend his funeral and spent the following month sequestered behind the walls of Casa San Marco. Slowly, mainly due to Lydia's patience and encouragement, Florencia began to function in a more normal fashion, venturing out on shopping excursions or for long walks in the park. The two women saw their bond grow stronger through this tragedy, and they became virtually inseparable as time went on.

In truth, it was Lydia's strength that allowed the whole family to function in a more or less normal manner. She took charge not only of the household, but the family business matters as well. Peter had not been a keen businessman. He had preferred, instead, to let professional investment advisers oversee the distribution and allotment of the millions of dollars that the liquidation of Lonfranco's ventures had garnered. Lydia remained the person to whom these men would report, and she continued to handle the task of dealing with the 'suits' in her usual, self-confident manner. The investments flourished, ensuring the family's comfortable lifestyle would go uninterrupted.

The eleven years following Peter De Seta's death passed without major disruption or trauma in the lives of the four De Setas. Several suitors would make proposals of marriage to Florencia, who was still an extremely attractive, and now very wealthy, single woman. She had rebuffed them all, preferring instead to center her attention on her sons and charity work for underprivileged children. She ensured that Peter's camp in Tigre was maintained and periodically expanded to keep his dreams alive. Most notably, she had little to do with the society set, other than when it benefited one of her charitable causes.

By 1977, she and Lydia had the right to feel justifiably proud of the job they had done in raising the two boys and managing their financial affairs in a diligent and efficient manner. Neither of the ladies had any way of knowing that the storm clouds gathering on the horizon in December 1977 would soon cause drastic upheaval in each and every one of the De Seta family's lives.

CHAPTER NINE

"Lonnie, are you crazy? Mama will tan your hide. You haven't moved from where I left you a half hour ago. What are you doing?" A freshly showered, nattily attired Renaldo De Seta inquired of his older brother. Lonnie awoke with a start, disoriented for the first few seconds.

"What? Holy shit! I must have dozed off in the sunshine. What time is it? How long do I have?" He was up and into the casa on the fly, tearing off his pajama top as he ran. The same question that had kept him awake all night and had resurfaced once he was alone on the patio kept running through his mind. What is Celeste up to? What was going on with her and her two brothers?

He had been trying to come up with some logical answers to these questions when exhaustion finally overcame him as he sat alone in the warm morning sun.

Celeste Lavalle had not been marking term papers as Lonnie had implied. Her two brothers, Jean Pierre and Serge, had arrived in town the day before. As was always the case, Celeste had canceled their Saturday night date at the last minute to attend to what she described as "family business matters."

Lonnie had never met the two men from Tucumán, and Celeste was always extremely secretive and uptight whenever they appeared on her doorstep, usually without prior notice. He knew that if his relationship with her was to go anywhere at all, she would have to answer the questions that were eating away at him. For now though, it was the other woman in his life, his mother, that he had to deal with.

He dressed quickly, without showering, ran his electric razor over his morning stubble, slicked back his straight black hair with pomade, and was down in the entrance foyer before his mother descended the sweeping staircase.

Lydia had taken up early residence at Buenos Recuerdos that spring, for even at age seventy-seven she preferred to be on hand for the spring breeding session. She still controlled almost every aspect of the family's business interests and remained personally involved with matters effecting the Pergamino operations in particular. Hector Brown was still the resident manager of the estate, although his son Oliviero handled most of the labor to which his father once tended.

Now that her grandsons were fully grown, Lydia preferred the tranquility and fresh air of her country estate to the stifling humidity and pollution of the city. Her mind seemed freer there to wander back to the enchanted days when her husband had first introduced her to the Argentine Pampas. It was the happiest time of her life, and there wasn't a day when the memory of her Latin lover didn't enter her thoughts. She felt truly blessed that she had known and loved him as she had.

Sunday mass had become one of the few occasions for which Florencia De Seta would venture out in public. She still derived a great deal of pride from showing off her two handsome sons to the other society matrons and their adoring daughters. Although she liked Celeste Lavalle well enough, Florencia would be the first to admit that she was very much a snob as far as choosing the proper wives for her sons. The girl from Tucumán lacked certain social graces that were necessary to survive in the rarefied air of Porteño society. And all that political nonsense! The change in Lonnie had not gone unnoticed by his mother, and she much preferred the macho athlete he used to be to the firebrand debater that he had become. There was nothing but trouble to be had by speaking out against the powers that ruled Argentina in these times. Even in the old days, Lonnie's grandfather knew that premise well and practiced it with great skill. Keep a low profile and make friends, not enemies, of government officials.

Lonnie had always been such a hothead, but at least when he was playing rugby, he had a sensible outlet for his pent-up emotions. Now, this Celeste had turned him into a deep thinker, a political philosopher. Florencia wanted Lonnie to be more practical in his course selection, to get his business degree and continue on to law school. It was about time that a male member of the De Seta family took the helm of their corporate enterprises!

Renaldo would, in all likelihood, follow in his father's footsteps, for he had a vocation for the sciences, and she thought him too mild-mannered and introverted to develop the killer instinct that a great businessman needed.

No, it would be her strong-willed Lonfranco that would ascend to the president's chair of De Seta International SA one day. The private family holding company had, for the time being, a figure-head executive made up bankers and accountants. Lydia was the nominal president, but she was getting on in years, and Florencia knew that she would be more than happy to pass the mantle to her grandson, provided he had obtained the proper academic credentials. Now, if only she could find him the proper young debutante to tame his unpredictable spirit and keep him in line!

In this regard, Florencia made sure that she and her sons lingered after mass to exchange pleasantries with the appropriate young ladies and their well-to-do parents. The boys were polite, but disinterested. Renaldo could think of only two things: Astor Gordero and the possibility of him keeping his promise of a future meeting and his bed, for he was exhausted to the point of nodding off during the sermon. Lonnie was consumed by Celeste and her whereabouts. He had telephoned her flat before departing for the basilica, but there remained no answer. He was confused rather than jealous, for after all, these men that were depriving him of her company were her brothers. Had it been anyone else, Lonnie would have taken the bull by the horns, confronted his competition, and settled the matter once and for all. The only thing he could do now was wait and wonder.

Oli was sent to awaken Renaldo at ten a.m. the following morning. It was Monday, and because his school term was finished, he had been allowed to sleep late. He had, in fact, slept almost twenty hours. There was a phone call for him from Señor Estes Santos, Oli said. Hearing his coach's name cleared the cobwebs from the boy's head instantly. *Santos must have talked to Astor Gordero*, he thought.

"Renaldo, the man is true to his word. We have a meeting with him at noon on the twenty-second of this month. Will you still be in town?" the older man asked excitedly.

"I am not sure, Estes. We usually go to Pergamino for Christmas, but we haven't set a departure date yet. I suppose for something this important, I could always stay behind and arrive separately. Who did you talk to? What exactly was said?"

"Gordero wasn't in his office yet, but when I left my name with his secretary, she put me through to his executive assistant, one Wolfgang Stoltz. Herr Stoltz is as Teutonic as his name sounds, very proper, very, very German. He had been informed by Gordero to expect a call from us, and we were given the first appointment that was open. So you better make an effort to stay in town, amigo. Chances like this don't pop up every day."

"The twenty-second is almost two weeks away, Estes. By that time he probably will have forgotten who we are. The whole thing seems like a waste of time to me. I bet you that the meeting will be either delayed or canceled by his German friend."

"Don't be such a pessimist, Renaldo. What have you got to lose by staying in town a few extra days? You told me that you planned to stay the entire summer in Pergamino, anyway. The man kept his promise about arranging a meeting, so let's give him the benefit of the doubt until the twenty-second, at least. Come on, the man hasn't lied to us yet, has he?"

"No, I guess you are right. But I don't put much faith in anything beneficial ever coming out of this. You are a dreamer, Estes, if you think that there will."

"I've never been hurt by dreaming, my boy. That is what got me into professional football in the first place. Dreams of being a big league keeper. Without dreams, you might as well go to that estancia of yours and breed cows for the rest of your life. Doesn't that sound exciting? Anyway, I must go. I will call you in the next few days. Work on your arrangements and try to stay in town for the twenty-second. Oh, by the way, that was a very brave, and I might say foolish thing, you did in Cordoba, Saturday. Tell me, why didn't you just leave The Fat Man and save your own hide in the alley back there?"

"I don't really know. It all happened so quickly. I guess I wanted to be just like you, Estes. A leader of men and an opportunistic dreamer," he laughed into the receiver as the last phrase passed his lips. "Good-bye. Estes, stay in touch."

Lonnie had already left Casa San Marco by the time Estes Santos called Renaldo. There had continued to be no answer at Celeste's flat all day Sunday and up until midnight, when Lonnie had torn the telephone from its socket and hurled it against the wall. He had slept fitfully, rehearsing over and over what he was going to say to her when he finally made contact. He had decided that he must confront her in person to get the answers to the questions that were driving him to distraction. He was shocked when she opened her door, still half asleep, attired in one of his dress shirts.

"Lonnie, what a surprise! I wasn't expecting you this morning. Why didn't you call? I could have made some breakfast for . . ."

"Where on earth have you been Celeste? I have been worried sick about you since you canceled our date on Saturday. Where are your brothers? Are they here with you now, or did they really come to town at all?"

Lonnie pushed past her into the flat, half expecting to find a naked lover lying on the bed. He stormed around the small rooms looking for any sign that indicated another man had been there over the last forty-eight hours. Other than Celeste's rumpled bed, there was nothing askew.

"Get out, you bastard! You don't own me! No man has the right to interrogate me in my home. Get out!" The force of her words and the hatred in her voice stopped Lonnie in his tracks.

"Celeste, I'm sorry. It . . . it's just that you have been acting so strangely the past week or so, I just want to know what is going on in your life."

"Why? What's it to you? Just because I fuck you a few times doesn't mean that I have any feelings for you. It's just sex. I have nothing in common with you, anyway. You are the embodiment of everything that I have always hated. You've never had to work a day in your life. You've never been hungry or had to deal with real poverty and misery. You and your fancy family just drive out to your country estate if the inner city becomes too noisy, or humid, or God knows what else for your bourgeois blood. I despise you and everyone like you. Now get out of my sight!"

Lonnie didn't move. He was aghast at her verbal assault and stood staring at her in disbelief. She stood by the open door, contempt burning in her eyes. Finally, he muttered his plaintive reply,

"Please, Celeste, don't do this to me . . . to us. I know that I am hotheaded sometimes, but you have no idea what you've done to me. I am a changed person. You opened my eyes to things I have never seen before or was too blind to see. The political injustice that has been going on in this country for decades, benefiting the likes of my own family. I have changed, Celeste, and I want to do something about our social and political injustice. I just don't know how to go about it. I don't know what to do on my own. Please don't cast me aside like I am the wrapper off some candy bar! Let me prove to you that I can help make a difference! I will do anything, anything you tell me. I am lost without you. My life has no meaning without you. All the money, the luxuries that my family has accumulated over the years, they mean nothing to me. They got my father nowhere except an early grave. I can make a difference. You will see, if only you give me one chance to prove myself."

Lonnie was sobbing uncontrollably by the time he finished the last sentence. The girl from Tucumán knew that she had him in the palm of her hand. Her plan had worked to perfection.

"Stop your sniveling! You say you are a man that is ready to make a difference, yet you stand here before me crying like a baby. I don't think you are man enough to be a part of what I must do. Get out."

"Celeste, if you make me go, life will be empty for me. Tell me what to do. I love you so much, I will do anything. Don't waste my life without benefiting from my help, because if you make me leave now, I have nothing to live for. I know . . . I know that I will do something, something violent and stupid! I would be out of my mind over losing you. Let me help you do whatever it is you must do. Let me meet your brothers. Let them decide about me. You can trust me! Put me to work, because my life is in your hands!"

Celeste kept her eyes locked on his and slowly closed the door behind her. This would be easier than she had anticipated. The tutor crossed the room to where Lonnie stood, took his hand, and led him into the bedroom. She made him sit on a small wooden chair that she pulled from beneath her makeup table. It was barely sturdy enough to hold his massive frame.

The half-dressed woman wanted her visitor to be uncomfortable and on edge. She climbed onto her double bed and sat cross-legged, staring at him for several minutes without saying a word. Finally, she spoke.

"That chair is not comfortable for you, Lonnie, is it? You would like it much better if you could join me here on the bed, wouldn't you? You had better get used to being uncomfortable if we let you join us. Your present life is like this bed: soft, warm, and inviting. Your new life will be like that chair, hard and unyielding. Are you strong enough to endure the hardships that will surely accompany your new life? Do you think you can take it without running back to Mama at the first sign of trouble? Once we let you in, the only way out is in a casket! Does that scare you, my petit bourgeoisie?"

He didn't even feel the chair beneath him. He was so exhilarated with the thought that he would finally be able to make a difference, to do something useful with his life, to be with her!

"No, I am not scared. The only thing that scares me is losing you, Celeste. I have fought many demons in my life, but none like the ones I would have to cope with if I could not prove worthy of your love. I am ready to follow you anywhere!"

"Forget about your past brawling and macho bullshit. That was schoolboy stuff compared to what I will ask of you. Have you ever fired a handgun or rifle? Do you know anything about explosives? How about killing a man with a knife so that he doesn't make a sound? These are the kind of things that you must learn, the kind of things that I will ask of you, if you stay. You had better get it through that cement head of yours right now that I am not joking about any of this."

Celeste rose from the bed and went to her dresser. From the top drawer she took two objects, and when she turned to face him, tossed a spherical object into his lap. Lonnie caught it just inches away from his groin. He looked down at his hand in amazement, but didn't flinch. He was holding a military issue hand grenade. When he looked up at her, she was pointing a cocked pistol directly at his head. A broad smile appeared on her pretty face.

"So, cowboy, do you still want to play my game? It is a deadly game, be certain of that. This is your last chance to say adios, or you will be in for the rest of your life. Now, what will it be, stay and play, or run and hide behind the high, safe walls of your family's mansion?"

"I'll play your game, Señorita. I am not afraid to die. All I am afraid of is losing you. Teach me. Teach me to use these things and I will do your bidding. Just like in your tutorials, you will see that I am a fast learner."

Lonnie could feel his own weapon growing hard under the coarse denim of his blue jeans. Celeste looked incredibly sexy standing there in his dress-shirt, the revolver in her hand. She must have felt the sexual tension as well, for she straddled his legs and sat down on his lap. She pressed the barrel of the pistol to his temple, then thrust her bare love nest rhythmically against his swollen, straining member.

"Don't fuck with me, Lonnie, or I'll make sure that you will be both coming and going at the same time. You understand me, you big stud?"

He said nothing, simply placed his mouth on hers and kissed her passionately. Rising from the chair, he carried her the few steps to the bed, her legs wrapped around his waist, the pistol still held to his temple. He had never been so sexually charged in his life. It was only during her orgasm as he feasted on her sweet delights that she finally dropped the deadly object, moaning and writhing in ecstasy. Lonnie then used his own concealed 'canon' on her, with similar results.

He was in charge now, and for once, it would be him that controlled the tempo and flow of their union. He was insatiable, taking her several different ways before exploding all over her breasts, face, and hair. It was nearly two hours since she had tossed the grenade in his lap.

Their moans and sighs intermingled as they lay in each other's arms. Lonnie could not see the sly grin on Celeste's face as she rested with her head on his shoulder. *This will be fun*, she thought. *Training a new martyr for the cause, and getting fucked like that at the same time. This is a bonus that I hadn't counted on.*

Two days later, Lonnie was hastily summoned to Celeste's flat. She had made certain that her infatuated lover would return immediately to the scene of their most recent union by using her sexiest voice, saying that she had been horny ever since their last tryst. She had informed him that she was consumed by an uncontrollable need to be taken roughly again, to be dominated and pleasured into submission.

Lonnie didn't need an engraved invitation. His mother had been tormenting him about his summer plans all throughout their noon day meal together. She was insistent that he take some extra business courses at the university while doing volunteer work at No Se Preocupe on weekends. The trust fund that Lydia had set up for him paid out a healthy monthly allowance, and Florencia was well aware that her eldest son did not need to supplement his income by taking some meaningless job just to occupy his time. He had told her that he would go by the registrar's office that afternoon to find out whatever he could about summer courses. That is where Florencia assumed he was going when he left Casa San Marco in a big hurry shortly after luncheon had concluded.

Lonnie's erotic anticipation waned as soon as he entered Celeste's flat. She was fully clothed, and the icy tone of her voice told him that there would be no carnal games played today.

"Sit down on the couch, Lonnie. I have someone here that wants to meet you." Her voice and manner were completely detached and businesslike. "First, however, I must blindfold you for security purposes.

I hope you don't mind, but if things go well, the blindfold will not be needed again."

She moved behind him, taking a black silk scarf from the side table. Lonnie was both excited and terrified. He hoped that she hadn't noticed the sweat on his brow as she tightened the scarf around his head. He sat in total darkness now, unable to see a thing.

The student was aware of movement behind him, and what sounded like two or more people entering the living room. He was tempted to tear the blindfold from his eyes and confront these mystery people eye to eye, man to man. But he had told Celeste that he was man enough to play her game, so he remained seated and silent in his blacked out dungeon.

"Lonnie, my two brothers are in the room with us now, and be forewarned, they are armed with handguns equipped with silencers. If you make a move to discard your blindfold, or if your answers are not honest and true, they will not hesitate to use their weapons. Be careful what you say."

Celeste spoke to the men in French for a few seconds, then there was silence. Lonnie could once again feel movement in the room, adjacent the couch where he sat. *Are they circling their prey for the kill?* he thought. The blindfolded visitor was surprised at how soft and articulate the voice was that finally broke the silence.

"Señor Lonfranco Ernesto De Seta, it is a pleasure to finally meet your acquaintance. I apologize for the necessity of the blindfold, however. One can not be too careful in these times. I am Serge Lavalle. No doubt Celeste has told you a bit about my brother and me. Jean Pierre is here in the room with us as well, but I will be the only one addressing you this afternoon.

"Celeste has apparently had quite an effect on your political philosophy, Señor De Seta. She has told us that you are ready and willing to try to make a difference in our beloved country's political future. Frankly, I am surprised that you would risk your considerable fortune to attain martyrdom, for make no mistake, Señor, that is the only place our actions will lead us. It is only through our actions and our blood that Argentina will achieve its true destiny. A nation where all people share equally in the bounty of our great and prosperous land. Not just the wealthy, the military, the corrupt, but all the people! That is the way our great leader and founder, Juan Domingo Perón would have made Argentina forever, had not certain satanic forces worked to promote his downfall and ultimate death.

"The three of us are Montoneros, Señor De Seta, and as such, there are death warrants on our heads. Each of us, even Celeste, has killed for the cause, and it is precisely what we expect of you as well. These are not childrens's games we play, Señor. We have had two brothers killed already in our fight for justice. It is their martyrdom that makes us relentless in the pursuit of our goal. Nothing will stop us. Not even the bullets of the government lackeys."

Lonnie sat listening intently to every word that Serge Lavalle said. He was given a lecture on the history of the Montonero movement, the greatness of Juan Domingo Perón, the diabolical corruptness of the succession of leaders that vowed to remove Perónism from Argentina's political structure, and a forecast on just how the rebel organizations would one day band together and realize that Perónism was the only true form of political freedom for the people of Argentina. Lavalle spoke with a passion and insight that had reminded Lonnie of his first private political debates with Celeste. It had been necessary for her to be extremely guarded in her statements then, but Lonnie could now see the same political undertone running through Serge's monologue.

What it all came down to was the use of force, extortion, murder, and widespread civil disobedience as a way of showing the general populous that the current political and economic situation was bankrupting the country, benefiting only those at the very top of the hierarchy.

Inflation had reached astronomical proportions in the last few years, well over three hundred percent per annum at times, and the current junta had removed protective tariffs on imported goods, flooding the local markets with cheap imports and driving many local manufacturers to bankruptcy. The offshoot of this economic policy was that more workers were unemployed, reducing their influence as a political force. Cattle and grain had, once again, become the only real exports of value to the Argentine economy. As such, it was the members of the old oligarchy friendly to the junta that prospered the most.

Serge Lavalle rhymed off several of the past holdings of De Seta International SA, making it clear to Lonnie that this man knew a lot more about the De Setas than he had ever expected. It was also made clear to Lonnie that the Montoneros included his family as part of the same oligarchy that was profiting the most under the current economic climate. It was becoming very clear to Lonnie why he would be such a prized disciple of the Montonero cause if he were allowed to join them. He was, as Celeste had told him, everything she had grown to despise about the current political landscape. Her coup had been recruiting and transforming an oligarchist into a populist. The fact that her ex-student was in love with her had certainly made the job easier.

Celeste had never used the term 'Montonero' in any of her discussions with Lonnie, whether in private or publicly in her tutorials. She had only referred to the subversives as 'revolutionaries.' Even so, Lonnie was well aware of the violent and chaotic events for which this particular cadre of 'revolutionaries' had been responsible.

Over the past twenty years, hundreds of people, from high-ranking government and military officials to local police and judicial authorities had felt the wrath of these cold-blooded killers. Innocent people often got in the way of their murderous schemes, and the outrage of the general populous against the continuing terror tactics of the Montoneros caused ruling military powers to not just react, but to overreact. Pitched military battles combined with sweeping arrests of anyone with mildly leftist views had wiped out all but the best organized and most secretive of the 'revolutionary' cadres by 1977.

The Marxist E.R.P., or People's Revolutionary Army, had lost their charismatic leader Mario Roberto Santucho in a wild gun battle in July of 1976. The military junta that had deposed Juan Perón's widow, Maria Estela Martinez De Perón, from the presidency four months before Santucho's death proclaimed that they would stop the terrorism through a policy known as 'the PRN' or the Process of National Reorganization.

In reality, the PRN was nothing more than a thinly veiled antiterrorist guise that allowed the junta to revoke virtually all civil liberties throughout the entire country. They even encouraged the formation of their own antiterrorist guerrilla group, a ruthless band of right-wing cutthroats called 'the A.A.A.' or the Argentine Anti-Communist Alliance. It was little wonder that present-day Buenos Aires often resembled a town right out of the American Wild West. Exactly who was responsible for the latest bombing, kidnapping, or shootout was often never resolved. Suffice it to say that many a cowboy died with his boots on in the name of whatever cause held his favor at the time.

The Lavalles must have been both smart and lucky to still be alive in December of 1977. The blindfold around Lonnie's head could attest to their caution, and Serge's lecture on the political forces of the day was only the precursor of many tests that Lonnie would be forced to endure before they would trust him as one of their revolutionary brothers.

After what seemed like an eternity of sitting and listening in his dark obscurity, Lonnie was finally asked his first question. He welcomed a chance to respond.

"So you see, Lonnie, our life is not one of glamour, fame, and material riches. Rather, it consists of hatred, infamy, and at times, scurrilous poverty. Quite different than what you have been used to up to now. You will have to work very hard to convince us that you won't go running to the authorities to turn us in and save your own neck at the first sign of trouble.

"We will give Celeste two weeks to teach you, to indoctrinate you, to brainwash you into our way of life. Be assured that you will be watched constantly during that time. Know this as well. As of this meeting, there is no escaping from our grasp, except by man's ultimate destiny. Do not disappoint us, Lonnie, for we have great plans for you. Do not disappoint Celeste in particular, for I know that her plans for you are of a more, shall I say, exacting and intimate nature than Jean Pierre and I had in mind. You have stepped over the line by coming here today, Lonnie, and there is no stepping back. Now tell me, are you man enough to not only survive, but thrive in the heat of this political cauldron you have just plunged yourself into?"

Lonnie sat motionless for several seconds, the thoughts swirling through the rapids of his mind. When the words came, they were from his heart.

"All my life, I have been seeking a way to express myself. For a long time, I thought that sports was the perfect outlet for the hostility that I felt inside. But after my father died when I was eleven, throttling a weaker opponent was no longer the thrill that it had once been. The questions that I needed answered were still rattling around in my head. I had so much hatred trapped inside me. Where it came from, I still, to this day, do not know. It is still there though, I can assure you of that!

"The rage that I felt the other day when I thought that Celeste was seeing another man, I would have killed anyone who I had found in here, perhaps even you and your brother. Celeste has changed me, though. She has made my mind work for the first time in my life. She has opened my eyes to many, many things that were always there to see, but I was too ignorant to notice them.

"I will be honest with you. I cannot say for certain that the political doctrines that you espouse are the best ones for Argentina or even for me, personally. But I do know this. As far as I am concerned, my life before I met Celeste was going nowhere. My mother wants me to become a lawyer and run the family business. She is sentencing me to a necktie and business suit for the rest of my life. I would most likely assault the first advocate that disagreed with me in court, and end up a defendant instead of an attorney. I am in love with your sister. That I know to the bottom of my heart. There is nothing else in this world that matters to me now. Celeste is my future. Do with me what you will, as long as I can fight by her side, I will follow her anywhere and do your bidding."

Once again there was silence, broken only when Celeste finally spoke to her brothers in French. It was a language that Lonnie had discarded from his studies early in high school. At this moment, he wished that he had pursued it further. There was movement in the room again, sounds of items being stuffed into haversacks perhaps, then farewell embraces and the traditional two-cheeked kiss. Certain words he remembered, au revoir, bonne chance, good-bye, and good luck. Again it was Serge that addressed him directly.

"My brother and I must be leaving now, Lonnie, but we will meet again, you may be certain of that. You have a lot of work to do, and I hope that you have listened carefully to my dissertation. Celeste will guide you from this moment on, and she has specific orders that you must follow exactly as she says. Do not disappoint us, Lonnie, or this will be your fate. Adieu, 'til we meet again."

As Serge's last word hung in the darkness, something landed in Lonnie's lap. He grasped the object in his hand, and there was no mistaking its identity. It was a bullet, quite a large caliber judging by its length and weight. He could hear the door open, then close quickly. They were obviously gone, for there was silence in the room once again. Where was Celeste? Had she gone with them?

A great temptation to tear off the blindfold and race after the two brothers, just to get a glimpse of them, had to be resisted. He was amazed at how much he really wanted their approval, to be one of them, to be with Celeste. He sat motionless on the couch, waiting. After a considerable amount of time, Lonnie was startled to feel her soft hands deftly undoing the knot in the scarf. She did not speak.

It took several seconds for Lonnie's eyes to adjust to the afternoon sunlight that still managed to find its way through the drawn curtains. When his eyes finally focused, she was standing in front of him. *How beautiful she is*, were his first thoughts.

"I will give you one opportunity to leave and never say a word about this meeting and never set eyes on me again. I lured you here today under false pretenses, I know that. I want your mind, not your erection, to make your final decision as to what you will do. There is the door, walk through it now and you can go back to the world you are used to. Stay here in this room, and you will never be able to return. I have to use the toilet. If you are still here when I get back, we can get to work. If you are not, well, you've been a great fuck." She was gone in an instant, before he could say a word. He was still sitting where she had left him when she reentered the room.

"You have balls, Señor De Seta, that is for sure! Unfortunately for both of us, I will not be playing with them during the course of your indoctrination. You must be singular in your purpose and actions. There will be no distractions whatsoever. Don't think of trying any funny stuff. You will use your brain over the next two weeks. The rest of your anatomy can wait until you have proven yourself to be worthy. You can stand up and stretch now, use the facilities if you need to. I will get us a cold drink, then we will get to it."

The remainder of the afternoon and into the early evening resembled one of Celeste's tutorials. They sat at her desk together, studying transcripts, documents, and texts on the Montonero movement in Argentina. Any passage that was anti-Montonero in stance was boldly highlighted in marker pen, and Celeste would offer a firm rebuttal to the 'lies' that the junta forced into publication.

Lonnie was an attentive student, although Celeste's proximity to him proved distracting at times. He had the urge to take her in his arms, throw her on the bed, and ravish her several times. She, however, was nothing but business. When Celeste realized that his concentration was waning, she told him to go home and get a good night's sleep. He asked her if he could take some of the documents home with him, to refresh his memory as to certain particular facts. Her answer shocked him.

"Lonnie, you could be imprisoned or worse just for having these transcripts in your possession. If someone in your household found them, a maid, your mother, whoever, you would have far too much explaining to do. If you were to be stopped by the police on your way home and they found any subversive literature on you, there would be hell to pay. You are not properly versed on our methods of denial yet. What to say if and when you are stopped, and believe me, you *will* be stopped. One of your first visits will be to a dentist who is friendly to our cause. He will perform certain dental surgery on you that will provide you with an escape mechanism should you be caught and tortured. A hidden cyanide pill under one of your molars. All of us have them. Believe me, it is better than living through the hell that they inflict upon their prisoners.

Both my brothers that were here today have been tortured. Did you wonder why Jean Pierre did not speak to you? It is because a local police captain in Tucumán thought it would be funny to cut off his tongue when he still refused to talk, after two days of beatings and torture. I took care of that bastard personally. He never lived long enough to torture anyone else. My other two brothers, whom Serge referred to, were lucky. They were blown to bits instantly when a government tank sent a shell through the front door of my parents' home without warning one night a few years ago. We must always be on guard. One never knows who one's friends are, or who the informants are.

Tomorrow we will talk of our immediate plans. I will tell you this much now, though. You will need a fair bit of money at your disposal. You will get your own flat, nondescript, in one of the working-class barrios. You will also need a car, something used that will fit into your new surroundings. And your clothes...no more designer fashions for you, my preppy clotheshorse. You are a man of the revolution now, and you will dress the part. Go home, get some rest. I want you here at twelve noon tomorrow. We have a lot to do. Oh, by the way, the other new thing that you will need is a new name. Think about that. See if you can come up with a good alias for yourself. Nothing too cute, though. Now get out of here. I'm tired!"

Celeste left him standing at the entrance to her flat without so much as a handshake. She disappeared into the bedroom and shut the door forcefully behind her.

CHAPTER TEN

Señor Gordero will see you now, gentlemen." An immaculately tailored business executive stood before the two visitors that waited anxiously in the posh reception hall of A.R. Gordero and Sons, SA. *The man's warm smile is meant to relax us,* Renaldo thought to himself. But by this time, the whole atmosphere surrounding the anticipated, yet unexpected, audience with Astor Gordero had frayed the boy's nerves to the point of physical illness.

Even as Renaldo and Estes Santos entered the Gordero Building, a beautiful Parisian-style edifice on the corner of Santa Fe Avenue and Avenida Nueve de Julio in the heart of the capital's financial district, they still could not believe that this meeting was actually taking place. Renaldo had awaited the news informing him of its cancellation with every ring of the telephone over the past fortnight. But such tidings were not forthcoming. So now he and Estes had donned their best business suits and proceeded to walk over fate's threshold. What awaited them there was something that neither man had foreseen.

The beautiful receptionist and her stunning assistant who served them coffee during their forty-five-minute wait for some word from the inner sanctum only added to the overwhelming atmosphere of monied savoir faire. Had these women been in any other situation, Estes would have been all over them, trying his macho charm on for size. Not here, though. He sat staring at the same page of the morning newspaper for the entire interlude, perspiration dotting his brow. The appearance of the nattily dressed executive had ended their tedium, but at the same time had increased their terror.

"I apologize for the delay, gentlemen. Please come this way. Señor Gordero had some last-minute details to attend to. I am Herr Wolfgang Stoltz, Señor Gordero's executive assistant. I trust the ladies were attentive to your needs while you were waiting?"

Stoltz led the two men through a single doorway leaving the reception area behind, then down a long mahogany paneled hallway covered with priceless artwork. Not a single window or door interrupted the continuous flow of fine art on polished wood as they proceeded toward an ornate double portal at the end of the corridor. It was just outside this entranceway that Herr Stoltz stopped and addressed the two visitors.

"Let me say personally, gentlemen, how grateful I am for your actions that day in Cordoba. To risk your own lives to save Señor Gordero was an act of true heroism. I assure you that neither Señor Gordero nor I will ever forget that. Normally, I would have been there, at his side. I handle all Señor Gordero's affairs, both corporate and private. I am also a great fan of the game of football. We never miss a Prefect match together. Unfortunately, I had come down with a severe case of influenza only the day before the championship final and was, therefore, indisposed. Luckily, you gentlemen performed my usual task, which often involves getting my employer out of uncomfortable situations. For that, once again, I am truly grateful!"

Renaldo stood silently in the hallway accepting this stranger's words of thanks. The man spoke in precise, clipped sentences, flavored with a heavy German accent. Herr Stoltz was, perhaps, in his mid-fifties, around six feet in height, his thinning blond hair cropped short and styled to perfection. He wore an expensive, double-breasted grey suit, rimless metal-framed glasses, and had nurtured a blond, pencil-thin mustache, again trimmed just so. *A handsome, efficient man*, Renaldo concluded*, with a touch of Teutonic arrogance thrown in for good measure.* His words of gratitude having been extended, Herr Stoltz turned and led the two nervous saviors through those portals of destiny.

"Gentlemen, gentlemen, come in, please. It is so good to see you again."

With that, Astor Gordero broke into a verse of the Prefect fight song that had caused them all so much trouble in Cordoba. He stopped singing as he embraced each man in turn, and again welcomed them to his "humble establishment." Neither Renaldo nor Estes had noticed the person sitting in the high-backed chair in front of Gordero's desk.

"And now, gentlemen, allow me to introduce you to Miss Simone Yvonne Montana Carta-Aqua. You, perhaps, know of her more prominently by her stage name, Symca. My dear, please meet Señor Renaldo De Seta and Señor Estes Santos."

The lady extended her hand toward the younger of two men in the traditional Latin greeting, but the boy did not attempt to grasp it. He simply stood there awestruck, unable to move or speak.

"Allow me, Señorita." Estes Santos quickly reached for the lady's gloved hand, raised it to his lips, and caressed it ever so gently. "I am afraid my young friend is afflicted with a severe case of idol worship, Señorita. It is a malady that has consumed the vast majority of his peers as well. And if the truth be known, even a man of my age is aware of the fact that you, Señorita, are the number one recording star in all of Argentina. It is an honor to make your acquaintance." Estes continued to hold her hand as the charming rhetoric flowed from his lips.

"Thank you, Señor, you are most kind. I hope that the young man will be alright, though. Señor Gordero has promised to take us all to lunch once your business is concluded, and I would hate for him to miss a meal the likes of which the Jockey Club will provide for us. Perhaps you could bring him some water, Wolfgang! Astor, I will now make those phone calls you requested from your other office. Don't be too long, gentlemen, for I am famished, and it is not polite to keep a lady waiting."

Only Renaldo's eyes followed the lady's sultry walk as she left the room, for he continued to be unable to move. It was The Fat Man's insistent prompting that brought him back to his senses.

"Please, gentlemen, please be seated. I have some interesting news for you both."

Astor Gordero gestured to the chair that his female visitor had just vacated and its matching adjacent clone. He nestled his large body into an oversized swivel chair that sat behind his mammoth antique desk. Wolfgang Stoltz made himself comfortable on a small couch to the visitors' right, notebook and pen in hand.

"I am sorry that this meeting could not have been held sooner, but that in no way diminishes the gratitude that I extend to you both for saving my life in Cordoba. It is only due to your swift and unselfish actions that I am sitting here today at all. I wanted to make sure that I could show you my appreciation to the fullest extent possible. It was only yesterday that I became certain that I could give you both what you so richly deserve.

"Gentlemen, this is a great day for Argentina. It will be announced later this afternoon that FIFA's World Cup Organizing Committee has agreed to fully sanction the World Cup Tournament here in Argentina, commencing in June. As you are no doubt aware, there has been much criticism of our National Organizing Committee's accomplishments and progress to date, both from the international press and from the competing foreign football associations as well. Those Brazilian bastards have done everything that they can to steal the tournament away from us. And those European crybabies, the Dutch and the English, they say that their insurance companies won't take the risk of insuring their players if they come to Argentina because of the rampant political terrorism here. What bullshit! When is the last time you saw anyone gunned down on the streets of Buenos Aires? Anyone that didn't deserve it, I should say."

He paused to catch his breath and also to laugh at his morbid little joke. "Well, all this subterfuge didn't work. FIFA president João Havelange, the only decent Brazilian on the face of this earth, is staking his career on our promise that we will be ready on time, and we will! I am on our organizing committee, and I know the daunting tasks before us. But the junta has declared the tournament to be of national importance. Economically, more than eighty thousand well-heeled visitors will arrive here to spend their hard-earned cash. Nothing will stop us from taking it from them, nothing! We will be ready!"

Again, Gordero paused to catch his breath. This time he studied the reactions of the two men in front of him before proceeding. When he was certain that his words were making the proper impact, he continued. "Unfortunately, while I am one hundred percent certain that our stadiums, hotels, and communications facilities will be in peak working form next June, I am much less certain about the readiness of our national football squad. The Argentine people will accomplish everything asked of them off the playing field. It is, however, what the eleven men chosen to wear our national colors accomplish on the playing field that will ultimately determine the success or failure of this entire undertaking. It is in that regard that I have news for you both.

"The entire program has been in absolute chaos for over a year now. Management has been accused of taking bribes from corporations to ensure that certain players, who, by coincidence, happen to endorse their products, receive a starting position on the team. Coaching and training techniques have been at odds with our financial capabilities to support them. Several world-class players just don't want to play, and for the most ridiculous reasons! Worst of all, most of our best players are still under contract to European teams that won't release them until the end of their current season, if at all. It is a nightmare, worse than you could ever imagine."

A sorrowful look of despair fell across The Fat Man's jowly face. Then, with perfect courtroom timing, a broad smile suddenly returned to his countenance and the soliloquy continued.

"I do see a glimmer of hope at the end of this very dark tunnel, however. For one thing, Octavio Suarez has agreed to take control of the entire on-field program and he intends to clean house, bring in his own people, and start from scratch. Everything will be his way, and only his way. No bribes, no sacred cows, no interference. That is the only way he would agree to take the position of manager of our national team. He has been guaranteed a substantial sum of money by the junta to make all the training preparations he requires. First class all the way. And Señor Havelange has agreed to turn up the heat on those damned Europeans to let our boys come home in time to train with the team. Then there are some particular matters of interest concerning the two of you . . ."

Once again, a pregnant pause for the dramatic effect. Gordero swiveled his bulk to face Estes Santos. "Octavio Suarez has asked for you to be the national team's goalkeeper coach, Estes. He knows you, and is impressed with your teaching ability and leadership skills. He wants to meet with you right away. It will be quite a feather in your cap, Estes, especially if you can help to make the team respectable. Championships are never won without great goalkeeping, and besides, it will look good on your résumé. National Team and World Cup coach. A good stepping-stone to bigger and better things to come, I am sure! As for you, my guardian angel . . ."

He paused again, and turning slightly, fixed his gaze directly on Renaldo this time before proceeding. The boy squirmed visibly in his chair, anticipation written all over his face.

"You will be the new Pelé, if Octavio Suarez has his way. He has seen you play the game. I told you that on the train from Cordoba. Remember, 'head and feet as one?' Those were his words, not mine. He has told me that the team needs new blood, someone young and charismatic. An hombre gol, a goal scorer that can bring people to their feet. Pelé did it for Brazil in his first World Cup when he was only seventeen. You, my boy, will have a few more years experience than the Black Pearl did when he made his debut on the world stage. Your time is now, Renaldo! The whole country is looking for a hero. Someone to make them forget, someone to let them dream. Octavio Suarez says that you are that someone. I, for one, agree with him!"

Renaldo's mouth was as dry as sandpaper, his face flushed, and the palms of his hands clammy with sweat. He could feel the blood pounding in his temples. It took a concerted effort for him to mumble some response.

"Señor Gordero, with all due respect, I have never even played in one professional first division game. I am flattered by your confidence in my abilities, but to compare me in the same breath as the great Pelé . . . I am just a schoolboy. For me to be the savior of the National Team is, is, crazy!"

"The idea is not crazy at all, Renaldo," Estes Santos interjected before Gordero could make his rebuttal. "I have been your coach for a full season now, and during my career as a premier league goalkeeper, I played both with and against the best players this country has ever produced. I have never, in all those years, come across a player with your natural talent, at any level! But this goes beyond just natural ability. There is an intangible that all great athletes have, no matter what their chosen sport. A je ne sais quoi, as the French say. You are a leader, Renaldo. You have the ability to anticipate, and then to act. You saved all of our lives in Cordoba by getting us out of that stadium. You acted instinctively, and you led us to safety. The only reason you have not been playing professional football to date is your mother's insistence that you obtain your high school diploma. I do not argue with that philosophy at all, but you have achieved that goal now. What lies before you is the chance of a lifetime! Do not turn your back on it, grab on to it and run with it. You still have to earn a place on the team, and that will not be easy. But you have nothing to lose by trying, and in Octavio Suarez, you have the best coach in the business. Besides, if what Señor Gordero says is true, it looks as if I will be along for the ride, to keep you on the straight and narrow path to glory."

Shock and disbelief still shrouded the young man's face as he tried to comprehend what was happening to him. It was now Astor Gordero's turn to reassure his teenage guest.

"Very well said, Estes, and I must say, my sentiments exactly! Do not sell yourself short, Renaldo. Your talent is there for everyone but yourself to see. Believe in yourself. Do not doubt what is God-given, for it is only self-doubt that will deprive you of greatness. I have set up a meeting for you both with Octavio tomorrow morning at nine out at River Plate Stadium. After that, both of your fates will be in his capable hands. Now, gentlemen, I believe that we are keeping a very pretty, not to mention famous, young lady waiting. Let us not extend this discourtesy any longer. We can continue our discussions over luncheon. Shall we be off? Wolfgang, would you please inform Señorita Carta-Aqua that we are ready for her to join us."

The word 'overwhelmed' did not do justice to Renaldo's feelings at that moment. Did he not have enough to digest without the added discomfort of being in the presence of the nation's most adored and sought-after show business personality? A poster of Symca's scantily clad form adorned the ceiling above his bed. He would stare for hours at the suggestive jacket covers of her albums while he fantasized that she was singing her love songs to him alone. It was one thing to have a dream girl, but to meet her in the flesh and act like a total Neanderthal was another. What an imbecile she must have thought him!

The party of five was ushered to Astor Gordero's private table in the rear of the Jockey Club dining room. The expedition through the packed club was equivalent to reading the who's who of Buenos Aires. Corporate luminaries, military officers of the highest rank, government ministers, and monied society dandies rubbed shoulders with one another while playing the game of see and be seen. None of them, however, could compete with the young lady that the rotund lawyer escorted through the throng on his arm.

As the party passed through the various rooms, the diners literally froze the instant that Symca came into view. Part of the reason was that ladies were allowed only in the dining area of this most revered and legendary Porteño establishment. As was so often the case, on this day, there were very few of the gentler sex present for the noon day meal. After the initial shock of seeing such a gorgeous celebrity in their midst, the tongues started to wag. Astor Gordero milked the situation for all it was worth, introducing his famous guest to any of his acquaintances whom he deemed worthy of such a reward.

At twenty-one years of age, Symca had acquired the poise and public relations savvy that could only have been attained through a lifetime in the entertainment business. She had been a child star in countless Argentine movies during her adolescence, switching to television soap operas and record production in her teens. It was said that she was one of the wealthiest women in all of Argentina. Her public appearances and live concerts had, more often than not, led to riots by overzealous fans. Even the strict decorum of the Jockey Club was being strained to the limits by her presence, as the rich and powerful craned their necks and strained to catch a glimpse of her.

The procession seemed to take forever before Renaldo was able to find asylum in the corner seat of Gordero's table. He hoped more than anything that he would not make a fool of himself again. The meeting at The Fat Man's office had passed from his memory, replaced only by the thoughts of her beauty being more overpowering in person than in any photograph or poster he had ever seen of her. He barely heard Wolfgang Stoltz address him.

"So, Renaldo, are you a fan of Señorita Carta-Aqua's?"

"Sorry? Oh, yes, most definitely! I have her entire collection of recordings. She is the number one heart-throb at my school. Many of my friends won't admit to it, but we hardly ever miss her weekly television soap opera. You must excuse me, Herr Stoltz, but I am a little overwhelmed to be in her presence. What is Señor Gordero's connection to her, if you don't mind me asking?"

"Not at all. It is no secret. Señor Gordero is her attorney and manager. He is also a longtime friend of her father. Señor Gordero was responsible for the young lady entering show business when she was very young. He is, I suppose you could say, her guardian. She is a very sweet lady, very down-to-earth. Do not be intimidated by her. Simone is a very warm person, as I am sure you will find out."

Estes Santos was commenting on the young lady's obvious beauty when she and Gordero finally reached the table.

"Well, that was a marathon, my dear. I thought we would never make it here. You caused quite the uproar, as usual. Now, let us turn our attention to our raison d'être."

He motioned to the captain standing by his side, menus at the ready. "Filmon, bring us two bottles of Dom Pérignon right away, and drop those menus on the table. We have cause for celebration today, and I, for one, have a powerful hunger!"

The luncheon lasted over three hours. Most of the time was consumed by Astor Gordero pontificating on whatever subject caught his interest at any particular moment. Sports, politics, sex, show business, all the bases were covered. He would, from time to time, allow each of his guests to express their personal opinions on any given subject, after which he would control the flow of the conversation as if he were the conductor of a great symphony orchestra.

Renaldo, for his part, had very little to say. He was more concerned about exactly how he was going to ask Symca for her autograph before they went their separate ways. He was totally under her spell. Her smile was unlike any he had ever seen. Her lips were so full, her hazel eyes so deep and seductive. She wore her auburn hair in long ringlets down past her shoulders, and as for her figure, the skintight crimson minidress that she wore barely covered her assets. Her voice was deep, almost husky, and many of Renaldo's friends had commented that it was that voice, more than any of her other attributes, that made them crazy with macho desire.

Estes Santos was trying all his most charming lines on her, the ones that he was too nervous to try on Gordero's secretaries., the younger man thought. It was when the conversation turned to the gala fundraising event to support Argentina's World Cup program, an event to be held at the world-famous Colon Opera House with Symca as the star attraction, that she finally addressed the young Porteño directly.

"If you would like to come and see my show at the gala, I can arrange a backstage pass for you. Would you be interested in something like that, Renaldo?" For once that day, the boy didn't hesitate to answer.

"A backstage pass to one of your shows? There is nothing in this world that would make me happier, Señorita." His youthful enthusiasm caused the older men at the table to break out in spontaneous laughter. Embarrassed, Renaldo sank back in his chair. Symca grasped his hand and looked him directly in the eyes.

"Don't let these old baboons cause you any discomfort, Renaldo. If it weren't for people with enthusiasm like yours, I might still be in university studying anthropology or some dreadful thing. And Señor Gordero would not have lined his pockets with the steep legal and management fees he charges me."

"Touché," was Gordero's only comment, delivered with an innocent half-smile with his large hands overlapped against his heart.

"In any event, I hear that the entire National Team will be introduced to the public on the opera house stage that evening, and Astor has informed me that there is a very good chance that you will be one of those being introduced. In that case, you won't need a backstage pass. Just come and knock on my dressing room door when you arrive."

"In deference to Señor Gordero, Señorita, I will accept a backstage pass, if the offer is still open. So much has happened to me today that the only thing of certainty would be to acquire a tangible piece of paper. At least that way, I could prove to my friends that I actually met you."

"Very well, then, I will have Astor arrange to have one sent to you. The gala is on the evening of January fourteenth. I believe that is the same day that the World Cup pool draw is taking place to see which countries are grouped together in the tournament. It should be a very exciting time, don't you think?" Her smile held him spellbound. Again the words did not come easily to him.

"If you are on the stage, then for certain it will be exciting. I heard you open for the Rolling Stones at River Plate Stadium last year. My seats were so far from the stage that you looked like a miniature doll, but your music was amazing! I have collected all your recordings and your television show is a weekly ritual. My friends and I never miss an episode."

He was speaking so quickly and with so much enthusiasm that the other three men at the table interrupted their discussion concerning the astronomically high price of the World Cup Gala tickets to listen to Renaldo sing the praises of his celebrity dining companion.

"That Raul Espling is such a snake-in-the-grass on your TV show. You are always getting hurt by him and turning the other cheek. My friends and I want to tar and feather him for the things he does to you. Is he that bad in real life?"

Symca didn't have an opportunity to respond before the next question left Renaldo's lips. "How about Anita Corazon? What is she like in person? Next to you, well, there is no contest, but she is still a very attractive lady that can really dance. That hot tango scene in the episode last month was incredible!"

He had to stop for a moment to catch his breath. "Your life must be so exciting. You do so many different things, and you do them all so well. I still can't believe that I am sitting at the same table with the amazing Symca. My friends will die with envy. That is, if they believe me at all."

"Well, Renaldo, let's give them some proof then." She reached for her small handbag and retrieved an oversized business card and a small felt marker. The outer flap of the card was embossed with a pouting, steamy color head shot of herself. She raised the flap and wrote several words with a flourish, then pushed the card across the linen tablecloth into Renaldo's hand.

"It's a private message. Don't look at it until you are alone. You wouldn't want these old dinosaurs to tease you about it. They would just be jealous."

Howls of mock protest greeted her last remark. Renaldo slid the card into his jacket pocket without a glance, although the anticipation of seeing what she had written was already driving him crazy. It was Astor Gordero that made him shift his thoughts to the other unbelievable news of the day.

"Now if I could have your undivided attention for just a few minutes, Señor De Seta, we have some logistical matters to finalize before we go our separate ways. Firstly, as I mentioned earlier, I have arranged a meeting for you and Estes with Octavio Suarez in the morning. I know that this is the holiday season, and Estes has told me that you are to be in Pergamino by tomorrow evening. I would not postpone the chance to meet with Señor Suarez in person, if I were you, Renaldo. He will be inundated with endless tasks of reorganization, and one cannot be certain when he will be able to schedule you in again. The meeting will be brief, I can assure of that. I'll tell you what I can do. Let me pick both of you up by eight o'clock tomorrow morning. We can go in my limousine to the stadium, see Octavio, and then, I will have my private Learjet at your disposal to fly you to Pergamino. You will be there even earlier than expected. What do you say?"

There was nothing that he could say. The presence of Symca had allowed him to temporarily forget the ridiculous notion that he would be a member of Argentina's World Cup team. The thought of such a thing rendered him temporarily mute.

"Come on, Renaldo, at least come with me to meet Señor Suarez." Estes Santos was leaning across the table, an earnest look on his face as he addressed the younger man.

"Your mother is already at Buenos Requerdos, and the train that you were scheduled to take would not have gotten you there until the late afternoon. You told me that you have already packed and completed your gift shopping, so there is absolutely nothing to stop you from accepting Señor Gordero's offer."

Again Renaldo was unable to respond. It was Symca that interceded to show him the way.

"Renaldo, fate works in very strange ways. Sometimes it can choose people for greatness even against their will. Fate chose me for stardom, and now it seems it has chosen you for something very special as well. I have been in the entertainment business since I was very young. Can you imagine for a moment what it must have been like for me as a five year-old to walk out on a stage and perform before a live television audience? I can still remember how terrified I was. But I knew that I loved to sing and dance, and everyone was so nice to me, telling me how talented I was, how pretty I was. It seemed as if the only one that had doubts about my ability was me.

"You are in the same situation right now. You are the only one that is doubting what you can accomplish. The professionals, Señor Suarez and Señor Santos here, have expressed their feelings that you have the talent to make a contribution. Don't deny yourself the chance to see if their faith in you is justified. If they prove to be wrong and things don't work out . . . well, look at you. You are young and intelligent, not to mention extremely handsome. You are also well-educated and wealthy, from what I understand. It is not the end of the world if you fail to succeed in making the team. But I for one would be very, very disappointed if you did not at least try to live up to the expectations of the men whose job it is to capture the World Cup trophy for our country. Please go and see Señor Suarez, for me, if for no other reason. Believe in yourself, Renaldo, the way you see others already believing in you!"

She had spoken with such sincerity and passion that he was helpless to resist her request.

"Alright, Señorita, for you and you alone, I will see Señor Suarez tomorrow. But that is as far as this whole thing might go. It is my mother I worry about more than anything! You see, my father was killed attending a soccer game in England many years ago, and she absolutely hates the sport and anyone associated with it. Estes here can tell you about my mother and soccer. It was only if I kept up straight 'A's in school this past year that she would even allow me to lace on a pair of boots. She actually thought that I was still playing on the high school team instead of on the semiprofessional under twenty-one team. When she found out the truth, it was Estes who caught an earful from her. Thank God that Señor Santos is a charmer with the ladies of world-class proportions, or I might have had to give up the sport forever. So, we will see what transpires. I am curious about one thing though, Señorita. It sounds to me like you are a football fan yourself. You speak of the game with such enthusiasm. Is that the case?"

Symca smiled seductively at her young admirer, as if she had a deep secret that she was about to reveal for the first time.

"Well, Renaldo, the truth of the matter is that the very first man I ever dated was Roberto Camacho, the striker with River Plate. I was only fifteen at the time, but I fell head over heals in love, not only with Roberto, but with the game in general and the River Plate club in particular. I am sorry to say that even after Roberto and I stopped seeing each other, I remained a fierce supporter of that team. Meeting you and Señor Santos today, however, might convince me to shift my loyalties to Newton's Prefects. That is a lady's prerogative is it not, gentlemen?"

Hearty laughter greeted her closing remark. Renaldo sank back in his chair, deep in thought, as Estes Santos picked up the conversation with Symca. Renaldo was surprised that she had been involved with the great Camacho at such a tender age. The man was a legendary player, to be sure, but also a fabled womanizer.

But that was past history. Right now, the young player was intrigued by the fact that she seemed to have more than just a passing knowledge of his background, and why the inspiring interest in his future? What had Gordero said to her about him? Perhaps there was more going on here than met the eye.

It took only one glance at the lady's smiling face to make him forget everything except the card that she had signed for him earlier. The card that continued to rest close to his heart in the inside breast pocket of his suit jacket.

Astor Gordero and party were the last patrons to depart the Jockey Club dining room that afternoon. The waiters and bus boys were busily resetting the tables for the evening throng that would begin arriving in a few hours. The maitre d' and captains remained attentive to Señor Gordero and his vivacious companion up to and beyond the entrance foyer of the club. It seemed that a few of the less discreet patrons who had departed earlier had let the word slip out that the famous Symca was dining there that day. A crowd of over one hundred admirers now lined the sidewalk awaiting her departure.

The maitre d' had arranged for Gordero's limousine to be waiting at the curb, but his table captain offered the lawyer the services of the club staff to form a human wedge as a means of escorting the lady and himself through the crowd to the safety of his automobile.

"That will not be necessary, Filmon," Gordero said with a smile while eyeing the expectant gathering outside. "It is these people that have made Señorita Symca the star that she is today. We will not deprive them of a chance to glimpse their idol. Renaldo, Estes, I will see you tomorrow morning, bright and early, before eight o'clock. I hope you have enjoyed yourselves today, gentlemen. Adios! Thank you, Filmon. Everything was superb, as usual. Are you ready, my dear? Well, then, Wolfgang, lead the way! Come, my little beauty. We are off to meet your makers!"

With a loud laugh and a wave of his arm, they disappeared through the revolving glass doors. Delighted screams and chants of "Symca, Symca, Symca" greeted them instantly. Gordero took as much pleasure from all the adulation as did the young lady for whom it was meant. They took time to sign several autographs and answer questions about her next album or tour. When they had finally departed in Gordero's white Mercedes limousine, the sidewalk in front of the Jockey Club was littered with flowers and promotional photos that had gone disappointingly unsigned by the star whose likeness they bore.

Estes and Renaldo were able to slip out into the afternoon sun, completely unnoticed. They walked half a block before hailing a taxi. Once in the confines of its rear seat, Estes embraced the younger man with a passion that startled the cabby and embarrassed the recipient.

"Didn't I tell you that The Fat Man would come through for us, Renaldo. I knew it! I knew that he would. God, he has given us both the opportunity of a lifetime. I am still in shock. A coaching position on our World Cup team. And you, the new Pelé! I can see the headlines now. 'Renaldo leads Argentina to World Cup supremacy.' You will not disappoint us, my friend, I am certain of that." Renaldo struggled to free himself from his coach's bear hug.

"Cut it out, Estes! Let go of me! Look, I am very happy for you. It is a position that you richly deserve. You have the experience and the talent to make a contribution. For my part, this joke ends tomorrow. I am sure that the luncheon with Symca was my reward for looking out for Gordero in Cordoba. I will be a celebrity just for being able to tell my friends the story of what happened today. That is enough for me, because that is reality. I prefer to live in the real world, Estes, not someone else's fantasy."

Estes Santos just shook his head and stared at his charge for a moment. Suddenly he addressed the cabby.

"Driver, pull over right here for a moment, please." He then turned to his backseat companion.

"Well, I have some 'business' to attend to right now. Sitting with that lovely señorita all afternoon has made me . . . Well, you know what I am talking about. Anyway, Renaldo, don't forget what your sexy idol just told you back there during lunch. Believe in yourself, the way others do, and there will be no stopping you! Remember that, my friend. I will see you in the morning. Take care."

He was out of the cab and into the lobby of the Hotel Presidente in seconds. Renaldo was thankful to finally be alone. After telling the driver to proceed to Casa San Marco, he pulled his new treasure from his jacket pocket. He stared down at the sultry picture on the cover for several seconds. Slowly then, with trembling fingers, he raised the flap to reveal its hidden message.

A smile came to his face as he read the inscription.

"To Renaldo. We will meet again, you can count on it! Believe in the future! Love, your new friend, Symca."

He was delirious with joy as he told his assembled amigos of that day's unbelievable adventure. They had been hastily summoned to Casa San Marco for beer and pizza, as well as the promise of a story they would not soon forget. Renaldo did not disappoint his schoolboy peers, although by the time the party broke up in the early morning hours, he was chagrined to find that Symca's momento had collected some additional pizza-stained fingerprints as a result of being passed among the unbelievers all evening.

It was fortunate that he remembered to set his alarm clock, for the early morning meeting had been relegated to the back of his mind by his preoccupation with the charms of the beautiful Symca. The new teen celebrity had not related that portion of the day's events to anyone. He lay partially clothed, semi-inebriated, and totally elated on his bed, staring up at her poster.

No matter what happens with Octavio Suarez in the morning, he thought grinning broadly, this has been the most memorable day of my life!

CHAPTER ELEVEN

A shiver ran the length of the worshipper's spine as he left the darkness of the vestibule and walked the twenty or so yards to the edge of the vast expanse. Standing now in blinding sunlight, he shielded his eyes, then raised them to view the upper reaches of the sacred temple. Silence cascaded down around him. The spirits were there, though, he could feel them.

He walked further into the open space, trying to imagine the events of six months hence. How different the temple would be then. Seething with emotion, deafening in its enthusiasm, a literal sea of humanity.

Would those worshippers be elated or deflated? That was the ultimate question!

Now he was inside the circle where it would all begin. Would he be here again in June? Down here on the pitch instead of up there in the pews of the temple? He had thought it ridiculous before this very moment, ridiculous to think that there was even the faintest possibility that such a thing could happen. But somehow now, standing here inside the midfield circle of River Plate Stadium, standing on the exact spot were the first touch of a black and white ball would commence the greatest sporting event known to man . . . now he knew in his heart that he wanted to be a part of it.

He was all alone. The thousands of workers that were racing against time to complete the renovations of what had been known as 'Monumental Stadium' were gone for the Christmas break. The cranes and massive machinery stood silent in the sun.

Monumental is a name befitting of this place, he thought as he scanned the entire circumference of the upper terraces. Seventy-five thousand hearts would beat here in unison, hoping that the spirits of past champions could help their current-day heroes in what everyone knew was a 'monumental' task . . . becoming champions of the world!

He turned his attention to the playing surface itself. New sod had been laid and not a single cleat had desecrated the beautiful green turf, one hundred and twenty yards in length from goal line to goal line. Eighty yards in width from touch line to touch line. The worshipper was mystically drawn toward the goal area. As he walked the righteous path to glory, the same path that he hoped to travel at full speed in only a few months, the field markings came into view.

First, the penalty arch, beyond which no player could venture preceding that moment of high tension, the penalty shot. Then, the dreaded penalty area itself, running along the goal line for eighteen yards from either side of the two upright goal posts, then extending eighteen yards out onto the pitch to form a large rectangle. It was within these markings that unsportsmanlike conduct was punished with instant and often dire consequences. The yawning goal net beckoned him closer. Eight yards wide from inside upright to inside upright. Eight feet high from the pitch to the underside of the crossbar. So invitingly large when empty, so terribly small when a world-class keeper stood defiantly under its shadow. He came upon the penalty spot next, twelve yards from the goal line, in the dead center of the field. The place of ultimate drama, shooter versus goalkeeper. One on one, matching wits, nerve, and luck. Glory for the triumphant, agony for the vanquished.

"Renaldo, it's time! He is ready for you now!"

Estes Santos had to yell at the top of his voice to enable his message to carry from the entrance tunnel to where Renaldo stood at the penalty spot. Astor Gordero had taken Estes in to meet Octavio Suarez first, immediately upon their arrival at the stadium some thirty minutes prior.

Before he headed toward the sideline, Renaldo considered taking a small divot of turf as a lucky memento, but thought better of such sacrilege when a gust of wind blew open his jacket and tossed his necktie over his shoulder. This was a sign. Respect this holy place, and respect may just be offered in return. He turned from the spot and jogged to Estes' side.

As usual, it was Astor Gordero who made the formal introductions as Renaldo stood cautiously in the manager's doorway.

"Good, good, come in, my boy. Renaldo De Seta, I would like to introduce you to Argentina's newly appointed World Cup team manager, Señor Octavio Suarez."

The boy stepped forward and held out his hand to Suarez, who remained seated behind an old metal desk heaped with piles of manila file folders and newspapers. The manager slowly extended a limp arm to meet that of the younger man. The handshake was impersonal and without enthusiasm.

"Would you gentlemen excuse us for a few minutes, please. I would like to talk to Renaldo in private, if you don't mind."

The visitor's young heart sank when he heard Suarez request privacy.

This is it! he thought silently, *The game is over. How could I have ever let myself think for an instant that there was the slightest chance of joining the team? Damn, what a gullible fool I have been.*

Renaldo studied the man behind the desk as Gordero and Santos made their departure. He must have been at least fifty years old, with long, thin, greying hair hanging in straggles and strands down past his shoulders. His face resembled that of a horse, elongated, with small, darting eyes behind black, horn-rimmed reading glasses.

He looked more like an absent-minded professor than the most victorious manager in the history of the Argentine Football Association. A career of almost twenty-five years had garnered fifteen First Division Championships, seven Libertadores Cup titles for the best club side in South America, and two postings to Argentine World Cup staff as Assistant Manager in 1966 and 1974.

He was an obvious choice to head the contingent in 1974, but he was known as an outspoken individualist who would not always toe the association line. His players loved him, and he, in turn, would go to bat for them, but bureaucrats and football executives drove him crazy. His appointment to the 1974 team came only after a virtual player revolt on the eve of the Munich competition. Wisely, the association had not waited until the very last minute to give him full and absolute control of the national program for World Cup '78.

A cigarette hung from the headman's lips, and judging by the overflowing ashtrays that were scattered throughout this dank, poorly lit cubicle of an office, he must be a chain-smoker. Styrofoam cups of coffee, many half empty with cigarette butts swimming in them, were also a prominent decoration. Suarez continued to rummage through a stack of files strewn helter-skelter over the desk. Renaldo could see his frustration growing by the second until miraculously, out of the bottom of the mess, he retrieved the errant folio.

"Aah . . . good, here we are. Pull up a chair, son. Just throw those files on the floor."

Suarez motioned to a barely visible chair in the corner of the room, stacked to its limit with more of the same folders that covered his desk. By the time Renaldo had moved the chair and was seated, Suarez was deep in wordless thought, studying the contents of his newly found document.

Several minutes passed before he abruptly closed the folder, lit another Marlboro, and focused his attention on the visitor.

"I have seen you play many times, son. You are good, very good! But as you know, you have never faced the kind of competition that we will be up against in the World Cup."

He paused to take a long drag on his Marlboro. Renaldo noticed that his demeanor had changed once he started to talk about the tournament. Those darting eyes seemed to come to life, and there was a new enthusiasm in his voice. He gestured around the tiny room with a sweep of his arm.

"The organizing committee has promised me a proper office and support staff right after Christmas, but the whole situation is in such a shambles that I decided to start the day they hired me. This was the only room that they could give me. I've been here for three days and nights now. I suppose I will have to go home for Christmas or my wife will kill me. I can only tell you that things are even worse than they are reporting them to be in the press. The program is in disarray!" Suarez paused to look in several white cups for a sip of coffee. There was none to be found.

"I have players squabbling about money already. How much will they make if they grace us with their presence on the National World Cup side? 'I demand to be paid more than so and so, because I am a better player,' or 'I have more international caps,' or 'I am being paid more by my club team,' or 'I have laid more girls, so you had better pay me more than anyone else or I won't come.' "

That was a great imitation of a spoiled, whiny, little girl, Renaldo thought.

"I have no idea who will be released from the European teams in time to train with us," the boss continued. "We open training camp on February fifteenth in Mar del Plata. That gives me a little over a month to pull this mess together! Already I know of a few barracudas who are just waiting for me to slip up, so that they can walk in and take over the manager's position. Barracudas after only three days! Three days on the job and the vultures are circling already. Well, fuck the whole bunch of them!"

His face was flushed with anger at the thought of someone hunting for his scalp already. He tried to compose himself and force the unwanted thoughts from his mind. He sat silently studying his guest for several seconds, then continued.

"Luckily, no one in the press knows where to find me. I insisted that the organizing committee tell them that I wouldn't officially take over until the twenty-seventh of the month. So I bought myself a few days anyway."

He stood up and stretched his lanky frame. Renaldo recalled how tall the man was from some of the clinics he had attended in the past. At least six foot three, maybe taller.

"I need new blood, Renaldo. New faces with a fresh attitude. I will not field a team of prima donnas. The old guard will find that out soon enough. I know that you are young and untested, but if you are willing to work for me without bitching and moaning, then we will see what magic I can craft with you. Gordero and Santos are very high on your ability. They told me there might be some problems with your mother, however. Are they solvable? It would be a shame to let an opportunity like this pass you by on that account."

Suarez lit another Marlboro, then walked around to the front of his desk. He then abruptly sat down on the edge of its metal top, only inches from Renaldo's chair. His voice took on a more fatherly tone.

"We all have to cut our mother's apron strings sometime, my boy! What do you think? Can I count on you to show up here on January fifteenth for the initial team meeting and medicals?"

Suarez was right. He had to follow his own destiny, and he might as well cut the apron strings sooner than later.

"Yes, Señor Suarez, you can count on me to be here on the fifteenth of next month. I will have dealt with my mother by that time. Thank you for having faith in me, for giving me this chance. I suppose I have been my own worst enemy as far as doubting myself. I have had a secret dream for many years, since the death of my father. I now realize that you have just given me the means with which I can make that dream reality. For that, I am most grateful. I will not let you down, Señor Suarez."

Tears welled in the boy's eyes as the emotion of the moment overcame him. Octavio Suarez stood and rested a fatherly hand on his shoulder.

"I am thankful for that, son, for I will need an abundance of help myself to make my dreams into reality. The road will not be smooth, and the glare of the lights will make weak men run for shelter. Be strong, have faith, and dreams may just become reality!"

He walked over to a large cardboard box in the corner of the room, stooped down and pulled out a thick binder.

"This is your training manual. It will be your bible for the next six months. Guard it with your life, for without its knowledge, your life is worth nothing to me. Start on the training regimen tomorrow. I want you in good physical condition by the fifteenth. Follow the dietary instruction stickly and don't do anything stupid with the young ladies. I have lost more than one potential superstar with a case of the clap. Keep your fly zipped up until next July! Now, I believe that you have a plane to catch, so I will see you on the fifteenth. I am going to keep Santos here for the day to help me sort out this mess. That's it! Off with you now, and Merry Christmas."

Renaldo rose from his chair and again shook the manager's hand. It felt totally different this time, strong, confident, and reassuring. The two men walked out into the corridor that connected the bowels of the stadium.

"What is the weather like outside? I haven't seen the sun for days," the older man laughed. They made idle chatter as they snaked their way through the subterranean labyrinth, then up into the entrance plaza where the two other men waited by Gordero's limousine.

Farewells and good wishes for the holidays were exchanged, then Renaldo and Astor Gordero climbed into the rear of the Mercedes, while Estes Santos and Octavio Suarez disappeared into the darkness of the stadium. Renaldo opened his window and stuck his head through the opening to get a last, inspiring glimpse of the temple before it faded from sight.

What history will be written within its towering confines six months from now? he wondered silently. *And will I be there to help write a chapter or two? Only time will tell.*

The loud 'pop' of a cork brought him back inside the cool interior of the limousine with a startled, curious look on his face.

"I take it from the binder you are holding that there may be cause for celebration. Is that the case?"

Gordero extended a full crystal goblet of his trademark Dom Pérignon to the younger man, a sly, inquisitive grin etched on his face. Renaldo sat back in the seat and reluctantly took the goblet. He had forgotten about his early morning hangover in the excitement of the hour. No sense in refusing the liquid gold that his host was offering, though. After all, things had worked out exactly as Gordero had predicted with Octavio Suarez. No cruel joke had been played on him, and yes, he was going to be a member of Argentina's World Cup team, at least at the outset of training. Yes, damn it, there was cause for celebration!

"Cheers to you, Señor Gordero. You are a miracle worker, to be sure. Never in my wildest dreams did I think something like this could happen to me. I am in shock! Señor Suarez told me to report back to the stadium on January fifteenth for the initial team meeting and physicals. I still can't believe what you have done for me!"

"All that I have done to date still does not amount to saving a life, Renaldo, which is exactly what you did for me in Córdoba. Now it is what you can do for your country that really matters. So 'cheers' to you, my boy. Help bring the World Cup trophy to this great land of ours!" He downed the entire goblet in one mouthful, and then refilled both vessels with the bubbly essence.

"What about your mother? You will have to deal with her right away. Perhaps Estes or I could come up to Pergamino to have a word with her, if necessary. Try to convince her what a splendid opportunity this is for you."

"That will not be necessary, Señor Gordero. I will handle that situation myself. As Señor Suarez just reminded me, we all have to cut the apron strings at sometime or another. That time is now, for me. I will be here on the fifteenth with or without her blessing. I will let her have a peaceful Christmas day, and then discuss the matter calmly and rationally a day or two afterward. It will mean delaying the start of my university education for a few months, but the school will still be there when I am ready to attend it. I am confident that I can win her approval without breaking her heart."

"I am glad of that, Renaldo. I have met your mother several times at various charity fundraisers. She is a charming, hardworking lady. I know that she has only your best interests at heart, but I can tell you that the prospect of what you are about to tell her will not rest lightly on her shoulders. Especially after the tragic incident with your father."

A strange use of words, Renaldo thought. He had only ever heard of his father's untimely death being referred to as an 'accident,' never an 'incident.'

Surely just a champagne-induced slip of the tongue. He put the matter out of his mind, as Gordero continued his oration.

"I also have your best interests at heart, Renaldo, for I am the one responsible for leading you to the edge of the cauldron that you are about to be thrown into. Your life will change totally for the next six months, maybe forever. It will be like living under a microscope. The press, the fans, they will want to know everything about you. Your privacy will disappear. There will be so many distractions, so many temptations. A clean-living young man such as yourself has no idea what is in store for you. That is why I want to stay close to you, to look after your affairs for you. I can keep the distractions away as much as possible while you concentrate on one thing. . . football!"

Renaldo's partially fogged mind was having trouble figuring out exactly to what the older man was alluding. He simply listened in silence as the presentation continued.

"I have handled many other players in the past, but you are the only one I am interested in now. There will be an assortment of sleazy hangers-on that will come knocking at your door the instant that you are named to the preliminary team. These people are professional bloodsuckers. Your name becomes their calling card for an endless string of shams and rip-offs. I want to keep you from falling prey to these people. I will negotiate your contract with Suarez. You cannot expect a great sum of money, initially. But once you have proven yourself on the world stage, well, then, the sky is the limit! Huge contracts are being offered to Argentine players to play the game overseas. Combined with lucrative endorsement deals with worldwide corporations, it boggles the mind to even think about the possibilities. The one thing that is imperative in this whole equation is that your public image, your reputation as a man of character, remain unsullied in any way. You must be a saint in the eyes of the public. Then, and only then, will the major corporations open their vaults to you."

The Fat Man stopped talking long enough to replenish his goblet. His passenger's had remained full and untouched.

"Renaldo, I can guide you down the right road. I know that the money is not what really matters to you now, that you are wealthy in your own right. But it is the public's perception of you at such a young age that can be shaped and contoured to your maximum benefit. We have had players on our World Cup teams compete under the shadows of horrendous personal scandals. Game fixing, wife beating, extra-marital affairs, even homosexuality! The foreign press in particular will dig up any dirt that they can to throw us off our game. They are absolutely ruthless people, especially the closer a team gets to the championship game.

"I am offering my services to you as a sort of, let's say, guardian of your career. I have at my disposal the means and the wherewithal to keep the public perception of Renaldo De Seta on the straight and narrow. And should, heaven forbid, a small indiscretion occur on your part, well, let's just say that I am a man of many contacts in the less glamorous side of the business world as well. Sometimes, events need a little cosmetic surgery to keep a career wholesome. Almost anything can be arranged for a price. But I know that none of that will be necessary as far as you are concerned. Allow me to tell people that you are represented by Astor Gordero, and I promise you smooth sailing right up to the victory podium, where you will hold aloft the World Cup trophy!"

The man has delusions. He is a dreamer of the grandest scale. I cannot take this piffle seriously, Renaldo's mind was saying.

Nevertheless, the more Gordero talked and the more Renaldo drank, the more legitimate seemed the reasons for entrusting his future to the Buenos Aires lawyer. Gordero had done everything that he said he would do for Renaldo. He had the connections, the esteem, the knowledge. He also had a certain young actress/singer as a client. The distractions would be tremendous, he knew that. Who else was there to turn to, to guide him, to show him the path to glory? The limousine was now approaching Ezeiza Airport. Gordero persisted.

"Think seriously about what I have said, Renaldo, while you are relaxing in Pergamino over the holidays. Talk to Estes Santos about the potential of my representing you. I trust his judgment. But once you return to Buenos Aires in the New Year, it will be decision time. You must have dealt with your family matters by then, as well as come to an understanding about my participation in your future. I can help you, Renaldo, make no mistake about that."

The Mercedes had entered the private aviation compound and was pulling astride a sparkling white Learjet, the graphics "A.R. Gordero and Sons" prominently displayed on the fuselage. The chauffeur popped the trunk, then ran to open his employer's door.

The pilot and an attractive flight attendant stood at the bottom of the plane's staircase. Gordero greeted them warmly, then introduced Renaldo to them both. The chauffeur handed the boy's luggage to the flight attendant, who disappeared into the aircraft to stow it away for the flight. As was often his habit, Astor Gordero had a surprise to bestow upon his guest before they parted company.

"Oh, by the way, Renaldo, I almost forgot this." He reached into the inner pocket of his sizable white linen jacket and brandished a pink envelope in front of the departing passenger's face. "You made quite an impression on a certain young lady at our luncheon yesterday. She insisted that I give this to you without delay, and I was advised to tell you that she expects you to follow the enclosed instructions succinctly and to the letter of the law. That's legalese for 'you better do as I say!' So, have a good holiday and come back ready for your new life. Here is my business card with my phone numbers on it should you want to talk about anything, anything at all, over the next fortnight. Have a safe trip. Adios, my boy."

He embraced a startled Renaldo and kissed him on each cheek. Then his bulging torso withdrew as he motioned to the pilot with a wave of his hand.

"Please join us, Señor De Seta, and we will be on our way to Pergamino." The pilot gently touched the boy's shoulder and motioned to the stairway.

Renaldo mumbled a barely audible "thank you" to Gordero and accompanied it with a wave and a smile as he ascended into the jet. Within minutes they were airborne, an orange juice and black coffee resting on a tray beside him on the overstuffed couch where he sat.

A very functional piece of furniture, he thought. *I could not see a man with Astor Gordero's prominent credentials, namely his stomach, trying to fit into a regular airline seat, even a first-class one at that!*

He was now alone in the cabin, the attendant having gone forward, pulling the privacy screen behind her. He gently held the pink envelope to his nose, searching for her scent. He swore that he could detect the same perfume that he had basked in the day before. Slowly, lovingly, he opened the envelope and pulled out its contents.

The two-inch high florescent red letters spelling out 'Backstage Pass' leapt out at him. Set on an elaborately designed black felt background, the pass was inscribed with the name of the event, the venue, and the date of the World Cup Gala Concert. Attached to the back of the pass was another of Symca's oversized photo cards. This one, however, contained a totally different pose than the one from the day before. This pose was even more sensual than the first, exposing part of her left breast. Renaldo strained his eyes to decipher the outline of her nipple under the sheer leopard skin material. He became aware of a stirring in his trousers and was forced to readjust his posture, lest the flight attendant suddenly appear.

Under the flap awaited a message that would cause him increased discomfort in his midsection.

'Dearest Renaldo,

Meeting you was the highlight of my day yesterday. I have sent the pass as promised, but I can't wait that long to see you again. Here is my home number. Call me as soon as you get back in town. Happy Holidays. Thinking of you. Love, Symca. tel: 555–7399'

This is unbelievable! She wants to see me? Why me? The lady could have any man she wanted in the entire country! Heaven help me!

A cloud suddenly appeared on his previously unblemished horizon. His brow furrowed. *Oh, sweet Jesus, what am I going to tell mother about Symca? She will think that this is all the Devil's hand.* He could hear her prayers for divine help already.

"Hail Mary, sweet Mother of our Savior Jesus, I ask your help in my time of need. The rock-and-roll star has seduced my precious son into becoming a football player. My sweet, sensitive, scholastic son, turned into a football player! Better a murderer or a rapist." Renaldo intoned the mock prayer to the empty passenger compartment.

What a predicament I have gotten myself into, he mused, a half-smile on his lips. *Best to keep quiet about Symca for the time being. No sense giving Mama a stroke for a Christmas present. Besides, her interest in me will be fleeting at best.*

It was with mixed emotions that he pondered, in turn, a great lustful adventure, followed by his eventual dismissal from the superstar's romantic considerations as the jet descended into Pergamino.

CHAPTER TWELVE

"How could things have gone so terribly wrong? Especially after the holiday reunion had started off so nicely?"

Florencia De Seta sat staring out her bedroom window at Buenos Requerdos, pondering the unsettling events that had ruined her holiday merriment. She had spent most of the past two days in bed, fretting about the future of her newly wayward sons. Even though Lonnie had not arrived until late Christmas Eve in a state of agitation and with very little good cheer, Christmas Day had been splendid. The boys had bought both her and Lydia very thoughtful gifts, excluding the book on political change in Argentina by some left-wing author who was currently rotting in a state penitentiary. Lonnie had suggested that it would be 'enlightening' reading for both her and Lydia over the holidays. She much preferred the exquisite leather handbag that was also a gift from her eldest son.

Oli had prepared her usual holiday feast for the family, and the Christmas meal turned out to be a happy, boisterous gathering with all the participants in a festive mood. She had actually gotten a little tipsy as the family sang a variety of songs and carols to Renaldo's guitar accompaniment. Even Lonnie seemed to be enjoying himself, and there was no mention of politics the entire evening. The tidings of good cheer carried over into the following four days. The boys took to their horses and explored the outer reaches of the estancia while she and Lydia relaxed in the warm glow of the holiday spirit.

Then, after dinner on the twenty-ninth, things changed for the worse. Lonfranco and Renaldo had come to her together and asked to have a family meeting. Lydia's inclusion had foreshadowed their need of a sympathetic ear. The elderly lady was sometimes too much of a free spirit for Florencia's liking, and the boys knew this all too well.

Florencia still did not believe the things her sons had said to her in the heat of that moment. She had not slept well the past two nights, ever since the fateful family council meeting on the twenty-ninth. Here it was, New Year's Eve, and her mood was anything but celebratory. What was upsetting her at this moment, more than any of the news her sons had to tell her, was that the knot had reappeared in her stomach. She hadn't felt its dull pain since Peter's death.

Is this an omen of foreboding? she ruminated, silently staring at the late afternoon shower that swept over the Pampas. *Am I to lose someone else, another loved one?*

Lydia had been no help, whatsoever. She had actually encouraged the boys to "follow their hearts." What absolute nonsense! *Have I raised two worthless dreamers as sons? It would certainly appear so. Lydia has refused to even consider the idea of cutting them off from their trust funds until they come to their senses and return to school. She is the only one empowered to revoke the trusts that she established for the boys after their grandfather's death. The country air has made her brain go soft!*

The grandmother had called it "quite sweet" that Lonnie had decided to take the summer off and travel around the country with his girlfriend. *What about the extra courses he needs to get into law school? It is that girl from Tucumán that has poisoned him, turned him in to a great political philosopher. A dope-smoking hippie bum is more like it!*

During some of the discussions at the dinner table, the rhetoric that he was espousing had been nothing short of political treason. If her eldest son had been younger, she would have washed his mouth out with soap for preaching such anarchy against the state. He was blaspheming against the very institutions that had made their family's net worth triple in the past three decades. But even worse were his solutions to the country's problems: civil disobedience and guerrilla tactics against the state.

"It is all that damned Celeste Lavalle's doing," she cried out in anger.

The pain grew sharper in her stomach. She really did have to see a physician about this problem. She couldn't keep sloughing it off as just nerves.

And young Renaldo! Who on earth had gotten hold of him to fill his brain with such inane thoughts? Argentina's World Cup soccer team? He is just a boy, barely shaving. Now he comes to Pergamino with this ridiculous notion that he is a world-class football player. Why, he cried for me at the first game he ever went to!

Florencia clutched a hand to her aching midsection. It was raining harder now, vast sheets of water tumbling down from a dark grey sky. The weather outside was an exact barometer of her inner disposition. She continued to ponder the future as she reclined on her bed.

The world has gone crazy. What on earth is happening to my boys? Young Renaldo acted as if some woman had gotten her hands on him as well. The signs of romantic infatuation are there for all to see. Loss of appetite, manic swings in temperament, elated and outgoing one moment, moody and withdrawn the next. Constantly staring at the telephone, as if hoping with all his heart that it will ring for him. Locked in his room, playing the guitar and trying to sing those silly love songs for hours on end. What, sweet Jesus, what, did I do to deserve this? I was going to have one son a lawyer and the other son a doctor. How those society bitches would have eaten their hearts out then!

Now neither of them wants to go back to school. At least Renaldo's dream of joining that stupid football team will be short lived. He said that they open training camp in February. I cannot stop him from going because he is still on summer break, but with any luck, he can still enroll in his first semester after he is cut from the team. How could he ever think that he was anywhere near the caliber of player to do such a thing? It must be that scoundrel Santos. I'll have a word or two with him when we get back to town. And what about the lack of respect for their mother's feelings that they both had displayed? That hot head Lonnie storming off the estancia, saying that he was never coming back. That he preferred the company of real people to, to…what did he call us? "Petit bourgeoisie.' The nerve! At least his brother had the manners to stay here as planned.. That means I still have an opportunity to convince him to give up this whole business. He must go back to school where he belongs and forget these childish football dreams. That damn sport killed his father, and if there is anything that I can do to prevent it from doing the same thing to my son, I will do it! Tomrrow, I will go to the chapel in the village and light two candles for their lost, pathetic souls. Please God, help me show them the way…

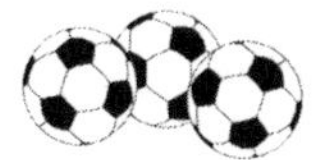

Renaldo had noticed the change in his brother the first night Lonnie arrived at Buenos Requerdos. There was something different about him, about his mannerisms, his speech. The brothers had not crossed paths the two weeks prior to arriving at the estancia, Lonnie preferring to stay at Celeste's flat before they separated for the holidays.

Florencia had taken early leave of the capital due to unusually high humidity and pollen counts above normal, which were causing her some discomfort. Lonnie's whereabouts the ten days before Christmas had not been under scrutiny for that reason.

Renaldo had suggested that they ride the range together the day following Christmas. He told his brother that he had some important news to tell him out of earshot of his mother and grandmother. Bright and early on a cloudless twenty-sixth, the De Seta brothers took the food and wine that Oli had prepared for their trail lunch, saddled up their mounts, and left the main buildings of the estancia in their dust. The siblings had ridden extensively with their father when they were young. Their teenage summers were spent under the tutelage of the senior gauchos, learning the ways of caring for a herd of prized beef cattle on the Pampas. Renaldo took to this life with great enthusiasm. Lonnie, after a few summers at Pergamino, decided to spend his holidays in Tigre, working on his grandfather's ferry boats and helping out at No Se Preocupe. He still loved to ride the plains though, and it didn't take much coaxing for him to join his younger brother for the day's outing.

They rode through the flat agricultural lands first, corn and wheat interspersed in checkerboard fields. Further on, the great herds of cattle were visible in the distance. Renaldo had always likened his first glimpse of the herds to the experience of the American Indians of the last century as they rode over the crest of a hill and confronted the immense herds of wild buffalo that roamed the plains. The brothers stopped to drink maté, the native herbal tea, with a few of the gauchos who were tending the herd. Then it was on to their favorite destination of years gone by, 'Lake Lonfranco.'

In reality, the 'lake' was little more than a large pond shaded by mature jacaranda and tipa trees, but their grandfather had brought their father to the very same location years before. He had told a very young, very gullible Peter De Seta that the pond was really just a small part of a huge underground lake that he had discovered while mapping the area for settlement years before any other civilized human had ever been to this particular part of Argentina. Lonfranco had subsequently named the lake after a famous plainsman and great explorer . . . himself! But what he hadn't told Peter was that the lake was also the scene of some of the most romantic liaisons he and Lydia had engaged in during her first visit to Argentina years before. It was only the sanitized version of the family folklore that had been passed down to the two brothers who now swam in the invitingly cool water. For several precious moments that beautiful summer day, all the world's problems and turmoils disintegrated into a fond remembrance of their youth.

Over the sandwiches and roast chicken that Oli had prepared for them, accompanied by two bottles of a local white wine called 'Torrontes,' Renaldo broke the first piece of news to his brother.

"I have been asked to join the preliminary lineup for our World Cup team. Isn't that crazy? I am still in shock! The day I arrived here, that morning, I met with Octavio Suarez, the newly appointed manager. He talked about how he is looking for some new faces, because of all the trouble with the veterans, and . . ."

Lonnie almost choked on his drumstick as he listened to his brother's news. He was quick to taunt his younger sibling, cutting him off in mid-sentence.

"You? On our National Team? A skinny little kid like you on Argentina's World Cup team? What have you been smoking, brother? Give me some, too, so I can make the team with you! It must be primo shit! God help you, the Brazilians and Germans will eat you alive!"

The older brother was writhing on his back, holding his head in disbelief when he suddenly sat up, threw the half eaten chicken bone at his hurt-looking companion, then pounced on top of him.

"You little son of a gun, I always knew you were good! Right from those first days when you could keep the ball away from me in the garden at home. The only way I could get that damned thing back was to beat the crap out of you. Congratulations, little brother! Now, you had better get me some damn good tickets to your games."

He rumpled Renaldo's long, curly hair, then pulled him upright into a sitting position and embraced him with sudden tenderness.

"What about Mama? Have you told her yet? She will shit! Don't let her talk you out of this one. I want those tickets! This is great news. I can't believe it. . . my little brother playing for Argentina in the World Cup. Amazing!"

"I have to make the team first, Lonnie, so your tickets are still in doubt at the moment. And no, I haven't told Mama yet. I thought you might have some pointers for me, you being the one that is always in trouble, always giving her bad news."

He threw the chicken bone back at his brother, then reached for the open wine bottle and took a healthy swig.

"I have some other news that you might find just as interesting. I had lunch the other day with Symca, the rock star and television actress," he commented nonchalantly, a large smile planted on his face.

"Now I know you've been toking up. Who helped you make up these fantasies? Maybe it's LSD that you've been experimenting with. No grass is powerful enough to give you these hallucinations." Again the doubting tone of voice and mock disbelief shrouded Lonnie's face.

"Believe me, it's true, all of it. The whole thing started in Córdoba. I tried to tell you about it that Sunday that Mama made us go to mass together, but I was so tired that I crashed when we got home. The next morning, you took off to Celeste's before I woke up. Anyway, I helped save a man, a very influential man it turns out, from being hung, drawn, and quartered by a mob of pissed off locals. So once we were safely in the hands of our military escort and on our way to the train station, this bigwig says to Estes Santos and I that we have saved his life, that he is indebted to us, and please would we ride back to Buenos Aires in his private rail coach. That's what started this whole thing."

The storyteller stopped long enough to soothe his parched throat with the local vintage, then continued to illuminate his spellbound listener.

"So Estes and I get a phone call to meet this guy for lunch ten days later. No big deal we think. A free lunch, then the permanent kiss-off. But no, we walk into this guy's office, and who should be sitting there but Symca in the flesh! She goes to powder her nose and The Fat Man, the guy we saved, says to Estes that Octavio Suarez has asked for him to be the goalkeeper coach of the World Cup team. And Suarez also wants me to try out for a spot in the lineup. Well, you could have knocked me over with a feather!"

Renaldo brushed his right hand past his face and fell languidly backward to emphasize his point. The wine and sun were making him feel very good. He raised himself up on one elbow and continued.

"Then it's off to lunch at the Jockey Club no less, and for three hours I just sit there, staring at the most beautiful woman I have ever seen. It was like I had died and gone to heaven. She is an absolute angel, a very sexy angel."

He was talking so quickly that Lonnie had to have him repeat several details, especially about Symca's short minidress.

"Man, oh man, for a schoolboy you sure have had an exciting few days. What about Symca? Are you going to tell mother about her? She will really freak out about that one! Well, look at it this way. If you become a doctor, you can be a celebrity doctor that handles only football stars and entertainment personalities. Renaldo De Seta, doctor to the stars." He fell back on the cool grass, laughing with great gusto.

"The best part is that Symca wants to see me again. She wrote me this note before I came here." Renaldo pulled the photocard from the inside pocket of his blue jean jacket and handed it to his now thoroughly incredulous brother.

"Oooooh la la, this picture! What are you, some super stud or something? I thought that I was the one that was good with the señoritas, but nothing close to this has ever happened to me. Are you going to call her?" The leer on Lonnie's face left little doubt about the real meaning of his question.

"I don't know. She must be just toying with me. I don't understand girls at all. You know me. I've only had a handful of dates all through high school. Those were ones that Mama arranged so that I could go to the social functions that she thought would be good for our family image. I'll admit it, I'm lost!" The anguished look on his face left little doubt that he was telling the truth.

"I have this feeling, one I've never had before. It is so weird. I can't stop thinking about her, yet I know that she will break my heart if I give her the chance. What should I do, my wise and sexually experienced brother?"

They talked for over an hour, and through it all, Renaldo could feel that Lonnie had something of great urgency that he wanted to get off his chest. The younger brother had confided his innermost secrets to his older, more worldly sibling, but now it was time to turn the tables and search the depths of Lonnie's soul. When a break came in their fluid discourse, Renaldo seized the opportunity and struck with uncharacteristic bluntness.

"You have changed, Lonnie, I've noticed it ever since you arrived at the estancia. Something is going on with you. Feel like opening up to your little brother? I am a good listener, and I can keep a secret. What do you say? Is it something to do with Celeste?"

Lonnie sat silently, deep in thought, all the while staring at his brother. *He is a good kid, kind, and honest. None of this mess is his fault. How can I tell him that I am about to try to change the only values he has ever known? The values that have made this family part of the ruling oligarchy, part of the wealthy bourgeoisie that I despise so much. How can I tell him that I will stop at nothing, even the most violent acts, to bring social change to Argentina?*

Celeste had done her job well. In the almost two weeks that they had spent together since his interrogation by her brothers, the tutor and student had worked an exhaustive schedule of eighteen-hour days. They only left the flat to shop for food and other necessities. A strict regimen prohibited the consumption of alcohol and drugs, as well as abstinence from all physical contact.

Lonnie slept on the couch in the living room, the same couch where she had first seduced him. This fact did not go unnoticed by its occupant during the solitary, sexually repressed nights that he spent on it.

During their working time, Celeste gave him documents and excerpts from textbooks and newspapers to read and memorize. She would then test him on the material. If she was not happy with his progress, he was forced to address the subject in question over again.

Lonnie, never a great scholar, took to this quest for knowledge with newfound enthusiasm. He asked many insightful questions of his tutor, and with each answer, learned a little more about the woman with whom he was so deeply in love.

He had learned that her family had not joined the E.R.P., a militant organization that was actually founded in their hometown of Tucumán, because of its Marxist philosophy of class struggle and antinationalist leanings. They, instead, threw their lot with the Perón-inspired Montoneros, who espoused a fairer redistribution of the nation's wealth.

The central policy was dubbed 'Justicalism,' the giving of social justice to the long oppressed workers by redistributing the reserves and assets of the state to the workers, all within a nationalistic framework.

Celeste's eldest brother, Yannick, had attended university in Buenos Aires with Mario Firmenich, the current Montonero leader, who was at that very moment, either in exile or dead. Not even Firmenich's most ardent followers knew of their leader's fate.

Yannick had participated in the kidnapping and assassination of ex-president Pedro Eugenio Aramburu in May of 1970. Aramburu was the man that had forced Juan Perón into exile in 1955, and as such, was the target of a blood vendetta by the Montoneros. It took the rebels fifteen years to attain their retribution, but when they did, Yannick Lavalle was there to see it happen in person.

The violence did not end there, however, and in the end, those responsible for Aramburu's murder were hunted down and eradicated. Yannick and another brother, Patrice, were blown to pieces right inside the family home in Tucumán.

This personal tragedy for the Lavalle family only strengthened the resolve of the remaining members to attain their goals of social justice through the most violent means possible. The blood of their martyred brothers had not turned cold before revenge had been exacted. And so it continued, right up to the present.

The problem was that the government forces were winning the war, if not all the battles. Not only were known members of the antigovernment forces being systematically hunted down and incarcerated or executed, but their family members, friends, and even their acquaintances were being dragged from their homes and tortured until they surrendered at least some form of information.

The right-wing terror group, the A.A.A., declared outright war on any individual or group that entertained leftist leaning. Community centers in communist neighborhoods, upper-echelon trade unionists, and even members of congress were targeted. The E.R.P. and Montoneros struck back by robbing banks and food depots, in addition to assassinating police and military officers that they believed were responsible for the deaths of their comrades.

Whether in the provinces or in the heart of Buenos Aires itself, the terror squads from both left and right plied their deadly trade with cool efficiency and little or no regard for human rights. Many an innocent victim was sacrificed in this unprecedented orgy of violence and destruction.

Lonnie was an easy convert to the cause of the Montoneros. Having no political ideology before he met Celeste left him vulnerable to both her dogma and her womanly charms. His pent-up emotional frustrations could be channeled into acts of aggression that were beneficial to the cause.

But more than anything else, Lonnie's primary value to Celeste and her brothers was his sizable bank account. Money to buy state-of-the-art weapons, rent safe houses, and acquire a fleet of automobiles for car bombings and escape vehicles.

Celeste had been careful to ask only very impersonal questions about her lover's financial status at first. She would accompany him to his bank and watch him make various transactions. She was even introduced to his bank manager on one occasion.

Lonnie's income was derived from a trust that his grandmother, Lydia, had established in his behalf. The amount of annual capital and income dispersed was determined by the trustees of the trust, according to his need.

On Lonnie's twenty-first birthday, a payment of two hundred thousand American dollars was made to his account under the terms of the trust. Another payment of two hundred thousand dollars was to be made at age twenty-five. The trustees had the discretion to accelerate that payment date upon request from the beneficiary. The full trust was to vest in Lonnie at age thirty. That sum was estimated in the range of twenty million American dollars.

Celeste was saddened slightly by the knowledge that Lonfranco De Seta would never live to see the ripe old age of thirty. The tigress from Tucumán knew that there was already a bullet out there with his name on it. She just had to keep him alive long enough to make sure that his monetary assets were diverted to the proper location, the private bank account she had set up under an assumed name to channel funds to her Montonero brothers!

By the twenty-fourth of December Lonnie was wound up tighter than a top. He was ready to prove himself worthy of the cause and pleaded with Celeste to give him a mission that would display that he was more than just a textbook warrior.

She had refused his request, insisting that he go to Pergamino to keep up relations with his family. She knew that he must be encouraged to keep the ties strong with family members who controlled his purse-strings. She also devised the ruse of their traveling together for the summer in order to explain his sudden disappearance to the family.

It would probably also be the last time that they would ever lay eyes on him. Even though Celeste hated people like the De Setas and all they stood for, she was not so cruel as to deny them a final Christmas with their prodigal son. After he returned to her, she would give him his sought-after trial by fire.

So she packed him off to the Pampas with a kiss on the cheek and a gift box wrapped in Santa Claus paper. The sexual tension was written all over his face, but he was told that if he studied hard while they were apart and passed the final test that she would administer to him on his return, then she promised to make his wait very worthwhile.

Once he was in his Mercedes 350 convertible on the road headed to Pergamino, Lonnie reached over to the passenger seat and ripped open the gift. He almost swerved onto the shoulder of the highway as the sun reflected off the chrome-plated barrel of the revolver that Celeste had used to make him a convert to the cause two weeks earlier.

The hand grenade that he had caught an inch from his groin accompanied the revolver. He shoved the package under the passenger's seat and reduced his speed to the legal limit. This was one time he would not be caught for speeding.

The student tore open the flowered envelope that the tutor had placed in the box, then held up the note it contained so he could read it. He smiled lustily at its message.

"To my soldier boy. Keep your weapon well-oiled and clean, for it will be put to exhaustive use when you return. *Viva la revolution!* All my love, Celeste."

How much of this can I disclose to Renaldo? Lonnie's tormented mind pondered. Probably none of it! Why worry the kid half to death when he had so many positive things happening in his life right now. No, he must never know what I am about to do. I owe him that much.

"So, are you going to tell me what is bothering you willingly, or will I have to steal your clothes and pony? Then you will have to walk back to civilization stark-naked and barefoot."

Lonnie had to think fast, blurting out the thoughts as they came to him.

"Well, little brother, it has to do with our mother, and her expectations of me, I guess. She wants me to go to law school, become a lawyer, and take over management of the family business. She thinks that I should take extra courses this summer to accelerate my progress toward the faculty of law. At one time I would have probably wanted the same things, but Celeste has changed my perception of many things, especially people and their values."

There was a strange look in Lonnie's eyes as he spoke, something that Renaldo had never noticed before.

"She has opened my eyes to the plight of the working people in this country, their hardships and suffering. She wants me to travel to Tucumán and the provinces with her next week. We would visit her home and meet her family, then continue on to the Andes. After that, we plan to turn south to Patagonia."

Was it pain? Anger? Self-doubt? Renaldo sensed that it could have been any or all of these emotions that surfaced as his brother spoke. It certainly wasn't the infatuation of a new romance! Renaldo knew that, just by looking in a mirror. He was head over heels in love, but not Lonnie! Lonnie was, different, and the message that his older brother conveyed sent shivers up the younger boy's spine.

"Celeste says that I have never seen how real Argentines live, never understood their tragedy. It is shameful that there is so much suffering by our less fortunate brothers and sisters in this country today. Only when the common people unite for social reform will there ever be a free and just Argentina."

Lonnie caught himself just as he was about to launch into the Montonero indoctrination sermon. He had to stifle the political rhetoric or Renaldo would never believe his story.

"Anyway, this trip will be of great benefit if I continue on in the political philosophy and sociology courses that Celeste has picked out for me next semester. So you can see that I am in the middle of a tug of war between the two women in my life. Why do they always want to control men?"

The final look of sadness on his brother's face led Renaldo to believe that Lonnie still was struggling with his ultimate decision.

"Don't ask me. You're supposed to be the expert! So what will you do? It can't be an easy issue to resolve?"

"It's no contest. I am going with Celeste, of course! Just knowing her as a student in one of her tutorial classes started to change my values, but once we fell in love with each other, well, I can't stand to be away from her. I guess that's why I haven't been in the holiday spirit too much lately. I will probably move into her flat when we return to Buenos Aires for the start of school, mainly to save me from Mama's badgering. So I won't be seeing as much of you, little brother, in the future either. But it sounds like you have a busy enough agenda of your own. I will be calling for my football tickets though. You can count on that!"

Lonnie was confident that Renaldo had accepted his story, and together they concocted the family council meeting to confront their mother in unison with their plans. There was no sense in dragging the bad news out all week. They would get everything out in the open at the same time, and let the cards fall where they may. Neither brother was prepared to back down from taking his own destiny in his hands, and that process might as well start with their relationship with Florencia De Seta.

For the next three days the brothers returned to Lake Lonfranco to refine their plans for the meeting that they had set on the twenty-ninth. It also gave them an opportunity to be together for what Lonnie sensed might be the very last time.

A hint of melancholy crept into the mood of their final outing to the lake on the afternoon of the twenty-ninth. Although the brothers were expected to stay at Buenos Requerdos until after the New Year's celebration, Lonnie had a premonition that the meeting would not go well that evening. If his fears were realized, he would be gone from the estancia by the next sunrise, probably forever. He had become very close to Renaldo these past few days, and losing that bond was the only regret that Lonnie had as they prepared to mount up and return to civilization.

"I want you to know how much being able to talk to you like this has meant to me, Renaldo. I will never forget these days we have spent together here." With that, he grabbed his younger brother and embraced him, kissing him on both cheeks, then holding him in his arms. Renaldo could not see the tears flowing down Lonnie's face as they stood in silent contemplation for several seconds. The older brother then released his grasp and without turning to face his sibling, leapt onto his mount. He dug his heels into the pony's flank calling over his shoulder, "Race you to the cattle herds! Last one there has to tell mother his news first."

"Mama, I want you and Gramma to know that I have been invited to try out for our National World Cup soccer team, and I would like your blessings to explore this great opportunity over the next few months."

Renaldo stood in the center of the parlor, addressing the two seated ladies. Lonnie, who had won the race to the cattle herd, stood behind his brother, leaning against the large stone fireplace.

They had given the ladies no warning of their intended gathering, simply stating at the evening meal that they both had matters of great importance to discuss immediately following supper. Oli served coffee and cakes in the parlor, and once the ladies were settled in, Renaldo took the floor.

He remained there for the next thirty minutes, facing a continuous barrage of searching questions from his disbelieving mother. Lydia kept her counsel to herself, until out of frustration, Renaldo asked for her opinion, hoping to take some of the wind out of his mother's sails.

"I think you should give it a go! It is a marvelous opportunity for a young man to experience, even if you don't make the team. If training camp starts in February, you should have a pretty good idea of where you stand by the time university starts in March. Your summer plans were to stay here at the estancia and help with the cattle herds. You have done that the past three summers, so you are really not missing out on anything special if you return to the capital. It is up to your mother, but I see no harm in you following your dreams, at least until university starts."

Relief was written all over Renaldo's face. The icy stare that Florencia was directing at her mother-in-law did not go unnoticed by him however.

"I cannot give you an answer on this matter right away. You have caught me totally off-guard, Renaldo, and therefore, it is only fair for you to let me ponder the question for a time. You know how I feel about that sport and the lecherous people involved in it. You have such a bright academic future ahead of you. It really is a mystery why you would want to get involved with that peasant's game at all. I will consider the matter!"

The lady's stare would have melted a block of ice as she turned her attention to her eldest son.

"Lonfranco, what do you have to say to us tonight? I hope it is a more constructive plan than your brother's."

"No, Mama, I don't think that you will consider what I have to say to you constructive at all."

Lonnie had been doing a slow burn listening silently to his mother interrogate Renaldo as if he were a five-year-old. He was barely able to hold his temper when it was his turn to be heard.

"I will not be taking any extra courses this summer, Mama. Celeste and I are going to Tucumán to meet her parents, then we will be traveling for the balance of the school break. I do not ask for your blessing, for I am not a young child that needs it. I am strictly informing you of my intentions, that is all."

His tone of voice was off-hand, almost hostile. Even Renaldo was taken aback at the forcefulness of his statement. So much for the well rehearsed, kid-glove approach they had each agreed to take. Florencia was flushed with anger, unable to form a response for several moments.

"How dare that little whore ruin your life! And you, you thickheaded imbecile! Can't you see that she is just a social climber after your money?"

Florencia glanced over at her mother-in-law, hoping for a supportive gesture. When it was not forthcoming, she leveled both barrels at her son.

"Men! One sniff of a woman and they become useless. Their minds all turn to manure. I had hoped for much better than this for you, Lonfranco. You are a great disappointment to me!"

"Whore? How dare you call Celeste a whore! Why she has more brains in her baby toe than you have in that bourgeois head of yours, Mama."

Renaldo feared that his brother was on the verge of physical violence. He acted instinctively to head off further unpleasantness.

"Lonnie, calm down a minute, just wait! Mama, it is only for the summer that he is talking about. He will still be going back to university. What is the harm of him seeing a bit of the country for the summer?" Florencia was beyond listening to reason though.

"You don't know about women, Renaldo. Just wait until you fall in love. Then you will probably come to me with some hairbrained idea like this, too. Where is the respect for your family, my sons? Where is your respect for me?"

"At least we had the courtesy to have this talk with you, Mama. The way you put Renaldo down, though, you're lucky I even stayed around to tell you what my plans were. You have to let us go, Mama. We are not children anymore. There is a whole world beyond the high walls of your beloved Porteño society. It's a pity you will never let your petit bourgeoisie facade down long enough to experience it."

One could have cut the tension in the room with a knife. All of the brother's best made plans for a 'civil' family chat had blown up in their faces.

"I am going now, and I won't be back! When I return to the capital, I will send for my possessions. I wish you were not so set in your ways, Mama, for it will bring you nothing but heartache. And if I ever hear you call Celeste a whore again, I will kill you! Do you understand me?"

Lonnie was shaking with rage as he turned and fled the parlor without saying another word. Renaldo watched in total disbelief, too shocked to make amends for his brother's lack of tact.

Lydia tried to reassure the younger woman not to put much stock in her impetuous son's passion-driven insults. Florencia rose slowly from her chair, looked at the two remaining family members, shook her head sadly and started toward her bedroom. When she was almost out the doorway, she turned to address Renaldo and Lydia.

"This is a sad day for our family, a very sad day! I had so much hope for my sons. Now, now things will never be as I had dreamed. I have failed as a mother! When my own flesh and blood threatens to take my life, I have failed as a mother. This is a black, black day!"

CHAPTER THIRTEEN

Astor Gordero speaking. Is that you, Renaldo?"

"Yes, Señor Gordero, I am back in Buenos Aires, and I thought that we might talk about you handling my affairs while I am with the World Cup team."

"Certainly, my boy, let me check my schedule here. Just one moment. Oh . . . um . . . let's see. With the World Cup draw only a few days away, things are quite hectic, as I am sure you can imagine. Aah, can you be at my office at eight tomorrow morning? I can have breakfast sent in for us. How does that sound to you?"

"I am at your disposal, Señor Gordero. Eight o'clock is fine for me."

"Good boy, Renaldo! I am thrilled that you have called me. I look forward to seeing you tomorrow. Good-bye till then."

Astor Gordero wasn't the only one that was thrilled. After the week that Renaldo had spent in Pergamino, he was beginning to believe his mother's rantings about his own ability and his right to even set foot on the same turf as Argentina's proven football heroes.

She had never let up. Each time that mother and son had come into contact, the lady would start to harangue her offspring again. Luckily, she was not feeling terribly well and kept to her bedroom for extended periods.

Even at that, Florencia looked terrible when she did make an appearance. It was as if Lonnie had put a pistol to her temple and pulled the trigger. His words and actions had struck at the very core of her being, and Renaldo knew that the excessive abuse he was enduring now was a result of a mother's broken heart.

He was the only one left to take out her frustrations on, and Florencia was not about to make things easy for him. When he had approached his mother about his plans to return to the capital, Florencia told him that she and the staff would be staying in Pergamino indefinitely. When he had asked permission to return to Casa San Marco to tie up some loose ends, he was informed that other than a cleaning lady and a part-time gardener, there would be no one there to care for his needs.

"Go if you must!" was her abrupt farewell. She did watch, however, from her bedroom window as Olarti drove her youngest son down the tree-lined entrance drive and out of sight, away from her influence and out of her life.

The rattle and shake of the old Ford pickup seemed to symbolize the upheaval in Renaldo's young life as he headed for the Pergamino train station. His heart was heavy with sorrow for his mother's lament, and yet buoyant about his own personal opportunities. He had cut the apron strings, but he had also made a silent pledge to make the person that wore the apron proud of him.

The phone call to Astor Gordero had been the easier of the two calls that Renaldo intended to make upon arriving at Casa San Marco. The second call, the one he really dreaded, seemed to take too much effort. How many times had he dialed the first six digits of her number, 555-739 . . . only to hang up the receiver before touching that feared number '9' a second time to complete the call?

What if she rejected him? Or was cool and offhand with him? He must stay focused on his football preparations. He had been following the regimen in Octavio Suarez's binder to the letter. Training exercises, diet, even shooting balls into the old goals that his grandfather had erected ages ago on the Buenos Requerdos soccer field.

It was when he tried to immerse himself in the sections of the binder which dealt with the manager's weighty football philosophy that his mind kept wandering back to her essence. Renaldo's mental preparation was proving to be much more challenging than his physical preparation. He just couldn't get Symca out of his thoughts. But actually phoning her was an even harder task to accomplish.

In the end, he simply rationalized that one successful phone call was enough for the first night at Casa San Marco, and that if things went well with Señor Gordero tomorrow, he would be sufficiently elated to consummate the dialing of her number.

Again, it was Wolfgang Stoltz that met the young player in the reception hall of A.R. Gordero and Sons at eight a.m. sharp the following morning. Renaldo was not kept waiting for more than thirty seconds this time.

They passed down the same mahogany hallway as before, then were greeted by two waiters in white waist coats and black ties as they entered Astor Gordero's office. The Fat Man was nowhere to be seen at the moment, but judging by the appearance and aroma of the foods that completely covered the board table, Señor Gordero was about to make his entrance momentarily.

Sure enough, before a cup of coffee could be handed to his guest, the host made his entrance through one of several doorways leading out of the main office. As usual, the gentleman was quite a sight.

He was attired in blue silk pajamas, complimented by a matching silk bathrobe. His feet were covered in slippers of the same print, and the whole ensemble was offset by a contrasting red ascot and pocket puff. A freshly cut red rose adorned the robe's lapel. Gordero made his way directly to the seat at the head of the table, all the while greeting his guest and asking the two men to join him. The smell of talcum and cologne overpowered the aromas of the breakfast delicacies. He saw the puzzled look on his visitor's face and laughingly addressed him.

"No, no, my boy, I do not come to work in my pajamas! I have a suite of rooms behind that door. This is my residence in Buenos Aires as well as my office. Saves me precious travel time while putting me right in the middle of the action, night and day. Usually, I do not book appointments before ten o'clock, but these days, well, there just aren't enough hours to get everything done. I've even had to cut my morning massage time in half. Now that is a sacrifice that no man should be asked to make."

Gordero laughed heartily at his own little joke, at the same time filling his plate from the trays and baskets that the two waiters paraded past his chair.

"How was your holiday, Renaldo? You look fit. Did you stick to Suarez's bible? No overindulging?" The Fat Man did not wait for a reply.

"I wish I could say the same. The parties and galas were excessive this season, all part of the World Cup arm twisting. Thank your lucky stars that you only have to worry about playing football, young man. The headaches of trying to get this operation off the ground are staggering!" A jam-laden croissant was being wagged at the boy as the older man continued his dissertation.

"Not enough first-class hotel rooms, outdated communication systems, terrorist threats, not enough ticket sales. Why, the last financial breakdown I saw yesterday had us losing up to eight hundred million American dollars on the whole event if we fail to entice more tourists to Argentina. Stadium construction, oye! Let's not even talk about that topic. It will turn me off my breakfast. Now, eat! Eat up, then we will talk business. Wolfgang has everything prepared for you!"

Renaldo was famished! Not having Oli at the casa was the only thing he didn't like about being there alone. He was making up for his home cooking experiments when Gordero popped 'the' question.

"Have you been in touch with Miss Carta-Aqua since your return?" The sudden mention of her name caught the diner totally off-guard. He had trouble clearing the frittata and croissant from his mouth, enabling him to reply.

"No, no, Señor, you are the only person I have called. I really can't see what possible attraction I could be to someone as famous and lovely as Señorita Simone, but I plan to call her tonight, hopefully to find out once and for all."

"Don't sell yourself short, my boy," Gordero mumbled, his mouth overflowing with Spanish omelette. "Um, she . . . one moment . . . there! Simone told me that she found your innocence and enthusiasm very appealing. The young lady is constantly surrounded by show business people. Most of them are full of shit! Just 'hangers-on,' looking to feather their own nests."

The look of disgust on the attorney's face was one Renaldo could easily imagine being put to good use in a courtroom rebuttal or scathing cross-examination. His host's demeanor brightened suddenly with the recollection of one word.

"Refreshing! Yes, it was definitely 'refreshing!' That was the word she used to describe her luncheon companion the other day. She was talking about you, son. So call her, Renaldo. Don't let this woman slip through your fingers or you will regret it the rest of your life."

"I will, Señor Gordero. I really plan to call her. It is, well, I guess that I am just a little star-struck, being such a fan of hers for so many years.

"How do you think the draw will work out? Everyone is sitting on pins and needles, waiting to see who our first round opponents will be." A look of enthusiastic anticipation was directed toward the knowledgeable one.

Better to shift the conversation away from Symca and the accompanying embarrassment to a subject that Gordo can expound upon at great length, Renaldo thought swiftly.

"Oh, what a headache. Those crybaby Dutchmen insist that they should be seeded fourth, ahead of Italy! The Italians have already won two World Cups and been runners-up another time. But the Dutch feel that because they were finalists in Germany four years ago that they should get the seeding. It is a plum posting which allows the chosen team to play all its games in Mendoza. Mendoza will be like paradise for any team lucky enough to be based there, with its clean Andean air and very few distractions."

Another pregnant pause ensued as the 'El Hombre Gordo' changed plates for the fruit and cheese course. A sip of coffee, and on he pressed with further enlightenment.

"The committee is leaning towards giving the Dutch what they want. Then, to keep the Italians happy, we will have to put them in Group One with us! That is their preference, playing Argentina instead of Holland, Germany, or Brazil in the first round. Hopefully, you and your new teammates will make them regret their decision to be grouped with Argentina!"

One could not blame the Italians, Renaldo thought. The facts were that Holland, Brazil, and Germany would all be heavy tournament favorites, while Argentina and its reconstructed football program would almost certainly be taken very lightly by the foreign competitors and press. The insult did stir some resentment in the rookie player as the lawyer kept up his diatribe.

"There is so much at stake in this draw! We would much rather have put Italy in Mendoza to assure high attendance figures in the provincial venues, but the consolation is that the Argentina-Italy game will be in Buenos Aires now. That game should set both attendance and television viewer records.

"Oh, and let us not forget those other international crybabies, the Brazilians. We have gone out of our way to make sure that they will be pleased with their facilities. Their first choice for a location was Mar del Plata. So where do we put them? Mar del Plata! Then last month they go whining to FIFA that they are worried about the climate there in December. Too harsh to suit their refined playing style. Well, screw them! Luckily, it was the only city outside of the capital that had enough hotel rooms to meet their quota. So there they stay!

"The organizing committee meets today at two o'clock to finalize the seedings and select which urns the other countries' names will be put in. We have to mix up the strong and weak teams, as well as divide them up geographically. At least no one will be able to accuse the person that draws the names out of the urns of cheating. It is going to be Señor Havelange's three-year-old grandson that will make the draw. Let the Brazilians accuse him of cheating! Ha! He is one of their own."

Renaldo was, in turn, fascinated and relieved sitting at this early morning feast and listening to Astor Gordero's privileged information. He had no idea of the behind-the-scenes politics that went on prior to an event such as the World Cup. He was also happy that Symca's name had faded from The Fat Man's memory. When Gordero had consumed his fill at the table, he motioned to his desk on the opposite side of the room.

"Gentlemen, shall we discuss some business?" The two waiters helped to pull back the oversized chair from the end of the table, allowing its occupant to escape and waddle slowly across the room. Once seated for a second time, he opened a folder and nodded to Herr Stoltz.

"Do you mind if I don't dress for the formal part of our meeting, Renaldo? I would stay in pajamas all day if I could get away with it. I find clothes so restricting, so hard to buy the proper coordinates, for obvious reasons. That Hefner man that started Playboy has the right idea. He never gets dressed, just lies around, smoking his pipe in silk pajamas and servicing all those gorgeous rabbits."

"I do believe they are called 'bunnies,' Señor Gordero," Wolfgang Stoltz interjected in his precise German accent.

"Whatever, Wolfie, but I'll bet you they all screw like rabbits!"

Renaldo almost broke out laughing when he heard the very proper German being referred to as 'Wolfie.' The confusion about rabbits and bunnies also put a smile on his face. The multi-paged document that Herr Stoltz handed him brought his train of thought back to more pressing matters.

"What you have been handed by Herr Stoltz is a standard player-agent contract that I have used several times in the past. We can go over it page by page and clause by clause, if you like, or I can give you the most pertinent clauses to look at and mark right away. Needless to say, this agreement is only valid if you make the final cut and stay on the team. If you succeed, then certain bonus clauses, additional money paid to you, that is, come into effect. Up until the final team is announced, no funds will be advanced to you, but I retain the right to handle all your publicity, public appearances, media interviews, etcetera."

Gordero paused long enough to get a nod of comprehension from his perspective client, then continued with the contract's summary.

"Things will be primarily general image making at this point. I will not charge you for my time in this regard, as it is unlikely that there will be much attention focused on you as an untried rookie, at least in the early stages. I will handle the negotiations of your final contract fee with Octavio Suarez. As I mentioned, that sum is not payable until the final cut is made. Once it is announced that you are on the World Cup squad, my meter starts ticking. As your agent, I take ten percent of your gross salary. Also ten percent of any endorsement or public appearance fee. There is no telling the financial range that these items could fall into at this time. Play well for your country, and they could be substantial, astronomical even!

"Now, there are also certain morals clauses that you must adhere to, probably similar to the regulations that you found in Suarez's bible. Again, they are image makers, and I cannot stress these enough! I want you clean-shaven in public at all times! That should not be a problem with your background. Also, jacket and tie are required at all media gatherings. Thank God you went to a private school. Some of my football clients from the provinces didn't even own a tie when I met them, let alone know how to make a knot properly."

Renaldo knew this point to be true, as some of his under twenty-one club teammates still needed his help to tie their neckties before facing the press. He thought of those players and what they would think of him trying out for the national team. Just as his mind started to wander from all the regulations and legal jargon, Gordero mentioned a subject that snapped the boy back to full attention.

"Stay away from bars, brawling, and broads. They are all off-limits until next July. I have had this discussion with Señorita Carta-Aqua as well, so should the two of you decide to get together for an evening out, I am afraid that it will have to be with my approval. In any event, we are putting Symca to work as a goodwill ambassador for the World Cup Tournament, and she will be on the road touring almost nonstop between now and the opening game. So that is not a great concern to me."

Gordero continued to list off clauses and restrictions concerning Renaldo's deportment, but the boy's mind was now ruminating on the comment about Symca being on the road until June. Not wanting Gordero and his assistant to know how much that news had taken the wind out of his sails, he tried to nod approval whenever he thought it was necessary. From that comment on though, he really didn't hear a word that they were saying. All that he could focus on was one act . . . calling her right away, tonight!

"Well, those are the important clauses, Renaldo. Now, because of your age, I would not be insulted if you wished to take this agreement to a lawyer of your choice. Someone that you have known for a while, someone that handles your family business matters. It is up to you. How did your mother take to the news of you joining the team? Is there any input that you would like her to have in this regard?"

"No, Señor Gordero, I have cut the apron strings, and I would prefer that none of my family advisers have any knowledge of my personal matters from this moment on."

Renaldo paused for an instant, and Gordero thought that he saw tears welling in the young man's eyes.

"I believe that I told you on the train from Córdoba of my secret pledge, my driving desire to do something in my dead father's memory. You have opened the door for that pledge to become reality, Señor Gordero. You see, until I met you, I had no hope of fulfilling my pledge, certainly not at this point in my life. It was only in my dreams and fantasies that I was able to accomplish what I had hoped to do, to play for our National World Cup team and help win the championship for Argentina. My father was such a fan of the sport. It cost him his life, but he had a passion for the game that was totally out of character for the man. My mother used to say that he was always so logical, so controlled, until you put him in a soccer stadium. It is you that have given me the opportunity to make my pledge a reality, Señor Gordero. For that, I will be eternally grateful. I do not need to see another attorney before signing this agreement. As I have said, you have opened doors for me already that I never thought could be opened. My fate is in your hands, Señor, so if you have a pen, I am ready to sign!"

Do it now, right now! All seven digits, 555-7399. There, OK. It's done. It's ringing, so take a deep breath and try to sound calm and cool. Three rings . . . no answer yet, she must be out.

He had sat staring at the phone for over an hour. Looking, but not touching, as if it were a poisonous serpent.

Believe in yourself, believe in yourself! Come on, do it! Now it was too late. There was no hanging up, no turning back. He half wished that the phone would continue to ring, that she would truly be out. At least he would have the consolation of knowing that he had been man enough to try and reach her. The sudden click of the receiver on the other end of the line startled him.

"Ola, darlings, you have reached Simone, but I am not here to talk to you in person. So please leave me a brief message with your phone number included, and I will get back to you pronto. Stay cool, and we will chat soon. Ciao, darlings."

A damn answering machine! I hadn't expected something like this. What do I say? Oh, damn it! Renaldo was frantic, totally unprepared to talk to an electronic device. The beeping tone of the machine came and went, and he knew that he had to say something that instant.

"Hello, Simone . . . this is Renaldo De Seta speaking. We met at Señor Gordero's office and had lunch together at the Jockey Club before Christmas. Señor Gordero delivered your card to me. That is how I received this phone number. If you remember who I am and would like to talk to me, my number is 555-2619. Thank you very much. Have a nice evening. Good-bye."

He replaced the receiver onto the body of the telephone and stood there in the living room of Casa San Marco shaking.

Good God, how did I sound? I have never spoken to a machine before. I bet I sounded like a real idiot. What did I say? I bet I'll never hear from her after that. Women! How can they make a man feel like a little boy? The whole thing is crazy. I should be thinking of nothing but football, but here I am, gaga over some woman I have only spoken to once. A woman that could have any man in Argentina! Why me? I must stop this. Call some friends, go to a movie, go for a walk. Do something!

But he did nothing. He sat and stared at the phone for another hour. It was becoming his worst enemy, tormenting him, enslaving him. He finally grew tired of the game and made his way to his second-floor bedroom, discarding his clothes en-route to the double bed that would be his sanctuary. Sleep came with surprising alacrity, for he had risen early that morning after a fitful night. Too many things on his mind.

After what seemed like only a few moments of sleep, he became aware of a distant ringing that seemed to persist. *What was it? Why doesn't it stop?* He sat up with a start.

The phone! What time is it? He glanced at the bedside clock as he leapt out of bed, then stumbled to the door and out into the hall where the damned black tormentor continued to beckon. *Three twenty-three a.m. There must have been an accident. Someone must be hurt. Mama? Lonnie?*

"Hello, hello!"

"Could I speak with Renaldo De Seta, please?" There was no mistaking her husky voice.

"This is Renaldo speaking. Is that you, Señorita Symca?" He was out of breath, his throat dry, and his voice hoarse.

"Yes, yes it is, Renaldo. Call me Simone. That's what my friends call me. Did I wake you? I am sorry to call so late, but I just arrived home from the television studio, and I have to be back early in the morning. Well, ten o'clock. I guess that's not early for people who keep normal hours. Anyway, Renaldo, can you have dinner with me tomorrow night? Nothing fancy, because I have to go back to work again. We are taping all the remaining episodes for the season before I go out on tour. The schedule is hell, but I would love to see you, even for a short while. What do you think? Can you make it? Do you have other plans?"

"If I did, Señorita, I would cancel them right away. Where and what time?"

"Great! Let's meet at Café Guerrin on Corrientes Avenue. It's close to the studio. We break for dinner at nine. Is that OK?"

"Perfect with me. Simone, I can't believe you called. I am in shock."

"Well, I will wear something special for you tomorrow night, to shock you all the more. Good night, Renaldo."

The receiver went dead, but he didn't put it down immediately. Instead, he held his old adversary lovingly, kissed it several times, then screamed at the top of his lungs, "I am going to have dinner with Symca tomorrow, alone! I can't believe it! I can't believe it!"

The hours passed with a mixture of anticipation and dread for Renaldo that day. What should he wear? Would he look too much the schoolboy beside the famous starlet? Would he act mature enough and not embarrass himself?

He spent the entire day at Casa San Marco, going over his evening wardrobe several times, then sitting down to listen to her recordings while staring hypnotically at the jacket covers. When time seemed to drag and impatience got the best of him, he put himself through a rigorous workout behind the high walls of the casa's garden. Images of his father and brother were constantly in his mind. Waddling like ducks, then leaping in the air as high as they could. *Froggie, froggie, froggie!*

How simple life was back then. Not a care in the world. A happy family. Now what was left? A father that was gone forever, a mother that thought her two sons were on the road to self-destruction, and an older brother that may never come home again. Some family! Then Lydia flashed into his mind. She was really the rock of the family, always steady, very constant in her temperament. Renaldo was hopeful that she would have the strength to calm his mother down, to make her see that her sons were not going to turn out to be vagrants or beggars.

He was covered in perspiration when the cleaning lady came to tell him that there was someone to see him at the front door of the casa. He grabbed a towel, and with only his sweat shorts on, disappeared into the darkness of the casa.

Renaldo didn't recognize the attractive woman standing inside the entrance foyer. As he approached her, it became evident that his scant attire was having an unusual effect on the lady. Her eyes widened and a large smile came to her lips. It was the same lustful leer that he had seen on Estes Santos' face when he entered the railcar and saw the two putas aboard in Córdoba. Her expression stopped the sweaty athlete dead in his tracks.

"My, my, you have been keeping yourself in good shape." She was looking him over as if he were a prize bull at Buenos Requerdos.

"I don't believe I have had the pleasure, Señora . . ."

"Oh, believe me, the pleasure is all mine, Señor De Seta. And it is Señorita, Señorita Adelina Viamonte. I am Octavio Suarez's private secretary. Very private, especially to the press. They do not know about me, about the work I do for Octavio behind the scenes. Now, I have an envelope for you, the contents of which are absolutely secret. You are not to discuss them with anyone. That is why he has sent me to hand deliver them to all the prospective players that are in the capital."

She paused for a second, the tone of efficient authority fading from her voice. It had dropped two octaves and was dripping with innuendo when she spoke again.

"Well, I am sorry that I have to be on my way now. I would love to stay and watch you work out. You have a fantastic physique." She stepped close to him and ran her hand lightly down his chest, stopping just above his navel.

"This job does have fringe benefits, however. I am certain that we will see each other again. I hope that you do well with the team." The voice changed back to its business mode. "Now, do not leave that letter lying around. Read it, then hide it. We will see you soon. Good-bye, and keep up the good work."

The leer returned to her pretty face for a second before she turned and walked through the front door.

Whoa, mammazita! She just about ate me alive. He temporarily forgot about the envelope that he was holding as his eyes followed her out past the front gate. Her short sundress and spiked heels highlighted a set of shapely legs to perfection.

Ola! What a set of wheels. It's time for a cold shower!

Once she was out of sight, his thoughts returned to the contents of the envelope. He tore it open and stood staring at a sheet of stationary embossed with the official World Cup '78 logo. He read its contents silently.

'Attention all prospective National Team Members for the World Cup '78 Argentine squad. Your presence is required at the Velez Sarsfield Stadium in Buenos Aires at 10:00 a.m., sharp, on Monday January fifteenth, 1978. We will be meeting in the Governor's Reception Lounge. Enter through east gate number seven. Representatives will meet you there to assist with directions. Bring your official team binder if you already have one in your possession. Be on time! The gates will be locked at 10:05 a.m. No excuses accepted.

Do not discuss these arrangements with anyone! The press is not invited to attend this preliminary meeting. It is essential for team security and planning that they, in particular, know nothing of this.

Viva Argentina!

Signed, Octacio Suarez'

Well, at least Suarez hasn't forgotten me, Renaldo mused as he made his way to the shower. He was aware of Suarez's distrust of the working press. They had often vilified him in their papers and television commentaries. Secrecy had become a well-known obsession with the National Team manager, who operated with only a few close associates. The aspiring player wondered what Señorita Viamonte had done to endear herself to him. It wasn't hard to imagine.

Renaldo was half an hour early for his evening rendezvous. His purpose was to carefully select a table that afforded the maximum amount of privacy. A small booth with a banquette and two chairs suited his requirements. He tipped his waiter in advance to be on the lookout for a specific celebrity who might be joining him and to keep this information confidential. A look of disdain told the nervous patron that the server found it hard to believe a national treasure such as Symca would have nothing better to do on her break than join him. He ordered a Coca-Cola, sat back in the booth, and tried to relax. Three cokes later and it was almost ten o'clock. No Symca. Each time the waiter passed he would flash a sarcastic smile Renaldo's way.

I shouldn't have said anything to that bastard. If she doesn't show, I will ask him for my money back.

At around ten-thirty the noise level in the busy café suddenly diminished to almost total silence. Wondering what had happened, Renaldo pulled himself up, out of the banquette, and stood in full view at the front of his booth. She was standing just inside the front entrance, and even with a scarf over her hair and dark glasses on, there was no mistaking this lady. There was also no mistaking the two behemoths that stood on either side of her. Bodyguards!

Oh, God! Were they going to occupy the other two seats at the table? It would be like having dinner with two gorillas watching! The disappointed suitor envisioned the scene.

The maître d' had started to lead the three new arrivals to a table in the opposite direction from where Renaldo was standing when he noticed his waiter run up and whisper something in his superior's ear. The maître d' stopped immediately and looked directly at Renaldo, who was being pointed out by the now-beaming waiter. A chance to serve the fabulous Symca had made his aloofness disappear. Her eyes followed the waiter's arm and she was at Renaldo's side before the rest of the group had moved a foot.

"Renaldo, I am so sorry to be this late. The shooting went overtime. I was afraid that you would leave, thinking that I had stood you up."

She took his hand and kissed him on both cheeks as if they had been friends for years. Simone had been right. Her outfit was amazing. A black leather miniskirt, black fishnet stockings, black stiletto pumps, and a black, rhinestone-infested halter top, with clearly no bra underneath.

"Dynamite!" was the only way he could respond. She laughed in her deep, throaty way. It seemed to set him at ease. By now, the four men that she had left at the door were at her side.

"Would the Señorita care to change tables to your usual location?" the maitre d' inquired.

"I usually call ahead for a table that is out of the way before I come here. I also need a table for the boys that is close by, in case some fan gets a little too enthusiastic. The one you selected seems just fine, though. No Ramon, we will stay right here. The boys can take that table over there. Is that alright?"

"As you please, Señorita. Enjoy your meal."

They were seated side-by-side on the banquette in an instant. The now-attentive waiter asked the lady if she desired anything right away.

"I need some cold white wine and a salad. How about you, Renaldo? You must want something more substantial than a salad. It's OK. Their steaks are very good here."

"Alright then, bring me a vacio jugoso and a glass of domestic red wine."

"A glass of Pouilly Fusée for me, please, and you can bring the wine right away," she smiled at the waiter.

They were tucked away, out of view from all but two tables, one of which was occupied by her burly employees. Their unwelcoming stares kept any would-be autograph seekers at bay. Symca, finally feeling relaxed enough, took off her dark glasses and let her hair free of the confining black kerchief. The auburn ringlets fell to the point where her halter top met the bare flesh of her upper breast. Renaldo was, once again, captivated by her beauty, but he was determined not to be a mute for the rest of the evening.

"You must be exhausted with the hours you are keeping. Tell me exactly what is going on in your life right now." He was proud of himself for starting off the conversation.

She took his lead and ran with it. The next twenty minutes were taken up discussing her hectic schedule. By the time her salad and his rare porterhouse steak arrived, accompanied by a second glass of wine for each of them, Renaldo felt not only very informed, but very relaxed in her presence.

"Do you like my outfit? I picked it out especially with you in mind. I would love to wear this out to the clubs, dancing with you, but it can't be tonight. Between the studio's schedule and Astor's insistence that I become the goodwill ambassador for World Cup '78, it doesn't look like we will be able to have much time together. As soon as we finish the last episode of the TV show, I head to all the venues that are holding World Cup games: Mar Del Plata, Rosario, Córdoba, and Mendoza. Promotional appearances and concerts in each city. Then it is back to the capital for rehearsals for the World Cup Gala at Teatro Colon on the twelfth. Do you still have the backstage pass I sent you? Now that is one night we might be able to go out dancing!" Simone touched his hand, stroking it ever so gently as she beamed with optimistic enthusiasm.

"Right after the show, come to my dressing room. Astor usually parades his special guests in to see me after an event such as this, but with any luck, I can feign illness and get out of there in a hurry. So you won't forget, will you?"

She was being so sweet to him, so attentive. It was as if they had been lifelong friends or even lovers. What she saw in him, he still could not figure out, but he was now beyond questioning the whys and the wherefores. The fact was that he, Renaldo De Seta, was sitting next to the famous Symca, and no other man in Argentina mattered to her at this moment.

All too soon one of her escorts came to the table to humbly interrupt their tête-à-tête.

"I am sorry, Señorita, but the director gave us strict orders to have you back at midnight. It could mean our jobs if we fail to heed his bidding."

"I understand, Carlo. There is no end to this business. I want you to meet my friend, Renaldo De Seta. He is going to be on our World Cup soccer team."

Renaldo took the man's large hand and noticed the puzzled look on his face. The protector was obviously a soccer enthusiast, and one that had definitely never heard of a player named 'Renaldo De Whatever' on any team, let alone the National World Cup team. Carlo was polite enough to wish Renaldo good luck in front of Symca, then he withdrew so that the two new friends could say their good-byes.

"Oh, I wish we had more time. I've been doing all the talking and there is so much about you, and what is happening with the team that I really want know. Can I call you if I get a minute? It might be late at night. Is that all right?" She smiled sadly at the thought of their forced estrangement, then gently took his hand in hers.

"Don't worry, Simone. You can call me anytime. I have been fascinated by your stories. Nothing at all has happened with the World Cup team yet, and besides, I have been sworn to secrecy by Octavio Suarez, the team manager. Are you going to watch the draw on television this Sunday? It will answer a lot of questions for everyone. Señor Gordero said that we will probably have Italy in our group for the first round. Oh, yes, there is one piece of news you should know. I signed on the other day as one of Señor Gordero's clients. He is willing to handle the business affairs relating to my football career. What do you think about that?"

The shadow that fell across the table prompted him to remove his eyes from hers for an instant. The two bodyguards were now standing directly opposite them, clearly in a state of agitation.

"Señorita, please. We must . . . "

"Yes, boys, yes, right now! I will stay in touch with you, my darling Renaldo. I like spending time with you. You are so unlike any of the others."

She tightened her grip on his hand and leaned over to him quickly. Her lips pressed against his ever so softly at first, then suddenly with more pressure and explosive passion. He tried to reciprocate by leaning the full force of his weight against her, but when he felt her tongue dart into the warmth of his mouth, his mind lost all coherence. It was over too quickly. She was up and gone, with only her final words as his souvenir of their evening together.

"I will call you, Renaldo! Think of me. Ciao, bello."

He slumped back against the rear of the banquette, his mind reeling. Had she really kissed him like that, or was he just imagining it? The stiffness in his groin convinced him that he was not dreaming. Luckily, no one in the café had witnessed the kiss, as a result of the two gorillas blocking out the view.

He sat alone now, transfixed by the memory of her beauty, her scent, her voice, her eroticism. He didn't hear the waiter ask him if he required anything further. Renaldo was unable to reply. The waiter stood for a few moments, then walked away. He was vaguely aware of hearing her name now and again in the din of conversation that swirled around the café.

"That was Symca that just left," or "Symca was dining here tonight with her producer," or "Did you see the outfit on Symca? What a stunning woman she is." Symca this, Symca that. But she had been with only one man tonight. She had kissed only one man tonight. He sat silently for almost thirty minutes before he summoned the waiter, left him an additional tip when he settled his account, and walked, still mystified, out into the humid night air.

The San Martin Cultural Center in Buenos Aires was overflowing with officials and press on the afternoon of Sunday, January 14, 1978. Security was extremely tight, with three different sets of pass gates that anyone entering the center had to clear.

Military vehicles had blocked all the approaches to the center as well, preventing any suicide car bombers from gaining access to the immediate vicinity of the cultural center. The precautions were certainly warranted. Police and antiterrorist authorities had received several threats of violence aimed directly at Argentina's World Cup movement ever since FIFA had given their final approval.

Communiqués from the Montoneros and the E.R.P. had stated clearly that the huge sums of money that were being spent on this international showpiece should be spent on providing food and shelter for the country's poor and dispossessed. "The common working man can not afford a single ticket to a single match, so what good is all this extravagance doing him?" they argued.

The junta responded in the press by saying that "World Cup '78 belonged to all the people of Argentina, and that every citizen should take great pride in hosting the finest football teams in the world and welcoming the eyes of every nation that would be watching this spectacular event."

No matter whose rhetoric one chose to believe, the fact remained that the threat of violence was very real, and the people inside the cultural center were very thankful for the military's strong showing.

Astor Gordero was one of those people inside the cultural center that Sunday. His job was primarily one of handholding FIFA President João Havelange and his three-year-old grandson, Ricardo Teixeira, who would actually perform the drawing of the balls from the urns. To keep the young boy relaxed and happy until he made his way to the podium to commence the draw, Gordero had brought along his private secretary, Señora Melendel, who was the mother of two small children herself and who came supplied with toys and games.

The seedings and the placement of all the countries had been arranged to the satisfaction of the organizing committee, if not the other countries involved. Now the final placement of the teams was in the hands of young Señor Teixeira.

There was also great concern regarding the new communications equipment. Would it function on cue without causing international embarrassment to the host country? This was the first time that a live, worldwide satellite feed had ever been transmitted from Argentina. It was critical that everything go off without a hitch.

The expectation and tension were almost unbearable as President Havelange finally made his way onto the stage. Astor Gordero knew, as did every other member of the organizing committee, that the international football community was poised to abandon Argentina and move the tournament elsewhere if every detail of this day did not proceed without a hitch. Gordero felt confident that no detail had been left to chance, that no item, however minuscule it may seem, had been overlooked. The day now rested in the hands of the Gods and a three-year-old boy.

The Italians had backed off their demands and had allowed Holland to be seeded fourth, heading up Group Four. This put the Italians in Group One with Argentina, along with two teams to be determined by the draw. In all, eleven nations remained to be pulled from the urns.

Total silence greeted young Master Teixeira as he stepped up to urn 'A,' dressed in his Little Lord Fauntleroy outfit and withdrew a capsule containing the name of the first team to be placed. He handed the capsule to his grandfather, who opened it, then stared directly at the television cameras and pronounced,

"The first team selected in the World Cup '78 draw is . . . Poland."

Polite applause filled the theater. The Polish contingent did not join in, however. There was shock and dismay on their faces. Master Teixeira's selection had placed them in Group Two, head-to-head with their perpetual nemesis, West Germany. No one in the Polish camp had forgotten the bitter defeat that they had suffered four years earlier on a rain-soaked pitch in Frankfurt. It had been the World Cup semifinal game, a game that held so much promise for the Cinderella Polish side, promise that was washed away in a torrential downpour that left the field of play little better than a quagmire. The tight scheduling of the tournament forced the game to proceed, and even impartial onlookers still commented to this very day about the strange bounces that the ball took off the saturated pitch.

The game was, nevertheless, magical, with Herculean efforts given by both sides. The West German home side was inspired by their vocal, horn-blowing followers, but the Polish defense was equal to the task . . . almost.

Tournament scoring sensation Gerd Mueller was, once again, the man of the hour, placing the ball in the back of the Polish goal behind their brilliant keeper, Tomaszewski, late in the second half. Had the game been played under proper conditions, well, the result could have been much different, according to the Poles. But the result stood, and the West Germans advanced to the final, while the valiant underdogs would now play for the bronze medal.

What upset the Poles about their particular placement in Argentina '78 was that not only were they grouped with the West Germans again, but they would have to face them in the opening game of the tournament, in River Plate Stadium, on June first. Not an appealing proposition at all. The deed was done, however, and like all the rest of the participants, the Poles had to play with the hand that young Master Teixeira had dealt them.

Spain and Scotland followed in succession. By the time the draw was completed, everyone in the building breathed a collective sigh of relief.

Argentina's opponents, along with Italy, would be France and Hungary. The two latter teams were considered by most experts to be unknown quantities, but at least the host nation would be playing against three European teams that all prescribed to a similar style of 'continental' football. The draw and its international transmission had gone exceedingly well, and Astor Gordero was the first one to open a bottle of his favorite champagne and offer a glass to President Havelange, in celebration.

The two men engaged in lively conversation as they stood at the foot of the giant marquee that was now decorated with the names of the sixteen participants that would strive to make the World Cup trophy their own. The board, so critical to each country's aspirations, was demarked as follows:

Group One	**Group Two**	**Group Three**	**Group Four**
1. Argentina	5. Poland	9. Austria	13. Holland
2. Hungary	6. West Germany	10. Spain	14. Iran
3. France	7. Tunisia	11. Sweden	15. Peru
4. Italy	8. Mexico	12. Brazil	16. Scotland

Not everyone was happy, but there could be no finger-pointing and accusations of a 'fix.' President Havelange was a powerful and extremely influential figure in the world of international football. To even imply that there had been the slightest irregularity would be considered a personal affront to the president. It was also opportune that he was Brazilian by birth, a fact that helped to gag Argentina's most vocal critic.

Now the guessing was over. The torch was ready to be passed to Octavio

Suarez, allowing him to assemble and prepare a team that could sweep Argentina past their first three European opponents and into the second round of the tournament.

CHAPTER FOURTEEN

Everyone be seated, please, and I will try to get you out of here as quickly as possible. Some of you I have only met on the opposing sides of a soccer pitch. To those people, welcome! I am Octavio Suarez, National Team manager of Argentina's World Cup '78 squad. I have had the opportunity of at least conversing with all of you on the telephone, if not in person. To those of you whom I have met with, welcome also. I am glad that our attendance is one hundred percent. That does not count the three players who are still being held hostage in Europe. We will discuss them at a later point in the meeting.

"I would now like to introduce you to the remainder of my National Team coaching staff. Estes Santos, of Newton's Prefects Under Twenty-One squad will be our goalkeeper coach and defensive strategist. Ubaldo Luque, from River Plate F.C. will handle physical conditioning and offensive strategy. But not to confuse the issue, I will have the final say on everything. The team is my show, no one else's. I personally will take the blame, while you the players, if we are successful, will take the credit. That is how it works. My word is the final word, the only word. Defy me, and you will be gone!"

Suarez was attired in a navy blue blazer and grey slacks. On the breast pocket of the jacket was sewn the golden crest of the Argentine Football Association, the black letters 'AFA' clearly visible. *The manager is surprisingly well-groomed and relaxed compared to our first meeting almost a month ago,* Renaldo thought.

"There are any number of rookies and veterans waiting to take your spots. Some of the faces in this room are not household names, yet! Others among you have reputations to live up to. Reputations of being fine football players and also unmanageable prima donnas! Make no mistake . . . this team will be a dictatorship, not a democracy. I will purge any and every ego I see standing between us and ultimate victory. If anyone has a problem with that, there is the door, use it!"

Not a soul attempted to rise from their seats. Each and every man assembled in the room wanted to be a part of the greatest experience in Argentina's history. Suarez waited almost a full minute, peering into the faces of his attentive audience. When he was satisfied with the reaction of his charges, he proceeded.

"We know who our first round opponents are now. We open against Hungary on June the second in Buenos Aires. It is fortunate that there will be no traveling for us during the first round. That allows us to settle into our training facilities and maintain a routine schedule. France is our second test, and they will be tough, as will the Italians. Only the top two teams go through to the second round, so every game, every goal, every save, and every tackle, are all of the utmost importance."

Everyone present, even the most experienced of veterans, knew that Suarez spoke the absolute truth. The fight for possession of the championship trophy would be grueling and unforgiving.

"Those of you that have not received your training manuals, I refer to them as your 'bibles,' raise your hands and the coaches will distribute them. We do not officially open training camp in Mar del Plata for another month, but I cannot stress enough the importance of arriving there in top condition, both mental and physical. We will have at our disposal, thanks to the generosity of the organizing committee, a host of doctors, nutritionists, physiotherapists, and psychologists to cure whatever ailments you bring with you. But in the meantime, be sensible! Train according to the bible, eat properly, get the right amount of sleep, stay away from booze, and for God's sake, unless you are married, keep your fly zipped shut!"

There was sporadic laughter at the last comment, mostly from the younger players. Renaldo, having heard the same lecture during his first meeting with the boss, managed to stifle any amused reaction that he otherwise might have displayed.

"Don't laugh, my little ones! Some of you are just like children. You must be told a frightening story before you believe the dangers that surround you. Four years ago in Germany I had to send one of my best players home because he got the clap so badly he couldn't pee. Got it in Argentina, during training camp! He came home in disgrace, to waiting divorce papers! Some of you know the man I am referring to. Needless to say, he is not in this room with us now."

Not even a smile was to be found in the room after the manager's graphic example.

"We have eight, maybe ten exhibition matches lined up. Three against European teams that are not in the tournament, but who will still be able to educate us in the continental style of football."

Suarez paused for a moment, as if there was something important that he had forgotten to reveal to his new 'family.'

"I want to clear up one matter, with regards to my starting game rosters. Many of you who know me are aware of my philosophy on substitutions during a match. Basically, I don't believe in substitutions unless it is a case of disabling injury. What I am looking for, the thing that I always seek in my starting lineups, is an intangible harmony between the eleven men on the field. It is a 'feeling' that I hope eleven of you will develop over time. A 'feeling' that will spur you to fight each other's battles, on and off the field. I don't know who the eleven are yet. We have months of preparation to determine that. But let me say in all honesty, that your actions will speak much louder than your reputations in determining whether or not you are included in that special group. Everyone starts with a clean slate in my plan. Rookie, veteran, it doesn't matter. True harmony and unselfish spirit are what I am seeking. I want eleven of you on the pitch from start to finish, fighting each other's battles, together as one group of players, a true 'team!'"

Absolute silence greeted Suarez's last word. The manager had been strongly criticized in the past for this same strategy of not using substitutions, but only when his teams failed to capture whatever prize they were pursuing. On the occasions when Suarez was triumphant, and the latter far outnumbered the former, the manager would always say that the 'spirit' of his eleven starters was responsible for the team's success. Not a man listening in that room at Velez Sarsfield Stadium was willing to offer a dissenting opinion.

"The full team roster and the list of fixtures will be handed out separately at the end of the meeting. The coaches and I will now meet with each of you individually for a few short minutes to get reacquainted. The last point that I want to stress to you all is about the working press and our relationship with them. I am the only spokesman for this team. Be very clear on that! All press releases and press interviews will be set up and controlled by me. If I hear that any one of you has spoken to the press without my prior approval, you will be gone faster than shit through a goose! Do you understand me? Good! No information that has been discussed here today will be divulged to anyone, for after all, this has been a private meeting that never took place according to the press. How could it have, if they didn't know about it?"

Laughter filled the room for the first time since the manager started his address. Even Suarez had a broad grin on his face at the thought of pulling a fast one on the despised media vultures.

"The formal introduction of the National Team will take place at a gala fundraising event on February the twelfth at the Teatro Colon. It will be carried live on national television, and you will all have your moment in the limelight then. The press will be all over you between the gala and our departure two days later for Mar del Plata, so remember to clear all interviews with me before you open your mouth. Until the moment you walk on that stage on the night of February twelfth, no one is officially on the National Team. I refuse to have the press or anyone else run this program by second-guessing my decisions. There will be time enough for that in the future.

Also, be aware that there are three players still playing in Europe who I want for this team. When they will become available to me, what kind of shape they will arrive in, and whether or not they will fit into my system remains to be seen. But their personal jersey numbers, '7,' '10,' and '15,' will be given up by the players who are prescribed those numbers on the first roster list the moment these men return to Argentina. Understood? You will all have a fair and equal opportunity to achieve a starting position on the team. Work hard, do your best, and don't worry about your competition. Keep focused on what your job is, on what I have asked you to do, and you should succeed. So, that is it for now. Good luck, stay healthy until we meet again, and keep your lips sealed. I will start the individual meetings in the interior office now. Estes, check the list and bring in the first gentleman!"

Renaldo De Seta took a deep breath and sat back against the folding chair that was one of thirty-odd arranged in rows for the players. He looked around the room self-consciously, for he knew that he was truly a babe in the woods among seasoned veterans. Men whom he had watched play ten years ago were seated next to him, legends of the game in Argentina, some with the experience of two World Cups under their belts.

Ubaldo Luque was circulating around the room, handing out binders and rosters and engaging in friendly banter with the players he was familiar with, which was almost everyone. When he came to Renaldo, he smiled warmly and held out his hand.

"We have never met before, have we, son? You must be Renaldo De Seta. It's not hard to pick you out in this crowd of old men. I see that you already have your bible. Here are the roster lists and the exhibition match schedule. You are number seventeen on the list, so you will have a little time to kill before you go in to see Octavio. Relax, socialize with the others. There are coffee and soft drinks being brought in right now. Nice to meet you. Good luck."

He handed Renaldo two sheets of paper stapled together and moved on to the next man. It was evident from scanning the lineup that the boy from Newton's Prefects Under Twenty-One team was the youngest player on the roster by four years. He tried to place the players on the list with the faces in the room. His eyes ran down the names one line at a time, then searched the room for the corresponding countenance. Octavio Suarez's hopefuls included:

Argentina's World Cup '78 Training Roster

# Name	Height	Age	ClubTeam
Goalkeeper:			
1. Junior Calix	6' 1"	27	Huracan
2. Angel Martinez	6' 2"	27	River Plate
Backs:			
3. Julio Paredes	5' 10"	25	San Lorenzo
4. Jorge Calderone	5' 11"	27	Newton's Prefects
5. Ignacio Suazo	6' 4"	24	River Plate
6. Luis Anariba	6' 0"	22	Unattached
7. Francisco Guity	5' 9"	28	Racing Club
8. Juan Chacon	6' 5"	28	Independiente
9. Daniele Bennett	5' 10"	29	Union Santa Fe
10. Victor Ciro	6' 0"	24	Huracan
Halves:			
11. Humberto Velasquez	5'6"	25	Talleeres Córdoba
12. Leopoldo Anariba	6' 0"	22	Racing Club
13. Miguel Cruz	5' 11"	22	Independiente
14. Ricardo Arzu	5' 9"	25	Independiente
15. Francis Argueta	6' 1"	25	Independiente
16. Carlos Castillo	6' 0"	30	Talleres Córdoba
17. Renaldo De Seta	6' 2"	18	Newton's Prefects U.21
Forwards:			
18. Ramon Vida	5' 11"	22	Boca Juniors
19. Ruben Gitares	6' 0"	24	Newton's Prefects
20. Caesar Castro	6' 1"	28	River Plate
21. Nicolas Pastor	5' 10"	26	Talleres Córdoba
22. Enrique Rios	6' 0"	24	Independiente

Several surprises, but on the whole a fairly competent group of professionals, Renaldo thought to himself. Most of the surprises stemmed from names that were not on the list at all. The three players still in Europe had already been explained. The problem was that if they were unable to join the team in the near future, the consequences of their absence would certainly be felt down the road.

Defender Réné Dolmo playing with Real Madrid in Spain, and halfback Americo Galvani, currently with St. Etienne in France, had abundant international experience that was bound to be an asset to the team. But more critically, the nation's all-time leading goal scorer, Nicodemo Garcia, was at this moment plying his trade for Catalonia in the Spanish league. Garcia was the one impact player who Octavio Suarez was really counting on to make his team a true contender. Without 'Nico's' leadership by example and deft touch around the goal, the Argentine squad would resemble only a shadow of the team that they could have been, had forces outside Argentina not conspired against them.

There were some shocking names omitted from those players who were now in Argentina. Long-time international goalkeeper Hugo Bravo was said to have retired after a well-publicized spat with Octavio Suarez. Former National Team captain Dante Capurro had refused to report because his wife was due to deliver their first child the following June, right in the midst of the tournament. Capurro's leadership and savvy would be sorely missed, but Octavio Suarez had been unable to change his mind.

Other names that were omitted seemed to fall into the 'prima donna' category that Suarez would not tolerate. Without the return of the European players, however, Renaldo wondered how long Octavio could resist the pressure to forget the conflicting egos and field the best team available. So many questions remained to be answered over the next few months. The press, relentless in their quest for information, would hound the team's manager day and night until they received those answers. The list of exhibition fixtures were scheduled as follows:

March 4, 1978	vs.	Uruguay	at Mar del Plata
March 19, 1978	vs.	Peru	at Buenos Aires
March 23, 1978	vs.	Peru	at Lima
March 29, 1978	vs.	Bulgaria	at Buenos Aires
April 5, 1978	vs.	Romania	at Buenos Aires
April 19, 1978	vs.	Eire	at Buenos Aires
April 25, 1978	vs.	Uruguay	at Montevideo
May 3, 1978	vs.	Uruguay	at Buenos Aires

It looked like a fairly rigorous schedule that Octavio Suarez had devised for his charges. The good thing was that it gave them a good taste of both

European and South American competition. Two Copa Roca games were also tentatively scheduled against Brazil in March, but confirmation of the dates and locations of those fixtures had not yet been resolved.

All in all, it was an exhilarated Renaldo De Seta that sat waiting for his turn in the inner sanctum with his new mentor. The other players had seemed to all break off into their club team cliques, Independiente players in one huddle, River Plate players in another, and so on. Calderone and Gitares from the Prefect's professional team made no effort to welcome their young understudy, so Renaldo remained seated and alone.

"Hi, man, I'm Ramon Vida, from Boca Juniors. You must be De Seta. I can tell because none of those assholes have come over to welcome me either. I'm the only one from Boca Juniors left now that Bravo quit and Capurro won't report. I'm afraid that our manager might paint me with the same brush just because we were on the same club team. I follow you on the list, so I thought that we might as well wait together and get to know each other."

Vida held out his hand, which Renaldo shook from a half standing, half sitting position. The Boca player was shorter in stature than Renaldo, standing just under six feet. His body was svelte, almost wiry, and his black hair was worn short and combed straight back into a cute little duck tail. That was the only thing 'cute' about Ramon Vida. He exuded Latino self confidence, and while his face bordered on handsome, it also contained several small scars from past wars. And those eyes, dark mysterious pools that could easily be read to say, "Don't mess with me, or else . . . "

When both men were seated, Vida asked the question that was on the minds of all his new training mates.

"So, how did you manage to get yourself selected to the training roster? Is it true that you have never played a first division game?"

"Yes, it is true. The Under Twenty-One side that I played on won the National Championship, and when Señor Suarez contacted me, he simply told me that he was having trouble with several of his veteran players, and that he wanted to look at some 'new blood.' I had taken some clinics from him over the years, and he remembered me. So here I am, for the time being, anyway."

"Well, don't feel badly. I sat on the bench my first two years with Boca watching Nico Garcia tear up the league. Luckily, he got a fat check to go to Spain this past season, and that was the break I needed. I guess I fit into the 'new blood' category, along with you."

Renaldo was starting to warm up to Vida. He had an easy manner and a quick smile, and having just turned twenty-two, was the closest player on the roster to his age. At least he had been friendly enough to introduce himself and keep Renaldo from looking like the solitary wallflower of the group.

"So, what do we have over here? How many caps, or maybe we should say bonnets, baby bonnets, do you two infants have for your country?"

The two young players looked up from their conversation into the distorted, hideous smile of 'Killer' Juan Chacon. 'Killer' was a legendary fullback for Independiente, tough, ruthless, mean-spirited. He had been booked more times than any player in the history of the Argentine first division. He never shied away from physical contact, perfecting his style of play to the point of being known as 'the king of the cheap shot artists' in the Argentine first division. If 'Killer' became incensed with a rival player, he was more than willing to use his fists to drive home his point.

It was said by those who opposed him on the field of play that his greatest defensive asset was his supreme ugliness. A face that was severely disfigured after biting into an electrical cord as a toddler seemed to give him a persona with which to identify. Add to that his dominating physical presence, standing six foot, five inches tall, and one could see why he relished taking on all those hotshot, pretty boy forwards that earned three times his salary. Let them dare to bring the ball into his territory on the pitch!

Legend had it that one self-centered dandy of a forward who bleached his hair and fancied himself as a matinee idol once made a comment on 'Killer's' nightmarish looks to the press before a game. He described Chacon as the 'ugliest man on earth,' and stated that no woman would ever want to spend a night with such a hideous creature. The scene was set for all-out war the following day.

As the grudge match unfolded, however, the handsome boaster went out of his way to keep a good distance from the ugly defender. But the Independiente fullback would not be denied his revenge. With the clock running down to the final minutes and his team hanging on to a one-goal lead, 'Killer' Chacon finally had an opportunity to extend his greetings.

A corner kick in the Independiente end had brought all the opposing players to the goalmouth to try for the equalizer. As the ball floated high in the air, making its way with an outward curve to the spot where 'Señor Handsome' waited to volley in the tying goal, 'Killer' Chacon leapt with perfect timing and headed the orb away from his goalmouth. Unfortunately for 'Señor Handsome,' the full force of Chacon's knee hit him square in the face. It would be El Blondo's last professional soccer game. The braggart had suffered a broken jaw, a broken nose, and the loss of several teeth. Now it was debatable just which of the two antagonists was the ugliest following their tryst. The Football Association reviewed the matter and agreed with the referee that fair contact had been made with the ball by Chacon, and that the injury had not been deliberate.

Not one of 'Señor Handsome's' teammates had come to his aid or accosted

'Killer' Chacon immediately following the incident. No one on that field of play wanted to pursue the matter. The man was too ugly, too ferocious, too 'loco' to risk personal injury. The 'Killer' Chacon legend had grown from that day on, and now Renaldo and Ramon were staring at 'His Ugliness' himself.

"You babies can't speak either? We can order in some formula bottles instead of coffee, if you like. I don't believe what they have given us to play with here. A combination of has-been old men and wet-behind-the-ears rookies. You, you there! Did your mama have to write you a note to let you come and play with the big boys?" He was addressing Renaldo, a fierce look of contempt on his loathsome face. His teammates from Independiente had formed a circle around the two younger players.

"Why don't you fuck off and leave him alone. He doesn't know you, and he certainly hasn't done anything to deserve this shit!" Ramon Vida had risen to his feet in defense of his new friend. He still could not believe how truly grotesque the man was, especially from only inches away.

"That's alright, Ramon. It is an honor to meet a legend like Señor Chacon in person. Without a man of his stature on our team, I am sure that our opponents would take liberties with the likes of you and me. We can rest assured that they won't with 'Killer' Chacon on the field. It is my pleasure, Señor."

Renaldo grasped the stunned defender's hand and shook it with enthusiasm.

"Well, now, here is a man that knows true talent when he sees it! But go to hell anyway! I hate all pretty boys, and you look like a real sweetheart. Big blue eyes, such nice long curls. You're too cute to be a real man. Maybe you should try out for the women's soccer team. Or maybe you should pull your pants down and show us that you belong here with the men. What's your name anyway, my gorgeous little chicken?"

"Renaldo De Seta, Senor Chacon. And this is Ramon Vida from Boca Juniors."

"I know this pissant already. How many goals did you score against me this year, rookie? Not even one, right? We kicked Boca's ass every time we met this season. Maybe you'll find the Brazilian defense more to your liking, rookie!" Chacon was literally spitting the words out only inches from Vida's reddening face when suddenly his wrath was diverted. "Oh, look over there, it's the retarded Anariba twins. They say one of them can only tie shoelaces while the other one can only do up buttons. They have to dress each other every day. Let's go have some fun with them."

With that, the five players from Independiente focused their attention on the unfortunate twins seated together across the room. The Anariba brothers had played well together for Racing Club two seasons earlier, until a knee dislocation had forced Luis to the sidelines early in the 1976 campaign. When his rehabilitation took much longer than hoped for, Racing Club let the somewhat 'dim' player out of his contract. He had remained unattached to any club right up until Octavio Suarez had to prepare his invitations to training camp. Rumor had it that Luis was ready to make a comeback, however, and the National Team manager had nothing to lose by offering the twins a chance to rediscover their past competence with his squad. Thus, the two introverted brothers were there at Velez Sarsfield that day.

"Man, you sure handled that ugly bastard with ease. I thought he was going to give us a full dose of his tough-guy shit. I've seen him do it before. I still have a scar on my calf from his personal 'welcome' to the big leagues early last season. You're some cool cat, Renaldo. I was all set to kick the ugly cocksucker in the balls if he didn't lay off."

"It's nothing, really. My father used to call it the 'bee' rule. He used to say that 'You can catch more bees with honey than vinegar,' even big, ugly bees, it seems."

Luckily for the Anariba twins, Juan Chacon was called in to see manager Suarez only moments after they had descended upon the unsuspecting brothers. Without their fierce leader, the rest of the Independiente men dissipated to various corners of the room.

Every now and again, a player from one of the smaller, less represented teams would come over and introduce themselves to Renaldo and Ramon. They would stay and exchange pleasantries until they, in turn, were called for their audience. Finally, it was Renaldo's turn. He said good-bye to Ramon Vida, telling him that he would watch for him on the night of the gala, February fourteenth. Then it was into the lion's den.

The manager and two coaches greeted Renaldo with enthusiasm.

"It seems you have already made a very good impression on Juan Chacon. He came in here singing your praises. How on earth did you manage that? I have seen him reduce rookies to tears with only a stare," laughed Octavio Suarez.

"I just decided that I didn't want that same stare directed at me any more than was necessary. There was no sense in antagonizing the man, so I made him feel like I respected his rather dubious talents."

"Be careful, son. He is a very mean customer, and he can turn on you in an instant. Don't ever let your guard down when you are around him. But in the meantime, let's hope you can sidestep the opposing defenders as well as you just deflected 'Killer's' known dislike for untested newcomers," coach Luque interjected.

"Renaldo, I know you are used to playing the forward line, but I want you to start out as a center halfback for now. I have a feeling that if your ball-handling skills are as deft as I think they are, you may just end up being the general of our attacking forces. You will have more room to demonstrate your considerable talent at halfback. My main problem, as I perceive it, will be communication between the backs and the halves, and then the halves and the forward line. A truly great halfback can play the transition game from defense to offense with uncanny skill. That is the role that I want to train you to fulfill. If, heaven forbid, Nico Garcia is unable to join us from Europe, then I will have to reconsider and put you on the forward line. For now though, you will be my transition halfback.

We will start out playing a 4-3-3 formation, with two outside attacking fullbacks to assist in the thrust forward. We will be expected to play offensive football by our supporters, and that is what I intend to do. We need to score goals, and for that reason, I am putting you at center half. You can use the whole pitch as your canvas to create a masterpiece from that position, Renaldo. Whenever I have seen you play, I have always thought that you could make your feet do exactly as your brain desired. Prove it to me. Stay in shape, train hard, and keep out of trouble. We will be together again on the twelfth of next month, for the introduction of the team to the entire country.

My assistant will be in touch with you a few days in advance of that with the final details of the evening. Here is a sheet of phone numbers to use if you have to contact any of the three of us for whatever reason. Well, I guess that is all. Look after yourself, and I will see you on the twelfth."

Octavio Suarez shook Renaldo's hand, as did Luque. Estes Santos just gave the boy a sly wink as the rookie player exited. Alone in the corridor outside of the meeting room, one thought kept racing through the boy's mind.

Your feet do exactly as your brain desires. Head and feet as one, isn t that the way Gordero phrased it on the train from Córdoba? He remembered The Fat Man and the way he had twisted his fingers like a pretzel. He stood there in the hallway, absent-mindedly twisting his fingers, trying to duplicate the feat he had witnessed on the train.

"Whoa, Renaldo, baby, are you alright? What did they do to you in there? Torture you or something? What's with the fingers? Somebody slam a door on them?" Ramon Vida had watched his new friend doing digital contortions for several seconds before proceeding down the hall to meet the coaching staff. An embarrassed Renaldo De Seta smiled bashfully and shrugged his shoulders as he disappeared around the corner of the hallway.

"Damn fingers, they still have minds of their own!"

CHAPTER FIFTEEN

Señor Figueroa, there is a message for you here."

Lonnie stopped dead in his tracks as he started to ascend the poorly lit staircase. It was the first time since he had rented the small room in the Versailles district on the outer limits of the capital that anyone had spoken to him. His eyes strained to see who was addressing him from the shadows.

To his relief, the old janitor shuffled into sight, his arm outstretched, clutching a piece of paper. The old man had rented Lonnie the room a few weeks earlier. He had been a good source of information regarding the other tenants and the general layout of the neighborhood.

The building was occupied almost exclusively with migrant workers who were either employed temporarily or seeking employment in one of the many industrial complexes in the area. People came and went with great frequency, and the turnover in rooms was never ending. It was exactly what Celeste had told Lonnie to find. No friendly neighbors snooping around, and no one tracking his comings and goings.

He had arrived in a battered Chevy Corvair, giving his name as Marco Figueroa. He was seeking employment in one of the several oil refineries that were only a few blocks from this dilapidated tenement. Lonnie had told the janitor that he had no idea how long he would require the room, but he paid the man four weeks in advance to allay any questions of his financial stability. It was not unusual for tenants to disappear in the middle of the night with all their belongings and money owed on their accommodations. That is why the old man worked the night shift, his main job being to catch any 'fly-by-nighters.' The payment in advance had put Lonnie in his good graces, and the custodian had given him a toothless smile the few times that they had crossed paths.

The new resident thanked the janitor as he took the note and hustled up the stairs to his room. There were no telephones in the building, so any contact with the outside world had to come via the pay phone at the cantina down the street. He would usually meet Celeste around the corner from the bar at a designated time after receiving her call there. This was the first time that a written communication had been transmitted to him. He found it strange that she would take such a chance.

He unlocked the door to his room and flicked on the interior light switch. The now-familiar yellowish-white walls greeted him again. The only decorative touch on their peeling surface was a faded portrait of the Virgin Mary over his less than comfortable bed. A wooden chair and dresser completed the adornments. It had been necessary to purchase an electric fan to make the fetid room bearable in the humid February air. The washroom was down the hall, shared with the other tenants on that floor.

Lonnie found it perversely humorous that he was now residing in 'Versailles,' for he had visited the French palace a few years past on his summer vacation. The comparison between his new residence and the fabled home of the French monarchs reassured him that he had truly cast aside his monied upbringing and was now living the lifestyle of the oppressed working man. Celeste had been right. He did have to live their pain to understand it. Just hearing the stories of the unemployed day after day as he sat in the cantina was enough to convince him. The despair and hopelessness that many of the men exhibited convinced Lonnie that the junta would do nothing to improve their plight.

Millions of dollars were being spent on military hardware, but relatively nothing on job creation and social assistance. He had been totally oblivious to the predicament of the working class while living within his ivory tower and swanky Palermo mansion. Celeste Lavalle had changed all that. She had opened his eyes to the injustice and made him feel like he could make a difference.

The boarder sat down on the bed and opened the note. The handwriting was Celeste's. He had waited for three hours at the cantina that night for her call, but it never came. By closing time, he had consumed so many beers that he was feeling no pain at all. It was probably a good thing that she had not contacted him during that last half hour or his slurred speech would have given him away. He stared at the piece of paper. Its message was brief.

'Call at ten a.m. tomorrow. Hotel Bolivar, room six. 555-5344.' It was signed with a simple letter 'C.'

Something's up, he thought. The change in routine must be for a reason. He had not phoned her flat since he arrived in Versailles. *Why is she staying at Hotel Bolivar? Maybe there was finally going to be some action.*

God knows he had trained hard enough to be put to the test. The entire month of January had been spent at a secluded Montonero training facility north of Tucumán near the town of Taft Viejo. The cool Andean air had proved both mentally and physically invigorating to Lonnie. In the shadow of those towering mountains, he had engaged in everything from classroom studies of the great left-wing visionaries, to hand-to-hand combat, small arms training, and high explosive assembly and detonation. The instructors were known only by colors, never by their given names. In doing so, Señor Verde, Señor

Rojo, and Señorita Azul protected their real identities from infiltrators and counterterrorists who might have gained access to their inner circle.

As a graduation present, Lonnie was presented with a nine millimeter Spanish-made Llama handgun. Its thirteen-shot clip rendered it a very deadly weapon in the hands of a trained shooter, and Lonnie had scored the highest points for marksmanship among the new trainees. His reward for this feat was a German-made Merkel twelve-gage shotgun. The camp's munitions expert, Señor Amarillo, balanced this over-and-under beauty to perfection as he sawed off the stock and barrel to suit Lonnie's grip and upper thigh length. A special leg strap holster for his two-shot widow-maker completed the transition of this former schoolboy into a walking human arsenal.

Itching to put his diploma to use, Lonnie returned to Buenos Aires with Celeste to arrange for his false identification. They then set out to scrounge up enough secondhand clothing to make his new identity believable, bought the old Chevy Corvair with money Lonnie gladly donated to the cause, and rented the room in Versailles.

The newly indoctrinated terrorist was able to spend a week at Celeste's flat while all the arrangements were being completed. This allowed her to fulfill her part of Lonnie's graduation present.

Initially, their passion was purely animalistic. Lonnie was left drained and handcuffed to her brass headboard to fall asleep that first night. He awoke the next morning to find his manhood in the process of being completely devoured by her sensuous mouth, and when it had risen to its full majestic splendor, she straddled him and rode him as if he were a stallion at a Wild West rodeo.

When he finally gained freedom from his metal captors, he returned the favor in kind, working her swollen clitoris until she begged for his cock to be thrust deep inside her. He did not oblige, but left her still handcuffed to the headboard just short of orgasmic splendor. He rose from the bed, looked down at her writhing form with disinterest, went to the refrigerator to get a beer, then turned on the television. The sound of the announcer's voice prompted a stream of expletives from the bedroom. Lonnie's impatient response was immediate.

"Shut up, you little commie puta. The boxing match is about to begin. Now be a nice, quiet little slut, and I might decide to come and fuck you between rounds. Otherwise, I'll just leave you there and go out for pizza with some of my university friends. Maybe I'll bring them all back to work over that little terrorist pussy of yours. Now be quiet, or I'll be forced to gag you."

It was all bluff, of course, for he had no intention of leaving her now or ever again. Their brashness could quickly turn to tenderness, and they would make love as if they were society newlyweds on their consummation night, cautious, nervous, and yet curious about the wonders each other's body possessed.

He hated to leave her when his forged documents finally arrived, for he had no idea when they would be able to spend time together again, in such a carefree manner.

Lonnie De Seta was about to step over the brink, leaving his old life behind him with the distinct possibility that he would never be able to return to it again. His family, the privileged upbringing, society status, all those women, and yes, the money . . . they meant nothing to him now. He was a soldier of the people's revolution, and he had a feeling that he was about to cut his teeth with the phone call that he would make at ten the next morning.

"Are you ready to stop playing games and see what you are really made of? If so, bring your car and your gifts and meet me at Café Ultimo on San Martin Avenue at noon. We have work to do."

The receiver went dead. She was all business again, no more honey in her voice. Cold, strictly business. Well, he was man enough to stop playing games. He ached to prove himself to her once and for all.

The gifts that she referred to were the weapons that he had received upon graduation at Taft Viejo. They were hidden in the trunk of his car, and he now brought them to his room to clean, in preparation for the activities to follow. He did not shave, for he wanted to look as rugged and fearsome as possible. Blue jeans, old beaten-up cowboy boots, a torn short sleeve shirt, and an oversized baseball cap completed his wardrobe.

He stood staring at the reflection in the mirror, quite proud of himself. He looked exactly like any of the thousands of transient, unemployed laborers milling around Buenos Aires that summer. Nothing set him apart from the restless hordes now. No one would suspect that only two months before, he had dressed in the finest designer jeans, wore only Gucci loafers, ate at the capital's priciest restaurants, and squired his dates around in a Mercedes.

His dumpy Corvair was the crowning touch to Señor Marco Figueroa's new identity. It was so ugly that no one had given it a second glance, not even the young car thieves that roamed Versailles at night. Ugly on the outside, but under the hood she was supercharged for action. A mechanic friend of Celeste's had retrofitted the engine so that the four-speed manual transmission was performing to its maximum efficiency. The grease-monkey had told Celeste that, while the car could be quickly overtaken on the highway, in city streets with lots of turns and quick braking and acceleration, it would have no equal.

The room in Versailles had been chosen primarily for the easy access its location provided to all parts of the capital, and if necessary, westward into the hinterlands. Avenida Juan Justo was a major artery running from the city limits on the west, straight into the heart of Palermo. It intersected the capital ring road, Avenida General Paz, only a block from Lonnie's new home. He had driven the streets of Versailles many times, learning their nuances and directions in case of an incident involving police pursuit. A small garage had been rented from an elderly woman who no longer had an automobile as a safe hideout for the Corvair. The Montoneros had been very thorough in their preparations, and it was finally time to show the oligarchy and the junta that the revolution was still very much alive.

Lonnie arrived half an hour early at the café, but he remained in the parked Corvair across the street. He had been taught to never make himself noticeable in any situation where someone could give a description of his appearance. A waiter, another café patron, anyone. Celeste arrived exactly at noon and noticed the parked Corvair before she even set foot inside the café.

"Good job, Lonnie! I half expected you to be sitting in the sunshine sipping on a beer," the lady smiled as she climbed into the passenger seat. Celeste was wearing a realistic, shoulder-length red wig.

"I'm not some dumb cowboy, Señorita. Don't forget, I've been to terrorist school. Nice hair. Sexy redheads always get my cock stiff!"

"Drive! Head north." Her voice was suddenly steely, all business. "Take General Paz up to Avenida del Tejar, then turn south. Do you know where the army headquarters is by General Paz Park? All the top military men do their banking at a large branch of the Banco Nacional across from the park. We are going to make a withdrawal from that branch and leave that scum a message they won't forget."

Lonnie noticed that his palms were perspiring as he held on to the steering wheel. Beads of sweat also dotted his forehead.

"You look nervous, cowboy. Don't worry, we are not pulling this off alone. Serge and Jean Pierre are meeting us in the park. They have cased the whole scene. Just follow Serge's orders and you will be fine. We are going to arrive at the bank when it is about to close at three p.m. You are the official getaway-car driver, so you won't be inside on this job. I hope this piece of junk you're driving is up to the task."

"Piece of junk? You helped me select it, and it was your mechanic that overhauled it! Both the car and I will do our jobs just fine!"

Lonnie was consumed by a strange sensation of relief, intermixed with disappointment. He wasn't going to be on the inside, but he rationalized that his role was crucial to the success of the operation, basically ensuring that they all escaped.

"Does your brother have an escape route mapped out? I haven't been up in the Villa Urquiza district in a long time."

"Of course he does. Serge is very thorough. You will have time to drive the route before the actual job commences. Stop worrying and relax."

Lonnie followed Celeste's directions until they found themselves alongside of General Paz Park, one block east of their intended final destination. The park was lush with flowers surrounding the statue of General Paz, who was mounted on a fine charger. Beyond the park, just out of view from the public eye, sat the complex of buildings that housed the Argentine army headquarters and its chief personnel. Security around this facility was always extremely heavy, and it would be considered nothing less than a suicide mission to try and attack the complex itself.

But to strike a blow for the revolution in the army's own backyard, right under their very noses, that would send a message neither they, nor the Argentine people could ignore!

Celeste had Lonnie pull the Corvair over to the curb. They had barely come to a full stop when the rear doors were flung open and two men entered the vehicle, one from either side.

"Hey! Qué pasa? What's going on here?" Lonnie was half turned in the driver's seat protesting the intrusion when Celeste put her index finger to his lips.

"It's OK. Drive west past the park and keep going."

He had no idea who the two men dressed in business suits were, or why Celeste didn't let him draw his concealed Llama pistol and get rid of them. He looked at her incredulously, but her nodding gesture to proceed convinced him to put the car in gear and drive.

"It's good to see you again, Lonnie. Celeste has told us that you have done very well with your training and studies. Congratulations! I hear as well that you were the best marksman in your training group. Excellent! Maybe you will have an opportunity to demonstrate those skills this afternoon. Now, I have a map for you to study. It is our escape route. Pull into this parking lot for a moment and take a look at it."

There was no mistaking that voice. Although he had never laid eyes on Serge Lavalle or his brother, that voice propelled memories of their first encounter to the forefront of Lonnie's brain. The blindfolded lecture that he was forced to endure, ending with the .45 magnum bullet being tossed in his lap. It seemed like such a long time ago, and yet that voice, there was no mistaking that voice.

He pulled the Corvair into the parking lot directly across from the Banco Nacional. It was a large, impressive building, with two tiers of steps running past the four massive Ionian columns that supported the sloping entrance façade roof. Both military and civilian personnel could be seen scurrying to and from the bank, trying to make sure that their transactions would be completed before closing time. Serge Lavalle leaned forward so that he could help Lonnie decipher the handwritten map.

"You will drop us off right here in this parking lot, Lonnie. The three of us will proceed across the street and into the bank. Once we have disappeared through the front doors, you will wait exactly three minutes, and then you will pull across the street and sit directly in front of the bank with the motor running. Stay in the car, but open the right side doors, front and back, leaving them ever so slightly ajar. This will ensure easy entry into your limousine, for I anticipate that we will be in quite a hurry! Do you understand everything so far, Lonnie?"

"Yes, I think so. Three minutes after you disappear, pull in front of the bank, stay in the car, motor running, open front and back passenger doors slightly. Yes, I've got it so far."

"Good, now do it. Pull across the street and stop for just a second in front of the bank. I will tell you when to stop." Lonnie put the car in gear and waited for a break in the traffic.

"Good, right here. This is where you will wait. Between the third and forth column. Now drive on east and check your map. We turn right off the main thoroughfare at the first intersection, cross the railway tracks, and then left. Drive past Pirovano Hospital and onto the entrance ramp to Avenida del Tejar. Then it's back to Avenida General Paz and on to your rented garage in Versailles. Now here is the first turn, take a right."

They drove the whole escape route to the point where they were to enter del Tejar again. Serge told Lonnie that speed was only important in making the very first turn. Once they were out of the sight-lines of the curious onlookers, not to mention any guns that were pointed at them, Lonnie should drive at the speed limit so as to not attract attention. Unless they were being pursued, that is.

They were now back in the parking lot, in front of the bank. It was eight minutes to three. Serge and Jean Pierre clicked open their briefcases and slapped ammunition clips into their Uzzi submachine guns. They cocked the breech levers, sending the first bullet into the chamber. Celeste, who was wearing a pretty pink sundress, pulled a Heckler and Koch .45 caliber pistol equipped with a silencer from her native Indian handbag. She, likewise, loaded and cocked her weapon, then returned it to its original location. Serge then handed her two grenades, which she quickly placed with the pistol.

"You had better do the same, Lonnie. Where is your shotgun? If anyone tries to move you from in front of the bank, stall for time until you see us coming, then waste the bastard. Use your pistol first, if your assailant is only one person. But if more than one, use the shotgun. Are you loaded up and ready?" Lonnie was ready, having loaded both his weapons before leaving Versailles.

"Yes, I'm all set. The shotgun is under my seat, ready for action. The nine millimeter is in my shoulder holster right here. I'm ready. Good luck!"

Celeste bent forward and kissed him tenderly. "Good luck, my terrorist cowboy. Promise you'll wait for me. I'll be back soon."

"I'll wait, you can bet your life on it." He returned her kiss, then she opened the car door and stepped out. Serge again leaned forward from the rear seat and held out his hand for Lonnie to take.

It was the first time that the driver had a chance to study the man's features. His eyes were hidden by reflective sunglasses, but the rookie terrorist thought that he saw a flash of something, compassion, sorrow, empathy, something, through those dark lenses. Serge's bearded face was foreboding, traces of scars evident beneath the growth. His teeth were somewhat crooked and yellow, and the overall impression of this man was of someone not to mess with.

The voice seemed strangely out of context with the person. So practical, reassuring, and full of knowledge . . . like a schoolteacher or priest. But it was totally at odds with his rugged, almost terrifying physical appearance.

Lonnie grasped the man's hand, then the three Lavalles were standing together in the parking lot. Jean Pierre was the surprise. He had simply tapped Lonnie on the shoulder twice as he exited the Corvair. A mute sign of approval, Lonnie figured.

He was young, tall, and handsome in appearance, with none of the outward signs of torture that his brother exhibited. He could have been a fashion model, dressed in his navy blue Italian suit, his brown hair parted in the middle and swept long to either side. Boyish good looks that concealed the heart of a terrorist, ready to die for the cause. Celeste suddenly broke ranks and stuck her head in through the front passenger window.

"Here, take one of these. It might come in handy if things get sticky." She tossed a pineapple-shaped grenade onto the front seat beside Lonnie's right thigh, smiled, blew him a kiss, and joined her brothers, who were starting their walk to the curb.

"I'll add it to my collection!" he called out after her. There was no acknowledgment of his last remark.

Here we go! thought Lonnie. He reached under his seat and adjusted the Merkel shotgun for easy access. The driver observed his comrades cross the street, stride up the two tiers of steps, and disappear into the bank. He looked down at his watch. "Three minutes to Hell," he said out loud.

The three Lavalles entered the bank and immediately went to their assigned locations. Celeste ignored the long line and went directly to the teller nearest the door. Serge went to the narrow desk used to fill out withdrawal or deposit slips, opened his briefcase and waited for his cue. Jean Pierre strode up to the armed security guard standing just inside the entrance and handed the man a note. The customer's clean-cut appearance, along with the contents of the note, set the guard at ease temporarily.

The small piece of paper contained the following message: 'Good day, Señor. I am unable to talk, having recently had my tonsils operated on. Could you kindly direct me to the manager's office, for I have a three o'clock appointment.' As the guard raised his arm to point in the direction that this young businessman should proceed in, Jean Pierre slid his right hand into his suit jacket pocket. He grasped a set of brass knuckles firmly, then smashed his armored fist into the unsuspecting security officer's nose.

The guard dropped like a stone, blood spurting profusely from the cavity that used to be his nasal passage. Jean Pierre relieved him of his military issue revolver, pulled a set of handcuffs from his other jacket pocket, rolled the guard over on to his stomach, and cuffed his hands behind his back.

As Celeste pushed her way to the front of the queue, several of the people she had passed objected vigorously. One military colonel in particular asked, "What gives you the right to have your affairs dealt with before the people that have waited patiently for their turn at the teller's window?"

She smiled sweetly at the officer, then slowly withdrew the handgun from her satchel.

"This, Señor Colonel, gives me the right, and the authority, to do anything I want to do. Now, hand me your wallet for starters, and the rest of you people, down on the floor."

Serge's cue was the felling of the guard. The instant he saw Jean Pierre drop the unfortunate man, he pulled his cocked Uzzi from the briefcase and blasted several rounds into the bank's ornate cathedral ceiling. Screams of panic filled the banking hall, followed by a strange silence. Once again, it was Serge that did the talking.

"Everyone lie down on the floor right now and you will not get hurt. This bank is being liberated by the people's movement of Argentina. We are Montoneros, and we have come to remind all of you that the revolution lives. It will never die until justice and equality for the working man is realized. The junta uses the money in this bank to buy weapons to oppress the common people. We will use this money to buy food and shelter for the common people. We are asking every one of you to make a donation. Take out your wallets and pocketbooks and lay them on the floor beside you. Each of the donors will receive a letter of gratitude in the mail. The people of Argentina thank you."

Since dispatching the security guard, Jean Pierre had leapt behind the teller's counter and was systematically emptying the cash drawers of their coveted pesos. Celeste was filling her handbag with the personal property of the bank's unlucky patrons, while Serge continued his oration on the evils of the military government and the hope of equality for the working class through violent revolution. Their work completed, Jean Pierre and Celeste joined their elder brother a few feet inside the entrance way.

"Savor this moment, my brother and sister. See the scourge of this nation groveling at your feet, begging for mercy. It makes my heart soar with pride." He took a longing glance around the austere room, then turned his attention to address the prostrate throng.

"Now, do not move or try to follow us. We have planted explosives at the door to the bank. They will be detonated if anyone leaves this building. Stay where you are if you want to see another sunrise. Viva la revolution!"

Those words had barely passed Serge's lips when the three 'liberators' turned and flew through the entrance doors and down the first tier of steps. On the landing between the two flights they halted as one, Celeste delving into her handbag and retrieving a can of fluorescent red spray paint. Since she was the artistic member of the family, she proceeded to spray the word 'Montoneros' on the lower five steps of the top tier. It all took a matter of seconds, and when the pretty terrorist had completed her artistry, she reached into her satchel for one last important object.

Tucked safely in a side pocket so as not to become lost in the jumble of wallets and other paraphernalia, the rippled metal of the hand grenade felt cool in her palm. Her brothers were waiting for her, and as she stood erect clutching the deadly sphere, the three, in unison, pulled the safety pins and hurled the lethal pineapples toward the entrance doors. Without waiting for their devastating effect to occur, the Montoneros turned and fled in the direction of the idling, rust-colored Chevy Corvair.

Lonnie had done his job to perfection. No one had interfered with the unseemly little car as it sat in front of the majestic establishment. He had been parked less than a minute when the Lavalles came running down the steps past the columns.

The driver was shocked to see them halt, however, and it was only upon witnessing Celeste's artistic talents that he began to comprehend what they were doing. The baseball-like throw to home plate startled him once again, but his compatriots were safely inside the vehicle and half a block from the Banco before the first explosion and repercussion shattered the mid-afternoon calm.

They had turned the first corner of the escape route and eased up on their speed before anyone spoke.

"Good job, Lonnie. I knew we could count on you. Is everyone alright?" Big brother Serge was still in control, always the leader, always the protector. Celeste leaned over and kissed Lonnie's cheek.

"A piece of cake, wasn't it boys?" she laughed. "I think that there will be a lot of soiled trousers inside the Banco Nacional this afternoon. I wish that I owned a dry cleaning establishment in the area." Lonnie and Serge laughed heartily.

"Did you like my message, darling?" Celeste squeezed Lonnie's thigh.

"I can't believe you had the balls to do that! Oops, wrong choice of words, I guess." They all laughed again, except for Jean Pierre, who slapped the back of the driver's seat to show his approval.

Serge continued to monitor the road behind them as well as Lonnie's speed and direction. There was no pursuit, and the foursome made it unmolested back to the safe garage in Versailles. There, they laid out the contents of the day's take on the hood of the Corvair. When the final tally was done, the take amounted to over sixteen million pesos, or two hundred thousand U.S. dollars. The Montoneros celebrated with a bottle of local champagne that Serge had brought along, then the three Lavalles changed into outfits similar to that of Lonnie's. Working class apparel had previously been stored in the garage for this occasion. They removed the stolen license plates that had been mounted on the Corvair just for the heist and affixed the original plates registered to Señor Marco Figueroa. Once he was satisfied that everything was in order, Serge addressed the group one final time.

"You should all be very proud of what we accomplished today. Not only did we succeed in showing the whole nation that the people's movement is still alive and strong, but we garnered an incredible sum of money right from under the noses of the military, without the loss of one human life. That is something to tell your grandchildren." The leader stopped to take a large swallow of the champagne in celebration. Wiping a few errant drops from his beard, he cautioned his followers.

"We must be extremely careful from this moment on. The search for us will be massive. Lonnie, I would suggest that you and Celeste take a vacation together. Is there somewhere safe that they know you? Somewhere that no one will be suspicious when you suddenly show up? I would advise you to re-adopt your past lifestyle. Nice clothes, the Mercedes, all those things you used to do last summer. That should divert attention from your present guise. Can you do that?"

"I think it shouldn't be too hard to accomplish," Lonnie said with a grin. "I preferred driving my Mercedes to the Corvair, to tell you the truth. I guess the people's revolution still has to work on my materialistic values some more. As for the rest of it, well, I told my mother that Celeste and I were traveling for the summer, but most years I work at my father's camp for terminally ill children in Tigre. I don't think anyone would be suspicious if Celeste and I showed up there to lend a helping hand for awhile. How does that sound to you?" He directed the question to Celeste.

"Fine with me. You have told me so much about the camp, I would really like to see it. How long would we have to stay?"

"It all depends on the heat," replied Serge. "Usually they round up hundreds of suspects when something like this happens. Our escapade will prove to be all the more embarrassing for the junta because of the 'peaceful nation' and 'nonexistent terrorists' bullshit they are spewing to the press. Security and a calm atmosphere for the World Cup has become their top priority. Well, we just showed the entire world that the people of Argentina want social justice, not some football circus." The leader spat out his final words contemptuously.

Another pull on the bottle, then he revealed his own plans. "Jean Pierre and I are going to Mar del Plata to get lost in the summer crowds. We have already rented a flat, and we just plan to disappear. Write down the address of the camp in Tigre for me, Lonnie, and I will contact you when we are ready to strike again. My brother and I will drop our bounty off at the local cadre headquarters, then head directly out of town. I suggest that you two leave Buenos Aires as quickly as possible, for the roadblocks are bound to go up around the capital in a matter of hours, if not sooner. Any questions?"

The room was silent, then, one by one, they embraced and said their goodbyes. Serge and Jean Pierre left the garage first, carrying the spoils of battle in an old duffel bag that matched their change of attire. Jean Pierre had a knapsack slung over his shoulders that contained the two Uzzis and several more hand grenades, but to those that they passed on their walk to the bus terminal, they looked just like any other transients in this down-on-your-luck part of town.

"So, do we head to your casa to get the car and new clothes?"

"The Mercedes is stored at the dealership, so that's no problem," Lonnie responded to Celeste's query. "As for going home, I would rather not. Too many questions to answer, especially if I run into my mother. I have my real identification in a safety deposit box at my bank. Tomorrow we can retrieve it, take out some money, and go shopping. You can pretend that you are my socialite girlfriend helping me spend all my hard-earned cash. Who knows, you might even have fun and cast aside the powers of the revolution for the powers of the almighty American Express card." Lonnie shot his lover a sarcastic grin as he pulled her tight against his muscled torso. The excitement of the day's activity had stirred his manly urges.

"Where will we stay tonight, your place or mine?"

"I'm way ahead of you, my preppy hero. I have already vacated my flat for good. End of school term you know. My things are at a storage facility. We can pick up what we need tomorrow. I am sure that I will find your accommodations up to your usual five-star standards. Let's go. I can hardly wait to order up room service."

CHAPTER SIXTEEN

Nijinsky, Pavlova, Stravinsky, Strauss, Bernstein, Caruso, Callas, Toscanini, Nureyev, Barishnikov, the list goes on and on. Each one had performed their artistry on the great stage of Teatro Colon, and very shortly, Renaldo De Seta was going to be standing on that exact same stage. He would not, of course, ply his particular trade among the gilded boxes and mauve velvet armchairs. There would be no football played beneath the great seven hundred-bulb chandelier. But there was no mistaking the reason that close to four thousand souls had filled every nook and cranny of this venerable theater.

The elite of Argentine society, as well as the nation's most powerful military and political figures, had come to see and be seen at this extravagant, yet culturally rich fundraising gala. But the magnet that drew them to the fabled opera house was not drama or music this time . . . it was football! The eyes of the world would be focused on their turbulent homeland in a few short months, and fifteen other nations would be their guests at a very special party, the FIFA World Cup of Football.

A call, one could say almost a plea, had gone out to all Argentines regardless of social standing to pull together to make the games of the eleventh World Cup the best that had ever been staged. The junta had promised all its native sons and daughters a spectacle that they would never forget, as long as the organizers were allowed to focus on the athletic concerns and not on terrorist threats or acts of sabotage.

The recent bank robbery near the army headquarters in Buenos Aires had outraged not only the military leaders, but also many left-wing supporters, including trade unionists, students, and the leftist-working press. They were in sympathy with the government-inspired editorials that vilified the perpetrators. The vast majority of both Porteños and Provincials saw this mindless act of violence as a blight on their country's concerted effort to show the world that Argentina was a safe and sane land, a land where tourists from around the world could come and enjoy the most popular sport on earth in comfort and safety.

Now three misguided zealots had blasted their way into the world headlines, severely undermining much of the credibility that the junta had tried so hard to establish. The fact that the robbery occurred in broad daylight across the street from Argentine army headquarters reflected badly upon the whole national security program. 'Heads were rolling' in the corridors of power, and on the streets. Heaven help anyone that got caught in a police sweep without letter-perfect identification.

But on this night, Saturday the fourteenth of February, all the tensions seemed to melt away once the patrons were seated inside the plush amphitheater. No one without a valid ticket could get within a city block of the teatro, and all the guests and performers were electronically screened and searched upon entering the building. Not even the society matrons objected to this inconvenience, so great was the outrage at the thought that their country was perceived as a breeding ground for thugs and violent revolutionaries.

Six people had been killed by exploding hand grenades as they tried to follow the Montonero thieves from the Banco Nacional.

Colonel Xavier Rodrigues Borges, the country's senior antiterrorist strategist, was among those slain. Argentines from all walks of life wanted an end to the cold-blooded insanity. This night at Teatro Colon was to be their new beginning, a new focus on the spectacular events to come. Three thousand military policemen ringing the opulent Greco-Roman structure in the heart of the capital were there to ensure that nothing would disrupt the gala evening.

The program was artistically enchanting, covering all aspects of Argentine music and folklore, from ancient times to modern day. Native Indians were playing the Quena and Charanga, mournful melodies played on a great, long instrument called an Erke. Gauchos were performing their Milongas, Estilos, and Cifras, always rousing and immensely entertaining. Then, of course, a tribute to the late Carlos Gardel, the celebrated innovator of the tango, the national dance of Argentina. The legendary Argentine composer Hector Panizza was honored with a moving selection from his greatest symphonic works. A host of other talented singers and musicians complimented the program.

The pièce de résistance for the young generation, however, was the performance, late in the show, of the nation's number one pop star, Symca. She was to be followed directly by the much anticipated unveiling of the National World Cup Football Team.

This gala evening was being broadcast live over state radio and television, and listeners were constantly encouraged to mail donations to the World Cup Organizing Committee's capital fund. A letter of gratitude and a poster of the National Team would be sent to all donors.

By positioning the vivacious Symca near the conclusion of the schedule, the producers ensured a national audience until the very end of the festivities. Astor Gordero had arranged the entertainment and structured the acts to receive maximum exposure vis-à-vis mail-in donations. The introduction of the National Team, followed by a spirited and emotional rendition of the national anthem, was anticipated to bring tears to the eyes, not to mention pens to the checks, of millions of patriotic Argentines.

Renaldo De Seta sat watching the musical feast on one of several television monitors placed in the banquet hall, where the National Team waited impatiently. He, like all the other footballers, was attired in his new navy blue blazer, the breast pocket adorned with a luminous gold crest, which offset the black letters 'AFA,' (Asociacion Del Futbal Argentino). Lightweight grey flannel slacks, black Ferragamo loafers, and a powder-blue and white-striped tie completed the ensemble for all the National Team hopefuls.

The youngest aspirant cut a resplendent figure, one that would make almost any lady feel weak at the knees. But at this very moment, his thoughts were of one lady in particular. The subterranean structure of the Teatro Colon extended for three stories, with seemingly miles and miles of corridors, salons, reception rooms, and general work areas. The football players were told to stay in their designated area, but because they were the last group to go on stage, it didn't take long for many of them to become restless, despite the fully stocked bar and endless procession of hors d'oeuvres. Two armed soldiers and two civilian security guards had been placed outside the banquet room with strict orders that absolutely no one was to enter or leave the room.

The guards were only human, of course, and somewhat in awe of these national heroes. As a result, they were easily persuaded to turn a blind eye when required. An autograph, a handshake, or a brief conversation with one of their idols seemed to provide sufficient distraction for several of the players to simply disappear.

Renaldo was able to deftly slide through the door and down the corridor without being noticed or missed. *Sometimes being an unknown commodity has its benefits,* he thought gleefully as he set out to find his lost treasure.

That treasure, buried somewhere in the cavernous depths of Teatro Colon, was to be found in a remote, tiny room, two stories below where the musical history of Argentina was being woven and spun with great passion.

A star, a solitary star, much like the one the fabled wise men of years gone by must have followed, marked the end of his search. Emblazoned within its glittering five silver points was one word, a word that set his heart racing, 'Symca.'

"Come in," was the response that greeted the footballer's knock on the door. Renaldo paused for several seconds. "Come in! It's alright, I'm decent." Peering into her makeup mirror, she tried to focus her eyes on the handsome figure that now stood just inside the cramped closet. "Renaldo, my God, is that really you?" Dressed in a rose-colored satin robe, she let out a little girlish squeal of delight and leapt into his arms, kissing him full on the lips. He was taken aback by her enthusiasm.

"Easy, easy, or we will ruin your makeup. You look absolutely ravishing. How have you been?" The athlete was suddenly aware that his reaction to her greeting had awakened a sleeping giant. He pretended to show interest in the beautiful pink roses that adorned a side table, managing to stand with his back toward her.

"These are lovely. From a secret admirer?"

"Not so secret. A mutual acquaintance actually, Astor Gordero."

She was at his side now, running her fingers through the long curls that fell past the nape of his neck. A tremor flashed up his spine. He turned, intent on removing her hand and freeing himself from any physical contact, lest he lose all control.

Instead, the chanteuse again pressed her lips to his once their eyes met. She leaned against his torso, and he simply melted into her arms.

Even with his eyes closed and his heart pounding, he was still aware of the firmness of her breasts against his chest, not to mention the inflamed heat of her womanhood as the robe parted under the pressure of his concealed, unyielding organ.

The embrace had unleashed a pent-up passion the young man never knew he possessed, and his mind surrendered to the spell of her feminine sensuality. His right forearm held her tightly to him. His strength and hardness took her breath away. Their tongues excitedly explored uncharted waters, entwined in a romantic dance of their own.

When she finally found it necessary to disengage and step back a few paces to collect herself, her eyes were glossy and temporarily unfocused. She then locked on to his massiveness and licked her lips with unconcealed lust.

"You may be just a boy in age, Renaldo, but you are more of a man than I have ever felt. Look at you! Those trousers are about to rip at the seams. It's unbelievable! I never would have thought . . ."

He had turned scarlet in color and was trying vainly to conceal his passion from her devouring eyes. Renaldo found it impossible to regain his composure, however, for she stood in front of him with the robe askew, her lovely breasts and light-brown bush fully exposed.

"I'm sorry, Simone, I should have been more discreet. It's just that I have never been . . ." She was at his side once more, her fingers pressed to his lips.

"Do not be sorry, Renaldo. Football is obviously not the only gift that God endowed you with. There is no cause for embarrassment. I am totally in awe!"

Her hand softly traced the outline of his straining member for a fleeting moment. Her eyes traveled from his midsection to his handsome face and back again several times before she abruptly stopped her explorations and addressed him in a more controlled tone of voice.

"Now, we must regain our composure, my love. Just look at me! You have ruined my makeup, and I still have to dress for the show. I was not counting on such a distraction to my normal pre-stage routine. So off you go. I don't trust myself in your presence anymore. Do you have the backstage pass that I gave you?"

Renaldo was unable to form a coherent response for several seconds. He could only stare at the embodiment of eroticism that stood before him. It was only her look of mock annoyance that transformed him from his mute state.

"Yes, yes, most certainly. I slipped it into my jacket pocket just before I left home tonight. I didn't know if I would find you before the show, and there was no way that I was going to be locked up in a room full of men while you were on stage, World Cup Team or not! We went through our whole stage ceremony this afternoon at the rehearsal. There is nothing to it, just line up in order and walk out into the lights when they call our names. I'll risk a tongue lashing for being late to see you perform live any day."

"I will sing just for you then. When you leave this room, display the pass right away, for the area next to the stage is swarming with security. You won't be able to get close to it unless they see the pass. Can you come back here after the show?"

The look of exhilaration suddenly left his face, replaced by almost painful disappointment.

"Simone, I'm sorry. I know that you had hoped that we could go out dancing, and I would love nothing more in the whole world than to spend the evening with you. But Octavio Suarez, the team manager, is fanatical about security and secrecy when the whole team is together. The only reason I was able to escape to visit you now is that he was off inspecting the security precautions throughout the teatro before we go on stage. In any event, he has informed us that we are being loaded on a bus immediately following our presentation, and then taken to an unknown hotel to spend the night. It is as though we are a bunch of boy scouts. The man is obsessed! But we don't leave for Mar del Plata until the day after tomorrow. Do you have any time at all before then?"

He could see a similar disappointment in her eyes.

"No, my darling, I fly directly to Rio tomorrow to start a two-month promotional tour for the World Cup. This was our only opportunity, and it is lost. I suppose by the time I get back to Buenos Aires, you will be locked away with your teammates. All we can do is wait for another chance to be together. But know that you will always be in my thoughts, my Renaldo!"

She pressed tight to him again, her tongue flicking quickly over his hot lips.

"Go now, my love. Find a place stage right, as close to the front as you can. I will try to find you. There is one song that I will sing especially for you. Now, you must be off."

She turned from him and crossed the room to her makeup table. Without looking at him again, she proceeded to rectify the damage their hot embrace had done. Renaldo stood and took one last lingering look, then without saying a word, disappeared into depths.

As he sat in his private box just off stage left, Astor Gordero could not help but feel proud of his latest accomplishment. The gala had been his idea, an idea which he had nurtured and coddled through to fruition.

His assurance that he could deliver the nation's hottest star in Symca, convinced the local World Cup organizing committee that the event could be both a financial and artistic success. Some of the older members of the committee objected to the playing of rock music on the hallowed stage of Teatro Colon, but Gordero insisted that the evening would be a cultural bonanza showcasing all forms of Argentine music. To further persuade the dissenters, the cunning lawyer showed them the latest projected loss figures on the staging of the World Cup.

Those figures still ran into the hundreds of millions of dollars. That was the deciding factor. The vote was unanimous to present 'Musicale Argentina '78,' with Astor Gordero as its artistic director.

If the truth be known, it was Wolfgang Stoltz that had spent the last month pulling things together. His job was made easier by the fact that nationalistic pride and enthusiasm had never been more evident. It took very little persuading to secure all the entertainers that Gordero had placed on his 'A' list. For after all, what entertainer could refuse a national radio and television audience, as well as an association with World Cup '78?

In the end, Stoltz was inundated with offers to perform in the gala. Advertising and sponsorship by major corporations had covered all the broadcast and staging expenses. The revenue pledged by this soccer mad nation, a nation which was about to be whipped into a frenzy by the country's most stimulating personalities, would surely exceed all expectations. So now, with the evening unfolding without a hitch, Gordero was ready to sit back and watch as his well laid plans became reality.

The lawyer had talked to his newest client at the afternoon rehearsal. The boy seemed remarkably calm and self-assured, if not just a little bit distracted by the whereabouts of the evening's headlining act. Renaldo had mentioned how disappointed he was that the team would be spirited away right after the show, revealing that he had hoped to spend some time with Simone that evening.

"Now is the time to think about football, my young friend, not matters of the heart. There will be plenty of time for romance once you have made the team and secured the World Cup trophy for Argentina."

Renaldo knew that The Fat Man was right, but it didn't diminish his longing for the stunning female vocalist.

What Astor Gordero did not tell his protégé was that he had secretly met with the boy's mother a few days earlier. Wolfgang Stoltz had been sent to Casa San Marco for the express purpose of personally delivering Gordero's letter of introduction. This was how proper society people made contact, and Florencia was duly impressed. The salutation was suitably humble and flowery, yet it contained the notion that the weighty lawyer wished to enlighten her about some serious matters of business concerning her son, Renaldo.

Florencia De Seta accepted Señor Gordero's invitation to discuss her son's future, primarily due to the persuasive charm of Herr Wolfgang Stoltz. She was quite taken with the handsome German from the minute she laid eyes on him, and eventually the lady found courage enough to ask if he would be attending the planned meeting. Stoltz did not miss the smile on her face after answering in the affirmative.

The meeting took place at the 'Hippodrome Argentino,' the posh race track in Palermo. Gordero had a thick file on Señora De Seta, and he slyly deduced that she would welcome a chance to 'strut her stuff.' His front row table in the exclusive Turf Club section of the track was a perfect venue for the reclusive, yet extremely attractive widow to do just that. He was not disappointed. Even though Florencia ventured out in public infrequently, she considered the races just the sort of opportunity that would give her both entertainment and some escorted exposure.

Gordero had learned that the wealthy widow had not completely given up hope of remarrying, or at least finding a gentleman companion. Florencia was very old-fashioned, however, about being seen at social functions unescorted. An acceptable male consort had been hard to come by of late, for the society matchmakers had given up on her long ago, after she had rebuffed all their handpicked suitors. The story now being spread by the Palermo gossipmongers was that Florencia De Seta had become so disenchanted with her two sons that she had thrown up her arms in disgust and said "to hell with them!"

Those two sons had strayed from Florencia's deemed course, and the society tongues were wagging. One had supposedly left home in a rage a few days after Christmas to wander mindlessly around the countryside with his communist girlfriend. The other had dropped out of school with the ridiculous perception that he could pursue a professional football career. These actions had shattered Florencia's motherly aspirations to such a degree that she had returned to the capital, intent on living her life for herself.

This meant kicking up her heels and exploring a lifestyle that she had previously never considered. She had done away with her staid wardrobe and ultra-conservative attitudes and quietly leaked the word to the 'hotline' that she was interested in enjoying some male companionship.

While Florencia considered Astor Gordero far too obese and grotesque to be of romantic interest, she was certainly aware of his power and influence. *Perhaps his connections could be as beneficial to me in the long run as they might prove to be for Renaldo,* she mused.

The appointment had started on a congenial note, with an impeccably prepared meal and a few winning horses. Astor Gordero was a warm and compassionate host, relating his great respect for the De Seta family and conveying his sympathies for the tragic death of her talented and caring husband.

He followed by complimenting her on what a fine job she had done raising her two sons, at the same time dealing with the pressures of running the family business. Gordero described his relationship with Renaldo, and exactly what it would mean to the boy if he actually qualified for the final team.

It was at this point that Florencia turned icy. She had bluntly refused an offer of gala tickets, turning down a chance to see her own flesh and blood in the national spotlight. Instead, she gave the lawyer a long tirade on the evils of football. The lady informed her host of how upset she was with her youngest son for wasting his time with such foolishness. The lonely widow had gone so far as to express her hope that Renaldo would be among the first players to be dropped from the team.

"That would enable him to enroll in university at the start of the next semester and get on with his medical career," Florencia had stated emphatically.

Again, Renaldo's agent tried to enlighten Señora De Seta as to the material benefits that could accrue, should her son be successful in his quest to make the National Team. But she would have none of it.

"The boy does not need material benefits derived from that 'filthy occupation.' My son was meant to be a doctor, just like his father. After he gets this distracting malady out of his system, I am certain that he will repent and proceed on the true course his life was destined to follow!"

Gordero was forced to turn the charm level to maximum while trying to be nonchalant about the Renaldo's football ambitions. It was imperative for his future plans that he not aggravate an obviously delicate situation.

The barrister politely informed Florencia that her son had signed a contractual agreement with A.R. Gordero and Sons that covered only matters pertaining to his football career. The seemingly sincere lawyer assured the boy's mother that he would tear up the document the instant Renaldo was released from the team. He also assured her that he would persuade the boy to listen to his mother's better judgment and pursue a career in medicine, whatever the outcome of his present situation.

This seemed to set the lady's mind at ease, and she warmed to her dining companion, becoming more relaxed and open. By the time they parted company, Señora De Seta had actually admitted that she was happy to have a man of Astor Gordero's stature looking out for her son's best interests.

"Should, heaven forbid, my son continue to be a part of this 'national sickness,' I will rest easier knowing that a man of compassion and feeling is by Renaldo's side."

Gordero left it to Wolfgang Stoltz, who had joined their table during the latter part of the afternoon, to return the lady to her residence. It was, to a great degree, Herr Stoltz's warm smile that helped to melt Florencia's blustery demeanor. The widow's attitude changed perceptively once the suave European arrived on the scene.

Astor Gordero parted company with Señora Florencia De Seta totally satisfied with his performance that afternoon. He could tell by her eyes that she trusted him implicitly by the time the dessert course arrived. It was a game that the obese attorney liked to play while dining with business associates. *How many courses of a meal will be completed before I convince my prey that the Gordero way is the only way?*

The weak and pandering gave in before the appetizers even hit the linen. Florencia had been a workout, remaining immovable until well into the main course before succumbing. As usual, Gordero knew he would eventually win the day, and by dessert he was confident that he had the lady in the palm of his hand. Wolfgang Stoltz would simply close the deal, as usual.

The blackness in the great auditorium was suddenly pierced by a battery of ultraviolet lights emanating from the broadcast scaffolds at the front of the house. From vents on both sides of the stage and behind the raised, chrome-plated drum kit wafted clouds of dry ice fog, enshrouding both the silhouetted musicians and their instruments. As the billowing whiteness traveled into the first few rows of the audience, the drummer let loose with an up-tempo backbeat. The riveting rhythm was picked up thirty seconds later by an electric bass player. Congas, timbales, and other Latin percussion instruments joined in. The result was a pulsating, finger-snapping, toe-tapping groove that had the entire hall clapping their hands in unison.

The gala's master of ceremonies could be heard over the PA system giving a brief but rousing introduction.

"Señoras, Señoritas, and Señors, Musicale Argentina '78 is proud and honored to present the number one pop sensation in the entire country! The beautiful! The amazing! The unbelievable! Sssyyymmmcaaa!"

As the last syllable of her name passed the announcer's lips, the band suddenly stopped playing and the ultraviolet lights disappeared, leaving the stage in total darkness. It was as if someone had pulled the power switch. All that remained were the cheers and screams for "Symca," along with the rhythmic clapping of four thousand pairs of hands.

Then, without warning, a burst from the four banks of powerful Klieg lights illuminated the star for whom they had all been waiting. Standing center stage in a silver-sequined minidress, black fishnet stockings, and incredibly high black pumps, the vocalist literally oozed sexuality.

With her long legs planted astride and her head bent forward resting on her chest, she stood motionless, drinking in the adulation. Right on cue, using the musician's sixth sense, the entire band came to life, and the sultry star launched into an upbeat version of her current chart topping hit.

The staid Teatro Colon went berserk. People were dancing in the aisles, gyrating to the beat in their seats, rushing the stage, and hooting and shouting for more. The sound was unbelievable. The twelve-piece band had been handpicked by the diva, and the ensemble had a musical cohesiveness that was without equal. Guitars, keyboards, horns, rhythm section . . . individually and collectively, they were the best that Argentina had to offer. The results of their tightness were audibly evident.

From where he was perched on the bass drum's hard traveling case at stage right, Renaldo De Seta had a spectacular view of the proceedings. He could not believe what he was hearing or seeing. To listen to her records or to hear her outdoors in giant stadiums was one thing, but here in acoustically perfect Teatro Colon, he was blown away!

Never before had the young man heard a band play with so much force and clarity. Each instrument could be picked out individually, and yet it melded perfectly with the overall effect.

The light show was something from outer space, or so it seemed. Special effects that Renaldo hadn't even seen at her outdoor spectacles were used here. But more than anything else, the sound, the lights, the atmosphere, it was the singer that held the focus of everyone's attention.

She glided about the stage, using every angle to make the audience feel that she was singing especially for them. Her dance moves were agile and fluid, ranging between ballet and gymnastics. Her deep voice was in peek form, displaying a lusty sensuality and yet capable of hitting all the octaves from baritone to soprano.

Mesmerizing was the only word that came to Renaldo's mind. He was in a trance. He cared for nothing else at this moment, for the lovesick boy was truly under Symca's spell.

Her performance was almost exclusively up-tempo, and there were no pauses or dialogue in the whirlwind performance. She did pause before her last number though, and in a heartfelt plea, urged her fellow countrymen to give their support generously to the World Cup '78 movement. There was hardly a dry eye in the audience when she suddenly turned stage right and looked squarely at Renaldo. Their eyes locked for several seconds before the soulful siren turned back to the television cameras and her adoring audience.

"Señors and Señoras, I would like to finish my portion of tonight's show with a very special new song, a song that was written just for me. It will be released as a single very shortly, and I am singing it this evening for someone very special. It is entitled, 'My Love Will Wait for You.' I hope you like it."

She turned again stage right and blew the invisible someone a kiss. Instantly a haunting melody filled the teatro, and there had never been a more tender, more passionate love song sung on that revered stage. The standing ovation that followed the tune's conclusion lasted over three minutes, and cries of "Symca!" "Symca!" "Symca!" rose to the rafters.

From his vantage point, Renaldo blew the object of his affection a kiss as she departed the stage into the opposite wing. Simone paused momentarily, giving her admirer a fleeting glance before disappearing.

Renaldo was numb, exhilarated, and depressed all at the same time. *When will I see her again? She was so spectacular, so gorgeous, so erotic! Could that last song honestly be meant for me?* How every part of him ached with confused, infatuated joy!

Reality beckoned, however, and the MC's announcement that the World Cup team would take the stage within a very few minutes jolted the dazed teenager back to his present predicament. It was now time to face a different kind of music.

"De Seta, where the fuck have you been? What do you think I'm running here, a church picnic excursion? Do you realize that we are about to appear in front of a national television audience, and where are the National Team players? Out chasing pussy! You'll get all the ass you can handle if you make this fucking team, Señor Hotshot, but while you are under my direct control, you had better learn to follow orders and follow them to the letter!"

The manager's face was no more than an inch away from Renaldo's as he vented his fury and heaped scorn on all those assembled.

"This is a team we have here, Señors, not a group of individuals and prima donnas. I won't tolerate any of this shit, ever again! Do you understand me? Do you, you bunch of self-centered idols? Because if you don't, I have a whole list of players that would gladly fill your shoes and heed my bidding!"

The veins were bulging on Octavio Suarez's neck, and his face was bright crimson from screaming at the top of his lungs. With all the smoking the manager did, Renaldo worried that he might keel over from a heart attack on the spot. The youngest player took solace in the fact that while the initial reprimand had been meant specifically for him, the tirade gradually expanded to encompass the entire group.

"I am sorry, Señor Suarez, it won't happen again," was the meek apology that Renaldo tendered.

"It damn well better not happen again, or I'll have you enrolled in university just like your mother wants before you even set foot on a soccer pitch. Now find your place in line!"

The sting of the last comment found its mark on Renaldo.

There is no reason to bring my mother into this, or my future plans either. Some of these players can't even read, or so I have been told by Gordero. They let their feet do the talking on the field of play. That is all I want, too. My mother and university . . . shit! That was a low blow, Renaldo smoldered silently.

Many of these men had grown up in the slums and shanty towns of their birth places, and football was a way out, a means of escape to a better life. They didn't need a high school diploma, they needed to eat and support their families. Now with Suarez's biting remark, they would think of him as some scholastic mama's boy. He hung his head forlornly as he stepped in front of Ramon Vida in the line.

"Hey, don't worry, man, I snuck out, too. Sure was some grade A pussy on that stage. The bitch was so hot, I thought this old place was going to burn down. Bet those longhairs have never experienced anything like her before."

The blood started to boil in Renaldo's temples when Vida made his off-color remarks about Simone. Luckily, he was able to keep himself in check by biting his lip and keeping his back to the Boca center forward without speaking.

To say anything in her defense or to act personally offended by Vida's remarks would tip his hand. He did not want anyone to know of his relationship with Simone. Besides, he felt certain that he was going to take enough ribbing from his teammates as it was. There would be time later to defend Simone's honor if necessary. Right now, it was better to simply hold his tongue.

Within a few seconds they were being escorted through the winding corridors to stage right. There was the familiar drum case that had been Renaldo's orchestra seat. The lights had dimmed and a great fanfare accompanied each player's introduction as they walked individually into the floodlights. A brief biography was given as the athlete stood alone in the national spotlight, being scrutinized by millions of people.

Then the lights would dim again, followed by the fanfare and the next name. Down the list, closer and closer the MC narrated. Soon enough it was the youngest hopeful's turn, and the blinding glare temporarily disoriented the terrified rookie as he stepped out onto the vast expanse. The routine had been exactly the same at rehearsal earlier that afternoon, but so much had happened to him in the last hour. He found himself lost in a haze of overpowering sexual tension augmented by pure and utter panic.

The master of ceremonies smoothly ushered the stage-struck novice to the appropriate spot as the fanfare ended and Renaldo De Seta's biographical notes were read to an enthusiastic yet curious audience. Who was this unknown boy among the greatest football names in the country? What had he accomplished to be worthy of sharing the stage or the soccer field with the national heroes from River Plate, Boca Juniors, and the rest?

As his eyes grew accustomed to the bright lights and to the intense scrutiny, Renaldo seemed to become visibly more relaxed and confident. Hearing the list of his athletic accomplishments being transmitted across the nation brought a warm smile to his initially nervous countenance. He raised his right hand and waved to the people in the front rows. The smile grew broader. A particularly vocal response was floating down from a private box on Renaldo's right. The boy glanced up, and there, just beyond the footlights, was Astor Gordero's mammoth silhouette.

The handsome teenager's smile, combined with his mentor's vociferous ovation, melted away much of the skepticism that lingered in the minds of the watching millions. Like the tide rolling over the beaches of Mar del Plata, he could hear a buzz of curious excitement and acceptance sweep over the audience.

"He is very cute. What is his name again?"

"He should be a fashion model, not a football player!"

"That smile could launch a thousand ships, all overflowing with lusting Porteña women."

These were only a few of the whispered comments that could be heard rippling through the once staid hall. The reaction was much more blatant and forceful when it came to the national television audience. Before the boy with the long curls and the radiant smile had even left the stage, the telephone lines at the National State Network switchboard were lit up like a Christmas tree.

"Who was that player, number seventeen on stage, the young one? How do you spell his name? How can we contact his fan club? Where do we get posters and information about him?"

Of the twenty-two players that were introduced that evening, it was the unknown and untested rookie who captured the hearts of the public. If only his athletic prowess could come close to matching his startling good looks, Argentina would have a new matinee idol!

That test was imminent, for within forty-eight hours, all the talking and posturing would cease. The game was the thing, and these twenty-two were about to learn how to play it all over again, from the beginning. It would be the Octavio Suarez way or the highway!

CHAPTER SEVENTEEN

Their elation lasted until they read the headlines of the Clarín morning paper. La Nacional, La Prenza and the Buenos Aires Herald screamed similar reactions.

"Montonero Bloodbath!" "Damn the Terrorist Assassins!" "Six Die in Vicious Terrorist Attack!"

"Six people dead? Those fools must have tried to follow us. Idiots! We told them that there were explosives outside the bank. They wanted to be fucking heroes. Well, look where it got them! Look, this fat little colonel that bought it tried to give me a hard time when I went to the teller's window. Look, here is his picture. I'm sure it's him. Fat little shit. I should have wasted him right there as he stood in line!"

Celeste's initial shock that people had actually been killed during the bank robbery had given way to an aloof fascination. There was no remorse in her voice. Instead, a morbid exhilaration swept over her as she read and re-read the names and occupations of the men who had died. Four were army personnel, the other two, off-duty policemen.

Lonnie De Seta felt extremely nauseous as he poured over every reported detail in the papers Celeste was not reading aloud. *What am I afraid of? Why have I started to shake?* His stomach soured even more as he absorbed the morbid results of his first act of terror. He had been trained to expect bloodshed, even desire it. But his role had been so removed from the action that he never got a chance to look a stranger in the eye from the business end of an Uzzi. Not like Celeste.

Paper after paper called for the death penalty for these cowards. People from every sector of society, government, clergy, even unionists, condemned their scurrilous deed. Army and police forces were on total mobilization to assure that the killers would be apprehended quickly.

Killers? He had hoped to be referred to as 'revolutionaries,' or 'the people's army.' At worst, they would be described as 'terrorist bank robbers,' but 'killers'? The dogma of the Andes training camp seemed very hazy to him at this moment. *Why are we doing this, killing people?* The answer had temporarily escaped him. *Celeste will tell me why again, when she is finished reading,* he rationalized.

"All of this drivel is controlled by the junta. We will not be lauded as heroes until the underground and student papers hit the streets. Do not let this garbage sway your mind, Lonnie. Our cause is just, and thousands of people will have food and clothing because of the money that we liberated yesterday."

She could tell that he was upset the moment that she put down the final paper. He looked pale and confused.

"It is the people, Lonnie, the people in the streets who will sing our praises. And when they rise up and shake loose the yoke of military oppression, they will remember what the Montoneros did for them! Do not worry about those six. Many more will die before this is over. The people will not be lied to and cheated anymore!"

Her words were meant to reassure him, and while they provided some comfort, he knew that he had truly stepped over the brink. *Killers!* It was time for Marco Figueroa to go underground immediately. Lonfranco De Seta would be reincarnated that morning. He called the dealership to have his Mercedes serviced and awaiting pick up later that afternoon.

One of the newspapers had promised composite sketches of three of the terrorists in a special late edition dealing entirely with the Banco Nacional attack. Lonnie was certain that absolutely no one had gotten a look at him driving the Corvair that afternoon, and there was no description of the getaway car, or its driver, in any of the papers.

"All I have to do is shave and scrub up a bit, then it shouldn't be hard to make it by taxi to my bank," he told Celeste. The cab ride would be the only time that Lonnie would be carrying Marco Figueroa's identification. Once he was safely inside the bank, he could exchange it for his real documents from the safety deposit box. Cabs were a much safer means of transport than buses as far as police spot checks were concerned. Cabbies were experts at avoiding road blocks, and no one thought it too suspicious if a short-fused, impatient cab driver pulled a U-turn to find an alternate route rather than sit in line waiting to be interrogated. Time was money! All Lonnie had to do was find a good cabbie and make it to his bank.

The sun shone brightly as Lonfranco De Seta emerged from the Banco Rio de la Plata on San Martin Avenue. Everything had gone off without a hitch, the cab driver skirting the one road block that they had the potential to encounter. *My first purchase is going to be a pair of new sunglasses,* he thought. A short walk to his favorite men's store, Gino Bogani, to pick up some new threads, then he would head directly to the dealership. He felt totally relieved at having his old persona back again. He felt invincible. How dare anyone accuse Lonnie De Seta of being involved in a terrorist bloodbath! He was a man of privilege, of breeding, a true Porteño!

The society playboy liked the fact that he could have a dual identity. It was his alter ego, Marco Figueroa, who was the terrorist, the murderer, the wanted man. Lonnie De Seta was going shopping, not to jail!

It was necessary to make one last trip to Versailles to pick up Celeste and their possessions before heading to Tigre. While Lonnie was away, she had cut her hair into a short bob, then dyed it blonde.

It doesn't look half bad, the former brunette assessed. She had been unable to leave his shabby little room since walking there after dark the night before. Lonnie had been the one to go for food and newspapers that morning, as Celeste was concerned about being recognized. Now all she had to do was make it into his Mercedes and she was virtually guaranteed a safe escape to Tigre.

The rumble of military vehicles outside her window jolted her sense of security. She pulled back the tattered curtain and looked down upon a sea of drab grey trucks disgorging a steady stream of olive-clad national guardsmen. People on the street were being lined up against the buildings, or, if they showed the least bit of resistance, made to lay prostrate in the middle of the gutter. Celeste brought her left hand to her throat, as if she could feel the noose tightening.

The buildings were being systematically searched, with certain tenants being brought down to street level for further interrogation. She had only her real identification in her knapsack, the one saying that she was a visiting associate professor from Tucumán University. The word Tucumán would be enough for the police to interrogate her for certain. She had given her false identification to Lonnie for storage in the bank vault. It would have been perfect. Sandra Necochea, café waitress from Buenos Aires. A full set of working permits and a letter from her supposed employer made the documents nearly foolproof. Now they were locked away, of no use to her whatsoever.

The intruders were on the floor below her now. She could hear their loud pounding on the doors, their feet on the stairs, their shouts for everyone to come out of their dwellings. For Celeste, there was no way out. She must act now!

Suddenly there were three loud thuds on her door, the call to open up and make yourself seen, then the crash of a jackboot smashing through the flimsy locking devise. Three guardsmen fell into the room, carbines at the ready. One glance told them that the room was unoccupied. There was nowhere else to look, no bathroom, not even a closet. Only a chair and a dresser. They moved on down the hall.

Being slight in stature sure has its benefits. This was Celeste's first coherent thought after she heard the guardsmen move on. *How stupid they are,* was her second thought. They had looked under the metal cot to see if someone was on the floor, but that was it. The junta's lackeys had failed to search the dresser, which would have yielded them Celeste's knapsack with her ID in it. But more importantly, they hadn't looked behind the dresser, where the petite terrorist had been holding her breath to save her life. An artistically beveled baseboard adorning the dresser had been enough to shield the cute contortionist's feet from view.

It was over an hour before the room's occupant was able to move from her cramped position, but as long as she could hear the commands and screams from the street below, she was perfectly content to endure a little claustrophobia. When Celeste finally freed herself, the only sounds that could be heard were the sobbing and wailing of the relatives left behind. Their loved ones had been taken away, away on a journey to Hell.

Lonnie tore up the steps and into his former tenement. The door was still ajar, the locking mechanism lying on the threshold. Celeste was sitting by the window, a surprisingly placid look on her face. Lonnie did a double take when he saw the blonde lady. He looked at the number on the door. It was his room, and that was Celeste, but Celeste as a blonde.

She had told him that she planned to cut her hair, but the color?

"Are you alright? I heard on the street that the National Guard searched every building. How did you avoid them?"

Without saying a word, she pointed to the dresser. He walked over and looked behind it.

"You were able to fit behind this thing, and they didn't see you? My God, you are the smartest, luckiest, not to mention the sexiest little blonde terrorist that I have ever met. Now get your things. We have to go quickly. I've always been horny for blondes, and since you had to throw away that red wig, I thought I was stuck with a brunette. They say blondes have more fun, and if we don't get moving I will want to have my way with you before we even start our journey to Tigre. Once we make it there, well, I have a private little cabin down by the river that I think you will find more conducive to romance than our present surroundings."

He took her in his arms and kissed her gently. She was trembling. Lonnie had thought her incapable of fear. The crying from the room across the hall made it painfully evident just how close she must have come to joining the ranks of those who would soon be known as 'The Disappeared.'

Mar del Plata. Argentina's Riviera. World-famous beach resort mentioned in the same breath as Cannes, Miami Beach, and Rio's Copacabana. Five miles of beaches, chock-a-block with brightly colored umbrellas. The most exclusive private beach clubs known to man. The largest casino in the world. Seventy thousand hotel rooms. A population that swells from three hundred thousand people in the off-season, to close to two million in January and February.

Nonstop night life in a playground by the sea. An adult fantasyland of sun, surf, and sex.

Unfortunately, none of the twenty-two hopefuls for Argentina's National World Cup team would have a chance to sample any of these pleasures. Octavio Suarez was no fool. He had chosen the team's initial training site for one reason. Climate!

Cool, moderating winds blowing in from the Atlantic sent soft summer breezes onshore, a welcome relief from the oppressive humidity and pollution of the capital. Thirty miles southwest of Mar del Plata, the small family resort town of Miramar offered the same climatic conditions without all the distractions that the larger city provided. Particularly appealing was the total lack of nightlife, which the city elders encouraged to promote safe, family-oriented vacations. Just the kind of 'vacation' that Octavio Suarez wanted for his charges.

A secluded resort, Empresa Rio de la Plata, had been selected as the team's headquarters months in advance, and millions of government dollars had been invested in updating the facility to enable it to welcome its distinguished guests. Security precautions were of the utmost concern. Therefore, the resort was cordoned off with a twenty-foot high, electric barbed wire fence around its entire perimeter. Continuous patrols by special canine commando squads of the elite Compania 601 Special Forces Squadron were in evidence even before the team arrived. Concrete barriers blocked all entrances to the compound, and an elaborate telecommunications and surveillance system was installed to monitor the activities in and around the facility.

Once inside the compound, the atmosphere changed drastically. Beautiful wooded glens offset the two training pitches that had been lovingly and painstakingly leveled and sodded over the past year. They were sodded with the same turf that would grace the newly renovated forty-two thousand seat Mar del Plata Stadium. The entertainment facilities for the team were extensive. Televisions in every player's room, pool and ping-pong tables, a fully stocked library, massage and physiotherapy rooms, swimming pools, tennis courts, basketball hoops, bocce courts, and hundreds of board games.

The kitchen had been modernized to provide the best nutritious fare that the top-flight chefs could offer. Nothing had been left to chance. Every detail had been checked, and double-checked. The press center was a building just inside the perimeter, close to the main entrance. It was far enough away from the players' quarters to ensure that the scribes would not be a constant bother, and it was the only building that the working press had access to inside the compound. The rest of the facility was restricted, off-limits by orders of Octavio Suarez.

This news was not at all well received by the hacks, for as much as the press was locked out, the inmates were certainly locked in. Players could not leave the compound unescorted under any condition. Written approval for leave had to be obtained from the manager himself, and no one else. This was a bitter pill for the media, for it meant that there would be no exclusive interviews with this player or that player at a local cantina or restaurant.

Wives and families were encouraged to visit the players on Sunday afternoons, but there were no overnight conjugal visits. Eight weeks of abstention. Not a real problem for Renaldo De Seta, for the memory of his embrace with Simone was enough to keep the fire burning in his heart until they met again. But for some of the veteran players, eight weeks was an eternity. As Renaldo learned on his very first night, even some of the younger players thought it the most draconian and undemocratic of rules.

"Man, how am I going to sneak some pussy into my room? I will never last. I will be cut from the team due to sexual frustration. My balls will be so big from lack of use that they will drag behind me as I try to run down the field. I can't stand this. It's only the first night, and I'm going crazy."

Ramon Vida was pacing around Renaldo's room. "I wish I had a cigarette. Damn! How about you, man. You got a girlfriend yet?" Renaldo blushed slightly, not knowing what to say.

"Well, not exactly. There is one girl who is very special to me, but nothing has come of it yet."

"Don't worry. Just wait until you're a big star, a World Cup champion. Then they will all fall on their knees before you. My girl, oooo la la, did she give me a going away party! Toni is her name. I have a picture. Here, take a look."

He tenderly pulled the photo from his wallet. To Renaldo's amusement and stimulation, it turned out to be a full frontal nude picture leaving nothing to the imagination.

"She is very pretty, and well built it seems."

"Man, you can't even see her best asset. She just loves to give head, can do it for hours. God, I'm going to miss her. I think I'm going crazy already. How about some music?" With that, he was gone, soon to return with his oversized portable cassette machine, the Bee Gee's "Staying Alive" pumping from the speakers.

"Hey, baby, do you know how to disco? These Bee Gees are amazing. They just make me want to get down!" He was strutting and twirling around the room. Then he cranked the volume switch without missing a beat. "Stayin' Alive, Stayin' Alive, Ah, Ah, Ah, Ah, Stayin' Alive, Stayin' Alive."

The music had attracted other players from the single-level complex. Soon, Renaldo's room was jammed with his would-be teammates, singing, dancing, clapping, and laughing through the entire album. Ramon even gave disco lessons to a few of the more cement-footed onlookers.

Renaldo was an unwilling participant in Señor Vida's school of modern moves and received good-natured jibes about the necessity of being more proficient with his feet for the morning's dancing lessons. For those, Octavio Suarez would be the dance instructor, and the ballroom floor would be the newly laid green carpet outside their dormitory windows.

Estes Santos was the first sight Renaldo focused on at 6:45 a.m. the next morning.

"The adventure begins!" Santos shouted at the top of his voice as he entered the room. There were no locks on the doors at the Empreza de la Plata. Octavio Suarez was a firm believer in curfews and bed checks. In Estes' case, it was more likely that he would break the rules than be in a position to enforce them. But the goalkeeper coach had undertaken his new position with a serious, workman-like attitude. He knew that this would be his one chance to grab the golden ring. Renaldo looked at his watch.

"You are early. I've still got fifteen minutes to sleep. Go away and leave me alone," he moaned.

"The early bird gets Señor Suarez's favor. He is already in the dining hall waiting to see the order and state of alertness that you Nañdus show up in. He watches everything. Start off on the right foot, my friend. Get down there!" He yanked the covers off the naked player. "Now!"

Renaldo groaned as the image of the scrawny Nañdu bird flashed through his mind.

Sure enough, Octavio Suarez sat in a corner of the dining hall, chain smoking, drinking repeated cups of coffee, and scribbling intermittently in his binder. No one spoke to him or acknowledged his presence.

Number seventeen was not the first player to make his way to the dining room. Four other veterans were already half finished with their light meal of fruit, juice, high fiber breads and cereals, topped off with gallons of piping hot coffee. The cafeteria-style facility appealingly displayed its bounty for all the pampered patrons. Coffee, juice, and a slice of toast was all the extra baggage Renaldo felt like carrying today. He took a table by himself after being ignored by the older players. The room slowly filled up, with Ramon Vida and defenders Daniele Bennett and Julio Paredes joining Renaldo at his table.

All were dressed in new light-grey sweat suits that had been distributed the evening before. These togs would be the standing uniform of the camp. Long sweatpants and grey sweat tops at all meals, meetings, and training sessions. Personal clothing could be worn only in the dormitories during leisure hours and on visitor's day. Powder-blue and white-striped National Team jerseys and dark-blue soccer shorts could be worn on the training pitch during actual on-field play.

Control! Octavio Suarez was in total control here, and every man in the compound knew it.

"Good morning, gentlemen. Señors Luque, Santos, and I welcome you all and wish you all the best of luck in your upcoming audition. You have all had ample opportunity to digest the theory and tactical analysis laid out for you in your training bibles. Today, we are going to transfer what is written on paper to poetry on grass. You will see, if you have absorbed the written material, that theory will become tangible physical movement, and tactics will become a flowing art form!"

It was evident by the squirming around the room that the professor's students were having trouble making sense of his cerebral philosophy. The puzzling stares made Suarez redefine his lecture strategy.

"In short, we will be using a 4-3-3 formation with two lateral attacking backs. Let us not worry about who is present here today and who is not. Just do the job that your position demands, while keeping focused on our system and the goals of the team. I repeat, the goals of the team, for this is, and always will be, a team!"

Rules, regulations, schedules, and procedures were reiterated to the assembled mass. The rest of the morning was spent with the team doctors on an individual basis. General practitioners, physiotherapists, psychologists, "everything but proctologists and gynecologists," one player was overheard saying.

Those pronounced physically fit were told to report to the playing fields to commence their individual physical evaluation. This included timed sprints, timed laps, sit-ups, push-ups, footwork drills, and finally, an obstacle course. The players were then sent to shower and have a light lunch, followed by two hours of siesta time. At three o'clock, they were to assemble once more in the dining hall, which would become a multipurpose classroom, lecture hall, auditorium, and of course, gastronomic gallery. When everyone was present, they would be led by their coaches in a ceremonial walk down to the training fields to commence the first group workout of Argentina's 1978 World Cup Soccer Team.

Renaldo had little trouble with any of the sessions. He much preferred the physical trials to being poked, prodded, and pounded by the medical men. The psychologist had worried about his youthfulness. Would he miss his mother, his family, his dog? Could he stand to live with real men, many of whom were less than paternalistic in their outlook on life? The egos, the tempers, it was all part of what he was about to experience in the next eight weeks. He had thanked the doctor and assured him that he would confide his innermost traumas, should any arise.

The only trauma that the youngest player in camp was experiencing at the moment was one of anticipation. After so much waiting, so much talk, so much speculation, just what would it be like when he finally took the field with the best players in Argentina? Would he embarrass himself? Would he find out that he was in over his head as his mother had suggested? Would he be sent packing with his tail between his legs?

Three o'clock. The moment of truth had arrived.

Drills commenced with limbering up and callisthenic routines. This sequence would be repeated in the same order through to the end of the tournament. Ball drills were next. Short passing, long passing, dribbling, corner kicks, free kicks, penalty kicks. Next, defensive marking systems were discussed, and finally, the twenty-two were divided into 'A' and 'B' squads, two full teams of eleven men each.

Renaldo was placed on the B squad along with Ramon Vida. The A squad members were the veteran players, or the perceived first team. Players that manager Suarez had seen play many times, players that were known quantities to the headman. The B squad was comprised of the young, unproven players plus the old, perhaps too-long-in-tooth veterans.

The style of play would emphasize ball control. Short, controlled passes resulting in a slow offensive buildup, complemented when appropriate, by the attacking outside backs joining the push forward. There would be one deep back, known as the libero, whose job was purely defensive. This player's primary duty was to sweep the ball upfield and out of harm's way when his territory was threatened.

The tempo and flow of the game would be dictated by the ball's proximity to their own goal. The further away the ball traveled, the more leisurely and artistic the players could become. But when the black-and-white globe was in their third of the field, an aggressive defense was expected to clear the ball from the danger zone.

Initially, the defenses would concentrate on man-to-man marking while perfecting their offside trap. The outside halfbacks were primarily defensive feeders to relay the ball up the field to the forwards. They could join the attack, but only if the man they were marking defensively could not turn into an offensive threat during a counterattack. The center half had much more latitude. He often became the instigator of the attack by creating space for others to run into by means of his deft dribbling. Ideally, he would then hit one of his teammates with a precision pass. He was the quarterback, the man who most often controlled the flow of the game, if everything was going well.

The forwards, well, they were simply the forwards! The money men, the goal scorers, the headline grabbers! They were usually the most temperamental group on any team, and they could either become overpowering or overanxious in the heat of a tight contest. A striker on his game is an awesome sight to witness. As awesome as it is pathetic when the perfect setup is misplayed, then an accusing finger is pointed at everyone but himself.

Nervous anticipation was the predominant emotion as the players lined up for the first actual scrimmage. The A squad field chart lined up as follows:

Position (age)
(club team)

Forwards (strikers)

Pastor (26) Talleres Córdoba	Rios (24) Independiente	Gitares (24) Newton's Prefects

Halfbacks (halves)

Castillo (30) Talleres Córdoba	Cruz (22) Independiente	Velasquez (25) Talleres Córdoba

Fullbacks (defenders)

Bennett (29) Union Sante Fe	Chacon (28) Independiente	Suazo (24) River Plate	Calderone (27) Newton's Prefects

Goalkeeper

Calix (27)
Huracan

This lineup combined both the obvious and the subtle. Junior Calix in goal had just finished an outstanding season with an absolutely horrible Huracan team. His composed and unselfish effort had not gone unoticed, and he was manager Suarez's choice to replace the absent Hugo Bravo.

The four defenders were very solid and experienced. Juan Chacon would act as the sweeper and general of the defense. Calderone was an exacting passer, Bennett a tenacious tackler, and Suazo stood six feet four inches, giving the back line some additional height to clear dangerous balls out of the air.

There seemed some room to maneuver at halfback. Humberto Velasquez was a good defensive half, coming from a very defense-oriented team in Talleres Córdoba. Whether he could change the flow of his game to find the fleet-footed strikers that Suarez had assembled remained to be seen. Miguel Cruz at center half looked very solid, if he could control his temper.

The oldest player on the roster, Carlos Castillo, had been reunited on the left side with longtime teammate Daniele Bennett. The two had sparkled together a few years earlier at River Plate, and now, in the twilight of their careers, they had returned to their respective hometowns to play out their remaining seasons.

Octavio Suarez had coached both men at River Plate, and he needed their maturity and steadiness. The two amigos had developed a sixth sense in relation to each other's whereabouts on a football pitch over their years together, and Suarez was counting on them to renew that intimate bond.

Castillo's teammate at Córdoba, Nicolas Pastor, was given his familiar left side forward slot. The feeling was that Pastor, Castillo, and Bennett had an excellent opportunity to really communicate well and make things happen.

The right side was locked up by league leading goal scorer Ruben Gitares of Newton's Prefects. The center forward position was being held for the arrival of Nico Garcia from Spain, but in the meantime, someone had to fill the spot. To provide a semblance of continuity up the middle, Independiente's most prolific marksman, Enrique Rios, was slotted into the glamour position. This formation gave Chacon, Cruz, and Rios an Independiente run up the center of the field.

Everyone knew that this lineup was not etched in stone, especially with the pending return of the three European players. But it seemed to manager Suarez a logical place to start, and he had time to see if his logic was correct or not.

Renaldo's counterpart at center half on the A squad, and the man he would have to beat out to make the starting lineup, was a cocky spark plug of a player named Miguel Cruz. Cruz made up for what he lacked in refined talent with a bulldog tenacity and a whirlwind style. At twenty-two, he had already played three seasons with Independiente's first division team, and his quick development was often linked to the tutelage of his mentor, club-mate, and brother-in-law by marriage, 'Killer' Juan Chacon.

Number seventeen knew that he had his work cut out for him in playing against the often explosive-tempered Cruz, not to mention his terrifyingly ugly relative lurking in support on the back line.

Well, no time like the present to find out if this whole thing is a joke or not, he thought to himself as Ramon Vida directed the ball onto his right foot with a short back-pass to start the scrimmage.

From the beginning, he seemed a marked man. It was almost as if Octavio Suarez had told the A squad to test the rookie to the limit. Players swarmed all over him. Every touch of the ball invited two 'touches' to his person. The Under Twenty-One player was pulled, pushed, tripped, elbowed, and even cleated by the infamous Señor Chacon. Disorganized frustration could best describe the B squad's efforts that first afternoon. A 4-1 drubbing was actually a compliment to their defensive resiliency.

The veterans had surged at their defense in continuous waves, unrelenting and unforgiving. There was, however, one bright moment for the underdogs. Up 3-0, the A's seemed to get off their tempo for two or three minutes. B striker Caesar Castro hit the upright with a booming thirty-yard rocket. Seconds later, Renaldo miraculously found some space.

B halfback Victor Ciro stripped the ball from his opponent, Pastor, and right-footed his prize perfectly to the waiting rookie center half. No one approached Renaldo as he gathered in the pass heading diagonally upfield. Angling toward his opponent's deep sideline, he picked out Ramon Vida making a parallel run thirty yards upfield. The defense seemed content to let the rookie run out of real estate to make his play in, and once he was trapped in their web, they would descend upon him and simply relieve him of the ball.

As Vida was crossing the penalty arch some twenty yards out from keeper Calix, Renaldo fed him a perfect pass that he, in turn, one-timed into the lower left-hand corner of the net. Both B players had been running on an angle past and away from the A squad goal, and the last thing Junior Calix expected was a shot back to his right side, against the flow of play. He didn't move a muscle as the back of the net bulged with Vida's hard drive.

'Killer' Chacon was immediately in Renaldo's face.

"Fucking schoolboy, don't you every pull a stunt like that in front of me again. The next time you come down here, I will introduce my elbow to your front teeth! Now get back on your half of the field and stay there."

The final word was emphasized with an unfriendly shove to Renaldo's right shoulder. The rookie stumbled back two paces, only to be embraced by the jubilant Ramon Vida, who had sought Renaldo out to offer his thanks for the setup.

"Nice pass, hotshot! The Ugly One is pissed, though. Let's get out of here." He steadied his teammate, then turned him around and led him back over the half line.

"Fucking babies! Don't come back again!" was 'Killer's' farewell.

It turned out that Renaldo never had the opportunity to cross back into hostile territory. Rueben Gitares retaliated for the A's less than half a minute after the ensuing kickoff, and Suarez blew the whistle ending the session. He had seen enough.

A standard post-scrimmage routine was unveiled that first day. Shower, steam, massage, and physio time were allotted before assembling for the evening meal. An informal team meeting would accompany dessert and coffee, then a first-run movie was shown in the lounge. There was an hour or so of free time before room check and lights out.

Players would gather in small groups in one room or another, and once Ramon Vida heard Renaldo play his acoustic Gibson guitar, he made sure that his new friend and the instrument were always available for an impromptu sing-song.

Classically trained with a profound knowledge of the abundant guitar heritage of Argentina, the rich melodies and intricate finger work that Renaldo preferred to play were always saved for his private moments. His teammates wanted up-tempo pop songs, meaning disco, or perhaps something from the Swedish group, Abba.

Always a good improviser with a keen ear, once the introverted guitarist had heard the melody on Vida's tape recorder, he could pick it up and craft a Bee Gee's tune in minutes. After several nights as the extroverted Vida's instrumental sidekick, Renaldo's painful shyness seemed to subside with the acceptance of his musical skills by his peers.

Ramon Vida had become the vocalist in the new duo, saying that the guitarist's voice reminded him of fingernails scraping on a blackboard. Renaldo was fast warming to the brashly outspoken player from Boca, and the two seemed to spend most of their free time together, rehearsing new songs to entertain their teammates. Ramon's earthy sense of humor and his constant yearning for female companionship kept Renaldo not only thinking of Simone, but fantasizing vividly about their last encounter.

The bond that made the 'R&Rs,' as Ramon named their act, a tight duo musically, was also evident on the training fields. As players shifted back and forth from the A squad to the B squad depending on manager Suarez's fancy, the R&R duo seemed to find each other and create dangerous opportunities, if not goals, on every occasion that they were teamed together. The musical combo continued to draw the ire of 'Killer' Chacon, who did not partake in any of their free-time jam sessions, and who also insisted that the rest of his Independiente followers stay away from the 'fucking mamas' boys.'

The R&Rs were undisturbed by this rebuff, and it was evident that the two B squad Independiente players, Arzu and Argueta, would have liked to join in the fun that the dynamic duo provided the rest of the team.

While he grudgingly played the showman for Ramon and his teammates, it was the few solitary moments alone in his room that Renaldo cherished the most. He would sit on his bed, softly strumming staccato cords while he hummed or half sang the words of his most revered composer-lyricist.

His father had first introduced him to the bossa nova rhythm from Brazil when he was a small boy. Sergio Mendez and João Gilberto melodies soon became musical mainstays in Casa San Marco. But it was the songs and lyrics of the incomparable Antonio Carlos Jobim that truly inspired the boy. His "Girl from Ipanema" single was a commercial success on all five continents, even though it was popularized in much of the world by a Sergio Mendez cover version. Antonio Carlos Jobin had collaborated in the recording studio with some of the greatest names in modern music, from Brazilian jazz pioneer Laurindo Almeida, through bossa nova creators Gilberto and Luis Bonfa, to legends like tenor sax great Stan Getz and guitarist Charlie Byrd. His musical coup, however, was the recording of a landmark album in Los Angeles in 1967 with Frank Sinatra.

Arranged and conducted with full orchestration by the meticulous Claus Ogerman, the 'Francis Albert Sinatra-Antonio Carlos Jobim' album was an international chart-topper that popularized the Brazilian's velvet melodies and lamenting vocals to millions. That particular album remained Renaldo's all-time favorite, and he carried the cassette tape of these two musical virtuosos in his guitar case. It was as cherished as the instrument itself.

Thoughts of Simone flooded his mind as he played and softly sang the master's gifts just for her. The melody was never a problem for him, but the singing voice . . . it was more of a whining croak. His speaking voice had been deep and mature since puberty, no problem. But once he changed its normal pitch or key, dogs started to bark. So he kept it soft, barely a whisper, as he longingly played "Insensatez," "Corcovado," or his favorite, "Desafinado."

"Sensuous Symca Fills Maracana!" blazed the headline in the Rio paper that Simone had clipped and sent him. She had written twice, which Renaldo found flattering, considering her nonstop touring schedule. Filling immense Maracana Stadium with two hundred thousand people was no small task, but the Brazilians were morbidly curious, as well as confident, that this foreigner would not live up to the preshow hype. Swept up in their own World Cup fever, they came in droves to see the host nation's number one sex symbol. Many of them were prepared to have a bit of fun at her expense in a boisterous, pep rally-type atmosphere.

Arriving on stage in only a yellow Brazilian football jersey with matching yellow spiked heels, the sexy singer embraced the audience, blowing kisses to the throng, backed by a pulsating samba beat. She had the crowd eating out of the palm of her hand before she even sang a note.

Symca was the toast of Rio the following morning, and the influx of tour orders for World Cup '78 that flooded travel agencies the next few days were directly attributed to Argentina's hottest football ambassador.

Renaldo reread her letter and tried to translate the newspaper article from Portugese to Spanish, but he never mentioned their existence, nor his relationship with the most famous woman in Argentina to anyone. Not even Ramon Vida.

His personal life was no secret to the two nonplayer guests who, from time to time, would drop by his room for a quiet chat. One of them, Estes Santos, would lustily ask for any details of his young friend's courtship of the starlet. Knowing Estes as he did, Renaldo did not take offense, rather he would shift the topic of conversation to criticizing his performance on the soccer pitch. He had asked Estes to keep his relationship with Simone a private matter, and the goalkeeper coach did not betray his vow of silence. Santos would also ask of news from home, of Florencia, even Lonnie. How was his mother coping as the start of the university semester drew closer? With the first international exhibition matches about to commence, it was out of the question that he would be available to start the school year, barring injuries or outright dismissal from the team, of course.

Renaldo responded that his mother seemed surprisingly calm about the situation. In fact, it was never mentioned at all in her sporadic letters. By the tone of her missives, she seemed in particularly good spirits. Lonnie and Celeste had been working at No Se Preocupe the last few weeks, and the older brother had promised Florencia that he was going back to school. That would make his mother happy, but not as euphoric as parts of her letters seemed to be. No, there was something else going on in the life of Florencia De Seta that her youngest son could not put his finger on. *Better euphoric than depressed,* was the boy's overall attitude as he thanked heaven for small mercies.

The other visitor that knew of his romantic yearnings was none other than Astor Gordero. The attorney's family had owned a mansion on the beach in Mar del Plata for years, and Astor would take the sun and surf each summer like countless others, albeit much more lavishly. The selection of the seaside resort town as the team's training headquarters had been spearheaded by The Fat Man, and now that they were in residence, it afforded him the opportunity to keep an eye on how things were proceeding. He was also able to titillate his young client with news of the boy's famous heartthrob. Renaldo enjoyed Gordero's visits, not only for the insights on Simone, but also for the firsthand knowledge that he always acquired on everything from the team and its composition, to the activities of the organizing committee and the preparedness of the facilities.

Astor Gordero had a willing and enthusiastic audience in the bright, curious schoolboy, and Astor Gordero was one man that loved to hear himself talk. Renaldo was amazed by the politicking and arm twisting that took place in the committee rooms, which the visitor described down to the most minute of details. As the two talked, one could sense a bond of friendship and trust developing, at least on the younger man's part. He would look forward to 'El Hombre Gordo's' visits, for the player always felt that he was the guardian of secret or privileged information after a tête-à-tête with his knowledgeable agent.

But Astor Gordero was not one to tip all his cards in the great game of life. There was always some angle, something hidden up his sleeve. In this case, it was his current orchestrations regarding his client's mother, Florencia.

Since their initial meeting at the race track, Gordero had spoken to Señora De Seta several times on the telephone. Initially making contact on the pretext of having information on her youngest son's progress in Miramar, Gordero soon discreetly maneuvered the conversation to the topic of financial planning for Renaldo, should he become successful in his attempt to make the National Team.

Florencia was mildly flattered at the incredible amount of fan mail and requests for Renaldo's poster that were arriving daily at the National Team mail depot, according to her new large friend. The Teatro Colon appearance on national television had given the señoritas a fresh face to dream about at night, and it was the simple name 'Renaldo' that appeared on the envelopes of hundreds of inquiring letters.

Her son was handsome, and she knew that it was more than just maternal pride that allowed her to say that. She voiced concerned, however, that this newfound attention would somehow distract him from his toils. Gordero assured her that fan mail would only become available to the players after training camp was over. Only immediate relatives and close friends had the direct address to the Miramar training facility. There were secretaries sorting and organizing the requests on the players' behalf at this very moment. Those that made the team would spend time back in Buenos Aires on days called 'press days,' signing autographs and promotional material such as fan mail, posters, flags, hats, and much more.

At this stage, Renaldo had no inkling that he was fast becoming Argentina's new mystery sensation, and Octavio Suarez was bound and determined to keep it that way.

"My concerns for your son deal with addition, not adulation, my dear lady," Gordero exclaimed. "As I have told you previously, the boy stands to make millions of dollars in salaries and endorsements, even if he plays only a year or two. It is my desire as his attorney, and I feel, close friend, to make sure that every potential financial windfall is investigated and acted upon with extreme diligence. It is a swamp full of alligators out there, and there are many unscrupulous individuals just waiting to prey on a new, unsuspecting victim. I do not want Renaldo, or yourself, Señora, to fall victim to these scoundrels."

A look of remorse was the perfect accompaniment to the revelations of a cruel world. A pause for effect, then Gordero continued.

"To prepare a proper business plan for your son, however, I feel that it would be prudent for me to survey the boy's entire financial picture. In other words, for me to know his total asset base, as well as details such as when legacies or other inheritance benefits accrue. This will enable me to stagger the payments to your son and reduce his overall tax consequences. It is a sad matter, but have no doubt, Señora, the tax payments will be substantial on anything he makes in this country."

Florencia was impressed with the lawyer's thoroughness. The technicalities of the various trusts and estates were something that she, for the most part, left to the executors to sort out. There was always more than enough money at her disposal, but she now had to face the reality that her youngest son's financial independence was imminent, football career or no football career.

If Renaldo truly trusts this man, would it not be best to consolidate his assets as Señor Gordero suggests? she mused as the lawyer kept up a constant monologue on the other end of the telephone.

"Señor Gordero, perhaps you could drop by Casa San Marco in the near future and we could discuss this matter in person."

"I am at your disposal, Señora."

Two days later, Astor Gordero was seated in Figueroa San Marco's old office.

"If these walls could talk, Señora De Seta, I believe they would be able to relate the whole story of the modern industrial revolution in Argentina. Between your late father-in-law, Señor Lonfranco, and General San Marco, this room has hosted presidents and diplomats from all over the world. It is a historically rich and fascinating place. I feel honored to be here."

"Thank you, Señor Gordero. It is true, this room has a different feel about it than any other in the casa. My late husband used to come in here, close the door, and just sit for hours behind that desk when he needed a place to think. He would say that the ghosts would help him decide what to do, that the history in this room held the answers for him. Perhaps you and Herr Stoltz will add to that history."

Wolfgang Stoltz had been brought along by his employer because of his special facility for untangling complicated estate matters. He also had a special facility for undressing attractive, wealthy widows. It was this particular skill that brought him to the attention of Astor Gordero's father, years earlier.

As a young lawyer, Stoltz had specialized in estate law. After being hired by A.R. Gordero and Sons to fill a vacancy in their trust and estates division, it quickly became evident that the novice German barrister had a knack for unleashing pent-up romantic emotions in the frustrated, lonely ladies that were most often the beneficiaries of the estates he oversaw. Wolfgang Stoltz played his role as faithful employee and diligent counsel to perfection, and the client roster of A.R. Gordero and Sons quickly swelled with the names of most of the single financial heiresses in the capital.

Discretion in high places was mandatory, and Herr Stoltz's reputation was never tarnished by his extra-legal liaisons. Quite the contrary, he became the most sought-after attorney in all of Buenos Aires. His intelligent, reassuring manner of explaining and simplifying complicated estate documents always seemed to put his wealthy, usually attractive, clients at ease, so much at ease, that the majority of Stoltz's work was carried out in opulent hotel suites at all hours of the day and night. He was well rewarded by both his clients and his firm for his deft touch, and he had never entertained thoughts of striking out on his own or settling down with one special woman. Wolfgang Stoltz loved variety, and his profession afforded him an opportunity to use his special talents on a variety of appreciative clients.

Florencia De Seta was now experiencing what a legion of similar Porteña señoras had experienced before her. She was smitten by the handsome German, there was no denying that!

During their conversation that afternoon in the office at Casa San Marco, Florencia could sense a more than a purely business interest on his behalf as well. It was, in particular, the way he looked at her. She could feel his eyes upon her, asking mute questions, searching beneath her exterior guise for a more intimate connection as she tried to simplify her family's financial structure for her two guests.

"The two family real estate assets, this home and the land and estancia in Pergamino, are held in a trust set up by my mother-in-law, Lydia De Seta. Upon her death, sole ownership rests with her grandsons, who are, of course, my sons, Lonfranco and Renaldo. If she dies before Renaldo reaches twenty-one years of age, those two properties are held in the estate until his twenty-first birthday. Once Renaldo is twenty-one, the hard assets vest in the two boys, and they have the option of maintaining both properties, or one brother can buy out the other using a loan from the undistributed portion of his personal trust. The personal trusts were also set up by Lydia, and they vest in the boys at age thirty."

The widow paused to make certain that her guests were following her train of thought. A warm smile and a nod from Herr Stoltz confirmed that she could proceed.

"There are two preliminary payments of two hundred thousand dollars each at ages twenty-one and twenty-five. So you see, gentlemen, one of my sons, Lonfranco, has already received his first payment of two hundred thousand dollars, and is due to receive another in two years. Renaldo's first payment will be in May of 1980. Both boys have the option of taking loans from their trusts after age eighteen. The current trustees are accountants with the firm Martinez-Riachuelo, and they report to the boys and me on a quarterly basis. Lonfranco took some money from his distribution for his personal use, but left most of the cash in the trustee's hands to invest on his behalf. Am I making sense so far, gentlemen?"

"Very lucid and precise, Señora, please continue," Wolfgang Stoltz replied in a soft tone.

"It is my sincere hope that by the time the boys inherit the bulk of their assets, they will have obtained not only an education, but the business acumen that will enable them to handle their own investments. That is why I feel so strongly about Renaldo not wasting his time with this football foolishness. He has the mental capacity to not only attend medical school, but also to learn about the world of finance and commerce. He is a very bright boy, and I will not have him sidetracked for long, Señor Gordero!"

"Once again, Señora De Seta, let me assure you that the financial benefits of a professional football career can be maximized in a very short time, with the right person overseeing the deal-making. If your son has the athletic potential that I and several others feel he does, he will be a very rich young man in a very short time. One other thing, Señora, is that he will have done it all on his own, and not through an inheritance or a trust. That self-esteem is something Renaldo's family fortune cannot give him at this stage of his life."

Gordero sat back in his chair, pleased with himself at parrying the widow's latest anti-football thrust.

"I suppose there is something to be said in that regard, Señor Gordero, but I worry about him so much. He is just a boy, suddenly living in a man's world. He has always been so shy in the presence of strangers. I fear he will be overwhelmed, taken advantage of. Do you understand a mother's fears, Señor?"

"I am sure Señor Gordero is sympathetic to your misgivings, Señora De Seta," Stoltz interjected, "but your son has found in Señor Gordero not just an attorney, but a trusted friend and confidant as well. It is our intention to provide Renaldo with the very best legal and financial advice, while at the same time educating him in the ways of contracts and agreements, so that he can use that knowledge in future business dealings. That will, at least, give him an introduction into the world of commerce and finance, as you so justifiably wish."

She found that his precise Germanic accent softly, yet authoritatively reinforced the logic of his words. Herr Stoltz seemed to be in calm control of the world around him, unlike so many of the hotheaded Latin businessmen she had been forced to deal with in the past. *I can trust this man!* she thought. As their discussions proceeded, she felt inclined to relate her own financial details to her guests, in case the two legal minds could offer her any suggestions in one way or another.

"My husband, Peter, and I were also the beneficiaries of two trusts established by my mother-in-law. On Peter's death, the assets of his trust became my property through his will. I draw a monthly income from my personal trust that more than covers my living expenses, for the real estate is still owned and maintained by Lydia. I also have investments that are a result of my family in Tigre. After both my parents passed away, the ferry business and our family home were sold at considerable profit. That money was divided among their surviving children, and that sum, alone, could have afforded me a comfortable lifestyle. The same accounting firm that act as trustees handle my personal investments, primarily for the sake of convenience. I sometimes wonder, however, if I should not take the assets that are under my direct control elsewhere. Having one accounting firm know everything about my financial situation is unsettling at times. Perhaps you, gentlemen, could take a look at my portfolio, at a later date."

It was difficult for Astor Gordero to keep the Cheshire cat grin off his face. This was exactly what he had set out to accomplish when he first contacted Señora De Seta. He had known that the family wealth was vast, but exactly who the controlling parties were and how the assets were distributed was a matter of delicate inquiry. As Wolfgang Stoltz confidently reassured the lady that A. R. Gordero and Sons specialized in managing some of the nation's most prominent families' financial portfolios, Astor Gordero already knew that Florencia De Seta could be convinced to do anything he desired of her.

While it was clear that using his trump card was not necessary to gain the information he had sought, Astor Gordero decided that its use would add some excitement to the proceedings. Yes, he would allow it. He would allow Wolfgang Stoltz to court and seduce Florencia De Seta. That done, it was appropriate to turn his attention to the timely demise of Lydia De Seta, so that all the family assets would flow through to Florencia and her sons. The total control of their family fortune would not be long in coming once Lydia had left this world.

It has been a very successful meeting, very successful indeed! an enthused Astor Gordero thought to himself as he waddled through the front gate of Casa San Marco and into his waiting Mercedes. Herr Stoltz would now close the deal, in more ways than one.

CHAPTER EIGHTEEN

Early March brought cooling winds to Mar del Plata, and flying in on those winds came the National Team of Uruguay, intent on giving the local heroes their first bitter taste of international competition. The fixture could not be played in the main stadium due to several construction mishaps which had severely delayed completion of the renovations. More importantly, one of the near disasters was the collapse of the player's tunnel leading to the pitch. Luckily, the tunnel was deserted at the time, and the popular joke in town was that no laborer could ever be hurt working on the sight because they were always having lunch or a coffee break.

The situation was so bad at the Mar del Plata Stadium that the Brazilians had cancelled their participation in the Copa Roca, saying that the venue was unfit for use. Octavio Suarez was livid at the rebuff, but most of his ire was directed at the local organizing committee for allowing the stadium debacle to occur in the first place. Assurances were given by the National Organizing Committee that work would be stepped up, and the National Guard was called in to supervise the pace of construction. In reality, the stadium workers became little more than slaves, working under the watchful eyes of armed guards.

The Uruguayan match was played in the smaller municipal stadium, under cloudless blue skies, in front of a noisy, capacity crowd. There was some pretty football played at intermittent intervals, but for the most part, it was a lackluster, tentative ninety minutes. Octavio Suarez chose to go with the entire A squad, without substitution, right up to full time. The crowd became restless when the veterans failed to produce a goal after sixty minutes, and there were calls for substitutions as well as jeers for the coaching staff. But Octavio Suarez stuck to his original game plan. Not one B squad player made it on to the field that afternoon. A 0-0 result was not well received by either those present or the national press. Suarez's rebuttal was one word . . . "Stamina!"

The following two weeks saw many experimental changes to the A squad in preparation for the upcoming matches, hastily arranged with Peru. The Ramon Castilla Cup was conceived at the eleventh hour to replace the failed Copa Roca. Two games would be played, the first on March nineteenth in Buenos Aires, followed only four days later by the return fixture in Lima.

The initial National Team game in the capital coincided with the relocation of training camp to an all-new facility on the outskirts of Buenos

Aires. The just completed National Training Center would be the player's home for the next three months or so, and the organizing committee had spared no luxury in making sure that the idols of the nation would train in first-class surroundings.

While there was comfort to be had off the practice fields, it was a different story out on the green turf. Octavio Suarez ravaged his charges for their lack of discipline and imagination. The manager hounded those men that he thought had performed poorly, and no reputation or past press adulation could save a player from a Suarez browbeating, if the boss set his sights on him.

Wholesale changes to the A squad were made on a daily basis, but when the team took the field in River Plate Stadium on the nineteenth, it was the original eleven A squad players that lined up against the Peruvians. The visitors scored an early goal, but Suarez would still not substitute. Whistles and expletives rained down from the galleries as the team descended into its refuge at the interval and, again, as they took the ball to kick off the second half.

A cheer arose from the crowd when the public address announcer proclaimed that the home side had used its two substitutions. Standing over the ball at the midfield spot was Ramon Vida, and ten yards to his rear stood the other half of the R&Rs, Renaldo De Seta.

From the whistle, the Argentines seemed a different team, pressing forward, always running, shooting at every opportunity. Within minutes, a beautiful give-and-go between old teammates Castillo and Bennett worked the magic for which Suarez had hoped. A twenty-five-yard blast from Bennett's attacking left foot found the back of the net. Tie score!

Several solid scoring opportunities followed for the men in the powder-blue and white-striped shirts. Surprisingly, it was often the youngest player on the pitch spearheading the attack with a precise pass or a dazzling run. The game winner came off the head of Jorge Calderone, who used his license to come forward with the play to redirect in a perfect lob from the captain of the day, Ruben Gitares.

Renaldo was generally pleased with his performance that evening, but one nagging incident lingered in his mind. It had occurred during a Peruvian corner kick late in the game. The rookie was back in Argentina's goal mouth, marking his opposite number on the Peruvian side. As the ball arched its way in the air toward the Argentine net, Ignacio Suazo and Juan Chacon leapt to head it out of harm's way. Suazo was able to make contact and clear, but as 'Killer' Chacon returned to earth, his well-placed elbow collided with the side of Renaldo's head, sending the boy sprawling.

"Stay on your feet, pansy. You're no good to anyone down there." Renaldo looked up at the apparition that had felled him, rolled over, and headed upfield with the play without saying a word.

"And don't get too comfortable in that position, sweetheart. It belongs to my brother-in-law!" were the words that followed him.

It seemed that in the future, Renaldo would have to face both the opposition and 'Killer' Chacon to earn his place in the starting eleven.

The twenty-third of March found the entire National Team high in the Andes Mountains, inside Nacional Stadium in Lima Peru. With eighty thousand rabid supporters cheering them on, the Peruvians were expected to make up for their lackluster showing in Buenos Aires. Drawn into group four with Holland, Scotland, and Iran, this aging, but experienced team had its work cut out for it to advance to the second round of the championships. At the moment, however, they were using these warm-up games to try to blend some inexperienced, but fresh legs with those of the slower veterans. It did not come together well on this day in Lima.

Again starting his original A eleven, Suarez's men took a quick two-goal lead that they then defended for the rest of the half with great authority. It was, by far, the best forty-five minutes the A's had played to date. Miguel Cruz and Ruben Gitares were the marksmen, and it was Cruz's strong showing that kept Renaldo on the bench for the entire match. Ramon Vida replaced Enrique Rios in the second half and scored a beautiful goal on a setup from Cruz late in the game. A decisive 3-1 victory for the Argentines made the return trip to Buenos Aires a high-spirited event for most of the team. One exception was Renaldo De Seta.

"Come on, man, you'll show them your stuff next week against the Bulgarians. Don't sweat it," chirped an elated Ramon Vida as he tried to bring his friend out of a depressed state.

"How can I show them anything, Ramon, if I don't even get on the field? The way Cruz played today, my chances don't look good to see any action next week, or ever."

"Oh, man, you sound like a sick old lady. Stop that feeling-sorry-for-yourself shit. Come on, I feel like singing. Get your guitar down from up above and the R&Rs will rock and roll, baby!"

Renaldo obliged, and soon the whole entourage, including the coaching staff, was joining in the course of Donna Summer's "Love to Love You, Baby." Ramon was right, of course, there was no sense worrying about someone else's performance. Renaldo could not control how well Cruz played. He could only make certain that he was ready to play his best whenever given the opportunity.

To the surprise of the entire team as well as the seventy thousand faithful that filled River Plate Stadium on the afternoon of March twenty-ninth, it was the eleven B squad players that took the field against the visiting Bulgarians. The Europeans had failed to advance to the World Championships, but Octavio

Suarez wanted to give his team a good dose of how football was played on the continent, especially as they faced three European teams in their own World Cup group. The Bulgarians fit the bill in that they played a style similar to the French and Hungarians. It was hoped that they would not treat their sojourn to South America as a tourist trip, but rather as a serious football excursion and play with attitude and intensity.

Whatever the case, whether it was too much local talent or too much disinterest on the part of the guest team, the home side ran roughshod over their iron curtain adversaries. The rhythm was there for all to see, beautiful, melodic, electrifying. Ramon Vida set a tenacious tempo, being everywhere the ball was in tallying two goals and an assist in a 3-1 Argentina victory. The crowd chanted "Vida, Vida, Vida," from the heights, and it looked like the nation had itself a new football hero.

Defender Julio Paredes had the other home side marker, set up nicely by Renaldo on a give-and-go. The rookie's critique of his game fell into the so-so category. No goals, one assist, and a scraped shin, courtesy of 'Killer' Chacon, who had been substituted in at the start of the second half. The Ugly One had unnerved him somewhat, and the Bulgarian goal came off a corner kick that Renaldo's mark volleyed into the net. The young center half had been tripped as the ball was in the air, leaving his man uncovered and able to convert. The boy could have sworn that the leg that sent him to the turf had a white stocking with light blue rings on it. A 'friendly' leg, perhaps belonging to Juan Chacon?

On the positive side, the Europeans were very loose in their marking, enabling the rookie to control his team's offensive flow. The crowd loved it, and the young player's performance earned him considerably higher esteem in the eyes of his manager than in his own self-estimation. The success of the B squad would certainly make the training sessions more competitive, which is exactly what Octavio Suarez had hoped.

One week later, another communist block country arrived in the capital to test the locals. Romania, like its predecessor Bulgaria, had not qualified for the big event, but their style of play mimicked that of the Italians. That is, severe defending, with a packed defense in a 1-3-4-2 lineup. Three backs, with one deep central defender playing the sweeper or catenaccio. This 'get the ball upfield' at any cost' role was carried out behind four halves, who were mostly interested in defending, and only two men up front on the attack.

For the first time, a mixture of A and B players took the field. Ramon Vida started at center forward, Miguel Cruz at center half. The host nation came out of the gate lethargically. Some pretty soccer here and there, but no finishing skills and not much intensity or drama. Tied at nil after the first forty-five, the two substitutions that Suarez made were certain to cause some resentment in the locker room after the game. Little-used Luis Anariba, the recovering but still tentative twin, replaced Juan Chacon at central defender. That was not so bad in itself, for 'Killer' was guaranteed a spot in the final lineup and Anariba was on his way out the door. It was the second substitution that would inflict the discomfort. Cruz out, De Seta in.

The Independiente clique would be very vocal in their disapproval of the withdrawal of Cruz, who, they felt, was not being given enough playing time after his stellar match in Lima.

For forty-five minutes, though, Renaldo was free to concentrate on his skills without looking over his shoulder for the ugliest man on earth. He knew that he would have to deal with the consequences later, but for now, football was all that mattered.

The massed defense of the Romanians that had once seemed impenetrable surprisingly started to crack within a few minutes of the second half whistle. Ruben Gitares and Ramon Vida cut swaths through the loosened marking, time and time again, finding space to make their magic. Only an acrobatic keeper in the visitors' goal kept the score knotted.

It was B striker Caesar Castro, playing on his home club turf at River Plate, that put the first one away after a scramble in front of the Bulgarian cage. The second home side goal was sure to have repercussions.

Substitute Anariba, who had not been severely tested by the offensively impotent Romanians, managed a swift clearing pass to Renaldo, who, in turn, headed upfield with his gift. Looking for a teammate to feed the ball to, he noticed that the center of the field seemed to open up and part like the Dead Sea. Vida and Gitares were taking their markers to the outside, and the Argentine center half had an unobstructed run up the middle, until he was three yards inside the penalty area.

At that point, the now overzealous defenders descended upon the young one and sent him unceremoniously crashing to the ground. The Columbian referee pointed to the penalty spot immediately. Ramon Vida was at his prone teammate's side at once.

"You OK, man? Check to make sure your dick is still there. That's all that matters!" His friend's offhand and unexpected comment made Renaldo laugh, even as he rubbed his aching hamstring muscle.

"Take the shot, man. It will look good on your résumé if you make it," Vida asserted.

"How will it look if I screw up, Ramon?" the center half replied while being lifted upright by his vocal partner.

"You will look like the pansy that Chacon says you are, my friend. Just imagine smashing the ball into his ugly mug. That's good for a guaranteed goal!"

Sure enough, as Renaldo stood at the spot eyeing an extremely nervous keeper, he visualized the hideous visage of his antagonist in the upper left corner of the net. The rest was easy. A swing of his powerful right leg, then swoosh. Goal! A perfect canon of a shot, upper left corner.

He turned and trotted toward the centerline without any show of emotion. An enthusiastic Ramon Vida joined him.

"Man, you must have really seen his face up there the way you let that one go. Ugly cocksucker! I wish it really was right there, right where you put that ball! Watch yourself, my friend. That Independiente scum will be pissed off."

"Maybe it would have been better for you to take the damn penalty. You could have imagined some pussy in the top corner. Guaranteed goal, right?" Both men chuckled as they resumed their positions.

A 2-0 victory lifted the national spirit throughout the length and breadth of Argentina. Its team was undefeated in their last five international matches, and talk of a world championship was quietly circulating in the cafés and bars around the country.

The players had two weeks to rest and recharge their batteries before facing their next opponent, Eire, or as some preferred, the Republic of Ireland. River Plate Stadium and the host side would prove daunting obstacles to the men of the Republic. They would need more than shamrocks and shelaighlees on this day in South America.

On the home front there was optimism at all levels, with the possible exception of the Independiente players currently with the National Team. This group of men had only one task, one goal to achieve. They set about making life as difficult as possible for the young center halfback that had been critically acclaimed in the press after his last two outings. Chacon's crew wanted the rookie gone, and the prospect of the 'pretty boy' throwing in the towel and leaving camp spurred them on their miserable way.

Two weeks in hell would be an apt description of Renaldo's life, following the Romanian fixture. Both on and off the training field, Chacon and his buddies were relentless in their baiting and badgering of the team's youngest player. Rough treatment on the pitch and psychological warfare off it seemed to be the order of the day. Ramon Vida pleaded with his friend to take his case to manager Suarez, "to have those poisonous thorns removed from your feet!" Renaldo would have none of it.

"Everyone is just trying to make this team and they don't care how they go about it," he had responded to Vida. "I won't go bellyaching to Suarez like some mama's boy. That's already what they think I am. I can handle it. What I do on the field will state my case! All that other shit, well, don't worry. I won't give them the satisfaction of breaking me."

All that other shit included the ransacking of his room on several occasions, for there were no locks on the doors at Suarez's behest. Renaldo's equipment was tampered with, causing him to report late to the training pitch more than once, but the most serious offence concerned the cleats of his soccer boots, which just happened to have an unauthorized adjustment. The resultant bleeding and blistered feet were not a pretty sight. The verbal abuse was constant, with most of it coming from Chacon and Cruz. Renaldo would just turn the other cheek and walk away.

The Independiente players also presented him with several on-field trophies for his troubles. A blackened right eye, delivered personally by Señor Chacon, a lovely gouged shin, with love from Miguel Cruz, and an assortment of bumps and bruises from the supporting cast. The cooler Renaldo remained, the more livid Ramon Vida became.

"We have to do something about those assholes, man! They are driving me crazy, and it's you that they are attacking," Ramon implored as he once again, lifted his teammate upright after another rough encounter.

"Don't get involved, amigo. They are not out to steal your position on the team," a winded, aching Renaldo advised. "They only want to make sure that Cruz gets his! They won't break me, Ramon. You can count on that!"

Estes Santos finally visited Renaldo's room one night to talk about the Independiente problem. The situation hadn't gone unnoticed by the coaching staff, but so far, Octavio Suarez had not intervened.

"Are you alright, my captain? They've been riding you fairly hard, I understand. Can I do anything to get them off your back? Suarez is impressed with you, in case you didn't know. Every position is still wide open as far as he's concerned. The boss has been testing you with this, to see how far you'll let them push you. Some say you will pack your bags and go home to your mother. But I don't think so! And more importantly, neither does Suarez!"

"Estes, thank you, but I'm not going anywhere! Unless I'm released from the team, that is. In that case, I won't have to worry about the rotten apples in the barrel, will I?"

"Renaldo, you're not going to be cut from this team, so you'll have to deal with this situation right now. It won't go away until you do. In order to earn the starting center half position, you'll just have to tough it out in Suarez's eyes. We both know that is your goal, isn't it? The starting position, not riding the bench." Their eyes met at that moment. Old friends, teacher-student, a special relationship. Santos smiled warmly, then continued.

"But these guys are pussy cats compared to butting heads with the Italians or Brazilians. Rough treatment isn't all that bad a thing for you to get used to on the training pitch. It's all the off-field shit that I want stopped. You'll let me know if the heat gets too intense, won't you?"

"Again, thank you, Estes. I'm OK, really! There are some good players on this team. It should do pretty well. There are some nice guys, too. New friends, friends like I've never had before. Interesting people, all of them." Renaldo smiled back reassuringly at the older man. "I have to get through this myself, Estes. I knew when I came to camp that this would be the toughest thing I had ever done in my eighteen years, and it is! But it is also the most exciting thing that I have ever done. To stand at center field in River Plate Stadium and start the second half representing my country against the Peruvians was an indescribable feeling. Goose bumps. Every young Argentine's dream. When I was little, playing in our garden at the casa, I was always playing for the National Team in my mind. The dream became reality, Estes, and I want to keep that reality alive. So don't worry about me. Besides, Ramon Vida says he's going to 'fucking kill the ugly cocksuckers' if they lay a hand on me again. I bet that tough bastard would, too. He grew up on the streets of Boca as a gang leader. He's told me some stories . . . Anyway, how are things going with you?" Renaldo thought it time to deflect the conversation somewhat.

"It's a bitch, to tell you the truth! After all this time, five international games, Calix and Martinez have allowed the same number of goals with exactly the same amount of playing time. Calix should be the starter, but his feet have turned to cement a few times and his clearing has been erratic. Martinez is cockier. I think he wants it more. I like his style better, too. More vocal, a real field general. Calix never says boo unless someone is breathing down his neck. At this point, I don't know, it's a coin toss."

They said their good-byes with the coach promising to keep an eye out for his former captain, but the matter was never discussed again.

Lady Luck was not with Octavio Suarez in the days leading up to the fixture with Eire. One of the first permanent changes to the A squad roster was to be the inclusion of ex-patriot Americo Galvani at wing half, replacing the defensive-minded, often lead-footed, Humberto Velasquez. The fleet Galvani had returned to his native Argentina from St. Etienne of the French league in enough time to dress for the Irish encounter. On the seventeenth of April, two days before his first international appearance in two years, Galvani received a phone call from St. Etienne saying that his wife and two daughters had been hurt in an automobile accident. A distraught Americo Galvani phoned Octavio Suarez from the airport minutes before his flight to Paris took off. He bluntly informed the manager not to figure him into the National Team's plans. Suarez was calm and reassuring to the departing husband and father, and insisted that his spot would be held for him if he could make it back, no matter how long it took.

The manager was a realist, though, and he knew that the talented halfback would not don a National Team jersey in the foreseeable future. It was deflating news, news that would force him to rethink his midfield strategy.

The word was no better up front. Center forward Nicodemo Garcia remained mired in a cesspool of politics and intrigue, with Catalonia demanding outrageous compensation for his release. The Spanish team had booked a summer tour in the United States to play several of the new North American Soccer League teams such as the Cosmos. They claimed that Garcia was their marquee player, and that gate receipts would suffer if he was not a participant in the tour.

The fact that the tour was a hastily booked ploy was known throughout the soccer community, and diplomats, presidents, and even royalty were caught up in the soap opera saga of freeing Nico Garcia from Spain. Octavio Suarez remained confident to anyone that would listen to him. Garcia would return and in time to train before the opening of the tournament. The center forward spot was his to claim. All he had to do was show up.

In the meantime, the battle for Garcia's backup was leaning toward young Ramon Vida. Independiente's Enrique Rios showed flashes of danger, but his play had so far been mostly uninspired. No one could say that about the one-man hurricane named Vida. He made things happen, and what was more, he was a deadly closer.

The crowds that saw Vida play certainly loved him, but the entire nation awaited the return of Nico Garcia to lead them to the Holy Grail. Privately, Octavio Suarez had a nagging feeling that he would never lay eyes on the nation's most capped player in his dressing room. Only time would tell.

The Eire match was little more than a walk through for the home side. An easy 3-1 Argentina victory over a weak opponent seemed to make the press and public restless and grumpy rather than elated over remaining undefeated in the warm-up games. "The opposition has been of a low caliber in each of the matches!" the Clarín daily newspaper declared. Some felt the team had yet to be tested seriously, and that blame fell on the doorstep of the hated Brazilians. Their cancellation of the Copa Roca matches had robbed the Argentines of the type of world-class adversary that they needed to play against.

The score should have been 7-1, taking the clear scoring chances that the powder-blue and white stripes missed. The need for Nico Garcia's finishing skills had never been more evident. Miguel Cruz hit two posts, but also managed a goal in a confident showing. Ramon Vida scored once after being substituted in at the half, but he was frustrated with a few missed passes and some bad line calls. A yellow card for talking back to the referee didn't improve his postgame demeanor.

"At least you got onto the field, Ramon. It was pretty painful to watch that effort from the bench," was Renaldo's way of lifting his friend's spirits.

"You should have been in there, man. That Cruz is a jerk. He wouldn't pass me the ball if the goalie had given me an engraved invitation to score on him. Twice I was wide open, waiting with an open goal in front of me, and what does he do? Shoots the ball himself, the pig! Missed the fucking net altogether on one of them. No one sets me up like you do, my friend. The boss should have put you in at the half as well. Sometimes, I wonder if even Suarez knows what Suarez is doing."

With only two substitutes allowed per game, Octavio Suarez had to pick his lineups, and their potential replacements, with great skill and care. Where would such and such a player make the most impact? Who had shown the flashes of brilliance in practice that deserved to be displayed against world-class opponents? Each position had a different factor to weigh, and different men fighting for a starting role.

Renaldo's failure to play did not reflect on his talent, Ramon Vida proclaimed after he had stopped ranting about Miguel Cruz. It was just a numbers game, and everyone had to wait their turn. The only positive repercussion of Renaldo's bench riding was that the hazing from Chacon and Cruz subsided to a small degree. It did not, however, make up for Cruz' increasing arrogance in proclaiming to anyone who would listen that the center half job was his for certain, sewn up, a lock, no problem, no contest!

Cruz and Ramon Vida came close to fisticuffs on several occasions following the Irish visit. Renaldo De Seta just waited for his time to come.

Six days and an overnight ferry ride across the Rio de la Plata later, the rookie found himself, once again, on the bench as his teammates faced off against the Uruguayan National Team. One hundred thousand people jammed beautiful Centenario Stadium in Montevideo to get a firsthand look at the undefeated World Cup host nation's side. With their own team having failed to earn a berth in the global tournament, the Montevideans were expecting to be dazzled by their Latin neighbors. On this day, however, it would be their own native sons who would steal the show. The men from across the estuary would be soundly drubbed! If it was a bad day for the Argentine team, it was a horrendous day for their youngest player.

The Uruguayans took to the attack from the opening whistle, and only the diving, leaping saves of a surprisingly vocal Junior Calix kept them at bay. The keeper pleaded with his mates for help, for closer marking, better clearing, more communication. Another surprise for Octavio Suarez was the lionhearted play of the almost deposed halfback Humberto Velasquez. He patrolled his wing, albeit almost totally in the defensive half of the field, like a man possessed. No foe would beat him one-on-one. He forced six throw-ins single-handedly. His upfield clearing passes always found their mark, and he twice headed the ball to safety on dangerous corner kicks. Suarez rated him the only player on the field to be worthy of the National Team jersey at the postgame press conference. After that, it was all bad news.

The training roster of Argentina's National Team had remained remarkably free of debilitating injuries up to their arrival in Montevideo. The usual aches, sprains, muscle pulls, and bruises were always in existence, but not one player had been forced to sit out an international game due to injury. That would change in the first minute after the South American neighbors commenced play.

Argentina kicked off with Miguel Cruz taking a lateral pass from center forward Enrique Rios. Ramon Vida sat with his musical partner on the bench. Cruz was set upon at once by two aggressive Uruguayan forwards, but he managed to slide the ball through to Carlos Castillo on the left wing. There was no one within twenty yards of the halfback from Talleres Córdoba, and the whole left side of the pitch was clear of opponents all the way to the penalty area. Castillo's peripheral vision caught Daniele Bennett streaking up the field from his back position, and things looked perfectly set for the old give-and-go. The pass to Bennett was perfect, but as Castillo planted his kicking foot to turn upfield and join in the attack, a sickening crack that was loud enough for the approaching Uruguayans to hear echoed from the Argentine's ankle. The visiting player fell to the turf instantly, shrieking in agony. The Chilean referee had heard the joint snap as well, and wasted no time in summoning the doctor and stretcher bearers onto the pitch.

Octavio Suarez agonized on the bench. Another halfback! First Galvani goes, and now this. Castillo had been a huge part of this team. A steadying influence who had played the most inspired football of his career. He was truly irreplaceable!

The job of substituting for the thirty-year-old Castillo went to twenty-two-year-old Leopoldo Anariba. Suarez was giving up eight years of international experience, but he had no other option at this point. Anariba looked like a fish out of water after only two minutes of play, and the host nation set out to exploit his inexperience with relentless thrusts up his wing. The substitute was beaten cleanly and left sprawling on the green grass as his opposite number potted the first tally after eleven minutes.

Argentina had left its offense back across the river it seemed. Miguel Cruz was invisible on the field after Castillo went down, and Suarez could tell that the injury had unnerved his entire team. The visitors were lucky to escape the first half down only 1-0. With only one substitution available, Suarez inserted De Seta for Cruz, hoping that the boy could turn the flow of the game around with some of his magical passes. As the team lined up in the passageway to the field before the second half, Juan Chacon gave Renaldo a piece of advice.

"Hey, baby face. You think you can do something that my brother-in-law couldn't? You better have eyes in the back of your head then, because you have more than the Uruguayans to worry about if you do. Keep your head up, my beauty!"

The word 'beauty' was accompanied by a powerful squeeze of the younger man's cheeks and jaw by The Ugly One. Renaldo instinctively batted Chacon's fist away from his face with his outer forearm. A toothless, hateful laugh was the only reaction of the antagonist.

Uruguay kicked off the second half and went right to work where they left off, straight at Leopoldo Anariba. Calix was called on early and often to keep the visitors from falling further behind, and the continued play in their defensive zone brought Renaldo into constant contact with his nemesis.

"What the fuck are you doing out here anyway, De Seta? Shouldn't you be back in grade school by now?" was just a sample of the friendly chatter that Chacon would scream for all to hear during a pause in the action. He never let up. Every stoppage was greeted with some words of wisdom from the deformed defender.

The Uruguayan players could not believe what they were hearing at first. None of them wanted to provoke 'Killer' Chacon into one of his savage moods, but the home side had never imagined that one of Chacon's own teammates would be the butt of his stinging slurs. Eventually the comments got so outrageous that the Uruguayans started to break down laughing whenever Chacon opened his mouth. The referee warned the Argentine defender that he would be booked for delaying the game and unsportsmanlike conduct if he did not button his lip right away. That forced 'Killer' to adopt a new tactic.

Renaldo was able to find a small amount of room every so often to take the ball across the centerline, but once on foreign turf and without Ramon Vida to work with, it seemed that there was never any support. Where was center forward Rios? Had he dug a hole to hide in? Gitares was on the bench, Suarez not wanting to waste his best forward on a day that he had had a premonition about. It told him things would go poorly across the river, so he acted accordingly and sat down several A squad players.

Every advance the visitors could muster was stymied and turned aside. The play remained almost exclusively in the Argentine end. A Uruguayan free kick from thirty-five yards out at the seventy-first minute brought more trouble. Juan Chacon dared the young center half to join him in the wall to block the ball's path. The rookie took the dare, lining up ten yards from the ball, arm and arm with the 'Killer.'

"So what are you going to protect with your hands, my beauty, your balls or your face? You wouldn't want to get la pelota smacked against your pinup good looks, would you? Here, let me hold your balls with one of my hands so that you can play hide and go seek."

Renaldo felt the defenders hand brush against his shorts in a mock attempt to grab his privates. He twisted his torso to avoid the exploring fingers. At that instant, the ball struck the player's shoulder who was locked onto number seventeen's right arm. As that player, big Ignacio Suazo, recoiled from the direct hit, he pulled the smaller rookie off balance before they could unlock themselves. Renaldo felt totally out of control. Chacon maintained his lock hold on the left side, and Suazo was falling to earth and taking him along on the right side.

The twisting tumble was bad enough, but just as the center half hit the ground, a piercing sting shot through the back of his left heel. Chacon gave the boy a less than affectionate shove to free himself and headed back to his defensive position. Suazo pushed Renaldo off his chest and scrambled to his feet. The rookie tried to right himself and rise, but as soon as he put pressure on his left foot, the heel exploded once again. Renaldo called out in anguish.

"My heel! Someone . . . you bastard, Chacon! You cleated my Achilles' heel! I can't get up. Damn . . . someone, help me up!"

Play had been halted, and for a second time, the stretcher bearers were forced to do their frightful calling. Ramon Vida had to be physically restrained by his teammates on the bench. The boy from Boca had sensed trouble the minute De Seta and Chacon had lined up side-by-side in the wall. But he was not the only one to witness the foul deed that had transpired after the kick.

Octavio Suarez was, for once, powerless to avoid this disaster. These two men were teammates for the National Team of Argentina. The manager had idealistically hoped that they would temporarily put aside their petty differences and play together for their nation. No such luck. Chacon was indispensable on the back line, and the boy had real talent, even if it was in a substituting role. They had to learn to play together, or so Suarez had hoped up until the free kick. Chacon wanted the younger man gone, banished from the team, and it looked as if he had achieved his goal.

There were tears in Renaldo's eyes as he was carried off the pitch to the stadium infirmary. Ramon Vida was at his side, clutching his friend's right hand.

"I'm going to kill that animal. Don't worry about a thing. If you can't play in the World Cup, he sure as hell isn't going to play either. I promise you, amigo. I will set things right!"

"Don't, Ramon, please don't do anything stupid. You can make this team. Don't do anything that would jeopardize your chances of that happening. He's not worth it!"

"I've come up against scum like him before, man, and do you know where they are now? Six feet under the ground! That asshole doesn't scare me. He's just an ugly bully. I have a thirty-eight magnum that I'm going to introduce him to. We'll see how brave he is then. The stupid cocksucker!"

"That's smart, really smart, Ramon. So instead of being on the field at River Plate Stadium next month, you will be in a jail cell or worse. Don't do this, my friend. It is craziness!"

"People like him don't deserve to live, man. They make a beautiful sport as ugly as they are. You forget about him and get your foot back in shape. I'll spare his miserable life if you can get back on the field by the start of the tournament. But if you're gone for good, I'll waste the bastard. On the Holy Virgin's name, I swear it!"

Eight days later, back across the Rio de la Plata, the final act in Renaldo's downward spiral was played out. The medical news had been bad. He had a partially torn Achilles' tendon, not ruptured, thank God, but still painful enough to necessitate crutches. There was no active cure to speed up the healing process, no surgery, no miracle antibiotic, nothing! Only rest and painkillers.

"Stay off that foot for the next two weeks," the team orthopedic surgeon had told him. And so he had. Away from the training facility, his teammates, and the game he loved. Octavio Suarez had sent him home, home to his mother, as many had predicted.

"I do this to cleanse your mind, as well as your body. Away from the afflictions that you have been forced to suffer at the hands of those who would pretend to wear the National Team jersey with honor and good sportsmanship," Suarez had said as the boy slipped out of the compound unseen, on the night after their return from Montevideo. Coach Luque was to drive him directly to Casa San Marco. Only Astor Gordero had been apprised of the move. He had concurred with Suarez's decision.

"I am not blind, son. I am aware of everything that has gone on here. But in sport, as in life, it is better to fend for yourself without external interference. Respect will be your ultimate reward. If you can concentrate all your energies on the recuperation of that heel without having to play their mind games, then I think that we will see you back here before the tournament begins. The physio specialist will see you on a daily basis. Work hard, concentrate. Do not let yourself get distracted by hatred. I will call you in a week. Good luck."

With that, he shut the back door of the car and disappeared into the shadows, for he had his own demons to deal with.

The 2-0 loss in Uruguay had turned the whole nation on its collective ear. Not only was their team no longer undefeated, but the naysayers, doubters, and pessimists were jumping off the euphoric bandwagon at a frantic pace. No matter that two players were carried off the field on stretchers, both with possible career-ending injuries. No matter that the home side had played ninety minutes of flawless football in front of a vocal, supportive crowd.

'Pretenders' blared the headline of the Clarín. La Nacion trumpeted 'Without Garcia, We Are Doomed.' The bubble had burst, and everyone was second guessing Octavio Suarez. There were even calls for his ousting by some of his old, but still influential detractors. Luckily, cooler heads prevailed and nothing was changed, thanks largely to some vigorous behind-the-scenes lobbying by Astor Gordero.

It pained Suarez greatly to send his youngest player home. While Renaldo had remained stoic and never complained to anyone of his treatment at the hands of the Independiente roughnecks, the manager knew that there was a much better chance of Renaldo returning to full form if he didn't have to put up with any of their bullshit. The game movies were inconclusive in laying the blame for the center half's injury at Juan Chacon's doorstep. All that could be seen was a man in the defensive wall, Ignacio Suazo, lurching backwards after the ball had struck his shoulder, and in doing so, twisting the unfortunate De Seta to the ground. Chacon's legs and feet were not visible to the camera because of the falling torsos that blocked the view.

'Killer' had gotten away with another one, or so he had bragged to his club team compatriots. Octavio Suarez had witnessed the blasphemous act with his own eyes though. He didn't need movie film. The manager would wait and pick his opportunity to have a little heart-to-heart with his feared defender. Maximum effect. That's the way Octavio Suarez operated. Wait until you can achieve maximum effect. Then fire away with both barrels!

"I never realized how much I wanted to be a part of all this until it was taken away from me," a downcast Renaldo mumbled to himself as he sat alone, transfixed to the tiny black-and-white images on the screen.

His mother had welcomed her youngest son home with a 'I told you so!' attitude. Florencia De Seta was elated that the timely injury had come just as the university term was getting into full swing.

"A bright boy like you can make up for the work you've missed in no time. I have kept in touch with the registrar, and a small donation to their scholarship fund has surprisingly kept one placement open, just for you."

There was no need to argue with her at the moment, for any talk about returning to the team would seem like nothing but fantasy. Especially as he was still unable to put any weight at all on the extremity. What he was about to watch on the television screen that afternoon did nothing to lift his spirits or make his return to sporting glory more likely.

This was a vastly different Argentine eleven, even though most of the names were the same. Somehow, they had been transformed. They were now fluid, poetic, deadly. Gone were the tentative bumblers of Montevideo. In their place stood men who demonstrated the pace and rhythm at which the game was meant to be played. Attacking football, beautiful football!

The stadium crowd roared its approval after the first home goal at the six-minute mark, and the noise never subsided from that point on. It was as if the fans considered this match to be a dress rehearsal for the big show that was still a month away. No carnival in Rio could be more raucous than this!

A second goal at thirty-four minutes and a third at sixty-seven made the final tally 3-0 Argentina. The naysayers would be crawling all over each other trying to jump back on the bandwagon after this result. What had Suarez said to them? What rabbits had he magically pulled out of his hat to provoke such a first-class display? Renaldo wished with all his heart that he could be a part of it again.

A look at the score sheet was further reason to worry. All three goals had come off the feet of Miguel Cruz, who, even before the television broadcast went off the air, was being heralded as "The New Argentine Scoring Machine." Cruz had been lucky, if not all that deadly. He was put through on a breakaway by Jorge Calderone, when a poorly organized offside trap went awry on the visitors. He then eluded a diving keeper and waltzed home the last ten yards with no one in pursuit. Two strange bounces off defensive players landed the ball at the Independiente player's feet with the gaping goalmouth unobstructed for his second. But Cruz's third marker could be attributed directly to the muscle of his brother-in-law, 'Killer' Chacon.

Ramon Vida had played effectively at center forward the entire game. While he hadn't figured in the first two goals, he had barely missed several good chances and was a constant thorn in the Uruguayan defender's side. With just over twenty minutes left to play, Vida was set free up the middle, again by the precise foot of Jorge Calderone. Three strides inside the penalty area, two visiting defenders converged to foul the Argentine. The referee pointed immediately to the spot.

Vida was on his feet at once and walking toward the ball to complete the task when Chacon latched onto his left arm.

"I want my brother-in-law to score a hat trick today, amigo, and if you really think about it, that is what you want, too," the ugly defender suggested to Vida as he led the smaller man away from the penalty spot with an iron grip.

"Fuck you and your brother-in-law! That is my penalty, and I am going to take the shot."

The Boca player tried to wrench his arm free, but the grip was unflinching.

"I said, I want Miguel to take that shot! Now shut up, you little shit, or you'll end up like your girly friend, Renaldo."

"You ugly bastard, I'll fix your . . ."

Their conversation was drowned out in the exultation of Cruz's third goal. The center half hadn't hesitated, simply stepping up to the spot as if it were his divine right and blasting the ball past a stationary Uruguayan goalkeeper. Done, hat trick! Welcome the 'New Argentine Scoring Machine.'

For Renaldo De Seta, it was the bleakest of moments. Cruz did have a lock on the center half position. Sewn up, no problem, no contest! Everyone would be singing his praises come the morning, talking about what a team he and Nico Garcia would be. The invalid's heart ached as he hobbled up the stairs to his bed that evening. He had come so close. Now, there was little reason for hope.

Renaldo took breakfast alone in the garden the next morning. Florencia had already departed on her day's agenda by the time the former National Team member emerged, showered, and dressed. As he sat in the warm solace of the late fall sun, his thoughts drifting between school and football, there was a tapping sound on the glass door behind him.

"Señor Renaldo, excuse me for interrupting, but may I have a word with you?"

"Yes, of course. What's on your mind, Oli? What is it? Come and sit down." He pulled his body upright in the lounge chair as the elderly maid approached.

"Thank you, Señor Renaldo, but I will stand. I hope that you do not think me too forward, but Olarti said that I should talk to you."

"Don't be shy, Oli. We have known each other too long for that. What is it?"

"You see, Señor Renaldo, my people, the Querandi Indians . . . my people grew up on the Pampas. That is where we flourished and multiplied. We were able to hunt without barbed wire fences and soldiers on horseback with guns."

Renaldo sensed a faint tone of bitterness and disgust in the old woman's voice that he had never heard before. He nodded for her to continue.

"My people did not have horses, only our bare feet in the beginning, and our feet had to serve us well. They were our only means of transportation. I remember my grandmother anointing my grandfather's feet with oil and massaging them for hours. Even by the time wild horses became plentiful on the Pampas, many of my people still relied on their feet to hunt and to fight. When a warrior had a problem with his feet, the medicine elders of the tribe would put him on a strict diet of certain herbs and juices, and place a secret poultice on the painful area. Many times I have seen them do this, Señor Renaldo, and many times the area of pain is on the back of the heel, the same as you. Olarti knows of a man, a man who still practices his medicine and lives on the Pampas near Pergamino. Olarti thinks that you should go with him to see this medicine man. Olarti thinks that he can help you, make you well again for the football."

Renaldo was flattered by her concern for his condition, but dismissed the idea offhand as something associated with black magic or witch doctors. He thanked her warmly, but stated that he had at his disposal the most up-to-date technology and research on his injury. His healing would be supervised and administered by the most knowledgeable doctors Argentina could assemble, the doctors of its National Soccer Team. Oli did not seem upset at this rebuff and simply wished him good luck with a caring smile, then cleared away his breakfast dishes.

The morning talk with his old and trusted servant kept reappearing in his mind throughout the balance of the day, however. Olarti had brought the daily newspapers for Renaldo to read, and a front-page picture of Miguel Cruz with the caption, 'Señor Goal' did nothing to raise his spirits. Florencia had reappeared at siesta time with a list of medical texts and the first-year medicine course outline. She had obviously paid another visit to the Newton Academy's medical registrar, who, once again, had been most helpful, providing her with the literature to allow Renaldo to commence his studies at home while convalescing. She instructed her youngest son to complete the marked forms and check off the list of course options. Olarti would pick up the required texts at the university bookstore tomorrow.

Florencia once again told her son how happy she was that he was finished with 'this football business,' and informed him that she would be out that evening at the theater and dinner with Wolfgang Stoltz. In a light, almost euphoric tone of voice, she suggested that he invite over some of his old school friends for dinner.

"This will provide you with some company, and also an opportunity for some scholastically oriented conversation," she had quipped. The lady didn't wait for a response to her suggestion, but simply pecked the boy on his cheek as he lay on the sofa. Then she was gone, and Renaldo was alone again.

After being with people constantly the past two and a half months, the solitude of Casa San Marco was unnerving for the ex-National Team player. His mother was hardly ever home, a development brought about by the sudden romantic interests of Herr Wolfgang Stoltz. That she had reciprocated with her own unbridled enthusiasm was another shock to Renaldo. His mother had been the classic grieving widow following her husband's death. While her youngest son was pleased with the lady's uplifted spirits and joie de vivre, he also found the association between his mother, Wolfgang Stoltz, and Astor Gordero to be an amazing coincidence. Over all though, he was pleased for his mother and he admired the efficient Herr Stoltz.

Astor Gordero had dropped by Casa San Marco on the boy's first morning home to cheer him up and give him some encouragement. He started their conversation, however, with the topic of Herr Stoltz and his mother.

The attorney offered his apologies and humbly stated that he preferred to "bring any doubts or ill feelings about this development to light immediately, so that the proper measures could be taken." The inference was that Gordero would allow nothing to interfere with their attorney-client relationship, not even his association with Wolfgang Stoltz. Renaldo assured The Fat Man that as far as he could tell, his mother was in the best frame of mind that he had seen her in for ages, and that he had no problem with Herr Stoltz 'paying a call' to Casa San Marco. He did confide in his attorney that her attitude about his returning to school was a major source of discomfort. Gordero suggested that perhaps Herr Stoltz could be of subtle assistance in that matter, but first the boy had to get back on his feet and start building up the strength in his foot. Ubaldo Luque had sent along a list and descriptions of certain exercises that Renaldo could perform while convalescing to keep his overall body condition close to top form. The physio trainer that would be visiting Casa San Marco daily would instruct him in their proper execution.

"Octavio Suarez wants . . . no, *needs* you back on the team, young man. You must devote all your energies to strengthening your limb. You will be attended to each day. Suarez will be apprised of your progress. Things with the team are still extremely unsettled. The Nicodemo Garcia situation is by no means resolved. We have faith in your resiliency, Renaldo. We know that you will come back to us!"

The truth of the matter centered around the potential loss of millions of dollars in the coffers of A.R. Gordero and Sons should their recent star acquisition became 'yesterday's has-been' before the World Cup Tournament even commenced. It was Gordero that had insisted on the intensive recuperative program that the boy would receive at home. He was not about to let this Roman candle become a dud without first experiencing its skyrocketing glow!

The imperative thing was to keep the boy in shape, keep his spirits up, and give him the best medical attention. Even with all that, the prognosis was grim. If Renaldo attempted too much too soon, he stood the possibility of rupturing the weak tendon completely. Rest and small doses of massage and physio were the only safe solution. An agonizingly slow solution.

Astor Gordero could be of personal assistance on the spiritual level, however. He delivered an item to the downcast youth that had the desired effect.

"Before I depart, Renaldo, there is one last thing. This correspondence crossed my desk the other day, and I thought you might be interested in it." He pulled a legal-sized manila envelope from the inside pocket of his flowing white linen suit jacket. "I will stay in touch, my boy. Get that foot in shape, or no more mail delivery!" he chuckled as he made his way from the parlor.

Inside the envelope were several newspaper clippings that contained reviews of Symca's shows in various South American cities. The promotion had been a phenomenal success, and bookings for World Cup tour packages were selling out in a hurry. It seemed like each foreign city had more glowing things to say about the Argentine chanteuse than the previous venue. Renaldo only glanced at the headlines briefly, for wrapped inside the articles was an envelope addressed to Renaldo De Seta. The script was her hand.

The missive had been written before his unfortunate gift from Juan Chacon, so the mood was up-tempo. While Simone had been unable to watch any of his games on television, she had scoured the local newspapers for details following each match. She also called Astor Gordero from time to time, for more detailed inside reports.

The singing sensation revealed that the pace of her tour was exhausting, but nevertheless exhilarating because of the warm reception that greeted her at each stop. Renaldo devoured every line of the newsy letter, but it was a final personal message that caused him to blush;

'I think constantly of our last embrace in my dressing room at Teatro Colon. The power of your touch, the feel of you against me . . . it was overwhelming! Never have I lost my senses as I did that night. I pray for God to keep you safe and well, and to place me in your arms again soon. I await our reunion, breathlessly! All my love, Simone.'

He reread her note and the newspaper articles until late in the afternoon, eschewing lunch, and only rising from his recliner when the physiotherapist arrived to commence the healing therapy. Renaldo ate supper with his mother that evening, then retired to his room to play the guitar and pour over Simone's words once again. The therapy had been excruciatingly painful, but Tito, the therapist, had been friendly and as gentle as possible. He told Renaldo that the two of them had to develop a relationship of trust for the therapy to be beneficial. There would be pain, but the pain and anger that Renaldo was about to experience should be focused positively on a quick recuperation, not negatively, toward Tito, the therapist.

For the next several weeks, Tito would become a daily fixture at Casa San Marco, a fixture that scheduled his visits around times when the lady of the house was absent. Any awareness on Florencia's part of a lingering association with Argentina's National Soccer Team was sure to produce an adverse reaction.

Astor Gordero had been the one to suggest that Tito be 'spirited' into the residence when his mother was away tending to her active schedule. That proved not a hard matter to arrange by simply sneaking a peek at the lady's daybook in advance, and so it was to be. On the afternoon of Tito's first visit to his new patient, the pain of the therapy would be dulled by the euphoria of young love and the dreams that had been delivered in a manila, legal-sized envelope.

It was now the fourth of May, eight days since Simone's stirring note, eight days since Tito's initial session. Renaldo still could not put pressure on the inflamed heel, still could not stand without crutches, still could not walk, let alone run or jump. It was taking too much time. There were only twenty-seven days before the opening kickoff in River Plate Stadium. "This is too slow, far too slow," he lamented.

That evening as he sat alone, staring blankly at the television screen, Renaldo De Seta came to the conclusion that he had nothing to lose by talking to Olarti about native medicine. He rang the small, sterling silver bell that brought Oli from the kitchen.

"What can I do for you, Señor Renaldo?"

"Oli, I've reconsidered what you told me about your native healing methods. I would like very much to talk to Olarti about the medicine man he knows. The other doctor's medicine is not working quickly enough to enable me to play football again. I must do something, anything! But please, Oli, do not mention a word of this to my mother. If she ever found out that you had helped me for this purpose, I am afraid that there would be dire consequences."

"I understand, Señor Renaldo. Would you like me to summon Olarti now, or in the morning?"

"Well, I'm not going anywhere, Oli, so if he doesn't mind spending a few minutes right now, then I would love to see him."

The two men talked for over an hour, not as employer-employee, but as old friends would talk. Renaldo was fascinated about the possibility of meeting a man such as Copiapo, the native holistic healer. No one knew his exact age, Copiapo having outlived all of his contemporary tribesmen. His reputation as a miracle worker, according to Olarti, was known throughout the Pampas. Both natives and whites, primarily gauchos and plains farmers, were counted among his followers.

The legend was difficult to find, for even as an elderly man, he pursued his ancestor's nomadic lifestyle. He was even more difficult to actually see, for the healer was very selective in choosing on whom he shone his light. Olarti was certain that he could track Copiapo down through his contacts at Buenos Recuerdos, and as soon as there was news of the healer's whereabouts, a visitation would be requested.

As sketchy as the information seemed, it did give Renaldo reason to hope. A thin thread of hope, but still hope. There were several logistical problems to work out if he was able to obtain an interview with Copiapo. Not the least of these was the fact that Renaldo was, at the moment, an invalid in Buenos Aires, not riding the Pampas in Pergamino.

For some reason, his grandmother, Lydia, came to mind. He had not seen her since departing Buenos Recuerdos shortly after the new year, although she had written him two encouraging and supportive letters urging him to 'live his dreams.' A weekend trip to visit her, with Olarti driving because of his injury, would be just the diversion that his mother would never suspect. To cover himself and reduce Florencia's suspicions, Renaldo turned his attention to the university forms that had been left for him. He completed all the documentation necessary and placed them on her bed with a note inscribed "Mother knows best. Your loving son, Renaldo."

He could play her game! Show an interest in returning to his studies, then just before plunging into the textbooks, request a weekend visit with his grandmother to clear his head. He knew the ruse would work. Now it was up to Olarti to find Copiapo.

An unexpected phone call summoned Renaldo from his bed the next morning. It was the morning of his nineteenth birthday.

"Señor Renaldo, your brother, Lonnie, is on the telephone. He was wondering if you could talk to him," Oli stated from the half open bedroom door.

"Tell him I will be right there, as fast as I can hobble to the phone."

There had been no word from his older brother since the beginning of March, when Lonnie had informed their mother that he was not returning to university. He was taking the semester off to continue his travels with Celeste and would decide about school at a later time. Florencia, needless to say, was incensed with her eldest, and had told Lonnie that he and that 'communist slut' he had taken up with were not welcome at Casa San Marco until he came to his senses and decided to get his life in order. In other words, get rid of the girl and go back to school.

Lonfranco's name was forbidden to be mentioned in the casa, and for all intents and purposes, he ceased to exist in the mind of Florencia De Seta. Her new, self-fulfilling attitude, as well as the attentions of Herr Stoltz, made it easy for her to put the wandering vagabond out of her mind.

"Hello, Lonnie, are you alright? Where are you?"

"I'm in better shape than you are, little brother, if what I read in these week-old newspapers is true. Happy birthday, by the way. Now that you are an old man, is your body giving out on you? What happened? I saw one of your games on television, the one against Peru in Buenos Aires. You looked terrific! How badly are you hurt?"

"Well, I still can't stand on my foot, but I haven't lost hope. Where on earth are you?"

"We are in Bariloche, in the lake district. I have never been down here, so we are going to explore the National Park. You know, mountain climbing, hiking, the works. You should see the glaciers. They are breathtaking! How is Mama? Oli told me that she was out at the moment, so I figured that I could spend a few minutes talking to you. What are your plans?"

"You know what Mama wants me to do. She already has me registered in medical school. But to be a part of the National Team, that was the experience of a lifetime! I want to make it back there, to play in the World Cup. It will be a struggle though, both physically and mentally, with Mama overseeing my every move. Oh, by the way, she has a new suitor, a man by the name of Wolfgang Stoltz. He's a lawyer who works for Astor Gordero. Seems like a decent man. Anyway, Mama is on cloud nine these days. But what about you? When are you coming back to town?"

"No plans, little brother. I'll tell you one thing, though. If you make it back to the World Cup Team, I will be in Buenos Aires expecting to get really prime seats from you. So don't let me down. Get back there with the team. Medical school can wait, just like law school. I better go now, these phones are expensive. Good luck, kid, I miss you. I will bring back your present from my travels. Happy birthday and get back on that team!"

"Thanks, Lonnie, I miss you, too. It was a big help to have you to talk to over Christmas. Give my regards to Celeste. Please call again, when you get the chance. Good-bye for now."

As the receiver went dead Renaldo felt a pang of remorse shoot through him. There he stood, alone in the second-floor corridor of his ancestral home, memories of the happy times flooding his brain. Childhood memories of the perfect family life. A loving, respected father, a devoted mother, a rough and tumble older brother. Lavish birthday parties and expensive gifts from years gone by. A perfect childhood, a perfect family.

Those times were history now, alive only in his fond recollections. They had been a complete family for only seven years, from his own birth to his father's death. Seven years! Not long enough to savor the joys of family, not long enough at all!

CHAPTER NINETEEN

It was fortunate for Lonnie De Seta that the national telephone service, Entel, was performing to its usual poor standards during the call to Casa San Marco. The truth was that Lonnie was not in Bariloche, but in Barracas, a working-class barrio on the south side of Buenos Aires. The poor connection had made him seem hundreds of miles away, which is where he wished he was at that particular moment.

He moved quickly out of the pay telephone kiosk and disappeared into the dark, narrow alleys of the local marketplace. He would pick up the staples of his existence, then return to the room that he had shared with Celeste for almost a month. It had been a month of living in hell.

Lonnie De Seta was a changed man. He had stepped over the line and there was no going back now. No second-guessing. The revolution was all that mattered. The revolution and Celeste, of course.

He was now a true soldier, for he had struck a coup alone and earned his warrior's feather. Three words told the whole story. Three words that affirmed that he would be a fugitive until the end of his days. Three words . . . Miguel Tobias Panizo.

It was Señor Panizo's unfortunate fate to be the under secretary for economic coordination and a labor specialist at the beginning of April, 1978. It was also his unfortunate fate to be targeted for assassination by a dissident cadre of the Montonero movement. The evolution of this terrorist splinter group threatened to disrupt the plans of the junta for a peaceful and bloodless World Cup Tournament. The same evolution also disrupted the plans of Lonnie De Seta.

The splinter group was formed the instant that the three grenades exploded outside the Banco Nacional in February. That six people would die had been unexpected, but the public outrage and condemnation of the 'barbarous act' had exceeded anything seen in modern Argentina.

An official day of mourning was proclaimed by the junta, and all the dead were given full military honors. The press uniformly called for stepped-up antisubversive action on the part of the military, and Lonnie knew that he had been lucky to escape the sweeping police dragnet. That was not the worst of it, however.

The most shocking after effect of the Banco Nacional job was the complete denial and disassociation of the Montonero leaders from any knowledge of, or responsibility for the 'tragedy.' The very men to whom Serge and Jean Pierre had dropped off the bank's bounty had called a local radio station that same night to disavow any relationship to those responsible. The man that made that call, Adolfo Bertoni, had reaffirmed his earlier pledge of abstention from violent acts in preparation for, as well as during, the World Cup tournament. The problem was that Adolfo Bertoni was a two-faced liar.

The Banco Nacional heist had been his brain child. He was a born and raised Porteño, and he knew the workings of the city like the back of his hand, especially the military workings. He had been a radical student leader at the university before graduating into the Montonero's finishing school. He had worked his way up from foot-soldier, to cadre leader, to self-proclaimed spokesman for the entire movement.

It was evident to Lonnie that Serge Lavalle held Bertoni in great regard. They had worked on many of the same assignments together. Now, here was this very man proclaiming that there were hundreds of small-time terrorists who aspired to be like the Montoneros, but who were pathetically foolish and bloodthirsty in their attempts. He called the Banco Nacional job 'amateurish' and swore to find out who those responsible were, through his own sources.

Bertoni had his own very personal reason for wanting the Banco Nacional job to go down, in spite of his public pronouncements to the contrary. He had become heavily involved in the capital's flourishing cocaine trade as a sideline and was expecting a large shipment to arrive by mid-February. Payment for the drugs would be courtesy of the good depositors of the Banco Nacional. There was no humanitarian rationale that could justify the death of the six men on the bank's steps. No aid or welfare group would see a single peso. Not one destitute worker would get the slightest benefit from the actions of Serge Lavalle and his cohorts on that February afternoon. The only beneficiary of that afternoon's activities was Adolfo Bertoni, who had lined his pockets with gold, just as he would soon be lining his nostrils with the purest cocaine.

The transfer of funds between Lavalle and Bertoni was cordial, but swift. News of the robbery and subsequent murders had not been broadcast by the time the two men parted ways. Serge and Jean Pierre were able to board the bus to Mar del Plata without interference and departed the outskirts of the capital only minutes before all the major arteries in and out of the city were shut down by road blocks. They arrived at the safe house in Mar del Plata unmolested, and undisturbed. The brothers were ready to enjoy a month or so of anonymity in the sea and sun, but the newspaper that Serge picked up on his first morning stroll set the alarm bells ringing in his head.

"Six Die In Terrorist Bank Attack. Montoneros Deny Responsibility!"

Six dead? How can that be? Those fucking heroes, they must have tried to follow us. To stop us, were the thoughts that raced through his mind as the headline screamed at him. He hurried back to the house and roused Jean Pierre.

"Look at this. This is blasphemy! That bastard Bertoni swore to me that there would be a statement of affirmation released to the press immediately after the job was concluded about how this money was going to help the starving and homeless. How the Montoneros were willing to do anything in their power to help the needy of Argentina. There is none of it here. Only denials. He calls us 'amateurs.' The bastard says that he is going to find out who is responsible and deal with them himself. What bullshit! He says 'The Montoneros are dedicated to peaceful attainment of civil liberties and the rights of the underprivileged. As well, no disruption will take place prior to or during the World Cup Tournament. I give the nation my word on this, and I will see to it personally that such barbarism will not occur again.' I don't believe it!"

Jean Pierre then asked the pressing question to his brother using sign language. Serge replied hesitantly

"Yes, I think that we are safe here for the time being, but I must speak to Bertoni. I will be able to tell by his voice if he is lying to me. I have heard him lie before. His voice changes slightly. I will be able to tell if he has sent someone to take care of us or not. He likes the blood-sport. He might just do it to make himself look like a hero. I don't know. Keep the door locked and your weapon ready. I will return when I have spoken to our two-faced friend."

Two hours later, Serge Lavalle returned to the safe house.

"Grab your things. We are leaving right away."

Jean Pierre gestured with both hands in his confusion. "I think that Bertoni has turned on us. He says that the pressure from the military is devastating. Thousands of people have been pulled in for interrogation, and very few have been released. The backlash against the Montoneros because of this is enormous. The press and the people are calling for our heads. They are worried about losing their precious football tournament!"

Serge threw up his hands in exasperation. He paced the room for several seconds before continuing.

"Bertoni told me that we should stay where we are. Not move around and change locations. He said that the army has vowed to revenge the deaths of their brothers-in-arms. The six deaths changed everything, according to Bertoni. I think the lying bastard is out to get us. Once we are turned in or eradicated, the junta will call off the dogs, as long as there is no further trouble. Bertoni blames the negative reaction against the Banco Nacional job on the World Cup Tournament. This damn football is interfering with the politics of the country!

It's totally emotional. There is no rationale for this kind of reactionary behavior. Everyone is freaking out because of this stupid football!"

The academic philosopher from his university days temporarily resurfaced in Serge Lavalle. He had always been the most cerebral of his terrorist ilk, and the thought of football interfering with the people's movement for civil liberties was unthinkable. The masses were thinking football, not politics. Fools!

Serge gave a running dialogue to his brother as they gathered up any evidence that would show that they had been there. "We have to warn Celeste and Lonnie. We are going to Tigre. There are excursion boats that run up the coast to Buenos Aires, then on to Tigre. I have booked us a private compartment. It wasn't hard. The tourists are still arriving and no one is going home yet. We don't have to get off the boat when it docks in the capital, and hopefully, the authorities will not have the boat searched. If we can make our way to Lonnie's camp, I think that we will be safe for a while. Bertoni thought that all four of us would come to Mar del Plata and stay in the safe house. I never did tell him of Lonnie and Celeste's change of plans. If someone is sent here to kill us, they will waste a lot of time looking for three men and a woman. It will give us a bit of a head start. That's it, grab your bag. We're gone!"

That they made it safely to Tigre was nothing short of a miracle. There were military guards aboard the vessel as part of the stepped up security program. The guards had the authority to detain anyone who looked mildly 'interesting,' and the Lavalle brothers subsequently spent the entire voyage locked in their stateroom. More military personnel greeted the boat's arrival in Buenos Aires, and from their porthole window, Serge was able to witness firsthand the detention of several of the disembarking passengers.

Luckily, Tigre was free of inspecting officers, with the exception of several jeep loads of national guardsmen who passively watched the tourists funnel off the pier. Serge made his brother strap a camera over his neck just as he had done, to enhance the 'enthusiastic visitor' appearance. There were no problems, and the brothers arrived at camp No Se Preocupe by taxi less than thirty minutes after the boat had landed.

Jean Pierre remained in the cab out of sight while his older brother set out to find Lonnie. He was successful at his first stop, the camp office.

The blank stare that greeted Serge's muted greeting told the visitor that Lonnie could have been blown over by a strong gust of wind, so amazed was he at the sight of the figure standing before him.

"Could I speak with you about the camp in private, Señor?" was Serge's opening remark to the good looking man sorting papers at the front desk.

"Why, yes . . . of course. Would you like to see the facilities while we talk?"

The two camp secretaries hardly glanced up from their toils as Lonnie led the visitor out the office door, shouting over his shoulder that he was going on a tour and would be back shortly.

"My God, Serge, what are you doing here? What has happened? You were supposed to be in Mar del Plata!" Serge gave his compatriot a very quick rundown on the events of the last two days, while emphasizing the safety of Tigre to his very nervous friend.

"Jean Pierre and I need accommodation right away. Some place out of the way. Anything, a cabin, a third-rate hotel. Anything where we won't be seen, or at least noticed. How is Celeste? Is she here?"

"Yes, yes, she is down at the beach with some of the children. She is marvelous with them, you know. Is that your cab? Stay in the cab and I will make some fast phone calls. I'll be right back." With that he disappeared into the camp office, emerging less than five minutes later with a slight grin on his face.

"I have just the spot for sports fishermen to stay a few nights. Cabbie, take these gentlemen to the Arrayan Cabins on Paso Alto. They have guides, tackle, and boats for rent. I have known the owner all my life. Just ask for Jorge Gonzales. Good luck with the fish. Call me at this number if I can be of any further assistance."

He handed Serge a piece of paper with the words, 'eight p.m., your cabin,' printed on it. Lonnie then headed for the beach as the cab sped through the front gates of the camp.

To say that Celeste was shocked at the news Lonnie brought her that afternoon would be an understatement. Nevertheless, eight p.m. found the four co-conspirators seated around the circular dining table in the spacious fishing cabin that Lonnie had arranged.

"So, that is the story as I see it. I am certain that we have been double-crossed by Bertoni, but there is no way of proving it, unless we expose ourselves to him. That could be a deadly mistake. I suggest that we continue our fight for the cause of the people on our own, from a new headquarters, maybe even here at this fishing camp. Buenos Aires is all gaga about that silly football tournament. Everyone wants the Montoneros to go away until it is over so that they can have their soccer fix. Well, I say it is a perfect time to draw attention to our movement, to the people's plight! Lonnie, can you get your hands on some money, say ten thousand U.S. dollars?"

Serge's question jolted Lonnie. "Well, yes, that shouldn't be a problem. What do we need that kind of money for, Serge?"

"Material . . . plastic explosives, weapons, ammunition, a car. The usual items. Is it a problem?"

"No, not at all. I just didn't think that we would be going to the mattresses this soon."

Lonnie was referring to the old Mafia custom of family soldiers holding up in a dormitory-fortress style existence if there was a gang war in progress, or if one of their own was being sought by the police or an assassin.

"There is nowhere to go except to the mattresses, Lonnie. If Bertoni is looking for us, you can be assured it is to turn us in and ease the pressure on the rest of his organization. I knew the man was a coke head. I should have never trusted him as I did. We go back so many years, though. It's because he is a Porteño. He is caught up in the fast life. Always has been. He doesn't know the hardships of the common people in the provinces. He is not one of them, like we are. The working people of Argentina deserve their civil liberties, not to be thrown in jail and detained without explanation. I want to keep going, to show the people . . . Hell, the world, that true Montoneros don't stop pressing for justice just because of some irrelevant soccer games. We will work as a unit again and strike independently for our cause. There is no going back. I did not anticipate six people dying at the banco, but I was ready to lay down my life and fight my way out of there if I had to. We have all lived to continue our righteous work. That is an omen. We can never go back now, only forward, for the people."

That stirring piece of rhetoric cemented the formation of the outlaw gang which was to become the most hated and hunted terrorist cadre in Argentina's history.

Preparation leading up to the first act of enlightenment by this splinter group took almost six weeks to complete the procurement of the necessary explosives and finalization of plans. Serge and Jean Pierre were moved to a nondescript rooming house in downtown Tigre. An extended stay at the fishing cabin would have provoked questions once the season drew to a close. Everything had to be arranged with the utmost of secrecy and caution.

Lonnie had withdrawn ten thousand U.S. dollars from his private account and turned the funds over to Serge. He and Celeste continued their work at the camp as usual, with the exception of sporadic meetings at the rooming house. It was the Lavalle brothers that would handle all the planning and purchasing. By the twenty-sixth of March, Serge was ready to reveal the first strike plan.

"I want to hit the middle class first. I want to make them wake up and realize that we haven't gone away. These bastards are still thinking about their fucking football tournament. I want to bring them back to reality. This is

Argentina, home of the powerful and corrupt. The world must see that someone still cares about the people who can't even afford a ticket to a football game. So, this is what we are going to do."

Two days later, during the morning rush hour in the southern part of the capital, a main commuter railway bridge was destroyed by plastic explosives. No one was injured in the blast, but the disruption kept many an irate businessperson away from work that day. Celeste had, once again, left her artistic handiwork at the scene, and the florescent red 'Montoneros' painted on the side of the trestle left no doubt in anyone's mind just who the perpetrators had been.

Serge wanted to act quickly and consummate as many operations as possible in a short period of time, then change headquarters and lay low for a while. The second sortie involved the bombing of a police station in northwest Buenos Aires. This particular station was acknowledged to be one of the most brutal detention and torture centers in the entire country. It took Serge until April sixth to replenish the supply of plastic explosives after the railway bridge job. They hit the station that same night.

An old clunker of a car that Lonnie had bought a few days earlier with his false identification was parked in front of the target and left for several hours while the operatives kept the comings and goings of the station under surveillance. They were waiting for the arrival of the new internees, the ones destined to be tortured or killed. Jean Pierre had memorized the times that the armored police vehicle arrived at the station each night with its load of freshly rounded up subversives. The plan was to coordinate the detonation of the car bomb with the opening of the police station gate.

In the ensuing confusion, it might be possible to free some of the prisoners before the compound was resecured. The assault was risky, but Serge had concocted this plan as an act of defiance, an act to show the military and the police that the Montoneros were an ongoing force with which to deal.

Celeste continued to preach her terrorist dogma throughout the initial planning stage of the cadre's new operations. That Lonnie was so thoroughly brainwashed into the cause of the people's revolution was, in part, due to her oratorical skills and, in part, due to her oral skills. Rhetoric was always followed by passionate lovemaking, and she knew that it was her skill as a lover more than his passion for politics that kept Lonfranco De Seta a member of the Montonero movement.

Lonnie never doubted any of the plans that Serge came up with. He was like a big pussy cat, except for one nagging matter. The fledgling terrorist wanted to prove that he was a worthy warrior, personally. The police station operation seemed tailor-made for Lonnie to draw his first blood.

The armored police personnel carrier arrived at its destination right on schedule. Serge sat behind the wheel of the getaway vehicle, half a block away from the front gates. On his lap lay a remote control detonator. Celeste was covering the left flank on foot, thirty yards down the street from the car bomb. Jean Pierre had taken up a similar position on the right flank. Lonnie was sitting at the bar in a small café, directly across the street from the police station gates. He wore a hat and dark glasses, concealing his face further by engrossing himself in the daily newspaper. When he saw the police vehicle approaching, he turned his back to the window in order to avoid flying glass. The blast was deafening. Café patrons hit the floor as the walls of the old building shook from the percussion. Lonnie was out the front door and across the street in an instant, his Llama nine millimeter pistol at the ready.

Celeste and Jean Pierre converged on the armored vehicle at the same time that Lonnie arrived. While the blast had been loud and devastating to nearby buildings and passenger vehicles, it had only seared some paint off the side of its intended target. The dazed driver and guard refused Lonnie's threats to get out of the cab and open the rear prisoners' door. The cab's doors and bulletproof glass were intact, and there was no way that the two men on the inside were setting foot on the outside. Jean Pierre was trying to force the rear door open and having very little success when a frustrated Lonnie joined him.

"The driver has locked himself inside. I can't get the keys. Ten seconds, and we are out of here."

His mute companion nodded in agreement. Celeste was busy with her can of spray paint, while waiting for the first police reinforcements with her cocked Uzzi ready for action. She didn't have long to wait.

Just as the lady artist had completed her standard calling card on the exterior wall of the prison, three uniformed officers rushed from inside the compound toward the back of the vehicle. As soon as they opened fire on the partially concealed terrorists that were trying to force the prisoner's door ajar, Celeste cut loose with her own automatic weapon.

It was no contest. The standard issue .38 caliber handgun that the officers possessed was like a peashooter compared to the Uzzi. All three of the constables fell in Celeste's hail of lead. But there were more men on the way, too many policemen to ward off. The prisoners' door would not budge, and now it was time to flee so that they could fight again.

Serge had pulled up in the getaway car, and the three pedestrians piled through its doors. The squeal of rubber was intermixed with the pop-pop-pop of the police revolvers. While they had been unable to rescue any of the 'Disappeared' from the clutches of the corrupt authorities, they had, at least, managed to block the entrance to the compound with the armored vehicle. It would be several minutes before the police could follow in pursuit. Celeste took one last glance at her handiwork as the car turned a sharp corner.

"One thing's for certain, they know who was here!" she smiled.

The four revolutionaries abandoned the first escape car, then drove a second vehicle casually to the boarding house in Tigre. Their mood was sullen and the air was thick with frustration. It was the nonfamily member that finally vocalized his dismay.

"Well, as I see it, we didn't accomplish a damn thing today. No freed prisoners, no cash, just three dead policemen. That is sure to bring the heat down even harder. The people's movement isn't really benefiting in a tangible way from our little escapades, are they? And I have done fuckall to help! We have to do something that will make a difference. There must be something I can do to make a difference!"

"Lonnie, remember that we are soldiers of the people, fighting against terrible odds. Especially right now, with the security forces on the alert. We have let them know that we exist, and that we are ready to kill and be killed for the people. But I understand your frustration. You are a young Turk, anxious to lose your virginity, draw your first coup. Well, I have just the job for you. I will explain everything back at the boarding house." Serge Lavalle spoke in an almost fatherly tone to the anxious young buck.

As promised, less than five minutes after arriving back at their headquarters, the cadre leader summoned his troops.

"Sit down at the table."

Serge had retrieved a folder from the secret compartment of his suitcase. The others joined Lonnie at the dining room table.

"Miguel Tobias Panzino, under secretary for economic coordination. Here is his picture. Take a good look at it, study it. His job, Lonnie, is to distribute funds to various government agencies, including the military and social services. In other words, it is this man, and this man alone, that decides if the army gets a new tank or farmers in a flood-stricken village get emergency aid."

"Guns or butter, Lonnie! Remember, just like in my tutorials," Celeste interjected.

"That is right, guns or butter," Serge continued. "But this bastard has been in the pocket of the junta since they took power. Look at the military spending increases in each of the last two years. Not only that, this man is lining his own pockets. He is on the take. Government contracts also pass his desk. They are available for a healthy deposit to the bank of Miguel Tobias Panzino. Welfare and social benefits have been halved under this arrogant pig. The people are suffering as a direct result of this man's actions. Now, if he were eliminated, the person replacing him might be inclined, primarily out of fear for his own life, to reconsider those allocations. The voice of the people will be heard, Lonnie, and I am giving you the opportunity to be their spokesman."

An electric current surged up Lonnie's spine. This was it! A chance to make a difference by simply squeezing the trigger of his Llama pistol. A hit! A contract! An assassination! *Viva la revolution!*

He was euphoric as Serge detailed the particulars of their next exercise. It would be necessary to change their base of operations immediately following the hit, for the two brothers had already stayed longer than most guests at the boarding house in Tigre. To remain would only arouse suspicion.

There were already composite sketches of the Banco Nacional murderers circulating the capital. The sketches were poor quality and bore no resemblance whatsoever to the physical appearance of Serge and Celeste. He had cut his full beard and was now clean-shaven. She had discarded the red wig, then cut her natural dark curls and used peroxide to turn her remaining hair blonde. Only Jean Pierre's likeness was even close to the way he had appeared, and at that, it was still highly flawed. But to stay in Tigre would be a mistake. The odds of fooling the authorities and the townspeople were getting slimmer by the day.

The next morning's newspapers were full of the horrors of the police station bombing. The three officers had all been killed, a testament to Celeste's proficiency with a submachine gun. There was the usual outrage from high officials, but there was also another denunciation by Adolfo Bertoni. Speaking on behalf of not only the Montoneros, but for all people's revolutionary activists, the part-time coke dealer swore to wash his own dirty laundry and rid the country of these killers.

The two-faced bastard! were the words that came to Serge Lavalle's mind. Bertoni reaffirmed that his own people were hot on the trail of these 'rebels,' and that they would shown no mercy if the real Montoneros found them first.

"We will do the job on Friday the eleventh, four days from now," Serge announced at their evening meeting. "It will be the start of his weekend. He should be relaxed, off-duty, and somewhat off-guard. You will hit him in front of his residence. He lives on a quiet street in Recoleta. We have four days to perfect our schedule, memorize his routine, and find new accommodations for us after the fact. Lonnie, we will need more money for cars and necessities. We can go to your bank this afternoon, right after we do our first drive-through Panzino's neighborhood. Lonnie and I will set this one up alone. It is too dangerous for us all to be in the capital together. Any questions?"

The excitement of his first real revolutionary act clouded the fact that Lonnie was being used for exactly the purpose Celeste had recruited him for. The new soldier just could not see the facts. He was financing the entire operation through his personal bank account. He was now going to take the fall if anything went awry with the pending assassination. Celeste had molded him into exactly the person that she had set out to create. She was aware of the tremendous physical power she had over him. If football and politics didn't mix, no one could say the same for sex and politics!

At exactly five-thirty p.m. on Friday, April eleventh, the unfortunate Miguel Tobias Panzino happened to step out of a brand-new Mercedes sedan in front of his residence on Callao Avenue. Señor Panzino had a taste for fine automobiles, and he had declined a chauffeur on this day to drive the vehicle by himself. The spacious, walled casa was situated directly up the street from Recoleta Cemetery. At that moment, the under secretary had no idea that he would be taking up permanent residence there very shortly.

Panzino's usual police escort, a precaution afforded to all high-ranking government officials because of the recent surge in terrorist activities, had been reduced to one police car. Serge had been right. The unsuspecting official must have figured that a quiet weekend lay ahead, free from state or public business. No need for extra security. A brief ride through the downtown streets from his office and he would be safely home.

Serge Lavalle sat behind the wheel of the latest 'terrorist taxi,' as he called the escape cars. Lonnie De Seta had moved from behind the large shrubs that bordered the entrance drive to Señor Panzino's casa. Serge could see the under secretary wave the police car goodbye as he collected his briefcase and personal effects. Lonnie, having seen the cruiser depart from his hiding place, was now twenty paces up the driveway, quickly approaching his target.

Panzino was stooped over the backseat from the rear driver's side door. When he stood erect and turned to enter the house, his arms full of folders and a large leather briefcase, he came face-to-face with the barrel of Lonnie's Llama pistol.

Miguel Tobias Panzino was not a brave man, and he was not above begging for mercy in order to save his life. The official started to tremble, and a warm wetness ran down his trouser leg.

"Please, Señor, do not shoot me. I have money I can give you, anything you want! Stop, in God's name. Do not shoot me. I have children. Oh, Holy Mother of Jesus . . ." Panzino's voice was rising in volume as he pleaded for his life. The under secretary was virtually screaming by the time he uttered his last word.

"This is for the poor people of Argentina, you military lackey. May your soul rot in Hell!"

Lonnie was almost sorry that he had to pull the trigger. He was enjoying the self-serving puppet's discomfort so much. The single report of the pistol reverberated throughout the neighborhood. The shot hit Miguel Tobias Panzino squarely between the eyes, from a distance of six yards. The force of the gunshot hurled him backwards into the rear door frame of the Mercedes, then rebounded his near lifeless body forward, directly into the arms of a surprised Lonnie De Seta.

The terrorist noticed that there was very little blood evident on Señor Panzino, only a peso-sized entry hole above the bridge of his nose. As he tried to free himself from the dying man's grasp, a screaming Señora Panzino came flying through the front door of the casa.

"Assassin, you have shot my Miguel. Assassin!"

She was fast approaching the Mercedes. Lonnie turned the pistol on her. The lady stopped dead in her tracks.

The temporary diversion was costly to the people's soldier. With his dying spasm, Miguel Tobias Panzino raised his right arm and managed to dislodge Lonnie's dark glasses and baseball cap. The shocked killer stood staring, unmasked, at the newly widowed Señora Panzino.

"Assassin! I have seen your face! I will remember your face to my dying day. Shoot me now, for I will never rest until I see you tortured and hanged!" She spat on the drive in Lonnie's direction.

Lonfranco De Seta could only stare blankly at this shrieking apparition. His finger only had to squeeze the trigger once more and he would be rid of this vile, threatening woman. The blast from Serge's car horn shattered the temporary silence.

"Soldier, get in the car, now!" Serge called out through the passenger side window. Lonnie's trigger finger seemed frozen, unable to react. He knew that he should waste the bitch. She could now identify him. She could ruin everything! But the rookie murderer could not kill a second time. He simply lowered the Llama, turned, and walked slowly to the car.

The assassin's last image of the scene in the Panzino driveway was of Señora Panzino sobbing uncontrollably as she cradled her dead husband's body. *That woman could be my undoing,* Lonnie thought to himself as Serge hit the accelerator.

The 'terrorist taxi' traveled only a few blocks until it was abandoned in favor of another vehicle. That car then headed south on Del Liberator Avenue straight into Boca. The rush hour traffic and early Friday night revellers made it easy for the two people's soldiers to meld in. The first stop was a pay telephone booth, where Serge made a brief call to a local radio station.

"Listen to what I have to say and don't talk. I am a member of the Montonero cadre that has just assassinated the under secretary for economic coordination, Miguel Tobias Panzino. He has been slain because he was a member of the antipopular economic team of the military dictatorship. He has committed economic atrocities against the underprivileged masses. The people will rise against injustice. *Viva la revolution!*"

The next stop was the room in Barracas, where Celeste would be waiting.

"You did a dangerous thing back there by not killing that woman, Lonnie. She saw your face, she can identify you. Man, you should have blown her away!" Serge Lavalle lectured his neophyte killer.

The soldier sat pensively looking at his general. They were parked in front of the nondescript transient hotel in Barracas that had become Lonnie and Celeste's new home. While Serge's words echoed eerily through the small vehicle, Lonnie's thoughts were fixed on the words of the recently widowed Señora Panzino.

"But you did well, Lonnie, you made a clean hit. The people of Argentina will make you a hero for this. You are a true revolutionary now, so take pride in your achievement."

For some reason, Lonnie could find little solace in the praise of his leader. Serge continued to address him.

"Be very careful now. Do not go out until you talk to me again. The heat will be intense because of your actions. I will be in touch in a few days. Here, take these. They will hide your face as you make your way to Celeste's room. Do not look at anyone, do not speak to anyone. If my guess is correct, your likeness will be on the front cover of every newspaper in the country tomorrow morning. Start to grow a beard, right away. Let your hair grow as well. Above all, take care, my friend. Power to the people!"

With those words, he handed Lonnie an old slouch hat and a pair of dark glasses, then sped off as soon as his rider had stepped onto the curb. The new guest made it to room number thirty-two without being noticed by anyone, as even the desk clerk was having an impromptu siesta.

Celeste had outfitted their room for a considerable stay, stockpiling staples and necessities that would enable them to be exposed to the public as little as possible. They would cook their food by means of Coleman stoves, and keep those items that should be refrigerated cool by using ice inside portable coolers. Only Celeste would venture out to the market and newsstand on infrequent occasions as needed. The only items that Lonnie had at his disposal for entertainment were an old television set with uncertain reception and a small portable radio.

Serge had been correct. Lonnie's likeness was pasted on the front page of the Clarín, as well as every other newspaper and television news report the next morning. The police artist must have worked all night with Señora Panzinos to capture the traits of her husband's murderer while they were still vivid in her mind. It was a vaguely accurate representation, but it could have been almost anyone. The widow had used the phrase 'attractive, with a rugged, manly appearance' several times in describing the assailant, and the press picked it up and ran with it. The 'Attractive Assassin' became a media sensation overnight, and again Serge was correct, the heat was intense.

Hundreds of innocent people were rounded up and interrogated. Many were never seen or heard from again, but the 'Attractive Assassin' remained at large. He was confined to his own small world, but he was still a free man.

Celeste was the only one in contact with her brothers, and the news that she brought back to Lonnie after seeing them was always the same. "Sit tight, it is still too hot to make a move to another hideout, let alone plan another operation."

For almost a month he had 'sat tight,' but even Celeste's womanly charms were starting to wear thin. He was beginning to act like the caged animal that he felt he was becoming. Several times, his volatile temper got the best of him, often over insignificant matters. It was only Celeste's warning that the desk clerk might call the police that settled him down.

He was also starting to feel that he was all alone in his troubles. Celeste had been reassuring enough, but she and her brothers were, after all, family. They would stick together, no matter what happened. Blood was thicker than water. Likewise, it was his own sense of family duty that compelled him to take to the streets for the first time on the morning of May fifth.

Celeste had gone to the market and then to see her brothers, so if he was both swift and lucky, she would never be the wiser to his temporary absence. If his mother had truly disowned him, then he only had one relative left that really mattered. It was that relative's nineteenth birthday on May the fifth, nineteen hundred and seventy-eight, and Lonnie desperately wanted to hear Renaldo's voice again.

He had taken Serge's advice and grown a lush, full beard. Combined with his straggly long hair, he bore absolutely no resemblance to the 'Attractive Assassin.' Lonnie encountered no problems on his clandestine journey to a secluded pay telephone. He was buoyed by his younger brother's spirit, despite a possible career-threatening injury. The assassin wished that he could have told Renaldo the truth . . . that he was in huge trouble and just wanted to come home. What on earth had he done with his life? What on earth had he turned into? The older brother's eyes were filled with tears as he skulked back into room number thirty-two.

Celeste was late returning from her excursion, but it wasn't her tardiness that upset Lonnie when she finally arrived. It was her state of mind. She was nearly hysterical, so much so that he had trouble understanding exactly what she was trying to say between the gasping sobs that raked her body.

"Je . . . Jean . . . Pi . . . Jean Pierre, is . . . dead! Oh my God, he's dead! I went to their rooming house . . ." She paused to catch her breath, then in one heartrending outburst from the depths of her soul, she cried out the tale in sheer anguish.

"There were police and people everywhere. I overheard two policemen talking. They said that there had been a killing, but that the police were not involved with the actual murder. That it seemed from some of the posters and notes found in the dead man's room that this was an act of terrorist revenge . . . a settling of accounts. The landlady had said that there were two men sharing the room, and that the other man was unaccounted for at this, oohhhhh . . . time. Serge, I . . . I . . . don't know what happened to Serge!" she gasped for breath, tears streaming down her cheeks.

"I managed to shove my way to the back of the ambulance, just as they were carrying Jean Pierre out on a stretcher. They hadn't covered him up with a blanket or anything. I saw his face. It was horrible! The medic told the driver not to hurry, that it was only a, ohhhh . . . a . . . 'stiff!' He was dead, Lonnie! Jean Pierre, oh God . . . my baby brother is dead!"

CHAPTER TWENTY

Two days after Jean Pierre's assassination, Renaldo De Seta was seated in the parlor of Buenos Recuerdos sipping tea with his English grandmother, Lydia. The family matriarch had been thrilled that her grandson was paying a visit so soon after his birthday. This enabled her to present the young man with her own gift, a beautiful, native leather briefcase. The visit also enabled the lady to give her grandson some old-fashioned doting and tender loving care.

"Renaldo, I know that if things work out the way you hope, there will be no need for an attaché case for a while. At least not for medical texts. But even football players need something to carry their team documents in, don't they?" Lydia had joked.

The lady looked fantastic. The Pampas air and open spaces certainly agreed with her. She was still very active in the management of the estancia and had slowed down very little considering that she was now in her seventy-ninth year.

Grandmother and grandson talked at length of many things, both old and new. Stories from the past and hopes for the future. Renaldo touched briefly on the subject of his mother's new beau, but gave no concrete details. He knew that Peter De Seta was the only man that Lydia cared to hear about in connection with the former Florencia Robillar.

Renaldo did relate that the new man was very pleasant and also polite and attentive to his mother. He went on to describe the unusual birthday gift that the nameless gentleman had presented to him.

The three of them had dined together at Casa San Marco on the evening of Renaldo's birthday, at which time Herr Stoltz had unveiled an engraved sterling wine bucket with a bottle of Dom Pérignon resting inside. Four matching crystal flutes completed the gift. The card that hung around the neck of the bottle read, 'Do not open until the World Cup is ours!'

"I hope that I do not have to wait another four years, or longer, before opening this bottle, Herr Stoltz."

"I am counting on it being opened in just over a month's time, Renaldo. I am also hoping that you will be partly responsible for that happening."

Florencia's icy stare curtailed the prospect of further discussion on the subject. It was known to all parties that Herr Stoltz had a conflict of interest as far as Renaldo's future was concerned. Loyalty to his employer would dictate hopes for a speedy return to the lucrative world of international soccer. Loyalty to Florencia would dictate a return to university and a medical career.

In Florencia's mind, the matter had been settled by divine intervention in the guise of her son's injury. It was a sign, a beacon showing him the true course of his future. The Senora would allow no talk of football in her household!

She had given Renaldo an engraved Mount Blanc pen and pencil set with his name and the date inscribed. To rub salt into his wound further, the words 'Good luck at university' were written prominently on the card that accompanied the gift. The evening was cordial, but not overly cheery.

Renaldo told his mother nothing of the phone call from Lonnie that morning. He did inform her of his wish to go to Pergamino to see his grandmother and 'clear his head,' before the school term commenced. Florencia thought that it was a good idea for her son to get away for a few days and readily offered Olarti's services to act as chauffeur and attendant. The plan had worked exactly as Renaldo had hoped.

It was arranged with Lydia that Renaldo and Olarti would spend their second day on the Pampas touring the operations. Lydia declined to accompany the two men, much to her grandson's relief, stating that she had just completed a similar tour herself the previous week and thought her time best spent attending to other matters. The two men departed on their scheduled rounds, but deviated from the stated course and ended up in the small village of Tuerto, two hours' drive from Buenos Recuerdos.

It was there that one of Olarti's local contacts had found Copiapo. It was there that Copiapo had agreed to see Renaldo De Seta.

The native healer was everything Renaldo had expected: weathered skin the texture of leather from years in the broiling sun, long grey hair tied in a pony tail, with the ends braided into decorated ringlets, a toothless grin below eyes that were feeble in vision but all-seeing in knowledge.

He was seated cross-legged on the floor of the shanty that served as his temporary home when the two men were shown in to the single-room structure. The ancient one seemed to have several followers attending to his needs, but they were all congregated on the outside of the dwelling. Copiapo sat meditating in solitude as his guests waited patiently for him to acknowledge their presence.

It was necessary for Olarti to translate the proceedings, for the healer spoke only in his native tongue. His first interaction was little more than a two-syllable grunt. Renaldo looked to his attendant for enlightenment.

"Take off all your clothes, including the brace," Olarti commanded.

"Everything? Even my shorts?" was the boy's stunned reply.

"Everything!" Olarti responded firmly.

With that, he unbound the leather ankle brace that Tito had fashioned especially for support of the heel area. The swelling and inflammation had subsided in time, allowing for the application of the brace. Pressure was kept on the tendon to provide for support and promote healing. Daily therapy in Tito's capable hands had provided some strengthening, but progress had been slow.

The old man pointed to the brace that lay on the ground in front of its owner. Olarti, who was supporting his employer so that the younger man could undress without using his crutches, knelt and handed the device to the medicine man. Copiapo inspected the object with great interest, turning it in every direction. When he finally looked up, Renaldo stood before him, supported by Olarti, naked as the day he was born.

The healer gazed at the boy's physique silently for several minutes, then motioned with his arm for him to turn around. Again, several minutes of silence followed. A second mumbled series of grunts was translated to mean that the patient was to lie on his back, resting his damaged limb in front of the aged healer.

Searching hands fondled the entire foot, caressing, probing, but never causing pain, even when exploring the tenderest areas. At the conclusion of his examination, the healer locked eyes with his young patient. Time seemed to stand still, but Renaldo did not feel uncomfortable and never broke the contact. Another grunt ended the intimate exchange.

From a leather medicine kit, Copiapo retrieved several pouches and a vial of amber-colored liquid. He then rang a small bell that had sat unnoticed by his side. Instantly, an attractive native woman entered the shanty and proceeded directly to squat by his side. Renaldo reacted to his vulnerability in the presence of a female by groping for his shirt and covering his privates. The natives were amused by the Porteño's discomfort, exchanging broad grins before conversing. Their dialogue was totally one-sided, with the old man mumbling instructions, the woman nodding affirmation, and Olarti a mute witness. When Copiapo stopped talking, the woman picked up the articles that he had pulled from his kit, rose to the upright position, then announced in perfect Spanish that the session was over and that they should follow her out as soon as Renaldo was dressed. Both men mumbled their appreciation in their native tongues. It was as if they had been afflicted with the old man's voice, so hoarse and unintelligible were the croaked thank-yous.

Quinta was the native woman's name, and she ran through Copiapo's instructions in a soft, patient manner. Renaldo was to continue to use the brace, as well as all his current treatments. He was to make a compress of the plants and powders contained in the pouches, combining them with the oil in the vial. He was then to apply the mixture and bind it tightly to the damaged area by means of a lambskin cloth. That was all that was necessary according to the holistic guru.

"Copiapo says that your wound will heal," Quinta whispered gently, touching the boy's forearm. "He says that you have fine structure, as well as an intense will. You can go now. I wish you both good spirit."

"Something strange on the telephone report sheet from Casa San Marco this morning, Astor. It might bear checking out," Wolfgang Stoltz announced as he entered his employer's inner sanctum on the morning of May sixth.

"There was a call to the casa yesterday morning from Lonfranco De Seta, the eldest son. From my privileged position, I am aware that Lonfranco has been in his mother's disfavor since he refused to return to school in March. The boy claims to be traveling the country with his girlfriend, Celeste Lavalle. The call was a routine exchange of birthday greetings between the brothers. Nothing controversial was discussed. The incongruous part is that Lonfranco told his brother that he was calling from Bariloche, in the Lake District, but the call was actually placed from a pay phone in Barracas, only a few miles from the casa. Why, if he were so close, would he not just get in his car and wish his brother happy birthday in person?"

Astor Gordero looked up from the plate of eggs and peppers that he was devouring.

"That does seem strange, quite out of character. The brothers are very close. I know that for a fact. Only some kind of disagreeable circumstance would keep Lonnie away from the casa on his brother's birthday. And why would he lie about his location?"

"Perhaps it was fear of his mother's attitude that kept him away, fear of confrontation on his brother's special day. She never utters his name in my presence. It would seem as if she has totally disowned him."

"The lady is given to uttering no one's name but yours these days, from what I hear. That is because she thinks of nothing other than your big, uncircumcised cock, Wolfie!" Astor Gordero chuckled as he shoveled in another forkful of food. A sly grin was firmly planted on Wolfgang Stoltz's face.

"Wait just one moment. Barracas? Barracas! Look at this." Gordero held out a copy of the morning Clarín to his associate.

"That terrorist was murdered in Barracas yesterday. This could be mere coincidence, but on the other hand, there could be a lot more to it. Look, look at this. It says that the act was clearly an assassination, that the dead man was tortured before he was killed. There were several revenge notes found at the scene from another left-wing group. There were also several sets of identification found, but it does not say what the man's real name was. Let's see if they have identified him yet."

A huge, jam-stained hand reached for the telephone receiver and dialed in several numbers. "I want to speak with Colonel Clavijo right away. This is Astor Gordero speaking."

Police Colonel Rafael Clavijo was an old crony of The Fat Man's and was one of the Newton's Prefect celebrants on Gordero's private rail car that had traveled to Cordoba.

"Colonel, Astor here. Tell me, have you made a positive identification on that terrorist in Barracas?"

"Yes, yes, of course. The police department is very efficient, and in this case, very lucky. Two sets of identification were found bearing the same address in Tucumán, a terrorist hotbed. We checked them out and they came up positive. The documents belong to a pair of brothers, it would seem. Lavalle was the dead man's name, Jean Pierre Lavalle. The other man, Serge Lavalle, is still unaccounted for. He may be a hostage, or he may turn up in some ditch. It certainly is nice when this scum eradicate their own. Gives me more time for the finer things in life. I will keep you posted, Astor. Anything else I can do for you?"

"You have been most helpful, as always, Colonel. We will dine together soon. I will see to it! Good-bye, Rafael."

"Lavalle, Celeste Lavalle's brother! Florencia always refers to her as 'that communist slut,' for she makes her leftist leanings very clearly known. The university had alerted the police about her," Stoltz enthused as his precise mind assembled the pieces of the puzzle.

"Then it would seem that Lonfranco De Seta has made the acquaintance of the Lavalle brothers, and perhaps they have converted him to their terrorist ways," Astor added. "Get some men down to Barracas right away and see what else you can find out through our other sources. If Lonnie De Seta has turned into a terrorist, it will make his elimination even easier than we expected. I want to see Rojo Geary as soon as possible. Not here, but at the usual location. Good work, Wolfie! Make sure you give the wire tap operator a raise for his fine work."

Astor Gordero threw his linen napkin down on the table and rose from his breakfast. He patted his enlarged girth with both hands and smiled contentedly to himself.

"Isn't it funny how life works out sometimes, Wolfie? I was expecting to have a lot of trouble removing the elder De Seta brother from the family structure, but if things unfold as I suspect, we will have less work to do on him than any of the others. If the police don't find him, Rojo Geary will. Then it will be 'rest in peace, Señor Lonfranco De Seta.' The family fortune is falling into our hands even more easily than I had anticipated. This good news calls for some champagne! Herr Stoltz, would you kindly crack a bottle of our finest, while I call down for some hors d'oeuvres? Fate really does work in strange ways! Come, let us toast the pending acquisition of the De Seta financial empire!"

CHAPTER TWENTY-ONE

London, England. May 6, 1978.

"Two fingers for Sir Reggie!" someone yelled above the din.

"Two fingers? Bloody hell, crack the jeroboams!" was Sir Reginald Russell's retort.

Instantly the sound of corks popping reverberated throughout the dank, cramped confines. Paper coffee cups were filled to overflowing with Moet & Chandon's finest bubbly. Mud-splattered, half-naked players rubbed shoulders with gentlemen in Savile Row overcoats and suits. The air was thick with cigar smoke, sweat, and backed-up latrines. Sir Reggie gulped down the contents of an entire vessel in one swallow.

"More! Fill it up again, Monteith, and keep filling it up until I bloody well fall on my keister." Another paper chalice was drained in a heartbeat. "Again, Monteith. Be spry with that bottle, you old sod!"

Archibald Monteith reacted to the request with a steady hand that spilt nary a drop of the precious liquid. Replenished, Sir Reggie allowed himself to slump against a dirty brick wall.

"Forty years! Forty bloody years! We're back now though, we're really back! Monteith! Keep the cup filled, man. Is that too hard a task to perform?"

Monteith knew his retainer too well, though. He could always find some trivial matter to busy himself with that would allow him to ignore his Lordship's requests for more alcohol. The ex-Royal Marine medic was now absorbed in topping up some of the board of director's cups. Sir Reggie understood. The two men had an unspoken agreement, the result of many years spent in each other's company. When Sir Reginald Russell began drinking, Archibald Monteith assumed the ultimate control of how much and when to holler 'enough!' This had enabled his Lordship to avoid countless embarrassing situations.

"Two fingers, huh! I prefer the taste of the bubbly. Think I could get used to it, too," Sir Reggie mumbled to himself as he drank in the atmosphere of the fetid cavern. Two fingers of his favorite Glen Moray single malt Scotch had most often been consumed to dull the pain of frustrating defeats during the long climb back to the top. 'The top' being a return to the first division ranks of the English Football Association.

Today they had made it back, back after forty years in the shadows. "The Canaries are back!" he shouted to no one in particular. That was certainly cause enough to crack the huge bottles of champagne that Monteith had hidden in the dressing room after the interval. The score had been tied at nil, but Sir Reggie just had a feeling. All they needed was a tie, one point, to clinch promotion. The Canaries did better than that, though. They won, 2-0, sending the home crowd into a long-awaited frenzy.

"The Isle of Dogs will be howling tonight!" he laughed out loud.

Now the real work would begin, and Reginald Russell knew it all too well. It was one thing to attain promotion to the FA first division, but it was a totally different thing to represent yourself well and avoid being embarrassed by the 'Gods of English football.'

Manchester United vs. Canary Wharf in a first division fixture? Surely some people would take it as a misprint, a jest. Those poor souls didn't know their FA history. Canary Wharf had been there many times, to Old Trafford, to Highbury, to White Hart Lane. The Canaries had competed since 1897, never missing a season. There had been many peaks and valleys . . . deep, deep, valleys, but now they were back. Back where Sir Reggie wanted them, back where they belonged.

Someone in the crowd called for a few words from their patron, and with that, Sir Reggie tried to disappear into the shadows, heading for the therapist's door.

"Come on, me Lord. All's they want is a few words. Just tell them how proud of them you are. Come on, here he is, here's Sir Reggie for you."

Monteith led the chairman of the board of directors to the trainer's wooden crate and gave Sir Reggie an arm up.

The assembled mass cheered wildly. Sir Reggie motioned for them to stop, only encouraging them further.

"Please, gentlemen. Gentlemen, please! Thank you, thank you. Allow me a few words of thanks. To the board of directors for their judgment and support, to the working press for remembering history, to manager Randal Horton and his staff for a fine strategy and the perseverance to see it bear fruit, and last, but certainly not least, to you, the Canary Wharf players. You were the ones that made our dreams come true. Thank you, thank you all. Now gentlemen, a toast to the Canaries! Three cheers, hip hip hooray, hip hip . . ."

As he was partway through the cheer, Sir Reggie remembered one person who he had forgotten to thank, the person perhaps most responsible for the team, and himself, being where they were today. He whistled loudly for silence as the last hooray echoed above the unusual scene.

"Gentlemen, your attention for one more moment, if you will. There is a very special person that I forgot to acknowledge, and I think you all know the influence this person has had on me. For obvious reasons, this lovely creature is not in the room with us at the moment, lest she be scared out of her wits by those dangling participles that seem to escape their towels every so often. However, my daughter, Mallory, is the one person who instilled in me the will to bring the Canaries back to the first division. I can tell you in all honesty that it was her unflinching spirit and daily enthusiasm that transformed me into a man possessed with accomplishing this feat. Now, Monteith, get me a full cup, for I am going to find the lady and give her some of the celebratory reward. Carry on, gentlemen!"

To the sound of a hearty "here, here," Sir Reggie leapt from his pedestal with two full cups of cheer, Monteith having relented and given his Lordship a cup of his own with which to join his daughter in celebration.

It was an arduous journey to the exit, numerous well-wishers and story seekers blocking the way. The English press had been full measure in their support of the Canaries ascension, for tradition and history were what made English football so unique. The Canaries were one of the old-guard teams, and as such, were shown the respect Sir Reggie felt they should be accorded. Each scribe seemed to want a personal word from the chairman as he struggled toward the door. Reggie politely sidestepped all requests and pushed onward, but he stopped dead in his tracks when he came upon Lawton MacRae.

The man cut a striking pose, sitting astride a dust bin, a Marlboro cigarette and bottle of Bass Ale keeping him company. He was stripped to the waste, but had retained his match shorts, stockings, and cleats. A large, toothless grin was plastered on his weathered face.

He was the eldest of the lot. Their captain. Experience personified! Thirteen seasons with the club, all in the netherlands of the charts. Third division, then second. Really never a thought of the big league, not until Mallory Russell got involved. Then it all changed, and Lawton MacRae was there to see it happen.

"Lawton, hail fellow, Lawton. How does it feel, man? We made it, made it to the big time again!"

"Aye, gov'nor, it feels right smug, it does at that!"

"There'll be a bonus in your stocking, Lawton! Enjoy yourself, you've earned it."

Then it was on through the crowd and finally out into the passageway.

She stood in the shadows, almost invisible. The body moved first, intercepting the intruder.

"Right, Sir Reginald. Lady Russell, it's your father."

With that, the plainclothes Marine sergeant withdrew to the shadows himself. According to proper military protocol, the sergeant should have addressed his superior officer by his rank, Lieutenant Colonel, but Reginald Russell forbade military decorum when he was in civilian clothing.

"Reggie, isn't it wonderful? They're tearing up the turf, and the singing . . . it sent shivers up my spine."

The commotion from the pitch was still reverberating down the player's tunnel as a triumphant father and daughter stood relishing the moment. Sir Reggie gave his daughter a loving smile.

Even in the half-light there was no mistaking her beauty. Her long blond hair was tucked neatly into a tam, accentuating her fine cheekbones and flawless complexion. Her eyes remained a mystery, however, hidden behind dark glasses that afforded her the anonymity she felt she required on occasions such as these. It was false security, for everyone in the football circles knew or knew of Mallory Russell. Sir Reggie's favorite, the real brains behind the Canary Wharf revival, the best-looking and shrewdest woman connected with football in all of Great Britain! This was really her moment, and Sir Reggie knew it well.

"Mallory, darling, I've brought you some good cheer, and a heartfelt 'hoorah' from the gentlemen inside." Sir Reggie embraced his only daughter, trying not to spill his champagne all over them.

"You're to blame for all of this, you know," he chastised her ruefully. "All this noise and mess. And now, what are we going to do? I can see the headlines already in August . . .'Notts Forest Feasts On Canaries,' or how about, 'Liverpool Makes Canary-Paté Out Of First Division Pretenders!' There are no legs left in there, darling, although I must say, there are several other parts of the body that seem in excellent condition! Oh, sorry." Sir Reggie never missed an opportunity to instill some of his famous bawdy humor into a discussion.

"Father!" Mallory recoiled in mock disgust. "Their legs will be fine, the good ones, at least. As for the rest, it's up to us to bring in some new blood, real footballers. We'll use the best we've got, but if we have to play with the rest of this lot, heaven help us!"

It was at that moment that the seed was planted, the seed of an idea that would change their lives. It had to do with the 'new blood, the real footballers.' Neither of the Russells could know that Mallory's comment would cast the die on a long, arduous journey. The events that were about to unfold had their conception in that dimly lit passage.

"The board will have to meet early next week to plan a strategy, and we'll want to have that architect there with the plans for the east stands. What was his name?"

"Hughes, father, John Hughes," Mallory replied impatiently.

"Right, Hughes! You would think that I could remember that after all this time. Well, it looks as if it's a go, the expansion of the Bird Cage. Neville Strathy had a word with me at the final whistle. The financing is all in place. With board approval, we can start construction this month!"

He embraced his daughter once more, positively beaming with enthusiasm and good cheer.

It had all come together so nicely. The years of frustration had given way to the feeling that the Canary Wharf Football Club was now poised on the brink of its new destiny. Sir Neville Strathy, chairman of the National Westminster Bank, had been a schoolboy chum of Reginald Russell's at Eton in the 1930s. The old boy network came in handy at times, and Sir Reggie had kept all his banking, accounting, and legal business with fellows that he knew from the 'old days.'

It was Strathy's financial clout that was about to allow the Canaries to expand their ancient home stadium, lovingly known as the Bird Cage, to standards expected of a first division football team. Strathy had been a Canary supporter ever since the two men had met, but he had always told his friend that it was necessary for the team to achieve entry into the English league first division before he could be of any real assistance. That time had come, and Sir Reggie was about to call in his marker.

The Canary Wharf Football Club had been founded in 1897 by Reginald Russell's grandfather, Sir Arthur Grainger Russell, thirteenth Earl of Weymouth. It had been a gentleman's wager with shipbuilding magnet Arnold F. Hills, proprietor of the Thames Ironworks, that prompted young Arthur to form a semi-amateur team made up of stevedores, dock workers, tugboat crewmen, and ferry sailors. These men were all employed in the area of Canary Wharf, situated on the Isle of Dogs in London's east end.

The arrogant Mr. Hills had formed his own club two years earlier, primarily to give his shipbuilders a heightened sense of pride in their company. Mr. Hills also believed that the sport could be a healthy outlet for his employee's physical and mental well-being. The popularity of the team astonished its founder, with thousands of people turning out to watch the amateurs at Browning Road, East Ham.

Hills, an ardent Victorian capitalist, saw a chance to increase the prestige of his company's name, as well as make a tidy profit from this football enthusiasm. He set out to find a location for a proper stadium that would capture the imagination of the entire nation. His quest for a site ended in 1897, when Hills announced that he would construct the most magnificent recreational complex in all of England at a site in West Ham. The 'Memorial Recreation Ground' was to house a stadium with a capacity for over one hundred thousand spectators, as well as facilities for cricket, tennis, and cycling.

When the grounds opened on the sixteenth anniversary of Queen Victoria's ascension to the throne, it was everything for which Hills had hoped. The London press trumpeted that the facility was 'good enough to hold the Football Association Cup final in.' However, there were problems from the outset.

Hill's football team became more competitive each year after moving into their own posh grounds, and both the players and their fans were anxious to join the ranks of the professional leagues in order to continue their improvement. Hills looked upon professionalism as a form of prostitution, for he strongly believed in the purity of amateur sport. He reacted by throwing the would-be professionals out of his facility in 1904, then promptly reformed a truly amateur squad which had the exclusive use of the Memorial Recreational Ground. The displaced team was forced to relocate to a cabbage patch next to Boleyn Castle in Upton, a short distance from their former home. Here, they merged with Boleyn Castle F.C. and became known as West Ham United F.C. They adopted their nickname and symbol from the shipbuilder's tool, and thence became the 'Hammers.' This team continued to draw the majority of its support from those involved with the shipbuilding trades. The Thames Ironworks amateurs and the Memorial Recreation Grounds faded into history, along with their authoritarian patron.

Back in 1897, though, Arthur Russell had no such delusions about the evils of professionalism as he put together the very first Canary Wharf side. After accepting Hill's challenge and the obligatory wager on a match between the shipbuilders and the 'sea rats,' as the Thames Ironworks owner referred to Arthur's ragtag charges, the younger man set about town to hire a few 'ringers.'

Emotions ran high among the hundreds of fans that had turned out as the two teams took to the barely passable playing field on Hermit Road in Canning Town. Hills was certain that his squad, with two years experience under their belts, would wallop the upstart 'dockies,' but that was not to be the case. Arthur Russell had spent his money wisely on three Southern League players, a keeper and two classy forwards. He plugged his defense with rugged, burly bruisers that manhandled the shipbuilders at every opportunity. The two professional forwards earned their wages that afternoon, each scoring twice to give the 'sea rats' a 4-1 victory. Arnold Hills left the grounds in a rage after learning that he had been duped by young Russell and defeated by those 'professional whores.' He refused to pay over the wager money to Russell, even though there had never been any discussion about the use of such players. The two men never spoke again after that day.

Local support from the cockney residents on the Isle of Dogs was so fervent that the team never did disband, joining the Southern League for the following season. A site was needed for their own home field, and this prompted the enthusiastic twenty-eight-year-old Arthur to ask for an audience with his father, Reginald Eastwyck Russell, to resolve the matter.

Sir Reginald was a no-nonsense businessman who did not suffer fools gladly. He had served in the Royal Marines in his youth, as was the family tradition, and then had joined his father, Stuart Ridley Russell, in the family's lucrative import-export business. The heart and soul of that affair was located on the Isle of Dogs, four miles east of Buckingham Palace.

The Canary Islands Trading Company had been founded by a consortium of prominent bankers and businessmen to capitalize on the rich and exotic bounty that was found in the islands off the west coast of Africa. Thomas Stuart Russell, young Arthur's great-grandfather, had not only been one of the consortium's founding members, but had been the man most responsible for convincing the Londoners that there were huge profits to be made from trading with the islands.

Thomas Russell had spent all of his formative years at sea, initially as a Royal Marine, and then as the captain of his own merchant vessel as he sought to reap the benefits of his earlier nautical education. The riches of the world lay at Thomas' feet, and he was determined to capitalize on his knowledge and good fortune.

Of all the places that he had weighed anchor, none so impressed him as the Canary Islands. Due to their relative proximity to England, Russell felt that there was a far better chance for trading success in the Canaries than in the West Indies, which were several times the distance from London. Rich in wine, tropical fruits, spices, sugar, and tobacco, the islands were, at this time, a Spanish protectorate. But the King of Spain was anxious to open up commerce on the islands. He accepted Thomas Russell's proposal almost immediately, and armed with a trade agreement signed and sealed by his majesty the King of Spain, Russell sailed first to the Canary Islands to fill his ship's hold with wondrous cargo, and then on to London to show off his wares and raise the capital required to open up this new frontier.

Thomas Russell had come by his seafaring nature quite honestly. The family roots could be traced back to the late fourteenth century, when the Russells were thriving wine importers, distributors, and traders. The family had settled in Weymouth, Dorset, which was an active mercantile port at the time. The Russells were also involved in local politics, sending family members to parliament on several occasions.

In 1506, John Russell, a young, well traveled, multilingual lad with a charming disposition, was sent to the Court of Henry the Seventh to act as a gentleman usher. The royal court quickly became enamored of young Russell, and when seventeen-year-old Henry the Eighth ascended the throne a few years later, he entrusted his most important affairs to the talented, yet discreet, young man from Weymouth.

John Russell served his Majesty as a soldier, courier, and intelligencer during the wars with France that commenced in 1513. He gathered valuable experience and made many important contacts. He lost an eye in combat at Morlaix and was subsequently knighted for bravery by the Earl of Surrey.

Ever trustworthy, Russell's real work lay in the subtle, unprincipled world of international diplomacy. He was increasingly employed as a special envoy of the king, handling the most delicate affairs of state. His faithful service to the erratic Henry continued with flawless tact, and in 1539, John Russell was raised to the peerage as Baron Russell of Weymouth and made a Knight of the Garter.

Baron Russell continued to serve his master in any capacity required of him, including traveling to the continent with Henry's armies that were constantly warring with France. Through the years, he had acquired many estates and tracks of land in his native Dorset, and it was to his beloved home county that he returned to be by the sea as his health failed in the summer of 1554.

His career had spanned four reigns as a trusted courier, soldier, diplomat, and administrator. When John Russell died in March 1555, he was accorded a state funeral befitting a man of his standing and prominence. The first Earl of Weymouth had an immense fortune, as well as his good name to pass on to his descendants. Much of the family remained close to their roots by the sea, developing a reputation as merchant mariners, traders, and when duty called, officers and gentlemen of his Majesty's Royal Navy.

Two hundred and forty-three years after the death of the first Earl of Weymouth, Thomas Stuart Russell, the tenth Earl of Weymouth, arrived at the London dock yards with his tropical treasures. His reputation as a stalwart businessman and global navigator allowed him to assemble a consortium of enthusiastic entrepreneurs that were eager to invest in such a venture. A site for dockage and warehousing was secured on the Isle of Dogs and named 'Canary Wharf' after the source of their expected riches.

The Canary Islands Trading Company flourished almost immediately, and three generations later, the Russell family was still in control of the lucrative operation.

Now Arthur Russell sat facing the corporation's chairman, his dour father, Reginald. The elder Russell was devoid of any interest in the sport itself, but news of Arthur's sea rats' thumping of the shipbuilders had the whole community abuzz. His son's passionate plea for the continuation of the team and what it would mean to the men that toiled on Canary Wharf was not lost on Reginald Russell. The team spirit had already given the locals a focal point, a sense of belonging, a community source of pride.

The work on the docks was thankless, backbreaking toil that could easily wither a man's body and soul. "Football could give the workers strength through pride in their team," Arthur had told his father. Much to the younger Russell's surprise, the elder Russell agreed with him.

The corporation held a long-term lease on several acres of reclaimed marshland southeast of the Wharf, about ten minutes' walk from where father and son sat formulating the future. Despite his enthusiasm, Reginald Russell told his son that all he could do was bring the matter up at the next director's meeting for discussion. He did, nevertheless, assure his son that he personally would speak favorably for the proposed 'Canary Wharf Football Club.' That was more than Arthur had hoped, for he knew that his father was held in great esteem by the other directors. Arthur was certain that those men would be reluctant to deny their chairman such a request.

Two weeks later, Arthur Russell was called into his father's office.

"Pack your bags, my boy. We are taking a trip north to Glasgow. There is an engineer up there by the name of Archibald Leitch. He specializes in stadia design and construction. You have your team, Arthur, and soon, you will have one of the finest stadiums in London to play in as well."

With a howl of delight, the younger Russell embraced his father. Their journey to Glasgow was a great success, with the engineer proving both approachable and professional. A design was settled on consisting of one main covered grandstand in two tiers housing roughly nine thousand seats. This section of the grounds would be reserved for people of the carriage trade, gentlemen of wealth and influence and their families.

The main grandstand would have a multi-span roof with the individual letters of the word 'Canaries' painted on the front of each gable. Reginald Russell had chosen the name for the team personally, and also insisted that the colors be black and yellow, in deference to their namesake. The balance of the stadium would consist of standing terraces on three sides, all uncovered and accommodating some fifteen thousand patrons. These were the working man's vantage points, for it was from the terraces that true football fans watched their heroes play, or so was the popular belief of the time.

Total cost for the work was estimated at fourteen thousand pounds, a hefty sum in that era. But the Canary Wharf directors were caught up in the enthusiasm of their new project and the attention that it was drawing to their company in the London press. Leitch, seeing this enthusiasm firsthand on a trip to London, suggested to Reginald Russell that the ground be called 'The Bird Cage,' and sketched two distinctive cupolas resembling traditional bird cages on the end spans of the main grandstand roof. The chairman loved the idea, and 'The Bird Cage' became reality less than a year later.

One other item that arrived back in London with the Russells was a design for the Canary's team crest. Father and son had spent the entire trip home designing and refining the perfect logo. The end result of their collaboration centered around a bold, black, letter 'C.' Inside the initial proudly rested a black ship's anchor, representative of the team's seafaring roots. To add a dash of color, Arthur suggested that the anchor be set on a field of blue, as close to the color of the sparkling Atlantic Ocean off the Canary Islands as possible. When the graphic artists in London transferred the rough sketches and ideas produced by the Russells to finished form, the result was uniformly praised by the team's board of directors and adopted as the official team crest and corporate logo forthwith. The same crest would be worn on the Canaries' jerseys right into the last quarter of the new century.

That new century ushered in the Canaries' rise to the football league division two, and three years after that, promotion to the first division. The team had done all that was expected of it and more, giving the residents and workers of the Isle of Dogs a focal point that would shine some light on their dreary, workaday lives. The Canaries were the talk of the town, at least that part of the town, and sellout crowds became a Saturday tradition at The Bird Cage.

Young Arthur had proven to be a shrewd and resourceful manager. Each year, the team climbed steadily up the league ladder, until finally in 1913, the Canary Wharf Football Club won their first Football Association Cup. It was a triumph that would bring the last rays of sunshine to Arthur Russell's days in England.

With the outbreak of the First World War, the Canary Wharf manager rejoined his old Marine Battalion, the Fourth, and served his country for the next four years. Then, on April 23, 1918, during an attack on the German submarine base at Zeebrugge, Belgium, Major Arthur Grainger Russell was killed in action during the bloody, but successful operation.

The tragic news of Arthur's death was too much for seventy-nine-year-old Reginald, who suffered a stroke within hours of the telegram's delivery and passed away within a fortnight of his son. It had been the formation and ongoing operation of their beloved Canaries that had bonded father and son together, turning an icy, distant relationship into one of true love and warmth. The rest of the Russell family knew this for a fact, and in their honor, a bronze statue depicting the founding father and son team was erected outside the main grandstand entrance to the Bird Cage shortly after the end the war.

The family mantle was passed to Arthur's eldest son, twenty-eightyear-old Elliott Stuart Russell. The hostilities had also touched Elliott, who had been mustered out of the Royal Marines two years earlier after suffering the loss of his left arm, when his ship was sunk by one of the Kaiser's U boats.

The missing limb did not hinder Elliott Russell from fathering a son, born Reginald Arthur Nelson Russell, in the fall of 1919. Elliott had sired three daughters before the great conflict had commenced, and he was elated to finally have an heir to his title and business interests.

It was his business interests that totally preoccupied Elliott Russell, and the fortunes of his football team were left to hired managers. Working with a reduced budget and with minimal interest from the executive suite, the fortunes of the postwar Canaries soon hit the skids. They were relegated to the league second division in 1922, where they languished for the next nine seasons. Attendance suffered as a result, and the bottom-line attitude of their chairman, Elliott Russell, nearly caused the team to fold in the early 1930s. It was primarily the avid interest of Elliott's only son that convinced him to keep the team afloat, even though the world was suffering through the Great Depression.

Trade and commerce were severely affected by the global economic woes, and the profits of the Canary Wharf Trading Company were no exception. Thousands of workers were laid off from their jobs on the docks and from the seafaring vessels. But in spite of all this gloom, the amazing fact was that those same discarded workers turned to the football club to relieve their personal woes. Attendance at The Bird Cage actually increased in the first three years of the depression. By 1935, the Canaries were in a position to challenge for their old spot back in the first division.

Sixteen-year-old Reginald Russell urged his father to open the purse strings and acquire the necessary talent to gain promotion. While in boarding at Eton, young Reggie had formed a Canaries Fan Club amongst his peers. These youthful fanatics sent a petition to Elliott Russell, consisting of over two hundred signatures, pledging their undying support to the Canary Wharf Football Club.

While this did not translate into pounds and shillings, it moved the elder Russell to open the corporate coffers sufficiently to purchase a few class players that were available on the transfer market. Many of the other league division clubs were in dire financial straits, and they were more than happy to part with a player or two, just to keep the lights burning. The money was wisely spent, and the following season the Canaries, again, joined the ranks of England's football elite.

Gaining promotion was the easy part of the scheme. Competing with the likes of Manchester United, Leeds, Tottenham Hotspur and the rest of the league giants was another matter. The corporate balance sheet could not sustain the higher salaries that were demanded from first division players, and the old, but lovable Bird Cage was in great need of major refurbishment to bring it up to modern-day standards. The Canaries finished their first two seasons in the premier league in the lower regions of the table, avoiding relegation, but the writing was on the wall.

Without a major influx of capital, the team could not compete with their new adversaries for a prolonged period. While the Canary Wharf Trading Company had diversified into several different areas of trade and commerce before the Great Depression hit, the overall balance sheet was still extremely anemic by the start of 1938. The board of directors could not see the merit in pouring the corporation's capital into a venture that was losing money. The truth was that the football club had little hope of turning a profit without a larger, modern stadium that would warrant higher ticket prices. The funds for such a project were just not available in those belt-tightening times, and much to the dismay of his son, Elliott Russell refused to open his wallet a second time.

As a result, the Canaries sank to the bottom of the standings and were relegated to the second division at the end of the 1938 season.

The disappointed Canary Wharf supporters stayed away from the old Bird Cage by the thousands, taking their loyalties a few stops up the tube line to the home of the 'Hammers.' West Ham was enjoying a successful run at the top of the first division at the time, and the team still had strong links to the shipbuilding and seafaring community. The fortunes of his football team were insignificant to Elliott Russell, for he was astute enough to realize that there were far greater concerns facing the United Kingdom at that moment in time.

The news from the continent was chilling. In Germany, a country still despised by most Englishmen, a former corporal in the Kaiser's army was stirring the nationalistic passions of the Hun again. Adolph Hitler was a name that seemed to be in the news on a daily basis, and Elliott Russell knew full well where the rantings of this madman would lead. In early 1939, he obtained an audience with the War Ministry and offered all the resources of the Canary Wharf Trading Company to the service of his Majesty the King. Should war come again to the Empire, prime dock lands and their associated storage facilities would be of vital importance.

The gesture proved most timely, for when Germany invaded Poland in September of that same year, Great Britain found itself, once again, locked in deadly conflict with its old foe. The Canary Wharf Trading Company virtually ceased to exist during the six years that followed, and even the football team had to relocate its home fixtures due to the War Office's expropriation of the Bird Cage as a storage and training facility.

The Nazi air blitz on London that commenced in August 1940 pinpointed the shipping and marine facilities as primary targets, and both Canary Wharf and the Bird Cage suffered extensive damage as a result. It appeared to anyone who ever had been thrilled by the exploits of the yellow and black, that the once proud Canary Wharf Football Club would never rise from the ashes of Hitler's destruction.

But those people did not know Reginald Arthur Nelson Russell. The Canaries were never far from his thoughts, even though they had fallen on hard times and lost favor with many of their supporters. Young Reggie longed for the return to the glory years that were chronicled in the recently published team history, but he, like his father, had more pressing matters to attend.

After completion of his preparatory education at Eton, Reggie had enrolled in the Royal Naval College at Dartmouth. He had completed two years of training when the conflict broke out against the Axis forces in Europe. The lad was a gifted athlete who had been a championship swimmer at both Eton and the college. He had developed a striking physique from his pool activities and hours of canoeing on the River Dart. The early morning sorties up the Dart in his one-man Rob Roy canoe left him invigorated and ready to tackle the day's more mundane classroom activities.

Reginald Russell was a bright, energetic student. A voracious reader, he would tackle the complex questions of mathematics, astronomy, and naval warfare with an inquisitive mind. His shock of unruly blond hair was always distinguishable in the lecture halls, no matter how closely cropped the seaman's cut. Although he felt his appearance too angular to be considered handsome, the young ladies of Dartmouth obviously disagreed.

The aristocratic lad from London was the most popular of all the aspiring officers whenever college dances permitted female guests on the grounds. He was a spinner of yarns, and as smooth on his feet as he was quick with his wits. His years at the college were the happiest of his young life, but it was a lifestyle that came to an abrupt end when England learned the deadly meaning of the word 'blitzkrieg' in the fall of 1939.

The world was at war again, and every able-bodied man was needed to protect the Empire. After lengthy discussions with his father, Reggie decided to forgo the balance of his accelerated naval training and the assured commission as an officer upon graduation. Instead, he enlisted as a recruit in the Royal Marines, as was the family's military tradition.

Events moved quickly in Europe, and in a matter of months, the new enlistee was promoted to sergeant and put out to sea. His initial assignment, after completing basic training at the Marine depot in Deal, was protecting North Sea oil rigs aboard the corvette H.M.S. Wallflower. It was dangerous yet tedious work, and the new marine longed for action at closer quarters.

After the fall of Dunkirk and the withdrawal of the Allied forces from the continent in 1940, the high command decided that a special force was required to mount vigorous raiding operations against occupied Europe. Drawing personnel from the elite divisions of the army and the Royal Marines, the new units were to be called 'commandos,' after the Boer irregulars that had operated behind British lines in the South African war.

Using his father's influence with the War Ministry, Reggie obtained leave to attend the commando training center at Lympstone. His education here was the most taxing of any he had received to date, as he was trained in the many lethal facets of war that Marine commandos were expected to master. By chance, shortly before his stay at Lympstone was completed, a call for volunteers went out, seeking strong swimmers with canoeing experience. Within a week, the future Earl of Weymouth found himself on the Isle of Arran off the south west coast of Scotland, training with a new elite squadron called the 'Folbot Company.'

Named after their lightweight, collapsible, two-man canoes, this specialized group of individuals was to spearhead clandestine reconnaissance in several theaters of the war. The training was, once again, extensive and arduous. The days were spent swimming miles in frigid waters, paddling until 'one's arms seemed to go numb,' then being subjected to agonizing forced marches at 'double-quick' over the desolate, hilly countryside. It was a grueling, almost cruel education, but what excited Reginald Russell more than anything was the intelligence training that he was receiving.

This training entailed analyzing tidal currents, weather patterns, beachhead rock composition, and much, much more. It was this same intelligence work that could save the lives of thousands of soldiers. Reggie used his keen, analytical mind to decipher and assimilate the reams of pertinent data that was thrown at the recruits in those first few weeks.

The volunteers were summarily moved to Kabrit, on the northern end of the Suez Canal, without prior notice in January 1941. Here, their training continued under the combined operations group, which included volunteers from the army's Special Air Services, or SAS. Along with reconnaissance, the commandos were trained in the use of plastic explosives and underwater limpet mines, which were to be used in concert with their shore raids and anti-navigation expeditions. The unit's Folbot canoes had since been replaced by larger, more durable Cockle-type canoes.

Operating exclusively under the cover of darkness, the raiding parties would be launched from submarines several miles out to sea from their targets. The Cockles were then paddled silently ashore, hidden from sight, and the land-based operation carried out. The boat's ability to avoid coastal radar detection was their main benefit, their instability in surging tides and choppy seas their biggest drawback.

After successful small-scale reconnaissance operations on the occupied Greek island of Rhodes and the German-held Lybian coastal town of Badia, Sergeant Russell was chosen for a single-crew demolition raid in Axis Sicily. The target was a railway spur running from the coast to the capital of Palermo. Accompanying the sergeant was Lieutenant Brian Downs, originally a rower with the Cambridge University Heavy Eights. The men were launched from the submarine H.M.S. Utmost on a moonless June night, some four miles off the Sicilian coast. As they made their way toward the invisible shoreline, the commandos were aghast to find Italian fishing boats blocking the approach route.

Often these Italians toiled with armed German guards aboard, and should the intruders be sighted, all hell would break loose. The months of training in the techniques of silent paddling paid off, however, and the commandos skirted all the trawlers undetected.

Once ashore, still operating in total darkness, they hurriedly took samples of the beach stones for analysis, then proceeded inland. A visible line of telegraph poles that ran parallel to the rail spur helped guide the commandos to their objective. Having traveled no more than a third of a mile inland and with no enemy contact, the two operatives were able to plant their plastic explosives with weight-sensitive fuses under the tracks, cut the telegraph wires, and rendezvous back with the submarine as easily as if they had been on exercises.

As the two Englishmen were pulling alongside the navy vessel, the sky lit up with a telltale display of their destructive work. Exact confirmation of the damage inflicted was confirmed by a reconnaissance plane the next morning. The two commandos were presented with a black-and-white photo of a thoroughly demolished locomotive and several derailed box cars. A promotion to Lieutenant was Reggie's reward for a job well done.

Over the next two years, the 'Special Boat Service,' or SBS, as they had come to be known, took part in hundreds of operations in the Mediterranean and against Fortress Europe. The intelligence information and the destructive nature of the small-scale raids made the group invaluable to the Allied High Command. The section was overseen by the 'Special Operations Executive,' or SOE, a covert arm of the War Ministry that was, among other things, responsible for planting and retrieving secret agents from enemy territory. More often than not, the SBS was the main means of transport used to collect the operatives planted by the SOE. Reggie enjoyed these particular assignments most, for the gathering and decoding of intelligence was still his favorite pastime.

Lieutenant Russell was to spend a great deal of his time in 1942 attached to the Combined Operations Headquarters, where he personally took it upon himself to improve the equipment that was available to the SBS section. Better canoes, better waterproofing of equipment, and standardized training of recruits were only some of the recommendations that Headquarters adopted on the young lieutenant's urging. The High Command appreciated the value of small raiding parties, even if they acted only as diversions to pin down enemy troops in positions that often lacked any strategic importance.

With the Allies turning their attention to gaining a foothold on the 'Dark Continent,' the SBS curriculum was expanded to include active theaters of war. Reconnaissance of potential landing beaches on the North African coast were scouted by 'the Cockles' as to the type and density of sand or rock for supporting landing craft. Subsequently, the SBS canoeists were taught to act as channel markers with their infrared signaling beams to guide the landing craft ashore.

The fruit of all this preparation were born on the night of November 8, 1942, when the American task force, guided by SBS canoeists, landed in North Africa one hundred miles east of Algiers. Naturally, Lieutenant Reginald Russell was one of the SBS men guiding the way.

The Allies took a roller-coaster ride on the fortunes of war over the following two years. However, the commandos of the Special Boat Section, due to experience, better equipment, and diligent training, enjoyed a success rate on operations that was the envy of the entire military command. Reggie Russell, Captain Russell as of March 1944, continued to be at center stage both in the field and in the war council rooms.

Command of his own group of canoeists was an adjunct to the promotion, and his group 'R,' for Reggie canoeists, proved to be the most daringly proficient band of water rats in the whole section. The intelligence information that its commander was able to turn over to Headquarters proved invaluable. He had personally cracked several Axis code books that his commandos had captured during specific covert operations. By mid-1944, the former Eton student was back in England, having used both his garnered intelligence and the signals of his canoeists to assist in the Allied landings in France on a day forevermore known as 'D-Day.'

The Special Operations Executive had taken a real shine to Reggie Russell and his long list of achievements. The problem for Reggie was that he was becoming a desk commando, keenly sought after in the conference rooms for his knowledge of German intelligence.

Innumerable trips to Whitehall in London took him away from the front-line action, and he began to sense that he was more and more a Special Operations Executive man instead of a fighting commando. The captain had never feared for his personal safety and loved the rush of adrenaline that always accompanied close proximity to the enemy. His superiors, while not outright forbidding Reggie from going out on active operations, let it be known that he had become far too vital to their intelligence network to be risking his neck like some "wet-behind-the-ears" recruit.

Reginald Russell's sense of personal immortality was to change in early November 1944. A massive raid was to be executed against Walcheren, a heavily defended Scheldt estuary island protecting the approaches to the German-held port of Antwerp, Belgium. An amphibious landing was to be supported by Lancaster bombers. It was up to the Special Boat Squadron to secure essential preliminary landing information and act as marker guides for the main assault.

So great an importance did the High Command place on this operation, that they requested the very best men available be used by the SBS. That meant the popular Captain Russell would be unshackled from his desk.

What seemed like just another assignment had a special, ominous meaning to the young captain, however. It was on this same part of the Belgium coast that his grandfather had been slain in 1918, and that fact did not escape his attention. For the first time since joining the military, Reggie Russell was sick to his stomach before entering the frigid waters of the North Sea.

Under the cover of darkness, the SBS commandos secured their initial objectives after an uneventful landing and began transmitting information back to Naval intelligence. But something felt strangely out of sorts to the commanding officer of the detachment. Captain Russell couldn't put his finger on it exactly, but there was a feeling in his gut that he had never experienced on any previous operation. He tried to put the uneasiness out of his mind and carry on, but it dogged him throughout the damp, foggy night.

Just after dawn, a routine German patrol discovered one of the commandos who had slipped and broken his ankle some three hundred yards from the main Marine command post. Not wanting to alert the enemy of his presence, the commando had simply waited for daylight in hope that his mates would discover his predicament. As luck would have it, a German shepherd tracking dog picked up the poor fellow's scent first. The two Nazi handlers were shocked to discover the injured commando, but their shock turned to rage when the Englishman skewered their animal with his assault knife. A firefight ensued in which the commando and one German were killed, the second Nazi fleeing to alert his superiors of the unwelcome discovery.

The noise of the exchange tipped off Captain Russell to the fact that the jig was up, and he radioed intelligence that they had been discovered. The commander then took his Marines forward to assess the situation. They had advanced some two hundred yards when mortar rounds started dropping in their midst, one of the initial rounds exploding just to Reggie Russell's left. He had barely uttered the words "take cover," when he was propelled to the ground and knocked unconscious.

The commanding officer lingered in a haze-like state for what seemed an eternity. As he slowly regained his senses, he became aware of a sharp pain in his left temple. Voices were coming from somewhere close by, but Captain Russell was unable to discern what they were saying. He wanted to right himself, to assess the situation, but for some reason he could not move. The voices were closer now, but they were not English voices. These people were speaking German.

The mortars had ceased along with all small arms fire, and for the first time in his life, Reggie Russell felt terribly alone and scared to death. Where was his command? Had they surrendered? Were they all dead? He tried to keep his wits about him, but his mind would not function to its usual military standard. Intermittent rifle fire could be heard nearby, and suddenly the horrible truth dawned on the mission commander. The Nazis were shooting the wounded!

It was an outrage to be sure, but one that he was powerless to stop. He heard footsteps approaching, then felt a piercing blow to his rib cage as he lay face down on the muddy bog. The enemy was at his side now, poking and prodding. The Royal Marine clenched his teeth and stifled an urge to scream. Another blow to the ribs, but again he managed to keep silent. The only word that registered in his pain-racked mind was 'kaput,' meaning that the German soldiers had mistaken him for dead. His would-be killers moved on, leaving him where he lay, and it seemed a lifetime before he dared to open his eyes and attempt to assess the situation.

The pain in the left side of his head was excruciating now, pounding like a sledge hammer to the brain. Reggie tried to focus his eyes on something, anything, but his usually reliable vision just wasn't functioning. He touched the soreness with his hand, for his head felt wet and somehow different. Even with his failing eyesight he could discern the blood that covered his fingers. He felt the wound again, and was aghast to find that his scull had been split open down the middle of his cranium, similar to one of the coconuts that his father had often chopped in half back on the wharf many years ago.

Captain Russell still could not move his legs or lower torso, and as he lay there in the Belgian muck, he was forced to come to grips with his own mortal being. The commando had seen many a man die in battle, but he had developed a fatalistic attitude about the quick and the dead. It wasn't that he didn't care for those fallen patriots, it was just that he believed that death was their ordained fate. Reginald Russell's fate was to endure, to lead, to live a full and rewarding life! His fate was to be different than the poor departed souls that lay around him, or so he had thought until that very moment. The brave Marine captain was forced to accept the realization that he could do nothing except wait to meet either 'His Maker,' or the Royal Marines.

Fortunately, his 'maker' happened to be a medic in 41 Commando Brigade. The commencement of the main thrust of the operation coincided with the discovery of the SBS commandos by the enemy. Tracked amphibious vehicles as well as paratroopers were landing on Walcheren almost immediately after the sighting of the first injured commando by the unlucky canine. The mortar attack had been unleashed against what the Germans thought was the main assault force. Their short-lived reconnaissance expedition to collect trophies and the odd prisoner from the fallen SBS men ended quickly when the sky reverberated with the sound of the Lancasters above them.

The pounding that the German defenders took was horrible, but it also caused severe trauma to Captain Russell, who had to deal with the earth shaking furiously beneath his prone body. It seemed never-ending, one continuous roar of deadly ordinance from the heavens. As he lay in the midst of the apocalypse, Reginald Russell sang his favorite Canaries fight songs over and over to try to keep from going 'starkers.'

"Upward, onward, Canaries, soaring to new heights, thousands shout your praises, thousands fight your fights . . ." Over and over again Reggie kept the tunes coming. "Rule Canaries, Canaries rule the waves, yellow birds never, never, never will be slaves." Even the little ditty that had been a favorite on the terraces, but much too graphic for the gentle folk in the main grandstand. "I wish I were a Canary, 'cause I'd fly up in the sky, and find me- self a Hammer, and shit right in his eye."

It was this particular melody that attracted medic Archie Monteith of 41 Commando to the blood-covered form that lay in front of him. He was in the advance assault unit and preceded the amphibious landing craft ashore at the same location that the SBS had disembarked the night before.

Corporal Monteith was shocked to see the carnage that spread out before him as he and his fellow commandos made their way inland. At least ten Marine corpses littered the immediate area, and there seemed to be no evidence of survivors. The roar of the Lancasters and their deadly cargo had passed further inland by the time medic Monteith began inspecting his fallen brothers for any signs of life.

As luck would have it, Archie Monteith was a Cockney who had grown up on the Isle of Dogs, his father being a foreman on the West India docks. Archie had been an ardent Canary supporter through thick and thin, and when he knelt beside the badly wounded officer, he could scarcely believe his ears at what he was hearing. The captain's head seemed split in two, and there was blood everywhere, but here he was, alive and singing 'Rule Canaries.'

Corporal Monteith joined his injured compatriot in a hearty chorus of that particular tune to reassure the man that he was in friendly, knowing hands. Stretcher bearers were called up immediately, and Captain Reginald Russell was evacuated to a hospital ship lying off the coast. He was barely alive and still unable to move his lower extremities, but he was in friendly hands, and the war, at least as a combat commando, was over for him.

What the surgeons discovered aboard the Royal Navy hospital ship was not encouraging. The exploding mortar's shrapnel had not only fractured Captain Reginald Russell's skull, it had also lodged fragments close to his spine. Reggie was seven hours on the operating table, and the prognosis for a full recovery was very slim. He had lost a considerable amount of blood, and he lay perilously close to death for several days.

The captain clung to life long enough to be transferred to the Dreadnought Seaman's Hospital in Greenwich, where his family assembled by his side in an around-the-clock death watch. Fortunately, his condition stabilized, allowing two further operations to be performed to remove additional metal fragments from his back and skull.

Slowly, ever so slowly, he began to gain back his vision and some of the feeling in his lower legs. Intensive physiotherapy was commenced as soon as the head wound had healed sufficiently, and the young Marine captain showed amazing courage and fortitude in making slow but steady progress.

Emotionally, the most difficult thing for Reggie to deal with was the horrible scar on his shaved head. The surgeons had informed him outright that he should consider wearing a toupee from now on, for his hair would not grow in sufficiently to cover the wound. He was not a vain man, but he did not relish the fact that he would be disfigured the rest of his life. His sisters were most helpful in this regard, bringing to his bedside the latest in hairpiece fashions. They all had great fun trying out various styles and colors, sometimes with hilarious results.

Reginald Russell became quite a celebrity on his hospital ward, for his continuously changing 'rugs' were a diversionary source of amusement in those normally serious surroundings. Even women's shoulder length wigs were procured to entertain and uplift the other patients and staff. Reggie never lost his sense of humor throughout his painful ordeal.

Learning how to walk again was the worst part. Torturous hours were spent on the parallel bars trying to perform the most rudimentary leg functions. Stretching, bending, and weight training were also included in the tedious routine. But Captain Russell had two things for which to be thankful. Firstly, he was alive and making tangible progress, and secondly, his personal therapist was a doe-eyed beauty that had stolen his heart.

Emily Ladbrooke was the young woman's name, and she came from a titled family of merchants that had served the Royal Family for hundreds of years. Her father and two older brothers had served in His Majesty's Armed Forces during the present conflict, and it was the loss of her eldest brother's leg at Dunkirk in 1940 that had precipitated Emily's joining the Royal Nursing Corps as a rehabilitation therapist.

Her aristocratic background was in no way evident during the trying duties that she now performed for His Majesty's maritime warriors. While she was gentle and sympathetic to the physical limitations of her patients, she could also be a stern taskmistress. She was bluntly capable of shaming the injured men to push themselves harder and farther than they thought possible.

Foul language often filled the therapy hall, but Emily Ladbrooke would swear right back at them as if she had grown up in a bowery instead of swanky Knightsbridge.

The therapist pushed Reginald Russell particularly hard, and he, in turn, looked forward to their daily sessions of torture and profanity. It was really Emily Ladbrooke that brought out the baser side of Reggie's humor. They engaged in a small wager to see if the captain, before each session commenced, could recite to her a joke or story that would make her blush. If Miss Ladbrooke failed to take his bait and turn crimson, she would have the right to extend the therapy session an extra quarter hour. During this time, he would be forced to perform his least favorite therapy routine again. The primary reason for Captain Russell's remarkable progress, as he was later to admit himself, was that his beautiful therapist never once lost their wager. Within six months of his arrival, Reggie was able to walk with the assistance of a cane, a feat that astonished his surgeons.

The war in Europe was drawing to a close, and thoughts of the future were brimming in the Marine commando's mind. Reggie loved the order of military life, the spit and polish, the camaraderie, and the opportunity to educate himself in a well-defined environment. He had asked his father if there might be a position with the Marine High Command at Whitehall. As it turned out, the elder Russell was owed a few favors by Her Majesty's warlords. With their great killing machine being dismantled, there were thousands of young men in a similar position to that of Reginald Russell. But his family's long-standing service to the Royal Marines, not to mention the timely prewar tendering of the Canary Wharf lands to the Ministry by his father, were the salient points that made a difference. Elliott Russell managed to secure a posting as an intelligence liaison officer to the Ministry of Defense for his almost totally recovered son.

Reggie would have preferred a more active field commission where he might have been in charge of an actual team of commandos, but he had no delusions concerning his physical limitations. He resigned himself to the fact that he would likely be desk-bound for the rest of his tenure with Her Majesty's Royal Marines. If the truth be known, he did consider himself fortunate to be alive and able to work at all.

One astonished visitor near the end of Captain Russell's convalescence was Corporal Archibald Monteith, the medic who had saved Reggie's life. The young man had never forgotten the fallen commando who sang football fight songs to keep himself alive. Canary Wharf fight songs at that!

Monteith had made a point of keeping track of the captain's medical progress, and swore an oath that if he were spared during the conflict, he would look up this astonishing bloke when he was back safe 'over ome.' The reunion of the aristocratic officer and gentleman from the upper strata of

London society, and the Cockney corporal from Cubitt Town, Isle of Dogs, was emotional and poignant. When asked his plans for the future, Monteith simply shrugged. Instantly he was offered a position as the captain's adjutant to help him out in his new assignment. Reggie Russell never forgot a good deed, especially if that deed had been responsible for saving his life. After thankfully accepting the captain's offer, Monteith related that he could not believe his new employer's progress, particularly his ability to walk unassisted. At that point, Miss Ladbrooke entered the room, and after introductions had been made, the captain expressed that he held Emily Ladbrooke personally responsible for making him whole again. It was the first time he had ever seen her blush.

Their relationship had always been platonic, one of patient-therapist. But after Reggie had said his farewells and taken his leave of the Seaman's Hospital and Emily Ladbrooke, he realized that he longed for her company, for her forceful encouragement, and especially her ribald sense of humor. He had never met a woman like Emily Ladbrooke. In fact, he had never met any woman that induced the confusing mix of emotions that she inflicted upon him. The former patient found himself thinking of his therapist constantly and finally decided to take the bull by the horns.

Captain Russell subsequently moved into a small flat on Burney Street in Greenwich, only a few blocks from the Dreadnought Seaman's Hospital. He began to watch his obsession from afar at first, on her tea breaks in the garden, and as she entered and left the hospital. Always hidden, always from a distance.

Reggie was mortally afraid of unrequited love, afraid that she would find him humorous, but at the same time, physically hideous because of his head wound. He had found the perfect hair piece that was not only military regulation style and length, but also one that entirely covered up the nasty scar on the top of his crown. It was impossible to tell that there was any disfiguration at all under his new rug. But when it came to affairs of the heart, he felt less than whole and feared Emily Ladbrooke's rebuff more than anything in the world.

The SBS man became an expert skulker in the areas bordering the hospital. He knew from exactly which hidden vantage point he would be able to see Emily come and go, as well as observe her performing her daily tasks. Finally, the frustration and heartache became more than he could bear, and he arranged a chance meeting under the guise of a visit to his surgeon at the Seaman's Hospital.

Emily seemed profoundly happy to see him again and accepted his offer to join him for tea after her shift finished that evening. Tea turned into a full-scale dinner, then a cab ride to Whitehall to show her his new office and take in the moonlit wonders of Westminster and Big Ben. It was a thoroughly enchanting evening, and Emily's confession that she missed their naughty wagers allowed him the opening to proclaim that he wished he had not recovered with such haste.

He would have preferred, he admitted with great candor, to have her still inflicting her terrible tortures on his lower extremities, just so he could be near her again. Reggie delivered Emily home by cab just after midnight, and humbly asked if she would be willing to be his consort again. Her response was the sweetest, most tender kiss that any man could ever imagine.

There had been nothing in the commando's psychological training that could have prepared him for the totally foreign state of euphoric infatuation he was now experiencing. So distracted was Captain Russell over the next few days, that his co-workers at the Defense Department thought he had suffered some sort of mental setback until he joyously announced his engagement one week after that fateful moonlit night.

The nuptials took place on Christmas Eve 1945, and it turned out to be the social event of the early postwar era. The merging of two well-known entrepreneurial families was the talk of the town. The event itself, which took place in the chapel of the Royal Naval College in Greenwich, spared no cost, nor overlooked any detail of military pomp and circumstance.

A month-long honeymoon cruise to Nassau in the Bahamas allowed the newlyweds to escape to warmer, quieter climes, where they heartily went about consummating their new partnership. The result of their efforts was the birth of Nigel Arthur Thomas Russell in September of 1946.

Sir Reggie and the new Lady Russell settled into one of the several residences that his family had acquired in London over the years, this particular one being on Bolton Street in Mayfair. It was a lovely, three-story Georgian building that was situated just off Picadilly Street, two blocks from the Naval and Military Club, and in the heart of one of London's most exclusive shopping and entertainment districts.

The birth of their son settled the matter of whether or not Emily would return to her physiotherapist's job at the hospital. But it was not a contentious issue, as the Lady was quite content to stay at home and nurture young Nigel and her new husband. Captain Russell received a promotion to the rank of major on return from his honeymoon, and settled in to his posting as liaison officer for the Admiralty Board. Major Russell was certainly walking the corridors of power, for the Admiralty oversaw all naval operations and personnel, including the Royal Marines, for the entire Empire. The newlywed major's first assignment was to keep the Ministry of Defense informed and up-to-date on any peculiarities regarding the dismantling of Hitler's once-proud navy.

Other than his career and family, Reggie Russell allowed himself only one extracurricular activity, that being the preservation of Canary Wharf Football Club. The Yellow Bird's fortunes were sagging badly, and having been dislodged from The Bird Cage at the start of the war, the team resembled a band of gypsies wandering about the London suburbs, trying to find a suitable location for their home games. As Hitler's blitz on London intensified, the quest had become more and more difficult.

Elliott Russell was prepared to let the team disband during the hostilities, but doing so would mean relinquishing their Football Association charter, which Reggie opposed strongly. A phone call to the headmaster of his Alma Mater at Eton secured the temporary use of one of the school's playing fields, and it was there, under the shadow of Windsor Castle, that the Canaries home fixtures were played for the duration of the war.

Even with a semipermanent home base, the team was unable to mount much of a showing. Most able-bodied men were in the military, and few, if any, of those who stayed behind were encouraged by the thought of playing football for a displaced second division team. The end of the war found the yellow and black languishing perilously close to relegation out of the league second division into the even lower depths of the third tier.

There was no end to the obstacles blocking the Canaries return to the once-proud ways of their early days. Not only had the Bird Cage suffered heavy damage from the Hun's wrath, but the Defense Ministry had not relinquished their hold on the wharf and the surrounding lands.

Elliott Russell had taken ill with cancer during the winter of 1943 and left London to reside on the family estate in Weymouth. The Canary Wharf Trading Company had virtually ceased to exist as a result. With Reggie in the Royal Marines and the outcome of the war very much in doubt at the time, it looked as if the football club was on its last legs.

Only Reginald Russell's continued interest in salvaging the Canaries made it possible for them to survive. Without informing his ill father, the Marine captain had been sending funds from his personal account to outfit and pay the players. Fortunately, the last draft was sent just before the bloody mission to Belgium, and that allowed the team to carry on during Reggie's convalescence.

The end of the war found the sun once again shining on the family patriarch. Elliott Russell's cancer had gone into remission and his spirits were buoyant again. He was heartened by Reggie's speedy recovery from his wounds, as well as the boy's forthcoming marriage to Emily Ladbrooke. A few months later, the impending birth of his first grandchild gave Elliott cause to discuss his long-range future plans with his son. That discussion included the fate of the Canary Wharf Trading Company and its associated football club.

The corporation had divested itself of nearly all its hard assets at the outset of the war, and much of the resultant cash from the proceeds had been invested in foreign banks and real estate. While there was a sizable fortune at his disposal, Elliott Russell made it exceedingly clear to his son that he had no interest in operating a major trading company ever again. Due to the uncertainty of his physical condition, he preferred passive, liquid investments, backed by solid real estate holdings.

On the other hand, Elliott would permit his son to use their family influence with the Defense Ministry to try and obtain a lease for the land where the remains of The Bird Cage sat. Reggie's passion for the team and its survival were overpoweringly evident as father and son tried to map out the future that day. As a result, Elliott Russell agreed to set aside a certain amount of money for the refurbishment of the stadium if Reginald could secure favorable lease terms from the ministry. The younger Russell set about this task like a man possessed, and in short order, had secured not only a long-term lease for The Bird Cage, but also an option to purchase the lands outright should the ministry find that they were no longer of importance in the interest of national safety.

The Isle of Dogs was experiencing a postwar industrial rebirth with chemical plants, tea, and flour mills, fertilizer processing, and cement facilities all being rebuilt or renovated to replace the wartime destruction. Homes were being constructed for the men and their families who would work in these plants, and a whole new community seemed to be springing up from the ashes.

These people would be the next generation of Canary fans, Reggie Russell thought, and with this in mind, he set about reconstructing the main grandstand of The Bird Cage and patching up the adjacent terraces. The major would have liked to construct an entirely new stadium, but Elliot had made certain that only enough funds were available to bring The Bird Cage back to its prewar status, nothing more. The old man still considered the project extremely risky, and he wanted to be convinced that the continued operation of a football club was economically viable in postwar London.

The support of the local citizenry made the team's existence tenable from the first day they returned to The Bird Cage at the start of the 1947 season. It mattered little to the Cockney fans that this team was second division, for it brought to the workers and residents of the Isle of Dogs a focal point, a sense of community, a topic of discussion. The Bird Cage was filled to overflowing on Saturday afternoons throughout the next two decades, and although the Canaries never achieved promotion to the first division, their followers remained steadfastly loyal.

Family and career matters were also on the ascent for Reginald Russell as the new decade of the 1950s commenced. A promotion to colonel of Royal Marine Intelligence allowed Reggie to work more closely with his beloved former command. His planning, knowledge, and organizational skills had thrust him into the limelight at Whitehall during the Royal Marine's withdrawal from Palestine in 1948. Colonel Russell was directly responsible for the deployment of Royal Marines in Korea during the international conflict in the early 1950s. In 1953, he coordinated the internal security duties of the Marine commandos in the Suez Canal zone of the volatile Middle East.

On the home front, 1951 saw the arrival of a daughter, Mallory Elizabeth Russell, a blonde bundle of joy that brought great happiness to the entire family. As so often happens, however, the elation of Mallory's birth was tempered by the death of her grandfather, Elliott, two months later, as a result of his recurrent cancer.

Reggie had mixed emotions on his father's passing. On the one hand, he missed him dreadfully, but on the other hand, he did not want to see his painful suffering prolonged. Reginald Arthur Nelson Russell became the fifteenth Earl of Weymouth on his father's passing and acquired an immense fortune with considerable real estate assets. These included a host of industrial and commercial buildings, six estate houses in London proper, a residence in Nassau, an apartment in New York City, and several castles throughout southern England and Scotland.

Neither this inherited material wealth nor his new title seemed to affect Reggie in the least, for, as he would explain to anyone who cared, "I am just the same old chap, and besides, one can only reside in one place at one time." He was supremely happy with Emily and the children at their Mayfair residence and proceeded to sell off or donate the vast majority of his excess properties over the following few years.

Throughout the 1960s and 1970s, Colonel Reginald Russell was at the nerve center of every operation in which Her Majesty's Royal Marine commandos participated. Borneo, Malaysia, Kuwait, and East Africa were just a few theaters of operation that relied heavily on the intelligence that Reggie's operatives collected and transmitted to the active forces. His reputation for being painstakingly thorough grew with each success. He would not tolerate the loss of a single commando's life due to misinformation. Colonel Reginald Russell became somewhat of a legend within the Defense Ministry, and his services were called upon, once again, when the army ran into severe policing problems in Northern Ireland in 1969.

The only bone of contention in Sir Reggie's otherwise idyllic life was the perennial bridesmaid status of the Canary Wharf Football Club. Not once in the forty years since they were relegated to the second division did they manage to complete a season in the top three positions of the table. This was all that was required to gain promotion to the big league, but the Canaries always seemed to find new and innovative ways to finish no better than fourth.

Some years they would start with a tremendous run, then fade badly as the season closed. Other years they would open poorly, then make an exciting dash for third spot that would inevitably fall a point or two short. All these near misses drove Reggie to distraction, but it was the startling interest of his daughter, Mallory, in the team's fortunes that kept him from throwing in the towel completely.

The young lady had attended her first Canaries game at age five, and immediately took to the atmosphere and colorful characters that routinely filled The Bird Cage. She loved the singing of the fight songs and the hazing of the opposing players. She felt privileged to sit in the covered director's box on the center-field stripe, but asked endless questions about the people who stood and cheered on the terraces, even in the most inclement weather.

The flags, the banners, the scarves, all in yellow and black, gave each home game the atmosphere of a carnival. Mallory was elated after a Canary victory and equally despondent after a defeat. Through her teen years, she and her well-bred girlfriends would swoon over the more handsome players on the side, and fan-club letters often took priority over homework, much to the chagrin of her parents.

As time passed, Mallory Russell grew to be a beautiful woman. Her development into a statuesque blonde, with a full figure and haunting pale green eyes astonished her father. She had attended all the proper schools and would have perhaps gone on to a mundane career and then marriage had it not been for her consummate passion, football.

More than anything in the world, Miss Russell wanted the Canary Wharf Football Club to return to its former days of glory. She would frequently suggest roster and management changes to the chairman of the board of directors, her beloved father. Always dismissed offhand at the time of presentation by the exclusively male hierarchy of the club, these ideas of Mallory's seemed to make sense in retrospect, especially when another failed season was entered into the record books.

Her break came in the middle of the 1976 season, when the current manager, Tony Abbott, was forced to resign his post for health reasons. There was no love lost between Mallory Russell and the Canary's chauvinistic manager. It was a well-known fact that Abbott had several times threatened his resignation to Sir Reggie if his daughter didn't stop meddling in the team's business.

It was a problem with 'spirits,' and not personalities that forced out Mr. Abbott, however. Many years of frustration and lack of tangible improvement were said to have driven the manager to the bottle. He began to miss team meetings and practice sessions, but the coup de grace came when he was found in a drunken stupor under the main grandstand of The Bird Cage immediately before his team took to the pitch for an all-important match. Sir Reggie had no alternative but to dismiss the man who had been at the helm of the Yellow Birds for eleven seasons.

It was one of the saddest days in the history of the Canary Wharf Football Club, but it opened the door for the ascension of Mallory Russell to the board of directors, and her assumption of the reins of power. While a woman could not hold the actual position of manager in the eyes of Sir Reggie and the other directors, there was nothing to prevent handing the decision-making power to Mallory, and having her wishes conveyed to the team by a surrogate manager. This is precisely what transpired with the hiring of ex-Canary player Randal Horton as team manager and the election of Mallory Russell as executive vice president in charge of football operations.

Horton had been one of Mallory's poster boys years before, and the two had always been on the same wave length. As for Mallory's appointment, the rest of the directors figured that they had nothing to lose by giving the enthusiastic woman the reins, for attendance was falling at The Bird Cage as a result of the succession of mediocre teams. Having a beauty such as Mallory Russell in charge would, at least, guarantee increased press coverage.

While little could be accomplished for the balance of the 1976 season, the Yellow Birds did manage to improve substantially in the second half of schedule and came within three points of promotion. During the off-season, Mallory pestered her father to open the bank vault sufficiently to permit the acquisition of two top quality players who were on the transfer market from first division clubs.

The first was forward Georgie Steeves from newly relegated Tottenham Hotspur. His transfer fee of fifty-five thousand pounds was the most the Canaries had ever paid for a player, but in Mallory's opinion, he was just the offensive spark that the team needed.

The second acquisition was for a major league keeper, and in Scotsman Fraser MacTavish, the Canaries obtained a man nicknamed 'Stonewall' by his Glasgow Rangers supporters. MacTavish was a seasoned veteran, thirty years of age and only available due to a stable of young, energetic keepers that were trying to break into the Ranger's lineup. Fifty thousand pounds secured his services for the Canaries, but Sir Reggie had a stern warning for his daughter that this was the end of the spending spree. He also stated that there had better be a tangible return on his investment or she would follow in the footsteps of her predecessor, the unfortunate Tony Abbott.

The Canaries started the 1977-78 campaign slowly, losing several games that they should have won. It was relayed to Mallory by manager Horton that several of the holdover players lacked the real desire that was necessary to win. They had become second division floaters, content in their jobs and unwilling to give that extra effort needed to gain promotion.

Realizing that there was no more money in the till for further new blood, Mallory and Horton decided to give the most lethargic players there outright release and fill the void with untested amateurs that proliferated on the playing grounds of London. Two university players were plucked from their school teams, more for their enthusiasm than their proven ability. Horton was trying to field a team with the proper chemistry, and the impromptu shakeup and dismissal of several of the old-guard players had the desired effect on those who remained.

Team captain Lawton MacRae was squarely in favor of the purge, for he had the heart of a lion and hated the endless losing seasons. He berated his players for their lack of pride and self-esteem, then he and his mates gave manager Horton and the club executive a vote of confidence. The results of that vote were evident immediately on the second division playing fields.

The Canaries did soar to the top of the table, and could have possibly run away with the league had not several midwinter injuries to key players knocked them down into their familiar fourth place standing by the start of April. Luckily, all hands were back on deck for the crucial 'run for the roses,' and by early May, they had clinched promotion to the big league. The Russell family and the team's loyal followers were, at last, in a position to savor an accomplishment that had eluded the Canary Wharf Football Club for four decades.

The fact that it was all his daughter's doing and not that of a man, specifically his son, did not concern Reggie Russell. Nigel had grown to be special in many ways, most of them philosophical, spiritual, and nurturing. He was inseparable from his mother as a child and showed a scholarly, artistic aptitude at a young age. Theology at King's College, then an ordainment into the Church of England completed his formal education. But there was very little that was formal about Nigel Russell, and he immediately volunteered for missionary work in Africa. His mother, hating the thought of being so far away from her adoring son, became 'born again,' signed up as an aid worker, and traveled with Reverend Russell to Kenya. Over the past several years, she had spent less and less time visiting London, and nearly all the family reunions seemed to take place at some remote African village.

Neither Reggie nor Mallory seemed to mind the fractured structure of their family. All four were pursuing their own dreams, and with good spirit and best wishes from the others. Mallory and her brother had always been close. Their relationship remained so, but at this point in time, usually by means of transcontinental mail, as they were seldom on the same continent at the same time. For a free-spirited family like the Russells, it was a 'catch you later' existence.

Five days after 'the clinch,' the board of directors assembled in a private suite at the Naval and Military Club to chart the course of action for their newly promoted club. Architect John Hughes was also present by invitation. After a hearty luncheon and several congratulatory toasts, the board settled down to business.

Team treasurer Neville Strathy gave the financial report for the season just ended. A modest profit was realized due to the team's on-field success. One director mentioned that the coffers would be considerably fatter had the team not paid out over one hundred thousand pounds on the transfer market the previous summer.

An incensed Mallory Russell responded that without those two players, the team would still be in the second division, and they would not be sitting in their present posh surroundings discussing the future of the club in the premier league. The dissenting director had no rebuttal.

"Now, about the expansion of the Bird Cage. Shall we hear from Mister Hughes?" Sir Reggie smoothly shifted topics. John Hughes moved to an easel that stood at one end of the boardroom table.

"Ladies and gentlemen, as you all are aware, my firm has been working on the renovation and expansion of The Bird Cage for several years, always with the anticipation that the Canaries would gain promotion to the first division. That time has now come, and I am pleased to report that we have developed a phased scheme of expansion that will not put undue strain on the club's finances." Several of the directors responded to that comment with loud 'here, heres.' Hughes didn't miss a beat.

"The first step is to build a new, modern grandstand to replace the east terraces." At this point, Hughes flipped over the title page on his architectural plans to reveal an artist's conception of the new covered grandstand. "This facility will accommodate fifteen thousand seated spectators, twenty luxury boxes, office space that can be leased to other corporations, as well as the most up-to-date sanitary and concession facilities available in all of Great Britain."

This time, a rousing round of applause as well as 'here heres' filled the room.

"I am informed that the cost of phase one will be in the range of four million pounds. The second phase will take place when finances permit. The major task here calls for the construction of a mirror duplication of the new grandstand where the old west grandstand sits. The final phase will entail renovation of the end terraces to permit full enclosure of the grounds, with a ring of luxury boxes and the elimination of terraced standing. Total cost over five years is projected at ten million pounds. Any questions, gentlemen?"

As if to acknowledge the oversight, it was Mallory Russell that raised her hand.

"Oh, excuse me, Miss Russell. That should have been 'any questions, *ladies* and gentlemen?'"

"Thank you, Mr. Hughes. Your plans look most impressive. I worry about the loss of revenue from having the present east stands under renovation when we make our first division debut in only three and a half months. How quickly can phase one be completed?"

"An appropriate question, to be sure, Miss Russell. We anticipate that the club will be without the use of the east stand for the entire 1978-79 season. Construction, if started immediately, should take somewhere close to eight months. Allowances should be made for labor slowdowns and supply shortages, however."

There were many skeptical faces seated around the board table at this point. Hughes sensed that he had to take the offensive to reassure the wavering pinstripes.

"But there is a need to look at this project as a long-term benefit, not only to the supporters, but to the entire community. The Isle of Dogs has become something of an industrial wasteland, although there is much talk about major government-induced development in the near future. This new stadium could be the leading edge of that resurgence and accelerate a new dawn for one of London's most historic areas. All efforts will be made to parallel your construction with future government-assisted projects for housing, commerce, and transportation improvements. You will also be creating new interest in one of the oldest football clubs in the country, and by having only a limited number of seats available for your initial season in the first division, you will stimulate a tremendous demand for subsequent years."

Again, it was Mallory who responded. "The one overriding caveat that we have, Mr. Hughes, is our ability to remain in the first division longer than our initial season. We made it there with a combination of veterans, some of whom are on their last legs, and enthusiastic schoolboys, who surely will not measure up to first division standards. To make this expansion project viable, we must, once again, open up the purse strings and acquire the talent that will enable us to be competitive in our lofty new surroundings. Do not forget, gentlemen, that the bottom three first division teams will find themselves back in the second division a year from now. It is our job to find the men that will keep the Canaries out of that particular birdbath!" The assembled suits chuckled with amusement.

"Just where do you propose that we look for such players, Mallory?" Sir Reggie interjected.

"Argentina, father, that's where. In little over a month's time, the very best players in the world will be assembling in Buenos Aires. England's National Team will not be among them, as you are all well aware. The current state of our domestic football just does not measure up to world standards, gentlemen, whether you care to admit it or not. I believe most of the first division managers will stay at home and continue to naval gaze as is their sorry tradition. These men will not admit to the dismal state of our national sport." There was a muted rumble of disagreement with the young lady's sentiments that momentarily filled the air. Mallory leapt at once.

"There! That is exactly the attitude that I am talking about. If it's not British, it just doesn't measure up. Well, I say, horse droppings! There are hundreds of talented players about to be showcased in the largest football extravaganza that the world has ever seen, yet most of us are prepared to play ostrich, with our heads in the sand. Argentina, gentlemen, is where we can find the Canary's future, and I wager that we will be almost alone on this mission, if we dare to engage it." Stunned looks lined the faces of Mallory's counterparts.

"Do you actually propose to bring foreigners over here to play for us, Miss Russell?" one of them questioned.

"That is precisely what I am suggestin, Mr. Horrocks. We already have five Scots and three Irishmen on our roster, sir! What difference would a Brazilian or a Swede make?"

"But the chaps we have now are at least of British origin. I don't think the paying public would tolerate seeing a bunch of foreigners in our colors. Such a thing has never been done before. It's preposterous," Horrocks stated emphatically.

"I think not, sir." Reginald Russell was quick to come to his daughter's defense. "As you know, several of our nation's finest players have already departed for the continent because of the huge salaries that countries like Italy are willing to pay. I feel as Mallory does, that it should not be a one-way flow of talent. As long as they can score goals, I don't care if it is a Peruvian, an Iranian, or a Martian that tickles the twines for our birdies. We have nothing to lose and, perhaps, an awful lot to gain. I will think on your suggestion, Mallory, and report back to the board within seven days. Now, Sir Neville Strathy had best address the terms of his bank's most generous loan, which will enable us to not only to build our new stadium, but also sign players the likes of which the New York Cosmos have acquired in Péle and Beckinbauer."

Sir Reggie sat down with a wry grin on his face, his tongue planted firmly in his cheek. The board certainly had its work cut out for it, but Mallory's stimulating idea had given him a gut feeling that should they venture to Argentina, their voyage would not be in vain.

CHAPTER TWENTY-TWO

Buenos Aires, Argentina. June 2, 1978.

The day of reckoning had finally arrived. A nation held its breath, for the uncertainty of how its team would perform was at the forefront of every Argentine heart and soul. The events immediately preceding this day had been devastating and deadly for the host country of the World Cup Tournament. A black cloud had fallen over the sport of football in general, and the National Team of Argentina in particular.

Television news cameras had captured the final moments of four thugs posing as Catalan football enthusiasts as their plans unraveled in a small seaside town in Spain. It was in Calella, just up the Mediterranean coast from Barcelona, that the kidnappers panicked when their car was surrounded by an elite Spanish antiterrorist squad. Whether the detonation of their plastic explosives was intentional or not, it blew to eternity the five occupants of the vehicle, as well as the hopes of a World Cup championship for Argentina, in many people's minds.

Circumstances leading up to that cataclysmic deed began with the announcement that an Argentine football player would take a leave of absence from his Spanish club team to return home in preparation for the upcoming World Cup Tournament. While this news was greeted with euphoria on the western side of the Atlantic Ocean, on the European side, betrayal and rage were the predominant moods in a select number of bars and cafés around Barcelona.

Yes, Nicodemo Garcia would return to Buenos Aires in time to be the spiritual guide for Argentina. But Spain was also about to compete in World Cup '78. Where did Garcia stand? For Catalonia and Spain, his adopted home, or for Argentina, the land of his birth? Many of the more fanatical supporters of Catalonia F.C. in Barcelona considered his brief abandonment of their beloved team to be a breech of faith and an act of a traitor punishable by death. Dominated and derided season after painful season by their hated cross town nemesis F.C. Barcelona, the long-suffering Catalonia faithful could finally sense that revenge was imminent with the transfer of Nico Garcia from the Las Palmas club. A record amount of money had been paid for Garcia's services halfway through the 1977 season, and positive on-field results were instant for the upstart Catalans. The 1978 campaign was going to be their shining moment of glory, with Nicodemo Garcia in a starring role.

The only cloud on the horizon was the possibility that Garcia would forgo an idyllic Spanish summer and return to South America to play for his country in the World Cup. The president of Catalonia F.C. was extremely vocal in denouncing the preparations for, and the atmosphere surrounding, Argentina '78. Civil unrest, terrorist bombings and assassinations, economic chaos, and a lack of facility preparedness were the constant themes used in the growing swell of Argentina bashing. Garcia remained mute and out of the public spotlight once his season ended in early May. Nevertheless, the international drama continued to be played out in the committee rooms, and especially in the media. Shaking an angry fist into a television camera, Catalonia boss Rayo Vallencaro proclaimed that his new star would travel to Argentina "over his dead body!"

Thus ensued a high-level tug-of-war for the services of Nicodemo Garcia. Pressure from the Argentine FA was relentless and effective. The powers of FIFA came down on Señor Vallencaro to release his player for the World Cup. In the end, he would acquiesce rather than face stiff sanctions. But from the moment that Garcia stood before the press to announce his immediate departure for Argentina, sanity seemed to take a siesta. The player was stalked by a small fringe element of Catalonia supporters. His taxi was run off the road en route to Barcelona airport, and Nico Garcia became a victim of terror tactics not in his unstable homeland, but in the very country where Señor Vallencaro had assured him he would remain safe and unharassed. The irony was unmistakable.

For three days the kidnappers had eluded the most intense search and rescue operation ever seen in the region. The only clue relating to the crime had been found in the abandoned taxi, pinned to the shirt of the bullet-riddled corpse of the driver. A handwritten note informed authorities that Nicodemo Garcia would not be harmed. He would, however, be kept in detention until both he and FIFA agreed that under no circumstances would the player leave Spain. When the perpetrators and their prize tried to change hideouts on the third night of the crisis, they were betrayed by an informer. Surrounded by police, the fugitives panicked and were somehow blown to oblivion by their own hand. It would be 'the dead body' of Nicodemo Garcia, not Señor Vallencaro, who thousands of people would grieve over as it made its way home to Argentina.

A national day of mourning was declared in the land of the River Plate once their fallen hero arrived home. People wept openly over the casket as Nicodemo Garcia lay in state at center field of La Bombonera, his old home stadium with the Boca Juniors. What was to be the nation's finest hour was turning out to be its darkest moment. Grief and shock were supplanted by anger and despair when the size of void left by Garcia's absence was finally comprehended.

The one man who bore the brunt of the tragedy more than any other was the National Team manager Octavio Suarez. All of his preparations had focused on the prolific marksman being in the lineup. No one could take his place, no one could even come close to filling his shoes. It would be necessary for Suarez to devise a totally new strategy.

Everyone had an opinion as to what should be done. The press was often extremely negative, saying that there was now no hope of winning the championship. The recurring message seemed to be that "The Team's one goal should be to avoid embarrassing the nation."

Those that chose to be positive focused on the National Team's warm-up match record, as well as the talents of the new 'Señor Gol,' Migel Cruz. The cocky center half ate up the attention, saying on national television that "Although I am saddened by Nico Garcia's cruel death, it gives the true patriots of Argentina, those players who chose to stay and develop their skills in their native land instead of chasing the almighty peso, a chance to show their enormous talent to the world." As if this overt slight to the departed national icon was not enough, the arrogant Independiente player went on to proclaim,

"I, Miguel Cruz, the new 'Señor Gol,' will make the people of Argentina forget about Nicodemo Garcia very quickly."

Now, under a dark, early winter sky, seventy-five thousand people filled River Plate Stadium to overflowing. They were there to watch and to be given reason to forget.

At seven-fifteen p.m. sharp, the Portuguese referee raised his arm, blew his whistle, and pointed to Hungarian center forward Tibor Torok.

Words could not describe the atmosphere. The earth stood still for that moment, all eyes upon the mystic sphere. How could one solitary object bring so much joy and yet so much anguish? How could it have caused wars and split families, been responsible for suicides, and yes, even births?

The ticker tape that had cascaded down on the would-be national heroes had ceased. The multitude of patriotic singers and flag wavers stood inanimate on the terraces. Collective breathes were held for that fleeting instant. Then, with an ever so slight tap of his right foot, Tibor Torok raised the curtain on ninety minutes of nail-biting mayhem.

The Argentine National Team fielded by Octavio Suarez for this critical opening match contained several surprises in its lineup. Junior Calix had outlasted a strong challenge from Angel Martinez and was playing a vocal, confident style in goal.

There were no changes to the starting back four in Calderone, Suazo, Chacon, and Bennett. It was the half back line that had the most drastic overhaul.

'Señor Gol,' Miguel Cruz, patrolled his familiar center half territory, but due to the loss of Carlos Castillo in Montevideo and the glaring ineptitude of his replacement, Leopoldo Anariba, Suarez had decided to make wholesale changes. He sat down the defensive-minded Humberto Valasquez in favor of an all-Independiente half line.

B squad halves Ricardo Arzu and Francis Argueta, both 25, both from Independiente, were inserted into the A squad's roster immediately after the final warm-up match. Things worked well initially, the two new additions being used to working with Cruz on a regular basis with their club team. But there was dissension among the non-Independiente players over this perceived favoritism. The matter was made worse by the fear of Juan Chacon and his more arrogant than ever club-mates overhearing the disenchanted and taking personal retribution.

Daniele Bennett, the rock-solid fullback with Italian and English roots, had been appointed team captain by Octavio Suarez, but there was no doubting the fact that ugly Juan Chacon was the man to whom everyone in the locker room deferred. He ran the clubhouse as if it were his personal fiefdom and had his underlings from Independiente create whatever distraction or amusement for which he felt in the mood. Sometimes it was unyielding heckling of a National Team member that had made a bad play or had done something off the field that could be used against him. The Anariba twins were a constant source of low humor.

While Juan Chacon derived several hearty bouts of laughter at his unfortunate teammate's expense, the undercurrent of hatred and contempt felt by those not of his ilk was tearing the team apart.

Octavio Suarez was aware of the problem that the Independiente group was creating, but his job was to produce a World Championship team, not to babysit a bunch of whiners. He would let Chacon and his band have the limelight on the night of the opening match, but if any of them failed to perform, they would find themselves watching the contest from the pine rail.

Finally, the forward line, the place where Nicodemo Garcia would have worked his magic . . . if only! Goal scorer Ruben Gitares was a staple on the right wing, while Independiente's Enrique Rios retained his training camp center forward position by default. Newcomer Ramon Vida patrolled the left wing, which was a change of position for the confident shooter, but one Suarez felt was necessary to generate some of the lost offensive punch of which Garcia's death had deprived them.

Nicolas Pastor, the incumbent winger, had seemed like a fish out of water after his primary feeder and club-mate Castillo went down. Ramon Vida was given an opening during one practice scrimmage, scored three times, and never left the A squad. His presence in the lineup did not thrill the Independiente men, for Vida still carried a huge grudge over his friend Renaldo's misfortune.

The Boca Juniors player would mouth off at Chacon and company at every opportunity. He had pummeled Francis Argueta in a locker room dustup that saw him gain considerable respect, as well as distance, from his antagonists.

"Loco," was how Argueta described his vicious assailant. Vida could very easily have taken the Independiente's man's life, so savage was his display of temper. Rumors of 'The Loco One' having a .357 magnum handgun in his possession at the training facility further deterred any thoughts of settling accounts on the part of Argueta's cronies.

Ramon Vida's reputation as a Boca gang leader and street fighter had been picked up by the press during the course of his meteoric ride into the national spotlight. The other members of the Argentine National Team had read the stories as well, and they all knew that if there was one person on the team that was not going to take any nonsense from Chacon and his lackeys, it was their recently promoted left wing forward.

But the hour was at hand to put aside all the petty jealousy and childish games. It was only 'The Game' that mattered now!

The eleven men who had stood moist-eyed through a stirring rendition of the Argentine national anthem were about to cast aside their powder-blue warm-up jackets and step over the threshold into either ecstasy or agony. All of Argentina had waited years for this very moment, and these were the men who held the nation's pride at their feet.

The starting lineup for the National Team of Argentina was as follows on the night of June 2, 1978:

Forwards:

Vida (Boca Juniors) | Rios (Independiente) | Gitares (Newton's)

Halves:

Argueta (Independiente) | Cruz (Independiente) | Arzu (Independiente)

Backs:

Bennett (Union Santa Fe) | Chacon (Independiente) | Suazo (River Plate) | Calderone (Newton's)

Goal:

Calix (Huracan)

The Hungarians had shown flashes of brilliance in the qualifying rounds to get to Buenos Aires, defeating both Bolivia and the Soviet Union. It was said that they did not travel well and tended to be individualistic rather than a unified team. That assessment was the furthest thing from the truth during the opening ten minutes of the game.

The Hungarians sent four-man waves to attack the Argentine goal from the opening whistle. Torok was set loose up the middle on three different occasions by the precise foot of Attila Nagy. This lanky center half controlled the midfield to such a degree in the early going that Octavio Suarez thought that his side must be short one man.

Sandor Kovacs and Jozsef Laszlo on the red-shirted Hungarian's wings were a constant threat to pound home a rebound, and first blood was drawn by halfback Zoltan Kaiser utilizing that exact scenario. A half parried save by Junior Calix at the ten-minute mark found the attacking Kaiser with the ball at his feet and a wide-open net. He made certain of his shot and gave his countrymen the lead, 1-0.

Seventy-five thousand hearts sank, their voices no longer shrill, their banners and flags limp. What was happening? The powder-blue and white team had barely made it over the midfield stripe and had recorded no shots to their credit. Ricardo Arzu had been directly victimized by the goal, for Kaiser was his mark. The wily Torok had also left him clutching air on two occasions. Miguel Cruz had not touched the ball as yet, and what was worse, the constant pressure on the back line had led to finger-pointing and derogatory shouts of blame among the Argentine players. To slow the fleet Magyars down, the halves and defenders were constantly resorting to rough tackles, sweater grabbing, and in Juan Chacon's case, a few well-placed elbows. Free kicks were the Hungarians reward for their inhospitable treatment, and by the time Kaiser's blast entered the net, the home side was thoroughly dazed and confused.

Octavio Suarez was a patient man, however, and he realized that the tremendous pressure his charges were playing under would be certain to unnerve them initially. The manager would wait to make any changes. It was still too early to act.

Unfortunately, the remaining thirty-five minutes of the first half did nothing to reinforce that theory. The men of Argentina were dismal! It was only the acrobatic skills of Junior Calix that closed the door on disaster. There was no coordination between the backs and halves, no precise clearing passes, no stylish football, just bumbling miscues.

The Hungarians were everywhere, throwing even their sweeper, Ferenc Doza, forward into the attack on several occasions. A post and a crossbar came to Calix's aid on two occasions. Had it not been for the off-line clearing of six-foot, four-inch Ignacio Suazo and the brutal punishment being dealt out by 'Killer' Juan Chacon, the score could have reached double figures.

There seemed to be no help from the midfield whatsoever. In fact, they remained totally invisible, except when left prone on the ground after being beaten to the ball by a fleet red-shirt, or being reprimanded by the referee for an obstruction or a foul. Not one of the three Argentine forwards had touched the ball in the entire first half of play, a happenstance that Octavio Suarez had never encountered before. There was no flow, no rhythm, no attack. The manager was permitted only two substitutions, and he knew that the outcome of the game and perhaps his team's fate in the entire tournament rested on how wisely those selections were made.

It was clear that Independiente halfback Ricardo Arzu was out of his element on this night, and in his place, Suarez called upon defensive specialist Humberto Velasquez to stem the Hungarian offensive tide. His options were much more limited for the second substitution. How could he take out a forward when none of them had been tested yet? The back line was holding up well under severe pressure, so the only alternative was to add another new halfback.

Miguel Cruz had to stay in the game, for he was their leading goal scorer and a potential catalyst to ignite the offense. 'Señor Gol' had to produce in the second half, there was no doubt about that. The other wing half spot, currently occupied by Francis Argueta, had to be the second change. But who would go in to replace him? A look around the somber dressing room stopped at the player wearing number seventeen on his tracksuit.

That could be it! Brilliant, brilliant! thought Suarez as he called the player to his side. "If only that foot holds up, this might be our spark," Suarez commented under his breath.

"De Seta! Get over here!"

The occupant of seats 1 & 2, row 8, field level section 365, raised the field glasses he was holding to his eyes. It was fortunate that he had been able to persuade the army captain in charge of security in this section of the stadium that the metal armrest between his two seats should be removed in the interest of national security. He was, after all, a high-ranking colonel in the army reserves, with direct links to the president and the junta.

He had insisted the previous day that the armrest be removed, indicating that he would take full responsibility. The young captain had no recourse other than to oblige the colonel's request. Looking at the resplendently dressed tub of lard in all his finest military regalia conjured up images of his enormous girth blocking the escape route in an emergency. It also occurred to the captain that he would have to deal with this windbag for the entire tournament. It might be best to take heed of him in order to make the experience bearable.

That discussion had taken place on the afternoon of June first, just over twenty-four hours earlier. When the boisterous colonel and his entourage arrived to take their seats for the opening ceremonies and initial match of the 1978 World Cup, it was found that his militarily clad bulk would not fit into the newly renovated seats.

The colonel claimed that this was an outrage, that these same seats had been in his family for many years, and that there had been nothing wrong with the continual bench-style seat that had always been there. He had personally sat in seat numbers 1 and 2, right on the aisle, since the days of his youth. From here, he had been able to lead the cheers for the entire section and wave his huge blue and white flag with the Newton's Prefect insignia in place of the usual shining sun. A quickly located crowbar bent the armrest sufficiently to allow the colonel to half squat in his usual surroundings. But the oversized military man and his party left in a huff just before halftime when the dull, erratic game between West Germany and Poland made sitting in the cramped confines unbearable. A final word was had with the captain before departing, reminding him how serious the order to remove the arm rest was.

"If there happened to be a national crisis, I would be needed immediately at the Presidential Palace. Should I be delayed in the slightest by any 'inconvenience' at the stadium, it would be your head that would roll."

Yes, Astor Gordero was gratified that the captain had played the game properly. Other than the seat incident, he had thoroughly enjoyed the pomp and circumstance of the opening ceremonies. Massed military bands, dancers, balloons, and finally, doves for peace.

Cute, very cute, he had thought to himself. But all of it, even the seat incident, was insignificant today. Nothing that had happened prior to this day mattered now! It was the day of Argentina's first World Cup match. It was this team that mattered, all that mattered!

Two questions whirled in The Fat Man's mind as he scanned the Argentine players to pick out the substitutes as the teams returned to the pitch for the second half. Had he prepared young De Seta well enough for this moment, and had he planted the boy's name firmly enough in Octavio Suarez's mind?

Renaldo De Seta's recovery had been nothing short of miraculous, although his young client had only been back training with the team for six days and kicking a soccer ball for just three of those. Nevertheless, Astor Gordero was willing to take the lion's share of the credit for his protégé's unexpectedly quick return to the national side. After all, was it not he who had personally arranged for the top therapist in the nation to visit the boy on a daily basis? And was it not he, Astor Gordero, who kept the boy's emotional spirits high by delivering those silly love letters from Simone at precisely the right moment?

The urgency surrounding the boy's recovery increased dramatically when it became crystal clear that Nicodemo Garcia would never again wear an Argentine jersey. There would be an opening to fill in the starting lineup, and Renaldo De Seta was no good to anyone sitting on the bench. Forget the fact that it was highly unlikely one month ago that he would even be walking by this time. The Garcia incident must be exploited, and this colonel-lawyer-promoter knew just how to go about it.

Astor Gordero simply gave counsel to Octavio Suarez at every possible opportunity, apprising the manager of his young star's progress and helping to devise strategy and tactics. Suarez suffered The Fat Man's interference calmly, for if he had to share his thoughts with anyone in authority, Astor Gordero was the best choice. At least he knew something about football and the psyche of the Argentine people. It was also true that should things fall apart for the National Team, a friend of Astor Gordero's stature would be invaluable.

For once, Gordero was speechless when his binoculars picked up the handsome, curly-haired player who was removing his warm-up suit emblazoned with the number seventeen. 'El Hombre Gordo's' heart was in his throat.

Suarez is putting the boy in! Lady Luck is certainly sitting with me on this day, the rotund one thought to himself. He had come to the stadium for this game dressed, not in his military splendor, but in his favorite Prefect supporter,s garb . . . an oversized black leather jacket crested with the Prefect's logo, baggy blue jeans, and black, silver-tipped cowboy boots. A large powder-blue and white flag and a matching scarf completed the ensemble.

This prominent football fan was indistinguishable from scores of others on this night of nights, and that is exactly how Astor Gordero wanted it. His entourage this evening consisted of Wolfgang Stoltz and a handful of business and military associates similarly dressed down for the occasion. Argentina's pride and honor were about to be tested on the green grass of River Plate Stadium, and this battle called for real men to wear the attire of real football fans.

Once The Fat Man comprehended that his client had actually been substituted into the game, he was speechless. The only sound that he was able to mutter was a trilled 'R' that preceded the rest of the word 'Renaldo.' Herr Stoltz looked at his employer.

"What was that sound you just made, Astor? It sounded like 'RRRRRRRenaldo.'"

"Look, Wolfie. The boy is going into the game!" Gordero pointed a beefy hand in the direction of the Argentine bench. "He is truly going to play!

In my wildest dreams I didn't think it was possible tonight. RRRRRRRe-naaaaaaaallllldo. That's it! That's what I said! RRRRRRRenaaaaaaaallllldo. Come on, Wolfie, do it with me. Maybe it will inspire the boy."

Herr Stoltz looked a touch bewildered, but nevertheless joined his boss in a long, 'trilled R' version of number seventeen's name. The sound was inspiring. The Latin penchant for trilling their R's made the first letter of the boy's name escape the throat as an increasingly load roar. Standing in the aisle now, Gordero pointed to the young substitute's name on the scoreboard and goaded the surrounding spectators into accompanying him in the newly anointed salutation. As the expression picked up more and more support, it began to take on a haunting, pleading nature.

"RRRRRRRenaaaaaaaallllldo!"
"RRRRRRRenaaaaaaaallllldo!"
"RRRRRRRenaaaaaaaallllldo!"

Many of the faithful knew not what they were chanting or why, for Renaldo De Seta was, by no means, a household name in Argentina. Since his injury, he had been kept totally out of the spotlight by Astor Gordero, and the press continued to report the initial assessment of his injury. namely, that it was impossible for the boy to recover in time to rejoin the National Team. But here, against all odds, stood Renaldo De Seta on the pitch at River Plate Stadium, about to play the most important forty-five minutes of football in his lifetime.

Gordero thought of the strange Indian salve that the boy was constantly applying to his damaged heel. Tito had found nothing disagreeable in the mixture of plants, powders, and oil, so Gordero had allowed Renaldo to continue with the unusual remedy. Tito had come to Gordero's office after the first week that the holistic medicine had been used.

"The tendon has shown remarkable improvement, Señor Gordero. I have never in all my years seen anything like it. He claims that the salve was used by native warriors in the Pampas to soothe their bare and battle-scarred feet. If I were you, Señor, I would have the mixture analyzed and patented, for I have no other explanation for the progress that I have seen in these seven days. It is truly astonishing, Señor."

Never one to miss a potential marketing opportunity, Gordero had Tito bring him one of the used lamb skin bandages that was, in turn, sent to a chemical laboratory for analysis. Still extremely skeptical, Astor Gordero could only thank his lucky stars that something had enabled his client to be standing on this football field, instead of watching the game at home on the couch at Casa San Marco.

The foot felt adequately sound as Renaldo did short sprints and hops to limber up before the referee pointed to Enrique Rios and blew his whistle to commence the second half. He knew that the heel had never been tested in real action, but with any luck, the obscurity of the last month and his lack of previous international experience could prove to be a blessing in disguise. Surely the Hungarians new nothing about him. He had displayed only fleeting glimpses of his real talent in the few warm-up games in which he had participated, and hardly anyone had seen the magic that he and Ramon Vida could create when they were paired together.

Behind him, the fans were shouting "Argentina! Argentina! Argentina!" in a quick staccato clip, but from the opposite side of the stadium came a strange rumbling noise. The substitute could not make out exactly what was being said, so he quickly tried to turn his attention back to the tender limb.

The setting was awe-inspiring, but at the same time, somewhat distracting to the boy. Powder-blue and white banners and flags ringed the entire stadium. Ticker tape and confetti littered the warning track and often blew onto the pitch. One could feel that something dramatic was going to happen. It was in the air!

He remembered his dear father. How proud he would be of his son, if only he had lived to see this day. He wanted to play well for him, for the memory of Peter De Seta. He also remembered that day several months ago when he first met Octavio Suarez and stood on this same green carpet. That morning he had looked up to the Football Gods in the furthest reaches of the upper deck. Tonight they were still there, but they appeared in the form of fanatical, flag-waving human beings. He hoped that those Gods would be with him tonight.

The one major tactical adjustment for Renaldo was the fact that he was on the wing this time, not in the center of the field. Octavio Suarez had told him to simply patrol up and down the sideline initially, until he felt certain that he could run on the damaged foot. Suarez was taking a huge gamble on that heel. Should Renaldo go down, Argentina would have to play the remainder of the match with only ten men. There could be no further substitutions. The manager hoped that his youngest player would reaffirm his judgment and adapt under fire.

That proved easier said than done in the early going. The sideline was a new entity for Renaldo. He found it confining at first, an inflexible barrier controlled by the linesman's flag. The boy was a fast learner, however, and in this case, he was tutored expertly by the swift Hungarian wingers.

Twice his red-shirted opponents gathered in the ball and left the boy in their shadows.

"Wake up, you little shit!" was the warm greeting offered by Juan Chacon as Renaldo took his place in the goal area for the Hungarian corner kick that his second gaffe had produced. The third time a Magyar tried his wing, he was ready. He would use the sideline as an ally this time.

Anticipating the ball's path, Renaldo waited until the unsuspecting Hungarian had collected the sphere and turned to head up the line in full flight. Both men were within a yard of the boundary, but the Argentine had the preferable angle and more room to maneuver. The Hungarian could not proceed directly down the wing without contact. As the visitor turned slightly to look for a red jersey to pass to in the center of the field, a perfectly placed sliding foot knocked the ball back between the European's legs and within the reach of the approaching Ramon Vida. With play now progressing into the Hungarian zone, Renaldo felt reassured that the sideline worked the same for both teams. It was just as difficult for his opponent to work in the limiting confines of its shadow as it was for him. He must use it as a friend, respect it, and never take it for granted.

The undercurrent of the match began to subtly shift after about five minutes of play. The hard tackling of the Argentine defense, coupled with the brutal illegal punishment dealt out by Juan Chacon, was having the desired effect on the European guests. Chacon was an expert at avoiding the yellow card, for he would pick the opportunities to deliver his salutations only when the referee was occupied elsewhere. The rest of the time, a sneer, a growl, or a close-up look at his hideous countenance would be sufficient to intimidate an opponent.

The Hungarians began to shoot the ball from further and further out, seldom venturing near the monster of the back line. At the other end of the field, things were starting to jell. The Argentines were beginning to connect with their passes, which gave their offense a sense of rhythm. Much maligned Humberto Velasquez set up Ruben Gitares twice with pinpoint relays onto which he could run. The second of these led to a desperation foul by an out maneuvered Hungarian defender. The resulting indirect free kick for the host nation would be taken from thirty yards out. Eighteen minutes had elapsed in the second half.

The National Team had practiced several set plays for this opportunity, and Captain Daniele Bennett called on a piece using Miguel Cruz as the triggerman. Renaldo De Seta had not been included in any of the set pieces for obvious reasons. He took up a position at the edge of the box, just to the left of the Hungarian defensive wall. Ramon Vida trotted by on his way closer to the goal.

"Be ready for a rebound over on this side. That pussy Cruz won't score on the first shot," was his friend's advice.

At the referee's whistle, Enrique Rios ran directly over the ball from the left side. Three paces behind Rios came Gitares, who flicked the ball slightly to the right and onto the powerful foot of the waiting Miguel Cruz.

Cruz's low blast sailed unobstructed into the Magyar goalkeeper's arms, but Janos Toth, the keeper, was unable to find the handle. The ball squirted loose, sitting suspended in time for an instant in front of six disbelieving players. Suddenly, out of nowhere, came a solitary foot to tap the ball closer to the Hungarian net. That foot belonged to Renaldo De Seta, and his short pass landed directly on the toe of Ramon Vida's left foot. Not a soul stood between Vida and the back of the net, and that is precisely where the ball was deposited.

It was as if an explosion had gone off in River Plate Stadium. Roaring with delight, seventy-five thousand voices chanted in unison, "Argentina! Argentina! Argentina!" Ticker tape fell from the heavens. Ramon Vida stood with his arms outstretched to the Gallery Gods in thanksgiving as several of his teammates offered congratulations. Miguel Cruz was not among them. Renaldo waited until Ramon was finally alone before he approached the striker.

"Nice goal, hotshot," Renaldo offered with a smile.

"Nice pass, rookie. Didn't I tell you that Cruz would fuck up? Now let's go to work and show these Hunkies what you and I can really do."

The Hungarians were in no mood to allow their hosts to put on a soccer clinic, and they resorted to some blatant intimidation of their own to throw the Argentines off their game. The logic was that the hot-tempered Latins would lose their cool and open up opportunities for the visitors. That logic backfired.

The host nation's warriors kept their collective cool, and it was the visitors who became more and more frustrated as the clock wore down. Seldom did the red-shirts venture under the shadow of their opponent's goal posts, for there in all his ugliness stood 'Killer' Juan Chacon. The Argentines did not take the bait and retaliate, but something had to happen to sway the balance of the game before anarchy erupted on the pitch.

That something started with right back, Jorge Calderone. The twenty-seven-year-old from Newton's Prefects was having a career night, one in which he always seemed to be in the right place at the right time. His steadiness in the first half had reassured his defensive line-mates, and now with the Hungarians failing to press forward, he was able to use his considerable offensive skills to the team's advantage.

Time and time again, he would come upfield, spearheading the attack. His passes were perfection, and nearly all of the powder-blue and white sorties into enemy territory were the result of Calderone's newfound freedom. With just six minutes left to play, the versatile fullback again found himself deep inside Hungarian territory in uncontested possession of the ball.

Newton's Prefect striker Ruben Gitares received a laser-like pass from his club-mate as he was streaking diagonally across the field. In one motion, Gitares back-healed the ball to Miguel Cruz, who was making a parallel run, ten yards to the winger's left. Cruz gathered in the orb and strode straight towards the goal. Two defenders and the keeper converged on the center half, the keeper diving at Cruz' feet in an attempt to steal away the cherished object. Unfortunately for Toth, the ball once again squirted loose as he and Cruz tumbled to the ground in a heap. Only a few feet from this tangle of opposing players stood Jorge Calderone. The sphere was his and his alone. It was as if this one play was his reward for a stellar performance. With a gaping net twenty yards away, he made no mistake. 2-1 Argentina!

'Thunderstruck,' was the only word to describe the feeling that swept over Renaldo De Seta as the ball entered the net. The piercing burst of hysteria that enveloped those on the pitch was beyond imagination. Once again, the white streamers and confetti rained down from the heavens. The lengthy roar was eventually transformed into the bravado-induced chant "Argentina! Argentina! Argentina!" The initial outburst had actually startled Renaldo, for he had never before played the game at a time when so much was at stake.

The Hungarians would not roll over and allow the partisan fans to continue their celebration, however. Approximately six minutes remained until time, and the Magyars went for the equalizer with a bloody vengeance.

Possession of the ball became the battle cry, and the Europeans stretched the limits of fair play to make sure that it remained on their feet. Señor Garando, the Portuguese referee, was all over the field trying to calm tempers and keep play moving.

Torok and Nagy created several anxious moments in front of Junior Calix, for those two in particular would not be denied the ball. As a result, they found themselves in the thick of the rough-and-tumble play, and that meant having to deal with the ever-abrasive Juan Chacon.

It was the brave Torok that dared to defy the monster at the gate with a bold charge straight for the goal. The Hungarian center forward had gathered in a pass on the full run as he crossed the half line and was bearing down on number seventeen in powder-blue and white. In a split second, Renaldo had to decide whether to go after the streaking red-shirt or fall back and cover his opposing winger.

At that moment, Miguel Cruz buzzed into the picture and took a shot at disarming Torok. The Hungarian neatly slipped by the attempted tackle, but he was temporarily distracted. It was just the break that Renaldo figured he needed. The rookie Argentine set out after the Magyar, allowing Daniele Bennett to cover his mark. He worried about his heel for perhaps half a stride, then instinct took over.

The boy loved chasing down opponents and disarming them. He found it even more exhilarating than scoring goals, if the truth be known. Torok was thirty-five yards out when Renaldo left his feet. The hulking form of Juan Chacon loomed ahead. Torok had to either shoot or feint away from Chacon. The Ugly One was now advancing full speed at the intruder. A slight deke to his right brought the red-shirt one step closer to the outstretched right foot of number seventeen. That was all that was necessary.

The ball skittered harmlessly away after making contact with Renaldo's laces, and Torok, Renaldo, and of course, Juan Chacon, ended up in a three-man love-in on the turf. Surprisingly, Chacon's forearm seemed to find the Hungarian's chin somewhere in the entanglement, and in retaliation, Torok's elbow seemed to find Renaldo's nose.

Totally unexpected, the blow brought tears of pain to the boy's eyes as he sprawled on his back holding his broken, bleeding, proboscis. Fortunately, the referee had witnessed only the retaliatory act by the visitor. Once again, Juan Chacon's timing had been perfect. The red card was shown without hesitation to Torok, and his fervent argument that he was only defending himself fell on deaf ears.

The Hungarians, to a man, were irate. They swarmed referee Garando. He was cool enough to ignore their protestations as the training staff attended to the downed Argentine. As the two trainers knelt beside Renaldo, wiping away the blood, Juan Chacon stood directly over the boy offering kind words of sympathy.

"Get up, you little crybaby. The whole fucking world is watching you lay there getting your diaper changed. This is a man's sport. If you want to play with the big boys, you better be ready to take that shit. Now either get off the field or stand up and play!"

"I'll play, don't worry about me," was the boy's calm response as he pushed away the trainers and rose to his feet. The bleeding had not altogether stopped, and he was forced to wipe the stream of blood with his jersey. Ramon Vida was at his side now.

"Hey, man, you look great. Really nails. Those Hunkies won't come near you now! Your face is almost as scary as Chacon's! Let's go, tough guy."

Renaldo could always count on his flippant friend to make him laugh, even in the bleakest situations.

Less than two minutes remained until the final whistle, and despite having to play with only ten men, the Hungarians again pressed the attack. Unfortunately for the visitors, the tackling and interference by both sides was so vicious that no sustained offensive thrust could be mounted.

Under one minute remained when an exchange at midfield between Nagy and Cruz sent Señor Garando to his shirt pocket once more. In this case, it was a matter of well-misplaced kicks to each other's shins that saw both players shown the red card. The fact that the Hungarian had struck the first blow incensed the crowd, but Cruz's retaliatory offering was done with blatant attempt to injure, giving the referee no alternative. That did not mean that the volatile Cruz would depart in a gentlemanly fashion. He had several choice words for Señor Garando before Octavio Suarez ordered him off the field from the sideline.

The dilemma for Suarez was immediate. Because of his expulsion, Cruz had to sit out Argentina's next match against France. As the final whistle sounded, ringing in Argentina's initial victory in their quest for world football supremacy, Octavio Suarez was a worried man. He knew that the four days of preparation that his depleted team was afforded before battling the French was not nearly enough time to put the pieces together. There was no time for retrospection, and there was no time for savoring this victory. The future was all that mattered!

France had lost to Italy in a heartbreaking 2-1 game at Mar del Plata that afternoon. To avoid elimination, the French had to beat Argentina. Suarez knew that his charges would face a tenacious, determined opponent. Thoughts of Napoleon's gallant armies marching to victory after victory filled the manager's mind with anxiety. Luckily, the boss was able to conjure up the one thought that finally erased the scene from existence. It was the fact that there had been one Waterloo for the French already. Hopefully, the contest at the River Plate battlefield would be the second.

The eleven names that illuminated the giant scoreboard under the host country's name on the evening of June sixth provided ample cause for speculation. The starting lineup for this decisive match against France had been the best kept secret in Argentina. All press and visitors had been barred from the practice pitch, which had been shrouded in a twelve-foot high, solid wood fence. No one, players, coaches, or the manager himself, was allowed to discuss strategy during the inevitable interviews decreed by FIFA. The starting lineup tended to give credence to a rumor that had been circulating freely in the press. There was talk of a falling out between Octavio Suarez and his Independiente players, and the resultant purge by the manager had left only one of their number on the starting roster.

That player, the indomitable and irreplaceable Juan Chacon, had given veiled hints of his dissatisfaction with the player selection in an interview the day before the French contest. The real story had Chacon and Suarez almost coming to blows over the replacement of Arzu, Argueta, and now even Enrique Rios from the A squad. With Miguel Cruz's suspension, the number of Independiente players that started the tournament's second game for the home side fell to one. Five had started the previous game. Juan Chacon interpreted the action of the National Team manager as an affront to his club-mates and himself, and confronted Suarez in his office. Rumors abounded that 'The Ugly One' had to be physically restrained from attacking Suarez by coach Estes Santos.

The answers that the Gallery Gods were waiting for were about to be revealed as the Swiss referee blew his whistle and pointed to Ramon Vida. The young center forward was grinning from ear to ear as he nodded affirmation and flicked the ball back ten yards to center half Renaldo De Seta. The strategy of manager Suarez' game plan was now evident for all to see.

He had moved the 'dynamic duo' to the middle of the playing field, the location where they felt most comfortable. Enrique Rios had been removed from the center forward spot due to his indifferent play, and on the wing, Nicholas Pastor, the perennial A squad forward, was nowhere to be seen.

In his place stood veteran Caesar Castro, the River Plate winger who was on his home turf and patrolling the same terra firma that he owned during club matches. Suarez was gambling that the thirty-year-old Castro would feel comfortable in the well-known confines of River Plate Stadium. Vida and Castro had worked together as B squad forwards many times since the start of training, so they were well acquainted. Only Ruben Gitares remained on the front line from the original A squad eleven.

The half line held two surprises. One was De Seta, but the other was even more of a shock. Instead of either of the two Independiente halves available to him, Suarez had chosen to go with another B player in the often overwhelmed Leopoldo Anariba. Again, the manager was sending out the message that there were no secure postings on the starting eleven. Four B players now patrolled the Argentine middle and left side. Cruz's expulsion had opened the door for Suarez to regain control of his team. The eleven men in powder-blue and white stockings had received the signal loud and clear.

The red stockings of the French embraced legs that possessed startling speed, intelligent improvisation, cleverness, and imagination. France had scored on Italy after only thirty-eight seconds of their opening match. It was a goal that would stand as the prettiest and best executed end-to-end rush of the tournament. Italy had managed to regroup and emerge victorious, but Suarez was afraid that a similar opening flurry by the French would severely rattle his young charges.

Although Junior Calix was tested twice in the early going, the Argentines parried their opponent's opening assaults and then countered with a skillful attack of their own. The match had an energy level that Renaldo De Seta had never experienced before.

Gone were the clutch and grab tactics of the Hungarians. This was pure, fluid football, and the boy loved it. The navy-blue-shirted, white-shorted Frenchmen were every bit as cagey as Suarez had warned. The flow of play never ebbed for a moment as both teams played poker with their opponent's defenses.

De Seta and Vida had several bright moments together, none culminating in the sought-after reward, however. Castro and Anariba seemed to be holding their own, and as the last minute of the first half loomed, manager Suarez was generally pleased with what he had observed.

Renaldo's heel was holding up well to this point, and he had not seemed out of place among the artful French playmakers. The pace of the game had been hectic, with numerous fast-breaking counterattacks by both sides. Nevertheless, Argentina's youngest player remained stalwart in defense, managing to mark his opposite number with suffocating efficiency.

With the clock set to summon the two teams to the dressing room for the interval, the French mysteriously seemed to let up for a few moments. Ramon Vida was able to undress French defender Yves Herve from the ball deep inside the European zone and relay it to his young friend, De Seta. Renaldo gathered in the pass on the full run and beat a path directly toward the French goal. He was met inside the penalty area by France's captain, defender Christian Thiery. The powerfully built Thiery wasted no time in diving at his opponent's feet and sending both men sprawling to the turf.

The tackle had been legal, but as the Frenchman fell, his left arm seemed to make contact with the ball, sending it safely out of harm's way, over the touch line. Ramon Vida was instantly at the referee's side pointing to his hand and vehemently stating his case for a hand-ball foul. The Swiss official strode to the sideline to confer with his linesman, who had had a better vantage point from which to see the disputed play. Vida was on Mr. Raabsamen's heels the entire width of the field. He kept up a constant chatter as the two officials conferred and his persistence paid off.

Turning to make his way back across the pitch, the referee gave a slight flick of his wrist to indicate that he concurred with Señor Vida and ran directly to the penalty spot. The crowd erupted in sheer delight as league leading goal scorer Ruben Gitares stepped up to the ball and awaited the referee's signal. On the whistle, he deftly nestled the orb in the back of the French goal, blasting a shot in the opposite direction from the sprawling keeper, Jean-Marc Poullain. Referee Raabsamen again brought the whistle to his lips, this time signaling the half. The home side was ecstatic, the visiting Europeans stunned.

There were no substitutions for either side as the second half commenced. The French took to the attack like a team possessed, and well they should, for a loss would send them home disqualified. The Argentine defensive back line had remained intact after the Hungarian contest, and as usual, Juan Chacon was handing out his greeting cards to any French player who came close enough to collect one.

Twenty-year-old wing half Martín Palance was the heart and soul of the French offensive thrust. Time and time again, he defied the ugly Argentine with lightning sorties into the shadow of the powder-blue and white goal. He was rewarded for his dexterity in the sixty-first minute with the equalizing tally, converting a finely honed shot that had rebounded onto his foot off the crossbar. Countryman Didier Onze and two Argentine defenders were actually inside the net when the ball passed over the line. The great cliffs fell silent. The scoreboard did not lie! It was a tie game, and anybody's contest.

Among the advantages held by the home side at this particular point in the match was the fact that the starting French keeper, Jean-Marc Poullain, had to be carried from the field at the fifty-eighth minute. The unfortunate goalie had been injured by crashing his back into the upright post while making a particularly acrobatic save. His replacement, Michel Delaroche, was the older of the two men by five years. At age thirty-one, many thought that he had seen better days.

Despite this setback, Palance continued to be the spark that rallied the men in the dark-blue shirts. Forward, forward, like Napoleon's Imperial Guard, they wore the coq proudly. Didier Onze was to come the closest to being crowned the emperor when Palance set him free on a magnificent run. With only Junior Calix to beat, from twelve yards out he pulled the lanyard of his cannon. Calix sprawled to his left, clutching nothing but air.

The solid shot projectile hurtled unobstructed toward the enemy's headquarters. Onze followed its trajectory, confident in his ability as a master artilleryman. This would be the coup de grâce! The foe was finished. France would be victorious. But wait, what was this? For some unexplained reason, the shot misfired. His attempt wide by inches, the despondent Frenchman fell to his knees and grabbed his flowing mane in both hands. Agony!

There was action in the other goalmouth as well. The Argentines had adapted to the attacking French style, and the use of the offside trap allowed for some hasty counterattacks into European territory. Often the dark-blue-shirted midfield would be caught too far forward in attack to assist their rear guard.

It was the surprising Leopoldo Anariba that seemed to be constantly pressing forward. He had received yeoman's support in the first half from both Daniele Bennett in the rear and Caesar Castro up front, and now the rookie National Team member from Racing Club was gaining in poise and confidence. Chances were to be had continually. Vida hit the crossbar twice only two minutes apart. Gitares came close to putting the hosts back in the lead, but he was uncharacteristically inept in his finish.

Renaldo De Seta was more concerned about marking his man and not allowing the French an opportunity at his expense. He would feed strong balls to his teammates, but always with an eye on the gathering French hurricane. Less than fifteen minutes remained to play when the decisive moment arrived.

It started with a save by Junior Calix and a fast clearance out to Daniele Bennett on the left flank. Bennett looked upfield as the ball arrived and one-timed it thirty yards up the sideline to Leopoldo Anariba. The underrated halfback had acres of space since the French midfield was, once again, too far forward. Anariba made a run diagonally into the center of the pitch, and Renaldo De Seta, who was also unmarked, pressed forward ten yards in advance of his teammate.

Twenty-five yards from the goalmouth, Renaldo stopped dead, worried about a fast-breaking French counterattack should his line-mate cough up the ball. Anariba's run had, by now, drawn a crowd of French defenders, and from the left wing, Caesar Castro was making a strong push into the penalty area, distracting several more Frenchmen. All this activity left Renaldo momentarily alone and unattended.

As Anariba flew past number seventeen on his way toward the right-hand goal post, he delivered a true pass onto the surprised center half's right foot. So strongly was la pelota delivered to Renaldo that it volleyed off his boot to waist height. He watched it rise in the air and sit spinning almost in slow motion at the peak of its trip. The Newton's Prefect Under Twenty-one player remembered thinking what a great, strong ball Anariba had sent him, how he hadn't thought Leopoldo could pass with such authority until that very moment.

Renaldo then flashed on Astor Gordero's words, *Head and feet as one, head and feet as one!* With his peripheral vision, he could pick out the top left corner of the opposing goal. The French defense seemed frozen in time. No one came forward to challenge, and as the ball sat suspended at the vertex of its rise, number seventeen swung a powerful right leg up and made contact.

"There!" the boy shouted as the sphere arched on its journey. His right hand pointed toward the top left corner of France's goal, the preordained destination.

Head and feet as one! Come on, come on! This shot did not misfire, but was true to its mark. The French keeper had not expected a shot from such a distance, especially with powder-blue and white players streaming down the wings. That distraction and the resultant hesitation were his undoing. By the time he left his feet the ball was behind him, in the top left corner of the net!

Renaldo followed the flight of the ball, coaxing, pleading, urging it on its true path. He saw the back of the net bulge and Delaroche's futile dive.

Raising his arms upright was the boy's initial reaction. It was what he did instinctively any time he was fortunate enough to be rewarded in such a manner. He did not take to running wildly about the field, shouting praises to the heavens or falling to his knees while his teammates piled on top of him. Such demonstrations were for others. He had, at no time in his young life, scored a goal of this magnitude, however.

The stadium erupted in delight, and the heavens opened up with snow-like flakes of paper. Shouts of "Argentina! Argentina! Argentina!" rained down upon the players as they swarmed their newly anointed Wellington.

The goal scorer was finally freed from his human entanglements and began to make his way back across the center line when he heard it for the first time. The noise seemed to start low in the field level section of the stadium, close to where the boy knew that Astor Gordero was seated. It was a strange sound, somewhat like a low roar followed by a long exclamation. Ramon Vida was now at Renaldo's side.

"Do you hear that, man? You have your own cheer! Holy shit, listen to that, man. They're saying 'RRRRRRRenaaaaaaaallllldo.' That's you, man! You're a fucking hero with your own fucking cheer, my friend. Look at the scoreboard. Look at those giant letters!"

Mesmerized by the growing volume of the refrain, Renaldo cast his eyes upon the mammoth illuminated board. There, in huge letters, spread the graphics of his name. Several 'R's' in succession followed by 'E,' 'N,' several 'A's,' then several 'L's,' a 'D' and an 'O.' The entire stadium had picked up the chorus, and it was an extremely embarrassed, yet elated center half that took up his position for the final minutes of play.

On again came Napoleon's legions, undaunted by the odds against them. Fine, inspired football propelled the blue shirts forward in search of the equalizer. But Wellington's forces held their ground, and at the end of the day, left the field victorious.

The French must now retreat to Paris, empty-handed. Two games, two losses. A skilled, poetic team that just couldn't find their offensive form. Renaldo De Seta exchanged jerseys with French captain Christian Thierry, who expressed best wishes and admiration for his young opponent. The crowd was still in a state of euphoria as Renaldo De Seta left the playing field, stripped to the waist and listening. The Gallery Gods were loudly proclaiming him as Argentina's new darling of the River Plate.

The occupant of seat 3, row 8, field level section 365 had managed to contain herself through the first seventy-five minutes of the Argentina-France encounter. It had been an exceedingly difficult task, but the portly gentleman accompanying the young lady that evening had urged her to keep a low profile lest a riot break out.

They had arrived at the stadium early to avoid recognition, and sure enough, no one had given the girl dressed in the tight jeans, a brown bomber jacket, and midthigh leather boots more than an approving glance. The fact that her long, curly hair had been neatly tucked up under a powder-blue and white tam and her eyes were covered with oversized dark glasses made her discernible features even more obscure. Two of the five bodyguards occupied the seats immediately in front of her, two sat directly behind her, and the fifth beside her to the left. With Astor Gordero wedged into seats 1 & 2 to her right, Simone Yvonne Montana Carta-Aqua was surrounded by so much prime Argentine beef that she felt like a lovesick cow that had wandered into the bull's barn at mating season.

In the end, Symca's cover was blown with Renaldo De Seta's winning goal. She leapt to her feet along with the rest of the stadium, hugging the large girth of Gordero and squealing with joy. The Fat Man clutched his huge flag, and waving it to and fro, trilled a succession of 'R's' and then completed the expression with an 'E,' 'N,' several 'A's,' several 'L's' then a 'D,' and an 'O.'

"Simone, he scored, the boy scored! Did you see that shot? It was fantastic! Come, help me salute him. I've made up a cheer. You men there, all of you, help out. It goes like this . . ."

Gordero then led the faithful in a series of loud punctuated exclamations, each one gaining in length and volume. Others in the section followed suit, but when the young lady in seat 3 stepped into the aisle and doffed her tam, it seemed like that entire side of River Plate Stadium picked up the refrain. There was no mistaking the beautiful Symca as she urged the throng to join in with a spirited and sensual outburst of euphoria. Astor Gordero had been so pleased at his innovative cheer that he had paid the scoreboard operator one thousand U.S. dollars to visually display the boy's name should the definitive occasion occur.

True to the agreement, after the clincher had been netted, the giant blackboard spelt out 'RRRRRRR-e-n-aaaaaaaa-llll-d-o.' Now the entire gathering joined the chorus, and as the patrons close to field level section 365 gawked and craned their necks to get a glimpse of the nation's premier pop sensation, the entire stadium rocked to the haunting sound of the vocalized refrain saluting their new idol's name.

CHAPTER TWENTY-THREE

Lonnie De Seta held the small, portable radio tightly to his left ear. The reception in the basement room he and Celeste called home was terrible. Static cracked constantly, giving the hyperactive football announcer the effect of barking over the airwaves. Names were a blur, and the flow of the match impeded by noise pollution. Lonnie swore at the black rectangle in his hand.

"Goddamn piece of shit radio, smarten up and work, for Christ's sake!"

He smacked the side of the object and was about to put it down when he thought that he could make out the name 'De Seta' through the inaudible jumble. He put the box to his ear again. "De Seta scores!!! Renaldo De Seta scores to give Argentina a 2-1 lead with fourteen minutes to play!!!!!! RRRRRRRRRenaaaldo . . . De . . . Seta!!!!"

The goal scorer's older brother wanted to shout the boy's name at the top of his lungs. He wanted to dance around the room, embracing Celeste while whooping for joy. He could hear the commotion from the parlor above him in this moderately priced, moderately decent boarding house in the Boca area of the capital. But there would be no spontaneous outburst of any kind from the occupants of lower room number three.

They had resided in the small efficiency flat exactly one month to the day, when Argentina took the field against France. Outside their basement window, the football-mad residents of Boca were going crazy, and on the inside of that same window, so was Lonnie De Seta. Only it was a different kind of crazy.

Lonnie was well on his travels down the road to a complete mental breakdown. He was convinced that Celeste had already reached that destination.

So much had changed since Celeste's return to their room in Barracas on May the fifth, yet in many ways, so much had stayed the same. It seemed to Lonnie that he was making a lifetime commitment to living in flee-bitten rooms and scurrying about the outer world incognito, like some detested rodent. His roommate had been beside herself with grief since her younger brother's death, and at times, had remained in bed sobbing for days on end.

With a price on the 'Attractive Assassin's' head, Celeste should have been the one to venture out into the real world to buy staples and retrieve the newspapers, but in her state of mourning, she seemed either unwilling or unable to make that effort. The task fell to Lonnie to keep the pair alive, and when absolutely necessary, he would put on one of several disguises and slip out the basement window after dark to the late-night market nearby.

There had been no contact from Serge Lavalle whatsoever, and adding to Celeste's grief was the intuition that her eldest brother was no longer among the living. Lonnie could do little to search for the missing man, for he was 'the hunted one,' and his clean-shaven likeness still was pasted on the walls of many a building. The crazed, shaggy animal that Lonnie De Seta had become bore not a thread of resemblance to the word 'attractive' at all.

Nevertheless, extreme caution was the operative word. What little street talk Lonnie could acquire confirmed that certain unknown people were asking for information about any of the remaining cadre members from the Barracas terrorist assassination. The local newspaper vendor had been the most reliable source of information, but like most members of the Boca population, he wanted to discuss football-related matters only. The fugitive had to be careful not to seem overly interested in the terrorist roundup, so he would always open their dialogue with the topic that appeased the information vendor. Just as he was about to depart, Lonnie would ask his new friend if there was any late news on the terrorist killings.

The fear was real throughout the capital that the Montoneros or some similar dissident organization would disrupt the World Cup Tournament, so it was easy enough to steer the newsy onto the topic without raising an eyebrow. On the night of June seventh, as the terrorist ventured out to buy every printed word relating to Argentina's latest soccer victory, he was told that several different men had come by the kiosk inquiring after one specific person. The merchant showed Lonnie a poster that had been left with him. It bore the image of the 'Attractive Assassin.'

This news turned Lonnie's blood cold and caused his forehead to break out into a heavy sweat under his brown slouch hat. He felt weak at the knees as he made his way back to his semi-incarcerated existence. The questions raced through his mind.

Should they try to reach the bank, get some money, and make a run for it? Should they make a better effort to find Serge? Was it safe to move Celeste in her unstable state? And who were these people that were showing his picture around? Police? Montoneros? Assassins?

Lonnie wondered how much lower he could sink. He felt like sobbing in his mother's arms and repenting for all the bad little things he had done. But they were not little boy things these actions that had brought him to Boca. He had committed a cold-blooded killing, and his mother's love could not save him now. He was on his own, and he felt the noose getting tighter and tighter.

Orville Richard Geary Jr. liked to think of himself as a Porteño, even though he was born in Palo Alto, California. The offspring of a homesick U.S. Army colonel bound for Korea in April of 1950, and a fiery, red-headed Argentine exchange student at Stanford University, Orville Jr.'s namesake was killed in action before his son entered this world.

Carmela Gaspero claimed to have married the colonel two days before he had shipped out. Wanting to avoid a scandal, Orville Sr.'s distraught New England widow and family paid the extremely pregnant foreigner a tidy sum of money to make her disappear back to Argentina as soon as the baby was born.

Whatever documentation Carmela had obtained from Orville Geary during their brief romance was enough to convince the authorities to put the surname 'Geary' on her newborn baby's birth certificate instead of her own name 'Gaspero.' Little Orville would be an American citizen with an American-sounding name. That was very important to Carmela. She would always remember America, and she would always remember her handsome Colonel Orville every time she looked at her beautiful Yankee son.

It seemed that Carmela had a thing for men in uniform, for shortly after her return to Buenos Aires, she wed a young captain in the Argentine army. Orville Junior was raised along strict military guidelines by his cold and often abusive stepfather, but the boy reveled in the pseudo army-camp lifestyle. His birth father's military picture adorned the wall above his bed, and even his stepfather showed a certain amount of respect for the memory of his fellow soldier-at-arms.

Orville was sent to one of the finest military academies in all of Argentina by the time he was eight. It was there that he fostered the strong right-wing views that remained with him to this day. Loyalty to the country, the army, and to the family. That was all that mattered.

An officer's commission into the army upon matriculation was not enough to keep eighteen-year-old Orville content, however. He had become so enthused about things military that he wanted to put his classroom training to the test. In real life. On a real battlefield.

Orville Richard Geary Jr.'s American birth certificate was the passport to travel and adventure that he needed to accomplish this feat. His first port of call on what would turn out to be an extended four-year stopover was at Bien Ho, South Viet Nam, in December 1968. Orville had joined the U.S. Army to help stop the dreaded forces of communism from gaining a foothold in this lovely Asian country. The grunt with the Spanish accent was assigned to be a radio man in 'C' Company, Second Battalion, Twenty-Eighth Infantry Regiment of the First Infantry Division. Charlie Company of the Big Red One! 'Duty first, no mission too difficult, no sacrifice too great.' Orville Geary was in deep, and he loved it.

A transfer to Army Rangers and a promotion to sergeant followed the end of his first tour, then three more years of blood and guts. He had become a skilled, methodical killer who relished a 'clean hit,' 'large enemy body counts,' and 'firefights.'

It was a disillusioned and frustrated Orville Geary that returned to South America with an honorable discharge in early 1973. He could not shake the stinging humiliation of the shellacking that the U.S. forces were taking several thousand miles away. But it didn't take long for the former American combat soldier to find out that the political backdrop in Argentina provided a perfect venue in which a trained killer might ply his trade.

Left-wing advocacy had been on the ascendant during Orville Geary's absence from Argentina, along with increased civil strife, terrorist attacks against industry and state-run commerce, and a lack of respect for the ineffectual military. One seemed to have only two political choices, radicalism or Perónism. There was no right-wing military option at all, and that fact stirred Orville Geary into action.

The highly proficient killer took it upon himself personally to eliminate anyone that was obstructing the eventual return of a strong military junta to power. That was the only hope for Argentina as Orville Geary saw the situation.

There were many people to eradicate on his list, but each select 'hit' would carry the process a step further. Originally, Orville operated on his own, but as time passed, he found it useful to employ the services of other patriots that shared his philosophy. Supplies for his missions were always readily available, as were schedules and timetables of important targets. Ironclad alibis could be provided, if necessary.

The last item was never needed, for Geary was so good at his profession that the trail he left behind always turned cold. He drew around him a band of disillusioned military specialists, forming his own platoon of underground right-wing activists. Through the ensuing years, he played a large part in paving the way for the eventual bloodless military coup that took place in March of 1976. The country had witnessed the return of Juan Perón in June of 1973, his untimely death from pneumonia in July of 1974, the assumption of his office by his widow Isabel, and her eventual exile in 1975.

During all these events, Orville Geary was working in the shadows to strengthen the position of the right-wing military coalition. The ousting of Isabel Perón was the last stumbling block.

Her successor, President Italo Luder, declared a state of siege and immediately signed a decree ordering the army to annihilate armed left-wing subversives. With the economy stagnant and inflation at eight hundred percent, the general population was looking for relief from the civil strife and terrorism that rocked the country. Only the military could provide the strong, often ruthless, guidance so many sought, and President Luder read the writing on the wall.

After March 24, 1976, the country was run by men in uniform, and those men continued to hold Orville Geary in extremely high regard. His particular skills were constantly required, especially those which involved removing thorns from the junta's paws. Orville Geary and his platoon could be relied upon to handle the most delicate assignments, and Orville Geary always accomplished his missions.

While young Geary had inherited his military bearing from his father, he had just as significantly inherited a shock of red hair from his mother. It was a characteristic that would give him his lifelong nickname, *Rojo,* meaning 'Red,' in English.

Among his friends in Buenos Aires initially, then to his fellow grunts in ' 'Nam,' he was always ' Rojo' Geary, never Orville. It was the same Rojo Geary that Astor Gordero hired to track down Lonnie De Seta in early May of 1978. The trail, after a long, frustrating month, was now heating up nicely.

June the sixth had turned out to be a particularly rewarding day for Astor Gordero. The initial good news came via Wolfgang Stoltz shortly after eight a.m. Florencia De Seta had consented to A.R. Gordero and Sons handling her personal investment portfolio and estate matters, and she had promised to pursue the same arrangement with her seventy-eight-year-old mother-in-law Lydia immediately.

Stoltz had convinced Florencia that it made sense to consolidate all the asset supervision under one roof, considering Lydia's age. She alone controlled the De Seta empire, and it was imperative for Astor Gordero's plan to work that Señora Lydia De Seta be brought into the fold. Stoltz had pointed out to Florencia that it would be much better for the decision-making powers to be handed over to the future heir's financial advisors while the family matriarch was still living. That would ease the strain of bureaucratic paperwork for the bereaved family after Lydia's departure. Renaldo's grandmother had granted Florencia and Wolfgang Stoltz an audience in Pergamino one week hence to discuss the matter. Things looked very positive!

The second piece of uplifting news came by phone on Astor Gordero's private line shortly after nine a.m. Rojo Geary had been instructed to phone in once a week, using this constantly monitored and debugged line. He had relayed positive progress for the first time. It appeared certain that Lonnie De Seta was hiding out in the Boca section of the capital, and Geary was close to making the initial, and also the final, contact.

The beautiful Symca had accepted Gordero's invitation to accompany him to that evening's football match without hesitation once Gordero relayed the news that Renaldo De Seta would be in the starting lineup. Octavio Suarez had confirmed the boy's starting role in a noon telephone conversation with The Fat Man, who, in turn, relayed the news instantly to Señorita Symca. He would not tell Renaldo of the lady's presence in the stands, however, for fear that it would distract his concentration.

"We only need the boy running on two legs, not three!" he had laughingly told Wolfgang Stoltz. A stellar performance by his young client before a worldwide audience would certainly increase Renaldo's value on the open transfer market. Now all that was needed to make Astor Gordero's day a total success was an Argentine victory and a strong showing by his client. An extended lunch at the Jockey Club with Stoltz, then a few hours of sexual frolicking with two blonde, Dutch sisters seeking tickets to the tournament would kill much of the time until kickoff. As things transpired, June the sixth would be a very, very good day for Astor Gordero.

Renaldo De Seta's heart started to pound as his visitor to the National Team Training Center handed him a heavily perfumed envelope. There was no mistaking either Simone's handwriting or her fragrance. Thoughts of their dressing room embrace at Teatro Colon flooded the boy's mind. Her scent had made his head spin then, as it did now. He tore open the missive with shaking hands, unable to wait until he was completely alone to read its contents.

Astor Gordero smiled patiently as his client devoured Symca's words. She had written the note in the back of Gordero's limousine on their way home from the match the evening before, and while she would not let The Fat Man read her private jottings, she assured him that what she had inscribed would fill the recipient with courage . . . and passion!

Renaldo was no more forthcoming with the letter's contents than the author had been. Gordero was smart enough to give the boy his leave to go off and ponder the words and thoughts that preoccupied him at the moment.

Before parting company, however, Gordero again offered Renaldo tickets to the upcoming Argentina-Italy match for his mother and brother, Lonnie. The answer was exactly the same as it had been for the last month.

Señora Florencia De Seta had absolutely no interest in watching her son play his dangerous little games, and as for Lonnie, Renaldo had not heard from him for the last several weeks.

"I think he still must be traveling the country with his girlfriend, but he did express an interest in seeing me play if I made the team. He will probably show up before long. I just don't know when," Renaldo explained.

Gordero was careful not to make the boy suspicious by asking too many questions concerning his brother's whereabouts, so he dropped the subject. Wolfgang Stoltz had also inquired after Lonnie's locale in a discreet manner when the opportunity arose with Florencia, but the lady would turn to ice and make some offhand comment about her vagabond, communist son. The impression was given that there was no love lost between mother and offspring, and Stoltz would never pursue the topic after getting the standard response. There was no doubt that neither Renaldo nor his mother had the slightest inkling of Lonnie's whereabouts.

Astor Gordero was shocked by the foul humor that he found manager Suarez in as he entered the team leader's inner sanctum after leaving Renaldo. One would have thought that the thrilling victory over France the previous evening would have elevated Suarez temporarily to cloud nine, but the manager sat chain-smoking cigarette after cigarette as he picked up files that were scattered pell-mell over his office floor.

"Those bastards from Independiente. Do you know what they are trying to pull? Juan Chacon comes in to see me at nine a.m. sharp and informs me that I had better start Miguel Cruz at center half against Italy because he has served his suspension! That if I had other plans for that position, I should rethink them, for if Cruz is not in the starting lineup, all five of the Independiente players will leave the team in protest. Then he pushed me further into a corner. He insisted that his cohorts Arzu, Argueta, and Rios be returned to the starting lineup as well, or Chacon will refuse to play! How do you like that? The ugly cocksucker is trying to run this team!"

"So what will you do, Octavio? De Seta played so well against France, and on the whole, the lineup for that game was much more cohesive than the game against Hungary. You can't let the inmates rule the asylum!" Gordero responded.

"I know, I know, Astor, but I must have Chacon on the back line against Italy. He is the one player who sets the tone and tenacity of our defense. I am afraid that without him guarding the gate, the Italians will swarm all over our goal area."

"What does it matter?" an agitated Gordero screamed. "Both Italy and Argentina have already advanced to the second round. The game is meaningless. Call their bluff! If you give in to them now, they will own you for the rest of the tournament!"

Suarez's eyes narrowed, his face turned red, and the veins in his temples bulged.

"Goddamn it, Astor, no one runs this team except me, and you know that. I am not afraid to stand up to Chacon, no matter how badly I need him on the pitch, but this game is not meaningless! If we lose, we have to pack up our operation and play the second round in Rosario. I want to stay right here in Buenos Aires! Your boy De Seta had his opportunity and did an admirable job. Cruz wants the chance to win back his old position. After all, he did have an enviable record in the warm-up matches."

"One game, Octavio, one game is all that he excelled in. A lucky hat trick, and now he is untouchable? My boy can play circles around that little fagot, Cruz. I think that you owe the position to De Seta on the merit of his performance against France. Do you not agree?"

"Under normal circumstances, yes, of course, I do. But these are not normal times. We are in the middle of the biggest sporting event this nation has ever seen, and five of my players are threatening to pack up and leave! I must think on this subject for a while. Stand by me, Astor, for I might just have to give the Independiente players enough rope to hang themselves with."

With that, the beleaguered manager walked out of his office, en-route to the training pitch where his charges were limbering up for the first workout of the day. There were three days left to prepare for the contest against Italy, and Astor Gordero knew that they would not be good days to spend in the company of Octavio Suarez. He would leave the manager to his own designs and trust that he would make the right decision come the night of June the tenth.

The reaction of his bedraggled customer was startling. The news vendor could see the drifter's hands start to shake and his knees buckle slightly. Fear seemed etched in those black eyes for the first time since he had met the stranger. Señor Geary would be pleased. This was definitely his man.

The statement that someone was looking for the 'Attractive Assassin' had drawn an affirmative reaction. The two Argentina-Italy football tickets that had been promised as a reward for positive identification would be like manna from heaven to the newsy. He doubted that he would ever see his shaggy client again, but the tickets more than made up for the loss of a customer!

Rojo Geary had gone directly to the special investigative services branch of army intelligence to have the poster likeness of a clean-shaven Lonnie De Seta enhanced by computer to include a long beard and scraggly hair as detailed by the newsy. It was this updated version of Lonnie's countenance that Geary's agents showed to boarding house and hotel owners in the Boca district.

Once again, there was an affirmative reaction from one particular landlady, who confirmed that a person resembling the new poster image was a resident in her establishment. A wad of pesos freed up the information that this guest resided in lower room number three, and that he seldom, if ever, was seen by anyone.

It took less than an hour for Rojo Geary to arrive on the scene with two other heavily armed men. Swiftly and silently, they descended to the lower level, set their positions on either side of the door bearing the numeral '3,' then Rojo Geary sent a jackboot flying against the cheap door clasp.

The obstruction came crashing off its hinges, tumbling back into the room. The assassins, their heads now covered in black balaclavas, surged into the quarters beyond, fanning out and hitting the floor as soon as they cleared the portal. Not a single shot was discharged. Silence, absolute silence!

The intruders studied every corner of the fusty dungeon, their fingers gently stroking the triggers of their silenced Uzzis. The room was empty. The terrorist had eluded the assassin . . . this time!

Lonnie De Seta was well-known to the manager and staff of the Banco Rio de la Plata on Avenida San Martin back in Palermo. After all, he had been given a sizable inheritance on his twenty-first birthday. Branch manager Anthony Rodrigues was the man that personally designed the boy's investment portfolio. Rodrigues' father had been Lonnie's grandfather's banker, and this same branch also counted Florencia De Seta among their valuable clients.

The female staff at the Banco had their own reasons for noticing Lonnie. He had bedded several of them personally, which, in truth, was the reason he kept all his assets under Señor Rodigues' roof, rather than divesting the funds to some of the other financial advisers that he knew. The employees at the Banco Rio de la Plata were so accommodating!

Anthony Rodriques was also an acquaintance of Astor Gordero's. The two men had conducted many a transaction together. Rodriques was, nevertheless, pleasantly surprised to see the 'rotund one' filling his office doorway one early May morning.

"Señor Rodrigues, a minute for an old friend?"

"Señor Gordero, by all means, I am honored. What brings you to Palermo this fine day?" Rodrigues scrambled from behind his huge mahogany desk and extended his hand in welcome.

"I wish that it was for some idle chit-chat about our National Football Team, Anthony, but unfortunately, I come to discuss a very delicate matter with you." The Fat Man made himself comfortable on the plush sofa that sat against a tapestry-covered wall in Rodrigues' large office.

"It is a matter that should probably be handled by the police or the army, but I have been personally asked by the family to seek your cooperation discreetly and quietly. The authorities would tell the press if they became involved, and my team of specialists can ensure complete censorship of all activities. It could be our only chance to strike first before they know that we are on to them!"

Rodriques' face was puzzled as Gordero paused.

"Astor, what on earth are you talking about? Is someone in danger?"

"Anthony, forgive me. It is all so shocking, what things have come to in this country. You have as clients of your branch the De Seta family accounts, I believe?" Rodrigues nodded his acceptance of these facts. Gordero continued his explanation.

"Señora Florencia De Seta has reason to believe that her eldest son is being held hostage by a left-wing group of communist terrorists. She fears that they plan to extort money from his bank account and then kill him! Do you know the boy, 'Lonfranco,' or 'Lonnie,' as he is called?" Again Rodrigues nodded, this time a shocked look replaced his former puzzlement.

"I act for his younger brother, Renaldo, who is on the training roster of the National Team. A gifted young boy, that Renaldo! In any event, Señora De Seta, who is a longtime friend, is too distraught to talk to you personally, Anthony, so she has asked me to seek your assistance on her behalf."

Gordero paused for effect, eyeing a bowl of fruit that sat just out of reach. Rodrigues was quick to offer his guest some of the bounty, and The Fat Man accepted. Coffee was sent for, and the two men settled in for the details of Gordero's plan.

"You must freeze the boy's account temporarily, Anthony, and alert your staff to notify you if someone attempts to make a withdrawal in person from his account. I have pictures of his likeness for your staff, although if he is in captivity, he may look much more haggard than the photographs. You have modern surveillance cameras in this bank, do you not?"

"Yes, of course, the very finest available," was the manager's response.

"Good, good! I want to send a two-man team of special agents to monitor the activity in your branch. They are very discreet and will dress appropriately. I am certain you could find them a desk to make things look legitimate to the public. These men will be armed, however, and able to alert their team leader once they are notified that Lonfranco is in the branch, or that there has been activity on his account. Should he enter the branch, his abductors will likely be close by. My men will be instructed to detain Lonfranco for his own safety, and then the area will be swept by the team leader and additional agents looking for anything suspicious."

"Astor, this is very serious! Do you not think that the authorities should be brought in? After all, a kidnapping, and the threat of an armed confrontation in my bank, these are grave matters." Rodrigues felt ill as he hoped that this was all some sort of a joke The Fat Man was playing.

"Too many loose lips, Anthony. Believe me, Lonfranco De Seta's life depends on him believing that no one is aware of his predicament. If it is his money these scum want to get their hands on, then they will keep him alive until he comes to your bank to get it. Be assured that my agents are the very best at their profession. They are especially trained for exactly such situations. Trust me, Anthony, a young man's life is in the balance."

Astor Gordero gloated over his performance in front of Señor Rodrigues as he rode in the rear of his Mercedes on the way to the offices of A. R. Gordero and Sons. It had been a brilliant ruse, the kidnapping story.

Rodrigues was told to speak only to Astor Gordero about this operation, no one else. Should Florencia De Seta come by the branch on anything other than normal banking business, Gordero should be called at once. No information should be divulged to Señora De Seta until Astor Gordero was present, as to not cause the lady undue stress.

Rodrigues had not seen Florencia personally in almost a year, so Gordero thought it unlikely that the two would actually cross paths in the near future. The ruse had its risks, but those risks might just net Gordero the elusive Lonnie De Seta.

The fact that there had been no activity, whatsoever, on the De Seta boy's account by the end of a month's time had made Anthony Rodrigues even more anxious and fretful. He phoned Gordero, insistent upon having the two distracting agents removed from the branch, but was stonewalled for two more weeks by the persuasive lawyer. The bank manager had not received satisfaction. For the first time, he started to smell a rat.

Perhaps a discreet meeting with Señora Florencia De Seta would clarify the picture and allow me to find out what is really going on at my bank, the disgruntled head official thought to himself.

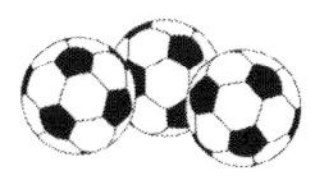

It did not take much to convince Celeste Lavalle that her lover was dead serious about departing their temporary home quickly and permanently.

"They are on to us. We are leaving, now! Get up and pack your bag. We are traveling light, so only necessities. And get your weapon ready. We may just have to use it today!" Lonnie was already stuffing his rucksack full of personal items by the time he had completed his instructions to Celeste.

"Who is on to us, Lonnie? Where are we going to go?" Celeste was near tears and trembling. "How will we ever find Serge if we leave? We haven't tried hard enough to help him! What are we going to do, Lonnie? Who is on to us?"

"The newsy knows for sure. He tipped his hand today, the way he looked at me when he showed me a poster of the 'Attractive Assassin.' I could see it! God knows who he is working for, but we have to go from here right away. We will hide at No Se Preocupe first, until I can get some money. After that, we will leave the country. As for the rest, I don't know, Celeste. Just stay sharp and in control. We can't help Serge if we are in jail, or worse!"

At precisely 7:15 p.m. on an unusually chilly June the tenth, Independiente's Enrique Rios stood over the white-and-black ball and awaited Israeli referee Cohen's whistle. A short lateral pass to Nicholas Pastor on the left wing got things going.

There was strong concern throughout the seventy-five thousand powder-blue-and-white-clad spectators about the radically alerted lineup. To start with, Angel Martinez had replaced Junior Calix in goal. That move might be understandable in the light of goaltender coach Estes Santos wanting to give his backup keeper some experience in the pressure cooker during the first round games. But what was Suarez thinking of when he penciled in the rest of his roster?

While the back four remained intact for the third straight game, only Ruben Gitares was on the pitch from among the forward six players that had started the French contest. The entire half line had changed. It was all Independiente now with Arzu, Cruz, and Argueta. Caesar Castro had been sat down from the wing position that he had played so competently in favor of Pastor, while Rios rounded out the changes. Six players on the bench who had played a large part in the victory over France! So much for continuity!

Thousands of armchair coaches in the noisy stadium hoped that Octavio Suarez knew exactly what he was doing.

Perhaps Astor Gordero was the only person present that night that really understood Suarez's strategy. The two had chatted earlier in the day, with the manager confirming that he would start all five Independiente players as Chacon had insisted. There would be other changes as well. Santos wanted to give keeper Junior Calix a rest. He had sprained his ankle slightly against the French, and the extra time to mend would serve him well.

De Seta would be on the bench for the entire game! Barring the necessity of substitution due to injury, Suarez planned to leave his starting eleven on the pitch for the complete ninety minutes.

"I plan to let the cards fall where they may tonight, Astor. If this lineup can bring us a victory against the Italians, well, I will be very surprised. But if they fail me, then all Hell will break loose, I guarantee you that! Chacon and his bum-boys will finally have the chance to put up or shut up, once and for all!"

The Italian team was one rich in experience and skill. They played a 1-3-4-2 tactical game, with tight defensive marking orchestrated by one sweeper with three defenders in front of him. A concentration of four players in the midfield was complemented by two counterattacking forwards. Ferocious tackling and relentless pursuit made their defensive zone hard to penetrate and next to impossible to score on with veteran Juventus keeper Enrico Sala between the posts. Up front, newcomer Paolo Martini combined with the poetic Romeo Nazzareno to strike fear into opposing defenders. It was a lineup that would overshadow their hosts for the entire evening of June the tenth.

Nothing seemed to work for the men in powder-blue and white. They could not get untracked against the disruptive pressure that the visitors applied constantly from the opening whistle. Angel Martinez was forced to be no less than brilliant in the Argentine goal. Martini, Nazzareno, Speza, and Giancarlo all tested the substitute keeper in the first quarter hour.

In the other half of the field, there was little about which to become excited. Only two clear chances were garnered by the host nation in the entire first half, Sala easily dispensing with these.

The half line was dreadful, Cruz never seeming to find the space he needed to get his game on track. With their center half teammate playing below par, the two other Independiente midfielders looked like wandering nomads. Moreover, Pastor and Rios had barely touched the ball by the time the interval was signaled. The faithful on the terraces were getting restless, and there was expectation throughout the throng that manager Suarez would make his two substitutions during the break. This team needed revitalization, and it needed it right away!

To the dismay of many, the original eleven players took the field for the commencement of the second half of play. Octavio Suarez had little to say to his laborers in the dressing room. A few words to an individual player here and there, but no reorganizational plans were discussed and no inspiring pep talk was offered. Fingers were pointed among the impatient players, and the mood was dark and somber.

The Azzurri pressed forward with the resumption of play. The blue of their jerseys seemed deeper, somehow, more vibrant, than the pale shade of the same color that the home side was attired in. The Azzurri blue ran even deeper and stronger when, in the sixty-seventh minute, the roof caved in on the Argentine defense.

Miguel Cruz was unable to apprehend the gifted Martini at midfield, and the Italian sent a twenty-yard pass laterally to halfback Giussepe Speza. The Fiorentina player paused to draw three defenders towards him, then softly placed the ball a further twenty yards upfield, dead on the toe of Romeo Nazzareno's right foot.

Nazzareno's volley to the streaking Paolo Martini was slightly off the mark, forcing the creative Azzurri striker to turn and come back to the ball.

By this time, Juan Chacon was all over Nazzareno, but he left his mark standing alone to pursue Martini when the fleet striker had to turn back after the ball.

I've got the little bastard now! 'Killer' Chacon envisioned in that split second. Miguel Cruz and Ricardo Arzu had come back to help out, and all three Independiente players were descending on the beleaguered Italian.

Martini's reception of Nazzareno's volley stunned millions. Instead of trapping the ball, he simply right-healed it behind him, upfield!

Romeo Nazzareno was a lonely man, his dear friend Juan Chacon having sought the affections of another temporarily. The slick veteran hit full stride and gathered in Martini's gift at the top of the penalty arch. After only a few paces, he pounded home the game winner from eighteen yards out, with a swing of his graceful right leg. Ignacio Suazo's long, sliding frame glided by too late to obstruct the sphere's flight.

Chacon knew he was in trouble when Martini's back pass rolled by him, just out of reach. As he tried to turn and chase the man that he was assigned to mark, his footing gave way, and The Ugly One tumbled directly into the oncoming Miguel Cruz. The two relatives watched Nazzareno's goal from the prone position, and Chacon wanted to dig a hole to hide in right then and there.

Octavio Suarez sat motionless in the dugout. No reserves pranced the sidelines warming up. There would be no substitutions this night, even though the fanatics were extremely vocal in their call for changes.

For the remaining twenty-three minutes, the visitors owned the ball. Their hosts could accomplish nothing, the theatrics of Nazzareno and Martini having thoroughly confused and demoralized them. The long-legged Italians reminded one of dashing thoroughbred ponies in the heat of a polo contest. Short, poetic strides, then a perfect exchange. Long, loping runs at the full gallop, then a well-taken shot!

The players exchanged jerseys and handshakes after the hard-fought game. Each one of them knew that before either team was crowned champions of the world, they might very well have to meet again, under much more intense circumstances!

"Chacon, in my office now!" Octavio Suarez tried to keep his temper under control. "Shut the door."

The manager spoke softly, his hands pressed against his desktop as he leaned over the object, his gaze staring down on its polished surface. He let the big defender stand squirming in front of him for almost a full minute before addressing him.

"So, that was not a very convincing performance that you and your compatriots gave out there tonight! As a matter of fact, you stank the fucking stadium out! Now listen to me, you ugly piece of meat. This is *my* team, and only *my* team. This game was meaningless in the big picture, so I gave you the rope you needed to hang yourself, and that is exactly what you did, you dumb fuck! Where were you when Nazzareno scored? On your fat ass, that's where! And where was your brother-in-law, Cruz? Right there beside you, rolling around on the grass like two fucking homos! You cost us this game, Chacon! Nazzareno was your mark. Asshole!"

Suarez tried to calm himself. He still needed Chacon's help if this team was to accomplish anything of substance in the tournament.

"So now it is time for you to make a choice. You can pack your bags and leave with the rest of your pathetic crowd, or you can stay and play by my rules, and my rules alone. Do that, and you keep your National Team sweater and a chance to help bring the world championship to our great country!"

The Ugly One was speechless. He knew that his manger spoke the truth. He had no rebuttal. Suarez eyed the sheepish defender with disgust.

"I will tell you right now. The lineup that started the French game will take the field in Rosario. Sorry, no more fucking friends and relatives along for the ride! And no more blackmail or you are gone! Try it, and I will disgrace you publicly. You will never play football in Argentina again! Do you understand me? Now, how will it be, Señor 'Killer' Chacon?"

CHAPTER TWENTY-FOUR

As the first round of World Cup competition drew to a close, the Argentine national psyche had been only slightly damaged by their heroes' loss to the Italians. There was still time to make corrections and adjustments, and moreover, the weak showing of the pretournament favorites was reason for cautious optimism.

Italy was the only team to advance to the second round of play with a perfect record. Three victories in three matches to top group one. Argentina also advanced from that group with two victories and one defeat. France flew home with a single victory over the hapless Hungarians to complete its South American visit with some semblance of respectability.

Group Two, consisting of Poland, West Germany, Mexico, and Tunisia, held one of the major surprises. The reigning champion of the world, West Germany, looked totally out of step and confused in their nil-nil encounters with Poland and Tunisia. A 6-0 shellacking of a terrible Mexican team did little to silence their critics on both sides of the Atlantic. Poland topped the group with two wins and a tie, followed by West Germany with one win and two ties. The very game Tunisians were a pleasant surprise but they were sent home along with the dismal Mexicans.

The despised Brazilians had been the favorites to top Group Three, despite their whining about having to play in the frigid seaside resort of Mar del Plata. But they had accomplished only two ties in their first two games, with only one goal to show for one hundred and eighty minutes of football played. It would be fair to say that the entire host nation was reveling in the misfortune of yellow-shirted prima donnas.

There was some merit to the Brazilian's claim of unfair treatment, however. They were the only team in the group forced to play all its fixtures on the horrendous pitch of Mar del Plata Stadium. Each of their three adversaries had been lucky enough to play at least one game in brand-new Velez Sarsfield Stadium in the capital city.

Judged the finest pitch in the tournament, Velez Sarsfield also afforded its competitors the moderate climate of Buenos Aires. The Brazilians were adamant that they needed a good playing surface to excel at their 'change of pace' style of play.

The soggy, rutted field at Mar del Plata resembled a groundhog's convention after Brazil's 1-1 tie with Sweden. To make matters worse, the chilling winds and biting rain that invited themselves to each of the Samba King's games made for plodding, disjointed contests.

These were not the Brazilians of Pelé and Socrates. The elements and the pitch had reduced them to mere mortals. A 1-0 victory over group winner Austria in the final game of the first round gave but slim hope for a resurgence to the form of yesteryear. It was a confused and troubled team that headed for Mendoza to open the second round against Peru. Spain and Sweden booked passage back to Europe as Austria and Brazil advanced.

Peru turned out to be the undisputed dark horse of the first round. Thought to be an easy adversary whose players were too old and too unfamiliar with each other's style, the Peruvians pulled the rug out from under Scotland's hopes in their opening match. An impressive three-goal comeback after Hamish MacPherson had given the Scots an early lead sent the Tartan army reeling. A scoreless draw with the Netherlands followed. Inspired by those two confidence-building games, the men of the Andes then thrashed Iran 4-1, achieving first place in Group Four. The Netherlands also advanced, giving game but luckless Scotland and Iran their leave.

Thus, the eight teams advancing for further battle were Italy, Argentina, Poland, West Germany, Austria, Brazil, Peru, and the Netherlands. Three South American teams, five European teams. A decent balance, and at this point, the Italians looked to be the class of the tournament.

The National Team of Argentina had been placed in Group B for the second round of play, along with Brazil, Poland and Peru. Each team would play the others in the group once. A complicated tie-breaking system would determine the winner of each group, should there be equal merit for the top spot.

Transposing the entire National Team operation to Rosario was a logistical nightmare that Octavio Suarez had hoped to avoid. There had been contingency plans made well before the fact, however, and the relocation was carried out in less than twenty-four hours without any major trauma. That left three days to adapt to their new surroundings and prepare for their opening second round match against Poland. On the bright side, the Italian victory had provided an opportunity to let fans outside of the capital city view their darlings in the flesh.

The move to this new home base posed logistical problems for more than just Octavio Suarez and his legions. Rosario was an industrial port city of seven hundred and fifty thousand people, some two hundred miles northwest of the capital up the Paraná River. The new host city for the National Team of

Argentina found its infrastructure strained to the limit once the world turned its eyes on the spectacle that was unfolding there.

Central Stadium, the venue for Argentina's games in Rosario, was the most intimate of all the facilities in the tournament. No moats or warning tracks separated spectators from their idols. The steep second tier of the stadium seemed to hang over the touch lines at an impossible angle. The problem was that only thirty-two thousand-odd hearty souls could be shoehorned into its tight enclosure. This was much less than half of River Plate's capacity.

Demand for first-class hotel rooms and tickets of any denomination were at an extreme premium. The flourishing local black market in 'beds, broads, booze, and a board,' the latter referring to the plank that one's derrière would cover in the stadium, managed to keep almost everyone happy, for a considerable brokerage fee.

With luxury accommodations all but nonexistent, the two finest suites in the Hotel Libertador had been booked for their respective guests using all the power and influence that they could muster. People of discriminating taste simply had to stay there. This prime billet was head and shoulders above all the other establishments in town. After all, they were the only ones to serve high tea at precisely four o'clock each afternoon. This fact would not be lost on the occupants of suite number 237, one Astor Armondo Luis Gordero and associates from Buenos Aires.

Similarly, the occupants of suite 358, Miss Mallory Russell and her father, Lord Reginald Russell of London, England, would luxuriate whenever possible in the lobby café over sandwiches, scones, and cakes. It was there, in the Café Inglaterra, that the two parties would make one another's acquaintance for the first time. It would be a meeting that would change all of their lives.

It had been necessary for Astor Gordero to delay his departure to Rosario by several hours to enable him to deal with a potentially embarrassing situation. On the morning of June eleventh, Wolfgang Stoltz had informed his employer of a telephone call that had been placed to Florencia De Seta by her bank manager, Anthony Rodrigues.

The wire tap operator had recorded the entire conversation. Luckily, Señora De Seta was not at Casa San Marco at the time of Señor Rodrigues' call. The female servant, Oli, had spoken to the banker briefly, the male voice stating in a blunt, agitated manner that his name was Rodrigues and that he would call again.

"That bastard Rodrigues!" thundered Gordero upon listening to a cassette tape of the conversation. "Alright, we have to act quickly, Wolfie. Get Señora Paz in here right now. Rodrigues takes his noon meal on the stroke of twelve every day. At twelve fifteen, Señora Paz will make her call. Can you get Florencia out of Buenos Aires sooner than planned? Your meeting with Lydia in Pergamino is on the thirteenth. Wolfie, you must find her right away and convince her that the capital is a terrible place to be right now. That you need some time away from the football madness, and that you both should take a few extra days and leave for the country sooner, like tonight! Do you have your presentation for Señora Lydia prepared so that you can leave?"

Gordero knew the answer to his last question before it left his lips. The ever-efficient German had been ready for weeks!

"Of course, Astor, everything is in order," Stoltz sounded hurt by the slight.

"Come now, Wolfie, I was just teasing. I knew you would have things set up perfectly, just like you always do!" The sparkle returned to the German's eyes.

At twelve fifteen p.m., Señora Carla Paz, the office manager of A..R.. Gordero and Sons placed her call to Anthony Rodrigues of the Banco Rio de la Plata. As Astor Gordero knew would be the case, Rodrigues was out of the Banco on his midday break.

"This is Florencia De Seta speaking. Could you kindly inform Señor Rodrigues that I returned his call, and that I am leaving Buenos Aires within the hour. Until this World Cup nonsense is concluded and I return to the capital, Astor Gordero is attending to all my business and personal matters. Señor Rodrigues should contact him exclusively concerning my affairs during my absence. Thank you very much, good day."

Señora Lydia De Seta could feel her blood turn ice-cold the moment Wolfgang Stoltz opened his mouth. Her right hand, which she had extended in greeting to her male visitor, was withdrawn after the faintest of touches. The lawyer from Buenos Aires sensed that he was in trouble from that moment.

The matriarch of the De Seta family sat in stony silence as Herr Stoltz gave a precise but lengthy speech on the merits of A.R. Gordero and Sons. This included a strong case for consolidating the family investment portfolio and asset supervision under one advisor. Any attempt at humor by the visitor was met with a dour stare from the hostess.

Even Florencia felt ill at ease with Lydia's demeanor. She tried to get the old lady to loosen up a bit by talking of her grandson's future security. In particular, the younger woman stressed the fact that Renaldo had already signed a management agreement with Stoltz's firm. When the presentation was finally finished, the elder Señora De Seta spoke for the first time.

"It is not my intention to be rude, Herr Stoltz, for you personally had no idea what you were getting into by coming to see me today. I do not blame you for that, but I must say that if Florencia had given me the name of the gentleman that she was bringing to Pergamino . . . well, I think we could have avoided this meeting and the uneasiness that it has caused me." Lydia paused for a moment, locking eyes with the stunned lawyer.

"My sincere apologies, Señora. What on earth have I done to offend you?" Stoltz stammered.

"I suppose an old lady should be able to forgive and forget, but I find myself unable to be that charitable. Herr Stoltz, did you take up arms against the United Kingdom in the last Great War?" Again Lydia's eyes bore down on the squirming guest.

"Yes, Madame, I must confess that I was a sailor in the German Navy. I was very young, still a teenager. The captain of my ship sought refuge in the port of Buenos Aires just before the end of the conflict. I have been in this country ever since. I obtained my Argentine citizenship in 1965. Is it my German background that is giving you discomfort, Señora De Seta?"

Again Lydia let the question linger in the frigid atmosphere of her parlor before responding.

"Yes, Herr Stoltz, that is precisely what is giving me discomfort. I lost a brother and a sister in the first war to your savage, imperialistic ambassadors of death. Another brother was gassed into a wheelchair to live a half-man's life. Two more of my brothers would perish as a result of your beloved Führer's unappeased bloodlust in the second Great War. Need I say anything further, Herr Stoltz?"

The old lady had to grasp the arms of her century chair, she was shaking so violently. Her voice was hollow and uninviting, and Florencia could not believe that this was the same person that she had known and respected for twenty-five years. Lydia fought hard to calm herself, then stood abruptly and continued to address a shocked Wolfgang Stoltz.

"Your accent alone is enough to make me want to vomit. I know that is not very ladylike at all, but I must be brutally frank with you both. I could never consider placing one peso of the family fortune under your care, Señor, for I would not be able to sleep at night with the thought of having a Hun overseeing my family's business affairs. Now, if you will excuse me, I must take my leave, for I feel that I am about to be ill. I am sorry, Florencia, but there is nothing more you can do here. I would ask you to take your friend and depart right away. Good day to you both." She was gone without a backwards glance.

The two lovers sat in a silent daze for several moments. Florencia had never heard her mother-in-law talk to anyone in that manner before. The lady never raised her voice, not even when trying to calm her robust grandsons. She glanced over at Wolfgang. The German looked crushed. Florencia swiftly moved to his side and grasped his hand.

"Don't worry, Wolfie, I will talk to her alone. I know I can convince her to change her mind. I had no idea that she harbored such strong feelings about the German issue. She must be ill, for I have never seen here act like that before."

"She was not ill, Florencia, and there will be no changing her mind," Stoltz replied, disbelief still ringing in his voice. "I thought foolishly that I would never have to confront that anti-Nazi prejudice again, but I was obviously wrong. I cannot undo what has been done, and I cannot make myself something I am not! No, it would be futile to try and convince Señora De Seta to reconsider my proposal. The lady's mind is made up! It is over! Kaput! Now let us be gone from this wretched place at once!"

"Hey, man, you are almost beautiful again. That swollen beak of yours looks pretty good today. Maybe a touch of makeup would help for those television close-ups after you score the winning goal tonight." An upbeat Ramon Vida had caught Renaldo De Seta inspecting his battered nose in the mirror as he burst into his friend's room at the National Team training center and headquarters in Rosario.

"I don't know, Ramon. It still is very swollen. I think I will let you score the winning goal tonight so that I don't offend anybody with my ugly looks. I will wait for the championship game to score again. By then, I should be back to my gorgeous self," Renaldo smiled as he gently patted his nose.

The two players then departed for their last practice session before the opening game of the second round. Poland was that evening's opponent, and Octavio Suarez had made sure that every player knew exactly what kind of lion-hearted men they were to face.

The manager had projected a film of the Poles 1-0 loss to West Germany in the 1974 World Cup semi-finals during the morning team meeting. Against huge odds on a leadened, drenched pitch, the men from behind the iron curtain had shown the world the meaning of true grit that day. Tonight, with two wins and a tie already to their credit in the 1978 tournament, the red-and-white-clad visitors would be no less formidable adversaries.

The Argentine National Team seemed to make the adjustment to their new surroundings and their new lineup with relative ease. Leaving Buenos Aires and the memory of the Italian fiasco behind them had given the players and management a chance to clear their heads of the past. While the future looked daunting enough with the likes of Poland, Brazil, and Peru as opponents, the six new Argentine starters for the Polish contest seemed to bring an easygoing sense of confidence to the practice field.

Calix, De Seta, Anariba, Velasquez, Vida, and Castro would all be on the pitch for the kickoff against the Poles, just as Suarez had promised.

So would Juan Chacon, who had held his tongue and his temper after the unceremonious dressing down he had received.

The other Independiente players were not pleased with the starting roster, particularly Miguel Cruz, but they kept silent about their feelings in public. For once, there was no doubt in anyone's mind that control of this team was back in the hands of Octavio Suarez.

The effects of the personal affront that Lydia De Seta had leveled on Wolfgang Stoltz were still evident when the German came face-to-face with his employer in Rosario the following afternoon. Stoltz had driven his two-seat Mercedes 350 SL at breakneck speed back to the capital immediately following his dismissal from Buenos Recuerdos. Originally, he had planned to take Florencia to a luxurious cottage on the Paraná River that was close enough to Rosario to allow him to attend the football games and do some business. It would have been perfect, for the location was far enough away from the continuous silliness of the World Cup that Florencia detested so.

But she would have no part of a romantic liaison after the visit with her mother-in-law. Florencia had never witnessed the always self-assured Stoltz in such foul humor, and the more he rambled on about his inability to change his past, the angrier she became with Lydia De Seta.

It is time to put the old witch in her place, Florencia thought to herself. She had told Stoltz that she wanted to return to Buenos Aires to compile all the trust and corporate documents that pertained to the De Seta family fortune. She would turn these documents over to A.R. Gordero and Sons, who would then assist her in wrestling control of the financial throne of the empire from the old lady in Pergamino. That was the only good piece of news that the humiliated lawyer had for Astor Gordero.

"Why that shriveled up old bitch! How dare she insult you in such a manner! Those English are made of stone, they have no feelings at all. Such arrogant people. I detest them! Don't worry, Wolfie. You will have your revenge. Many things can happen to the frail and elderly that are hard to explain. Illness, injury, robbery, who knows, even an untimely death! We gave the old bag a chance to do things aboveboard. Now we have to deal with her in a more heavy-handed manner. Believe me, Wolfie, nothing, absolutely nothing, is going to derail my plans to control the De Seta financial empire. By the way, I called Rodrigues personally to tell him that Florencia would be unavailable for the next two weeks. We must become more ruthless in our approach from now on. So, let us drink a toast to the timely demise of Señora Lydia De Seta!"

The familiar storm of confetti and white streamers greeted the national heroes as they emerged from the player's tunnel of Rosario Central Stadium on the evening of June fourteenth. The sea of powder-blue and white flags and banners duplicated the atmosphere and aura of River Plate Stadium.

The lineup changes were not the only thing that was different about the Argentine team. Octavio Suarez had insisted on his players wearing white shorts with powder-blue piping instead of the traditional black trunks. Something to do with an old superstition that the manager had, and one that he was unwilling to explain to anyone.

Poland kicked off and went on the attack immediately. Calix was forced to make two fine saves in the first minute of play. The home side defenders seemed nervous and tentative at first, but the half line played deep enough in their own zone to lend a helping hand in those crucial opening moments.

A Jorge Calderone clearance to Renaldo De Seta sent the boy streaming upfield on Argentina's first legitimate offensive foray. Although no goal resulted from this initial rush, one could see the confidence build in the powder-blue and white team by the minute. The Poles were ruthless in defense, and many an Argentine body lay prostrate on the pitch after an intimate exchange with one of the foreigners. The home side was able to give as well as take, however, and Juan Chacon was at his nastiest every time a red-stripped player came within range.

Renaldo was starting to feel at ease with the pace of the game by ten minutes in. He had space to maneuver, perhaps in part due to his relative anonymity. He had not played enough at this level to be scouted and feared.

All the better for me, he thought to himself as his runs upfield became more fluid, his passes more precise. Ramon Vida was experiencing the same kind of freedom for his part on the forward line. A cross bar was all that stood between him and pay-dirt in the twelfth minute.

The biggest surprise of all was the continued fine play of Leopoldo Anariba, who went after every Polish player that dared try his wing with the tenacity of a pit bull. In the fifteenth minute, the Racing Club halfback relieved Polish captain Kazimierz of the ball, then turned and headed up his wing. Ramon Vida was making a strong run up the middle, and was in a perfect position to accept Anariba's cargo. He hadn't traveled ten yards however, before he was felled by two visiting defenders. Because Vida was not in possession of the ball, no obstruction foul was called. To the disgust of the multitude, the referee motioned for play to continue.

Renaldo De Seta had swung wide to overlap the fallen Vida on his right. The defense was frozen for a split second, awaiting the referee's judgment on the tackle that felled the home-side striker. If the Polish defense seemed hesitant, Leopoldo Anariba certainly didn't. Deeper and deeper into foreign territory raced the Argentine halfback, until at last, he saw his opportunity to make a play.

Traversing the field toward the right corner, De Seta had only one man to beat as he neared the penalty area. Anariba had his wits about him, for he laid a perfect floating ball twenty-five yards upfield, directly on the handsome head of his still on-side youngest teammate. Renaldo De Seta's header on the dead run from seven yards out was true. Argentina 1, Poland 0 after sixteen minutes!

Thunder roared down from the Gallery Gods. The sky turned white with paper snowflakes set against an undulating powder-blue and white backdrop. A brilliant play! An astonishing goal! Ramon Vida was the first to embrace the marksman.

"Hey, hotshot, you said it was my turn to score the goals tonight. You're still too ugly to get that nose in the newspapers, man!" Vida had a grin on his face from ear to ear.

"I said the winning goal, Ramon. There is still time for you to show the world your stuff. Where is Anariba?"

At that moment, the man that made the goal happen joined the intimate circle of two.

"Bravo, Leopoldo, bravo! A perfect pass, and a fine, fine, run!"

Renaldo clapped his hands approvingly as he congratulated his playmaker. More powder-blue and white jerseys joined the gathering, until Swedish referee Johannsen had to reprimand the home team for delaying the game.

The Poles redoubled their effort to take the game to Argentina's doorstep. Renaldo's half line was forced to play deep inside their own zone in a defensive role for most of the next twenty minutes. The red team's break came when their star striker, Jerzy Wojciech, eluded Jorge Calderone just in front of the corner kick marking and headed along the goal line, directly at the Argentine net.

Defender Ignacio Suazo loomed quickly in Wojciech's path, but the agile forward eluded the more cumbersome defender and carried on his road to glory. The beaten Suazo was not above using his gangliness to his advantage at a time like this, however, be it legal or illegal. A long leg reached back and upended his adversary. The ball skidded safely out of play.

Suazo had wisely made certain that his foul occurred just outside the penalty area, but the ensuing free kick from the irate Wojciech proved to be trouble enough, especially for young Renaldo De Seta.

Wojciech's lofty service arched over the four-man Argentine defensive wall perfectly. An outstretched Junior Calix had to turn into a human pretzel to flick the ball over his head and away from the goalmouth. Unfortunately, the globe landed squarely on Juan Chacon's shoulder, just to the side of the near goalpost. The startled fullback could only nudge the ball back into play.

Chacon's half touch was good enough for Marek Tyc. The pint-sized whirlwind of a Polish forward needed only a slight touch of his head to send the object on its way into the gaping Argentine net. Only one obstruction stood in its path . . . player number seventeen in powder-blue and white.

Renaldo had initially lined up for Wojciech's kick on the goal line, some five yards behind his keeper, Junior Calix. He chose for his mark on the ensuing play the dangerous Polish striker Stanislaw Grzegorz. Big, blond, handle bar-mustachioed Grzegorz was lethal around the opposing goal, and Renaldo knew that he had to stick to him like a second skin.

The Argentine center half watched the ball's flight as it rebounded off his two teammates and was sent goalward by Tyc, all the while trying to keep one eye on Grzegorz. The Pole had dropped back several yards to await a rebound from a better shooting perspective, and the boy found himself mesmerized, alone, and the sole defender of his nation's honor.

Tyc's header came spiraling toward the open right side of the net. It was too high to deflect with his legs or torso, and in that split second, Renaldo's inexperience and youthful enthusiasm got the better of him. An outstretched right fist diverted the ball's flight to safety, but the consequences were instantaneous and dire.

The rookie knew that he had committed an unforgivable faux pas the instant he felt leather on flesh. Humiliated, he sank to his knees on the goal line. Juan Chacon had his usual words of encouragement.

"You stupid little shit! What the fuck are you doing out here? This isn't one of your fancy pants school yards you're playing in now, pretty boy! This is the World Cup! If you can't play the game, get off the field!"

A glassy-eyed youngster could only stare up into the ugliest face on the planet. Ramon Vida appeared at that moment and stood toe-to-toe with the insulting defender.

"Leave him alone, Chacon! It was your goddamned touch that put the ball right on that Polack's head. Without Renaldo on the line, you would have given them a sure goal. Now at least Junior has a chance to save the penalty!"

The veteran keeper joined the discussion at that point, hoisting De Seta to his feet.

"Don't worry, Renaldo. It was a sure goal without you there. Leave it to me now! Just play your game, and don't worry about this."

Laslo Kazimierz was the somewhat peculiar choice to take the red team's opportunity. Surely there were more adept marksmen on the Polish side than their aging midfield captain. Nevertheless, it was Kazimierz that stood some twenty yards away from the crouched Junior Calix as he began his run toward the ball.

In this game of cat and mouse, the keeper has to guess correctly in his directional moves or he is left alone on the turf clutching nothing but air. The bright yellow sun on the national flag of Argentina must have been shining down on Junior Calix this particular day, for he guessed correctly, and arose from his lunge grasping the treasured black-and-white sphere. Kazimierz's poor effort had landed directly in Calix's arms. The score was still Argentina 1, Poland 0, and the actions of Renaldo De Seta had been somewhat vindicated.

Octavio Suarez had nothing but praise for his men at the interval. There seemed to be the confidence-building within the starting eleven that he had hoped the lineup changes would foster. Some brief words of encouragement and a reminder not to get too anxious out on the pitch was the only advice offered to number seventeen by the manager.

Renaldo felt badly that he had put the team in that often lethal penalty situation, and he was certain that there was no one in the world more relieved with Junior Calix's save than the half back from Newton's Prefects Under Twenty-one team.

The final forty-five minutes of play were the most sparkling of the tournament to date. Both teams lunged and parried at a steady, gut-wrenching pace. The keepers were tested to the limit at each end of Central Stadium, and the dramatic tension built by the minute.

The Poles pressed the attack, seeking the Golden Fleece. Junior Calix barred the door on each occasion. Leaping, diving, sprawling, the goaltender would not allow his net to be violated.

Renaldo De Seta had drawn much closer marking immediately following his tally, but as time waned, he found himself with acres of open territory each time Argentina cleared the ball upfield. The offensive-minded red-shirts were susceptible to a fast-breaking counterattack.

At exactly the seventieth minute, Calix cleared a long, soft shot that he had trapped. His quick overhand throw was well-placed fifteen yards upfield, directly to a surprised Juan Chacon. It was lucky for The Ugly One that Calix's pass was on the spot, for Chacon had lost his assignment, the ever-present Polish striker Marek Tyc. The little whiz-bang Pole had left the plodding defender in his wake en route to the goalmouth. Even Chacon's attempted elbow to slow down his adversary had missed its mark, too high to strike pay-dirt. Now, 'Killer' stood alone in possession of the ball, with all the enemy attackers behind him awaiting the rebound that Calix never surrendered.

Space was not something Juan Chacon had seen a lot of that evening, for he had played an exhaustive role assisting his acrobatic keeper shut out the persistent Europeans. The Poles were not intimidated by his threats or his appearance, however, and they gave as well as they took in the trenches. For once, defender number eight had some room to take a stroll, and that is exactly what he did. There was no red jersey for forty yards in front of him.

The crowd cheered to see this rare sight. Every football fan in Argentina knew that Juan Chacon ran like a bull moose in heat. A distinctive half lope, half quick-waddle. Fans pointed fingers and broke into spontaneous laughter. Even the nearest Polish defenders did a double take upon seeing this most ungraceful of visions.

It was Octavio Suarez that ruined the fun. The second Chacon started his run upfield, the manager left the dugout. By the time he reached the sideline, Suarez still could not believe what he was seeing. He called out to the heavens for an explanation.

"Juan Chacon making a run upfield? Is he crazy? What the fuck is he thinking of? Chacon! Chacon! Get rid of that ball and get back where you belong! Who do you think you are, Franz Beckinbauer?"

The manager's reference to the multitalented, world-class German sweeper was laughable. Luckily for Suarez, his big defender was within earshot of the boss, and number eight suddenly realized that he was leaving a gaping hole in the defense behind him. The nearest player he could direct his treasure toward wearing powder-blue and white was number seventeen.

Renaldo De Seta graciously accepted his tormentor's gift. He had followed his deformed teammate upfield and was ten yards deep into the Polish half when the parcel arrived. Ramon Vida was on the move to his right, and the center half placed the ball directly at his friend's galloping feet.

Vida was poetry in motion. A swing of his hips one way, then another, kept the last line of Polish defenders guessing. Three Europeans closed for the kill twenty-five yards from the Polish goal line.

"Come on, come and get me!" Vida shouted as he plunged ahead. Over his right shoulder he could feel the looming presence of defender Antoni Wroclaw, whose outstretched right leg swept for the ball. Vida saw the flash of stocking as it approached and deftly sure-footed the prize six yards to his left.

"Oh no, not again. It's my turn this time! You said you would share, man. It's not fair!" Ramon Vida called out after his Argentine cohort who had trapped the pass. Vida lay on his stomach, facing the Polish goal twenty yards away, the defender Wroclaw sprawled underneath him. He was yelling at the black numerals 'one-seven' on the back of his teammate's jersey.

Renaldo De Seta was in the right place at the right time again. Dead center of the field, square on the penalty spot. Red-clad defender Jacek Poznan closed to intercept the intruder, but the boy turned to his right, then put on the brakes.

The Pole was running at full speed and could not stop when the Argentine feinted. Poznan overshot his mark, then made a vain attempt to reach back for the ball with a lunging left leg. A stationary Renaldo watched the twirling sphere rotate ever so slowly at his feet. He took one glance goalward, then merely let swing his own left leg.

Poland's keeper moved too late. His feetfirst dive at the ball resembled someone jumping into a swimming pool. The shot was past him to his left before he could get his arms in the outstretched position. Rising only inches off the turf, Renaldo De Seta's sure blast came to rest in the mesh at the rear corner of the Polish net. Argentina 2, Poland 0. An earthquake of jubilation shook the entire country.

Mallory Russell could only stare in awe at the spectacle taking place a few tables to her left in the Café Inglaterra. She had never seen one man devour so much food while holding what seemed to be some sort of continual press conference. People with notepads and tape recorders were shown one by one to his table, where they were encouraged to stand and listen to the gospel espoused by this terribly large and ebullient man.

Only the waiters who cleared and then restocked the table interrupted the dialogue. The regular morning diners had all but deserted the café's comfortable confines, and tables were being quickly reset for the noon meal, except for the two occupied by Mallory Russell, her father, and the much sought-after epicurean.

Mallory knew from the Spanish she was able to decipher that the man was connected with the World Cup Tournament in some way, but she had been unable to determine exactly how. Curiosity had gotten the best of Reginald Russell, who sought out the maître d' to reveal the hungry one's identity. He was all smiles when he returned to join Mallory at the table.

"You won't believe our luck, my dear. It seems that our breakfast companion is some big shot from Buenos Aires. But no ordinary big shot. The man is the chairman of Newton's Prefects, who happen to be the current Argentine first division champions. But it gets better! He is also the personal manager of that boy, De Seta. You know, the one that scored both the goals for Argentina last night. What was his given name? You wrote it on your notepad, didn't you?"

"Renaldo, Renaldo De Seta. Young, only nineteen. Has never played a first division game. Came to the National Team directly from their feeder system. There is next to nothing in the team's biographical information about him."

As usual, Mallory Russell had done her homework in her signature thorough fashion. She knew the names and statistics of every player who remained in the hunt for the sport's ultimate prize. The Russells were looking for a few diamonds in the rough to take back to England with them, and both Reggie and Mallory had spent hours of preparation prior to and following their arrival in South America. Both were determined that they would not go home empty-handed.

"I tipped the maître d' to get us an audience with Señor Glutton before he departs. Judging by the food still left on his table, we should have plenty of time."

Several minutes later, an impeccably turned out gentleman ventured to the Russell's table.

"Herr Wolfgang Stoltz at your service. I am Astor Gordero's executive assistant. The maître d' informed me that you have requested a few minutes of Señor Gordero's time. May I be of assistance, for as you can see, Señor Gordero is in great demand this morning."

A warm smile rained down upon the seated Anglos as Stoltz finished his introduction and glanced admiringly at his pontificating employer. Reggie Russell rose from his seat and handed the visitor his card.

"Sir Reginald Russell of London, England, Herr Stoltz. A pleasure to meet your acquaintance. This is my daughter, Mallory."

The gorgeous blonde lady extended her right hand. Stoltz held it tenderly and brought it to his lips. A slight click of his heels accompanied the respectful gesture.

"An honor, my Lady."

"Would you be so kind as to join us for a moment, if you can spare the time, Herr Stoltz?"

"My pleasure, to be sure, my Lord," responded the German as he drew another chair to the Russells' table.

"We were wondering, Herr Stoltz, as to the status of one of Señor Gordero's clients. The young soccer star, Renaldo De Seta. You see, Mallory and I operate a first division professional soccer organization in London. You may have heard of the Canary Wharf Football Club if you are a fan of the game. Are you a fan, Herr Stoltz?"

"Most definitely so, my Lord. I attended last evening's festivities. A triumphant occasion! I am also well aware of the great history and past glory of the Canary Wharf Football Club. Any student of the game would recognize that name. You are newly promoted to the top division, is that not so?"

Reggie Russell was reassured by the stranger's knowledge of things 'English,' and at the same time, put at ease by his comfortable manner and openness.

"Tell me, if you don't mind my Lord, what did you think of the atmosphere at the stadium? Did you feel safe attending the game? I am very interested to know your thoughts on our country, as well as on our football players."

The three soccer fanatics launched into a candid half-hour discussion on a myriad of topics. Football was always the cornerstone of each segment. Throughout the thirty minutes, the central theme would continually revolve back to the handsome Argentine footballer with the prolific scoring touch. Renaldo De Seta had been discovered!

Stoltz, for his part, was impressed with the gentleman's astuteness regarding Argentina's culture, politics, and sports. But it was the sculpted beauty of the lady's fine features and the cultured lilt of her accent that really enthralled him. It became evident to Stoltz that this woman was no vapid piece of fluff from the first time she opened her mouth to speak. The German found himself hoping that his employer would continue to lecture the two journalists that had become his latest attentive audience for a considerably longer period.

"I like to think of myself as a 'facilitator' more than anything else," a thoroughly satisfied Astor Gordero mused to his new English acquaintances. "It would seem that these days, I am forced to wear many different hats, but whatever function I am performing, I always strive to facilitate a conclusion that is of benefit to all the parties involved. I have spent my life putting people together and facilitating supply and demand. I practice law only to ease the transactions to their happy endings. That is my calling. That is what I enjoy most in life, the transfer of knowledge and currency. I have thought about entering politics many times, to perhaps facilitate on a grander scale, but in reality, I operate more effectively on the fringes of the system. Bipartisan, that kind of thing. A facilitator must always be flexible, ready to adapt to the moment."

Gordero paused to sip his cappuccino and pulled a chained pocket watch from his vest. His raised eyebrows attested to his sudden concern. He addressed his European guests once more.

"At this moment, my Lord and Lady, I, like yourselves, am consumed with the evolution of this football tournament. I have lingered far too long in the glow of last night's achievements. This country has a 'what have you done for me lately' attitude. There are many factors that combine themselves into making a championship team, and I operate by leaving as few of them to chance as I can manage. I must, therefore, be off to consult with manager Suarez. You are interested in young De Seta, is that correct? Herr Stoltz informed me briefly. A very fine choice of talent. Young, raw, impetuous, with great natural skills. He could be trained to adapt to your style of soccer. I have always said that he plays the game as if his head and feet are one!"

As The Fat Man attempted to stand, Stoltz appeared out of nowhere, grasped his employer under both arms from the rear, and literally hoisted him to his feet.

"Here is my card with my local phone number. I will be in Rosario until matters dictate a return to Buenos Aires. Perhaps we can have a cocktail together and further our discussions. Are you guests of this hotel?"

"Most assuredly so, Señor Gordero. We occupy suite 358. Allow me to present you with my card and credentials. To further our relationship, it would be our distinct pleasure to offer you dinner at the establishment of your choice. Shall we say tomorrow night?"

Lord Russell was quick to capitalize on the one weakness to which his new Latin friend obviously was prone.

"Dinner, tomorrow evening? Are we clear, Stoltz?"

The German produced a trim, leather daybook from his breast pocket, pulled the red ribbon marking the current week, and ran his index finger down the column for June fifteenth.

"General Ustedes requested an evening meeting to discuss stadium security at the local Officer's Club. Your acceptance is still pending."

Stoltz left the last statement dangling in the air.

"The Officer's Club, my God, I've dined there before. It's a miracle that I am still alive after eating the garbage that they pass off as food. Send my regrets to the general! Lord Russell, I would be more than happy to accept your offer. Shall we say Ristorante Borgo Antico at nine o'clock? It is on Avenida Ricardone. A short cab ride. I must be off now. Until tomorrow then, a pleasure my Lady, my Lord."

The maître d' and waiters had formed a line of revue past which their famous patron quickly departed. Stoltz, haven taken leave of the English, discreetly slipped an envelope stuffed with currency to the maitre d' as he followed his employer past the formally clad servers.

"A 'facilitator' is he now? What a fancy term for a fat tub-o'- lard," Reggie Russell commented half under his breath as the South Americans left the room.

"Easy now, father. Let's not form hasty opinions. Señor Gordero might just be the one man that could facilitate respectability for the Canary Wharf Football Club. Let's give him a chance to prove that he can do more than pack away the groceries." Mallory's warm smile and clear logic melted the old man once again.

"I suppose you are right. What have we got to lose? Why don't we prepare a short list of prospects that are acceptable to us and present them to the great facilitator tomorrow evening? If he truly loves to wheel and deal, we will give him ample opportunity to produce 'a conclusion that is beneficial to all the parties involved.'"

CHAPTER TWENTY-FIVE

Five days had passed since Lonnie and Celeste's arrival at camp No Se Preocupe in Tigre. They had been able to slip out of the capital by bus and train during the Argentina-Italy soccer game on the night of June tenth. Every living soul they encountered on their journey had only one focus that evening, 'the match.' No one gave the two fugitives a second glance.

Still, Lonnie was careful not to leave a trail directly to the camp. The part-time local resident had been insistent that he and Celeste walk from the train station in Tigre to their new hideout. Those people hunting the terrorists might ask questions of an unsuspecting cabbie. The train station could be staked out by any number of adversaries at this very moment.

They arrived at the camp shortly after midnight. June was a slow period at the facility, and Lonnie had no trouble breaking into a remote cabin undetected. Because of the football match, there was a good chance that the night watchman might be less observant on his rounds, if he chose to work at all. The old cabin was one of the original dormitories and still contained cots, mattresses, and blankets. With any luck, they could stay unnoticed for a day or two, long enough for Lonnie to snip and shave away the vestiges of his shabby former persona.

Celeste was not in good shape. She talked incessantly about a plan to find Serge, and Lonnie had to keep reminding her that their own survival remained the most pressing matter. To find her brother, they would have to expose themselves, and Lonnie knew one thing for certain. It was not Serge Lavalle that was being hunted as the 'Attractive Assassin,' it was Lonnie De Seta! His trail was getting hot, and it was all he could do to keep the two of them alive and free.

By June the fourteenth, four days later, they were still undetected by anyone on the campground. It seemed that the entire complex had been shut down for the World Cup Tournament. There was some activity during the day at the administrative office, but there were no patients, nurses, or other staff to be seen. Even the exterior maintenance men were nowhere to be found. Everyone in the entire country was focused on 'the show.'

Lonnie's physical transformation had been swift and startling. Clean-shaven and hair close-cropped, he bore no resemblance at all to any of his former identities. His hair had never been this short. He liked it, especially after the flee-bitten locks that he had worn for the last several months.

The fugitive had walked into town under the cover of darkness the night following their arrival, then had hidden in the bushes until the groceteria opened at eight a.m. He filled two rucksacks with essentials, then headed cautiously back to the camp.

He took to the woods wherever possible, keeping out of sight and avoiding all contact. His money was almost gone, and he knew that he had to think out the next move in this chess game for survival.

The one distraction that took Lonnie's mind off his own predicament was the amazing good fortune of his brother, Renaldo. The newspapers were singing the boy's praises, especially since the team had done so poorly against Italy without him in the lineup. It was certain that he would play against the Poles, or so the press was speculating. Strangely, there was almost as much ink concerning his good looks as there was about his football ability.

"Matinee Idol of River Plate!" screamed one tabloid sports page. There was a picture of Renaldo accompanying the story, and it was obvious that it had been taken prior to his run-in with Torok's elbow. The more current photos showed a somewhat swollen beak and dark circles under his eyes, which seemed to add a masculine roughness to the boy's features. The result was an even sexier young football star, according to many female fans interviewed in that same tabloid. Lonnie noted that Ramon Vida was number two with the ladies in the beefcake sweepstakes.

Renaldo and Ramon have a lot of high expectations to live up to, both on and off the field, Lonnie mused as he tuned in his erratic portable radio to the Argentina-Poland game from Rosario.

"I hope this little piece of junk doesn't let me down tonight! Come on, baby, be good to daddy. I went and bought brand-new batteries for you. Be a good baby and work for daddy Lonnie!"

The gentle coaxing achieved positive results, and an ecstatic Lonnie De Seta continued to cradle the radio's black form lovingly in his arms two hours later.

"Two goals! My God, I can't believe it! Two! I knew all along he was pretty good, but this, two goals for Argentina in the World Cup, unbelievable!"

He was talking to no one in particular, for Celeste had long since retired to the far end of the dormitory, his screams of delight having woken her twice.

Lonnie removed the cork from a bottle of cheap whisky that he had purchased in town and took another long pull. He lay down on his cot as the alcohol's magic swept over him.

"Good Lord, the papers will be full of him tomorrow. I'll have to go and purchase every one of them. My little brother is a fucking national hero! Amazing!"

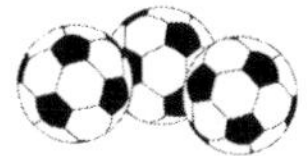

"Black pants and stockings! I want you to look as sinister as possible tonight against these 'Samba Sweethearts.' This isn't going to be any garden party out there. You must assert yourselves early and often. Don't give these bastards the space they need to execute their stylish fucking ball control game. I want you in their faces all night! I want your mother's maiden name tattooed on their asses by the time they come off at the half. Does each and every one of you understand me?" Octavio Suarez had a look on his face that told each of his charges that they had better not disappoint the manager or their time on the pitch would be short-lived.

Suarez would use every tactic available to promote an abrasive attitude on the field, and even changing the shorts and stockings from white to black was a ploy used to instill confidence and aggression.

The Brazilians had beaten Peru 3-0 in Mendoza four days earlier, and they seemed to be revving up their offensive machine now that they had left the inhospitable climes of Mar del Plata. That was exactly what Octavio Suarez feared the most, that the talented neighbors to the north would hit full stride this night in Rosario.

The starting eleven for Argentina contained one major surprise. Against all speculation, Miguel Cruz started at center half over Renaldo De Seta. Suarez's only comment to the boy wearing number seventeen was that he wanted keep the youngster fresh for the second half. This move would also temporarily relieve some of the enormous pressure and expectation that had come to rest on his shoulders.

Renaldo was disappointed with his mentor's decision, but raised no objection. What Octavio Suarez was most concerned about was that the Brazilians would go after his new scoring sensation's tender Achilles' heel in an attempt to drive him from the game. The manager had seen the yellow shirts use this approach before, and their wily defenders had developed the practice to an art-form. Better to let Cruz take a beating in the first half and see how the game developed.

The powder-blue and white sea of spectators, once again, showered their heroes in a white froth of streamers and confetti as they took the field. The Hungarian referee, Mr. Kukla, was all smiles as the two captains shook hands and took part in the ceremonial coin toss. His smile would fade quickly once he blew his whistle to commence the match.

Argentina had not beaten the Brazilians in eight years. That pressure, plus the intensity of this World Cup fixture, was evident instantly. Suarez's pep talk was taken to heart, and the hosts conceded their first free kick after only ten seconds.

Cheap shots abounded everywhere, and the stunned European official seemed incapable of gaining control of the match. Six fouls were called in the first three minutes, and there was no flow to the little bit of football that managed to escape the rough-and-tumble proceedings.

Scoring chances were initially scarce, but crafty Brazilian left winger João Batista started to exploit an overcautious Humberto Velasquez with short give-and-go overlapping thrusts, using the full support of his offensive-minded midfielders. These exchanges resulted in three almost identical saves at the top of his right goal area for Junior Calix in the space of five minutes.

Were it not for the continued ill-temper of the game with its lumbering pace due to stoppages, the Brazilians could have set the tempo to their Samba beat and done some real damage. As it was, they seemed more intent on defending their manly honor with every injustice offered them.

While the yellow shirts dominated what little soccer one could pick out of the first half, they went to their dressing room with nothing to show for it. Argentina's midfield had done exactly what Octavio Suarez had asked of them, but their 'in your face' execution had not produced one clear scoring chance for the home side. The consolation was that, at least, they had kept the visitors off the score-sheet!

Suarez was hoping for more ball possession from the rough play in the central part of the field. Nearly all the exchanges up to the interval had gone in Brazil's favor. Miguel Cruz had been adequate defensively, but he seemed caught up in demonstrating something other than football skills to his opponents. On more than one occasion, he had a clear chance to make a move upfield with the ball. Instead, he chose to deliver an ill-tempered thank you for any physical affront offered by an overzealous adversary. Suarez knew it was time to take a gamble.

"What do you mean you are taking me out of the game?" an incensed Miguel Cruz screamed across the dressing room at Octavio Suarez. "I've done everything you have asked of me. They haven't scored yet, have they? Check their forward Dos Santos' butt. You will see my mother's maiden name on it. I stuck to him just like you asked. I'll tell you another thing, too, that chickenshit is hurting a whole lot, thanks to me. Last half, I defend, this half, I score! You owe it to me. I must stay in!"

"De Seta starts! Let's get out there and play some offensive football this half," was Suarez' only reply.

"You little brownnosing cocksucker!" screamed Cruz at his replacement sitting on the other side of the room. "What did you do, pay him off to let you on the field? Well, I'm going to make sure that you don't look so good if you make it out of this room at all!"

In an instant, Cruz was on top of Renaldo De Seta, fists flailing and a stream of expletives spewing from his mouth. Estes Santos was the first on the scene, managing to pull the Independiente player upright and back a few paces from his startled adversary.

Just as Cruz opened his mouth to commence another verbal tirade, a closed fist came crashing out of nowhere, landing squarely on the restrained player's lips. The sickening sound that occurs when hard knuckles meet soft flesh reverberated throughout the suddenly silent confines.

The look of shock lasted only a second on Cruz's face before his eyeballs curled upward into their sockets and he collapsed backward, blood now running freely through the gaping hole where several of his teeth used to be.

"You should learn to keep your mouth shut when the manager tells you something, my friend. It is all for the good of the team, for the good of the nation. We want to win the World Cup, and we must listen to our manager. Maybe this little lesson will assist you in the future!"

There was no hint of anger in Ramon Vida's voice as he delivered his soliloquy to the fallen, unconscious Miguel Cruz. His tone was one of a soothing parent or teacher. Everyone in the dressing room was startled by the ferocity of the blow, and many could still hear its terrible sound inside their heads. It was up to the manager to refocus their thoughts.

"Alright, forget about this shit. We are here for one reason only. To play and win this football match! There is no room for personal rivalry. When this tournament is over, I don't care if you go out and shoot each other. But for the next week, I own your asses. If you want to be world champions, don't any of you ever forget that! Argu, Arguetta, stay here and clean your friend up. If he needs an ambulance, call the medics. Chacon, do you have anything to say about this?"

The Ugly One stood silently looking down at his fallen brother-in-law, shaking his head in disbelief.

"Good, now let's go show these half-breeds how the sport is played!"

Renaldo De Seta was about to become intimately acquainted with the current giants of Brazilian football, men he had read about in his adolescence. Legends backed by the incessant Samba beat. Those drums and whistles! What an amazing sound they made. And that beat! That beat always touched the roots of his musical soul, and he knew that it really did have a lot to do with the artistic beauty of the Brazilian game. He loved their music, their rhythm. But not now, not for the next forty-five minutes.

Suarez's fears for the rookie's health were realized within minutes. Number seventeen was sent to the turf seconds after his first touch of the ball. Never a pandering showboat when fouled, Renaldo tried to right himself instantly, but fell to the ground clutching his damaged heel. The offending Brazilian was nowhere to be seen.

But Juan Chacon was at the boy's side, for the foul had occurred deep inside Argentine territory. He said nothing, just looked at Renaldo with disgust, then took the free kick awarded for the misdemeanor. As the play progressed upfield into the Brazilian zone, the fallen warrior struggled to stand erect. He failed to see the retreating enemy forward that just happened to collide with his tender limb.

Down went the player a second time, his cry of pain piercing the night air. Again Juan Chacon was at Renaldo's side, only on this occasion, he was in Brazilian forward Aleixo Cabral's face. 'Killer' was all over his smaller opponent, pushing Cabral back several yards with his massive chest while verbally lambasting the yellow-shirt.

A linesman alerted the referee to the events behind the play, and the senior official hastily called time and ran to separate the two antagonists. Chacon was smart enough not to exercise his distaste for the foreigner under the watchful eye of Mr. Kukla.

A hideous smile and an unfriendly shove were accompanied by the words, "We will meet again, you yellow bastard!" as the two were separated. No foul was awarded during the stoppage, for the referee had not seen the incident take place. A trainer was now at Renaldo's side.

"How bad is it, son?"

"Ooohh, it's damn sore. Thank God his aim was off a bit. He got my ankle not my heel, but he gave me a good whack. I . . . I think the heel is alright, though. Here, take my hand, help me up."

"Stay there for a second and I'll give your foot a shot of aerosol freezing. Hold still now, that's a good boy."

A freezing cloud of relief dissipated on the halfback's heel and ankle. The pain retreated instantly, if only for a short time. The trainer checked the appendage in question for major damage and agreed with the player's assessment. His entire foot would be a black-and-blue mess in the morning, but for the present, Renaldo appeared fit to carry on.

'Carrying on' was certainly easier said than done. Every time he put pressure on his battered limb, the pain sent shockwaves to his brain. The substitute center half was reduced to hobbling about the midfield like some lost soul.

Octavio Suarez screamed at the boy from the sidelines to "work it out," and to "limber up." The fact of the matter was that his player could hardly stand up!

As play continued, a strange phenomenon unfolded all around number seventeen in powder-blue and white as he tried to patrol his sector of the pitch. The Argentine players seemed to treat Renaldo's designated part of the field with as much respect as their own goal area. They consciously kept the ball as far away from the boy's territory as possible. The home side now took to the attack, rejuvenated by the bad taste left in their mouths as a result of their comrade's pain.

Brazilian goalkeeper Oliveira had to be at peak form to keep his hosts from taking the lead. For a fifteen-minute span, the ball never crossed into Argentine territory, and their injured center half was allowed to play back in a static defensive role while he 'worked out' his injury and stood ready to blunt a counterattack.

Alas, there was to be no poetry on this day. The beat of the Samba and the staccato cheers of "Argentina! Argentina! Argentina!" were drowned out by a loud chorus of ugly, ill-tempered, retaliatory football. By the thirty-minute mark of the second half, the last true scoring chance by either side had been taken. The remaining fifteen minutes were reduced to anticlimactic hostilities.

'Killer' Chacon did manage to keep his promise and renew his friendship with Aleixo Cabral, however. The Brazilian departed the field with a souvenir black eye courtesy of his new amigo's infamous right elbow.

Both teams were battered and bloodied after ninety minutes, but under tournament rules, the goalless draw would stand in the record books. One point was awarded each team, and with one group game remaining for both countries, the future was anything but clear.

There were only three days to heal and regroup before Peru would take this same field against his warriors, and manager Octavio Suarez knew that he had his work cut out for him. It was highly possible that goal ratios would determine the eventual winner of their group, and at this point in time, Argentina trailed the Brazilians by a one-goal differential. Offense would be the key against Peru. Total offense, or there would be no tomorrow.

Renaldo De Seta wondered if he was the only one in the dressing roomed that sensed the difference in this team after the ninety minutes of bedlam. He had felt it first ascending the stairs to the pitch just after the locker room incident with Cruz. Chacon had held his tongue and his temper. His cocky, loudmouth brother-in-law had been put in his place, but more important than that, the words of manager Suarez seared his mind like a branding iron.

We are here for one reason only. To win this football match! That is what it all came down to . . . winning!

Nothing that happened off the field mattered once you set foot on that green carpet. Old club rivalries, personal disputes, even outright hatred had to be set aside. And tonight, for the final forty-five minutes of play, they had been. Renaldo De Seta knew that he had just witnessed the formation of a cohesive, unselfish football team.

It was a collection of small things that manifested themselves in their new attitude. The willingness to help each other, to stand up for each other, to protect each other. He had thought that Juan Chacon would have shaken Cabral's hand for laying the 'schoolboy' out. No one was more surprised in the entire stadium at the wrath The Ugly One showered on the Brazilian than Renaldo De Seta. No words were spoken between the disfigured defender and the injured midfielder during the entire second half, but the younger man sensed a new form of grudging acceptance from his caustic teammate, perhaps as a result of Suarez's words.

How they had helped each other during that last forty-five minutes! Renaldo had been virtually useless the entire half, unable to hit anywhere near full stride. Time and time again, his midfield mates pinched into his area to help out. Likewise, the defenders were constantly coming forward to lend advanced reinforcements.

While the match was no oil painting, it was a moral success for team unity and spirit, at least from Renaldo De Seta's perspective. A warm glow swept over number seventeen as he sat sipping a coke with his bruised foot in an ice bath. He knew that things would be different when they took the field against Peru. He was ready, his teammates were ready, the country was ready. *Victory is at hand! Viva Argentina!*

Esquela Perez had been the kitchen maid at Buenos Requerdos for just over two years. At nineteen, she had grown to be an attractive, even sensuous woman. Too sensuous for Nana Taseo, the long-time head housekeeper at the estancia. The gauchos and hired hands were always seeking her favors, hanging around the servants' entrance to the main casa in hopes of sharing a bottle of tequila after work.

The widow Taseo didn't trust anyone with such a low moral commitment and warned the girl of dire consequences should she slip up and find herself in the family way.

"Señora Lydia will not stand for anyone on her staff bearing a child out of wedlock, my little sugar bouche!"

Esquela could still remember that lecture. Now the words had come back to haunt her and panic had set in. She was three months late. The father could be any one of a host of men, and she was hardly able to conceal her growing proportions from Señora Taseo anymore.

She was desperate to keep her job at Buenos Requerdos, and that meant getting rid of the unwanted bastard she was carrying. The problem was that she had neither the money nor the knowledge needed to go about the tragic task. Beside herself with anguish, she decided to ask Pablo, one of the farm hands with whom she had been intimate.

Pablo drove the pickup truck into Pergamino several times a week, and confiding her dilemma to the comparatively worldly local hunk might get results. The stud had a reputation for getting girls into trouble, so surely he must know how to 'fix' things.

Wolfgang Stoltz was still fuming inside from the personal slight that the old English prune had levelled at him. He could not let such an insult go without rebuttal. Lydia De Seta controlled the empire that his employer sought to oversee. The arrogant Englishwoman had now become an obstacle to that end, and Stoltz was about to provide the means to remove that obstacle.

There had been a young German sailor who had landed in Argentina back in the forties with Wolfgang Stoltz. Paul Rheinhart had been a good friend, both in Germany before the war and at sea during it. The two men had kept in touch over the years, both settling in their adopted country.

Paul Rheinhart chose to continue his studies in the field of medicine and eventually ended up running the general hospital in Pergamino, of all places. When asked why he chose such a remote location to set up his practice, he always used to say that "Five years of bobbing around the Atlantic Ocean in a tin can had given him an overwhelming appreciation for the wide open spaces of the Pampas." Pergamino was where he settled and prospered.

Both these ex-Nazis still wistfully longed for the old days in Germany, and whenever they could, they reminisced about the past glories of the Reich. They held a mutual contempt for things and people not of German origin, especially things American or English.

Paul Rheinhart had felt the sting of Lydia De Seta's bigotry himself. She had refused to let him attend to her on several occasions during visits to his hospital, preferring instead a less experienced physician of Argentine origin. Dr. Rheinhart subsequently refrained from offering his services to the English bitch and had remained bitter about the affront ever since.

"Your call is very timely, Wolfie. I cannot believe the coincidence. That swine Englander frau has gone too far this time! Insulting a man of your stature, and in front of her daughter-in-law! I have exactly the substance and method you require. The poison is a mild arsenic extract that is tasteless, odorless, colorless, and if applied over an extended period of time in small doses, undetectable even by autopsy. It is perfect, but here is the best part. One of the local pimps works on the De Seta estancia. He sets me up with women for parties and stags when I have male guests come to visit. Remember the last time we were together here, Wolfie?"

"Very well, Herr Doctor, a marvelous time indeed, but do please continue," Stoltz urged.

"Well, this local worker named Pablo uses me for fast, no question abortions should one of his putas 'screw up,' so to speak. He came to me just yesterday saying that the kitchen maid at De Seta's estancia was knocked up, but didn't have the money to pay. As soon as I heard she worked for the English I told him that I would not help. No fucking way! But, on second thought, the kitchen maid would have access to the Señora's food and beverage. A few drops of my substance in the old fart's tea, and after a few days, the lady of the house would start to feel out of sorts. A few weeks and she will be gone forever. It's perfect. I'll do the abortion for the little tart, but in return, I will have Pablo instruct her what to do. There will be money needed to pay them both off, however. Is that a problem?"

"Not at all, but what about any implication or connection to her death on your part?" Stoltz queried.

"There won't be. The farmhand will handle everything. He has loyalty only to the almighty peso. I will pay him enough to keep him quiet, and believe me, Pablo is very appreciative. The girl we will pay off and send away, maybe to some Holy place from whence she will never return. Why leave any witnesses around, eh, Wolfie? As for covering our tracks with Señora De Seta, you are talking to the coroner of Pergamino District. I will conduct the autopsy on the deceased old witch myself. If, that is, the distraught family even desires to have one. So relax, it's perfect. My personal hatred for the woman overrides all sense of conscience, and besides, it is a great pleasure to be of service to my dear old friend!"

"You always were a genius, Pauli. I will bring you the money tomorrow, including a healthy honorarium for this medical consultation. I will be in Rosario while the tournament is here. Expedite the arrangements as soon as possible. I want Señora De Seta to begin her treatments immediately. The sooner the world is relieved of that snooty English whore, the better!"

"I've located Lonnie De Seta, Señor Gordero. I just wanted to confirm that you require the subject terminated. Are those still your instructions, sir?"

Rojo Geary stood outside the same Tigre groceteria of which Lonnie had become a patron. An operative in Tigre had been told to keep surveillance on camp No Se Preocupe and the nearest dry goods retailer. Geary's hunch had been right.

A suspicious stranger had shown up on the morning of the eleventh and returned four days later. He stood out to the groceteria owner as someone vaguely familiar, but the man never spoke a word or offered any information about his needs. The provisions that he had bought seemed to suggest that he was a camper, but the local campgrounds were closed for the winter. And there were no tourists in the area, especially during the World Cup Tournament.

The stranger's second visit was a carbon copy of his first. An issue of every newspaper in the store was picked up as his first order of business, followed quite literally by the purchase of everything from soup to nuts. Dark glasses and an old slouch hat obscured the visitor's true features, and the only dialogue was a grunt of thanks upon completion of the transaction.

That army intelligence agent must be notified at once! the excited retailer thought as he made his away to a private phone kept in the back office. *Where did I put his number? I hope he is still paying the reward for information that he promised!*

Geary's agent, posing as an antiterrorist intelligence officer, had arrived at the groceteria within minutes. The owner described the suspect's appearance and clothing, then pointed out the direction in which his customer had departed.

At nine in the morning there was next to no traffic on the road down to the river and camp No Se Preocupe. The agent drove his car cautiously along the gravel thoroughfare, stopping periodically to scan the woods with binoculars. As he slowly rounded one particular curve almost at the entrance to the camp, he saw the figure of a man sprint into the brush from the side of the road. It was his man, for there was no mistaking that hat! The subject was obviously using the camp as a hideout. The agent put his car into reverse and headed for the pay phone at the groceteria.

Geary's man relayed the double sighting to his superior, who, in turn, set out for Tigre immediately to confirm the report. The groceteria owner identified one of the original clean-shaven artist's sketches of Lonnie's likeness as being similar to the man that had entered his store twice. The slouch hat and sunglasses were added by means of overlays, and there he was. It was the same man, there was absolutely no question. The 'Attractive Assassin' was in Tigre, and Rojo Geary felt that familiar rush of adrenaline as he prepared for action.

Polite inquiries at camp No Se Preocupe from an 'old friend' of Lonnie De Seta's yielded nothing. A sweep of the camp was ordered for the following night. The commander summoned the rest of his platoon to Tigre, then called Astor Gordero in Rosario.

The hired gun had his team in position just after dusk on the night of the sixteenth. They would wait for total darkness to begin a search of the camp's buildings and grounds. Geary anticipated that it would be the faint glow of a propane lantern shimmering in the eerie blackness that would reveal his prey. Then, sadly for all concerned, the end would come quickly.

Sadly for the two fugitives because their young lives were prematurely ending. Sadly for Rojo Geary because he loved the game almost as much as the kill, and it was a 'kill' that Astor Gordero had confirmed in their phone conversation the previous day. De Seta had been a fairly challenging adversary. The soldier admired and respected that fact. He had seen many a fugitive go berserk from the constant strain of being on the run, and this always led to carelessness.

Lonnie had been smart until he showed up at that Tigre groceteria. Geary knew that the hunted man must have exhausted all his resources if he had to hide-out at his family's camp. The game was drawing to a close.

A faint beam of light from the Coleman lantern was barely visible behind the blanket that covered the unboarded window. 'Barely' was all Rojo Geary and his men needed. Once the old dormitory cabin was surrounded, the commander gave the signal. A single blow of a sledge hammer brought the padlocked front door crashing inward off its hinges. Rojo Geary was through the opening before it hit the floor.

Lonnie De Seta had become disenchanted with the musty world inside the dormitory. He frequently went for clandestine excursions around the property. His favorite place to think was down by the canoe shed on the dock. The squat, dark wood building afforded a perfect shield from unwelcome eyes, and the lapping of the water around the dock cribs soothed Lonnie's wound-up nerves. It was to this very spot that Lonnie had ventured to just before Rojo Geary and his men arrived to finish their cold-blooded assignment.

Celeste was threatening to leave him altogether if they didn't depart from their safe house and find her brother. Another heated argument sent Lonnie down to the dock to cool off. He had been there staring at the tide for several hours when the wrenching, crashing sound jarred him to his senses.

Lonnie sat some forty yards from the dormitory, but his vantage point afforded him a clear view of the padlocked doorway entrance and side window of the cabin. Suddenly, light spilled through the hole in the front wall where the door used to stand. He could clearly see the figures of several men hurtling into the sick yellow-green light. There was very little commotion and almost no noise. The fugitive stood frozen on the pier. He could do nothing.

In a matter of seconds, those same figures were outside in front of the cabin. One of the assassins, the one Lonnie took to be the leader, was visibly and audibly upset. He swore and cursed in loud English as the others followed him down to the river's edge.

Lonnie's heart pounded in his chest. He had his Llama pistol tucked into his belt buckle, but all his grenades and extra ammunition were in the cabin. He was virtually defenseless against those who stalked him.

The only means of escape lay overturned right beside the eyewitness. Someone had left one of the wooden canoes out on the dock instead of in the shed. Lonnie had noticed it on his first visit to the pier and had visualized exactly what he was about to now do. He had thought of the canoe as a possible escape vehicle in an emergency, and this clearly was an emergency.

Celeste was dead, there was no mistaking that fact! But Lonnie was shocked by his lack of emotion as a result of her death. He thought it strange that he hadn't raced to the dormitory with his Llama blazing. Strange that the thought of helping Celeste never entered his mind. He was tired, oh so tired. He would miss her, to be sure, but he would miss his beautiful, spirited lover, not the apparition that she had become.

Lonnie was also bitter. Bitter with Celeste for leading him down the road that shattered his once-prosperous, law-abiding life. How had she ever convinced him that terrorism could change anything? The only thing violence had accomplished was to ruin more lives, his own included!

No, he would not help her. She was beyond help. The deadly silence inside the cabin confirmed that. The 'Attractive Assassin' was thankful that his former companion had died swiftly, without torture or sexual abuse. A protracted, brutal death would have been unthinkable! That was all the remorse that Lonnie could muster for the passing of Celeste Lavalle.

He slid into the bottom of the canoe, grabbed a paddle, and pushed himself away from the dock heading silently downstream and out of sight from his pursuers. His thoughts remained with Celeste. Lonnie was comforted by the quickness of her killers' actions, for in his mind, he was certain that she had been put down by a silenced bullet within seconds of the forced entry.

Rest in peace, my dear Celeste. We will surely meet again in Hell!

CHAPTER TWENTY-SIX

The Group A qualifying countries for the second round of the World Cup Tournament were all from Europe. Italy, Holland, Austria, and West Germany took to the pitches in Córdoba and Buenos Aires to determine their representative in the final.

Italy had been heavily favored at the outset, but by the time they faced off against Holland in the final match of the round, they had scored only once in one hundred and eighty minutes of soccer. Their 0-0 draw with the Germans, as well as their 1-0 victory over the hapless Austrians had shown the Azzurri to be erratic in their finishing skills.

The West Germans had nary a victory to show for their first two outings. They were buoyed somewhat after holding favored Italy to a scoreless draw at River Plate, but failure to maintain the lead against their usual whipping boys, the Dutch, turned their camp into a hostile, finger-pointing compound. That 2-2 tie was an embarrassment bordering on disaster. An all-out effort against weak sister Austria was demanded by the German coaching staff and their disgruntled followers.

It was the men from the Netherlands that seemed to be hitting their full stride at the perfect time. An opening 5-1 blowout of Austria left no doubt in anyone's mind about the overwhelming offensive skills of the men who wore the orange and white. Moreover, their struggle to tie the hated Germans had removed a huge monkey from their backs. That outing had convinced their quickly growing legion of fans that the Dutchmen had acquired an abundance of true grit, as well as the determination not to lose.

Finally, in the early afternoon of June twenty-first, they stood in white shirts, orange shorts, and white stockings on the hallowed turf of River Plate Stadium. The men from Holland were tied with their opponent Italy in points, but they had played much more inspired football. A clear victory by either team would mean a berth in the World Cup final.

The Dutch got off a disastrous start. An own goal by defender Willie Brax after only nineteen minutes injured starting keeper Hendric Van Der Ven as well. The blond-haired guardian of the Dutch twines was carried from the game on a stretcher, not to compete in the tournament again.

The Italians sought to take advantage of their opponents' misfortune immediately. Substitute keeper Dirk Wilhelmus had to rise to the occasion time and time again. The young keeper was not the field general that his more experienced, more vocal predecessor had been. The Dutch defenders floundered, unsure of where their midfielders had gone. In truth, those midfielders were back on the defensive line helping out, so constant and unrelenting was the Italian pressure.

As young and inexperienced as Wilhelmus was, however, on this day, he was also lucky. Luck is always that intangible factor that every keeper hopes will be part of his bag of tricks. Today, the uprights and crossbar of his net were to give him the support in the early going that none of his teammates seemed capable of supplying.

Three times the men in the beautiful blue jerseys hit the woodwork. The Dutch, for their part, hardly tested the Italian keeper Enzio Sala. Where had the offensive skills displayed against the Austrians and Germans gone? That was the question on every Lowlander's lips as the whistle sounded the interval.

Mysterious things often happen to teams during the fifteen-minute intermission. Such was the case on this cloudless afternoon in Buenos Aires. The Dutch rediscovered their free-flowing style in that dungeon of a locker room. The Italians lost their calmness and teamwork in theirs. One would have thought that a compulsory changing of team uniforms had accompanied the changing of ends, so different was the style of play that both teams offered up in the early minutes of the second half.

The white shirts descended on the previously arrogant Italian defenders in waves. Shots were fired at Sala from all over the pitch. Long balls, scrambles in front of the net, corner kicks, free kicks, everything imaginable! The Azzurri defenders were wilting under the pressure, and who more appropriate to drive home the new Dutch superiority than the goat of the opening half, Willie Brax.

Only five minutes into play, a poor Italian clearance landed the ball on the pate of Dutch midfielder Pieter Thijssen. His responding header was relayed to the poll of fellow midfielder, Jan Johannes. The lanky Dutchman then directed the sphere downward onto the approaching foot of the offensive-minded Brax.

From just outside the Italian penalty area, he let go a rocket that exploded into the top left corner of the Mediterranean men's net. The Dutch were back on terms and soaring, the Italians, tied and slumping.

Patience seemed to be the keynote of the renewed Holland offensive. One could sense that the white and orange men felt victory inevitable now, all they had to do was continue to create chances. That they did, much to the disgust of the Italian defense and their frantic manager on the sidelines. Name-calling and finger-pointing had become part of the Italians' self-destructive strategy, and their game descended into a defensive quagmire.

The script reached its climax in the seventy-sixth minute. Once again, it was a Dutch midfielder that changed the scoreboard. So tightly packed in retreat were the Italian midfield and defense that the center of the pitch resembled uninhabited parkland. The acres of empty pasture gave the innovative Netherlanders the space to work their magic. Lady Luck then chose twenty-four-year old Kees Trelaan as the man of the hour.

A specialist in long, curving shots, he hit a beauty, unchallenged, from almost fifty yards out. Italian keeper Sala stood ready, watching the flight of the ball.

No problem! he thought. *This ball is going well wide of the mark.* Then suddenly, its trajectory started to curve inward toward the goalpost to the Italian's left.

Surely it will still pass wide of the net, was the last unconvincing thought that flashed through the keeper's mind as he realized, in desperation, that the shot was critically close to beating him.

Sala left his feet, lunging to the left. His outstretched right arm could only wave harmlessly at the ball as it sailed three feet above him. But disaster had not befallen the keeper yet, for just as he hit the turf, his ears reverberated with a sound that sent instant relief surging through his sprawling torso.

The 'thwack' of the black-and-white orb hitting the upright post was as sweet as any melody he had ever heard. These posts and crossbar were his allies now, just as they had been for the Dutch keeper in the first half.

But wait . . . something was terribly wrong. The orange-clad fans behind the Italian goal had erupted in delight. Sala raised himself on one elbow and stared disbelievingly into his unprotected net. There, in the far corner sat the dreaded object. One of the white-shirts was retrieving it, holding it joyously over his head for all the world to see. Disaster!

The shot had veered into the net once it struck wood. Nine times out of ten it would have rebounded back into the field of play, or better still, ricocheted out of play. Sala looked at his stunned teammates, then back at the fickle upright. Despair and desperation were etched on every Azzurri face. Only fourteen minutes remained to make amends.

There had been nothing to match the gut-wrenching drama of this game's last quarter hour in the entire tournament. Italy was Argentina's second team, the team that after the host nation, most Argentines had wished well for. Millions had reveled in the thought of an Italy-Argentina rematch in the final.

Now, the stadium, the bars, the cafés, and the living rooms across the nation were as silent as if they were witnessing a state funeral. Only the few thousand Dutch supporters behind Sala's goal made any attempt to dispel the wake-like pall that had fallen over Argentina.

The blue shirts tried gamely to find the equalizer, but the unyielding Dutch midfield would not allow them to get untracked. Martini and Nazzareno, so prominent and dangerous in the early stages of the match, were distracted and ineffective on the attack. So thoroughly smothered and turned back was each Italian thrust, that the ball rarely crossed into Dutch territory.

The clock was the real enemy. If only the Azzurri could hold back the clock and gain more time!

It was that same dreaded clock that put an end to the Italians' on-field misery, as well as their hopes of a place in the World Cup final. Seventy-five thousand people in River Plate as well as millions around the world beheld their agony. What had happened to the Azzurri of the first half? How had they allowed the Dutchmen to steal victory from their grasp?

The Italian players stood on the pitch, most with tears streaming down their anguished faces. They had come to Argentina with so much talent, so much promise! This was not the way things were supposed to end! There would be no tomorrow that mattered for these tragic warriors. But as they left the field of play, the thousands saluted them for their proficiency, their pride, and their sorrowful passion, now so openly displayed.

That same beautiful afternoon in Córdoba was to become one of the blackest days in West German football history. A German victory by a large goal differential, aided by a tie in the Italy-Netherlands match, could very well put the reigning world champions back in the final. Relentless offensive football was the order of the day. Unfortunately, the players were unable to carry out that order.

Things started off brightly enough for the green-shirted Germans. A goal in the nineteenth minute stood through the interval. But the dressing room gremlins played their nasty tricks on the men who held the lead. It was a different German team in attitude and ability that took to the pitch for the final forty-five minutes.

An own goal fifteen minutes into the second half brought the Austrians level, then five minutes later, the favorites found themselves a goal down to their European neighbors. The German's pride was severely offended, and they swarmed around their opponents' net, seeking to redeem themselves. It only took two minutes for their labors to bear fruit, and there still remained ample time to salvage a great victory.

The Austrians were not in an accommodating mood, however. There was nothing in this world that would temporarily erase past failures more thoroughly than a victory over their Teutonic cousins. They had repulsed the German blitzkrieg in the last half-hour of play and were now poised to storm the beaches in one final counterattack.

Under five minutes remained in this Prussian chess game when the checkmate occurred. Victory was placed on the doorstep of the Austrians and gratefully accepted. The winning tally in the eighty-seventh minute left no time for the Germans to regroup. They were unable to make even the faintest attempt at an equalizer, and one could sense that the wrath of an unforgiving and disillusioned nation would quickly descend upon their fallen heroes.

Wolfgang Stoltz and Paul Rheinhart had been on the terraces in Córdoba that afternoon. Matters at Buenos Recuerdos were proceeding according to plan, but the unpleasant business was hardly mentioned. This was a football outing, and the two old sailors from the Kreigsmarine were there to give all their support and encouragement to the current idols of German football.

Stoltz had found it essential to temper his enthusiasm for his 'Fatherland Favourites' in the company of his employer. Astor Gordero was a raving nationalist when it came to his love for Argentine football. The Fat Man would not tolerate discussion of the positive merits of any other nation's football program. Wolfgang Stoltz relished this one opportunity to cast aside the mantle of oppression and cheer heartily for his native sons.

Stoltz and Rheinhart would just as ardently drown their sorrow with pails of ale that bleak evening. By midnight, the lawyer from Buenos Aires had imbibed enough of the magic froth to convince himself that the German defeat had saved him from acute embarrassment and confrontation with his employer.

What if Germany and Argentina had met in the final as antagonists? What if Germany had beaten the host nation and reaffirmed their world dominance of the sport? He could imagine the horrible personal consequences, even with his alcohol-clouded brain.

No, he would feel better in the morning, despite the hangover that he knew would awake him. He would feel better for not having to hide his passion from Astor Gordero. He enjoyed his work, and his play, with the influential facilitator far too much to jeopardize his standing on something as trivial as the outcome of a football match.

Even so, the last image that Wolfgang Stoltz conjured up as he sank into a drunken slumber was of the West German captain holding aloft the World Cup trophy after having vanquished all the world's pretenders. *Deutschland Uber Alles!*

The second-to-last piece of the puzzle would be played out seven hundred and sixty-one meters above sea level in the foothills of the Andes Mountains. The city of Mendoza and a well-rested Polish National Team would welcome the traveling Brazilians back to the thin mountain air. It was the second time in less than a week that the yellow shirts had to traverse almost the entire breadth of Argentina to play their fixture.

Both teams had a technical chance of a berth in the final. The Poles, for their part, would go through if they were victorious and the Peruvians upset the host nation later that evening. The Brazilians needed not only to win, but to also run up the score, so that the critical goal differential was heavily in their favor should Argentina triumph.

A cloudless blue sky hung above the forty-seven thousand, six hundred and twenty expectant football fans that beautiful afternoon in Mendoza. It was part of the same high pressure front that brought identical weather to each venue that June day.

'High pressure' was an apt description of the atmosphere inside the stadium as well. The Samba beat was ever present, the crowd being predominately supporters of the South American team.

Four years earlier, these two teams had met in the 'bronze medal,' or third-place match in Munich. In that game, Poland had capped a brilliant World Cup showing with a 1-0 victory over the Brazilians. The men from the southern hemisphere did not take kindly to the comeuppance, for the unexpected loss had caused them all kinds of embarrassment on their return home.

To make matters worse, the Poles were officially considered the home team for this fixture, and as such, had the choice of uniform strips. They selected white tops, red shorts, and white stockings, forcing their opponents to don their secondary colors. The familiar yellow shirts of Brazil would be replaced on this day by ones of a royal-blue hue, along with white pants and white stockings. It was not what the Samba men wanted to play in, and the insult did not go unnoticed. Brazil had a score to settle, and it set about the task from the opening whistle.

The blue-shirts tattooed the Poles' woodwork with the imprint of the ball, and it was a thing of beauty to watch their pinpoint execution. The Samba beat, oh, that Samba beat!

A free kick taken by Brazilian gunner Emmerson Dos Santos eluded the Polish wall and tucked nicely into the mesh in the thirteenth minute. The Europeans were back on their heels and barely hanging together.

The South Americans pressed forward again and again. Fluid, always moving to space, a work of art in creation. Unfortunately, that creation did not include the ability to finish the piece. By the half hour, slight signs of frustration could be seen in the ranks of the crowd favorites, for the Poles had taken heart at having weathered the storm and were more confident and abrasive. The Brazilian surges dwindled in the face of Polish long ball counterattacks.

One minute before the half, Poland's newfound aggressiveness paid off. A scramble ten yards in front of keeper Oliveira resulted in a screened shot eluding all the defenders and knotting the score. Now which team would come back onto the pitch following the break with the confidence to play their style of football and win? Everything hung on the answer to this question.

Buoyed by their late success, the men in the white shirts and red shorts picked up their game where they had left off. The Brazilian defenders looked confused and disorganized in the early going, several near misses around their net undermining the confidence that was so prevalent in the first thirty minutes of the game.

It was left to the blue-clad midfielders to turn the current in the opposite direction. The midfield is considered the canvas that allows the Brazilian game to become an art-form, if things are going well. Slowly, ever so slowly, those men began to win more and more duels for possession. The precision passing of their halfbacks turned defense into offense, pushing the play forward, striving to find that Samba beat again.

They found the beat in the fifty-seventh minute when João Batista collected in a rebound and drove home the chance. One could feel the Poles wilt under the noise of the jubilant crowd. Several covered their ears to block out the harsh celebration. They had heard enough of the Samba beat, enough to last a lifetime.

The Europeans had nothing left to offer. A third South American marker followed five minutes after the second. The remaining time was a blur of blue and white on the run, a demonstration of style and tactics for which the Brazilian game is so famous.

The only problem was that, once again, the finish was lacking, and the men from Ipanema were unable to build their crucial margin of victory past the two goal level. A 3-1 final score in favor of Brazil entered the record books after ninety minutes of football.

This result meant that the host nation had to win by four clear goals against Peru to oust the Brazilians from the World Cup final. Four clear goals, almost an insurmountable task!

Barring a complete collapse of the Peruvian defense, each and every Brazilian player felt supremely confident that they would sport the yellow battle colors of their nation one more time in the most important game of their young lives. The World Cup championship final!

The Argentina-Brazil fiasco had proven to be a distasteful event for Sir Reginald Russell. He had so hoped to see the South American game displayed in its finest showcase. As it turned out, he was barely able to control his contempt for the stuttering, bullying football that the Latins offered.

"If we are supposed to be looking for a diamond in the rough, I'm afraid that we will never find it in this rubbish, darling!" the perturbed Lord snapped at his daughter.

"Sit down, daddy, and keep a sharp eye, now, that's a good chap. You are upsetting the patrons around you with your blathering on."

"I'm upsetting them? What about that crap down there? That's what should be upsetting them!" Reggie pointed to the pitch as he obediently took his seat again.

Mallory Russell kept her eyes glued on the player wearing powder-blue and white number seventeen. The player had been felled twice since entering the game as a substitute after the break. She knew for a fact that it was the same young player that had scored the two goals against Poland. The lady had been unable to take her eyes off him during that game as well.

Renaldo, Renaldo, she kept saying his name silently to herself. She was startled and disappointed to find him missing from the starting eleven against the Brazilians. Mallory Russell anxiously scanned the Argentine bench to make sure he was not injured. She was relieved to see him jogging and flexing on the sideline. The home side manager must know more than he let on to the news-hungry press. Managers always had that ability to confound the 'experts' with their player selection. Miss Russell sincerely hoped that the player she really came to see would make an appearance before the ninety minutes elapsed.

When Renaldo De Seta took to the pitch to start the second half of play, Mallory was not the only person in Rosario stadium that was elated. The trilled drone that started in the far corner of the amphitheater soon spread to the decks and terraces.

"RRRRRRenaaaaaaaallllldo? Yes, that's what they are saying! Yes, there it is again." The lady English football executive was duly impressed. She turned to her statistical form book and double-checked the boy's bio.

"Young!" she barely breathed the word. "So young to have his own cheer."

"What was that, love?" Reggie inquired.

"Oh, nothing, sorry." She must try to be more objective, to watch the entire field of play, not just that gorgeous specimen of a man wearing the black numerals 'one-seven.'

She felt her heart miss a beat when he was fouled in the early minutes. The bio had referred to an Achilles' heel injury, and there was no doubt that the Brazilians were privy to the same information. The boy basically did not participate in the majority of play after he went down a second time, but Mallory kept her binoculars trained on his form, particularly his damaged limb.

She was impressed with two things while the debacle of a game played itself out. Firstly, how the Argentine players seemed to rally around their stricken teammate and cover his space. Ramon Vida was a torrent, always coming back to help. Humberto Velasquez had steadied after his opening jitters and was now an authoritative force to be reckoned with. Leopoldo Anariba, for his part, gave up the hand-to-hand combat that had dominated his thinking in the first half. He now took more time with the ball, steering it away from the center midfielder. It was a vision of real teamwork!

Secondly, she was impressed with the strength of the injured player's limb. As the game progressed, she noticed that Renaldo De Seta seemed more and more at ease with the pain he must have been experiencing. He was always testing the foot's durability, performing quick sprints to work it out when the ball was safely away. Jumps and leaps for imaginary headers often followed a stoppage in the action.

At the cessation of hostilities, Mallory Russell kept her optical enhancers trained on number seventeen as he limped gingerly toward the tunnel steps, then hopped one-footed down out of sight. Her father was nattering on once again about the "pathetic state of South American football." She wasn't listening though, for her thoughts were in the future, three days in the future when she would again occupy these same seats and watch the young man from Buenos Aires ply his trade.

She gave a silent prayer that the boy's foot would be full measure by the time his team faced the Peruvians. It would take a good showing by her favorite to convince her father that Renaldo De Seta was, in fact, the diamond for whom they were looking. But then, she knew one thing for certain. No matter what her father's opinion, she had to have this handsome warrior for the Canaries . . . and for herself!

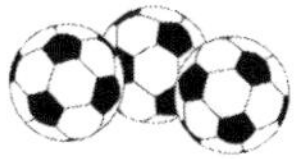

Whiling away the hours under such pressure was something new to Renaldo De Seta. Locked inside the team's secretive headquarters in Rosario, the involuntary confinement reminded him of an extra long detention back at the Newton Academy. The tension was evident throughout the compound as the National Team of Argentina gathered around a battery of television sets to watch their fate unfold that bright June day.

The two early games commenced at 1:45 p.m., while the all-important Brazil-Poland game kicked off at 3:45 p.m. Argentina would play, once again, at 7:15 in the evening. For fans throughout the country, as well as the players involved directly, this day was to be a football feast the likes of which Argentina had never experienced!

Renaldo preferred to stay by himself in the morning and early afternoon. He took a solitary jog around the practice field at 8:00 a.m., then retired to his room with a tray of fruit, juice, coffee, and breads.

The foot was adequate, adequate enough for Octavio Suarez to announce De Seta as his starting center half at the noon-day press conference.

The boy sat on his bed slumped over his guitar in a soulful connection. Softly strumming his favorite Jobim tunes, he would every once in a while add off-key lyrics to the melody. His 'do not disturb' sign hung on the outer latch, and for once, the world respected his request for privacy.

Strangely, Renaldo's thoughts were not of his injury or of football at all, for that matter. It was Simone's image to which he played his songs of love. He tried to recall how she looked, and especially how she felt in his arms when they were last together, so long ago.

He was desperate to drink in the scent of her, to listen to the sound of her, and hold her close to him once more. Not a soul knew of his anguish. Not a soul knew how his heart ached as only a young man's aches when he first tastes love. So bittersweet, so tender, so full of lust!

Renaldo was mistaken, however, as to the secrecy of his emotions. He had forgotten about one extremely obese 'facilitator,' who at that very moment ignored the posted request for privacy and knocked on number seventeen's door.

"Renaldo! Renaldo, it's Astor Gordero. I have something of interest that I was asked to pass on to you today. Please open the door and give your humble servant an audience."

Gordero rapped on the portal with his walking stick again. His client stood in the doorway before it was necessary to strike a third time.

"My profuse apologies if I am disturbing you from something earth-shattering, but I did feel that you might want to avail yourself of this as soon as you possibly could. I have a premonition it may be something containing 'inspirational stimulus!'"

He pulled a pink envelope from his portfolio and started to hand it to his client. The Fat One suddenly withdrew the offering and looked at the younger man.

"First, just a bit of business. How is the foot? You will be starting tonight, and I would be remiss if I didn't tell you that there have been inquiries as to your availability after the tournament. Inquiries from countries outside of South America." Gordero paused to let the last sentence sink in.

"Your future, my young friend, is starting to crystallize very nicely. A strong showing tonight could propel you into the economic stratosphere on the transfer market. At your age, with so much of life to experience for yourself, you would be crazy to let the opportunity pass you by." Again The Fat Man paused to make sure that his message was being understood.

"I will handle your mother and the education problem. One could consider what you will be doing as 'studying abroad.' The world can be at your doorstep, Renaldo. Tonight must be your night! Your foot must be strong, and your eye must be true. Remember, head and feet as one!"

And there it was again. That ham hock fist with those chubby fingers intertwined! Head and feet as one, head and feet as one!

The player assured his agent that the limb was close to top form, and affirmed that the obvious importance of the forthcoming fixture had not escaped him. As for playing abroad, that would mean leaving Argentina, his family, and Simone. The thought had never crossed his mind until Gordero mentioned it, and he found the notion unthinkable, even distressing.

The Rotund One pulled a chained pocket watch from the vest of his Brooks Brothers blue pinstriped suit. He was teasing the boy now, posturing on about football tactics while he knew that his listener had thoughts of the pink envelope alone.

It seemed an eternity to Renaldo before the figure large enough to block out the sun finally exited his room. The ceremonial handing over of the envelope had been Gordero's final parting gesture. The lovesick player inhaled the essence held by the pink folder before delving any deeper. His knees felt weak with expectation, and his sweaty hands trembled as he clumsily tore open the back flap. The perfume overwhelmed him, and he collapsed back on his bed, taking time to breathlessly focus on her written script.

'Darling Renaldo,

I am so proud of you! I have watched every game, every minute staring at the television for the slightest glimpse of you. Your performance against Poland made me weak with excitement and anticipation, anticipation of the moment we can be together again, alone!

I have been so busy with concerts and promotions and state dinners. It has left me exhausted. It is only the vision of your handsome face that lifts up my heart and carries me through.

I fear for your safety. The games seem so rough. When I saw you go down against Brazil, my heart stopped. Astor told me the next day that you were recovering nicely, but I am still worried for you. Astor also told me that the game against Peru could be a big stepping-stone in your career if you have a good night. He said you might be able to use some extra inspiration, so he has flown me to Rosario to watch you play tonight. How do you like that surprise?'

Renaldo had to stop reading. *"Simone, here in Rosario? In the stands tonight? Here to watch me play? My God, it's incredible!"*

He held the letter to his chest and imagined her cheering as he scored the winning goal. That would be heaven on earth.

"Simone, Simone!" He dared to let his eyes continue on their journey.

'I wish you all the luck in the world tonight, my love. Please know that I will be there to cheer you on. Hold that thought in your heart to give you strength and protection.

I would love to see you following the game, but I must return to the capital immediately afterwards. I now have to prepare for the special ceremonies preceding the World Cup final. They have told me that I will be performing in front of the largest television audience in world history! It makes me nervous even thinking about it.

Take heart, dear Renaldo. My thoughts are constantly with you. I will be praying for a victory tonight that will bring you back to Buenos Aires for the championship game and into my arms.

Until that moment, I await you anxiously,

Con amore, Simone.'

It was two hours later that Ramon Vida stood knocking on Renaldo De Seta's door.

"Hey, man, open up. Suarez sent me to get you. You're late for the team meeting, and the boss is pissed. What the fuck are you doing in there, man? You got some chicks in there or something? Come on, open up!"

A disoriented and disheveled Renaldo De Seta appeared in the doorway. Vida was past him and into the room in a flash.

"So, where is she, man? Where's the dolly, the quim, the puuuuussssyyyyy?"

"There's no puuusssy here, Ramon. I fell asleep and forgot to set my alarm. That's all. Come on, I'm ready to go. Sorry."

Number seventeen quickly buttoned and tucked in his shirt, slipped on his loafers, and stuffed Simone's letter in his jeans pocket.

The missive had sent him to a Utopian land of milk and honey, and he knew that he would be there still were it not for the rude knock of reality on his door. Astor Gordero's visit had thrown his studied pregame routine into a tailspin. Thoughts and images he never before imagined flew through his brain as he tried to concentrate on Suarez's instructions.

Simone was most prominently in his mind, but the unusual notion of cutting his mother's apron strings for fame and fortune in a foreign land kept recurring. Had Gordero struck a nerve at the right time in his young life? The thought was as compelling as it was frightening.

The Pandora's box of emotions was hard to exorcise to make room for the immediate task of the hour. It was only after the Argentine team bus pulled into view of Rosario Central Stadium with its flags, banners, and raucous fanatics that Renaldo was able to come to grips with the present. He felt that a good showing here tonight would allow him to take charge of his life, to become a man. A man that was worthy of loving the most famous woman in Argentina.

"So be it, head and feet as one!"

The burglar could still not believe his good fortune. He had been a resident at the comfortable summer home of the Jimenez family for five nights, and he had remained undisturbed as Peru kicked off against Argentina on the night of the twenty-first of June.

The large, two-story frame 'cottage' sat on the shore of one of the Delta's more fashionable islands, but as this was the off-season, it and all the adjacent summer retreats were boarded up and deserted. That suited the uninvited guest perfectly. No one had come by to make him take flight prematurely, for what the intruder needed was time. Time to make the assassins that were after his head give up their hunt in the Tigre area and move on to search elsewhere.

The cottage was adequately stocked with dry goods and canned foodstuffs. The electrical power had been shut down, and the visitor was careful not to turn on the main breaker switch unless it was to quickly cook some food or to watch the news and sports report on the old television set. He had made up his mind to move on in the morning, for extending his stay could prove to be hazardous to his health. No sense pressing one's luck, and besides, it was really the football match that had kept him in these cozy surroundings this long.

Yes, Lonnie De Seta considered himself lucky to be able to sit back and take in his little brother's starting performance against Peru. In fact, Lonnie considered himself lucky to be alive.

He had drifted out into the middle of the channel and floated downstream with the current that deadly night of the sixteenth. There was no attempt to follow his nautical course. Celeste's killers must have been so sure of their success that they had overlooked a maritime escape route and were unprepared to take to the waterways in pursuit. Lonnie rationalized that they may never have discovered that the fugitive had made his getaway by canoe. In any event, no one had come searching around the Jimenez cottage for him . . . yet.

He had spent that first night deep inside the meandering canals that snake through the Delta islands. Lush tropical foliage made it easy for him to paddle his canoe behind an outcropping of vegetation whenever he felt the need for complete privacy. There were no sounds at all that night as he lay on the floor of the canoe and tried to rationalize his situation. Tears of regret and anguish flowed freely down his cheeks as the events of the past months swept over him.

For the first time, the thought of ending the ordeal by his own hand passed through his mind. Yes, it was an alternative better than torture, or a life in one of those abysmal junta prisons. He still carried a cyanide pill in his hollowed out tooth for expressly that purpose. If all else failed, suicide could be considered, but not yet, not now.

There was still the chance that he could make it to his bank in the capital. Once he had made it that far without being detected, he could pick up his identification and credit cards from the safety deposit box, withdraw a substantial amount of money from his bank account, and flee Argentina forever. What Lonnie needed now was time to let his trail get cold, and that meant staying out of sight and away from any form of civilization.

He remained in his sylvan surroundings until darkness the following night, when he cautiously continued his silent journey. The fugitive knew exactly where he was headed, for he had been familiar with these waterways since his youth. He had dated a girl long ago that owned one of the seasonal retreats just along from the Jimenez cottage. There was a good possibility that one of those structures could afford him the sanctuary he so desperately required.

Lonnie's only possessions were crammed into his dirty chinos. A wallet containing false identification, the key to the safety deposit box, and a few hundred pesos lay in his back pocket. Under his belt buckle rested the Llama pistol. He hoped with all his heart that he would have to use only the contents of the wallet, not the pistol, to reach Buenos Aires and continue his flight to freedom.

For a fleeting moment, the pole atop Central Stadium bearing the national flag of Argentina stood perfectly silhouetted in the glaring full moon. It was the first sight witnessed by Renaldo De Seta as he took the field of play for this World Cup semifinal game.

A full moon with our national flag nestled inside it. Certainly a good omen, number seventeen thought to himself as he pranced nervously in his warm-up jacket prior to the national anthems being played. *Its bright beams will guide us to the mother-lode!*

Such was the unabashed confidence of the young and talented center halfback. And well it should have been, for 'the mother-lode' was exactly what the Argentine National Team needed to find on this bejeweled evening.

Four clear goals against any of the World Cup contenders was a tall order. Against Peru, the team that had dispatched the Scots from the tournament licking their inadequacies, overconfidence on the part of the home side could be disastrous. Even though the men of the Andes had already lost to Brazil 3-0 and Poland 1-0 in the second round, they were still a team to be taken very seriously.

The North American professional leagues had sent their scouts to the southern reaches in search of new heroes to help fill their stadiums. Several of the Peruvians had been mentioned in the press as being slated for a financially rewarding trip north. These men in red shirts and white shorts were playing for their futures, and instead of stars, they saw dollar signs in the sky that night.

It was black stockings and black shorts for the men in the powder-blue and white vertical stripes again. Octavio Suarez was impressed with the ornery attitude that his tactic had produced against the Brazilians, and he was hoping that the somber shade would have the same effect this night.

It was the Peruvians that stormed the barricades at the outset, however. Junior Calix was called upon to save the national pride three times in the opening minutes. There was a cocksure defiance to the red team's game. The Argentine defenders were cement-footed spectators to some of the most proficient passing of the whole extravaganza to date. Suarez bit his nails on the sidelines, waiting for the true home side to come out of the closet.

The manager would only have to wait ten minutes for the talent he knew existed in his charges to surface. The Peruvian attack became predictable, always the same players coming forward at the Argentine defenders. That meant a less than warm welcome from Juan Chacon, and he made short work of any red sweater that came within his range of contact.

The opening flurry by the visitors gave them a good taste of 'Killer' Chacon's style of hospitality. Octavio Suarez had seen the ensuing result in other games where the surly defender's opponents lacked true motivation and the 'victory at any cost' mind-set. It was not long before the men from the north tired of the physical punishment being dealt out by number eight of the host nation. As one quarter hour of play elapsed, the initial spirit and sheer love of the game seemed to have disappeared from the red shirt's demeanor. No longer did they venture under the shadows of the Argentine woodwork. Their passes started to misfire, and their shots were taken from an increasing longer distance.

The Argentine boss knew that The Ugly One had single-handedly changed the course of the match. The French referee was an unaffected onlooker to the punishment meted out by the grotesque back-liner. Juan Chacon had cast a sorcerer's spell on the Peruvian nationals, a spell that would last the remaining seventy-five minutes of football. It was a belligerent, bruising, one-man defensive spectacle that would prove to be the penultimate performance of his career.

Yet Juan Chacon's stellar showing would be overshadowed this night in Rosario. The seams in the visitors' defensive formations came apart the minute the red shirts started to lay back in the midfield. Challenges were now uniformly won by the hosts, and offensive thrusts deep inside Peruvian territory became more and more frequent.

The two Argentine outside defenders had been given permission to come forward with the play. This tactic would enhance the all-out offensive thrust that would be needed to produce four goals. Captain Daniele Bennett and Jorge Calderone used their new freedom with great zeal, and their timely runs and sure passes drew in the red defenders, opening space for the other powder-blue and white marksmen.

Renaldo's foot was holding up solidly after a few skirmishes. Tonight's opposition had not tried to drive him hobbling from the pitch as the Brazilians had. The longer the game went on, the more chance number seventeen had to test the limb's strength and resiliency. He could feel himself growing stronger and more confident with every touch of the ball.

At the twenty-minute mark, Humberto Velasquez undressed a Peruvian midfielder at the sideline and sent a nifty relay ten yards upfield to Ruben Gitares. The league-leading goal scorer beat a hasty path deep into the Peruvian corner, but found himself covered by three red-shirts. Center forward Ramon Vida was the closest player to Gitares, but there was an opponent shadowing Vida so closely that the winger delayed his pass for an instant.

Suddenly, a pale-blue streak appeared just beyond Vida, charging for the penalty area.

"There now, take this and fly, baby!" Ruben Gitares called out as he directed the sphere diagonally back across the pitch. Twenty-five yards away, Renaldo De Seta could see his gift arriving. He thought for a split second of Simone in the stands watching, but then it was down to business. As he gathered in the ball and strode toward the unprotected keeper, the phrase flashed in his mind like a neon billboard. *Head and feet as one! Head and feet as one!*

Vida and Gitares were bulling forward to the goal, drawing attention and creating diversion. Renaldo had a clear shot with only the keeper to beat. He was inside the penalty area now, but fearful of shooting too soon.

Hold it, hold it, let the keeper make his move! The young player's inner voice seemed to be guiding his every gesture now.

Watch for your opening, have a true eye and a strong foot. Easy, there it is. Now!

Fifteen yards out, the Peruvian keeper left his feet to lunge at the approaching attacker. It seemed a half-hearted effort to Renaldo, for the ball eluded this last defender's grasp by several feet. For a moment, number seventeen felt his stomach turn as his shot came perilously close to hitting the far post. But his aim was true, and the little bit of English that his right foot had put on the shot allowed it to tuck nicely just inside the upright. His thoughts flashed back to Simone as the scorer was engulfed by jubilant teammates. He realized then just how much he wanted to go back to Buenos Aires to play in the championship game and to hold her in his arms as his championship trophy.

Argentina had opened a crack in the door, but it was by no means sufficient to earn them advancement. The pressure had to be constant on the ambiguous Peruvian defenders, and the men in the powder-blue and white vertical stripes set about its application with abandon. It seemed as if every warrior on the home side wanted to add to the margin personally, for the surge forward, even by the fullbacks, was overwhelming. What the world was witnessing happened to be a South American team playing the overworked catch phrase, 'total football.'

'Total football' was thought to be the exclusive domain of the Dutch when it was introduced in 1974 in West Germany. The Orangemen had enthralled the world with their fluid, all-encompassing style of play. It was entertaining to watch, and the fact that the Netherlands fell two goals short of the World Championship had done nothing to diminish or dissuade its disciples.

Now, Argentina was throwing every man into the attack, and it seemed that only Peruvian goaler Jaime Allianza was interested in keeping the score respectable. The poor Allianza had little or no help from his leaden teammates as the home team gunners descended upon him.

Two minutes before the interval, a corner kick taken by Ruben Gitares curled twenty yards away from the goal line. Pursuant to the strategy of the day, six-foot-four-inch Ignacio Suazo had come forward to lend a helping hand. In this case, he lent his head to the cause, pounding the ball down to earth two yards in front of keeper Allianza. The Peruvian moved too late, and the precious leather was behind him into the goal before he hit the deck.

Suazo could not believe his good fortune, for he was not a polished scorer at the best of times. In fact, his 'near misses' had become a good-natured joke among his teammates. The team had practiced headers once with no keeper in the net, and Suazo had missed ten out of ten shots. They had presented the good-natured River Plate defender with a 'golden skull award' at dinner that evening, and the mood of mirth and camaraderie that the silliness produced was a tangible factor in their newfound cohesiveness.

Good things often come to those who suffer in silence, so now, Ignacio Suazo was being swarmed by his teammates and lifted aloft. He would go to the dressing room feeling more elated than at any time in his life.

Those moonbeams even helped Suazo! thought Renaldo De Seta as the home side exited the pitch. With half the game to play, Argentina was halfway to salvation.

The beautiful Symca had enjoyed the drama and atmosphere of the first half immensely, despite the fact that her focus had been strictly one dimensional. She could not take her eyes off of number seventeen in the powder-blue and white jersey. There were just so many things about Renaldo De Seta that had a disarming effect on her.

His traffic-stopping good looks were obvious. Then there was the way his body moved when he ran with the ball, so confident and graceful. His powerful strides exuded sexuality. His shyness in real life, his sensitivity, his youthful naiveté. His touch, and especially the enduring sensation of him pressed against her.

She had been with other men, but none of them had inspired her like this man. Her suitors had always been older, more experienced in the ways of love. But Simone had been a good student, and the fantasy of being the teacher for once kept her awake at night. She wanted with all her heart to be with him this moonlit night, but it could not be. Her solace was the fact that she knew they would be reunited in the capital within days, and she had conceived a plan to make the experience special.

Simone Yvonne Montana Carta-Aqua would pick her timing carefully for the opening of her new school. It would be a finishing school for her one student, and that student had only one goal to achieve in acquiring his diploma. The teacher would set an exacting curriculum, but in the end, the student would be finished with boyhood forever, for she was going to turn him into a man!

Octavio Suarez was on the alert for those invisible 'gremlins of the interval.' He sat with each of the starting eleven to gauge their strength and spirit. His team was still two goals shy of reaching nirvana, and he had options to consider regarding his two substitutions. Should he throw in fresh horses for the run down the stretch? Proven finishers Bottaniz, Pastor, and yes, even the newly dentured Miguel Cruz were available to insert.

Minutes before taking the field, the manager stood alone in his tiny office. He was out of sight, but with the door open. His arms were wrapped around his torso, head drooping on his chest, eyes closed, listening, listening. He had heard 'the buzz' before, 'the buzz' that a group of men that are harmonious in their destiny can make. Winners! It was in the dressing room right now. He could hear it as the voices intertwined to make 'the buzz.' He could feel its presence in that room.

"Winners!" Suarez mumbled. He raised his head, eyes now open and full of fire. "Winners!" he shouted above 'the buzz' for all to hear. The starting roster would remain unchanged!

The manager had some doubt about his good vibrations in the opening minutes of the second half, however. The Peruvians had refound their skills and panache during the break, and they pressed the game into the Argentine danger zone. Some fancy footwork and ball control confused the powder-blue-and-white-striped shirts for a time, but sooner or later, one had a feeling that number eight of the hosts would make his special presence felt.

Peruvian striker Hector Diaz had been pleased with his World Cup performance to date. He had scored twice against the Scots and wrung up another deuce against Iran in the first round of play. Furthermore, he had been praised by his manager and the press back home for his tireless showings against Poland and Brazil in the second round. He had no doubt that one more goal tonight against Argentina would etch his name in the minds of the North American talent agents.

Hector Diaz longed to play for the Cosmos in New York City. His dream was to be counted among the soccer elite of the world. Unfortunately, he would be counted out for the duration of the match after leaping for a header just a tad too close to Juan Chacon.

No one saw a blow struck or any impropriety committed at all by The Ugly One. The two players simply went up for the ball at the same time, became entangled, and fell to earth with the larger Chacon on top of the Peruvian.

No injustice was evidenced through the tangle of legs and bodies that surrounded the fallen warriors as the play swirled around them. Chacon was up almost at once, the red-shirted player remaining prone on the green carpet. Smelling salts revived the groggy striker, but he was carried from the pitch by stretcher after being unable to count to five. It would mark the end of the first and final offensive thrust that Peru would mount that second half of play.

At the forty-eight minute mark, Ruben Gitares lofted a free kick goalward from just to the right of the penalty area twenty yards out. Renaldo De Seta, the tallest man on the front line, trapped the ball on his chest and shrugged it toward teammate Ramon Vida. Four red-clad Peruvians converged on the center forward, but before any were within striking distance, the boy from Boca calmly flicked-on the volley with his right foot.

Number seventeen had faded to his left and dropped back a few yards to remain onside after the relay. He was in a perfect position for Vida's return offering. Clear of all obstacles, he stood alone, ten yards from the bewildered Allianza.

"One more time, head and feet as one! Now, do it!" Renaldo said aloud. The ball bounced once at his feet a yard out from the goal area. From seven yards, it was an easy left-footed shot into the near top corner of the twines.

The familiar trilled roar that swept through the grandstand surrounded the scorer as he took his spot for the ensuing kickoff. The scoreboard shone as brightly as its celestial cousin, Argentina 3, Peru 0!

One hundred and twenty seconds later, the world unfolded as every Argentine heart knew that it should. The padrone or 'old man' of the team, thirty-year-old Caesar Castro, would lay the foundation for the largest celebration Argentina had seen in years.

With the home side swarming around the foreigners' danger-zone, the red defenders tried jamming their goalmouth to keep the score respectable. As this critical play evolved on the fringes, the River Plate winger left his feet and flew into the midst of the Peruvian goal area. The airborne Castro then nonchalantly headed the cowhide toward the barn as he connected with a precise lob from the attacking Daniele Bennett.

Ramon Vida stood shoulder-to-shoulder with his red-shirted marker at the far goalpost. Up, up, up the ball arched after Castro's touch, spinning in slow motion toward the Argentine center forward. Vida had position on his defensive opponent, who seemed transfixed by the sphere's flight. Twirling and whirling as it calmly descended, the precious bundle was gently tucked into its woven cradle with the tenderness of a new mother. Ramon Vida had sprung up and took flight one yard from the goal line. Keeper Allianza failed to react at all to his soaring, affectionate, redirected header. This loving touch was to be the goal that put the host nation into the World Cup final!

CHAPTER TWENTY-SEVEN

Señor Gordero, how good to see you again, and Herr Stoltz, my compliments. Congratulations on your great victory tonight. It is fitting that the host nation of such a fine tournament be in the championship game. You both remember my daughter, Mallory?"

Reggie Russell was on his best behavior. He would bite his sarcastic lip as per Mallory's instructions, otherwise, he would be forced to suffer her unladylike wrath. His Lordship had his dander up, however, and it took all his self-control to keep from giving these arrogant South Americans a lecture on manners.

Sir Reggie was sick and tired of chasing the elusive Fat Man around Rosario. Sick of cancelled dinners and postponed meetings, sick of unreturned phone messages, but most of all, sick of pandering to his Kraut flunky for the opportunity of an audience.

Mallory had insisted that he calm down and concentrate on scouting the football players. The Brazil-Argentina fiasco had upset the old fellow so much that he was convinced he would see nothing inspirational three nights later as the home side met Peru. His daughter kept reminding him that they must have open minds and think positively, for there were no superstars waiting at The Birdcage back home on the Isle of Dogs. All they had were a bunch of has-beens and wannna-bees, not one quality player to build around. As usual, Mallory's pragmatism made the options crystal clear. Arrive home from South America with nothing in the fold and face annihilation from the likes of Liverpool, Leeds, and worst of all, their snotty London rivals.

Mallory had set the time and location of this rendezvous with Herr Stoltz herself. The venue would be the 'facilitator's' suggested restaurant, immediately following the Peru-Argentina contest. Miss Russell had paid the proprietor of Ristorante Borgo Antico several hundred American dollars to keep his staff late and attend to the needs of Señor Astor Gordero. The glutton was well-known in this cozy Italian establishment, and the tab for his visits always swelled to hundreds of thousands of pesos.

The game of cat and mouse with the English had worked to the Porteño's advantage. Once the Anglos had expressed interest in young De Seta, the games in Rosario became the boy's showcase. When his fine outing against

Poland was not duplicated against the Brazilians, it became advantageous for his agent to be 'unavailable.'

A strong performance against the Peruvians would increase the young player's value, and that, in turn, would make all offers received for his services more lucrative for client and agent alike. An excessive amount of money wasn't something Renaldo De Seta found himself in dire need of, but it was a good carrot to go along with the adventure and excitement of playing football abroad.

The astute attorney knew that he would need every possible incentive to lure the boy out of Argentina, and it was for that very reason that he had summoned Simone to Rosario. She was his 'ace in the hole.' The young stallion would eventually do as the beautiful and more worldly Symca advised him to do. Of that, The Large One was certain, for Astor Gordero never underestimated the power of 'pillow talk.'

"We want Renaldo De Seta and Ramon Vida for the Canary Wharf Football Club, Señor Gordero. Do you think that you might be able to 'facilitate' such a transfer?"

Mallory's bluntness startled the three gentlemen. The two new arrivals had barely taken their seats when the emphatic blonde lady tabled her wish list.

"My dear Miss Russell, you must forgive me, but I am truly famished. The crowds of people in the streets have delayed our arrival well past my usual mealtime. So please, allow me to order some fare from the kitchen, then we will proceed with business. I can never talk of financial matters on an empty stomach."

Why you bloated old cow! steamed Sir Reggie in silence.

Gordero milked the delay for all it was worth. The English had laid their cards on the table before the first draw. That gave the lawyer from Buenos Aires a chance to reshuffle the deck and play some bluff poker at their expense.

Luckily, the chef had been forewarned of The Fat Man's imminent arrival, and the antipasto and breads were placed on the table immediately. Platters of Italian meats and cheeses along with grilled vegetables were arrayed on a separate table that was drawn up beside the starving patron. A bottle of fine Italian Chianti was consumed before the soup course arrived. A second was sent for immediately. It was not until the lull preceding the pasta 'appetizer' that the well-nourished deal maker saw fit to address the desires of his European tablemates.

"You have made a very wise choice in the two players that you have selected, my Lady. They seem to complement one another very nicely on the football field. Off the field, they are friends and often roommates. I hear that they have even formed a musical duet of some kind. What you request could be a possibility, if only . . ."

An oversized bowl of pasta suddenly appeared in front of the speaker, and it was instantly evident that The Gross One's train of thought had been temporarily side tracked.

"If only what, Señor Gordero? If only what, for heaven sakes?" An impatient Reggie Russell was about to blow a gasket. He held his tongue, however, when he felt the point of Mallory's shoe pressing firmly against his shin under the tablecloth.

Several fork loads of fettucine were consumed before Gordero continued his dialogue.

"As you know, the De Seta boy is my client. The difficulty with his situation is his lack of worldly experience. His father died years ago, and he has been raised under the thumb of a domineering mother. The lady's only concession in allowing this gifted boy to stray from her clutches has been the semiprofessional football that he plays. In return for this allowance, he must keep his academic standing at the top of his class and accompany her to mass each Sunday to renounce his sins!"

A pregnant pause gave rise to the consumption of more pasta. A few moments later, the discourse continued.

"The good news is that Señora Florencia De Seta, the boy's mother, is also a client of mine, and it would seem that I have the lady's trust and confidence. I want you to understand that convincing Señora De Seta to give Renaldo her blessing to play football in England will be a Herculean task. But then, I feel in all modesty that you are talking to the only man in Argentina that could accomplish such a feat."

"Come now, Señor Gordero, the boy is nineteen years old according to the statistical records. In England, that means he is a man, free to vote, fight for his country, and fornicate as he pleases. Surely this Renaldo De Seta is able to make a decision with regards to his own future without running to mummy!"

The absurdity of the situation had gotten to be too much for Reggie Russell. Were they discussing a man that had already scored a handful of goals in the toughest football tournament in the world or some grade school sissy?

The aging British Marine was just like his daughter in many ways, straightforward and to the point. All he wanted now was the answer to a simple question. Was the boy available or wasn't he?

"Perhaps we Latins have a different sense of family, Lord Russell," Gordero mused. "Respecting the wishes of our parents is a lifelong obligation to us, and something that no Argentine takes lightly. Education is Señora De Seta's foremost concern for her son. His father was a highly respected doctor, and I know for a fact that she intends for him to follow in his footsteps. If we could arrange some academic liaison with a medical school in London, it would certainly smooth the process. The boy is as adept with a textbook as he is with a football!"

Mallory Russell did not want to seem overly enthusiastic about acquiring the services of the boy with the matinee idol's looks, but it took all the restraint that she could muster to remain calm. She hung on every syllable the oversized South American uttered. The medical school connection struck a nerve that brought her to the forefront of the conversation.

"That will work. I have it!" she blurted out spontaneously.

"My mother was a senior military nurse, specializing in rehabilitative medicine. That's how she met father actually. With our contacts, Sir Reggie's, in particular, with the Marines and the government, I'm certain that an exchange student visa could be arranged." Lady Russell sat back in her chair brimming with confidence.

"You bring up an interesting point, my Lady." Wolfgang Stoltz joined the discussion for the first time. He had been taking notes of the proceedings in his very precise manner until finally laying his notepad and pen on the table. His tone was polite, but slightly condescending.

"What would be the official status of our players in your country, if I might ask? Have you discussed this matter with your immigration authorities? Correct me if I am wrong, but to my knowledge, there have never been foreign players in the English first division other than those accepted as political refugees. How will your Football Association react to foreign nationals taking jobs away from native-born players? What about the players' union? How strongly will they object? Is it possible that there could be some 'unpleasantness' directed at these two boys for changing the balance of things in your country? It would seem that there are several obstacles to overcome on both sides of the Atlantic before a suitable conclusion can be consummated." The German picked up his pen and notepad and sat poised to transcribe the rebuttal.

"We have already talked to the bloody Department of Employment on this matter, and I can assure you that there won't be any frigging red tape if those two boys make up their own damn minds to come with us!"

Reggie Russell wanted to slug the pompous heinie. How dare he question their competency or the actions of the Football Association!

Unpleasantness! he had thought to himself before replying to The Fat Man's lackey. *The only unpleasantness will result from these mamas' boys not cutting the mustard in the English first division. They sound like a bunch of overprotected pussies!*

Again it was the chrome tip of Mallory's spiked pump that signaled the end to Lord Russell's soliloquy. His daughter picked up the flow without missing a beat.

"I appreciate your concerns, Herr Stoltz, but I can assure you that we will assume full responsibility for your players' health and welfare. We have discussed foreign players participating in English football for some time internally at the FA Level. There are no rules in our bylaws that prevent such a thing from happening, so therefore, we must assume that it is acceptable." She was looking Stoltz directly in the eye while she spoke. "The formalities will be looked after, gentlemen, of that you have my word." She looked at Gordero, then back at the German. "But your players will bring us much more than they take from us. Our football is stagnant. It is rotting from the inside out. Since we won the World Cup twelve years ago, our National Team program has achieved little or no success. The fact that we are not in this competition speaks volumes in itself. The game of soccer is changing, and we are not learning from the world around us. We are simply content to rest on past laurels. Yes, we were champions of the world, once. Well, that was too long ago for my liking, and I don't intend to sit idly by and never see England's name on the championship trophy again!"

Mallory could feel the passion that her favorite sport evoked flowing through her veins. She took a sip of the Chianti to settle her emotions, then pressed on.

"Your players are taught a different style of football from the time they begin to walk. They have different skills, different thoughts and patterns of action and reaction. If we can incorporate and blend these divergent strategies, well, English football will be forced to wake up and smell the coffee. That is what I want to accomplish, Señor Gordero."

The stylish lady crossed her arms and sat back in her chair, satisfied that she had spoken her case as articulately and earnestly as possible.

"There is another matter of concern regarding Ramon Vida's situation. I do not personally handle his affairs, and of course, you are aware that he is the property of the Boca Juniors Football Club." Gordero stopped speaking long enough to inhale the aroma of the veal medallions saltimbocca that had just been placed before his ever-expanding girth

The talented 'Boy from Boca' had increased his own worth tenfold when he notched his second tally of the evening in the seventy-second minute of the game against Peru. It would be the sixth and final goal for Argentina in their march to the championship final. Two goals for De Seta, two goals for Vida! The score-line had made the selection of the second player on Mallory Russell's list an obvious choice. Now what she needed was information on Vida's future plans.

"I understand that Ramon is a tough customer. A gang leader who was plucked right off the streets of Boca into their football program. It is said the only reason he is still alive today is that he is as good with his fists as with his feet!" Gordero revealed.

The medallions now became the primary focus of The Enormous One, and his three dinner companions were forced to amuse themselves while he attended to their disposal.

"Luckily, I have some 'favors' outstanding with Caspar Dominico, the president of the Boca Club. We are currently working on negotiations to move the Newton's Prefect First Division Club to Velez Sarsfield Stadium on the outskirts of the Federal District of the capital. That would leave Boca Juniors as the only major club team left in the Central District, or heart of the city. Without the competition our league champions would give him at the gate, Dominico feels that he could reassert his former popularity at the box office. The man is very keen to have us move, and I have informed him that the price for such a relocation on our part would be considerable. After all, Newton's Prefects are one of the oldest teams in Argentina, with years of tradition and all that nostalgic drivel. If the truth be known, I would be happy to leave that dilapidated bandbox of a stadium we call home. Velez Sarsfield is a magnificent facility, with a capacity three times our current venue!"

Another pause for the last few forkfuls to disappear.

"Señor Dominico is not party to these thoughts, however. Perhaps the transfer of Ramon Vida to Newton's Prefects, and thus under my control, would provide me with enough emotional comfort to allow me to part from the team's historic roots. Vida must still be convinced to go along with this plan, of course. He has no agent and makes all his monetary deals himself. That is good for us, for it means one less body to get in the way. In that regard, I know that one thing is for certain. If I am able to make arrangements with the Boca Football Club concerning Vida, and I present a proposition to both these players, they themselves will want to meet with you personally. The boys will certainly have questions, some of more relevance than others, which brings me to the topic of their remuneration."

A bowl of lemon ice to cleanse his considerable palate sat in front of the Buenos Aires lawyer. He pushed it aside, wanting instead to savor the symphony that had been played on his taste-buds. He called for the finest port in the house, as well as the humidor. Only Astor Gordero wrapped his lips around a sizable Havana cigar, the other gentlemen having declined the boxed gems.

"You see, perfect timing! It always seems to come down to money, doesn't it? Which is why I prefer to talk about money on a full stomach. Financial talk makes me famished, all those digits and numerals flying through the air." He smiled at his audience, pleased with his offhandedness. "Now, Lady Russell, I am sure that you and your father had a figure in mind when you opened these negotiations several days ago. I would be very interested in finding out what that sum amounts to."

The Fat Man's gaze bore down on the English Lady. She noticed an intensity in his stare that hadn't been evident before. There was a coldness, a tough sense of resolve that the word 'money' had draped over his false charm. This was serious business that they were down to now. There was no mistaking that fact for Mallory Russell after one look into the laser-like eyes of Astor Gordero.

"We were thinking in the range of two hundred thousand pounds sterling a year for each player, provided that they make the starting eleven, of course." Reginald Russell was sticking to their predetermined script of how the financial proceedings should commence.

"Not nearly enough!" the agent responded with a tone of dismissal. "I would be wasting my time trying to get either of those players to accept such an offer. Why, they could earn that sum right here in Argentina, without even leaving the capital city. After the fame that they have fashioned for themselves in this tournament, I expect that there will be others to follow in your footsteps." Gordero called for a new bowl of lemon ice, giving pause to let his words sink in.

"No, my newfound friends, you were smart enough to track me down in Rosario where your competition did not. Do not let your present advantage slide through your fingers. Once I depart for Buenos Aires in the morning, who knows what 'Angels of Destiny' will be awaiting my return, and with what kind of financial incentives to entice my client. No, I advise you to make your best deal right here, right now, or I am afraid we must terminate our discussions. There is much to do in the four days before Argentina becomes champion of the world, and I will not be distracted from that purpose."

Gordero motioned with a flick of his head that the meeting had drawn to a conclusion. He began to sway back and forth in his chair, as if to work up enough momentum to rise. Stoltz was at his side in the blink of an eye, the pen and pad dispatched to his inner jacket pocket.

"Señor Gordero, please, please, sit down!" Mallory Russell's pulse was racing. The thought of losing Renaldo De Seta was more troubling than she was willing to admit to anyone, except herself.

"Please, Señor, my father did not mean to be offensive or trite. Give us your figure. What would it take to deliver these players to the Canary Wharf Football Club?"

The rocking motion ceased. "Double your figure, and it's a deal. Two years guaranteed, no matter where they play. All visas, accommodations, motor vehicles, and sundries to be at the expense of Canary Wharf Football Club.

And, of course, admission into a medical school for the future Doctor De Seta. On the latter point, I will allow some 'poetic license' to be taken. All the other conditions must be met unequivocally. If you accept these terms, I will have the contracts drawn up and ready for signature in my office on the afternoon of June twenty-sixth. That is five days hence, and the day after Argentina wins the World Cup. I will guarantee delivery of those two players to the Canary Wharf Football Club under the said terms and conditions."

The lawyer leaned slightly forward and locked eyes with Mallory Russell.

"You see, dear Lady, while I am certain that I can 'facilitate' the delivery on my part, the consummation of this marriage now rests with you and your father. You have until I reach my limousine to give me your answer!"

Neither the chauffeur nor the finely turned out lady in the rear of the Rolls Royce noticed the man watching them depart Casa San Marco. The stranger stood concealed behind thick shrubbery on the opposite side of Calle Arenales from the only place he had ever known as 'home.' As soon as the car had disappeared from view, the scruffy looking drifter bounded across the street, threw open the wrought iron gate that Olarti had closed behind the vintage automobile, stepped up to the front door of the casa, and pressed a filthy finger to the buzzer.

He could hear Oli's footsteps on the ceramic tiles as she approached the entrance. She was uttering invectives in her native tongue, a trait that she practiced whenever her well-oiled routine was interrupted. The look of disgust on her face when she opened the small security portal and peered through told the visitor that his faithful servant and friend had not recognized him.

"Oli, it's me, Lonnie. Lonnie De Seta. Open the door!"

The servant remained steadfast, not moving a muscle. The puzzled expression on her face made it evident that she was trying to equate the man with the message.

"It's really me, Oli. Lonnie, you know, Renaldo's brother. Has he gotten so famous now that you have forgotten his older brother? Come on now, open up, or I will tickle you under your ribs until you cry for help. You couldn't have forgotten how I used to do that to you!"

"Lonnie, is that really you? My God, what have you been doing to yourself to arrive home in such a state?"

The small opening slammed shut, and there followed the sound of locks and bolts being released. The large metal door swung inwards on its hinges until it slammed against the inner wall. The tiny woman framed by the entranceway stood with her hands outstretched in welcome. Lonnie De Seta was home again, if only for a few precious minutes.

The native lady was full of questions about his health and well-being over the past few months. She commented on the pallid color of his skin, his weight loss, his filthy clothing, and his ridiculously short hair, all of this before they had reached the bottom of the staircase leading to Lonnie's bedroom.

"Celeste and I have been camping on the glaciers in Bariloche, Oli. We lost all our possessions during one particularly bad blizzard. I had to come home to pick up some fresh clothes and a few other things, for I am off on a boat cruise around Cape Horn in a day or two. There, are you satisfied? Now I am going up to take a shower and pack some clothes. Don't be scared, I know mother just left. I was watching from across the street. It has been such a long time since I have spoken to her. Does she ever mention my name, Oli?"

"No, Señor Lonnie, your mother is very busy with her new friends, particularly that German man. She seems quite sweet on him. She never talks of Renaldo either, if that makes you feel any better. She disapproves of his playing football and won't allow either of you to be discussed in the casa at all. But she is still your mother, and I know that in her heart, there will always be a tender place for you."

"I hope so, Oli, and I hope that one day I can make up for any pain I have caused her. But I am not in a position to patch things up today, and I don't want her to know that I was here. Is she gone for the day, or do you expect her home shortly?"

"She has a meeting with that famous lawyer, Astor Gordero, downtown at his office. I expect that she will be away several hours."

"Good, now maybe while I clean up, you could fix me some of your special eggs that were always my favorite. It has been a long journey home, and if you don't feed me, I will be forced to tickle you until you pass out!"

A tap on the fanny sent the woman on her way to the kitchen, then Lonnie strode up the grand marble steps to the upper level. He paused at his mother's bedroom door, something drawing him to turn the brass knob and enter.

A thousand memories cascaded over the fugitive as he inhaled the perfumed scent of Florencia's world. The room was exactly the same as he had remembered it ever since childhood. Rich burgundy and soft pink tones combined throughout the boudoir to offer a warm, inviting aura.

It all seemed so familiar. The times he had spent in that big bed when he was sick or frightened. The mahogany cabinet containing her precious Royal Doulton figurines. Florencia's crystal decanters in all shapes and sizes. The daily freshly cut flowers. The mirrored vanity with its sterling silver brushes, combs, and lady's knickknacks. Her large desk overlooking the front courtyard and gates of Casa San Marco. Everything in its place, just as he had remembered it.

He walked slowly to the desk and sat down in his mother's working chair. The room was like a museum to him now, full of precious artifacts and mementos of his once-pampered existence. Pictures of his father, his grandparents, and of his younger brother and himself in their adolescence. "So long ago, and so far, far, away," he muttered.

As he stood to leave these timeless surroundings, a goldleaf-embossed business card sitting on the edge of the desk caught his eye.

"Astor Armondo Luis Gordero. Barrister and Solicitor," read the bold script. The well-known lawyer had become very involved with his family's affairs since Lonnie's departure. He remembered reading in the newspapers about The Fat Man representing Renaldo's football interests, but he was unaware that his mother had been conducting business with the famous blowhard. He picked up the card, peered down at it for several moments, and then placed it in his wallet.

This man could be worth getting to know, Lonnie pondered solemnly. *Heaven knows, there is a very good chance that I will need a lawyer myself if things get out of hand. It might as well be a famous, well-connected attorney that already knows the De Seta family!*

He closed the door gently behind him as he exited into the hallway. *At least Mama's world has maintained its appearance of order and stability,* he reflected, *even if my world has collapsed around me.*

Lonnie's voyage to Casa San Marco this Friday, June the twenty-third, had been remarkably uneventful. The former terrorist had planned his escape from the Jimenez cottage down to the final detail, even allowing for the pounding hangover that he awoke to following his brother's two-goal performance against Peru. It had been very hospitable of Señor Jimenez to leave a fully stocked bar available to impromptu visitors such as himself. As a result, it was with great familial pride that Lonnie De Seta had imbibed almost a quart of the unknowing host's Chivas Regal Scotch in a tribute to his brother, Renaldo.

Nearly all of the private summer retreats in Tigre had an adjacent boat house down at the shoreline. A wide variety of nautical transportation such as sailboats, paddleboats, ski boats, and regular motor launches filled these lightly secured marine garages. Lonnie had been able to locate a suitable craft in which to navigate the Rio de la Plata downstream, under the cover of darkness.

The fugitive had always had a faculty for things mechanical, be it cars, motorbikes, or boat engines. He had discovered and made seaworthy one particular vessel during his nocturnal wanderings around the nearby Tigre estates.

There was no water in the bilge of the old Seabird cedar-strip launch that sat solemnly covered with bedsheets to keep bird droppings from ruining the varnished woodwork. The dry hold meant that she would not sink underneath him when they hit the first wave in the open water. The fuel gage registered three quarters full, and just for insurance, Lonnie took along several portable petrol cans that the old ark's captain kept in the shed for emergencies. The key to his successful escape sat trustingly in the ignition of his maritime accomplice, and it had been necessary to crank the engine over only a few revs to determine it was in working order.

These unknown part-time residents of Tigre had been very gracious to the stranger who was running for his life. Thanks to their foresight in leaving accessible everything Lonnie needed to survive, the much sought-after murderer was able to drift silently from his moorings and strike a course away from this deadly town. Using only the moonlight to guide him, he arrived well before sunrise at the long wharf of the Fisherman's Club in the northeastern suburbs of the capital. He was just a few miles from his home in Palermo when he abandoned his vessel and struck out overland on foot.

Lonnie lingered in the steaming shower for what seemed like hours. It was his first really thorough cleansing in months, and he had forgotten how good it felt. It was only Oli's summoning to the spread she had brought to his bedroom that lured him away from his watery pleasures. She was gone by the time he set foot in the bedroom proper, but the savory aroma emanating from the tray she had placed on his old desk reminded him of all the hearty, mouthwatering feasts she had turned out over the years.

His wardrobe held a special excitement, and yet, a certain amount of anxiety as well. After living in rags and tatters of late, the Gucci blazers and slacks, the custom-made silk shirts from Sulka, and the Feragamo shoes all seemed so incongruous. He had been transformed from the 'Ralph Lauren' playboy to the 'Charles Manson' murderer in a matter of months. How could he have been so stupid?

The drifter had precious little time to ruminate on the answer to his own question. It was Friday, which meant that he had only a few hours left to make it to the Banco Rio de la Plata in order to collect his passport, credit cards, and a mountain of cash, American dollars preferably. With all the foreigners in the capital for the weekend football festivities, the lineups could be horrendous. The banks were also known to run out of U.S. currency, even on a normal business day.

Lonnie knew that the expedition was fraught with danger. The bank could very well be under surveillance by any number of enemies. Although Lonnie De Seta's name had never been mentioned in the media in connection with a misdemeanor of any kind, one fact remained paramount. Someone was tracking him with 'malicious intent.' Lonnie remembered that stupid textbook term from one of his university law courses. "Bullshit!" he cried aloud in torment as he beheld his lost universe for the last time. Somebody was trying to fucking kill him, and he didn't know who or why.

Celeste's killers were not from the police or regular militia hunting the 'Attractive Assassin.' The men at No Se Preocupe were true assassins. Professionals! The police would have telegraphed their arrival in the silent Tigre night long before they reached the camp gates. Lonnie was outside, enjoying the beautiful night while keeping watch and listening on the dock. He had heard nothing until the sledgehammer fell!

With the exception of his roughly cropped hairstyle, Lonnie De Seta looked, for all the world, like a successful business executive in his blue silk double-breasted suit and Newton's alumni tie. A jaunty straw fedora solved the coiffure problem, and a pair of dark sunglasses further shielded his true identity. He had thrown an assortment of clothes and keepsakes in a folding leather club bag, then slowly made the heartbreaking walk to the main floor entrance foyer. His eyes darted everywhere as he moved, searching, reflecting, inspecting, remembering.

"Good-bye, dear Oli. I will miss you more than you will ever know. Now, make sure there is not a word of this visit to my mother, or I will be forced to break my vacation short and arrive unannounced again to tickle you for your indiscretions."

He bent forward from the waist and kissed the native woman on her cheek. In all the years of their friendship, it was the one act of affection that he had never thought of committing. The fugitive's eyes welled with tears behind his dark glasses as he turned and left the shocked lady muttering his name in the doorway.

It was an easy walk from Lonnie's home to the Banco Rio de la Plata on Avenido San Martin. He had devised a scheme in his solitary hours in Tigre that would allow him to circumvent the long queues at the teller's wickets and keep his public exposure to a minimum. That scheme was called Marla Gallego.

Señorita Gallego was an assistant to branch manager Anthony Rodrigue's personal secretary. She was a nicely wrapped package that Señor Rodrigues did not mind staring at through his office window. As a matter of fact, the top executive had reorganized his outer office in order to afford himself a better view of the young lady's long, velvety gams and tight curves.

Marla Gallego was as friendly as she was erotically stimulating. She would always strike up conversations with the bank clients waiting close to her desk for their turn to pay homage to the boss. One of those conversations with Lonnie De Seta culminated in the best fuck she had ever experienced. They had dated a few times, but Lonnie was too wild, and ultimately too moody for the marriage-minded Marla. That did not stop her from often fantasizing about their unions as she sat working at her desk near the marble-topped service counter.

"Marla! Marla, can I talk with you for a moment?" The pretty clerk looked up from her ledger at the stranger who was softly calling her name. She had no idea who was hiding under the fedora and glasses.

"Marla, come here for a second. I have to talk to you." The customer was now motioning with his hand for her to approach the counter.

Who is this man that knows my name? I don't recall him at all! she pondered.

More out of curiosity than courtesy, Marla finally gave in to the persistence of her admirer. Even as they stood face-to-face over the counter, there was no flash of recognition in her sweet mind.

"Marla, it's me, Lonnie De Seta. How have you been? You look good enough to eat!" The customer removed his dark glasses and doffed his hat momentarily while making his introduction. He was totally unprepared for the look of shock and horror that greeted the announcing of his name.

Marla's eyes almost fell out of their sockets, and she backed up several steps until she was flush against her desk. The sexy stenographer glanced around the immediate area to make sure that no one was watching, then stepped cautiously back to the counter. Her voice was barely a whisper when she finally spoke.

"Lonnie, are you in trouble? There are men here looking for you. They are not bank people. They have guns under their jackets! We have all been told to notify them if you or anyone else tries to make a transaction on your accounts. They have been here waiting for you for several weeks. I don't like them. They are rude and ignorant scum. What is going on, Lonnie? We have only been told that you may have been kidnapped, and that if you came here it would be to collect ransom money against your will. They have told us that the men with guns are here to protect you from your kidnappers. The longer those two swine are around here, the less I believe that story. Tell me quickly now, before they notice us!"

Lonnie De Seta had to grasp the bevelled edge of the counter for support. He had walked into the lion's den unprepared to tame the wild beasts. He just wanted a few simple items, one small transaction, that was it. His knees buckled and the remaining color drained from his face as Marla's words registered.

"Marla, you must help me! I am not being held hostage by anyone, but there are people who are after me. Those two thugs you speak of must be working for the people that want me dead. Marla, you must trust me now, and do as I ask."

He reached into his jacket pocket and removed his wallet. The safety deposit box key was then placed between them. Lonnie took a deposit slip and pen from the adjacent reservoir and scribbled several numerals. He then tore the piece of paper in two.

"Here is the key to my safeety box. I have written its number on the deposit slip. Write down your home phone number for me on this other half. When you have the chance, go and empty the contents of my box and take them home with you. I will call you tonight and make arrangements to pick them up. Please, Marla, I am desperate! I have also written a check on my account for some money. Take it, and try to get me whatever you can!"

"Lonnie, I can't access your account. It has been frozen by the computers. I can lend you a bit of money from my own account, but it will be nowhere near the sum of this check. As for the deposit box, I need your signature to . . ."

Marla's voice trailed off as her eyes focused on a figure approaching from across the employee's concourse.

"Lonnie you must get out of here now. One of those men is coming this way. Here, this is my number. Call me tonight. I will see what I can do. Now, go!"

She spun around quickly clutching the key and the piece of paper in her small fist. Marla Gallego was seated and pouring over her ledgers by the time the shadow of Astor Gordero's operative fell across her desk.

Lonnie De Seta had reacted with equal stealth, mostly due to the enormous amount of nervous adrenaline that was pounding through his veins. He moved swiftly, but he was cautious not to attract undue attention. He allowed himself one final glance back at Marla just as he was about to push the revolving door and make his exit.

The young girl was visibly upset, and in that split second, his eyes met those of the phony bank employee. The man shouted for his partner and reached underneath his jacket to reveal the butt of an oversized handgun.

The wanted man was through the door and down the steps of the Banco Rio de la Plata in a heartbeat. He barely felt the weight of his suitcase as he searched desperately for a means of escape. There was only one obvious choice.

It was fortunate for Lonnie De Seta that Avenido San Martin was a prosperous commercial street. It was also fortunate that due to the heavy demands placed on city's banks during World Cup Tournament, there was always a profusion of yellow and black taxis adjacent to these institutions. It was into the rear seat of one of these vehicles-for-hire that the desperado flung himself.

"Hurry, I have a train to catch. Constitution Station, pronto!"

As the cabby wheeled from the curb, he took a good look at his passenger in the rearview mirror.

"Hey, you're not some kind of bank robber or something are you? I saw you come down those steps in a real hurry. I don't want any trouble or anything."

"Relax, my friend, I'm not going to hurt you. Just drive quickly!" Lonnie's hand gripped the handle of the Llama pistol that protruded from his waistband under his suit-jacket.

"I had the misfortune of running into my lover's husband in the bank queue. It became a rather messy scene. He threatened to rearrange my anatomy right then and there, so I decided that discretion was the better part of valor, and I beat it! Now drive, amigo, for I must get out of the city for an extended vacation. The man is a monster!"

The lusty smile that greeted the tall tale reassured Lonnie that the cabbie was no longer a threat. He turned around to glance out the rear window.

"Don't worry, Señor. No one will catch us. I drive like a Formula One champion! Sit back, relax. I will take care of you."

What Lonnie De Seta needed now was to disappear and rethink his course of action. Everything rode on Marla being able to access his safety deposit box. It would be several hours before she arrived home from the bank, and he needed to formulate a contingency plan. The situation had gone from bad to worse, and if things continued to unravel, there were very few people left that could lend a helping hand.

Surrender was not even a consideration, for the stories of the barbaric treatment of prisoners emanating from such places as Olimpo Prison made it a moot point. He had to carefully plan his next move. It would have to be a plan he could use if the sexy little bank employee came home empty-handed.

Constitution Station serviced the southern routes to and from the capital city, and on this day in particular, the mammoth structure filled Lonnie's needs perfectly. Both the approaches and the passenger concourse were teeming with newly arrived football fanatics and weekend revellers, all in a party mood.

The atmosphere had a distinct Brazilian flavor about it, for thousands of the samba men's devotees had made the trip north from their headquarters at Mar del Plata. They were arriving en mass to spur their heroes on to victory in Saturday's third-place battle against Italy. It was as if an impromptu carnival had erupted, and each successive trainload of visitors added to the frivolous mood of merriment. The drums, the whistles, the music. The samba beat had reached the capital city for the first time in the tournament.

The man running for his life lurked in the shadows of the taxi's backseat. He kept a sharp eye on both the crowd and the cab's meter. It soon became evident that their progress would be slowed to a crawl by the surging throng that spilled out onto the main thoroughfares surrounding the station.

His freedom flight had been expensive. The fare of almost eight thousand pesos, or ten American dollars, virtually cleaned out all his financial reserves. He pondered the possibility of bolting from the crawling vehicle and dissolving into the crowd.

Lonnie knew that he would be slowed by the bulky club bag, and the last thing he needed was the notoriety of some irate cabbie screaming at the bystanders that he had been robbed or cheated. No, he was painfully aware that the only option here was the straight and narrow. He had enough money left to make a few phone calls and maybe buy a cup of coffee, that was it!

"Look at those stupid assholes!" the cabbie shook his head in disgust. "What the fuck do they have to celebrate? You would think that they were in the championship final the way they are carrying on. Go home! Go back to where you came from, you bunch of banana eaters!"

He was leaning out his driver's door window screaming at the bemused party makers. Lonnie threw a handful of peso notes into the front seat, slid quietly out the rear passenger-side door onto the sidewalk, and disappeared into the samba line. The loudmouth driver was now involved in a heated discussion with several men dressed in yellow Brazilian football jerseys, and the last thing that the hunted man needed was to become involved in an altercation.

The journey into the terminal proper was circuitous and boisterous to say the least. Lonnie didn't feel like dancing, but one glimpse of the olive green militia uniforms that ringed the party scene convinced him that the snaking samba line offered the anonymity he needed. The suitcase was a nuisance, but finally after about ten minutes of rhythmic shuffling, he walked through the open air portal and into the darkness of Constitution Station.

The national security forces were highly visible that weekend. Wherever there was a chance of large groups of people congregating, the men in uniform made their presence known. Police with dogs, mounted units on horseback dressed in full riot gear, armored vehicles with their terrifying water canons, and of course, scores of foot soldiers were all in attendance. As if that were not sufficient, busloads of reserves were parked on quiet side streets in strategic locations. The tournament had come off without any terrorist incidents thus far, and both the governing junta and the common people of Argentina were, for once, in agreement. A strong show of military muscle and an obvious preparedness to defuse any ticklish situations were the best deterrents. No one wanted it to rain on this parade!

Lonnie's heart was pounding heavily as he finally managed to locate a remote waiting area and plunk himself down on an empty wooden bench. He was drenched in perspiration from his impromptu samba lesson. A discarded newspaper became his shield from curious eyes as he opened it studiously and pretended to pour over its pages. His eyes were unable to focus on any but the largest headlines, however, for the thoughts racing through his mind dealt only with his own survival.

It was over one half hour before he dared to lower his pulp protector and scan the area for any overt interest in his being. Much to his relief, the festivities taking place outside in the open air were much more interesting than the now rumpled transient. No one gave the 'Attractive Assassin' a second glance.

By five-thirty in the afternoon, he got up enough nerve to try Marla's home phone number. The banks closed at four o'clock, so there was a chance that she might have had enough time to make it to her flat, which was not a great distance from the Banco Rio de la Plata. He knew that on Fridays, the employees seldom left the branch before six o'clock, but he was so bored, he figured that he had nothing to lose. To his amazement, his former lover answered the phone after just one ring.

"Hello, Marla, it's Lonnie. How are things? Are you alright?" There was dead silence on the end of the receiver.

"Marla, are you there? Can you hear me? It's Lonnie. I've been waiting for . . ."

"Lonnie, I can hear you, although the sound of your voice is like a nightmare to me. I am so confused and frightened." Her voice was a tearful whisper, barely audible over the stacic-riddled phone lines.

"Marla, were you able to get into my safety-deposit box? What did that man say to you after I left? How about the cash? Were you . . .?"

"Lonnie, listen to me. I don't know what kind of trouble you are in, but why did you have to involve me in your deceptions? I haven't seen or talked to you in over a year, then suddenly you turn up out of the blue one day and all hell breaks loose." Lonnie could sense the fear in her voice turning to anger. "I don't have anything for you tonight, and I won't be able to help you, ever! That agent wanted to know who the man was that I had been talking to. He said that he had never seen you before in the branch. The bank has surveillance cameras everywhere, especially in the vaults where the safety-deposit boxes are located. One of the men works the floor of the bank, the other one is in a back room monitoring the cameras. If I ever set foot in that area after today, they would know I was your accomplice. Frankly, Lonnie, you are not worth the risk to me!" She was talking so quickly now that she had to stop to catch her breath.

"Don't be frightened, Marla, just tell me what happened."

"Don't be frightened? Fuck you, Lonnie! They pulled me into Señor Rodrigue's office for over an hour and treated me like I was dirt! I won't be subjected to that kind of filthy language and lewd behavior for you or anyone else! Those men are the scum of the earth."

"I am sorry, Marla, really I am. You just don't know what I have been through the last few weeks. It is totally beyond comprehension. I will try to make it up to you one day, believe me, but for now, I have to know what you told them about me."

"I told them nothing about you. I said that the man was an old boyfriend who was still in love with me. I told them that we had broken up a few months ago, but now he had shown up out of nowhere to see if he could win me back with two tickets to the World Cup championship game on Sunday. I even made up some phony name to cover for you, Lonnie." She was crying now, more out of rage than self-pity.

"Do you think that they believed you, Marla? Is there any chance that they might find out that you were lying to them? What about the key and the piece of paper?"

"They didn't find them. I stuffed them inside one of the ledgers that I was working on as soon as I sat down. I was able to put them into my purse before I left the branch. I have them here with me now. I don't know if they believed me. They made me leave the bank right after the interrogation. Señor Rodrigues told me that they were going to review the surveillance videotape, and if they found any irregularities in my story, that, that I would be fired! Fired, Lonnie, goddamn it! I love my job, you know that. How could you ask me to put my whole life on the line for you?"

The fugitive had to be careful, for this girl was one of only a handful of people that he could count on now. He could not risk losing her friendship at this critical point in time.

"Marla, I swear that one day, I will make amends for all the turmoil I have caused you today, but as I told you, those people want me dead. They are probably watching my home, so I can't risk going there. I have no money or credit cards, and no place to hide. Could you find it in your heart to let me spend the night with you tonight?"

Her voice was cool, and the message not what he had expected from her.

"I'm leaving town in an hour for the weekend, Lonnie. I have a new man in my life, an investment banker who wants me to marry him. He happens to hate football and all the commotion that it has caused in the city, so he is taking me to San Roque Lake near Córdoba. I will not miss the insanity that has infested Buenos Aires one bit. I am sorry."

Lonnie felt his heart sink with disappointment and unspent lust. He had hoped that her tender charms and four secure walls would shelter him from the gathering storm for a few days. There was no chance of that scenario taking place now, but he had one last question and nothing to lose by asking it.

"Marla, I am up against a brick wall, and I can see the firing squad taking aim at me. Could I, as a favor to an old friend and lover . . . could I stay in your flat for a night or two? I promise you that I will leave on Sunday before you arrive home, and you will never have to see me or talk to me again. I promise you that on my father's grave!"

It was Lonnie who was in tears now, and he felt that he would break down totally if his lost love turned him down.

"Marla, I have no money, and there isn't a vacant room or an empty bed within two hundred miles of here. The football has seen to that. Marla, I beg you. Do this one thing for me, and one day, I will be able to repay you beyond your wildest dreams. You know me, Marla. You know my family and the assets behind us. I have made some bad mistakes lately, but when everything is settle, I will not forget you. On that I give you my solemn oath. My life is in your hands!"

There was silence on the line for the longest time. Finally, "You bastard, Lonnie. I don't want your gratitude or your money. I just want to be left alone. Two nights, that is all. If I arrive home Sunday and you are still here, the police will evict you. I will make certain of that myself. One more thing. Do not come to the bank again with the intention of talking to me, for I will ignore you or turn you over to those two baboons. I don't want you to try to contact me from this moment on. I give you these two nights because of what we once shared, Lonnie, but the slate is wiped clean as of Sunday. Forever! My key will be under the doormat, and your security box key I will leave beside the telephone. Understand me now, Lonnie. I will be gone by eight, so do not arrive until after nine o'clock. I can't afford a run-in or any questions from the man I am going away with. Leave the key where you found it when you go. Good-bye, Lonnie. I never want to hear from you again. Is that clear?"

The line went dead before he could utter his appreciation. Lonnie put down the receiver and shuffled almost trance-like back to his bench. He tried to look on the bright side of his dilemma, namely that if he could make it to Marla's flat, then he would be able buy a bit more time to work out his next move. He looked forlornly into his naked wallet. The emptiness of the leather billfold reaffirmed to the reluctant wanderer that time was about all that he could afford in his present state.

The 'Attractive Assassin' had no alternative but to strike out for Señorita Gallego's sanctuary on foot. When they were lovers, he had spent several nights in her lower level love-nest on Calle Viamonte. He knew it well, and he also knew that it would take the better part of the three hours he had to kill to make his way there.

He cursed the overstuffed club bag that was weighing him down and making his progress even slower. The streets overflowed with tourists and Porteños alike. The end of the working week always turned the streets of the capital into a vast parking lot, but the scene that Lonnie was witnessing was unlike any Friday rush hour he had ever experienced.

Carloads of Brazilians, Italians, Dutch, and especially Argentines blasted their horns in a symphony of patriotic noise. Men and women protruded through the automobile windows or sat atop their roofs, many with their faces painted in their national colors, flags waving to and fro.

All of this made it very easy for Lonnie De Seta to remain in the background of this strange ritual as he followed the route to Marla's flat. As dusk fell, the revelry grew in tempo and enthusiasm, fuelled by the large amount of liquor that was being consumed at every jam-packed bar and cantina Lonnie passed. It was close to ten o'clock by the time he finally stood in front of Marla Gallego's door. He was bone-tired, not having slept at all the night before during his boat ride from Tigre. The key was exactly where she told him it would be, for which he was greatly relieved. There had always been the possibility that she could have changed her mind and decided to be done with Lonnie sooner than later. Not leaving the key as promised would have taken care of that.

He stood inside the entrance of the tiny two-room flat. Everything was very much as he had remembered, although on several of his visits, he had been well into his cups and wanted to get down to business directly. Lavender and lace was the predominant theme, and he felt rather silly standing all alone in the midst of Marla's feminine world. It was, nevertheless, a safe world for the time being, and for that, he was exultantly thankful.

The weekend guest checked the refrigerator and found it only minimally stocked. He was not hungry at all, Oli's morning feast having sated his hunger pangs completely. The bar was the next object of his attention, and he found that there were enough spirits to keep himself tipsy for the entire duration of his stay, if he chose to do so.

It was obvious by the brands of liquor that the young lady kept in her abode that she entertained her new gentleman friend on the premises, just as she had entertained Lonnie. The investment banker must have been a Scotch drinker, he observed, which proved that the two men had more in common than just the horny little bank strumpet. He poured himself a hefty tumbler of Johnny Walker Black Label, then collapsed on Marla's soft double bed.

The Scotch had a soothing effect on the visitor as its warm glow spread through his body with every sip. Within five minutes, he was up for a refill, but this time, he brought the bottle back to the night table with him. He would worry about his future plans in the morning, but right now, all he wanted was to dull his senses enough to fall into a dreamless sleep. He conjured up memories of the passion that he and Marla had expended on this very bed, and he was saddened that he would never again taste the fruits of her bounty. He wondered if he would ever have the opportunity to taste those fruits with anyone. How his life had changed, and changed for the absolute worst.

"Fool!" was the last word he mumbled as sleep finally enveloped his clouded mind.

He awoke after noon the next day, Saturday, June the twenty-fourth. The Scotch had produced the desired effect, for he had slept like a dead man. His head was clear, however, and he lay on his back for a considerable time trying to analyze his options and formulate the next move.

Strangely, he kept visualizing his younger brother's face. Despite the terrorist's tenuous situation, all he could focus on was Renaldo. Tomorrow, the kid would be playing for his country in front of millions of spectators and television viewers. The enormity of that one fact dwarfed all of Lonnie's current problems.

How he would love to be there! To lead the trilled roar that had been customized to fit Renaldo's name. To see him hold the championship trophy aloft. That was his younger brother's reality. His own was much bleaker.

There was no money left to purchase a ticket to the match, even from a scalper. Unless he could steal one or rob a ticket holder at gunpoint, there was no way in the world that he would be able to witness his sibling's heroics in person. The truth of this dilemma forced Lonnie's thoughts to reluctantly drift back to the Banco Rio de la Plata.

He could not attempt another trip to the bank until Monday, and that trip could very well be the most dangerous and deadly transaction he had ever made. One certainty was that he would have to bypass the unstable Señorita Gallego and go directly to the vault custodian.

Lonnie had seen in a movie once where a bank robber wrapped his throat in gauze bandages and pretended that he was unable to speak due to a recent operation. All communication was done by written notes. The former Palermo playboy had to hope that whoever he was dealing with at that time would accept the box key and his scribbled instructions with signature as sufficient identification for access. This would be the initial plan, but he was by no means certain his act would work. An attempt had to be made though, for without funds, he could do nothing.

The Llama pistol would be tucked into his waistband for insurance. At the first sign of trouble, his simple request would evolve into an impromptu robbery to finance his escape. If that alternative disintegrated, then either the Llama or his cyanide pill would end everything. Those were his only options!

Still, there was Renaldo. How proud Lonnie was of him! He wished with all his heart that he could have been with him these last weeks, to help him, to support him as a brother. The boy had grown to manhood in the few months that they had been separated, and Lonnie had been forced to read about it in newspapers, not experience it firsthand.

His brother, the player, seemed untouched by the tremendous publicity that the idolizing press had laid at his feet. There had been no personal interviews. Octavio Suarez was the only person that spoke to the press directly, but all the articles and stories praised Renaldo's youthful enthusiasm, his natural talent, his stamina, and the ability to play, even when injured and of course, his beautiful maleness.

It was said that truckloads of fan mail addressed simply to 'Renaldo' arrived at the team's compound in Rosario daily. Again, Suarez interceded and refused to let the players be diverted from their purpose by such trivialities. After the tournament, there would be plenty of time to deal with the requests for autographs, pictures, sexual liaisons, and marriage. It was also said that the young center half could open his own lingerie boutique with all the ladies' undergarments that had been shipped to him in perfumed envelopes. All fan letters were screened electronically by x-ray as a security precaution, so it was very likely that the rumors were true about the 'gifts' sent to young Señor De Seta. All correspondence was packed away in a warehouse until after the championship final, but Lonnie smiled to himself at the thought of how embarrassed the kid would be with each package he opened. *Oh, to be a star!*

Hunger finally got the best of the weekender, and he rose from his deliberations to see if this pension provided breakfast with the bed. There was coffee, a bit of bread on the verge of outright staleness, and some extremely ripe fruit, enough to stop the rumbling down below for a while. There were also some canned meats and soups that would provide the evening feast.

Not too bad, not five-star fare, but passable terrorist provisions.

There was some time to kill before the day's premier entertainment event commenced. Lonnie didn't really care who won the third-place match kicking off at three p.m., but other than television, there was nothing to occupy his mind. The soccer game would provide a temporary diversion from his dilemma, so he tried to get excited about it. Besides, there might be an update or feature on the Argentine National Team, maybe even something on 'the kid.'

On one of his tours around the flat, he noticed his safety deposit key beside the telephone. He retrieved his wallet from the suit jacket that he had worn the day before and went to replace the 'key to his future' in its lonely confines. The white business card caught his eye.

"Astor Armondo Luis Gordero, Barrister and Solicitor." *Astor Gordero?* It was as if he had been struck by lightning. He was holding the business card of his younger brother's agent. A man said to have deep inroads into the inner workings of the Argentine National Team. If anyone could pull some strings and get the fugitive a ticket, that person was Astor Gordero!

Lonnie stared at the gold script. What were the risks of placing a call to the famous lawyer? Gordero was involved in some way with his mother, he knew that much from Oli. What were the odds that he could connect Renaldo's brother to any of his past terrorist crimes? Lonnie and his girlfriend were camping in the south after being banished by Florencia De Seta. That was the accepted story. If Gordero believed that, a request from Lonnie to see his brother play in the World Cup final might not arouse any suspicion at all. He had to be there to see Renaldo! He picked up the receiver and dialed the numbers on the card.

Might as well get to know this man sooner than later. He might end up handling my estate matters if things go badly. Lonnie smiled at his macabre sense of humor as he waited for some response on the other end of the line. Being Saturday, he knew that the chances of reaching Gordero were slim at best, but he had nothing to lose in trying.

"A.R. Gordero and Sons. How may I help you?" the voice crackled in his ear.

"Astor Gordero, if you please."

"Señor Gordero is not working today. This is his answering service. If you would like to leave a message, he will be in the office on Monday." Lonnie's heart sank.

"Is there no way of contacting Señor Gordero before Monday? There is some urgency to the matter I wish to discuss with him."

"Are you a client of Señor Gordero's?" the voice shot back, now slightly impatient.

"No, no I am not a client personally, but my brother is a famous client of Señor Gordero. Renaldo De Seta, the football player. And my mother does business with the Señor as well. It is really important that I reach him as soon as possible. Is there anything that you can do for me?"

"I am sorry, sir. If you were a client yourself, you would have Señor Gordero's private number, but I am under strict instructions not to give that number to the public."

"I am not the fucking public, you puta. I am Renaldo De Seta's brother. Thank you for all your help and please go to Hell at your earliest convenience!" Lonnie slammed the black receiver down, shaking with frustration.

"Goddamned slut! Who does she think . . ." He looked at the reverse side of the business card as he flipped it onto the nightstand. There was a second set of numbers written in ink.

"Son of a bitch!" His fingers dialed the number. The connection was crystal clear this time.

"Astor Gordero." The voice stunned Lonnie. He had never expected to actually be able to talk to the attorney in person. Now, he was mute with awe and trepidation.

"Astor Gordero! Is anyone there? Who is this? Please speak up. We must have a bad line." Lonnie took a deep breath and plunged in with both feet.

"Señor Gordero, it is a great honor to actually reach you. This is Lonnie De Seta speaking, Renaldo's older brother. I believe you have met my mother as well."

There was complete silence on the other end of the phone. At least ten seconds passed. It seemed like an eternity to Lonnie. He repeated his introduction before the older man could speak.

"I said, Señor, this is Lon . . ."

"Lonnie De Seta. Yes, yes, I heard you, my boy. This is a surprise!"

The Fat Man was frantically signaling Wolfgang Stoltz to tape record the conversation on the in-house wire tap and also to make sure that the line in was being traced.

"So, Lonnie, I've been expecting a call from you for weeks. Renaldo told me that you had promised to be back for the tournament if he made the starting roster. Quite frankly, I think your brother is disappointed that he hasn't heard from you. Where are you now, and what can I do for you?"

The solicitor looked over at his assistant, who held up his thumb and index finger in a circle to indicate that everything was in order.

"I am back in the capital, Señor Gordero, but in a rather sad state of affairs. I have been camping on the glaciers down in Bariloche with my girlfriend. The weather turned nasty, and we lost everything in a blizzard. Food, clothes, personal items, even my wallet. In truth, I am lucky to be alive. My girlfriend is at the hospital in Bariloche with fractured ribs and other injuries. She is going to be alright, but I had to come home to get money and clothing for us both. My arrival just happened to coincide with the World Cup final."

Lonnie took another deep breath and kept going. "I suppose you know why I am calling you this afternoon, and you must forgive my bluntness, but it would mean the world to me to be able to see Renaldo play tomorrow. Is there any way that you could secure me a ticket, Señor? I would be indebted to you for the rest of my life if you could achieve such a miracle."

There was a slight chuckle at the other end of the receiver.

"Lonnie, Lonnie, I have been known in the past as a miracle worker of some proportion, but this! This is something I fear the Savior himself would have trouble accomplishing. However, seeing as you are my star client's only brother, let me see what rabbits I can pull out of my hat. It will take some time to arrange things though. I won't have an answer for you until tonight. Where can you be reached? Do you have a number?"

Lonnie blurted out the number of Marla's personal line. The powerful Gordero had been cordial and sympathetic to Lonnie's initial request, so the bandit decided to go for broke and rub the genie's lamp twice more.

"With respect, Señor, I have no money to pay for a ticket if your search is successful. You see, as I said my wallet was lost in the storm and I arrived home after the banks closed last night. I am not staying at my mother's house, for we have had a strained relationship the last few months. Would it . . . do you think it would be possible to borrow a few thousand pesos until Monday when my bank opens? Then I will pay you for the ticket and the loan, with interest!"

"Well, let me see what I can do, Lonnie. I think there might be some loose change sitting around the office here. Don't worry, money can be taken care of. The ticket is the hard item to secure. It will be like finding a needle in a hay stack!" Again, The Fat Man's self-amused laugh filled the line.

"One last request, Señor, if you don't mind. Would it be possible for me to call Renaldo? To tell him I am in town, and that I am trying obtain a ticket to see him play? Could I please get his number at the training facility?"

The voice that answered the final question was totally different from the one he had previously heard. It had a hard edge, a certain authoritarian finality to its uttered reply.

"That is out of the question! Your brother has only one thing that he needs to think about, and you know very well what that is. I will not tolerate any interference or distractions as to our ultimate goal. After Renaldo is a World Champion, then and only then will you be able to congratulate him. I will contact you when I have word on the availability of a ticket. Stay right where you are, for I will only try to contact you once. Good-bye until then."

The abruptness of the termination startled Lonnie. It had been like talking to two different people. He supposed that the ability to change moods and personalities was an asset to a great theatrical litigator such as Astor Gordero. He had just been given a tutorial in the Dr. Jekyll and Mr. Hyde School of legal linguistics.

The fact that he now stood an infinitely better chance of seeing his little brother play the following afternoon was enough of a boost to displace the bad taste that the curt conclusion to their chat had left. What was more, his wallet might just be chock full of pesos if 'The Generous One' took pity on the poor, displaced camper.

Two out of three requests isn't bad for a complete stranger. Isn't bad at all!

Lonnie smiled with satisfaction as he poured some Scotch into the tumbler and made himself comfortable for viewing the Brazil-Italy pregame festivities.

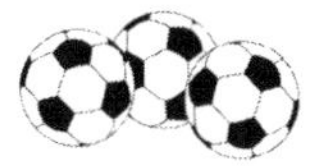

"My God, Wolfie, do you believe that? It is another sign, an omen boding well for us, and hopefully for all of Argentina. The planets are definitely aligned. I have been searching for that man for months, and he suddenly places himself in the palm of my hand. What more could I ask for?" Astor Gordero beamed with his good fortune.

"A victory against Holland tomorrow, of course!" was Stoltz's reply. "But it has been an incredible run of good fortune since we arrived home from Rosario," the German continued. "First, the flaccid English bow to your nonnegotiable terms regarding the two players."

"Then that mobster Dominico cedes his rights to Ramon Vida and signs over his transfer papers. You should have heard him squeal, Wolfie, just like the swine he is. He said that I was robbing him of his future superstar. I told him he will make so much money once Newton's relocates that he can buy the boy back in two years. He is lucky that I did not ask for more!"

Gordero was, of course, talking about the Boca Juniors situation and the dealing required to obtain the personal services of their star center forward. The Fat Man continued his discourse revealing more good news.

"Then, after two days of your adept romantic persuasion, Florencia De Seta arrives in this office to inform us that she is prepared to take her mother-in-law Lydia to court over control of the De Seta empire. She also states that such action will very likely be unnecessary, for the old woman has been bedridden of late with a serious undiagnosed malady!"

Mock concern shrouded the solicitor's face. "The Señora's daughter-in-law has been alerted by the staff in Pergamino that the situation is so grave that it might be necessary to fly the matriarch back to the capital to be hospitalized."

"The wrinkled old bitch won't live to see Buenos Aires again. Good riddance!" was Stoltz's caustic comment.

"But, Wolfie, the most touching moment of all was when Florencia informed me that you had personally convinced her to allow Renaldo to travel to England. When she said that, she realized she could not control his life anymore, and that as long as he was enrolled in a medical school while he played football, she would give the boy her blessing. That she now wanted to concentrate all her attentions on the control of the family business, counting heavily on your personal stewardship to guide her. My, my, you do work wonders with that magic wand of yours!" Gordero's belly shook from a bout of hearty laughter.

"I accept the compliment, Herr Chairman, for you know how much I enjoy my work." Stoltz had that mischievous grin of total satisfaction about him. "Now, what are we going to do about Lonfranco?"

The phone rang at that instant. Stoltz picked up the receiver, listened intently, then wrote down something on his notepad.

"That was the tracer. The call came from this address on Calle Viamonte. We have him!" He tore the piece of paper from the spiral binding and handed it to his employer.

"Good, very good! It is all working out so perfectly. With Lonnie and Lydia disposed of, Renaldo halfway around the world, and Florencia under your spell, we will have everything we wanted. Control of perhaps the largest private family fortune in Argentina."

The Fat Man rested his entwined hands on the crest of his ample belly.

"That tape of my conversation with Lonnie must be destroyed immediately. There can no link between us and him. Look after that right away."

"Of course. Anything else?" Stoltz stood ready with pen and pad.

"I feel generous, things are going so well! Poor Lonnie is out of money, nowhere to run and hide, his life on the line at every turn. And yet, all he wants to do is to see his brother play tomorrow. Of course we could hit him right now. He would never know what happened. But I think in light of the circumstances, we could give the terrorist a twenty-four-hour reprieve, don't you? Let him see his brother holding the World Cup trophy. Share in the triumph all Argentines have been waiting for. When that has been done, it can be good-bye forever." Gordero held up his right hand with his thumb and forefinger in the shape of a pistol, placed it against his temple, and dropped the thumb imitating the weapon's hammer.

"Boom. One less De Seta to concern ourselves with. Let's give Lonnie the satisfaction of meeting his maker after seeing his little brother play for the World Championship. It is the charitable thing to do. So, get me Rojo Geary on the red line and look after those tape recordings. My, how all this good news makes me hungry. Give me five minutes to talk to Geary, then send in Simone."

"Lonnie?" The blunt voice was all business. There was a pregnant silence on the other end of the line. Finally,

"Yes, it is me."

"You are a very lucky young man! I hope that your brother is equally as lucky tomorrow. I have secured you a press pass as a photographer. It will take a bit of play acting on your part, but my man will be with you to provide the essentials. You will be permitted on the field, behind the barriers at one end. Now listen carefully. Do you know the Café El Molino on Avenida Libertador? I think it will be as close to the stadium as the security forces will allow you to go without a ticket or a pass. My man will be outside the front door of the café at one o'clock. He will be wearing a black leather jacket with a Newton's Prefect crest on the front. You can't mistake this man. He has bright red hair. His name is Oswaldo, and he will stay with you for the afternoon. Oh, yes, he will also have an envelope full of currency. I am sure that you will find the amount to your liking. Do not be late, Lonnie."

The facilitator paused to let the voice on the opposite end of the line digest the information, then continued with a spiritual message.

"I expect a victory for our great nation in return for this favor. Think positively about your brother. Help guide him to the victory podium. You can call me next week when the celebrations end. Good luck and good-bye for now."

"Yes! Renaldo, my brother, I will be there for you now!" an ecstatic Lonnie De Seta screamed at the top of his lungs as The Fat Man bid him adieu. "And I will have money again, money to help me hide from the assassins until I can secure my identification from the bank. This is a great day, and tomorrow will be an even greater day for Renaldo De Seta and all of Argentina!" He grabbed the Johnny Walker bottle and replenished his tumbler. "Viva Argentina, viva RRRRRRRenaaaaaaaallllldo!"

An unusually cold, grey afternoon set the backdrop for the third-place fixture at River Plate Stadium. The impressive structure was filled to capacity, even though the host nation was still twenty-four hours from taking the field.

Both of the contesting teams would have preferred to be playing a day later as well, but their national pride was at stake this afternoon, and they put on a spirited and entertaining show.

The stadium seemed equally divided as to number of supporters. Thousands of Brazilians had made the journey to Buenos Aires to witness their heroes one final time. The Italians were by and large, supported by Porteños, whose hatred for the men in yellow had grown throughout the last few days by leaps and bounds.

The undefeated Brazilians had complained bitterly to FIFA officials that Argentina had been given a huge advantage by commencing their game against Peru after the outcome of the Brazil-Poland fixture had gone into the record books. The host nation knew exactly how many goals it needed to advance, a benefit not given to any of the other competitors.

Those FIFA officials stated simply that the fixture time had been set to allow the home side's followers an opportunity to see their heroes play. The country would have ground to a standstill if the match had been started at 4:45 p.m. on a Wednesday afternoon. They also claimed that knowing what was needed to advance did not guarantee that they would accomplish the required task. Brazil's protests fell on deaf ears, and the populous of Argentina interpreted these insults as just more sour grapes from a lesser opponent.

The Italians opened strongly and remained in control for much of the initial forty-five minutes. They were rewarded for their efforts with a 1-0 lead at the interval. Unfortunately, it appeared that they had left their confidence and offensive skills in the depths of River Plate when the whistle sounded to start the ball rolling again.

The Brazilians struck on two long blasts, the same type of shots that had undone the Azzurri against Holland. There would be Samba music in the streets of the capital again this night, for a 2-1 victory by the yellow shirts had earned Brazil the third-place finish in the 1978 World Cup Tournament.

At the national training center, the Argentine players tried their best to stay loose and enjoy themselves as the day of destiny approached. The four full days of rest and recuperation had done much to heal those physical and mental bruises that each player had accumulated over the course of the long, gruelling tournament.

To a man, they felt confident of the outcome that tomorrow would bring. This was due in large measure to the nurturing care and attention to detail provided by manager Octavio Suarez. His calm hand and gentle guidance were infectious. Gone were the days of the raving tyrant, the aloof, even hostile dictator.

This team had advanced further than the manager had ever imagined in his wildest dreams. It was now time to bond together for the ultimate test. Their strength would lie in their unity of purpose and their willingness to go the extra distance for each other.

The final evening in camp would feature no tactical meetings or pep talks. Instead, a talent show was organized to entertain and relax the warriors. Each team member had to participate. Ramon Vida and Renaldo De Seta would give their farewell performance as the R&Rs.

Number seventeen's sore foot was holding up well. The holistic medicine and the intense physiotherapy had paid huge dividends in what had seemed at first like a losing enterprise. The appendage was game fit, and Renaldo De Seta would start at center half in the World Cup championship game.

What terrified the youngest player in camp more than the Dutch was playing on stage in front of his peers that final night. The two rockers had rewritten the Beatles tune "Twist and Shout" to suit their particular purpose, and now they stood alone in the spotlight. The lyrics called for the guitar player to mimic the words of the lead singer, but singing was something Renaldo had not been forced to do in their previous performances. Vida was the showman. He always looked after the vocals and that was fine with his partner. Now the guitarist was being made to expose his inability to carry a tune, and it was one of the most frightening moments of his life.

During rehearsals, the 'Boy from Boca' had fallen to the floor clutching his sides while laughing at his compatriot's vocal tribulations.

"Man, if you want to score tomorrow, just start singing to the Dutch goalkeeper. You will drive him from the net for sure. Maybe even right out of the stadium. How can such a pretty face hide such an ugly voice?"

The guitar work was easy, so Renaldo strummed his instrument as powerfully as he could. Hopefully, the melody would drown out his off-key vocalizing.

Vida, the showman, was dressed in skintight black leather pants and was naked above the waist, except for a blue and white-striped Argentine scarf. Renaldo wore jeans and a National Team jersey. The singer strutted his stuff as if he were playing to a sold-out audience at Teatro Colón. After the guitar intro, the number unfolded as follows:

Ramon:

"Wellllll, come on, Argentina, now,
Shoot to score,
Wellll, little Dutch keeper now,
We're gonna shoot 'til you're sore,
Ya, you look so scared,
Standin' there all alone,
Don't know where your teammates are?
Well, they packed and went home,
So shoot it, shoot it, Argentina, now,
Shoot to score,
Gonna put some balls past them now,
'Cause we're the champs evermore!"

Renaldo:

"C'mon, Argentina,
Shoot to score,
Little Dutch keeper,
Shoot 'til you're sore,
Look so scared
There all alone,
Got no teammates,
Packed and went home,
Shoot, Argentina,
Shoot to score,
Put some balls past 'em,
Champs evermore!"

Luckily for Renaldo, the screams and cheers of his enthusiastic audience kept the sound of his strained vocal cords at an almost inaudible level. Ramon was all over the stage, making lewd gestures with the scarf between his legs and pumping his midsection in a suggestive manner. The players and staff loved it, and the R&Rs were forced to play the song over a second time as an encore.

Other acts included a film clip of Ignacio Suazo's greatest goals, narrated by Captain Daniele Bennett. The footage turned out to be his one and only goal against Peru repeated over and over again. Another highlight was a chance to win a date with an erotic mystery woman. This lovely damsel bore a striking resemblance to none other than Juan Chacon in drag. All six foot five inches of him was poured into a pink mini skirt, tight angora sweater with two large balloons as breasts, and the biggest pair of stiletto high-healed pumps that existed in the universe. Humberto Velasquez was the unlucky winner of the draw and was forced to give the hideous defender a kiss on stage.

The evening had exactly the desired effect on the players, and in the end, they all stood and sang the national anthem of Argentina with their arms locked together in a giant circle. Even the men that were not starting the championship game sensed the magic of the moment, and Octavio Suarez witnessed a scene of team harmony that he had never thought possible until that very moment.

There were tears streaming down the face of the large figure standing in the shadows of the assembly hall when the lights went up. What Astor Gordero had just witnessed was one of the most stirring moments of his life. These fine young men, the cream of the nation, idols one and all. To hear them sing the anthem with such passion and pride, that was worth waiting a lifetime for!

The agent sought out his client at the end of the gathering.

"Renaldo, I was wondering if we might have a few moments alone. Can you grab your friend, Vida, as well? There is something I wish to discuss with him in your presence. It shouldn't take too long. Go and get your friend and I will meet you both in your room."

Renaldo dutifully set out to find Ramon. Less than five minutes later, they found Gordero sitting on the edge of Renaldo's bed.

"I could not sit on that tiny piece of wood they call a chair. I don't think I would have fit into that thing even as a newborn. Come in, come in. This is your room after all, Renaldo."

The client was always shy initially in the presence of his enormous agent, but Astor Gordero possessed the ability to make the rookie open up and start talking after a few minutes. Ramon Vida had never needed any prompting to say what was on his mind.

"Hey, Señor Gordero, baby, nice to see you, man. Renaldo says that you wanted to see me. So, you want us to go on tour with Symca and open for her? I knew we were good tonight, but, man . . ."

The agent laughed aloud at the audacity of the street urchin.

"No, no, Ramon, as much as I enjoyed your performance tonight, I have a feeling that your future lies in areas other than the music industry, which is precisely why I wanted to have a chat with the two of you together. I have cleared my visit here with manager Suarez, so he is aware of what I am about to tell you both."

Gordero motioned for the two men to be seated before he revealed his startling news.

"Now, it seems from recent performances that the two of you complement each other very nicely in the center of a football pitch. You enjoy playing with each other, am I correct so far?"

"Ya, I like the kid, he's OK. Give me some time and I can teach him lots of things, both on and off the field." The former Boca player opened his mouth, stuck out his tongue, and waggled it disgustingly in Gordero's direction.

"Yes, yes, I am sure that you could, Ramon. But besides that, it seems that you very well may get the chance to keep playing together after the tournament ends. In England!" The effervescent Vida instantly became stone-faced in disbelief.

"What the fuck are you talking about, man? I never met anyone from England in my entire life," Vida shot back when the scope of the visitor's statement had finally registered.

"But I have, Ramon, and the people I have met want you and Renaldo to play first division football for them this season in England. For substantial remuneration, I might add."

As was his habit, The Fat Man paused to let his tiding have the maximum effect before revealing further information.

"Ramon, I have here your release papers from the Boca Juniors Football Club. They were signed by the club president Señor Dominico yesterday. You are now the proud possession of the Newton's Prefects Football Club. In other words, you will play for me next season."

The Newton's Prefects majority owner and chairman handed his new acquisition the legal documents. He could tell that Vida was having trouble comprehending the magnitude of the message.

All the better to baffle the crude ruffian and get him under my thumb right from the start, Gordero thought.

"As you prefer to deal with financial matters yourself, Ramon, I am in a position to negotiate with you directly. Here is the signed offer from the Canary Wharf Football Club in London, England. I have an identical one for Renaldo right here as well. The term of the contract is for two years. The team pays for all your lodging, transportation, and sundry expenses . . ."

The speaker could see a flash of anger in his new center forward's eyes as Ramon Vida interrupted his speech.

"That's it? Just room and board and a few bus tickets? What kind of fucking offer is that? Boca would have paid me big dollars to play for them as their World Cup star striker. I am not going anywhere for a few bus tokens and all the roast beef I can eat!"

"I concur with you fully, Ramon," Gordero nodded in sympathy. "How much do you think you could have gotten from Boca for your services after the World Cup?"

"I don't know, man, big money! Maybe one hundred thousand American dollars per year!"

"One hundred thousand is not bad, my young friend. Not bad at all for a second stringer from Argentina. But you are a star, Ramon. A starter for the greatest team this nation has ever assembled! And tomorrow, you will both be World Champions! World Champions receive their just rewards. The English are aware of your great worth, and they have signed contracts paying you both almost one million American dollars per year!"

The silence in Renaldo's small room was deafening. Both the young gentlemen could not believe the figure that they had just heard. Renaldo shook his head to clear his thoughts, but as usual, Ramon asked for clarification.

"Oh, man, you gotta be bullshitting us! Nobody pays that kind of money for two unknown punks from Buenos Aires. Try to come up with a better story next time before you waste your energy."

Vida started for the door. With surprising strength and accuracy, Gordero flung the contract at him. The new Prefect striker caught the document as it bounced off his forearm.

"Read the contract for yourself, Ramon. These people are noblemen, Peers of the Realm. Lord Reginald Russell and his daughter, the very lovely, Lady Mallory. They will pay you four hundred thousand pounds sterling apiece to play for them in London. It is all true, for even I would have trouble making up such a story."

Vida poured over the papers, trying to find the figures to verify The Fat Man's words. Gordero continued to reassure both his young charges.

"They want the two of you to be the saviors of English football. They are distraught that their team didn't qualify for this tournament, and they will stop at no expense to see that it never happens again. They expect you to infuse some style and skill into their home game. For that, they will pay handsomely, even exorbitantly!"

The two players looked at each other, still not fully grasping the coming change in their lives.

"Now, Ramon, I would like to discuss this matter in private with Renaldo, so if you could take your transfer papers and the contract to your room, I will be available in say, half an hour, to go over any questions that you might have. So please, excuse us now, and I will be at your door in thirty minutes. What is your room number?"

Renaldo had not reacted verbally to the information his agent had disclosed during the first part of their meeting. Gordero could see that his player was in a state of disbelief, so he motioned for the boy to come and sit at his side on the bed once Vida had left them alone.

"So, my young superstar, and at the price the English are willing to pay for your services, you certainly rank in the superstar category. What thoughts are going through your fertile mind right now? You remember that I did mention the possibility of playing abroad when we talked in Rosario, do you not?"

The boy nodded mutely.

"Well, your strong showing against Peru upped your value considerably. These people like what you and Vida do together. I am serious that they are expecting the two of you to have a positive impact on English football. These are not people who throw compliments, or their money, around frivolously. They believe in you, and what they think you can do for them."

Gordero was trying to gauge his client's silent reaction. There was doubt in the boy's eyes, but nothing to indicate that his answer would be an unequivocal 'no.' The Fat Man pressed on.

"There are also several personal matters that you should be aware of. Firstly, with respect to your mother, I met with Señora Florencia personally yesterday afternoon, and I am pleased to report that under certain conditions, she will give your adventure to Europe her blessing. Those conditions include your being enrolled in a legitimate medical school in London, so that you can continue your studies while you are abroad. This matter has been discussed with the English, and it was determined that they have the connections to arrange such a request."

Renaldo's eyes were wide with amazement, the latter piece of news seemingly more of a surprise than the former.

"Your mother realizes that she is beyond being able to control your destiny, but she wants to make sure that you have an education to fall back on once you 'grow up and stop playing that vile game,' as she puts it. Her immediate desire is to become more involved in the operation of your family business concerns. Also, I assume you are aware that she continues to see my assistant Herr Stoltz in a nonbusiness capacity. Your mother seems to be a very happy woman at this point in time, Renaldo, and from her perspective, now is as good a time as any for you to leave the nest and spread your wings!"

There were now visible signs of relief etched on the player's face, but still no verbal response. Gordero continued his soliloquy.

"This really is the chance of a lifetime for you, my son. You are a hero in your native country, no matter what the outcome of tomorrow's game. But there is a much larger venue out there. A golden ring that only a very few get the chance to grasp. It is yours for the taking, Renaldo. I will handle all your affairs both here at home and on the international front. You won't have to worry about a thing."

The lawyer was certain that this young man had a firmer grasp on the situation than his counterpart that had just left the meeting. The De Seta boy was no fool, but money alone would not be enough to make him accept the

English offer. There had to be a combination of positive factors that would all add up to a convincing, inviting scenario.

"I am certain that Vida will accept the offer and travel to England, so if you decide to go, you will have your friend with you. The important thing is that the two of you have just started to scratch the surface of what you can achieve on the football pitch. You have only really played together at your present positions for a handful of games and practices. But even a blind man can see the magic the two of you create. Your play together will only get better, and the English can see that!"

There was a glimmer of acknowledgment now on number seventeen's countenance, which gave the agent hope. The boy could not deny the fact that he and Vida were soul-mates on the field as well as off it. Now was the time to use his trump card.

"Also, let me make it clear that I am fully cognizant of the fact that a strong bond has been formed between yourself and a certain lady client of mine. This does not displease me at all, for life in the glare of the spotlight is difficult at the best of times. In my experience, I have found that kindred spirits always reach an understanding as to how best to deal with fame and fortune. That is why I put the two of you together in the first place. I knew that you could help each other, inspire each other to greater heights. Simone's concerts and feature performances have never been better since she has been corresponding with you. There is a certain 'passion' to her work that had been missing previously. Dare I suggest that you might have had something to do with that infusion of spirit? No more so than the effect that her support has had on your football performance, I suppose."

Renaldo could feel the flush of embarrassment that his agent's words were causing. There was no denying their truth. It was just a matter of dealing with that truth and hearing it spoken aloud that caused the boy discomfort. The Fat Man would not let his advantage slip, and he continued on with some revelations that the young player had not thought of previously.

"You see, my young friend, the two of you have been good for each other over the past few months. But should we win the world championship tomorrow, Symca's stock will rise as sharply as your own. She will be singing our national anthem prior to the opening kickoff. The largest television audience ever assembled will hear her every note. The exposure will be tremendous, and if the universe unfolds as it should, the young lady will be swamped with requests to perform worldwide."

There was now a strange look of admiration and unexploited lust about the younger man. The girl's name had struck a nerve.

"Simone must capitalize on this moment, Renaldo, just as you must. I have tentatively scheduled a world tour and several command performances in Europe for our mutual friend commencing immediately after the tournament ends. If you had been planning to fall in love, get married, settle down, and have babies . . . well, those plans will just have to be put on the shelf until my singing superstar is available. I guarantee you that such a thing will not happen during the next two years at least, and during those two years, you can be making a fortune and getting a start on your medical degree in England."

There was a flash of disappointment in the younger man's eyes as this latest theory sank in, but in truth, Renaldo had thought no further of his future with Simone than the eventual consummation of their relationship. She was still an unattainable commodity in his eyes, a fantasy that he considered beyond his grasp. Gordero kept up the one-sided dialogue, for he could see that his client did not fully accept his words of wisdom as gospel.

"You are both so young, the world is your oyster. Take the half-shell with both hands and drink down its succulent treasures. Life can too easily be full of regrets and missed opportunities. I can book the young lady into London venues during both of the years that you are contracted to the English. We can use London as a home base for her excursions to the continent. Believe me, Renaldo, I can arrange things so that you see much more of Simone in London than you ever would if you stayed here in Buenos Aires."

A large, chubby hand patted the boy tenderly on his thigh. Renaldo knew that his mentor spoke the truth, for as a longtime fan of the talented singer, he always thought that she had the potential to exploit her charms and talent on the global stage. She had outgrown the Argentine market. Her recent World Cup promotional successes were proof of that. Yes, Simone must drink from the half-shell with both hands, and if he believed his agent's musings to be true, so must he!

"So, there it is! That is all I can tell you about the future right now, my dear boy. Ahhhhh, I almost forgot. There are two more matters of relevance. Firstly, win or lose, you are aware that the entire team has a command performance at the FIFA closing ball tomorrow evening. All of you will be billeted at the Hotel Presidente, where the gala takes place. Simone has asked me to tell you that she will be there and is 'breathlessly' looking forward to seeing you." A fatherly smile adorned the facilitator's ample face.

"Secondly, the English have asked me to extend an invitation to lunch with them on Monday next. Vida is invited as well. Your decision must be made by then. I realize that all this is a lot to place on your shoulders on the eve of the most important football game of your life, but time waits for no man! You have been flung into the swirl of the tornado called fame. One look at the mountains of fan mail stacked away will attest to that fact. The time has come to deal with all these matters as an adult Renaldo, for you are no longer a schoolboy. So, I have talked too much! Do you have any questions for me, or should I just leave you the English contract to read and we can talk after the championship final?"

There was a pained expression on the center half's face as he spoke for the first time.

"My father was killed in England, Señor Gordero. After attending a football match. I really don't know if I can go there. What if there are too many ghosts in England for me to deal with? How will I cope?"

The boy's misgivings fell into the one area that the lawyer had overlooked. He had to think quickly.

"Renaldo, you have English blood in you. Your paternal grandmother Lydia is as English as the Union Jack. Your father's tragic death was an accident, an occurrence that could have as easily happened right here in Buenos Aires. You have a heritage in England, and I daresay, relatives as well. I can work with your grandmother to get you connected with these people. You will not be alone! You will have Vida, your extended family, and at times, Simone and me. There is also Lady Mallory Russell, the owner of the Canary Wharf Football Club. I think that you will be very impressed with her when you meet on Monday. Not only is she strikingly beautiful, but she is knowledgeable, down-to-earth, and extremely bright, for a woman. She has promised me that the club will look after your every need, and I believe the lady. Her father, Sir Reginald, is an eccentric old fop, but it is Mallory that really runs the show. You will see for yourself. So, do we have a luncheon date on Monday?"

Renaldo pondered the scope of all that he had been told. Slowly, almost cautiously, he nodded his head in the affirmative.

"I suppose that I have nothing to lose by going to lunch. Of all the things that you have told me, Señor Gordero, I find my mother's attitude the hardest thing to grasp. She has hated the English, even to some extent my own grandmother, ever since my father's death. For her to allow me to set foot on English soil is something that boggles my mind. But I will play this thing out, if that is what you wish, Señor."

"It is what I wish, Renaldo, because it is the best thing for you. Your mother is a changed woman, my son, because for the first time since your father died, she is in love again. Herr Stoltz has convinced her to cut the apron strings and let you soar to your own new heights. It is your life, and for the first time, she is aware of that fact."

Astor Gordero fumbled with his inside suit-jacket pocket as he attempted to rise from the bed.

"Oh, here, take this. I thought this little item might soothe and motivate you after I leave."

The agent handed his client a small manila envelope. Its contents felt hard and bulky in Renaldo's hand.

"You are a lover of classical music, I believe. Have you ever been to the opera?"

"Yes, Señor, many times."

"Good, I would have thought so. Then you might find this stimulating on two levels. It deals with tomorrow. The piece is 'Nessun Dorma,' from Puccini's Turandot. It has brought me to tears many, many times. I have translated the lyrics into Spanish on a piece of paper inside the envelope. Listen to them carefully. Allow the melody to carry you away. Allow the lyrics to give you focus on your true purpose. The song tells you what that 'purpose' is very clearly. Give your soul to this music, Renaldo, and it will reward you with true inspiration!"

It seemed that the pompous lawyer was near tears as he made his closing remarks to his puzzled audience.

"Now, remember tomorrow, head and feet as one! You have accomplished so much my boy, don't stop now. Viva Argentina!"

The agent turned to leave when his client's final question sent a chill down his spine.

"I don't suppose that you have heard from my brother, Lonnie, by any chance, Señor? I was really hoping that he would contact one of us to secure a ticket to the final game. Have you received any word at all?" Gordero turned slowly, allowing time to form the proper sad expression.

"Regrettably, I have received no word from Lonnie. But do not be disappointed. I am certain that he will be watching you, wherever he is. I know that you will make him a very proud older brother. Good luck, Renaldo. I want to see you on the victory podium tomorrow!" He held up one large hand, its fingers already meshed in the familiar pattern.

"Head and feet as one, my boy, head and feet as one!"

Finally alone in his room, the confused, lovesick player slowly opened the offering from Astor Gordero. Enclosed was an original, sealed cassette tape and the translation.

Renaldo unwrapped the cellophane covering, then slipped the black cassette into his tape machine. The usual hiss of a prerecorded tape sizzled on the speakers until the roll of a kettle drum and a sweeping flourish of strings sent the listener hypnotically backwards into the wooden chair. The tenor's plaintive voice fell across the stirring backdrop:

'Nessun Dorma! Nessun Dorma!'

The listener mouthed the translated lyrics as the symphonic sounds filled the room.

'None must sleep! None must sleep!
And you, too, princess,
In your virginal room,
Watch the stars
Trembling with love and hope!

But my secret lies hidden within me,
No one shall ever discover my name!
No, no, I shall say it as my mouth meets yours
When the dawn is breaking!
And my kiss will dissolve the silence
Which makes you mine!

Depart oh night! Set you stars!
Set you stars! At dawn I shall win!
I shall win! I shall win!'

Renaldo felt totally drained by the time the last riveting notes had subsided. He had given himself totally to the soporific combination of voice and instruments. The lyrics had made a profound statement, reinforced by that incredible melody. For the first time in his young life, he understood his destiny.

"At dawn I shall win, I shall win . . . the World Cup trophy and Simone!"

CHAPTER TWENTY-EIGHT

Millions of Porteños watched the sunrise that Sunday the twenty-fifth of June. The party had lasted all night, never stopping, never standing still. The central business district of Buenos Aires was clogged with traffic of every description. Movement, whether on foot or by some mechanized means, was next to impossible. The persistent staccato honking of car horns blended comfortably with the nonstop screaming of the word "Argentina! Argentina! Argentina!"

Powder-blue and white were the only acceptable colors to sport, and even many household pets, dressed appropriately, of course, joined the bubbling, throbbing masses on the avenues. There was no fear of the Dutch in these quarters. The final result was a forgone conclusion. No one would dare put a damper on the greatest party ever seen in South America. Not if they expected to leave Argentina alive!

Only as the witching hour approached did the streets start to empty. Those lucky enough to be the proud owner of a ticket snaked their way north to the towering River Plate. Those less fortunate, and they were the vast, vast majority, sought refuge under the bright beams of the nearest television set. By two forty-five p.m., fifteen minutes before kickoff, the once-infested streets of the capital were totally deserted. An atomic bomb could not have evaporated every human soul from those streets with such finality.

The morning had dawned brightly, but within a few hours, wispy clouds were often greying out the sun. Nevertheless, the mid-fifties temperature felt much warmer in the glow of euphoria that enveloped Buenos Aires that fateful day. The Argentine people, rich and poor, powerful and meek, old and young, sick and healthy, corrupt and pure . . . were ready for the Gods to deliver their just reward as faithful followers and devout disciples.

They would all spread the word of Argentina's greatness. They would shout it from the rooftops, the mountaintops, across the Pampas, through the rain forest, the length and breadth of their great nation. All that was needed was ninety minutes of total dedication to the ultimate goal. Victory!

"Oswaldo?"

"Ya! You must be Lonfranco De Seta. It's great to meet you. I am a big fan of your brother's. He has done some amazing things with that football during the tournament. I sure hope he has another big game today. How about you? Are you ready for a big day?"

The hunter and the hunted were finally standing toe to toe. Both searched silently for clues as they held eye contact for almost a quarter of a minute. As is usually the case, only the hunter knew the rules of the deadly contest in which the two men were about to participate.

Lonnie had watched the man for ten minutes from across the street before making a move. He wanted to be sharp, take precautions, and especially, stay alive. Not that Astor Gordero would have any reason to set him up. It was just that past experience had shown that these mystery killers had a habit of turning up when you least expected them. Out of thin air, silently, and with deadly result!

Gordero had been right though. There was no mistaking Oswaldo. A black baseball cap with the Newton's Prefect crest now covered his carrot-topped crown, but he had been instantly recognizable from twenty yards while bare-headed. His bright blue eyes were warm and friendly as he paid his respects to Lonnie's younger brother.

This man is alright, the elder sibling decided. *He likes Renaldo. Great! We will get along just fine.* The desperado relaxed a bit, ready to have a 'big day!'

The two press accreditations that had been bestowed upon Astor Gordero had initially arrived as a 'thank you' for the 'calling off' of government henchmen out to get the editor of a left-wing newspaper. Although the solicitor considered them only partial payment for the man's life, he had accepted the field-level photographer's passes several months before the tournament began, then filed them away until needed. That need had arisen with Lonnie De Seta's phone call.

"Here, put this on, then take this camera and sling it around your neck. This is your identification card. Stick it in your pocket, somewhere handy. We will have to show it several times before we get settled on the field."

Rojo Geary handed Lonnie a red photographer's vest with '38' emblazoned in large white numerals. That was the day's pass code, a well-guarded secret until just hours before game time. Geary had already been to the stadium and secured the two vests by the time he met Lonnie. Now they were ready. It was time to enter the palace of the Gods!

Lonnie De Seta had left no trace of his stay at Marla Gallego's flat. He had been meticulous in his efforts to not cause the lady any more discomfort. Actually, he didn't want the little bitch screaming at him that he had left his underwear in her bathroom sink when he attempted to discreetly visit the bank again. The flat would be exactly as she had left it, except for the consumed foodstuffs, and, of course, a few quarts of Scotch.

Lonnie had changed into blue jeans and a sweater. A brown leather bomber-style jacket and a very special accessory finished off his game clothes. That 'special accessory' was a white toque, with two powder-blue stripes circling around the turned-up headband. Above the stripes was written the word 'Argentina' in matching powder blue.

The toque had been a going away gift from Renaldo last Christmas. Both brothers had been set to embark on new adventures way back then. His little brother had told him to wear the toque only if Renaldo made the team, and Lonnie was there to see him play. That way, the toque would bring them safely together again.

It had been too precious an item for Lonnie to take away with him during his life as a terrorist and murderer, so he left it safely in his closet at Casa San Marco. The gift was the first item he had packed on his return home.

Lonnie's wallet, containing only the safety deposit key and Astor Gordero's card, sat in his rear jean's pocket. The Llama pistol rested against his waistband, concealed by the brown jacket. He had hidden his club bag behind some refuse cans in the rear of Marla's building. His plan was to return and collect his portable possessions later that evening.

As they came under the shadow of the mammoth steel and concrete home of the gladiators, Lonnie remembered his second request given to the genie.

"Did Señor Gordero give you an envelope for me, by any chance?"

Rojo Geary could see the hopeful anticipation on his new friend's face.

"Ya, he did! He told me the envelope contained important documents and to keep it locked up until after the game. It is stashed in the glove compartment of my car. I parked back there by the café. I didn't think I should risk bringing it out around this crowd. We can get it after the match, then I can give you a lift to wherever you're going."

Lonnie would have preferred to have the pesos crammed in his wallet right away, just in case anything unusual went down. But Oswaldo seemed like a straight up, responsible fellow. By the time the hunted man arrived on the floor of the swirling cauldron that was River Plate Stadium, he felt totally at ease in Rojo Geary's company, and he was ready to lose himself in Renaldo's glorious efforts.

By two o'clock, River Plate was overflowing, five thousand bodies above official capacity. Eighty thousand voices, eighty thousand faithful, believing voices! If there was a Dutchman in the crowd, he was to become invisible under the fluttering white storm of paper and ticker-tape. The national colors of Argentina were everywhere. One hundred-foot-long cloth banners, flags large and small, streamers, scarves, homemade signs. Everything under the sun that could be fashioned in powder-blue and white existed here. But most of all, it was the noise, the noise of those believing voices. Songs of national pride and heroic deeds rained down upon the green carpet. Surely no team in the world could conquer both the Argentine players and the Gallery Gods! This was Argentina's day! This *must* be Argentina's day!

At game time, manager Octavio Suarez remained in his office. His team had already been called to the field, but the man in charge told his assistant coaches to stall for time. He, and he alone, would give the word when to start down the path to glory.

For now, he listened, arms folded across his torso, chin resting on his chest, eyes closed, his back facing the door. He would not leave the room until he heard that sound, 'the buzz!' The sound of champions!

Goalkeeper coach Estes Santos sat on a small table directly in front of a large, orange plastic tarp. This strange item had appeared on one of the dressing room walls before any of the players had entered the facility. Santos was told by the manager to "guard that thing with your life. Let no man look beneath the orange shield." Santos had been steadfast in his resolve to carry out the boss's instructions, and he had managed to repel all curiosity seekers.

This had been a rewarding tournament for the former player-turned goalkeeper coach. Argentina's goals against statistics were the best in the tournament, and that was largely due to the strong bond that had formed between coach Santos and National Team keeper, Junior Calix.

The two men understood each other, and they had formed a mutual respect as teacher and student. Over the last three days, they had spent innumerable hours practicing together, defending against the curling long balls that the Dutch had used to sink every team they had played to date. By June the twenty-fifth, Santos was well pleased, and Junior Calix was ready to meet the orange onslaught!

There was a second request for the Argentine National Team to take the field. Ubaldo Luque, the assistant manager, vaguely described some small 'problem' that was holding the team back. He assured the uptight Austrian linesman that they would be along momentarily.

The players were wondering what was up! They were dressed in what had become their number one strip, starting with their alternating powder-blue and white vertically striped jerseys. Black shorts with five tight vertical stripes on the sides, blue, then white, then blue, white again, and finally a last stripe of blue, gave a sinister, aggressive posture to their uniform. Black stockings with three white horizontal rings on the fold complimented the shorts. They had never lost a game in World Cup '78 attired in this fashion. They felt comfortable suited up in this battle dress. They felt ready to play, and win!

But the waiting was getting to them. Each one, to a man, questioned what Suarez was doing in his office alone. Why had he not given his charges one of his patented inspirational lectures to propel them onto the field? Their voices rose in volume with impatient, nervous banter.

"There! There it is! 'The buzz' of champions. I have heard it! Champions!"

Octavio Suarez wheeled around, grabbed a cardboard box from the edge of his desk, and strode into the dressing area. Every voice in the room stopped in mid-sentence.

"Gather around this table, all of you. Thank you, Estes."

The goalkeeper coach stepped aside as the man in charge placed the box on the space he had vacated. Suarez turned and gave a hearty tug to the orange tarp. As it fell to the floor, the national flag of Argentina loomed in its place.

"La Bandera Immaculada, Señors. Our immaculate flag! This is the flag of the greatest nation on earth. A flag for all our people." Suarez took a nearby pointer and held it on the bottom horizontal blue band of the sacred object.

"Here, here is the blue of the great Atlantic Ocean that laps at our fair shores. In the middle, the white snow of the Andes Mountains, so pure and true. And here, the blue of the sky . . . breathtaking, never-ending! But it is here, right here in the center, that you will find the source that will light your way today. It is the sun, Señors! The sun that shines down from the clear blue sky, over the pure-white mountains, and glistens on the bright blue sea. The sun that always guides us, shows us the way, leads us to our destiny!"

The manager paused, looking into the glazed eyes of his players. He placed his hands on the lid of the box in front of him.

"Today, the sun will guide your way. Today, the sun will be with you every step that you take. The sun will keep your aim true and your heart strong. The sun will guide you to victory!"

Suarez cast aside the lid, reached into the rectangular crate, and held up a pair of stockings. White football stockings with three horizontal powder-blue rings on the fold. The boss extended his arms straight out in front of his body at shoulder height. He then made a slow one hundred and eighty degree sweep of the room with the precious article held lovingly in his hands. Atop the three powder-blue rings on the outer side of the stocking was a sewn-on patch. That patch was adorned with the smiling golden sun of La Bandera Immaculada.

"Here is the sun that will guide you to victory today! Now, each one of you step up here and take a pair. Change your stockings, now! All of you. Move!"

The pale blue sky as described on La Bandera Immaculada turned into a white downpour of paper products the minute the first Argentine player crested the top of the field-level stairway. There had been other impressive displays of support using the bleached pulp materials, but nothing, nothing at all like this.

The crowd literally disappeared from view as the paper torrent of affection and encouragement settled on the previously unsoiled green battlefield. The noise, the color, the atmosphere . . . it had to be experienced to be believed.

The National Team of Argentina had kept the Dutch waiting on the pitch for more than five minutes. The Europeans were seething as a result of the perceived insult. Strong words were exchanged as the two teams lined up for the respective national anthems.

The men from the Netherlands stood rigidly at attention as the strains of their homeland's chorus reverberated around the giant bowl. Despite the massed military bands with their musicians numbering in the hundreds, the Dutch anthem seemed too low in volume to be truly inspirational to her native sons. But then, the unyielding roar from the galleries made it difficult to hear oneself think at field level.

The public address announcer then instructed the eighty thousand witnesses to direct their attention toward the victory podium, which was set up on the west side warning track at center field. There, alongside junta leader and President Jorge Videla, stood a tiny figure dressed in a blue and white vertically striped jumpsuit.

"Señors, señoras, and señoritas, it is our distinct pleasure to present to you today, here to sing the national anthem of Argentina, the nation's leading vocal artist. Please welcome, the fabulous . . . Symca!"

The loudest roar of the day swirled around the amphitheater. Simone smiled confidently as she stepped to the microphone and waved enthusiastically to the thousands. She looked down the line of Argentine players that stood soldier-still in front of her.

Her eyes met Renaldo's as she passionately vocalized the opening bars of the melody. The crowd held its breath, many with tears in their eyes, as the beautiful lady sang this patriotic tribute from the depths of her soul.

When she was done, as the fanatical applause engulfed her, she paused for a moment to blow a kiss in the National Team's direction. Only number seventeen knew the true destination of her airy sign of affection. The kiss was for him, there could be no mistaking that. By nightfall, he was determined to replace that blown kiss with the real article. The touch of her ripe lips on his!

'Depart, oh night!
Set you, stars!
Set you, stars!
At dawn I shall win!
I shall win!
I shall win!'

Field level section 365, row 8, seats 1 & 2 were occupied by their usual subscriber, and on this occasion, Astor Gordero was, once again, attired in the full regalia of an army reserve colonel. This was going to be a day of great national pride and respect for Argentina, and he wanted the world to know that he had the rank and title to command respect as well.

The man of many hats also wanted to impress his distinguished guests, Sir Reginald and Lady Mallory Russell of London, England. As Gordero was now a business associate of the English visitors, he thought that they might also be impressed with his military bearing and well-placed junta connections.

Sir Reggie discreetly commented to his daughter that their host had enough material in his uniform to outfit an entire platoon of Royal Marines. Mallory was forced to stifle her humorous reaction with a sharp-eyed glare in her father's direction.

Wolfgang Stoltz sat in seat number six, in row eight. Seat number five had been left vacant, until the military escort arrived to deliver Simone from the podium to her designated viewing point. Introductions were made to the Lord and Lady, and then, with eighty thousand others, they turned their attention to the spectacle before them.

It was ironic that Simone and Mallory should be seated side by side. There was the usual polite small talk exchanged before the opening whistle, but if each of the women had confided in the other, they would have been shocked to find out that they both had really only come to see one of the twenty-two players on the pitch. Number seventeen in powder-blue and white!

By two fifty-eight p.m., the team photographs had been taken, the combatants had exchanged informal handshakes and hollow good wishes with one another, and the teams had saluted the multitudes with upraised arms. Now, finally, Italian referee Giovanni Patrizio stood over the ball at center field. Four years of preparations, qualifying matches, exhibition contests, scandals, name calling, and bitter rivalries had all led to this one moment.

The twenty-two world-class athletes that anxiously awaited each tick of the second hand would lineup as follows for this, the most important ninety minutes of their young lives.

For Argentina, clad in vertical powder-blue-and-white-striped jerseys with black numerals, black shorts with vertical powder-blue and white piping on the sides, and white stockings adorned with three horizontal powder-blue rings and the golden sun of La Bandera Immaculada on the fold:

#	Name	Age	Height
	Goalkeeper		
1	Junior Calix	27	6'1"
	Defenders (fullbacks, backs)		
4	Jorge Calderone	27	5'11"
5	Ignacio Suazo	24	6'4"
8	Juan Chacon	28	6'5"
9	Daniele Bennett	29	5'10"
	Midfielders (halfbacks, halves)		
11	Humberto Velasquez	25	5'6"
12	Leopoldo Anariba	22	6'0"
17	Renaldo De Seta	19	6'2"
	Forwards (strikers)		
18	Ramon Vida	22	5'11"
19	Ruben Gitares	24	6'0"
20	Caesar Castro	30	6'1"

For the Netherlands, turned out in their traditional orange jerseys with black numerals and three black pinstripes running across the shoulder and down the sleeve, white shorts with three vertical orange stripes as piping on the sides, and stockings in orange to match their jerseys, with three black horizontal rings on the fold:

#	Name	Age	Height
	Goalkeeper		
1	Dirk Wilhelmus	21	6'2"
	Defenders		
3	Nilis Hendrik	27	6'0"
4	Eimert Laurens	20	5'10"
7	Willie Brax	25	6'2"
14	Maarten Van Vlymen	29	6'0"
	Midfielders		
15	Jan Johannes	22	6'3"
17	Pieter Thijssen	28	6'3"
18	Kees Trelaan	24	5'9"
	Forwards		
19	Theodorus Oosterband	29	6'0"
20	Erny Jorgens	25	6'2"
25	Arturs Trelaan	27	6'1"

No European team had ever won the World Cup in South America. With several of their more experienced world-class players at home in Holland for various reasons, the Dutch had their work cut out for them. There was no fear in the eyes of the eleven starters, however, for they had played their best football of the tournament in the later stages. Each man felt that this team was capable of hoisting the World Cup trophy in triumph when all was said and done.

On paper, the final game was a contrast in styles and temperaments. The dark, hot-blooded Latins' short ball control game, versus the fair, cool-headed Europeans' 'clockwork orange' style of swirling, constantly changing, every-man-playing-every-position football. That was on paper. What unfolded in reality was actually quite different.

Holland came out tackling aggressively, marking the Argentine forwards with man-to-man coverage. This was a surprise to Gitares, Vida, and Castro, who had assumed that they would be given more space in the early going. They had been told that the Dutch would attempt to set up their well rehearsed offside trap, then storm back on the offensive with quick counterattacks. Not so!

The Dutchmen's style was 'in your face,' and defender Nilis Hendrik sent Ruben Gitares crashing rudely to the turf in under thirty seconds of play. The first of fifty-odd fouls the day would see had been committed. Many others were to follow in rapid succession.

Argentina was playing in an overlapping zonal defense, with midfielders and forwards falling back in a protective envelope as needed. The two outside defenders, Bennett and Calderone, were given leeway to push forward and add to the attack when an opportunity arose.

Renaldo De Seta felt ready. His foot was sound, and he had been truly inspired by both Octavio Suarez and the lovely Symca. He dared to glance up into the heavens before the opening whistle and proclaim, "Papa, this game, I play for your memory!"

While the Argentine strikers were tied up in knots from the first kick of the ball, number seventeen seemed to have more space than he had anticipated in the early going. Both on the defensive and in the attack, Renaldo had ample time to connect with his patent 'right on the mark' passes. He sent Ramon Vida charging into the penalty area in the third minute with a lovely chip shot, and Dutch keeper Wilhelmus had to soar to tip the streaking striker's volley over the crossbar.

Vida returned the favor two minutes later, setting number seventeen loose with a lovely back heeled pass. For fifteen yards, Renaldo ran as if he were poetry in motion, strong and straight, tearing at the heart of the Dutch defense.

There was no support for the boy on this sortie, however, and the over-enthusiastic Willie Brax was about to end this particular threat in a rather crude manner. As Renaldo cocked his foot to let fly a shot, Mr. Brax simply grabbed the waistband of his opponent's shorts and gave a firm tug. The threatening Argentine was pulled completely off balance, but still managed to make contact with the ball on his right foot instead of his left. The leather bounced harmlessly into the grasp of keeper Wilhelmus, but the foul resulted in a free kick.

Although nothing became of Ruben Gitares ensuing effort, the Dutch, in general, and Willie Brax, in particular, had been alerted to the skills of young number seventeen. They would have to pay considerably more attention to that handsome Porteño, or the damage he could inflict would show up on the scoreboard.

But offense wasn't the sole domain of the home team. The Dutch midfield was ever-present in the Argentine danger-zone, pushing forward, looking for a kill. Seven minutes in, big Pieter Thijssen took a run up the middle to head a free kick from Erny Jorgens inches wide of the near post. Two minutes later, a thirty-yard lob to the penalty spot was poorly cleared as a result of some confusion between Juan Chacon and Ignacio Suazo. There was Thijssen again, up from midfield to slam the misplaced ball directly at startled keeper Junior Calix. His desperate lunge managed to tip the leather skyward and over the net to safety, just as his counterpart had been forced to do minutes earlier.

A newfound aggression seemed to be instilled in the Dutch after Thijssen's two near misses on this grey afternoon, and the space that Renaldo had initially savored evaporated as the minutes ticked away. Each touch of the ball now attracted an orange jersey within seconds. One man in particular, blond, blue-eyed, number seven, the inconsistent Willie Brax, seemed to make the host's number seventeen his personal whipping boy.

Three times Brax tried to go after Renaldo's tender ankle and heel. Twice the gesture was ignored by both the recipient and the referee. By the third attempt, the official and the Argentine player had had enough. An unfriendly, two-handed shove to the Dutchman's chest was a gift from Renaldo to his suitor. That gesture was followed by Sigñor Patrizio reaching into his black shirt pocket to retrieve a yellow card for Mr. Brax. The European feigned innocence, but the frustrated referee simply wagged his finger at the offender and told him that such behavior would not be tolerated.

The incident did give the men in powder-blue and white a touch more space, for the only fear the Dutchmen had was for the two colored cards tucked inside the head official's shirt pocket. One could not inflict damage or score goals while sitting on the bench, and Brax's reprimand was taken as a warning that Sigñor Patrizio was unwilling to let the game slip from his grasp.

The current of the match flowed back into Argentina's favor by the time the clock indicated that one half hour of playing time had elapsed. Jorge Calderone had been masterful in his clearances from around the Argentine goal area. At each opportunity given, he would turn his possession of the ball into long, fluid runs up the flank. The Dutch were busy marking the home side's strikers, but with each successive sortie that defender Calderone orchestrated, the orange defenders became less stringent in their coverage of the powder-blue and white marksmen.

One such run by Calderone at the thirty-seventh minute drew both Dutch midfielder Kees Trelaan and defender Eimert Laurens away from their original assignments. There was a split second opening to be exploited, and the crafty Calderone knew exactly how to accept the Orangemen's gift.

Angling his run into the center of the field, the South American defender then turned straight for the goal at thirty-five yards out. Trelaan's sweeping right leg nicked the ball carrier's foot as the Dutchman sprawled to the carpet. Calderone left his feet an instant before contact in an effort to maintain his forward momentum. The Argentine knew that he was going down as well, but a heartbeat before hitting terra firma, he managed to right foot the object of attention past the onrushing Laurens.

The black-and-white orb rolled ten yards further upfield, untouched, until it was retrieved by the home side's number seventeen. Dutch defender Willie Brax was, as usual, glued to Renaldo's body, forcing the young Argentine to set his left leg solidly into the turf in hopes of making a play with his right foot. In the split second of time that he had available, Renaldo heard a familiar voice approaching quickly.

"Hey, man, over here!"

Ramon Vida roared into sight some eight yards away, heading diagonally for pay-dirt. Renaldo's pass was right on the money, and now it was all up to the 'Boy from Boca.'

Defenders Hendrik and Van Vlymen, as well as midfielder Johannes, loomed mere feet away, but they could not react swiftly enough to stop the darting Latin. Collecting the treasure and veering ever so slightly to his right, Vida split the outer two Dutchmen as he crossed over the white line marking the penalty area.

Johannes, the last obstacle before a clear shot could be taken, was a large, muscular specimen that could not be danced around in these close quarters. It was a time to use cunning instead of power, so the fleet striker simply slid to the ground and whacked the ball goalward with an extended left leg. The upright Johannes could do nothing but watch in horror as the ball squirted under the left arm of lunging keeper Wilhelmus and into the back of the net.

The heavens turned white in appreciation as the R&Rs were joined in their celebratory hug by several jubilant teammates. The giant scoreboard illuminated the result of their combined efforts for the world to see. Argentina 1, Holland 0!

For the Dutch, the goal sounded a wake-up call that reemphasized the urgency of their plight. The ball possession skills of the Argentine National Team had thrown them off their usual fluid game. The Orange-shirts had tried to be too precise, too pretty in showcasing their ample skills. They needed the football, and they set about acquiring it in the most direct of manners.

The remaining seven minutes of the opening half were as ill-tempered and nasty as any seen in the tournament to date. Signor Patrizio was impotent when it came to keeping the flow of the match moving. It seemed that he had spent the entire time between the host's goal and the interval admonishing one player or another. There was no reward to be reaped for the visitors as a result of their newfound belligerence, however, and they entered the bowels of River Plate at the break still down by that one large tally.

Manager Octavio Suarez was satisfied with his team's efforts in the first forty-five minutes of play. His charges had deprived the Dutch of their lethal long-range cannons by flooding the zones in anticipation of a missile being launched. Both Kees Trelaan and his elder brother, Arturs, had been kept without a shot during the initial segment. The fact that a pair of siblings had made the starting lineup of the Dutch National Team was definitely unusual, but these two men from Eindhoven possessed the most accurate and powerful shots on this team of renowned marksmen. That the brothers had been kept totally at bay this long was an accomplishment not overlooked by their opponents' manager. There would be no changes in the Argentine National Team's lineup to commence the second half of play!

Holland took the field after the intermission intent on equalizing quickly. There would be no more fancy flourishes that looked good on the highlight films, but failed to produce the desperately needed result. Their means to their desired end was direct, physical, even confrontational, football. They believed themselves tougher and more physically fit than the home side, and the plan was to wear down the men in powder-blue and white, then strike for the kill.

What the Orangemen had not counted on was having to deal with the likes of 'Killer' Juan Chacon each time they ventured too deep into hostile territory. The Ugly One's ill temper had been well scouted by the Europeans, and their initial plan of long-range shooting would have neutralized the hideous defender's effectiveness. But now, time was of the essence, and with the long ball effectively cut off by a swarming Argentine midfield and back-line, it was time to come head-to-head with the monster.

Chacon had his usual style of welcome ready for the 'golden boys.' The savagery that was meted out under the shadow of the Argentine goalposts was not the thing of beauty that football purists had hoped to witness. No, this was gritty, down and dirty, no quarter football, and with each successive infraction, the game slipped away from the ineffectual Sigñor Patrizio.

How could he card everyone? There would be no one left on the field to complete the match, so extensive was the use of blatant, unsportsmanlike conduct. It wasn't just the home nation. The Dutch gave back every tender gesture that they received in-kind. There was no pace, no flow, no tempo to the stuttering, pugnacious drama. High tension, yes, but skill and brilliant football were totally subservient to retaliation and vitriolic temperament.

Holland pressed forward in search of the elusive equalizer. Junior Calix met the challenge bravely, vocalizing instructions to his beleaguered defensive corps. The Dutch began to play the field laterally, moving ever closer to the Argentine goal using long crosses, sending four or five men in deep to try to maintain possession for the finish. There was brutal punishment rewarded to any Orangeman who dared to venture onto the sacred turf of the homeland, but the Europeans were more than willing to pay that price to achieve their goal. It was not in their disposition to turn the other cheek either. Frustrations mounted on both sides as time ticked away.

Twice the Dutchmen almost fell prey to their offensive enthusiasm. In the fifty-seventh and again in the seventy-ninth minute, clearances by the Argentine defenders resulted in lightning counterstrikes by powder-blue and white foot soldiers.

Humberto Velasquez sent Ruben Gitares blazing up the flank on the initial sortie, only to have the latter's shot pound off the woodwork and into touch. The second near miss saw Renaldo De Seta work his passing magic with Caesar Castro on the opposite wing. Yellow-shirted Dutch keeper Dirk Wilhelmus managed to get a flailing hand on the cannonading drive from the River Plate winger, tipping it ever so slightly out of harm's way.

Castro's near miss signaled the end of the home-side's offensive strikes for the remaining nine minutes of play, however. Back came Holland, jaws set with determination, eyes firmly focused on the mesh behind Junior Calix.

Dutch manager Hendrikus Arend had used his two substitutions in the fifty-ninth and seventy-second minutes of play. It was substitute center forward Frank Noordwijk that would finally silence the roar of the fanatical South American supporters and bring the Europeans to terms.

Noordwijk, at 6'4" in height, was the tallest of the Dutchmen in Argentina. He was not as proficient with his playmaking or shooting as starting center forward Oosterband, but in the air, there was perhaps no better finisher in the entire tournament.

Nine minutes from time, with orange jerseys streaking to and fro deep inside enemy territory, Kees Trelaan gained possession of the mystic sphere ten yards in from the touchline, some forty yards away from Calix's doorstep. The innovative midfielder started a false run down the sidelines, then faked a shot goalward. All this time a mesmerized, stationary Humberto Velasquez looked on from a mere two yards away. A call from brother Arturs sent the ball spiraling back into the center of the pitch, where the elder Trelaan had time and space to create some damage.

There was momentary confusion in the Argentine defensive ranks. Swift Erny Jorgens was making a run down the right sideline, calling for the ball. Captain Daniele Bennett screamed for an offside trap to nullify the threat, but there were already too many Orange-shirts blocking the defender's path. Trelaan's lob travelled twenty yards in the air, then bounced lightly, five yards in front of the wide-open Jorgens. The linesman's flag remained by his side, meaning Jorgens was still onside. With his path to the goalmouth totally unobstructed for a solo duel with Señor Calix, the wily striker chose, instead, to loft the ball high into the center of the pitch from twenty-two yards out.

Manager Arend screamed in dismay at the loss of what he perceived as a sure goal. But wait! There, two yards outside the penalty area, flying through the air, was substitute Noordwijk.

Higher, higher, the Dutchman leapt. Central defenders Chacon and Suazo were there to meet the challenge, but they were not airborne like their opponent. Jan Johannes was also mixed up between the two Argentine defenders to add to their confusion. Noordwijk connected with Jorgen's gift at the edge of the penalty area and sent the ball on its way.

Junior Calix in the Argentine net had run to the far post to cover the threat down the open wing should Jorgens try for the tally himself. The keeper moved too slowly to combat the centering pass that Noordwijk sent goalwards. Calix was little more than halfway back along his goal line when the net behind him bulged with the Orange-shirt's header.

Now, ten foreigners stood in huddled elation as eighty thousand looked on in mute dismay. Holland had come level, and the world order stood on the brink of collapse.

To make matters worse, the Dutch were far from content with their stunning accomplishment. They seized the emotional letdown and shock that their hosts were in the throes of and closed in for the kill.

On came the orange waves, sending the powder-blue and white defenders back on their heels in disarray. Try as they might, Argentina could not gain possession of the ball for more than a few seconds at a time before it was aggressively relieved from them. Eight minutes of relentless pressure culminated in the finest scoring chance of the day.

Less than a minute remained on Sigñor Patrizio's watch when the brothers Trelaan teamed up one more time. Again, it was Arturs who launched a deft chip shot thirty yards upfield, this offering coming to earth mere yards in front of his sprinting brother, Kees. Now it was Jorge Calderone's turn to be victimized by the onrushing Netherman. The Argentine fullback had given up the advantage of position, and short of a costly foul, there was nothing he could do except watch in dismay.

The ball came to earth at the edge of the goal crease, six yards out from Nirvana. Kees Trelaan was positioned perfectly to pounce on the waist level volley off the turf and jab the sacred object goalward with his left foot.

Keeper Calix made a futile stabbing motion with his left leg to divert the black-and-white globe from its damaging trajectory, but he narrowly missed making contact. The guardian of the gate could only look back in anguish as he and the onrushing Trelaan became entangled and crashed to the carpet.

The matter was out of everyone's hands now. The Gods would decide the outcome of the ball's pilgrimage to Mecca. The entire football universe gasped collectively as they followed its flight to the promised land.

Trelaan's touch sent the orb downwards again, then off the turf two yards out, volleying upwards at waist level. There were no other defenders close enough to interfere with its ordained destiny. No breathing, living, souls to save Argentina from a disaster that only minutes before had been unthinkable!

There remained only a certain white, six inch by six inch, upright wooden object to master. As fate would have it at this moment in time, it was the goalpost that would change the course of history.

The eighty thousand breathed a collective sigh of relief as black and white struck white. The benevolent sun of La Bandera Immaculada must have been shining down on the fortunes of her native sons, for the dreaded object rebounded back into play. It was then swiftly cleared from danger's doorstep by Captain Daniele Bennett.

There was no time left to strike again for the Dutchmen, no time left to redeploy for the Argentines. The last glorious opportunity had been decided by an inanimate object, totally impartial and oblivious to the emotional mayhem that it had created.

Sigñor Patrizio raised his right arm and gave three long blasts of his whistle. Regulation time had expired. The champion of the soccer world would be determined in extra time, or failing that, penalty kicks.

The tension inside the circular cauldron known as Monumental Stadium duplicated its namesake. Octavio Suarez had not been enamored by the play of his team in the final half of the contest. He had made no substitutions as yet, and during the five-minute break, he canvassed each of his starting eleven for signs of fatigue or mental letdown.

No one wanted to come out of the contest. Not one man was willing to give up his position. These were his shock troops, the best he had available, and Octavio Suarez would do or die with these same warriors. He gathered his charges in a tight circle around him just as the officials signaled for the players to take their positions.

"Señors, we have come a long, long way together. Too far to see things fall apart now! We are fortunate to be able to continue on in this game! You must take the battle to their doorstep immediately! Each of you, pull up your stockings. Let that shining sun guide you to your true destiny. Champions of the world! I have faith in each and every one of you. These multitudes looking down upon us have faith in each and every one of you. Have faith in yourselves, and you will stand on the victory podium in thirty minutes' time!"

Thirty minutes. Two fifteen-minute halves. No sudden death, just two fifteen-minute halves played to completion! The occasion called for the penultimate effort by each of the twenty-two men that lined up for the resumption of play.

Who would be equal to the task? Who would falter and bear the ignominious title of 'runner-up' for the rest of their lives? Those questions were about to be answered as the world watched and waited.

For Renaldo De Seta, there was no doubting the final verdict. He felt strong and mentally capable of carrying out the duty expected of him. He had taken only one direct scoring chance himself during the first ninety minutes of play. He was convinced that his opponents would, therefore, regard him in a lighter manner. This would translate into more time and space, which he could use to his advantage.

His role for the last forty-five minutes had been primarily defensive, due to the sustained dominance of the Europeans in the Argentine half of the field. But the bothersome Willie Brax had backed off from his persistently close shadowing as a result of the Dutchmen's offensive superiority. Number seventeen had seen room to create chances, if only the men in powder-blue and white could break down the orange dike and flow into the Lowlander's heartland.

Holland kicked off and went on the offensive immediately. Green shirted keeper Calix was called upon to stifle the orange crush twice before the ball crossed the center field line going in the opposite direction. But it was that first charge by the Latins that set the stage for things to come.

Juan Chacon's headed clearance in the third minute was trapped and controlled off the chest of Renaldo De Seta. With the Dutchmen pressed forward in search of the go-ahead marker, the midfield resembled deserted parkland.

Off tore number seventeen, straight up the field. Long, graceful strides kept eating up the green carpet. Closer and closer loomed the opposition's bank vault. There was only one way that he could be stopped, and it was left to retreating Dutch midfielder Jan Johannes to lunge desperately from behind at the mercurial feet of the intruder. Contact was made, and down went Renaldo De Seta, crashing to earth.

Sigñor Patrizio was on the spot instantly, displaying a bright yellow card deemed for Mr. Johannes. The fallen Porteño grasped his tender limb to inspect it for damage. He felt no unusual pain, and once convinced that there was no harm done, bounded to his feet, and raced upfield ready for the free kick that the foul had garnered.

Ruben Gitares took the set piece from thirty yards distance, and a diving Caesar Castro was able to redirect the ball with a precise header into Ramon Vida's path. The 'Boy from Boca' stood face-to-face with keeper Wilhelmus, but the shooter's angle was poor, and the Dutchman was able to parry Vida's blast over the touchline. Argentina had served notice that this segment of the contest was not going to be a carbon copy of the preceding embarrassment.

The ungentlemanly conduct had not disappeared with regulation time, and Sigñor Patrizio, again, had his hands full trying to keep things moving along with some sort of consistency. Chacon was cautioned, but not carded on two occasions for blatant fouls that normally would have brought a booking.

Perhaps the besieged official feared having to come into intimate contact with that deformed visage and foul temperament. He kept his distance as the frustrated Orange-shirts swarmed around him, pleading for justice. It was to no avail. Number eight in powder-blue and white merely shrugged his shoulders at the long-distance reprimand and went about his business.

The Dutchmen had made no adjustment in their offensive tactics, sticking with the same methodology that had produced their only reward thus far, long, cross-field buildups, followed by quick breaks toward the Argentine goal by any man who could shake loose of his mark. The deeper the Europeans pressed, the more susceptible they became to the fast-breaking Latins' counterattack.

One minute before the conclusion of the first extra stanza, a misplaced Dutch cross was trapped by Jorge Calderone twenty yards out from his own goal line. Turning upfield, the Newton's Prefect fullback spotted Humberto Velasquez with acres of space on the near sideline. Calderone's true pass sent the little halfback streaking upfield. As two Dutch defenders converged to relieve him of the ball, he calmly shoveled it off to Ramon Vida, who had drawn close to lend assistance.

Vida had some time to plan his next move, and he stopped dead in his tracks to seek out reinforcements. Out of the corner of his eye, he spotted the musical half of the R&Rs approaching rapidly on the full run.

"Go for it, man," were the words that accompanied his gift to the dashing center half. Three defenders had converged on Vida by this time, but none were fleet enough to catch the rampaging Renaldo. Vida split the opening between two of the Dutchmen with his pass, and onto the offering ran number seventeen.

Eighteen yards out, at the edge of the penalty area, Renaldo was forced to leap over the flailing form of Nilis Hendrik. But the ball stayed true to the Argentine's desired course as if it were on a string attached to his ankle. Straight ahead he propelled himself, closer and closer to his ultimate destination.

Now more Orange-shirts congregated to impede his progress. A slight feint to his left sent his old friend Willie Brax sprawling to the deck, clutching nothing but air. After that challenge, Renaldo was clear, and he raised his head to set his sights.

There, there it is. Right in front of me with only keeper Wilhelmus to beat. The Holy Temple of wood and mesh loomed larger than life.

Come on! Come on! Head and feet as one! Head and feet . . . The words swirled in his brain, but before he could react with his intended shot, Wilhelmus abandoned his upright stance and dove straight at the ball.

There was nothing that Renaldo could do. He leapt to avoid the outstretched keeper as Wilhelmus sprawled on the turf. Unfortunately, the leather didn't accompany the handsome intruder this time as he sidestepped the last Dutchman. Instead, it struck the goalie's elbow and floated upwards, twirling agonizingly in the air. The millions held their collective breath in slow motion torture. Where would it land? Who would it favor? That was the ultimate question!

The Argentine center half was now behind the prone Dutch keeper, watching, waiting for the spinning spheroid to make up its mind. Defenders Van Vlymen and Laurens had also sprinted behind Wilhelmus and were fast approaching to assist in the clearance. Even though Renaldo was still onside, there would be precious little time to act.

The object of attention dropped to earth two yards from the goal line, out of reach of the prostrate Wilhelmus, but dead in the midst of the two Dutch defenders and the sandwiched Argentine. All three made frantic attempts to caress the ball.

Head and feet as one! One more time, one more time!

The shining sun on Renaldo's left calf guided him home. The touch was ever so gentle, but it was all that was required. Down, down, the orb spun, hitting the green grass one yard from heaven, then bounding nonchalantly into the back of the net.

The goal scorer raised his arms triumphantly, but not believing his good fortune, sought out Sigñor Patrizio for confirmation. The black-shirt was striding full speed towards the net, his right arm outstretched, pointing to the ball now resting contentedly in the far reaches of the Dutch goal.

The usual celebration teemed down from the Gallery Gods, but along with the ticker tape came the trilled roar that was illuminated on the scoreboard.

"RRRRRRRenaaaaaaaaallllldo!"
"RRRRRRRenaaaaaaaaallllldo!"
"RRRRRRRenaaaaaaaaallllldo!"

The boy was elated by his good fortune, but there was no time to savor the moment. The home team was not out of the woods yet. These Dutchmen were not quitters, a fact that had been all too poignantly demonstrated by their ability to come back and tie the game in regulation time. There remained another full fifteen minutes of play on Sigñor Patrizio's watch, and the Europeans would fight until the last tick of the timepiece to avoid having the mantle of 'runners-up' bestowed upon their shoulders!

Argentina stacked its defenses and prepared for the onslaught. Try as they might, on this occasion, the visitors could not break down the impenetrable wall of powder-blue and white. Tenacious as pit bulls, the Latins were unwilling to relinquish this lead and risk the uncertainty of a penalty shoot-out. Each Dutchman was smothered at every touch, unable to find the space required to create an opportunity. Orange anguish escalated as the sands of time slid through the hourglass. All they needed was one true chance, one crucial opening to set things right!

The hosts were in no mood to accommodate the needs of their visitors on this fateful afternoon. In fact, there remained a taste for the kill on the palates of the Argentine forwards that would be savored six minutes from full time.

With the desperate Dutchmen throwing every man forward, an opportunity arose as a result of Leopoldo Anariba deftly cutting out and stripping defender Eimert Laurens of the ball. The Argentine halfback relayed the object of his handiwork twenty yards up the sideline to Caesar Castro, who, in turn, wasted not a second in connecting with Renaldo De Seta.

Just to the right of number seventeen flashed the 'Boy from Boca.' The R&Rs were together again, this time on a much larger stage, and they ran together stride for stride toward a different kind of golden record.

What developed was a form of 'after you, Alphonse' passing extravaganza, which revealed each man's desire to see his friend score the clinching marker.

Renaldo made the initial relay to his amigo, who collected the leather in full flight some twenty-five yards out. Too swift were these South Americans for the caught-upfield Netherlanders. At the top of the penalty arch, Ramon flicked the ball back at his chum, who had cut the distance between them to a mere five yards. The pass struck Renaldo on the right hip, and all the center half could manage at the speed he was running was a twist of his lower torso in his teammate's direction. Vida had slowed, expecting a return offering. He wasn't disappointed, for Renaldo's hip pointer struck him dead on the breast bone.

There was no time to stop and trap the orb, for both men were now half stumbling, half running to keep the threat alive. Off the Boca Boy's chest thumped the sphere, spiraling back at number seventeen only two yards until colliding with the top of Renaldo's right shoulder.

The ball seemed to rest comfortably for an instant in the crook of the younger player's neck. As Ramon Vida crossed in front of him some fifteen yards from the goal line, Renaldo carried the black-and-white passenger a few strides closer toward its desired destination. Vida's pick play had drawn the only remaining defender closer to the Dutch goal, allowing his friend to remain onside and blocking the Orange-shirt from challenging his partner. Renaldo was unmolested, so he took the time to carefully shrug the ball down to the turf directly onto his right foot.

One touch for control was all he needed before cocking his powerful right leg and letting fly. Dutch keeper Wilhelmus must have thought the bouncing ball show was going to continue. He stood his ground in the center of the goalmouth, keying on the approaching Vida in anticipation of a return pass.

The late-arriving Europeans frantically tried to gain position to interfere with Renaldo's unobstructed approach, but it was all to no avail. Even Wilhelmus knew that the jig was up, and his halfhearted kick-step at the rocketing missile ended up being too little, too late.

Astor Gordero's familiar catch-phrase flashed through Renaldo's mind as his right foot made contact. Off went the leather globe, sailing just out of Wilhelmus' reach, completing its voyage in the far lower corner of the Dutch net.

All doubts had been swept away with one swing of the boy's right leg. All the naysayers were silenced forever. The vast amounts of money and time spent by the host nation to provide a world-class showcase would pay the ultimate dividend. Argentina was about to be crowned champions of the world!

The remaining time elapsed as a mere formality. The heart had been torn out of the brave Lowlanders, and they knew that there would be no 'Dutch Masters' on this day.

The three shrill blasts of Sigñor Patrizio's whistle were the signal for all serious thoughts to cease throughout this South American madhouse. It was celebration time, and the largest, longest, loudest party ever seen in the southern hemisphere would commence before the final note of the referee's metal object had faded into the roaring dusk.

CHAPTER TWENTY-NINE

The Argentine security forces tried their utmost to maintain some semblance of order on the pitch. Each of the eleven victorious starters was given a two-man military escort to the victory podium as soon as the players had finished congratulating each other.

To Renaldo's surprise and amazement, he was hoisted off the ground from behind by two huge, muscular arms. As he tried to turn his head to see who was providing the impromptu elevator, the unmistakably gruff voice of 'Killer' Juan Chacon rang in his ear.

"Not bad for a snotnosed schoolboy, not bad at all! You did well, little one. I am proud to be your teammate!"

With that, the grip was loosened and number seventeen fell to earth. Still dumbfounded by The Ugly One's sudden amiability, Renaldo paused several seconds before realizing that Chacon had extended his right hand in an offering of reconciliation. The younger player grasped his former antagonist's huge fist and was instantly drawn to the larger man's chest in an affectionate bear hug.

"Thanks, Juan, it means a lot to me to have your faith and acceptance. You were the man that showed us all what 'true grit' really meant! I would rather have you as a friend than an enemy any day!"

Captain Daniele Bennett finally led his assembled compatriots up the steps and onto the podium where congratulations were extended by FIFA dignitaries and the junta leaders. Then, in the moment all of Argentina had waited and prayed for, the captain hoisted the golden trophy symbolizing world football supremacy above his head for all to see.

This simple act was greeted by the most deafening roar of unbridled euphoria ever heard in this soccer crazy country. They were the best, and their pride and passion was great enough to stir the souls of their dear, departed ancestors. This was a victory for all times, for generations past, present, and future!

It was difficult to say who the most elated observer was standing in row 8, field level section 365, seats 1 through 6. For Astor Gordero, the faith and guidance bestowed upon his young goal-scoring protégé would be richly rewarded in the months and years to come. The Fat Man felt that he and he, alone, was responsible for creating Argentina's new football superstar, and from that moment on, he was ready to let every living soul know it.

For Sir Reginald Russell, the performance of his newly acquired hired gunners partially erased his skepticism and the feeling of being taken for a sucker by the rotund facilitator. Reggie still felt that it was a ridiculously exorbitant amount of money that his daughter had forced him to commit to paying the two South Americans for their services in England.

We'll see how these warm weather Latinos react to playing a man's game of football in real soccer weather! thought the still unconvinced Englishman.

For Mallory Russell, it wasn't a matter of the money at all. The play of Vida and De Seta would be enough to keep her father off her back, at least for the time being. No, the money would be well spent. For her, there were two tangible things that exhilarated the fair-haired beauty.

The first was a chance to bring the South American style and skill to the paying English soccer public, and to use these two imports as a means of showing the Football Association that their navel-gazing attitude about how the game should be played needed a good dose of soul searching.

But most importantly for Mallory Russell, it was the opportunity to continue watching that gorgeous number seventeen ply his trade. To be close to him, to get to know him, to help him get adjusted to his new life in England, and to make him her lover!

For Simone, the day held a very mixed bag of emotions. She was thrilled for Renaldo and his success, but she knew that this same success would take him away from her. She was already aware of the pending deal that would send the object of her desire to another continent. Astor Gordero had informed her of all the particulars the day before the final. He had also informed the chanteuse that should there remain any doubt in the boy's mind as to whether or not to accept the English offer, that she was expected to 'close the deal' on his behalf. She was in no position to refuse her domineering manager's instructions, no matter how much her heart ached.

As the team and coaching staff left the podium for their victory lap around River Plate Stadium, Lonnie De Seta tried to seek out his brother to offer congratulations. He had been able to forget about his own predicament completely during the past two hours of high drama. Now with tears of joy streaming down his cheeks, he joined the ever-growing crush of press and supporters that were jockeying for position around their conquering heroes.

Rojo Geary's only instructions from Astor Gordero had been to make sure that the brothers did not come in contact with one another. Lonnie's subsequent disappearance would be too difficult to explain if Renaldo knew that his older brother had, in fact, been in Buenos Aires for the final game. Better he think that Lonnie had met his demise in the intended traffic mishap in Bariloche instead of the truth.

Gordero had already laid the groundwork for the ruse, and only the brothers coming face-to-face could disrupt things. Rojo Geary was a professional, and for that reason, Gordero had felt totally at ease that nothing would happen that wasn't planned. Let Lonnie see his brother play for the championship as a farewell gift. After that, his fate rested in the hands of the assassin.

Rojo Geary was truly touched by his companion's outpouring of pride and joy. Geary was also thrilled that Argentina was the champion of the world. He had admired the skills of Lonnie's brother, and thought that the two goals the boy had scored were a fitting tribute to his soon to be departed brother. Yes, Rojo Geary had enjoyed the emotion-packed afternoon immensely, but now it was down to business.

The stadium pitch was, by this time, a madhouse of uncontrollable Argentines of every description. People were tearing up chunks of turf as souvenirs or trying to carry away any stationary object that wasn't permanently secured. Water bottles, coolers, the team benches, and even the newly installed seats all fell prey to the pillaging hordes.

The more zealous fanatics tried to rip the game jerseys off the backs of their heroes as lasting mementos of the greatest day in Argentina's history. The players themselves were swarmed at first, then hoisted aloft and paraded around the pitch in triumph. Skipper Bennett kept an iron grip on his golden prize, lest it be swept away by the frenzied celebrants.

Lonnie De Seta tried to locate his brother in the swirling sea of powder-blue and white, but it was no easy task. So irrationally intense was the jarring turbulence of his fellow idol worshippers that nothing positive could be accomplished. Geary was ever at his side, trying to gently coax the terrorist into giving up his quest. There would be an easier means of paying his respects later that evening.

"Lonnie, this is crazy. I'm getting trampled to death here. I told you that Señor Gordero secured a pass for you to this evening's reception. You can see your brother there and actually talk to him. You won't even get close to him now! Let's go."

"No, no! I have to tell him that I am here, that I saw him play. I must! You don't understand. Look, there he is. Renaldo, Renaldo over here!"

Several yards away, riding aloft on a surging tide of ecstatic believers swept the day's scoring sensation. Renaldo thought that he had heard a familiar voice calling his name, but in the pandemonium that had enveloped his person, nothing could be certain. Number seventeen was actually more concerned for his physical safety at the hands of his boisterous admirers. All he wanted to do was work his way to the stairwell leading down to the safety of the National Team's dressing room.

Rojo Geary was prepared to take action right there on the pitch. The six-inch, spring-loaded, stiletto dagger that lay in the pocket of his leather jacket could do the job silently if the stubborn fugitive persisted with this idiocy. In the crush of people, Geary's trained hand-to-hand combat techniques would serve him well. No one would see a thing. When the mob had moved on, and Geary with it, only the recently departed Lonnie De Seta would remain behind.

Still, the assassin preferred to stick to his number one plan, and all it took in the end to keep things on the ordained course was an outstretched right leg that sent Lonfranco De Seta tumbling to the turf. Geary and several others fell on top of the tragic figure, and no one, especially Lonnie, was able to tell just who or what had felled him in the jostling crowd. By the time they had righted themselves, Renaldo De Seta had made it to the tunnel steps. With the help of the now very prominent security forces, number seventeen disappeared from the field of play to safety.

"Son of a bitch! I almost got to him. Damn, I wanted to see him so badly!" An exasperated Lonnie's eyes filled this time with tears of frustration.

"Don't worry, my friend. As I told you, I have your money and a pass for tonight's gala in my car. We must get out of here now and retrieve them. I can drive you to wherever you have to go to get cleaned up and changed."

Lonnie grudgingly gave in to his new acquaintance's suggestion. The two men slowly made their way for the nearest exit, still surrounded by victory-crazed Porteños.

The walk to the side street near Café El Molino took close to half an hour. Both men were constantly hugged and kissed by overjoyed citizens of both sexes. Rojo Geary didn't mind their playful celebrations, for he had all the time in the world to carry out his plan. It was Lonnie that seemed distracted, having little patience for this tomfoolery.

He was deep in thought about his next move. Had Gordero sent him enough cash to find a place to clean up, change his clothes, and make an appearance at the Presidential Gala? Would it be safe for him to go out in public in the first place? He had to see Renaldo one last time before he left the country, though. Only God knew how long it would be before he would have another opportunity to hold his brother in his arms and tell him how much he loved and respected him.

Yes, he would go to the Presidential Gala, and he would say good-bye to Renaldo. Tomorrow, he would make another visit to his bank, and if he successfully gained access to his safety deposit box, he could secure an airplane ticket and travelers checks with his American Express card. No one should notice him leaving Argentina among the general exodus of foreign football fans.

Lonnie would have the redhead drive him to Marla's, where he would retrieve his bag from the alley. Maybe the stranger would then deliver him to a nearby hotel. If he could have this one night to celebrate with his little brother, he would leave Argentina a happy man.

"My car is over here. Hold on. I'll unlock the passenger door for you."

Rojo Geary pointed to a little red coup parked near the end of a one-way side street. He slid behind the wheel, leaned over, and unlocked the black glove compartment, then lifted the chrome door-latch for Lonnie. Geary turned the key in the ignition as his passenger made himself comfortable.

"Man, it sure feels good to sit down after all that time kneeling on the grass at the stadium." Lonnie let out a sigh of relief. "So, where is the envelope that Señor Gordero sent for me? I can't believe he actually got me a pass for the gala tonight."

"It's in the glove compartment, my friend. I've already unlocked it, so go ahead, see for yourself."

Lonnie bent forward to open the compartment with his right hand. At the same time, Rojo Geary slid his left hand into his jacket pocket and grasped the ivory-handled stiletto. The assassin's right hand reached over and took a firm grip on the back of Lonnie's leather jacket collar. In one swift motion, Geary turned so that he was facing his passenger, pressed the release button on the deadly weapon, and thrust its entire length up under the unsuspecting terrorist's sternum, directly into his heart.

The solid grip on the dying man's collar forcibly calmed the convulsions of Lonnie's death throes, and within seconds, all was still and peaceful. Geary reached over to close the lids of his victim's shocked, disbelieving eyes, then extracted the murder weapon from its resting place.

A quick flash of the coup's high beams brought two men bounding out of the unmarked five-ton truck that was parked immediately in front of Geary's car. The men opened the rear doors of the lorry as Rojo Geary exited the execution vehicle, leaving the ignition running. He calmly strolled down the side street as one of the men slid behind the wheel of the red Fiat holding Lonnie's corpse. Geary didn't say a word or glance back as the four-wheeled coffin was driven up a ramp and into the rear cargo hold of the lorry. No one would see Lonnie De Seta again until he turned up, burned beyond recognition, in the wreck of that same vehicle, several weeks later in Bariloche.

Astor Gordero is a very thorough man, thought Rojo Geary as he climbed into his customized Jeep CJ4, parked just a few yards down the side street. Yes, The Fat Man always pays attention to details. That must be how he became so successful. Well, it has been a great day! Great for Argentina, great for Astor Gordero, great for everyone. Everyone except poor Lonnie De Seta!

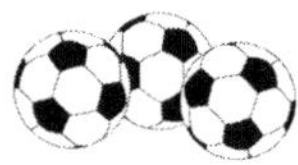

Octavio Suarez had given strict orders that only the players and their coaches be permitted into the National Team's dressing room immediately following the championship final. When everyone that mattered had assembled, Suarez commanded that the door be locked tight, then called for silence.

"Señors, I would ask that you join me in a silent prayer of thanksgiving and deliverance. A prayer giving thanks for the great achievement that you, the players, have accomplished today. A prayer for delivering us safely through the turbulent waters that we have travelled. Let us pray."

What had been a noisy chamber instantly resembled a mausoleum. Grown men bowed their heads, many with tear-filled eyes, to acknowledge their personal indebtedness to a higher being. Suarez was not known as a religious man, but no one was surprised at his sudden willingness to share the managerial spotlight with the Creator of all mankind.

In due course, he broke the introspective silence.

"My friends, thank you. Words alone cannot describe my pride and honor at being associated with each and every one of you in this room. I know that you have warmed the hearts of millions of people today throughout this great land. What you have accomplished here is more than just a victory in a game of football. You have shown the world that Argentina is, once and for all time, a unified nation. A nation that can rise above political and economic difficulties and meet any challenge laid before it, just as you have met every challenge laid before you."

Suarez's eyes were brimming with tears now, his complexion ruddy with emotion, his clothes soaked with perspiration.

"Think back, my noble gladiators, to when there was talk of taking the tournament away from Argentina. If we had not believed in the Organizing Committee, this triumphant day might never have occurred. Think back to when we lost to Italy in the first round. If we had not believed in ourselves, we would not have this golden symbol of world supremacy to look after for the next four years. I believed! You all believed! The entire nation believed! And here is the prize for our strength of conviction. The World Cup Trophy!"

The manager held the golden globe aloft for all to see. For the first time since he began to speak, the silence in the room was broken by hearty cheers. A two-fingered whistle from the manager silenced them instantly.

"Now, back to business. In a few minutes, the doors will be opened and we will be besieged with press and dignitaries. Remember that you are still ambassadors for your country and act accordingly. I will allow them thirty minutes, that is all. Then the room will be cleared while you shower and change into your number one dress. The bus will depart in one hour's time for the reception at the Hotel Presidente. It will be your last official function as a member of the Argentine National Football Team. Each of you has been assigned a room at the hotel for your personal use tonight, but I expect you to be present at the gala until I dismiss you in the farewell speech that I am apparently obliged to make."

The head man took one last triumphant look around the hushed chamber. His heart was in his throat when he continued.

"So, now you are the supreme champions, and I thank you for having faith in your coaching staff and advisors. All the world will remember what you have achieved here today. I am proud to say that I was a small part of your great success. God bless you all, and Viva Argentina!"

Octavio Suarez was flushed with pride as he nodded to Estes Santos. The goalkeeper coach echoed the manager's final exclamation as he let fly the cork on the first of several score of Mumm's Cordon Rouge champagne bottles that had mysteriously appeared. These were about to be both sprayed in celebration and consumed in honor of this great day.

Ubaldo Luque then unlocked the dressing room door and allowed the legion of impatient journalists into the inner sanctum. The air was filled with shouts of 'Viva Argentina!' over and over again as each of the newly arrived guests was given an impromptu shower with France's bubbly export.

Renaldo De Seta sat in front of his cubicle, stripped to the waist, his tender limb wrapped in an ice compress. He calmly answered questions from the scrum of journalists that transcribed his every word. It was his obligation to respond to even the most inane query, but the shy lad would have much rather that the attention be redirected elsewhere. All he wanted was to shower and dress in preparation for his rendezvous with Simone.

"Renaldo, are you aware that you have won the Golden Ball Award for the tournament's most valuable player?"

"Renaldo, what are your future plans? Will you stay in Argentina to play football or head abroad to Spain or Italy as rumored?"

"Renaldo, is it true that you had to have your foot frozen before each half, and that you pop painkillers like candy to keep going?"

"Is it true that you will demand five million American dollars to stay in your homeland to play this season, or will you give it all up to go back to school as has been speculated?"

"Renaldo, how about the ladies? Is it true that you have had several hundred proposals of marriage from complete strangers since the tournament began?"

On and on it went. Late arriving reporters repeated questions already asked. Flashbulbs from photographers' cameras constantly popped in the boy's face, to the point that his vision was blurred and spotted. The half hour could not have ended soon enough for number seventeen, and when Octavio Suarez finally demanded that the room be cleared, Argentina's goal-scoring maestro slumped back against the metal partition of his dressing area, too exhausted to move. Ramon Vida finally coaxed him into getting his act in gear.

"So, Señor golden balls, come on. We have to get moving. Estes Santos told me that there will be five gorgeous women for every team member at the gala. After being locked up for over a month, I think I will take on my five and then any that you have left over. So don't keep a horny man waiting. Get that cute little ass of yours into the shower and let's go!"

"OK, OK, Señor Casanova. Put a muzzle on that loaded weapon of yours until we get downtown, or I will be afraid to bend over if I drop the soap in there!"

Vida extended a hand and pulled his partner to his feet. For the first time since they were crowned champions of the world, the two men embraced.

"We did pretty fucking good out there today, amigo. Wait until those English get an eyeful of what you and I can do together. We'll be the crown princes of the empire! Pip, pip, jolly good! Isn't that how they talk?"

Renaldo smiled at his friend's attempted English accent and vocabulary.

"I guess so, Ramon, sometimes at least. I still haven't decided what I'm going to do about leaving Argentina. It is a heavy subject that will take some time to figure out." Renaldo could see the disbelief in his friend's eyes.

"Hell, man, you can't walk away from an opportunity like this. Forget about the money part. Just think about the experience of fucking all those lovely English girls. They all want to have hot Latin lovers. I will show them tricks that their uptight English men haven't even thought of yet. Pip, Pip, jolly good fuck old chap! Damn right!"

Renaldo laughed at the Boca Boy's gutter humor as he made his way to the showers. He had to admit that the urge to seek his fortune in another part of the world had been tugging at his heartstrings the more he mulled the possibility over in his mind. But right now, there was only one subject that he preferred to ruminate on, and his thoughts of seeing the vivacious Simone in an hour or so tugged at a part of his anatomy several degrees south of his heart.

What would normally have been a twenty-minute cab ride from the stadium to the Hotel Presidente on Calle Nuevo de Julio at Avenida Córdoba took almost two hours to complete. The National Team bus could only snail through the never-ending phalanx of powder-blue-and-white-clad vehicles of every description. Anything that had a motor and wheels was pressed into service as an unofficial motorcade for the men of the hour. The police escort was quickly surrounded and augmented by jubilant Argentines hoping to get a glimpse of their heroes.

The closer the procession got to their final destination, the crazier the party seemed to get. The streets were absolutely jammed with revellers utilizing every form of noisemaker known to man to demonstrate their elation. Ticker tape and streamers rained down upon the crowd from the high-rise towers, giving the effect of a northern hemisphere snow storm. But the real white stuff wouldn't have stood a chance of survival on the streets of Buenos Aires this Sunday night, for the atmosphere at ground level was hotter than Hades.

The National Team bus had been well stocked with liquid refreshments and food for the anticipated slow journey to the gala. All the players thoroughly enjoyed themselves, soaking up the sights and sounds of a city gone over the edge. Even an impatient Ramon Vida rationalized that it would give the lovely ladies waiting at the Hotel Presidente time to get 'really hot' for the objects of their desire.

At last, shortly after ten in the evening, the coveted coach pulled up to the rear service entrance of the hotel. The players were given a few minutes in the staff changing area to spruce up their appearances, and in some cases, to splash water on their already inebriated faces. They were then led to the backstage area, where they awaited their introduction by the evening's master of ceremonies.

The grand ballroom was filled to the rafters with everyone who was anyone in the national hierarchy. Over one thousand people were engaged in wining and dining on the finest delicacies available. No cost had been spared to salute the world champions this night. All the junta leaders, including President Videla, were prominently glad-handing their fellow celebrants, pressing the flesh as if confirming that their corrupt iron rule was responsible in some large way for the day's triumphant outcome.

While nothing could have been further from the truth, no one in attendance really cared in the slightest who or what had brought about the magnificent outcome of this day. All that mattered was that their nation stood singularly in the world's sporting spotlight, and everyone wanted to bask in its glow.

The signal was given to the orchestra leader for a drum roll and a grand crescendo of instruments. The MC, one of Argentina's leading movie stars named Vasco Caliente, stepped to the microphone and requested silence from the overjoyed partiers.

"Thank you, Señors, Señoras, and Señoritas, thank you. It is my great honor and distinct pleasure to introduce to you now, right here on this stage, the 1978 World Cup Champion Football Team. The National Team of Argentina!"

Thunderous applause turned into shouts of "Argentina! Argentina! Argentina!" as the men in navy blue blazers and grey flannel slacks were led by Captain Daniele Bennett out onto the stage and into the spotlight. The twenty-two men on the training roster were lined up after Captain Bennett in numerical jersey order, then each was introduced individually to a deafening response.

When it came time for number seventeen to step forward, the obviously nervous player bowed his head and took a small pace out from the line. The ear-splitting reaction caused the boy to raise his head and wave in a gesture of acknowledgment. This only heightened the crowd's response, and the self-conscious smile on the young man's face turned to a broad grin as he seemed to finally accept the adulation of his enthusiastic admirers.

"Stay right there, Señor De Seta," Caliente instructed. "I would now like to introduce the chairman of Argentina's World Cup Organizing Committee, Admiral Manuel Junin Melendez, who has a special presentation to make at this time. Admiral Melendez."

The uniformed admiral strode to the microphone, signaling Renaldo to step up to his side. Polite applause greeted the naval commander.

"Thank you. It is my distinct pleasure to present to Renaldo De Seta the Golden Ball Award of the 1978 World Cup Soccer Tournament. This award is emblematic of the most valuable player in the tournament, and Argentina's Renaldo De Seta, having played inspired two-way football that netted seven goals, is the winner of this coveted symbol of excellence. Congratulations, Renaldo!"

Thunderous applause replaced the limp display that had greeted Admiral Melendez. Shouts of "Bravo! Bravo!" and "Viva Argentina!" rang through the ballroom. As the embarrassed rookie center half accepted his reward and shook hands with the junta honcho, an explosion of flashbulbs was detonated by the photographers fighting for position to freeze this moment in time.

Temporarily blinded by the force of the newsmen's weapons, Renaldo shielded his eyes and turned away from the luminous onslaught. It was at that moment that he first heard the now-familiar refrain growing in volume and intensity.

"RRRRRRRenaaaaaaaallllldo!"
"RRRRRRRenaaaaaaaallllldo!"
"RRRRRRRenaaaaaaaallllldo!"

The entire room had picked up the anthem, and all the awed recipient could do was smile and wave his acknowledgment to the adoring masses. Admiral Melendez had left the boy's side. Renaldo stood alone in the glare of the spotlights, thankful for the adulation, but wishing with all his heart that he could be anywhere else in the world.

When all the players and coaching staff had been introduced, a nearly hoarse Vasco Caliente called for restraint and quiet from the guests.

"Señors and Señoras, please, please if you will. We have a special treat for you. Following her stirring rendition of our national anthem this afternoon at the stadium, it is a great thrill for me to introduce to you once again, the nation's leading vocal artist. She will now lead us in that patriotic ode one more time. So, without further delay, would you please welcome the beautiful and talented . . . Symca!"

Out of the opposite wing of the stage from which the team had made its entrance flowed the shimmering form of a stunning young lady. Simone had chosen a tight-fitting, floor-length, silver-sequined gown that was cut low enough from her shoulders to accentuate her ample cleavage. She was positively radiant as she stepped to the microphone, offering waves and blown kisses to the enthusiastic audience. The diva then turned to face the National Team members, curtsied in gracious respect, then broke into a soulful rendition of the Argentine national anthem.

There were several instances during Simone's impassioned vocalizing that her eyes met with Renaldo's. The singer was cautious not to make her feelings too obvious to those in attendance, but for the recipient of her longing glances, there was no doubting their meaning. When the last notes of the anthem had been supplanted by the same high-decibel reaction that had greeted the player's introductions, the sexy chanteuse smiled warmly to the faithful, blew a final kiss good-bye, then departed the stage.

It was left to manager Octavio Suarez to thank the president and dignitaries on behalf of the team in a relatively brief formal statement that he delivered with the use of prewritten cue cards. Polite applause followed the conclusion of the formal text, but as Suarez returned the cards to his jacket's inner pocket, he turned to his players and paused before the microphone.

"I would like to add just one more thing, if I may, Señor Presidente. This group of men on the stage here tonight have accomplished a feat that only a few weeks ago, the international soccer community, and even many in this room, felt was an impossible task. Señors and Señoras, these men standing before you have overcome more obstacles than you will ever know to reach the heights of Olympus. I must tell you all that there will never again be a group of individuals to wear our national colors with their heart and character."

There was a fierce pride resonating from Suarez's voice now. Those in the grand room who had not been privy to the man's passion were startled by the change in intensity from his written script. He turned to face them as he addressed his charges for the final time.

"Señors, you are the best in the world tonight, and no one can ever demean or diminish your accomplishments. God bless each and every one of you! Now, go and have some fun. There will be no curfew or bed check tonight! Viva Argentina!"

There was not a dry eye to be found standing on that stage as manager Suarez worked his way down the line of players, embracing each man in turn. The orchestra leader, picking up on the emotionally charged moment, lead his musicians in a spontaneous rendition of "Auld Lang Syne."

The entire ballroom stood in heart-tugging silence, reflecting on the magnitude of what they were witnessing.

Never again would this same group of champions be together as a unit, either on a stage or on a football pitch. The changes in their young lives from this day forth would be far-reaching, and in some cases, instantaneous.

This was truly a moment for all those present to savor, to cherish for the rest of their lives as the unsurpassed pinnacle in Argentina's history.

With the dawn, these young men would go their separate ways, and the quest to remain champions of the world would inevitably begin. But for these few sublime moments, time seemed to stand still for all those lucky enough to be in attendance at the grand ballroom in the Hotel Presidente.

Once the formal ceremonies and speeches had concluded, it was time for everyone to let their collective hair down. The orchestra picked up the tempo considerably, mixing the latest pop tunes with the more traditional favorites.

The National Team players were now free to mingle with the chosen guests and partake of the festivities that they, themselves, were responsible for creating. Estes Santos had not been exaggerating in his estimation of the quantity of female companions available for the pleasure of the guests of honor.

The task of finding the lovely things had been turned over to Astor Gordero, who had played a large role in planning the tournament ending fête for the Organizing Committee. Wolfgang Stoltz had personally handpicked over one hundred of the most attractive and exotic single ladies from all regions of the country. They included everything from debutantes to call girls, the latter's services for the evening being prepaid by A.R. Gordero and Sons to avoid any scandalous connection with the official organizers.

Each team member was a highly sought-after commodity, and all were constantly encouraged to join various tables of dignitaries for rounds of drinks and commemorative photographs. The mood of giddy excitement did not extend to Renaldo De Seta, however. He observed both Estes Santos and Ramon Vida squiring a bevy of young 'hostesses' from table to table, while he himself politely declined all offers of female companionship. There was only one lady that the young star had eyes for, but to his dismay, Simone had disappeared after leaving the stage. The only reason Renaldo put up with the pawing, pandering crowd of drunks was to locate the object of his desire. His frustration was growing by the minute when a familiar large figure summoned the boy to his side.

"So, Renaldo, how goes the battle? Are you enjoying yourself this evening? Quite a little party isn't it?"

The Fat Man was obviously enjoying himself, for his speech was slightly slurred, and there was a touch of imbalance to his portly waddle. He placed a heavy arm around his client's shoulder as he spoke. Renaldo could not help but notice that the champagne had given his breath an alcoholic bouquet.

"Yes, Señor Gordero, it is a great tribute to the National Team. But have you seen Simone lately? I was hoping that she would stay for at least some of the party."

"Oh, she is here, my young friend, but first, let me remind you of some pending business. You haven't forgotten that we have a luncheon appointment tomorrow, have you? One o'clock sharp at the Jockey Club! The English are extremely anxious to meet with 'Renaldo and Ramon.' I expect you to make sure that he arrives on time and with a clear head. By the look of things, he may have a little trouble extracting himself from tonight's commitments. But I am sure that you can have him focused on business by noon tomorrow. My car will be at the front door of the hotel for you at twelve forty-five. Don't be late. The English have a thing about punctuality!"

Ramon Vida was clearly enjoying himself in the company of several stunning beauties. His National Team tie had long since been discarded, and he sat mixing long swigs directly from his personal bottle of Dom Pérignon with lusty gropes and kisses. A few of the more amorous ladies had unbuttoned his shirt almost to his belt buckle and were fondling and nibbling on his chest and nipples. All sense of decorum and propriety had disappeared with manager Suarez's order to "go and have some fun."

"It would seem that I should have a few words with Señor Vida myself before he starts using that table as his personal casting couch. It would reflect on me personally if a client of mine became too exuberant in his celebrations. We can't have that in the midst a public gathering. I will remind Ramon of our meeting tomorrow, but I am depending on you, Renaldo, to make sure that he arrives with all his faculties functioning."

The agent knew perfectly well that he could count on his conscientious client to show up with Vida in tow, but more than anything, he was enjoying the game of cat and mouse that was obviously driving Renaldo to distraction. The anxious look on the player's face made it crystal clear that Simone was his only thought, and her whereabouts the only thing in this world that mattered to him right now. It was almost painful to look at the boy.

The image of young love suddenly and unexpectedly vanished from the agent's mind as the question of Lonnie De Seta's fate surfaced. It was the first time in hours that The Fat Man had conjured up that nasty business. If things had gone according to plan, there would be one less De Seta to contend with. Poor Renaldo. To lose a brother was a terrible thing.

Well, I will know about Lonnie's situation soon enough. Right now, it's Viva Argentina time! he rationalized, turning away from his audience. "Good night, Renaldo. Don't party too hard. I will see you in the morning."

"Señor, please, one moment. What news do you have of Simone? Where can I find her?" The urgent, almost tragic tone of the question brought a broad grin to the agent's round face.

"Oh yes, Simone! I almost forgot. Here, she told me to give you this." Gordero pulled a metal fob with a key attached from his jacket pocket, then entrusted it into the footballer's hand. Renaldo held it ever so delicately while reading the inscription.

'Hotel Presidente, Ambassador's suite,' read the engraved black script on the gold metal. The boy raised his head and looked at his mentor with a puzzled expression. The agent's response was fatherly in tone.

"My, my, we will have to teach you the ways of the world, won't we? Go, go to her! That is her suite tonight. She is waiting for you there now. Take the service elevator by the kitchen where you came in. That way, no one will bother you. The suite is on the seventh floor. Seven! A lucky number, so they say! Good night, my dear boy. I will see you tomorrow at one o'clock sharp."

Renaldo stood glued to the spot where he stood. His knees felt weak and the key almost slipped from his grasp, so sweat covered had his palms suddenly become. He watched the drunk facilitator stumble over to Vida's table, then glanced down at the key to paradise. As much as he had fantasized about this moment, he was now trembling with outright fear.

Simone, Ambassador's Suite, service elevator. The words kept repeating themselves over and over again in his mind. It was only the intrusion of an intoxicated army officer seeking the scoring sensation's autograph that snapped Renaldo out of his daze.

The player obliged the military man's request, declined an invitation to have a drink with the officer and his cohorts, then excused himself as politely as possible. Making it to the stage door was no easy task, as more would-be friends and souvenir hunters descended upon the boy at every turn.

Finally, he was clear of the mob and through the entrance to the service area. A startled, awe-struck waiter gave Argentina's newest hero directions to the service elevators, then offered to show Renaldo the way personally in exchange for an autograph. The player figured that a uniformed escort may just fend off other unwanted annoyances, so he readily accepted the employee's help. In little over two minutes' time, Renaldo De Seta was standing outside the door of the Ambassador's Suite, his heart pounding and his head spinning in anticipation of the treasures that lay behind that mystic portal.

He had been rendered physically incapable of using the key, and it seemed an eternity before his knock was answered. When she finally stood before him, he thought that he would faint. He could not move, only stare in silent apprehension and appreciation.

She was attired in a pink chiffon floor-length wrap, which was gathered at one shoulder and held in place by a golden clasp. Its semi-opaque material was meant to tease the beholder, but Renaldo's searching eyes were able to detect a cornucopia of feminine delights beneath the flowing mantle. Her matching pink stiletto pumps gave her added stature and allure.

Simone gently grasped her visitor's hand and pulled him into her private world. Not a word was spoken as their lips met in the most delicate of kisses. The boy had never tasted anything so sweet. Tenderness escalated into passion the longer their lips held the embrace, but before things could get out of hand, Simone gently freed herself from his arms.

"I am so glad you came to me, Renaldo. You don't know how I have longed for this night. Come, let's have a drink and get comfortable."

It was true. She had waited for this moment, and there was no way that she was going to rush things. She was in control, and she would set the tempo. Her finishing school for young boys was about to commence.

Renaldo followed her to the living room couch without saying a word. Simone's image flickered in the glow of countless lit candles as she walked. A grand piano adorned one corner of the suite's main salon, while a fully stocked bar enhanced another. Simone had thought of everything.

The stereo softly spun the familiar melodies of the Frank Sinatra-Antonio Carlos Jobim album that the boy loved so much, and beside the couch sat a beautiful Martin acoustic guitar. The drapes had been drawn to shut out the ongoing celebration that continued noisily on the streets seven stories below them. The mood that the singer had set was perfect. Perfect for love!

"What shall we have to drink? I've opened a bottle of champagne, but there is anything you could ever imagine here."

Renaldo could only drink in her beauty, nothing else. Her long brown curls fell below her shoulders, and in the candlelight, her enormous dark eyes and full lips had a richness and sensuality, the likes of which he had never imagined possible. All he could do was sit mutely, overwhelmed by her beauty.

"So, what will it be? Don't be shy. This won't hurt a bit. Here, let's have some champagne together. I'll add a fresh strawberry to sweeten things up."

"It could never be as sweet as you look right now." He was amazed that he was able to articulate the emotion pent up within him. "I mean, in my wildest dreams, I never imagined anyone could ever look the way you do tonight. I find this all very hard to comprehend. I have to pinch myself to make sure that I am really here, alone with you."

She seemed to glide across the room on a cushion of air as she carried the two crystal goblets to the couch.

"Here, have a sip of this. It will relax you. What a day you have had! You must be totally exhausted. Why don't you let me make you more comfortable."

She pushed her guest slightly forward and removed the team blazer from his shoulders, throwing it on a side chair when it was full extracted from his upper torso. His tie went next, followed in quick succession by the uncoupling of most of the buttons on his white cotton dress-shirt.

"There, that's better! Now, a toast to Renaldo De Seta, world champion!"

Simone entwined her right arm lovingly with his as the soft clink of crystal on crystal preceded their mutual imbibing. Their eyes were riveted to each other's as they slowly sampled the frothy nectar. The lady's lips then replaced the goblet's touch on those of her companion. Her perfume enveloped him as they explored the sweetness with their tongues. Simone sighed softly as she once again pulled away.

"Let me show you something that I know will turn you to putty in my hands."

She slid to the floor in one smooth motion, then removed his loafers in the blink of an eye. The dark socks that covered his feet also disappeared in a heartbeat.

"How is your injured foot? Does it still pain you greatly?"

Her hands felt incredibly soft as she massaged the soles of his feet. The boy had never felt anything like this sensation in his life.

"You should have been my physiotherapist instead of that roughneck they had working on me. God knows how many more goals I could have scored with this kind of treatment."

Renaldo's voice sounded calm and at ease. Simone smiled up at him as he stretched his body out to give her easier access to this new source of pleasure. Once his head reclined back against the soft cushions of the sofa, the teacher knew that she had her pupil totally under control.

"Quiet nights of quiet stars, quiet cords from my guitar, floating on the silence that surrounds us." Sinatra's lilting voice was a perfect backdrop for the total release that Renaldo was experiencing. Simone had been right, he was putty in her hands.

Renaldo had no idea how long she silently but lovingly attended to his aching extremities. All he was aware of was the tremendous sense of contentment and relaxation that had seeped into every inch of his being. It was another sensation, however, that shocked his manly urges into full awakening.

Along with her gentle manipulations suddenly came the soft blowing of warm breath on the tips of his toes. Then, one by one, each small protrusion was affectionately engulfed in the warmth of her mouth, where it was treated to the most intimate of introductions. This oral reflexology sent shock waves to the boy's brain, the resultant effect of which became prominently noticeable by his undeniable arousal. He was incapable of vocalizing his feelings, so intense was the reaction to her ministrations. The only response the pupil was capable of mustering was a succession of low, guttural moans.

The soothing, sweet-toned sounds of 'Corcovado' continued in the background.

"This is where I want to be, here with you so close to me. Until the final flicker of life's embers . . ."

She was aware of his confined acknowledgement, but did not alter her curriculum to suit his needs. This could not be rushed. These lessons required patience and control to bring the student to matriculation.

In time, when each of the ten had received the desired amount of attention, Simone slowly, ever so gently, started to caress her apprentice's inner calves. Working her way up to his inner thigh, it was impossible for her to not feel his need, so strained was the material of his grey flannels. Finally, she took pity on his discomfort, and while one hand explored the firmness of his hairless, exposed chest, the other silently uncoupled the leather belt buckle that constrained her reward.

The undergraduate was more than willing to assist his professor at this point, all caution and shyness having evaporated. The metal zipper was torn asunder in one swift motion, and a slight rise of the young man's buttocks allowed his instructor to discard the unwanted vestments.

Simone had closed her eyes, not wanting to gaze upon her treasure just yet. She pulled herself up beside him, so that his taunt nipple rested perfectly on her lips. With ever-mounting lust, she twirled the erect object with her tongue, then drew it into the warmth of her sweet mouth, just as she had done earlier with the tips of his body. She knew full well that he was experiencing immense pleasure, but offsetting this was the considerable frustration of her not focusing on the center of his newly blossomed desire.

In the end, Simone could no longer stand it herself. She set about kissing her way down that rock-hard chest, lingering with her tongue around his navel, then sliding to the floor between his legs. She allowed herself the sense of sight once she had settled comfortably there, and the vision she beheld silhouetted in the candlelight took her breath away.

He looked so beautiful sitting there in all his maleness. It was her turn to drink in his aroma, to revel in the aura of that immense object. She tried to grasp it gently in her hand, but her grip was too small. Two hands were required to continue this course of study, but the educator remained undaunted and pressed on with the lesson. Her tongue played an integral part in this passion play now, as did her lips, teeth, and full mouth.

Several times she perceived her disciple's white tears of love to be on the brink of expulsion, but the evangelist had learned how to control these urges. She was an expert educator, and class would not be dismissed until all her courses had been taught!

Finally, when her own desires became irresistible, she took him by the hand and led him to her boudoir. More candles decorated that chamber, which highlighted a king-sized, Louis the Fourteenth canopy covered bed. Renaldo was suddenly overcome with self-consciousness, his exposed manhood prominently on display for his adoring lover to gaze upon. Simone guided him to the bed, gently pushing him onto his back.

"Get comfortable, my love, and don't be shy. I will join you presently."

She stood at the foot of the giant playground, and with one touch of her hand to the shoulder clasp of the chiffon wrap, the confining article fell to the floor.

The boy had never conjured up such a vision of erotic pulchritude, even in his most stimulating of moments. Simone's height was accentuated by the stiletto pumps. Her smooth, long legs were caressed by the sheerest of pale pink stockings. From a lacy mid-length bustier of matching color extended ornately woven garters, which, in turn, clasped the sheer fabric encasing those beautiful gams. It was a breathtaking sight, one that brought the student to the verge of losing all control.

His administrator was attentive to his needs, however, and she joined him on the pillared laboratory for her introductory anatomy lesson. Their lips met once more, this time with some urgency, for the lady was aware that the heat of their passion had drenched her velvet cleft. Suddenly, she withdrew her lips and whispered in his ear.

"I want to teach you how to pleasure a lady, how to make her insane with abandon. We will start with a kiss on the lips, then work our way down to our ultimate goal. Don't be scared. I will show you exactly what to do."

Again she kissed him tenderly, then slowly, ever so lovingly, took his soft curls in her hands and guided his mouth to her breast. First one, then the other, while her sweet voice cooed instructions. Further south on this new journey, the traveler wandered, allowing his tongue to explore the hidden pleasures of her tiny navel. The texture and scent of her soft, silky skin combined to completely overshadow his own yearnings.

Further down past the equator, the adventurer roamed on his quest for knowledge, guided expertly at each step by his knowing tutor.

Ultimately, he beheld the center of her universe, and with it, all the joyous wonders contained therein. Softly, with her husky, soothing voice giving encouragement, the instructor nuzzled his features against her soul. She had waited so long for this . . . had thought of very little else each time she had laid eyes on him. And now, now she would teach him to be a man.

She was diligent and exacting in her enlightenment of the boy, making each semester last until she could resist no longer. The waves that eventually swept over her, driving her to a state of fretful convulsions . . . these were proof of his passing grade.

She had ushered him out of teenage adolescence and into that sacred realm that some men never achieve in a lifetime. She had given him this gift to bond their love, for she was fully aware that a more intimate union between man and woman did not exist!

The student could not believe his instructor's demonstrative reaction to his journey. He feared for a moment that he had caused her some physical damage, so violent was the reaction to his reaching the gates of Utopia. He was only reassured that she was whole by the loosening of her iron grip on his locks, and the hearty laugh that she emitted once composure found its way back into her spent existence.

He had swooned at her fragrance, almost unable to follow her urgings. Never could he have imagined such a sweet musk. He drank her in, his head swimming in the pool of her craving.

At the conclusion of this segment, the underclassman was congratulated for proficiency beyond expectation and escorted lovingly up once more to caress her northern lips. He would be informed that there was more on her course curriculum this night, however, and after a short recess, instruction began on the most essential of human functions.

His athletic prowess carried over into the domain of these lessons, and it was the teacher, not the pupil, who was amazed at the versatility and innovation which was abundantly displayed in class.

Time slipped away until the first hue of the coming morning made itself evident on the ceiling of the lovers' cloistered surroundings. They had not slept at all, preferring, instead, to drink the sweet wine of their newfound pleasures time and time again.

There was a sense of the supernatural under that canopied college. A sense of things and experiences beyond this world. Things too complex for the exhausted student to comprehend as he lay with the source of his enlightenment curled up in his arms.

So much had happened to him in the last twenty-four hours. Too much for his clouded, overwhelmed brain. He was aware of only one fact as his senses tried to etch this moment in his mind for all time. The worldly professor had been most appreciative of his attention to detail and unselfish research. While she would demand extended tutorials right up until he was forced to depart back through that mystic portal into the real world, she had revealed his term grade with a pink lip pencil on the smoothness of his chest. He would derive a sense of deep satisfaction each time he glanced down at the 'A+' that adorned his exhausted physique.

CHAPTER THIRTY

I'm sorry to say that I must leave you soon, my love. I have a business luncheon with Astor Gordero at the Jockey Club at one o'clock. I'll tell you all about it after I clean up and get dressed, but first I have to locate my personal belongings. They had everything moved from the training center to the rooms they assigned us in the hotel here. The key to my room should still be in my jacket pocket."

It was just after eleven o'clock, and Argentina's new football hero stood peering through the bedroom window at the never-ending procession of celebrants below him on Avenida Nueve de Julio. Simone had not stirred from their love-nest, wanting to prolong her rapture until the last possible moment. She knew that there were serious matters to discuss with this naked adonis strikingly framed in the window, but the essence of his virility made it hard for her to burst the sensual bubble the two of them had been floating in. Now the time had finally come to pay heed to Astor Gordero's bidding.

"Take a look in the closet here, my darling. I'm sure you will find everything has been delivered in tact. I even took the liberty of unpacking for you." She smiled coyly at her surprised lover.

"How on earth did you manage a trick like that?"

"Oh, a small word and a large tip from Astor Gordero can accomplish just about anything in this city. Surely you have come to realize that by now."

Renaldo opened one of the large French doors to the closet. Just as described, his wardrobe was perfectly displayed for inspection.

"I feel like the two of you conspired to seduce me last night. What if I had fallen for one of those 'hostesses' down in the ballroom and gone to my assigned room to sow my wild oats?" The smile on his face belied his mock serious tone.

"Then you would have been a horse's ass, my young stallion!" They both laughed as Simone threw a pillow at his pleasure parts. Her expression turned pensive all of a sudden as she addressed her amour in a more serious voice.

"Renaldo, I am aware of the reason that you are meeting with Astor today. He has watched us fall in love, and he didn't want me to get hurt by any decisions that were out of my control."

She paused while motioning for him to come to her on the bed. Once they were entwined in each other's arms, she continued.

"I know that there are people in Buenos Aires from England. People who want you and Ramon Vida to go back with them to London to play for their football team . . . for a considerable amount of money as I understand it!"

Renaldo was quick to interject, "Simone, my darling, I don't need the money, and one word from you will keep me in Argentina by your side forever! It would be impossible for me to leave you now!" She pressed a finger gently to his lips.

"Listen to me, my love. We do not control our own destinies anymore, you and I. We are both assets of an adoring public, and our careers are controlled by the same ambitious man. I know that you have signed a personal services contract with Astor, as have I. He is, therefore, in a position to do whatever he wants with us if we defy his wishes."

As she breathed the last word, Symca could feel the tension and anger build in his body.

"Nobody owns me, Simone, and I'll be damned if I'll let anyone run your life either. You are a star, the most famous woman in all of Argentina and . . ." Again she set her finger to his lips to calm him.

"Shhhhhh, just listen to what I have to say. Astor is not the enemy. We are both where we are today because of the faith he showed in us. He has big plans for both of us, plans that will allow us to be together more often than if you stayed right here in the capital itself. Because of your victory yesterday, and my close association with the successful tournament, Astor claims that I am now a very hot property on the international market. He wants to milk my new global status for all it is worth. That means an extended world tour, and he has already finalized many of the arrangements. I have very little choice other than to go along with his wishes, for Astor Gordero always gets what Astor Gordero wants, one way or another."

She paused to let the last phrase have the desired effect.

The chanteuse gave her lover a squeeze, then nibbled his muscular biceps ever so tenderly before reciting the obvious.

"That means that we will only be separated for six months at the most, as opposed to possibly two years if you remain in Argentina."

"I don't want to be away from you for six minutes let alone six months. It would seem like an eternity! Surely there is ample work for you here in Argentina!" His pained countenance only strengthened her resolve.

"My love, you know so little about the woman inside this body. I came from humble roots, starting with only the clothes on my back before Astor Gordero showed me the way. I swore that I would never be homeless or penniless again. I am an ambitious woman, a woman that wants to grab the golden ring while it is there for the taking. Maybe it is because you have never experienced poverty the way I have, maybe that is the reason you have trouble understanding why I am so driven."

He had no rebuttal to her last point, and she could see his pain and frustration mounting. Simone tried again to make him see the way their worlds were about to unfold. "Renaldo, you have reached the pinnacle of your chosen profession. I want to be the best that I can possibly be in my profession as well. If you really love me, allow me to be the best that I can possibly be. That is what true love is all about!"

She had taken considerable poetic license in relating her tale to the young athlete, but it was true that she was an ambitious woman, a woman who would not let her heart stand in the way of what she believed continued hard work could achieve.

"There is another reason I wish to leave Argentina, a reason that could have a terrible effect on us both. You know that Astor is very well connected with the ruling junta. Well, it is his opinion that the mood of euphoria that your victory has brought to this country will be short-lived. Argentina's problems have not gone away. They have only been obscured by this football mania. Each dollar that I earn here at home is eaten up by our astronomical inflation rate. It will be the same for you."

Her gaze was steadily searching for acknowledgement of these facts in his pale blue eyes. Simone could see that she was finally making headway. Renaldo's nod confirmed that he was aware that she spoke only the truth.

"The tournament did not help the starving and unemployed in the long run. When today's luster fades, the people will be left with a giant economic hangover. And who will be the voice of the people to express their pain and suffering? The same bloodthirsty terrorists that claimed to act on their behalf before they agreed to an armistice during the tournament! Renaldo, don't you see? The junta will react even more ruthlessly to keep their image from being tarnished now. The world has been watching us the past month, and we have passed the test with flying colors. What you and your teammates accomplished on the football field has glossed over our nation's violent fight for civil liberties and freedom of speech. But it is only temporary. People will start to disappear in the middle of the night again, and there will be more bombings and kidnappings and bloodshed."

As much as Renaldo did not want to hear such blasphemy against his beloved homeland, the land for whose very honor he had toiled so ardently for the past several months, he knew that her prophecy had far too great a chance of coming true.

"It will be dangerous to be a prominent figure in Argentina, according to Astor. It won't matter anymore if you are a government official, a general, a rock star, or a football player. If you are perceived as having wealth and stature by those who wish to make an example of you, then it won't matter who or what you are. I am scared to death about Argentina's future and my own personal safety, Renaldo, and I am going to leave as soon as I possibly can! Please, my love, take this opportunity to get away from here. Go to a place that is safe, where we can be together to watch what happens in Argentina from a distance. Astor knows what he is talking about, and he has convinced me that this country is not the place to be in the foreseeable future!"

There was real passion and fear in her voice now, not contrived play acting. She held him tightly in her arms while he tried to grasp the urgency of her current affairs lecture. Finally, he kissed her gently, then rose from the bed.

"Do you promise to come to London if I go? You won't disappoint me, will you?" He sounded like a lost little boy now, not the insatiable stickman that had driven her over the brink.

"Of course I do, my darling. Do you think that I would deny myself this for a second longer than I possibly had to?"

She was up off the bed and at his side now, grasping his sleeping giant in her tiny hand. Their lips met lustily, as if to confirm their devotion to one another even if they were thousands of miles apart. Simone grudgingly broke the embrace, her agent's instructions resurfacing in her passion-clouded mind.

"Go, go and take your shower. I will order some coffee and croissants from room service. Think about what I have just told you, Renaldo. We can have the best of all possible worlds, wrapped in each other's arms, far from the gathering storm."

Simone was pleased with her performance, convinced that her lover was still putty in her hands. It had not been a hard role to play, for she did believe much of the rhetoric that Gordero had given her as a script. What was more, she really didn't want to leave her eager stallion for any longer than she absolutely had to.

The streets of Buenos Aires resembled a giant wastepaper basket. Ticker-tape, confetti, and various other forms of paper jubilation were strewn from lamposts, trolley cables, trees, and buildings. It seemed that no one was working in the capital this glowing Monday, for the populous was either too hungover, or still too high on the adrenaline of victory to concentrate on their menial day-to-day tasks. Wandering bands of merrymakers jammed the sidewalks and often took over whole streets, blocking traffic to start an impulsive festival of football euphoria.

The general manager of the Hotel Presidente had been informed by Wolfgang Stoltz to contact both Renaldo De Seta and Ramon Vida no later than eleven o'clock that Monday morning. He was to personally relay the following message:

"Due to the congestion along Avenida Nueve de Julio, Astor Gordero's limousine will be at the rear service entrance of the hotel at twelve noon. Both the National Team players will be escorted by hotel security to the waiting vehicle using nonpublic areas of the hotel. They are expected to be on their way to the Jockey Club no later than twelve-fifteen." .

Renaldo had phoned down to his friend immediately upon finishing his shower to make sure that Vida had his priorities straight.

"Ramon, it's Renaldo. Did you get the message that there has been a slight change of plans?"

"Ya, man, some little shit in a tuxedo kept pounding on my door at a very bad time. I was just saying good-bye to one of my new friends. The asshole wouldn't go away. Estes finally had to get rid of him! Say, that old coach of yours is alright with the sweet young things. We kind of pooled our talents and bunked in together last night. As a matter of fact, he's still here going strong. The guy thinks he's twenty years old, for Christ's sake. Where did you go last night, man? I was looking all over for you. There were so many señoritas that wanted to meet 'The Great Renaldo.' You really owe me, man. I had to look after them all for you. I'm exhausted!"

"Well, Ramon, they were in the most capable hands on the National Team, of that I am certain! Now get your act together. We are being picked up in less than an hour. I'll see you then."

Simone had promised her new lover to be waiting anxiously for his return, for she had booked the Ambassador's Suite for the Monday night as well. A second evening of romance would be all that was required to cement their future plans together, in England!

It was only a six-block journey to the Jockey Club for the two National Team players, but the streets were alive with such irrational chaos that the forty-five minutes allotted traveling time would barely be enough. The R&Rs settled back into the tinted obscurity of the Mercedes to enjoy the sights and sounds.

"So, where did you get to last night, man? That was too good a party to just walk out on." Ramon had a lascivious grin on his face that belied his fatigue.

"Oh, you know me. I'm not much of a partier. It was a big day, and I couldn't stand all those drunken idiots wanting pictures and autographs. I just went to my room and took it easy." Ramon could not believe what he was hearing.

"Man, oh, man, I don't know about you, my friend. How are we ever going to live together in England if you don't want to get laid? I have my work cut out for me if we are going to be roommates." The extroverted Vida sat silently looking out the window for several seconds. "OK, so here's the deal. You teach me how to speak English, and I teach you how to act around the ladies. You are a star now, man, you have to start acting like one. That means, lots and lots of pussy! If you don't listen to me, Renaldo, the English will think that you are some kind of fairy, and we can't afford to have that kind of reputation over there. We are the great Latin saviors, come to rescue English football and fuck English women. That is our mission, my friend!"

Renaldo could not help but laugh at his outrageous companion. If, in fact, he did end up in London, life would certainly never be boring, not with Ramon Vida living under the same roof.

"I haven't made up my mind about going to England yet, Ramon. Everything has happened so quickly, I just don't want to act without thinking things through."

Vida simply shook his head in dismay.

"Well, you're fucking loco if you stay around here. For the kind of money they want to pay us, not to mention the experience of a lifetime, why on earth would you pass that all up?"

Renaldo wanted to blurt out Simone's name as his reason, for that was the answer his heart was screaming. But his mind was beginning to realize that Simone had been serious about leaving Argentina and about the dangers of staying in such an unstable environment.

He was unable to answer his friend's question. All that he could do now was to meet with the English and hope that they would make the decision easier for him, one way or another.

The table was the exact same one where he had first dined with Simone more than six months earlier. The memories of that unbelievable afternoon at the Jockey Club flooded back into Renaldo's mind. Now the same maitre d' led the two new arrivals through the packed dining room to Astor Gordero's preferred place of business.

While the patrons were impeccably dressed as usual, there was an air of spontaneous mischief about the private club, similar to the one that was so prevalent out on the streets. These affluent Porteños had every bit as much right to celebrate as their less well-off brothers and sisters, the only difference being their choice of location and the vintage of the liquid refreshment consumed.

The two football players had not made it halfway through the establishment when someone recognized them and called out their names. Even though both men were dressed in business suits instead of the number one dress of the National Team, there was no mistaking either of these two figures, so thoroughly had their likenesses been plastered over every newspaper and television screen the past few weeks. The diners seemed to rise as one, cheering, applauding, and straining for a better view of the 'dynamic duo,' as they had unimaginatively been coined in the press.

Astor Gordero and his guests were standing and had joined in the unrehearsed greeting. A phalanx of waiters gathered around Gordero's table, acting as a buffer against any overenthusiastic patrons who might just forget their manners and break the cardinal rule of this members' only club: 'privacy and discretion at all times!'

Ramon and Renaldo had acknowledged the accolades with smiles and waves before reaching their final destination, and that seemed to satisfy the masses. There would be no unbecoming behavior and no bothersome interruptions from that point on.

Introductions were made by the great facilitator himself. Renaldo had been so caught up in yesterday's 'affairs,' that he had forgotten that one of the people he was dining with was a woman. A stunningly beautiful woman at that.

He could only mutter a feeble "hello" using his rusty English. It wasn't that he had forgotten the language, it was more the effect of the strange feeling swirling inside his head. He had been here before with a similar group of people, several men and a beautiful lady.

Is this deja vu? Is this what I am experiencing?

But there was more! His heart was pounding, just like the first time he had beheld Simone. Now, the way the seating had been arranged, he was deemed to sit next to this exotic blonde creature. A natural blonde, of course, not the beauty salon type found locally. Those women changed their shade like chameleons. This species was pure and untainted.

He couldn't even remember her name after being introduced, so debilitating was the spell she had cast upon him. He managed to take his seat finally, but he was unable to comprehend any of the niceties flying around the table until the Venus spoke to him directly.

"Are you alright, Renaldo? You seem a bit disoriented. Are you feeling ill? Heaven knows that you have probably done a lifetime of celebrating in the last few hours."

He could not speak. All he could do was gaze into her eyes. If her physical appearance had been disarming, then her voice . . . her voice with that accent. That was the thing that rendered him totally inanimate.

He had never in his life heard any sound so sweet. Even his English grandmother did not possess such a melodious way of speaking. Years in Argentina had diluted the pureness of her English resonance. This sound, the sound of Mallory Russell's voice, had the effect of a snake charmer's flute, and Renaldo De Seta was her hypnotized cobra.

"Waiter, a glass of water for Señor De Seta, quickly, please."

Even though the English beauty spoke in her native tongue, a glass of sparking ice water appeared in seconds.

"Take a drink, Renaldo. Do you wish to postpone our meeting until later in the day?" Again he was mute, able only to hang on her every syllable and hope that she would continue to speak to him with that wondrous air. It was Ramon Vida's crass whisper in Spanish that crash-landed his floating thoughts.

"Hey, man, what the fuck's the matter with you? The lady is talking right to you, and you sit there like your mind has turned to shit. Wake up or you'll blow this deal for both of us!" Renaldo shook his head and took a sip of the ice water.

"I'm terribly sorry. I don't mean to be rude. It's just that I didn't get much sleep last night, and I guess I am a bit overwhelmed by everything that has happened."

"That's alright, young man. You have every right to be overwhelmed. For that matter, it would not be exaggerating to say that Mallory and I were overwhelmed by the performances that you and Señor Vida put on at River Plate yesterday. Don't give it a second thought." Reggie Russell smiled a fatherly smile as Renaldo focused in on the Englishman for the first time.

Funny hair, has to be a wig! the younger man thought.

"Thank you, sir. Your compliment is very gracious."

Renaldo had responded in English, which would become the language of choice at the table from that point on. Wolfgang Stoltz sat to Ramon Vida's left and acted as his translator for the balance of the meeting.

Astor Gordero had fallen abruptly silent after his opening salutations. *Did Renaldo know about Lonnie's now-confirmed demise? Was he about to expose this dark secret? Everything would be lost if that were the case.*

"What on earth is wrong with the boy, Wolfie? I have never seen him in such a state," an anxious Gordero finally asked his assistant. Stoltz's two-word reply put everything in perspective.

"The Lady!"

Now, reassured by this enlightenment and his client's verbal pronouncement, the host launched into a long-winded analysis of the championship game. That suited Renaldo perfectly, for it gave him the time he needed to collect his thoughts and focus on the business at hand. It was an impatient Reginald Russell that interrupted the corpulent lawyer to address the two younger gentlemen.

"Yes, yes, Señor Gordero, your team did perform magnificently yesterday, but I imagine that the young gentlemen would prefer that we get directly to the point of this luncheon. Shall we then?"

Gordero was a man not accustomed to being interrupted, but he did find one redeeming point in this inexcusable affront.

"By all means, Lord Russell. But you did mention the word luncheon, so I suggest that we order first, then continue on with business. By now you know that I have my little quirks about me, Sir, such as never discussing financial matters on an empty stomach. Filmon, we will order at once!"

The captain was at The Fat Man's side in the blink of an eye, while Sir Reggie sat back in his chair, full of barely contained disgust. One could almost see the steam emitting from the Englishman's ears.

Go ahead, you fat bag of dung, stuff some more groceries down your oversized gullet. Go on, do me a favor . . . eat until you explode, he smoldered silently.

"Right, shall we get on with it then?" Lord Russell was quick to pick up the ball as soon as the host had finished relaying his extensive gastronomic wish list.

"Certainly, my Lord. Now I will be able to concentrate to the best of my ability." Gordero's smile was self-indulgent. "As I told you previously, Lord Russell, both of these gentlemen have received a copy of your signed contract stating the terms and conditions of their proposed employment with the Canary Wharf Football Club. As I now represent both Renaldo and Ramon in the capacity of agent and attorney, I have been in a position to hold preliminary meetings with them individually to explain the contractual details. I must add, however, that there have been more pressing matters to attend to of late, but now that the tournament has drawn to a successful conclusion, we are able to turn our full attention to the future." Gordero paused to catch his breath before continuing.

"While the terms of both players' contracts are identical, it is, of course, up to each individual gentleman to decide if those terms are acceptable, and for that matter, whether or not he chooses to go to England at all."

There was an aloof matter-of-factness to the facilitator's last statement that brought Reggie Russell back to the point of boiling over, but one glance at Mallory's icy gaze convinced him to bite his lip one more time.

"I have received no final instructions from either Renaldo or Ramon due to circumstances beyond our control, and the purpose of this meeting was really for them to meet face-to-face with you and your daughter. I am sure they have questions to ask you, for it is a drastic change in lifestyles that they are contemplating. Why don't we turn the table over to them, and you can speak to their queries directly? Ramon, why don't you go first? Do you have anything you would like to ask Lord and Lady Russell about your playing for the Canary Wharf Football Club in England?"

Wolfgang Stoltz finished translating his employer's words for the Argentine striker, then sat ready to relate his response. Surprisingly, the Boy from Boca replied in fractured English.

"No, I have no . . . question?"

He turned to Stoltz and spoke rapidly in his native tongue. Stoltz nodded his head in affirmation to the several inquiries Ramon was obviously making. Satisfied with the answers that the German had given him, Astor Gordero's newest client looked directly at Mallory.

"OK, I go play football. In England. Nice women!"

Ramon's fragmented acceptance and compliment caught everyone at the table off-guard. Mallory Russell, far from being insulted, laughed graciously and extended a hand for the swashbuckling Latin to shake. Ramon grasped the delicate object rising to his feet, bent forward from the waist, and kissed it with a flourish. His contract, for all intents and purposes, was signed, sealed, and delivered. Laughter and a congratulatory round of applause greeted Canary Wharf's newest transfer as he returned to his seat.

It was Lady Russell that continued on with the negotiations. "And how about you, Renaldo? How do you feel about joining your friend in England? The two of you working your magic together in our first division would make a sight to behold. We have big plans for the Canary Wharf Football Club. Our stadium is under construction at this very moment. When finished, it will be one of the finest facilities in all of England! We want to field a team that will pack the grandstands by offering exciting offensive football. You and Ramon are exactly the players that can do that for us."

Mallory paused to see if she could read the young man's eyes for an indication of how hard a sell this was going to be. He was certainly transfixed on her every word, but she could decipher no clues as to his thoughts. She pressed on.

"Our ultimate goal goes far beyond just competing well in our newly promoted surroundings. We want to win the league championship, and of course, even the FA Cup is possible. But our ultimate goal is to be the champions of Europe. To win the European Cup as the premier club-side on the continent is the one feat that the Canaries have never achieved in their existence. That is our true goal, and you two gentlemen can help us to accomplish it!"

"An envious, but difficult goal to achieve, Lady Russell!" Wolfgang Stoltz made his first direct statement of the day to the gathering.

"Winning the first division championship in your own country will be a tremendous accomplishment in itself, something a newly promoted second division club has never done before, if I am correct. But to challenge the great teams of Europe such as Real Madrid, Athletico of Milan, and Bayern Munich? Well, do you not think that you are putting an unrealistic amount of pressure on these young gentlemen?"

Lord Russell was quick to respond to the arrogant German. "Herr Stoltz, it would seem that we have more faith in your homegrown talent than you do. What these 'young gentlemen' give us is an element of surprise. If we mold our team around their playing style, our English competition, frankly won't know how to react. Each and every one of them plays the same monotonous long ball game. There is little or no innovation, and the only thing that changes are the names of the players. We have missed two bloody World Cups because of this constipated philosophy, and Mallory and I want to show the Football Association that they need to adjust their tactics or remain perennial also-rans!"

"What about Liverpool's recent successes abroad? Have they not won the last two European Cups, the second less than a month ago?" responded Astor Gordero.

"True enough, Señor, but realistically, the team they beat, Brugges of Belgium, was not a great side. Add to that the fact that this year's competition was watered down considerably. Many of the club sides in the running were forced to give up their best players to their national teams competing in this tournament. The final game was also played in England, right at Wembley Stadium, of all places. It was basically a home fixture for the Reds. The truth of the matter is that those Mersey-Men should have won by four or five goals instead of just one!"

Lord Russell took a large gulp of the neat Scotch that he had hardly touched since the meeting began. The point of all this mindless babble was drifting away from his central theme, and he wanted to get the golden ball into his closet and be done with this whole business.

"No, gentlemen, we do not intend to put unbearable pressure on your players. That would drive them back across the Atlantic faster than any of us want. It will take time to build a team that is compatible with the new tactics we plan to adopt. The first season will be a learning experience for everyone. But, by the start of the second campaign, if things work out the way Mallory and I hope they will . . . well, Señor Gordero, by that time, with a lot of hard work and a bit of luck, all of us should be headed to the continent to take on Herr Stoltz's 'great teams of Europe.'"

The contempt directed at Gordero's assistant was thinly veiled. Stoltz pretended to ignore the comment and continued his translation for Ramon

Vida, but the German was seething with indignation internally. Patience had always been one of Wolfgang Stoltz's strongest attributes however, and he would be careful to choose the perfect opportunity to put this self-righteous weakling in his place.

Renaldo had listened politely to the verbal jousting going on around him without paying any of it much heed. He wanted the English lady to talk to him again, to personally reassure him that she would be accessible if he were to travel to England. That her warmth and charm were not just an act to lure him from Argentina. That her sparkling smile and incredible voice would rekindle the same newfound urges that had all but convinced him to sign the contract and fly to England.

Each phrase that she uttered throughout their two-hour luncheon brought him closer to the undeniable realization that he just had to be close to her. Simone had unlocked the vault containing his latent male sensuality, and the young man now wanted to capitalize on the unimagined riches therein. He had to constantly refocus his thoughts out of the carnal and into the current as he fantasized about their future together in England.

Reggie Russell had had his fill by the time the main course was all but consumed, both of the food and of the idle football gossip that had replaced the essence of the entire meeting. He wanted to force the issue by confronting the good-looking youngster that had not yet committed to playing in England. A simple answer would do. Are you coming or aren't you? Yes or no? Make up your bloody mind! It was time to play the trump card.

"Mallory, why don't you tell Renaldo about the phone call that we received from England this morning. Perhaps that news might help convince the lad."

"My word, I'd almost forgotten with all his talk of football and the like." Mallory focused her attention on the enamored gentleman to her left.

"Renaldo, Señor Gordero has informed us that your mother is most concerned about you continuing your education, specifically in the medical field. Well, we have many highly placed contacts in London, and with a little legwork, we received a call this morning from the Registrar of the University of London Medical School. He is an ex-marine corpsman that served in Europe with my father in World War Two. Apparently, if your grades are as good as Señor Gordero has led us to believe, he will be able to secure an undergraduate exchange student placement for you in the school's pre-med first-year program. We will need transcripts of your school records to send to England, of course, but if everything checks out, your mother should be pleased with this opportunity to combine football with your continuing education. How does that sound to you?"

The charmer still held the cobra in her hypnotic trance. Renaldo had only heard about every third word that Mallory related, so consumed was he by her presence. The embarrassing silence that followed her question finally prompted a response.

"That would be wonderful, I suppose. I must admit that my mind has not been focused on my education of late, but if enrollment in a medical course can be used to convince my mother, so much the better."

So what is your bleeding answer, you little pantywaist? Reggie Russell pondered while doing a slow burn. *Enough of this rubbish! We have kissed your mother's derrière, so let's have an answer. Come on, you little pansy, out with it. Make up your own mind for the first time in your life!* The words were on the tip of Lord Russell's tongue, but he managed to temper his question in deference to Mallory.

"So, young man, what shall it be? Adventure and an education abroad, or continuing to live under your mother's shadow here in Buenos Aires? We really must have your answer today, for Mallory and I fly back to London in the morning. Our season commences in less than a month, and if you decide to join us, we would require you to arrive in England in the very near future. Say a fortnight, at the absolute outside. I would like to retire to Señor Gordero's office now to work out the details. Things like flights, type of lodging that you require initially, a down payment of salary, everything that will make the transition to your new life in England as comfortable as possible. But we must have your answer. Now!"

"Perhaps Renaldo would like to take some time alone with me to discuss his future in private, Lord Russell." Astor Gordero did not appreciate the bluntness of the Englishman. It was a trait that he found tactless.

"No, that will not be necessary, Señor Gordero. I only have one question to ask of Lord Russell. Who actually runs the Canary Wharf Football Team, Sir? Who will Ramon and I be dealing with on a daily basis once we arrive in England?"

"Well, Randal Horton is our team manager, or coach, as you sometimes call them in South America. A splendid chap, old Randal. Used to play for the Canaries a few years back. Very bright and in full compliance with the change in tactics that we plan to institute if you and Ramon join us. There is also Mallory here. As team executive vice-president, she has taken an active, hands-on role in the club's operations. Far too active to suit many of the old chauvinist farts at the FA, I might add! And I will be around a fair bit as well. On the whole though, it's Randal Horton for 'on-field' matters and Mallory for 'off-field' matters. Does that answer your question?"

It certainly did! All Renaldo wanted to hear was that this vision of beauty seated beside him would be actively involved in his new career. That was enough for him to place his future into her hands.

"Yes, Sir, it does. I am prepared to sign your contract and to travel to England as soon as possible to play football for the Canary Wharf Football Club!"

"Good show, young man!" a triumphant Lord Russell bubbled with glee. Mallory Russell spontaneously leaned over and hugged her new center halfback, giving him a peck on the cheek. Her act made the recipient blush slightly, but Renaldo had no time to feel self-conscious. He was jostled vigorously by an exuberant Ramon Vida once Stoltz had finished translating his new Canary teammate's response. Astor Gordero offered his hardy congratulations, as did a more subdued Wolfgang Stoltz. The German then produced two sets of documents for signature from his portfolio.

'The Great Facilitator' presided over the official signing of the contracts as notary and witness, then called for a bottle of Dom Pérignon and the dessert menu to top off the closing of the deal.

When all the food and beverage had been consumed and it was time to part company, Renaldo still had not devoured his fill of the enchanting blonde creature. He wanted to sit right where he was and have her continue relating the funny little stories of her native land. She had become much more outgoing and at ease after his acceptance of their offer to join them in England. Was she flirting with him? Did he sense an interest that had nothing to do with football?

There was no way of knowing for sure, for Mallory reverted to her 'all business' demeanor as she and the new Canary Wharf center halfback shook hands discreetly when everyone at the table rose to part company.

"Gentlemen, we will see you in London!" Sir Reggie proclaimed proudly. "My daughter and I will work out all the finer details with Señor Gordero, who will then inform you of your departure date. Mallory will be at Heathrow to meet your plane on arrival and speed your entry through customs. Good luck until then and rest assured that neither of you will ever regret the decision that you have made here this afternoon!"

"Oh, man, did you get a load of that blonde piece of fluff in there? I took one look at her and decided that England was for me! And that one works all day in a man's business world. I wonder what the real English women look like, you know the ones that stay at home and pamper themselves so that they look really sexy in the clubs at night. I know I'm going to like London! I can feel it in my bone!"

Ramon Vida grasped the visible bulge in his trousers as he and Renaldo made their way back to the Hotel Presidente in the rear of Astor Gordero's limousine. Renaldo tried not to show the offense he took at his friend's slight of the lady.

"She was a very beautiful woman, and I think that there is probably more upstairs than 'fluff,' Ramon." Renaldo pointed to his head. "After all, for a lady to be a football executive in any country is something I have never heard of before. She would have to have a very sharp mind and thick skin to handle all the prejudice she must encounter."

"Not to mention great tits and long legs!" Ramon was doubled over in laughter at his irreverence. The champagne had topped him up, and he was ready to 'party on' back at the hotel.

The traffic was still barely moving twenty-four hours after the opening kickoff of the championship game. Nobody wanted to stop partying, and new revellers were arriving in the capital by the minute from the hinterlands around Buenos Aires to act as reinforcements for those too inebriated or hungover to carry on.

At last, the Mercedes pulled up to the rear entrance of the Hotel Presidente. The two National Team players thanked the chauffeur, then Ramon made his way for the staff entrance door.

"Hey, man, come on. You shouldn't stand out here too long. If someone recognizes you, you'll be mobbed."

"That's OK, Ramon. You go ahead. I'll talk to you later. There is something that I have to do now, so don't worry about me. I'll be alright. Go on. I'm sure that Estes must be exhausted by now. Go and rescue him. I will call your room when I get back."

"As you wish, my friend, but be careful out here. The streets are crazy. I don't want to lose my new English teammate, old chap!"

Renaldo waved reassuringly as Ramon disappeared through the doorway. He then walked briskly to the corner and hailed the first cab that he spotted.

"Avenida Arenales, near Calle Austria in Palermo, please, driver."

The trip to Casa San Marco took over forty minutes, but at least they were traveling away from the influx of celebrants that continued to flock to the downtown core. The cabbie paid little attention to his passenger, preferring instead to concentrate on the erratic traffic habits of his fellow drivers.

In due course, Renaldo was standing outside the wrought iron gates of the mansion in which he had grown up. Once past them, a ring of the doorbell brought the familiar shuffling sound from within, then Oli's squinting face at the security grate.

"Señor Renaldo! Mother of Jesus, is that really you? Olarti, come quickly. Señor Renaldo is home!"

The door swung back on its giant hinges as the little native lady flew into the outstretched arms of the returning hero. Olarti was with them only a few moments later, the three doing an impromptu dance of joy in the entrance foyer.

"It is so good to have you home again, Señor Renaldo. How is the foot? Oli and I watched every game that you played in! It didn't seem to bother you, at least not from what we could tell on the television." The man servant was beaming from ear to ear, as if he was the boy's personal therapist.

"It held up just fine, Olarti, thanks to you! Without your help, I probably never would have made it back to the team at all! I am deeply grateful, my old friend."

There was a flurry of questions directed at the new arrival, all of which Renaldo took the time to patiently answer.

"Should I stock the refrigerator with all your favorites, Señor Renaldo? Are you home for good now?" Oli wanted to hear an affirmative response, and the disappointment was evident on her weathered face when she received only a vague reply.

"I cannot say right at the moment, dear Oli. I have to talk to my mother first. Is she here right now?"

"Of course, Señor. She would not dare to venture out in this insanity. The streets are filled with drunken hooligans and madmen. And the noise! I could not sleep a wink last night for all the honking horns going by the house. Here in Palermo! It's unheard of. Your mother had a tough night as well. She is resting in her room."

"Thanks, Oli. Coming home is always special because I know that I have friends like the two of you here to greet me."

With that, he took leave of the elderly couple and ascended the circular staircase. He stood outside his mother's bedroom door, took a deep breath, then knocked ever so gently in case she was asleep.

"Come!" Her voice was strong and clear. Renaldo pushed down the brass lever and stepped inside.

"My eyes are playing tricks on me. Is that really you? All dressed up in your finest suit, looking so handsome. Whoever has been looking after you has been doing an excellent job! Come here, my son!"

Florencia De Seta arose from her bed and held her arms out to embrace her youngest. Renaldo was more than relieved at her warm reaction to his unscheduled visit. He only hoped that she would remain so affectionate after he divulged the true purpose of his visit to Casa San Marco.

"I have missed you, mother. You look even lovelier than I could have imagined. How have you been? Is everything alright with you?"

She was still stunningly beautiful, her figure full and shapely, her complexion unblemished and ageless. There was not a hint of grey in her long black locks, which at this moment fell straight to well below her shoulders. Her maroon robe complimented the color scheme of the room.

"I am fine, just fine. All this football nonsense has made me feel like a prisoner in my own home, however. But I must admit that I did break down and watch you play on television yesterday afternoon. That was quite a concession for an old lady like me. It would seem that you are some sort of national hero after your recent exploits. At least you weren't crippled. The kind of shape that you arrived home in from Montevideo last month, why I thought you would never walk without crutches again. You should say one hundred Hail Marys to show your gratitude!"

Renaldo smiled warmly as he led the lady back to her bed. Mother and son sat there together, hands entwined, while they caught up on each other's lives. Florencia seemed much more at ease and contented than her son had seen her in a long time. When he related this matter-of-factly, she was quick to put forth the reason.

"My new outlook on life has been brought about by the continued attention of a certain gentleman, Renaldo. The same gentleman that we dined with on your birthday, Herr Wolfgang Stoltz."

The warm smile and the sparkle in his mother's eyes left no doubt in his mind as to the truth of the lady's statement.

"You see, Renaldo, I was paid a visit by Astor Gordero shortly after you decided to let him handle your football career. A very knowledgeable and persuasive man, that Señor Gordero. In any event, our discussions got around to the family business concerns, and certain problems that I was having with your grandfather's executors. Our initial meeting led to several others, all of them attended by Herr Stoltz. To make a long story short, he asked me out socially, and I accepted."

Florencia bowed her head, then raised it with a slight look of regret and uncertainty replacing the previous effervescence.

"You know, my dear Renaldo, I have never looked at another man romantically since your blessed father passed away. But I found myself all alone, with you away playing football, and your brother traveling the land with that communist woman. I wanted a life with some personal fulfillment and happiness in it for a change, in a way that only a man can give to a lonely woman. One day perhaps you will understand my longing."

Her eyes seemed to be pleading with her youngest son for acceptance and empathy as he listened intently to her every word.

"I had done all that I could do to raise you boys to the best of my ability, but regardless of my feelings, you both went off and made your own decisions about the paths you chose to follow. Letting you go was difficult for me, Renaldo. I was very bitter for a time, but I know now that you had to act as your heart dictated. Herr Stoltz made me realize that you and your brother are not children anymore. That you have to spread your wings and find your true identities. Neither of you can continue to live under the shadow of my skirts a minute longer without hating me forever, nor would I wish such a thing to tear us apart. No, you must lead your own life, dear son. That is why you have come here today, to tell me that you have decided to go to England and continue on with your football career. Is that not so?"

The young man was dumbfounded. Female intuition was something he had only read about in magazines, but this, this was almost psychic.

"Mama, you shock me with your clairvoyance. It is true, I have just signed a contract to play in London for two years. It is for a lot of money, but more importantly, they have promised to secure me an exchange student's placement in a medical course at the University of London. I will be able to continue my studies at a world-recognized institution, as well as play football. For me though, the best thing is that I will be going overseas with my closest friend from the National Team, Ramon Vida. So I won't be alone, which should ease your mind a lot."

The Señora did have an air of acceptance about her, a warmth in her smile that was a far cry from the hostile barrier she would erect whenever her son had mentioned the word 'football' in the past. Relieved, the young man continued to supply the relevant information.

"So much has happened because of this football, Mama, it makes my head spin at times. Señor Gordero himself is the one that negotiated the deal, and I have just come from meeting the English team owners. They are very nice, very proper. I am sure that you would like them. The gentleman is a real Lord, and . . ."

"There is only one Lord, Renaldo. Don't ever forget that over there in the land of the heathens! Promise me that you will go to mass faithfully, that you will not let your church down and fall victim to the pressures of the unholy world. Promise me that, and you will go to England with my blessing!"

The pressures of the unholy world? Renaldo mused to himself. He thanked God that she could not read his mind, for it was awash with the erotic memories of his tryst with Simone not twenty-four hours earlier. Add to that the bawdy images which had turned him to stone as the melodious Englishwoman spun her oral web of seduction, and Renaldo had his first inkling of just how 'unholy' the pleasures of the flesh could be. He had already fallen prey to those pleasures, and he was both unable and unwilling to deny himself those newfound delectations. The good news was that by playing football in England, his mother did not have to be party to his newly discovered libido.

"Mama, you know me. You know that I would never do anything to upset you or disgrace the family name. I will honor your request while I am overseas and act in accordance with your wishes!"

Florencia De Seta embraced her son tenderly, satisfied that a pact of honor had been made. It was good that her youngest was going abroad, for heaven help her if Renaldo were to move back into Casa San Marco and chance to witness some of the 'unholy pressures' that she willingly succumbed to at Wolfgang Stoltz's bidding!

"Will you be staying home until you leave for England? How about dinner this evening? I can get Oli to go to the market and get a nice steak for us."

Florencia sensed a twinge of regret in her voice, regret that her baby would be leaving her soon and be living thousands of miles away. She wanted to spend every available minute with him until he had to depart for England. Letting this gorgeous boy spread his wings and fly out from beneath the shadow of her skirts was going to be more difficult than she had implied.

"Can we do it tomorrow night, Mama? I still have some team commitments this evening, but in the morning we are dismissed from all obligations and able to go home," Renaldo lied to his mother. His only 'commitment' was to spend the night in Simone's arms.

"Alright, if you promise to be here, then we will have a date tomorrow night. Just the two of us!" She smiled and gave her son another hug. When she pulled away, her expression appeared vaguely disturbed.

"You know, Renaldo, I wanted to have a similar talk with your brother, Lonfranco, and he was here at the casa only a few days ago. He didn't want to see me though. He arrived when I was out and told Oli not to tell me that he had stopped by. But Oli couldn't wait to tell me! She was really upset after he left. She said that he looked terrible. Thin and pale, dressed like a vagabond."

The color had drained from Florencia's complexion and fear of the unknown replaced the warmth that had danced in her eyes.

"That leftist tramp was not with him, thank heavens. Oli said that he showered and changed into a nice suit, then packed a suitcase. He told her that he was going away on a long trip. He claimed to have been camping in Bariloche, that he had lost everything in a bad storm and that the woman was in the hospital with minor injuries. Oli also said that she saw a handgun on his bed when she brought a tray of food up to his room. A handgun!"

The mother's hands started to shake uncontrollably in her son's grasp. The boy could not believe what he was hearing.

"Renaldo, I am scared for your brother! I think he might be in some terrible trouble, and I don't know what I can do to help him. I drove him away, out of this home and out of Buenos Aires. He didn't want to see me, Renaldo, and now I don't know where to find him to tell him that I love him and to come home, that everything is alright. I worry about him so much!"

Florencia was sobbing uncontrollably now. Renaldo held her tenderly, letting her rest her head on his shoulder. The news his mother had related had turned him cold.

The last time he talked to his brother, Lonnie promised to be back in the capital to see him play. If he had been in Buenos Aires just before the championship game, surely he would have known that Renaldo had been selected to be in the starting lineup for Argentina. How could he not try to reach him? A message at the training center, or even through Olarti, or Astor Gordero's office. Anywhere! But there had been no word, nothing at all.

Had Celeste brainwashed him to the point that he had abandoned his family completely? And why did he have a pistol with him? Lonnie had never owned a gun in his life. Their father had hated the detestable things and forbade them in his house. Renaldo had never even touched a firearm.

There were many questions and no answers. The only thing that he could do now was to comfort and reassure his mother. Renaldo the eternal optimist was confident that everything would work out in time.

"Don't worry, Mama. You know Lonnie. He has a mind of his own. Heaven knows that he can look after himself. I certainly wouldn't want to tangle with the big thug! I know that he loves you, Mama. He just didn't want to upset you by coming home unannounced. Why, I talked to him on the telephone just last week and he told me the same story that he told Oli. Celeste was hurt, a broken leg or something, and he was going to come home to get some money and fresh supplies. Don't worry, I know he has everything under control."

The son tried to sound as convincing as possible to his mother, but it wasn't easy. There was a terrible feeling gnawing at the pit of Renaldo's stomach.

"Do you really think so? Do you really think that he is alright, and that he still loves his mother?"

"Of that, I am certain, Mama! How could any son not love a mother like you? We will hear from him one day soon, when he is ready to contact us. Lonnie always likes to operate on his own schedule. So let's not worry ourselves sick about the big bag of bones. He is probably skiing down his favorite slope in Bariloche as we speak!"

The smile returned to Florencia De Seta's face once again.

"I suppose you are right. Lonfranco always was the wild one, hard to control. You, on the other hand, you were my angel!" She kissed him softly on the cheek.

"OK, Mama, OK. Your little angel has to fly off now and go about his heavenly business. Before I go though, there is one thing I would like to discuss with you. I hope this will not be too painful."

After the news about Lonnie, he had questioned whether or not to bring up the subject that had become an obsession since going to England was first mentioned several days ago. But there would be no time like the present. Right now, he could ask the question, then hopefully act on her answer. He simply had to know the truth before he set foot on a plane to London.

"What is it my son? Now you seem to be the one who is upset."

"It's about father. About what really happened to him in England in 1966. I need to talk to someone that was there with him,who saw what actually happened. If I am going to London, I need to know the truth, or else the unknown past will haunt me every day I am there. The explanation that you gave Lonnie and me about the traffic accident was fine when I was seven years old, but now for my own peace of mind, I have to know the hard facts. Can you help me, Mama? Can you give me the name of anyone who traveled to England with father in 1966? Please, I beg of you. Let me exorcise my own demons from the past. Then and only then can I get on with my future."

Her face had grown pale again, just as it had when she was talking about Lonnie. Florencia sat silently for several moments, staring down at her hands, which she had started to knead together. Presently, she stopped and looked up at her son.

"It is twelve years now, a very long time! I don't know if any of those men are still alive themselves or exactly where they are." Again she lowered her head as if to reflect on the past. Suddenly she looked up at her son, enlightened by a flash of rediscovered knowledge.

"There is one man, a doctor at the Children's Hospital with your father back then. He might be able to help you, if you can find him."

The pain in her son's eyes spurred her on. She could not bear the thought of him thinking that she had deceived him all these years.

"The story about the traffic accident is true, at least as far as I know. But I did not delve into the exact details. Your father was dead, and I would never see his smiling face or hold him in my arms again. That was my reality. How he died, by whose foul hand, it didn't make any difference. He was gone, gone to be with his Maker, and I trusted that he would find peace sitting at the hand of the Lord. That was my solace, that your father was in heaven and at peace. If you must know more, all I can give you is a name, Doctor Geraldo Quinquela!"

There was no flash of recognition in the boy's eyes. He had obviously never heard that name mentioned before this very moment. Florencia pressed on with the few details she had at her disposal.

"He was the chief pediatric surgeon at the Children's Hospital in 1966. He went with your father and the others to England. I do see him at the occasional charity function, so I know that he is still alive. Check the telephone directory or maybe the hospital itself. You may get some results there."

It seemed to Renaldo that his mother was about to collapse after she completed her final sentence. He held her in his arms lovingly, then helped her lie back on her soft pillows.

"Now, my dear boy, I must rest. Seeing you so fit and strong makes me very happy. But knowing that you are going away from me soon, and knowing the fear I have in my heart for your brother's safety, well, just promise me that we will dine together tomorrow night. That would lift my spirits immeasurably."

"Wild horses could not keep me from dining with the most beautiful woman in all of Buenos Aires tomorrow night. Have Oli prepare a feast, for I have had to put up with training camp food for far too long! I will be home by mid-afternoon, and I will stay with you here until my departure for England. Please don't worry about Lonnie or the other matter we discussed. Everything will work out, I promise you!"

He bent down and kissed her hand gallantly, mimicking Ramon Vida's actions earlier in the day.

"Good night, my love, till we meet again tomorrow!"

The Buenos Aires telephone directory made up in a large part for the inadequacies of the rest of the telephone system. It was thorough and precise in its listings, and the fact that Doctor Geraldo Quinquela's home address and telephone number were listed should not have surprised Renaldo. Nevertheless, he sat behind his father's large desk in the old office at Casa San Marco staring at the words and numerals.

Maybe this will be easier than I had anticipated, he thought as his finger dialed the required digits.

"Doctor Quinquela's residence, how may I help you?" The voice was obviously that of a maid or housekeeper.

"Would the doctor be available to come to the telephone at this time?" Renaldo asked in his most mature, businesslike manner.

"And who shall I tell the doctor is calling?" The positive response stunned the boy into temporary silence.

"Oh, um, my name is Renaldo De Seta. My father was a good friend and associate of Doctor Quinquela's."

"Very well, Señor, please hold the line."

Renaldo felt his palms growing moist from nervous anticipation as he waited. Several minutes passed until,

"Hello, this is Doctor Quinquela. Who am I speaking to, please?"

"Doctor, this is Renaldo De Seta. I believe that my late father was an associate of yours at the Children's Hospital. If this is a bad time for you, I can call back later."

"My dear boy, this is an honor above all expectation. Of course, I knew your father. He was a great surgeon. We were very close friends as well! Why, I was with him in England when he was . . ."

Renaldo could tell that the doctor was suddenly feeling some discomfort.

"Don't worry, Doctor. I know that you were with him when he was killed. It was my mother who gave me your name. I was wondering if you might have a few minutes to see me in the next day or so. There are some things that I would very much like to discuss with you on a rather personal level. I won't take up much of your time, say maybe half an hour."

"Renaldo, I have taken the last week off from the hospital to fully immerse myself in the tournament. As a matter of fact, I was at River Plate to see your dazzling performance yesterday. You were magnificent. Your father would have been very proud of you! Unfortunately, I must go back to a very heavy schedule tomorrow. I am now an administrator as well as a surgeon. But I could see you right now. Are you free to stop by my home in the next hour or so?"

The appointment was made without hesitation, then a second call was placed, this time to the Hotel Presidente.

"Hello."

"Simone, it's Renaldo. I was afraid that you would get bored waiting for me and leave. I'm sorry that things have taken so long, but I have one more stop to make before I return. Is that all right? Will you wait for me?"

"Of course, my love. There is nowhere in the world I would rather be than here with you tonight! Actually, I have quite enjoyed myself. After all the activity of the last few weeks, it is a treat to lay in bed watching television and ordering room service whenever I feel like it. We will have a romantic dinner right here in the suite when you return, so hurry and complete your business. I have many more things to teach you, my darling."

Renaldo sat staring at the receiver as the drone of the disconnected phone line hummed in his ear. Her last comment had rekindled the passions that she had awakened in him the night before. It was only the thought of his forthcoming audience with Dr. Quinquela that restored him to his normal 'state,' allowing him to rise from the desk and make his way to the kitchen to say good-bye to Oli.

"I am on my way, Oli. Tomorrow night, Mama and I will be dining together here at the casa, so put on your best spread, for I am a ravenous animal after being locked up for a month."

He gave the lady-servant a big hug, then grabbed a set of keys off one of the hooks by the kitchen door.

"I am going to take the MGB, so tell Mama if she asks where it has gone. I'll be home for a nice long stay tomorrow afternoon. See you then."

"You be careful driving, Señor Renaldo. The streets are full of crazy people!"

He was through the doorway and into the garage before she finished her warning. The thrill of sitting behind the wheel of the little red sports car was an unexpected rush. It had been over four months since he had driven any vehicle at all, what with being sequestered with the National Team, and then suffering his foot injury. He wanted to put the roof down and feel the wind flying through his hair, but Oli's parting caution had reminded him of his newfound celebrity status. *Besides, with all this traffic congestion, I would never get up enough speed to feel even the slightest hint of a breeze,* he rationalized.

He would leave the roof and windows up during his travels today. It was not worth being recognized and having a swarm of autograph-hungry fanatics climb all over his red beauty. There would be time another day for a ride with the roof down, perhaps in the country. Possibly a trip to Pergamino to tell his English grandmother that he was going to be living in London for the next two years.

'Maybe Grandmother Lydia would be willing to travel back to the old country and visit me once I get established. She could introduce me to those funny English relatives she used to tell stories about. Yes, a trip to Pergamino will definitely be on the agenda for later in the week!' His left foot depressed the clutch, and the red rocket bolted out of the garage and through the front gates of Casa San Marco.

As was the case with his brother Lonnie's fate, Renaldo had no way of knowing that he would never take that drive to Pergamino. At that very moment, his grandmother was being admitted to Hospital Rivadavia in extremely grave condition. It had been Nana Taseo, the head housekeeper at the estancia, who had insisted on the Señora leaving Pergamino to seek immediate medical attention.

Lydia had initially dismissed her strange malady as nothing more than a case of the flu and refused to have a doctor attend to her. But by the twenty-fourth of June, her condition had deteriorated to such a degree that Señora Taseo had alerted Florencia De Seta in Buenos Aires. The housekeeper had asked for emergency assistance to be standing by if her employer's health continued to slide downhill. The matriarch was barely conscious by the afternoon of the twenty-fifth, but she insisted on having the television set moved into her bedroom. There was no way that she was going to miss her grandson playing in the most important soccer game of his life.

Within an hour of the final whistle confirming Renaldo as a world champion, Lydia De Seta had lapsed into a coma. Nana Taseo had hoped that a good showing by Renaldo would lift the lady's spirits, as well as her waning constitution. For that reason, she had waited until after the match to make her report to Florencia. The instant that Argentina was crowned champion of the football universe, every telephone circuit in or out of the capital city was jammed indefinitely. Hundreds of the working press had to get their stories to the wire services. Thousands of ordinary citizens wanted to share their euphoria with far distant friends and relatives. Nana Taseo found it futile trying to get through to Florencia, and she would not sit idly by waiting for a miracle to happen. She conscripted Oliviero Brown to make Lydia's old, but impeccably maintained Bentley ready for a speedy trip to Buenos Aires. She then bundled up the elderly lady in warm blankets and had her carried to the waiting vehicle. With Oliviero at the wheel, and Nana fretting over her unconscious patient in the rear compartment, the makeshift ambulance sped off into the Pampas night.

The drive was unusually slow and arduous, however, due to the celebratory tidal wave that had engulfed the entire populous. Roads were jammed with overcrowded vehicles. These were more often than not piloted by extremely intoxicated drivers. No one was in a hurry, everyone wanted to party, and the whole country seemed headed toward Buenos Aires. The trip from Pergamino took over twenty frustrating, critical hours to complete, and the telephone lines remained overloaded that entire time.

Florencia De Seta would have no idea that her mother-in-law was in Buenos Aires until Oliviero Brown arrived at Casa San Marco bearing the news late in the evening of the twenty-sixth. Brown's message was blunt and to the point.

"Nana Taseo requests that Señora Florencia and a priest come to Señora Lydia's hospital bedside immediately. She doesn't have much time left!"

Luckily, Lydia De Seta was made of stern stuff. Even at her advanced age, she was fighter and would not easily succumb to the assassin's foul hand. She lay near death in Hospital Rivadavia for two days while the top pathologists in the land tried to analyze the source of her strange affliction. It was a visit from her grandson, Renaldo, in the evening of the twenty-seventh, that was unofficially credited with saving the lady's life. The sparkle seemed to return to Lydia's eyes when she suddenly awoke and recognized the handsome figure standing at her bedside. She then managed to raise herself ever so slightly from her prone position and whisper the word "champion" in his ear.

The young man stayed the entire night in her private room, and with the dawn of the twenty-eighth of June, the medical staff was amazed by Lydia's improved condition. She would remain in the hospital for a further two weeks to recover her strength and allow for further tests to be taken, and by mid-July, she was back at Buenos Recuerdos in much improved health and spirits.

The sudden disappearance of kitchen maid, Esquela Perez, while Lydia was in the capital never became connected to the elderly lady's illness. It would turn out that the grateful servant had been overzealous in her desire to please Pablo and the German doctor. She had increased the recommended dosage of 'medicine' threefold to speed up the desired results. That small gesture had sent the English lady spiralling downward much faster than anticipated. It also tipped Nana Taseo off to the seriousness of her employer's situation, thus saving her life. When word reached the Pampas that Lydia De Seta would survive her ordeal, Pablo was quick to rid the world of his sweet little accomplice. A simple note was left at Buenos Requerdos, informing the staff that Esquela Perez had eloped with a gaucho from a neighboring estancia. She would never be heard from again.

The young Porteño had never been this terrified in his life. The monster surged from behind, almost engulfing them at times. The red, white, and blue torrent was gaining on them, hurling insults along with rocks and bottles. He knew all too well what would happen should they be overtaken, for this monster was both human and inhuman.

"Father?"

Renaldo sat bolt upright in bed. His body was covered in perspiration. Simone, awakened from a deep sleep by her lover's terror-stricken cry, reached for the lamp on her night table.

"Renaldo, what is it? Were you having a bad dream? Are you alright? Tell me what I can do?"

She had never seen him so white with fear, his complexion as pale as the sheet that they slept on. Simone pulled the blanket around his shoulders and stroked his brow. He was shaking, but not because he was cold.

"I saw my father! Saw how he died! Simone, I never realized until the doctor told me. We both were chased by angry mobs leaving a football stadium. It happened to me in Córdoba last December. I was lucky and managed to escape. The same thing happened to my father in England back in 1966. Except he didn't get away."

He sat on the bed wrapped in the covers, swaying slightly back and forth from the waist. Letting out a deep sigh, he continued.

"He was leaving Wembley Stadium with his friends from Argentina after England beat us out of the World Cup competition. The game had been very rough. Our captain was sent off after an argument with the referee, but he refused to go. He had to be led away. The English hated our team, and our fans. They taunted my father and his friends the whole game, calling them 'greasy spics' and 'grease balls.' Some of the group from Buenos Aires took offense and tried to stand up to the hooligans. That only made things worse."

Renaldo's voice was hoarse, his speech little more than a strained croaking sound.

"When the game was over, even though England had won, a large gang of thugs waited for the men from Argentina outside the stadium. Then they attacked them!" He was sobbing now, coming to grips with all the bottled up emotions and fears that he had stifled since that terrible day. Simone was speechless, unable to comprehend who or what had turned her brave, insatiable lion into a frightened lamb. Renaldo tried to regain his composure, but managed only half sentences through the teary spasms that raked his body.

"The English . . . set upon him and his friends . . . and beat them severely! My father . . . broke free . . . but they ran after him yelling, 'spics out, spics out! Kill the bloody spics!' They had almost caught up to him again, when, he ran . . . between two parked cars. Right into the path of a large truck! Oh, God! My poor father!"

Simone held him in her arms, reassuring him that there was nothing to fear now, that his father was at peace, and that he would have been so very proud of his son's accomplishments.

"Who told you this terrible story, my love? Who would want to say such things on the eve of your great triumph? Who is this doctor you speak of? He must be some kind of sadistic madman to tell you these things!"

"No! No, I went to him. Dr. Quinquela, this afternoon. I made him tell me everything. He did not want to reveal how terrible things were in London that day. He was an associate of my father's from the Children's Hospital. He was at the stadium with him, he saw him die on that street!"

Renaldo had regained a large part of his composure now. Talking things out had calmed him considerably. He looked at Simone directly for the first time since awakening.

"I had to know! I had to find out the truth before I could ever set foot on English soil. My mother and everyone else had always sheltered me from the truth. I know now that she equated my father's death to everything connected with the sport of football. It is the reason she was so fearful every time I laced on a pair of football boots. It all makes sense finally."

"But how can you possibly go to England knowing what those insane animals did to your father? The same thing could happen to you as a player. The English hooligans have a terrible reputation, and you and Ramon will be the first foreign players to play in their league. You will be marked men!"

Now it was Simone who was trembling, tears welling in her eyes. She had done her duty as Astor Gordero had commanded, but she was truly in love with this gorgeous man and didn't want to see him in any danger.

Renaldo kissed her tenderly and told her not to fret. He was feeling better now, now that he had come to grips with the unanswered questions from his youth. Simone pulled him down to her and snuggled up under the bedding. Renaldo turned the light off as he felt the warmth of her skin once more beneath him. Together they lay in the silent darkness, reorchestrating their passion in thoughts, too spent now for actions. Concern for her young paramour's future evaporated as Simone drifted off to sleep, content in the knowledge that she had created a master lover.

They had explored unimaginable heights that second night together, and he had pushed her over the brink more times than she had ever thought possible. It was no longer necessary to instruct her pupil in the ways of love, for he had taken the initiative and embarked upon his post graduate thesis.

Simone had slept like a baby after her flame blew out the last candle and cradled her in his strong arms. That is, until his agonizing cry had shattered her tranquil euphoria.

Renaldo's sleep had been fitful at best. It wasn't the newfound knowledge that Dr. Quinquela had revealed. Not initially at least. It was the blonde vision and voice that kept appearing in his mind's eye. Even while making love to Simone, Mallory Russell's countenance kept flashing like a neon sign in the far reaches of his brain.

What was happening to him? Two days ago he could hardly talk to a woman without feeling self-conscious about his inexperience with the fairer sex. Now his long dormant hormones had manifested themselves in a plethora of salacious cravings. How could he make love to the most beautiful woman in the whole country while thinking of another? Did this mean that he was truly a man now?

Renaldo De Seta knew that the answers to his many questions about life and his future lay thousands of miles away, across the Atlantic Ocean. He had to travel to England to confront the real person living inside his body.

He had been convinced that Argentina held no further goals to accomplish at this point in his life. He was a world champion athlete, courting a world-renowned starlet. What more could he do here? His life had turned into a thing of which fairy tales and novels are made.

He had forged a peace with his mother, and while he worried about his wayward brother, there was nothing that he could do for Lonnie if Lonnie did not reach out for help.

Of course, unknown to his little brother, Lonnie De Seta was far beyond reaching out for anything, ever again!

Renaldo could deal with his father's death at the hands of the English, for he himself could have died at the hands of his own countrymen in Córdoba. He felt the need to visit Wembley Stadium in person, to see where his father's tragedy took place. After that, he was confident that those demons would be exorcised forever, and he could accept the English without fear or paranoia.

The future for Renaldo De Seta, world champion, had been rolled out in front of him as if it were a giant red carpet. It would soon be time to take the initial steps down that glorious road.

As the star of Argentina's World Cup championship stood on the threshold of the unknown, drifting back into a much calmer sleep, the words that had brought him success, fame, and fortune played over and over again in his mind.

It was like counting sheep. There was the jovial, jowled face of his mentor repeating his catchphrase. It was the phrase that had taken him to the highest echelon of the sporting world, and he hoped it would continue to keep him there, in his new endeavor.

Head and feet as one! Head and feet as one! Head and feet as one!

The End

AN INTIMATE EXPLORATION OF THE MEANING OF HOPE:

Without hope, Renaldo would never have been written. At a time in my life when despair could have easily overwhelmed me, I was driven to produce this story of a special young man living in a country that seemed to be without hope. As fate would have it, the events that actually happened in Argentina in 1978 gave an entire nation more hope than they had ever experienced.

There have been two events in my life that have shaped my destiny. The first was the sudden death of my mother, Myrtle, when I was nineteen and she was only forty–six. The second was the suicide of my wife, Carol, a week after her fortieth birthday.

In the first instance, I was the eldest of four children, my sister being only seven at the time. I felt that I must set an example and give my two brothers and sister hope that our mother had found eternal peace, and her spirit would always be with us.

In the second instance, I had two young daughters, aged ten and twelve, that needed constant reassurance and understanding that the life their mother had chosen to surrender was just too much to bear, and that she, like my mother before her, was now at peace, and in heaven watching over them every day.

It was the hope that I could make a difference in the lives of the people left behind that inspired me to carry on and shun despair. I left university shortly after my mother's death, and guided our family business for the next forty years. I am proud to say that we four siblings still communicate frequently, even though we are geographically many miles apart.

Shortly after my wife passed, a story I had been formulating in my mind during her painful illness began to pour onto the pages from my computer. This fictional story was something that I could control, and over the seven years it took to complete, writing was my therapy. This is why Renaldo came to be.

My young daughters are now wonderful, well adjusted women, the eldest living and working in London England, and the youngest having just given birth to a baby daughter. My hope for them as they were growing up was that they would not fall into despair after the loss of their mum.

We were fortunate to find an Angel, a beautiful woman by the name of Annie, who had also suffered an unthinkable setback. Annie had two children as well, and with love and hope for a future together, we merged our two stricken families and forged a union that has produced many joyous years, and at this point two granddaughters.

Hope... for a brighter day tomorrow, kept us all going, filled our lives with love and happiness, and allowed me to write Renaldo as a tribute to hope.

ABOUT THE AUTHOR

James McCreath...is the descendant of Scottish and Italian immigrants to Canada. His passion for the sport of soccer was ignited in the summer of 1966, when as an eighteen-year-old schoolboy, he toured Europe as England marched successfully to their World Cup championship. During his diverse business career, he has been involved in both the professional sports and entertainment industries. Mr. McCreath resides in his native Toronto, Canada. For further information, please visit website - www.renaldo.com and blog - renaldonovel.blogspot.com